THE NEW
SPACE
OPERA

**EDITED BY
GARDNER DOZOIS AND
JONATHAN STRAHAN**

An Imprint of HarperCollinsPublishers

This book is a work of fiction. The characters, incidents, and dialogue are drawn from the author's imagination and are not to be construed as real. Any resemblance to actual events or persons, living or dead, is entirely coincidental.

A continuation of the copyright page appears on pages 641–642.

EOS
An Imprint of HarperCollins*Publishers*
10 East 53rd Street
New York, New York 10022-5299

Collection, introduction, and story notes copyright © 2007 by Gardner Dozois and Jonathan Strahan
ISBN: 978-0-06-135041-2
www.eosbooks.com

First Eos paperback printing: September 2008
First Eos trade paperback printing: June 2007

HarperCollins® and Eos® are registered trademarks of HarperCollins Publishers.

Printed in the U.S.A.

10 9 8 7 6 5 4 3 2

For Jack Dann,
friend across two continents and two lifetimes,
and
for all those writers who have kept the paper spaceships
flying across the years

CONTENTS

VIII   CONTENTS

THE NEW
SPACE OPERA

INTRODUCTION

It's hard to imagine just what the world was like when space opera was born. There's a lot of talk in science fiction circles these days about the Singularity, the point when technological progress sweeps off the scale and the world essentially turns to magic. It must have seemed like the world was living through a singularity in 1900. Alabama turned on the first electric streetlights in 1882, Marconi filed the patent for radio in 1896, and the Wright brothers flew at Kitty Hawk in 1903: it was an exciting time when science and technology seemingly could take on and solve any problem. It was also a time of frontiers, of the full flowering of the British Empire, which was bent on "civilizing" much of the world, and of the settling of the American West. Jack Williamson, one of the pioneers of space opera, traveled west to New Mexico in a horse-drawn wagon in 1915, the same year that E. E. "Doc" Smith was writing the first great space opera novel, *The Skylark of Space*.

But we get ahead of ourselves. We should probably first touch on what space opera is, before we discuss it in any detail. *The Encyclopedia of Science Fiction* describes space opera as "colorful action-adventure stories of interplanetary or interstellar conflict," while Jack Williamson in *The New Encyclopedia of Science Fiction* refers to it as "the upbeat space adventure narrative that has become the mainspring of modern science fiction." And, perhaps getting closer to the feel of it, Paul McAuley in *Locus* refers to "lushly romantic plots and the star-spanning empires to the light-year-spurning space ships, construction of any one of which would have exhausted the metal reserves of a solar system . . . stuffed full of faux-exotic color and bursting with contrived energy." It is, in short, romantic adventure set in space and told on a grand scale. According to Brian Aldiss, writing in 1974, it must feature a starship, the most important of science fiction's icons, which "unlocks the great bronze doors of space opera and lets mankind loose among all the other immensities." It is the tale of godlike machines, all-embracing catastrophes, the immensities of the universe, and the endlessness of time. It is also, to go back to Williamson, the "expression of the mythic theme of human expansion against an unknown and uncommonly hostile frontier."

While proto–space operas like Garrett P. Serviss's *Edison's Conquest of Space* and Robert W. Cole's *The Struggle for Empire* were published as early as the late 1890s, and pioneered many of the tropes of space opera, it's difficult to make a useful connection between such works and what we know now as space opera. Instead we need to look at the pulp fiction magazines of the twenties and thirties for the first space operas. Ray Cummings, who'd worked with Thomas Edison as a personal assistant and technical writer, published one of the first space operas, *Terrano the Conqueror,* in 1925. He was soon followed by Edmond Hamilton, who published early space operas such as "Across Space" (1926) and "Crashing Suns" (1928) in *Weird Tales:* epic tales of alien invasion and cosmic adventure that were more interested in generating a thrilling sense of wonder than in the details of character and such. Perhaps the greatest of the early space opera writers, though, was E. E. "Doc" Smith, whose *The Skylark of Space* was published in 1928. It was followed by two sequels, and then by his hugely ambitious Lensman series, which featured ever larger spaceships, fantastically destructive weapons capable of wiping out entire galaxies, and even the first galactic empires. After Smith and Hamilton came John W. Campbell Jr. and Jack Williamson. Campbell, who would go on to greater prominence as the editor of *Astounding/Analog,* brought a new command of scientific language to space opera in the galaxy-spanning adventures *Islands of Space, Invaders from the Infinite,* and *The Mightiest Machine,* all of which were published in the early thirties. Williamson, who started publishing in 1919 and continued writing up until 2005, wrote a space opera flavored with an older kind of romanticism, turning to Shakespeare for the temple for Giles Habibula, the old soldier of space in his classic *The Legion of Space.*

The 1940s saw something of a sea change in space opera. In 1941 Wilson Tucker coined the term "space opera" to refer to "the hacky, grinding, stinking, outworn space-ship yarn, or world-saving for that matter." But, just as he did, more sophisticated, challenging work began to appear. Novels like C. L. Moore's *Judgement Night* and A. E. van Vogt's *Earth's Last Fortress* were better written, more complicated, and even more romantic. And certainly by the time writers like Leigh Brackett and Jack Vance were writing space opera in the early 1950s the term "space opera" referred to far better work than Tucker would ever have imagined.

It's here, with Vance, Brackett, Charles Harness, Poul Anderson, Alfred Bester, and others creating enduring works of high quality that still might be considered space opera, that Brian Stableford, for example, draws something of a line. Writing in *The Encyclopedia of Science Fiction,* he observed that by the late 1950s a number of the tropes of space opera, such as the galactic-empire scenario, had become a standardized framework available for use in entirely serious science fiction: "Once this happened, the impression of vast scale so important to space opera was no longer the sole prerogative of straightforward adventure stories, and the day of the 'classical' space opera was done." Throughout the early and mid sixties, the above-named writers, plus others such as James H.

Schmitz, Murray Leinster, L. Sprague de Camp, Gordon R. Dickson, H. Beam Piper, Brian W. Aldiss, Larry Niven, Ursula K. Le Guin, Roger Zelazny, James Tiptree Jr. and Samuel R. Delany (whose 1968 novel *Nova* can be seen as either the last important space opera novel of the sixties or one of the precursors of the New Space Opera of the nineties, depending on how you squint at it), would add an increase in both social/political sophistication and line-by-line writing craft to the form. Writers such as Cordwainer Smith, Alfred Bester (especially with his *The Stars My Destination*), Frank Herbert (whose famous *Dune*, in spite of a great deal of serious speculation about the future evolution of human societies, is fundamentally a baroque space opera on a scale not seen since the Superscience era of the twenties and thirties), and Delany took the form to new heights of complexity, flamboyance, and vividness, and radically upped the Imagination Ante for every *other* writer who wanted to sit down at the space opera table and credibly deal themselves into the game. Even Robert A. Heinlein, especially in "juvenile novels" such as *Citizen of the Galaxy, The Star Beast,* and *Have Space Suit, Will Travel,* could be said to be writing conceptually sophisticated space opera.

By the late sixties and early seventies, however, perhaps because of the prominence of the "New Wave" revolution in SF, which concentrated on both introspective, stylistically "experimental" work and work with more immediate sociological and political "relevance" to the tempestuous social scene of the day, perhaps because of the discovery of scientific proof that the other planets of the solar system were not likely abodes for life (and so, it seemed, not interesting settings for adventure stories), perhaps because the now more widely understood limitations of Einsteinian relativity had come to make the idea of far-flung interstellar empires seem improbable at best, science fiction as a genre was tending to turn away from the space adventure tale. Although it would never disappear completely, it had become widely regarded as outmoded and déclassé; the radical new writers of the generation just about to rise to prominence would collectively produce less space opera than any other comparable generational group of authors, and there would be less space opera written in the following ten years or so than in any other comparable period in SF history. By far the majority of work published during this period would be set on Earth, often in the near future—even the solar system had been largely deserted as a setting for stories, let alone the distant stars. Although stalwarts such as Poul Anderson and Jack Vance and Larry Niven continued to soldier on throughout those years, it was a common—and frequently expressed—opinion that space opera was dead.

But by the late seventies and early eighties, such new writers as John Varley, George R. R. Martin, Bruce Sterling, Michael Swanwick, Vernor Vinge, and others would begin to become interested in the space adventure again, reinvented to better fit the aesthetic style and tastes of the day, and, once again, the paper spaceships began to fly.

In 1975, M. John Harrison wrote *The Centauri Device,* a novel that turned the conventions of space opera on their head. It was, apparently, intended to kill space opera, or at least be an anti–space opera. What it was, instead, was the work that provoked others to pick up the cudgel and change things again. By 1982, when the British magazine *Interzone* published a "call to arms" editorial looking for radical hard SF, a new generation of writers had come along on both sides of the Atlantic who were ready and willing to produce just that. First among them was Iain M. Banks, whose *Consider Phlebas* was boldly, defiantly operatic in nature and scope, and yet very much leftward-leaning politically. His sequence of science fiction novels involving the "Culture" set both the critical trend and the commercial standard for space opera in the early 1980s.

This "new space opera," though, wasn't a technological fable of the turn of the century. By the beginning of the 1980s, when cyberpunk was emerging in the United States, it no longer seemed viable to tell bold tales of space adventure that looked to new frontiers where manifest destiny could be brought to the locals. Suddenly, the universe looked like a much darker place. Space opera was no longer looking to go out and take over the universe: it was looking to survive. This change can be seen in the work of Stephen Baxter, Paul McAuley, and even Colin Greenland. Retaining the interstellar scale and grandeur of traditional space opera, the new space opera became more scientifically rigorous and ambitious in scope.

Things really took off in the mid-1990s, until by now, here in the Oughts, it's possible to look around and spot legions of writers such as Dan Simmons, Alastair Reynolds, Charles Stross, Vernor Vinge, Orson Scott Card, Ken Macleod, C. J. Cherryh, M. John Harrison, Gwyneth Jones, Gregory Benford, Greg Bear, John Clute, Peter F. Hamilton, Walter Jon Williams, Greg Egan, Nancy Kress, Stephen R. Donaldson, Tony Daniel, John Barnes, Kage Baker, Robert Reed, Mary Rosenblum, Lois McMaster Bujold, Eleanor Arnason, the before-mentioned McAuley, Baxter, and Greenland, and a half-dozen others, who are producing major works of space opera that are literary, challenging, dark, and often disturbing, but also grand and romantic, exciting, fast-paced, set in space, and told on an enormous stage. And right behind these authors are coming new waves of space opera writers such as Neal Asher, Elizabeth Bear, Scott Westerfield, Karl Schroeder, John Meany, Sean Williams, John C. Wright, and others—all of which proves, to us, anyway, that *this,* right here, these days in which we swim, is the Golden Age of Space Opera.

This all too brief sketch gives you some idea of how we made the jump from Thomas Edison launching spaceships to Mars to slipping into a bar somewhere in the Kefahuchi Tract, wondering about being ambushed forty lights off the Galactic Rim. And yet, for all of it, the book you're now holding was never intended to be a dry historical or critical work. When we started work on *The New Space Opera* we weren't especially concerned about getting stories that met this definition or that, and we never once discussed how we might arrange the stories in the book to cumulatively make some argument or other. Instead we were looking for great new stories by some of the best writers working in the field. Back in 1974, Brian Aldiss wrote that "science fiction is for real, space opera is for fun." And that's what we did want. A book that would fuel our imaginations, our senses of wonder, and a book that would do that for you too. It's something we think the extraordinary group of stories here achieves easily. We believe you'll agree. And, we hope, we might do this again. Space is infinite, or close to it, and the scope for the space opera tale is just as inexhaustible.

SAVING TIAMAAT

GWYNETH JONES

One of the most acclaimed British writers of her generation, Gwyneth Jones was a cowinner of the James Tiptree Jr. Memorial Award for work exploring genre issues in science fiction, with her 1991 novel *White Queen*, and has also won the Arthur C. Clarke Award, with her novel *Bold as Love*, as well as receiving two World Fantasy Awards—for her story "The Grass Princess" and her collection *Seven Tales and a Fable*. Her other books include the novels *North Wind, Flowerdust, Escape Plans, Divine Endurance, Phoenix Café, Castles Made of Sand, Stone Free, Midnight Lamp, Kairos, Life, Water in the Air, The Influence of Ironwood, The Exhange, Dear Hill*, and *The Hidden Ones*, as well as more than sixteen young adult novels published under the name Ann Halam. Her too-infrequent short fiction has appeared in *Interzone, Asimov's Science Fiction, Off Limits*, and in other magazines and anthologies, and has been collected in *Identifying the Object: A Collection of Short Stories*, as well as *Seven Tales and a Fable*. She is also the author of the critical study *Deconstructing the Starships: Science Fiction and Reality*. Her most recent book is a new novel, *Rainbow Bridge*. She lives in Brighton, England, with her husband, her son, and a Burmese cat.

In the vivid and compelling story that follows, she proves that coming to really know your enemy may make your problems *harder* rather than easier to solve.

◐ I had reached the station in the depth of Left Speranza's night; I had not slept. Fogged in the confabulation of the transit, I groped through crushing eons to my favorite breakfast kiosk: unsure if the soaring concourse outside Parliament was ceramic and carbon or a *metaphor;* a cloudy internal warning—

Now what was the message in the mirror? Something pitiless. Some blank-eyed, slow-thinking, long-grinned crocodile—

"Debra!"

It was my partner. "Don't *do* that," I moaned. The internal crocodile shattered, the concourse lost its freight of hyper-determined meaning, too suddenly for comfort. "Don't you know you should never startle a sleepwalker?"

He grinned; he knew when I'd arrived, and the state I was likely to be in. I hadn't met Pelé Leonidas Iza Quinatoa in the flesh before, but we'd worked together, we liked each other. "Ayayay, so good you can't bear to lose it?"

"Of course not. Only innocent, beautiful souls have sweet dreams."

He touched my cheek: collecting a teardrop. I hadn't realized I was crying. "You should use the dreamtime, Debra. There must be *some* game you want to play."

"I've tried, it's worse. If I don't take my punishment, I'm sick for days."

The intimacy of his gesture (skin on skin) was an invitation and a promise; it made me smile. We walked into the Parliament Building together, buoyant in the knocked-down gravity that I love although I know it's bad for you.

In the Foyer, we met the rest of the company, identified by the Diaspora Parliament's latest adventure in biometrics, the aura tag. To our vision, the KiAn Working Party was striated orange/yellow, nice cheerful implications, nothing too deep. The pervasive systems were seeing a lot more, but that didn't bother Pelé or me; we had no secrets from Speranza.

The KiAn problem had been a matter of concern since their world had been "discovered" by a Balas/Shet prospector, and joined the minuscule roster of populated planets linked by instantaneous transit. Questions had been raised then, over the grave social imbalance: the tiny international ruling caste, the exploited masses. But neither the Ki nor the An would accept arbitration (why the hell should they?). The noninterference lobby is the weakest faction in the Chamber, quarantine-until-they're-civilized was not considered an option. Inevitably, around thirty local years after first contact, the Ki had risen against their overlords, as often in the past. Inevitably, this time they had modern weapons. They had not succeeded in wiping out the An, but they had pretty much rendered the shared planet uninhabitable.

We were here to negotiate a rescue package. We'd done the damage, we had to fix it, that was the DP's line. The Ki and the An no doubt had their own ideas as to what was going on: they were new to the Interstellar Diaspora, not to politics.

But they were here, at least; so that seemed hopeful.

The Ki Federation delegates were unremarkable. There were five of them, they conformed to the "sentient biped" bodyplan that unites the diaspora. Three were wearing Balas business suits in shades of brown, two were in gray military uniform. The young coleaders of the An were better dressed, and one of the two, in particular, was *much* better looking. Whatever you believe about the origins of the "diaspora" (Strong theory, Weak theory, something between) it's strange how many measures of beauty are common to us all. He was tall, past two meters: he had large eyes, a mane of rich brown head-hair, an open, strong-boned face, poreless bronze skin, and a glorious smile. He would be my charge. His coleader, the subordinate partner, slight and small, almost as dowdy as the Ki, would be Pelé's.

They were codenamed Baal and Tiamaat, the names I will use in this account. The designations Ki and An are also codenames.

We moved off to a briefing room. Joset Moricherri, one of

the Blue Permanent Secretaries, made introductory remarks.
A Green Belt Colonel, Shamaz Haa'agaan, gave a talk on
station security. A slightly less high-ranking DP administrator got down to basics: standard time conventions, shopping
allowances, access to the elevators, restricted areas, house-
keeping . . . Those who hadn't provided their own breakfast
raided the culturally neutral trolley. I sipped my Mocha/Co-
lombian, took my carbs in the form of a crisp cherry-jam
tartine; and let the day's agenda wash over me, as I reviewed
what I knew about Baal and Tiamaat's relationship.

They were not related by blood, except in the sense that
the An gene pool was very restricted: showing signs of other
population crashes in the past. They were not "married"
either. The Ki and the An seemed to be sexually dimorphic
on the Blue model (though they could yet surprise us!); and
they liked opposite-sex partnerships. But they did not marry.
Tiamaat's family had been swift to embrace the changes,
she'd been educated on Balas/Shet. Baal had left KiAn for
the first time when war broke out. They'd lost family members, and they'd certainly seen the horrific transmissions
smuggled off KiAn before the end. Yet here they were, with
the genocidal Ki: thrown together, suddenly appointed the
rulers of their shattered nation, and bound to each other for
life. Tiamaat looked as if she were feeling the strain. She
sat with her eyes lowered, drawn in on herself, her body occupying the minimum of space. Beside her, Baal devoured a
culturally neutral doughnut, elbows sprawled, with a child's
calm greed. I wondered how much my alien perception of a
timid young woman and a big bold young man was distorting
my view. I wondered how all that fine physicality translated
into mind.

Who are you, Baal? How will it feel to know you?

From the meeting we proceeded to a DP reception and
lunch, from thence to a concert in the Nebula Immersion
Chamber: a Blue Planet symphony orchestra on virtual tour,
the Diaspora Chorus in the flesh, singing a famous masque;
a solemn dance drama troupe bilocating from Neuendan.
Pelé and I, humble Social Support officers, were in the back-

ground for these events. But the An had grasped that we were their advocates: as was proved when they pounced on us, eagerly, after the concert. They wanted to meet "the nice quiet people with the pretty curly faces—"

They spoke English, language of diplomacy and displacement. They'd both taken the express, neurotech route to fluency: but we had trouble pinning this request down. It turned out they were asking to be introduced to a bowl of orchids.

Appearances can be deceptive; these two young people were neither calm nor cowed. They had been born in a medieval world, and swept away from home as to the safety of a rich neighbor's house: all they knew of the interstellar age was the inside of a transit lounge. The Ki problem they knew only too well: Speranza was a thrilling bombardment. With much laughter (they laughed like Blue teenagers, to cover embarrassment), we explained that they would not be meeting any bizarre life-forms. No tentacles, no petals, no intelligent gas clouds here; not yet!

"You have to look after us!" cried Baal. He grabbed my arm, softly but I felt the power. "Save us from making fools of ourselves, dear Debra and Pelé!"

Tiamaat stood back a pace, hiding her giggles behind her hand.

The last event scheduled on that first day was a live transmission walkabout from the Ki refugee camp, in the Customized Shelter Sector. In the planning stages, some of us had expressed doubts about this stunt. If anything went wrong it'd sour the whole negotiation. But the Ki and the An leaders were both keen, and the historic gesture was something the public back on the homeworlds would understand—which in the end had decided the question. The Diaspora Parliament had to struggle for planetside attention, we couldn't pass up an opportunity.

At the gates of the CSS, deep in Speranza's hollow heart, there was a delay. The Customized Shelter Police wanted us in armored glass-tops, they felt that if we *needed* a walkabout we could fake it. . . Pelé chatted with Tiamaat, stooping from his lean black height to catch her soft voice.

Baal stared at the banners on two display screens. The KiAn understood flags, we hadn't taught them that concept. Green and gold quarters for the Ki, a center section crosshatched with the emblems of all the nations. Purple tracery on vivid bronze for the An.

Poor kid, I thought, it's not a magic gateway to your lost home. Don't get your hopes up. That's the door to a cage in a conservation zoo.

He noticed my attention, and showed his white teeth. "Are there other peoples living in exile on this floor?"

I nodded. "Yes. But mostly the people sheltered here are old spacers who can't return to full gravity. Or failed colonist communities, likewise: people who've tried to settle on empty moons and planets and been defeated by the conditions. There are no other populated-planet exiles. It hasn't been, er, necessary."

"We are a first for you."

I wondered if that was ironic; if he was capable of irony.

A compromise was reached. We entered on foot, with the glass-tops and CSP closed cars trailing behind. The Ki domain wasn't bad, for a displaced-persons camp wrapped in the bleak embrace of a giant space station. Between the living-space capsule towers the refugees could glimpse their own shade of sky; and a facsimile of their primary sun, with its partner, the blue-rayed daystar. They had sanitation, hygiene, regular meals; leisure facilities, even employment. We stopped at an adult retraining center; we briefly inspected a hydroponic farm. We visited a kindergarten, where the teaching staff told us (and the flying cams!) how all the nations of the Ki were gathered here in harmony, learning to be good Diaspora citizens.

The children stared at Baal and Tiamaat. They'd probably been born in the camp, and never seen An in the flesh before. Baal fidgeted, seeming indignant under their scrutiny. Tiamaat stared back with equal curiosity. I saw her reach a tentative hand through the shielding, as if to touch a Ki child: but she thought better of it.

After the classroom tour, there was a reception, with speeches, dance, and choral singing. Ki community leaders and the An couple didn't literally "shake hands"; but the gesture was accomplished. Here the live trans. ended, and most of our party stayed behind. The An leaders and the Ki delegates went on alone, with a police escort, for a private visit to "Hopes and Dreams Park"—a facsimile of one of the Sacred Groves (as near as the term translates) central to KiAn spirituality.

Pelé and I went with them.

The enclave of woodland was artfully designed. The "trees" were like self-supporting kelp, leathery succulents— lignin is native only to the Blue Planet—but they were tall, and planted close enough to block all sight of the packed towers. Their sheets of foliage made a honeyed shade, we seemed alone in a gently managed wilderness. The Ki and the An kept their distance from each other now that the cams weren't in sight. The police moved outward to maintain a cordon around the group, and I began to feel uneasy. I should have been paying attention instead of savoring my breakfast, I had not grasped that "Hopes and Dreams Park" would be like this. I kept hearing voices, seeing flitting shadows; although the park area was supposed to have been cleared. I'd mentioned the weak shielding; I hoped it had been fixed—

"Are religious ceremonies held here?" I asked Tiamaat.

She drew back her head, the gesture for "no." "Most KiAn have not followed religion for a long time. It's just a place sacred to ourselves, to nature."

"But it's fine for the Shelter Police, and Pelé and me, to be with you?"

"You are advocates."

We entered a clearing dotted with thickets. At our feet smaller plants had the character of woodland turf, starred with bronze and purple flowers. Above us the primary sun dipped toward its false horizon, lighting the bloodred veins in the foliage. The blue daystar had set. Baal and Tiamaat were walking together: I heard him whisper, in the An language, "now it's our time."

"And these are the lucky ones," muttered one of the Ki delegates to me, her "English" mediated by a throat-mike processor that gave her a teddy-bear growl. "Anyone who reached Speranza had contacts, money. Many millions of our people are trying to survive on a flayed, poisoned bombsite—"

And whose fault is that?

I nodded, vaguely. It was *not* my place to take sides—

Something flew by me, big and solid. Astonished, I realized it had been Baal. He had moved so fast, it was so totally unexpected. He had plunged right through the cordon of armed police, through the shield. He was gone, vanished. I leaped in pursuit at once, yelling: "Hold your fire!" I was flung back, thrown down into zinging stars and blackness. The shield *had* been strengthened, but not enough.

Shelter Police, bending over me, cried: *what happened, ma'am, are you hit?*

My conviction that we had company in here fused into certainty—

"Oh, God! Get after him. After him!"

I ran with the police, Pelé stayed with Tiamaat and the Ki: on our shared frequency I heard him alerting Colonel Shamaz. We cast to and fro through the twilight wood, held together by the invisible strands and globules of our shield, taunted by rustles of movement, the CSP muttering to each other about refugee assassins, homemade weapons. But the young leader of the An was unharmed when we found him, having followed the sounds of a scuffle and a terrified cry. He crouched, in his sleek tailoring, over his prey. Dark blood trickled from the victim's nostrils, high-placed in a narrow face. Dark eyes were open, fixed and wide.

I remembered the children in that school, staring up in disbelief at the ogres.

Baal rose, wiping his mouth with the back of his hand. "What are you looking at?" he inquired haughtily, in his neighbors' language. The rest of our party had caught up: he was speaking to the Ki. "What did you expect? You know who I am."

Tiamaat fell to her knees, with a wail of despair, pressing her hands to either side of her head. "He has a right! Ki territory is An territory, he has a right to behave as if we were at home. And the Others knew it, don't you see? They *knew!*"

The CSP officer yelled something inexcusable and lunged at the killer. Pelé grabbed him by the shoulders and hauled him back, talking urgent sense. The Ki said nothing, but I thought Tiamaat was right. They'd known what the Diaspora's pet monster would do in here; and he hadn't let them down.

Perfectly unconcerned, Baal stood guard over the body until Colonel Haa'agaan arrived with the closed cars. Then he picked it up and slung it over his shoulder. I traveled with him and his booty, and the protection of four Green Belts, to the elevator. Another blacked-out car waited for us on Parliament level. What a nightmare journey! We delivered him to the service entrance of his suite in the Sensitive Visitors Facility, and saw him drop the body insouciantly into the arms of one of his aides—a domestic, lesser specimen of those rare and dangerous animals, the An.

The soldiers looked at each other, looked at me. "You'd better stay," I said. "And get yourselves reinforced, there might be reprisals planned."

Baal's tawny eyes in my mind: challenging me, trusting me—

The debriefing was in closed session; although there would be a transcript on record. It took a painfully long time, but we managed to exonerate everyone, including Baal. Mistakes had been made, signals had been misread. We knew the facts of the KiAn problem, we had only the most rudimentary grasp of the cultures involved. Baal and Tiamaat, who were not present, had made no further comment. The Ki (who were not present either) had offered a swift deposition. They wanted the incident treated with utmost discretion: they did not see it as a bar to negotiation. The Balas/Shet party argued that Baal's kill had been unique, an "extraordinary ritual" that we had to sanction. And we knew this was nonsense, but it was the best we could do.

One of our Green Belts, struck by the place in the report where Tiamaat exclaims "the Others knew it!," came up with the idea that the young Ki had been a form of suicide bomber: sacrificing his life in the hope of wrecking the peace talks. Investigation of the dead boy and his contacts would now commence.

"Thank funx it didn't happen on the live transmission!" cried Shamaz, the old soldier, getting his priorities right.

It was very late before Pelé and I got away. We spent the rest of the night together, hiding in the tenderness of the Blue Planet, where war is shameful and murder is an aberration; where kindness is common currency, and in almost every language strangers are greeted with love—dear, pet, darling; sister, brother, cousin—and nobody even wonders why. What an unexpected distinction, we who thought we were such ruthless villains, such fallen angels. "We're turning into the care-assistant caste for the whole funxing galaxy," moaned Pelé. "Qué cacho!"

The Parliament session was well attended: many tiers packed with bilocators; more than the usual scatter of Members present in the flesh, and damn the expense. I surveyed the Chamber with distaste. They all wanted to make their speeches on the KiAn crisis. But they knew nothing. The freedom of the press fades and dies at interstellar distances, where everything has to be couriered, and there's no such thing as evading official censorship. They'd heard about the genocide, the wicked but romantic An; the ruined world, the rescue plans. They had no idea exactly what had driven the rebel Ki to such desperation, and they weren't going to find out—

All the Diaspora Parliament knew was spin.

And the traditional Ki, the people we were dealing with, were collusive. They didn't *like* being killed and eaten by their aristos, but for outsiders to find out the truth would be a far worse evil: a disgusting, gross exposure. After all, it was only the poor, the weak-minded, and the disadvantaged who ended up on a plate. . . Across from the Visitors' Gallery, level with my eyes, hung the great Diaspora Banner. The populated worlds turned sedately, beautifully scanned and insanely close together; like one of those ancient distorted projections of the landmasses on the Blue. The "real" distance between the Blue system and Neuendan (our nearest neighbor) was twenty-six thousand light-years. Between the Neuendan and the Balas/Shet lay fifteen hundred light-years; the location of the inscrutable Aleutians' homeworld was a mystery. How would you represent *that* spatial relationship, in any realistic way?

"Why do they say it all aloud?" asked Baal idly.

He was beside me, of course. He was glad to have me there, and kept letting me know it: a confiding pressure against my shoulder, a warm glance from those tawny eyes. He took my complete silence about the incident in Hopes and Dreams Park for understanding. A DP Social Support Officer *never* shows hostility.

"Isn't your i/t button working?"

The instantaneous translation in here had a mind of its own.

"It works well enough. But everything they say is just repeating the documents on this desk. It was the same in the briefing yesterday, I noticed that."

"You read English?"

"Oh, yes." Reading and writing have to be learned, there is no quick neurofix. Casually, with a glint of that startling irony, he dismissed his skill. "I was taught, at home. But I don't bother. I have people who understand all this for me."

"It's called oratory," I said. "And rhetoric. Modulated speech is used to stir peoples' emotions, to cloud the facts and influence the vote—"

Baal screwed up his handsome face in disapproval. "That's distasteful."

"Also it's tradition. It's just the way we do things."

"Ah!"

I sighed, and sent a message to Pelé on our eye-socket link.

Change partners?

D'you want to reassign? came his swift response. He was worrying about me, he wanted to protect me from the trauma of being with Baal, which was a needle under my skin. I

liked Pelé very much, but I preferred to treat the Diaspora
Parliament as a no-ties singles bar.

No, I answered. *Just for an hour, after this.*

Getting close to Tiamaat was easy. After the session the four
of us went down to the Foyer, where Baal was quickly surrounded by a crowd of high-powered admirers. They swept
him off somewhere, with Pelé in attendance. Tiamaat and I
were left bobbing in the wake, ignored; a little lost. "Shall
we *have coffee,* Debra?" she suggested, with dignity. "I love
coffee. But not the kind that comes on those trolleys!"

I took her to "my" kiosk, and we found a table. I was impressed by the way she handled the slights of her position.
There goes Baal, surrounded by the mighty, while his partner is reduced to having coffee with a minder. . . It was a
galling role to have to play in public. I had intended to lead
up to the topic on my mind: but she forestalled me. "You
must be horrified by what happened yesterday."

No hostility. "A *little* horrified, I admit." I affected to hesitate. "The Balas/Shet say that what Baal did was a ritual,
confirming his position as leader; and the Ki expected it.
They may even have arranged for the victim to be available.
And it won't happen again. Are they right?"

She sipped her cappuccino. "Baal doesn't believe he did
anything wrong," she answered carefully, giving nothing
away.

I remembered her cry of despair. "But what do *you*
think—?"

"I can speak frankly?"

"You can say anything. We may seem to be in public, but
nothing you say to me, or that I say to you, can be heard by
anyone else."

"Speranza is a very clever place!"

"Yes, it is. . . And as you know, though the system itself
will have a record, as your Social Support Officer I may not
reveal anything you ask me to keep to myself."

She gave me eye contact then, very deliberately. I realized
I'd never seen her look anyone in the eye. The color of her
irises was a subtle, lilac-starred gray.

"Before I left home, when I was a child, I ate meat. I hadn't killed it, but I knew where it came from. But I have never killed, Debra. And now I don't believe I ever will." She looked out at the passing crowd, the surroundings that must be so punishingly strange to her. "My mother said we should close ourselves off to the past, and open ourselves to the future. So she sent me away, when I was six years old, to live on another world—"

"That sounds very young to me."

"I *was* young. I still had my milk teeth . . . I'm not like Baal, because I have been brought up differently. If I were in his place, things would be better for the Others. I truly believe that—" She meant the Ki, the prey-nations. "But I know what has to be done for KiAn. *I want this rescue package to work.* Baal is the one who will make it happen, and I support him in every way."

She smiled, close-lipped, no flash of sharp white: I saw the poised steel in her, hidden by ingrained self-suppression. And she changed the subject, with composure. Unexpected boldness, unexpected finesse—

"Debra, is it true that Blue people have secret superpowers?"

I laughed and shook my head. "I'm afraid not. No talking flowers here!"

Pelé tried to get the DP software to change our codenames. He maintained that "Baal" and "Tiamaat" were not even from the same mythology, and if we were going to invoke the gods, those two should be Aztecs: Huehueteotl, ripping the living heart from his victims . . . The bots refused. They said they didn't care if they were mixing their mysticisms. Codenames were a device to avoid accidental offense until the system had assimilated a new user language. "Baal" and "Tiamaat" were perfectly adequate, and the Meso-American names had too many characters.

I had dinner with Baal, in the Sensitive Visitor Facility. He was charming company: we ate vegetarian fusion cuisine, and I tried not to think about the butchered meat in the kitchen of his suite. On the other side of the room, bull-shouldered Colonel Haa'agaan ate alone; glancing at us covertly with small, sad eyes from between the folds of his slaty head-hide. Shamaz had been hard hit by what had happened in the Hopes and Dreams Park. But his orange and yellow aura-tag was still bright; and I knew mine was too. By the ruthless measures of interstellar diplomacy, everything was still going well; set for success.

If things had been different I might have joined Pelé again when I was finally off duty. As it was, I retired to my room, switched all the décor, including ceiling and floor, to starry void, mixed myself a kicking neurochemical cocktail, and applied the popper to my throat. Eyedrops are faster, but I wanted the delay, I wanted to feel myself coming apart. Surrounded by directionless immensity, I sipped chilled water, brooding. How can a people have World Government, space-flight-level industrialization, numinal intelligence, and yet the ruling caste are still killing and eating the peasants? How can they do that, when practically everyone on KiAn admits they are a single species, differently adapted: *and they knew that before we told them.* How can we be back here, the Great Powers and their grisly parasites: making the same moves, the same old mistakes, the same old hateful compromises, that our Singularity was supposed to cure forever?

Why is moral development so difficult? Why are predators charismatic?

The knots in my frontal lobes were combed out by airy fingers, I fell into the sea of possibilities, I went to the place of terror and joy that no one understands unless they have been there. I asked my question and I didn't get an answer, you never get an answer. Yet when I came to the shallows again, when I laid myself, exhausted, on this dark and confused shore, I knew what I was going to do: I had seen it.

But there always has to be an emotional reason. I'd known about Baal's views before I arrived. I'd known that he would hunt and kill "weakling" Ki, as was his traditional right, and not just once, he'd do it whenever the opportunity arose; and I'd still been undecided. It was Tiamaat who made the difference. I'd met her, skin on skin as we say. I knew what the briefing had not been able to tell me. She was no cipher, superficially "civilized" by her education, she was *suppressed* I had heard that cry of despair and anger, when she saw what Baal had done. I had talked to her. I knew she had strength and cunning, as well as good intentions. A latent dominance, the will and ability to be a leader.

I saw Baal's look of challenge and trust, even now—

But Tiamaat deserved saving, and I would save her.

The talks went on. Morale was low on the DP side, because the refugee-camp incident had shown us where we stood; but the Ki delegates were happy—insanely, infuriatingly. The "traditional diet of the An" was something they refused to discuss, and they were going to get their planet rebuilt anyway. The young An leaders spent very little time at the conference table. Baal was indifferent—he had people to understand these things for him—and Tiamaat could not be present without him. This caused a rift. Their aides, the only other An around, were restricted to the SV Facility suites (we care assistants may be crazy but we're not entirely stupid). Pelé and I were fully occupied, making sure our separate charges weren't left moping alone. Pelé took Tiamaat shopping and visiting museums (virtual and actual). I found that Baal loved to roam, just as I do myself, and took him exploring the lesser-known sights.

We talked about his background. Allegedly, he'd given up a promising career in the Space Marines to take on the leadership. When I'd assured myself that his pilot skills were real, he wasn't just a toy-soldier aristo, I finally took him on the long float through the permanent umbilical, to Right Speranza.

We had to suit up at the other end.

"What's this?" demanded Baal, grinning. "Are we going outside?"

"You'll see. It's an excursion I thought you'd enjoy."

The suits were programmable. I watched him set one up for his size and bulk, and knew he was fine: but I put him through the routines, to make sure. Then I took him into the vast open cavern of the DP's missile repository, which we crossed like flies in a cathedral, hooking our tethers to the girders, drifting over the ranked silos of deep-space interceptors, the giant housing of particle cannons.

All of it obsolete, like castle walls in the age of heavy artillery; but it looks convincing on the manifest, and who knows? "Modern" armies have been destroyed by Zulu spears; it never pays to ignore the conventional weapons—

"Is this a *weapons* bay?" the monster exclaimed, scandalized, on suit radio.

"Of course," said I. "Speranza can defend herself, if she has to."

I let us into a smaller hangar, through a lock on the cavern wall, and filled it with air and pressure and lights. We were completely alone. Left Speranza is a natural object, a hollowed asteroid. Right is artificial, and it's a dangerous place for sentient bipeds. The proximity of the torus can have unpredictable and bizarre effects, not to mention the tissue-frying radiation that washes through at random intervals. But we would be fine for a short while. We fixed tethers, opened our faceplates and hunkered down, gecko-padded bootsoles clinging to the arbitrary "floor."

"I thought you were angels," he remarked shyly. "The weapons, all of that, it seems beneath you. Doesn't your codename 'Debra' mean 'an angel'? Aren't you all messengers, come to us from the Mighty Void?"

"Mighty Void" was a Balas/Shet term meaning something like God.

"No. . . Deborah was a judge, in Israel. I'm just human, Baal. I'm a person with numinal intelligence, the same kind of being as you are; like all the KiAn."

I could see that the harsh environment of Right Speranza moved him, as it did me. There was a mysterious peace and truth in being here, in the cold dark, breathing borrowed air. He was pondering: open and serious.

"Debra. . . ? Do you believe in the Diaspora?"

"I believe in the Weak theory," I said. "I don't believe we're all descended from the same Blue Planet hominid, the mysterious original starfarers, precursors of *Homo sapiens*.

I think we're the same because we grew under the same constraints: time, gravity, hydrogen bonds; the nature of water, the nature of carbon—"

"But instantaneous transit was invented on the Blue Planet," he protested, unwilling to lose his romantic vision.

"Only the prototype. It took hundreds of years, and a lot of outside help, before we had anything like viable interstellar travel—"

Baal had other people to understand the technology for him. He was building castles in the air, dreaming of his future. "Does everyone on the Blue speak English?"

"Not at all. They mostly speak a language called *putonghua,* which means 'common speech,' as if they were the only people in the galaxy. Blues are as insular as the KiAn, believe me, when they're at home. When you work for the DP, you change your ideas; it happens to everyone. I'm still an Englishwoman, and *mi naño* Pelé is still a man of Ecuador—"

"I know!" he broke in eagerly. "I felt that. I *like* that in you!"

"But we skip the middle term. The World Government of our single planet doesn't mean the same as it did." I grinned at him. "Hey, I didn't bring you here for a lecture. This is what I wanted to show you. See the pods?"

He looked around us, slowly, with a connoisseur's eye. He could see what the pods were. They were Aleutian-built, the revolutionary leap forward: *vehicles* that could pass through the mind/matter barrier. An end to those dreary transit lounges, true starflight, the Holy Grail: and only the Aleutians knew how it was done.

"Like to take one out for a spin?"

"You're kidding!" cried Baal, his eyes alight.

"No, I'm not. We'll take a two-man pod. How about it?"

He saw that I was serious, which gave him pause. "How can we? The systems won't allow it. This hangar has to be under military security."

"I *am* military security, Baal. So is Pelé. What did you think we were? Kindergarten teachers? Trust me, I have access, there'll be no questions asked."

He laughed. He knew there was something strange going on, but he didn't care: he trusted me. I glimpsed myself as a substitute for Tiamaat, glimpsed the relationship he should have had with his partner. Not sexual, but predation-based: a playful tussle, sparring partners. But Tiamaat had not wanted to be his sidekick—

We took a pod. Once we were inside, I sealed us off from Speranza, and we lay side by side in the couches, two narrow beds in a torpedo shell: an interstellar sports car, how right for this lordly boy. I checked his hookups, and secured my own.

"Where are we going?"

"Oh, just around the block."

His vital signs were in my eyes, his whole being was *quivering* in excitement, and I was glad. The lids closed, we were translated into code, we and our pod were injected into the torus, in the form of a triple stream of pure information, divided and shooting around the ring to meet itself, and collide—

I sat up, in a lucent gloom. The other bed's seal opened, and Baal sat up beside me. We were both still suited, with open faceplates. Our beds shaped themselves into pilot and copilot couches, and we faced what seemed an unmediated view of the deep space outside. Bulwarks and banks of glittering instruments carved up the panorama: I saw Baal's glance flash over the panels greedily, longing to be piloting this little ship for real. Then he saw the yellow primary, a white hole in black absence; and its brilliant, distant partner. He saw the pinpricks of other formations that meant nothing much to me, and he knew where I had brought him. We could not see the planet, it was entirely dark from this view. But in our foreground, the massive beams of space-to-space lasers were playing: shepherding plasma particles into a shell that would hold the recovering atmosphere in place.

To say that KiAn had been flayed alive was no metaphor. The people still living on the surface were in some kind of hell. But it could be saved.

"None of the machinery is strictly material," I said, "in any normal sense. It was couriered here, as information, in the living minds of the people who are now on station. We can't

see them, but they're around, in pods like this one. It will all
disintegrate, when the repairs are done. But the skin of your
world will be whole again, it won't need to be held in place."

The KiAn don't cry, but I was so close to him, in the place
where we were, that I felt his tears. "*Why* are you doing
this?" he whispered. "You must be angels, or why are you
saving us, what have we done to deserve this?"

"The usual reasons," I said. "Market forces, political le-
verage, power play."

"I don't believe you."

"Then I don't know what to tell you, Baal. Except that the
Ki and the An have numinal intelligence. You are like us,
and we have so few brothers and sisters. Once we'd found
you, we couldn't bear to lose you."

I let him gaze, for a long moment without duration.

"I wanted you to see this."

I stepped out of my pilot's couch and stood braced: one
hand gecko-padded to the inner shell, while I used the instruments to set the pod to self-destruct. The eject beacon
started up, direct cortical warning that my mind read as a
screaming siren—

"Now I'm going back to Speranza. But you're not."

The fine young cannibal took a moment to react. The
pupils in his tawny eyes widened amazingly when he found
that he was paralyzed, and his capsule couldn't close.

"Is this a dream?"

"Not quite. It's a confabulation. It's what happens when
you stay conscious in transit. The mind invents a stream of
environments, events. The restoration of KiAn is real, Baal.
It will happen. We can see it 'now' because we're in non-
duration, we're experiencing the simultaneity. In reality—if
that makes any sense, language hates these situations—we're
still zipping around the torus. But when the confabulation
breaks up, you'll still be in deep space and about to die."

I did not need to tell him why I was doing this. He was
no fool, he knew why he had to go. But his mind was still
working, fighting—

"Speranza is a four-space mapped environment. You can't
do this and go back alone. The system knows you were with

me, every moment. The record can't be changed, no way, without the tampering leaving a trace."

"True. But I am one of those rare people who can change the information. You've heard fairy tales about us, the Blues who have superpowers? I'm not an angel, Baal. Actually, it's a capital crime to be what I am, where I come from. But Speranza understands me. Speranza uses me."

"Ah!" he cried. "I knew it, I felt it. We are the same!"

When I recovered self-consciousness, I was in my room, alone. Earlier in the day, Baal had claimed he needed a nap. After a couple of hours, I'd become suspicious, checked for his signs, and found him missing: gone from the SV Facility screen. I'd been trying to trace him when Right Speranza had detected a pod, with the An leader onboard, firing up. The system had warned him to desist. Baal had carried on, and paid a high price for his attempted joyride. The injection had failed, both Baal and one fabulous Aleutian-built pod had been annihilated.

Remembering this much gave me an appalling headache—the same aching awfulness I imagine shapeshifters (I know of one or two) feel in their muscle and bone. I couldn't build the bridge at all: no notion how I'd connected between this reality and the former version. I could have stepped from the dying pod straight through the wall of this pleasant, modest living space. But it didn't matter. I would find out, and Debra would have been behaving like Debra.

Pelé came knocking. I let him in and we commiserated, both of us in shock. We're advocates, not enforcers, there's very little we can do if a Sensitive Visitor is really determined to go AWOL. We'd done all the right things, short of using undue force, and so had Speranza. When we'd broken the privilege locks, Baal's room record had shown that he'd been spying out how to get access to one of those Aleutian pods. It was just too bad that he'd succeeded, and that he'd had enough skill to get himself killed. Don't feel responsible, said Pelé. It's not your fault. Nobody thinks that. Don't be so sad. Always so sad, Debra: it's not good for the brain, you should take a break. Then he started telling me that frankly, nobody would regret Baal. By An law, Tiamaat could now

rule alone; and if she took a partner, we could trust her not to
choose another bloodthirsty atavist. . . I soon stopped him.
I huddled there in pain, my friend holding my hand: seeing
only the beautiful one, his tawny eyes at the last, his challenge and his trust; mourning my victim.

I'm a melancholy assassin.

I did not sleep. In the gray calm of Left Speranza's early
hours, before the breakfast kiosks were awake, I took the elevator to the Customized Shelter Sector, checked in with the
CSP, and made my way, between the silent capsule towers, to
Hopes and Dreams Park. I was disappointed that there were
no refugees about. It would have been nice to see Ki children
playing fearlessly. Ki oldsters picking herbs from their win-
dowboxes, instead of being boiled down for soup themselves.
The gates of the Sacred Grove were open, so I just walked
in. There was a memorial service: strictly no outsiders, but
I'd had a personal message from Tiamaat saying I would be
welcome. I didn't particularly want to meet her again. I'm a
superstitious assassin; I felt that she would somehow know
what I had done for her. I thought I would keep to the back of
whatever gathering I found, while I made my own farewell.

The daystar's rays had cleared the false horizon, the sun
was a rumor of gold between the trees. I heard laughter, and
a cry. I walked into the clearing and saw Tiamaat. She'd just
made the kill. I saw her toss the small body down, drop to her
haunches, and take a ritual bite of raw flesh; I saw the blood
on her mouth. The Ki looked on, keeping their distance in
a solemn little cluster. Tiamaat transformed, splendid in her
power, proud of her deed, looked up; and straight at me. I
don't know what she expected. Did she think I would be glad
for her? Did she want me to know how I'd been fooled? Certainly she knew she had nothing to fear. She was only doing
the same as Baal had done, and the DP had made no protest
over *his* kill. I shouted, like an idiot: "Hey, stop that!," and
the whole group scattered. They vanished into the foliage,
taking the body with them.

I said nothing to anyone. I had not, in fact, foreseen that Tiamaat would become a killer. I'd seen a talented young woman,

who would blossom if the unfairly favored young man was removed. I hadn't realized that a dominant An would behave like a dominant An, irrespective of biological sex. But I was sure my employers had grasped the situation; and it didn't matter. The long-gone, harsh symbiosis between the An and the Ki, which they preserved in their rites of kingship, was not the problem. It was the modern version, the mass market in Ki meat, the intensive farms and the factories. Tiamaat would help us to get rid of those. She would embrace the new in public, whatever she believed in private.

And the fate of the Ki would change.

The news of Baal's death had been couriered to KiAn and to the homeworlds by the time I took my transit back to the Blue. We'd started getting reactions: all positive, so to speak. Of course, there would be persistent rumors that the Ki had somehow arranged Baal's demise, but there was no harm in that. In certain situations, assassination *works*—as long as it is secret, or at least misattributed. It's a far more benign tool than most alternatives; and a lot faster. I had signed off at the Social Support Office, I'd managed to avoid goodbyes. Just before I went through to the lounge, I realized that I hadn't had my aura tag taken off. I had to go back, and go through *another* blessed gate; and Pelé caught me.

"Take the dreamtime," he insisted, holding me tight. "Play some silly game, go skydiving from Angel Falls. *Please,* Debra. Don't be conscious. You worry me."

I wondered if he suspected what I really did for a living.

Maybe so, but he couldn't possibly understand.

"I'll give it serious thought," I assured him, and kissed him goodbye.

I gave the idea of the soft option serious thought for ten paces, passed into the lounge, and found my narrow bed. I lay down there, beside my fine young cannibal, the boy who had known me for what I was. His innocent eyes . . . I lay down with them all, and with the searing terrors they bring; all my dead remembered.

I needed to launder my soul.

VERTHANDI'S RING

IAN MCDONALD

British author Ian McDonald is an ambitious and daring writer with a wide range and an impressive amount of talent. His first story was published in 1982, and since then he has appeared with some frequency in *Interzone, Asimov's Science Fiction, New Worlds, Zenith, Other Edens, Amazing,* and elsewhere. He was nominated for the John W. Campbell Award in 1985, and in 1989 he won the *Locus* Best First Novel Award for his novel *Desolation Road*. He won the Philip K. Dick Award in 1992 for his novel *King of Morning, Queen of Day*. His other books include the novels *Out on Blue Six* and *Hearts, Hands and Voices, Terminal Cafe, Sacrifice of Fools, Evolution's Shore, Kirinya*, a chapbook novella, *Tendeleo's Story, Ares Express*, and *Cyberabad*, as well as two collections of his short fiction, *Empire Dreams* and *Speaking in Tongues*. His most recent novel, *River of Gods*, was a finalist for both the Hugo Award and the Arthur C. Clarke Award in 2005, and a novella drawn from it, "The Little Goddess," was a finalist for the Hugo and the Nebula. Coming up is another new novel, *Brasyl*. Born in Manchester, England, in 1960, McDonald has spent most of his life in Northern Ireland, and now lives and works in Belfast. He has a website at http://www.lysator.liu.se/^unicorn/mcdonald/.

In the brilliant story that follows, one with enough dazzling idea content crammed densely into it to fuel many another author's eight-hundred-page novel, he shows us that total war between competing interstellar races will be slow and bloody and vast, and, well—*total*. With no room left in the galaxy—or even the universe—for the losing side.

After thirteen subjective minutes and five hundred and twenty-eight years, the Clade battleship *Ever-Fragrant Perfume of Divinity* returned to the dying solar system. The Oort cloud web pulled the crew off; skating around the gravity wells of hot fat gas giants and the swelling primary, the battleship skipped out of the system at thirty percent lightspeed into the deep dark. Small, fast, cheap, the battleships were disposable: a football of construction nanoprocessors and a pload crew of three embedded in the heart of a comet, a comet it would slowly consume over its half millennium of flight. So cheap and nasty was this ship that it was only given a name because the crew got bored five (subjective) minutes into the slow-time simulation of Sofreendi desert monasticism that was their preferred combat interface.

The Oort cloud web caught the crew, shied them to the construction yards skeined through the long, cold loops of the cometary halo, which flicked them in a stutter of lightspeed to the Fat Gas Giant relay point, where the eight hundred habitats of the new Clade daughter fleet formed a pearl belly chain around the planet; then to the Cladal Heart-world herself, basking in the coronal energies of the senile, grasping, swollen sun, and finally into fresh new selves.

"Hi guys, we're back," said the crew of *Ever-Fragrant Perfume of Divinity* as they stepped from the bronze gates of the Soulhouse, down the marble staircase into the thronged Maidan of All Luminous Passion. Irony was still a tradable commodity on this innermost tier of the hundred concentric spheres of the Heart-world, even if not one woman or man or machine or beastli turned its head. Battleship crews knew better than to expect laurels and accolades when they resouled after a hundred or a thousand or ten thousand years on the frontline. Word of *Ever-Fragrant Perfume of Divinity*'s victory had arrived almost three centuries before. A signal victory; a triumph that would be studied and taught across the Military Colleges and Academics of the Art of Defense for millennia to come. A classic Rose of Jericho strategy.

Early warning seeds sown like thistledown across half a light-millennium had felt the stroke of the Enemy across their attenuated slow senses and woke. Communication masers hastily assembled from the regoliths of cold moons beamed analyses back to the Heart-world, deep in its centuries-long task of biosphere salvation: eighty thousand habitats on the move. The Clade battle fleet launched instantly. After two hundred and twenty years, there was not a nanosecond to lose. Thirty-five ships were lost: systems malfunctions, breakdowns in the drives that kept them accelerating eternally, decades-long subtle errors of navigation that left them veering light-years wide of the target gravity well, loss of deceleration mass. Sudden total catastrophic failure. Five hundred years later, *Ever-Fragrant Perfume of Divinity* alone arrived behind the third moon of the vagrant gas giant, which wandered between stars, a gravitational exile, and began to construct the rain of antimatter warheads and set them into orbit around the wanderer. A quick plan, but a brilliant one. A Rose of Jericho plan. As *Ever-Fragrant Perfume of Divinity* accelerated away from the bright new nebula, its hindward sensors observed eighty thousand Enemy worlds plow into the bow wave of accelerated gas at forty percent light-speed and evaporate. Twenty trillion sentients died. War in space-time is slow and vast and bloody. When the species fight, there is no mercy.

In the dying echoes of the culture fleet, the three assassins of *Ever-Fragrant Perfume of Divinity* caught a vector. The fleet had not been aimed on a genocidal assault on the Clade Heart-worlds clustered around the worlds of Seydatryah, slowly becoming postbiological as the sun choked and bloated on its own gas. A vector, and a whisper: *Verthandi's Ring*.

But now they were back, huzzah! Harvest Moon and Scented Coolabar and Rose of Jericho, greatest tactician of her flesh generation. Except that when they turned around on

the steps of the Soulhouse to bicker among themselves (as
they had bickered the entire time-slowed twenty-six minutes
of the transtellar flight, and the time-accelerated two hundred years of the mission at the black wanderer) about where
to go and do and be and funk first:

"Where's Rose? Where's the Rose?" said Harvest Moon,
whose rank approximated most closely to the historical role
of Captain.

Only two resouls stood on the marble steps overlooking
the Maidan of All Luminous Pleasure.

"Shit," said Scented Coolabar, whose station corresponded to that of engineer. A soul-search returned no trace
of their crewmate on this level. In this innermost level, the
heart of the heart, a sphere of quantum nanoprocessors ten
kilometers in diameter, such a search was far-reaching—the
equivalent of every virtual mouse hole and house shrine—
and instantaneous. And blank. The two remaining crew
members of *Ever-Fragrant Perfume of Divinity* understood
too well what that meant. "We're going to have to do the
meat-thing."

Newly incarnated, Harvest Moon and Scented Coolabar
stood upon the Heaven Plain of Hoy. Clouds black as regret
bruised the upcurved horizon. Lightning fretted along the
edge of the world. Harvest Moon shivered at a fresh sensation; stringent but not unpleasant—not in that brief frisson,
though her new meat told her that in excess it might become
not just painful, but dangerous.

"What was that?" she commented, observing the small
pimples rising on her space-black skin. She wore a close-
to-species-modal body: female in this incarnation; elegant,
hairless, attenuated, the flesh of a minimalist aesthete.

"I think it was the wind," said Scented Coolabar who, as
ever, played against her Captain's type and so wore the fresh
flesh of a Dukkhim, one of the distinctive humanesque subspecies that had risen after a mass-extinction event on the
world of Kethrem, near-lost in the strata of Clade history.
She was small and broad, all ovals and slits, and possessed
of a great mane of elaborately decorated hair that grew to

the small of the back and down to the elbows. The crew of the *Ever-Fragrant Perfume of Divinity* was incarnate mere minutes, and already Harvest Moon wanted to play play play with her engineer's wonderful mane. "Maybe you should have put some clothes on." Now thunder spilled down the tilted bowl of the world to shake the small stone stupa of the incarnaculum. "I suppose we had better get started." The Dukkhim had ever been a dour, pragmatic subspecies.

Harvest Moon and Scented Coolabar spent the night in a live-skin yurt blistered from the earth of Hoy. The thunder cracked, the yurt flapped and boomed in the wind, and the plain of Hoy lowed with storm-spooked grazebeastlis, but none so loud or so persistent as Harvest Moon's moans and groans that her long black limbs were aching, burning; her body was dying dying.

"Some muscular pain is to be expected in the first hours of incarnation," chided the yurt gently. "As muscle tone develops these pains generally pass within a few days."

"Days!" wailed Harvest Moon. "Pload me back up right now."

"I can secrete general analgesia," said the tent. So until the lights came up all across the world on the sky roof ten kilometers overhead, Harvest Moon suckled sweetly on pain-numb milk from the yurt's fleshy teat, and, in the morning, she and Scented Coolabar set out in great, low-gravity bounds across the Heaven Plain of Hoy in search of Rose of Jericho. This innermost of the Heart-world meat levels had long been the preserve of ascetics and pilgrim souls; the ever upcurving plain symbolic, perhaps, of the soul's quest for its innate spiritual manifestation, or maybe because of its proximity to the virtual realms, above the sky roof, where the ploads constructed universe within universe, each bigger than the one that contained it. Yet this small grassy sphere was big enough to contain tens of thousands of pelerines and stylites, coenobites and saddhus, adrift in the ocean of grass.

"I'm sure we've been this way before," Scented Coolabar said. They were in the third monad of their quest. Eighty days ago, Harvest Moon had discovered beyond the pain of exercise the joy of muscles, even on this low-grav prairie, and could now be found at every unassigned moment delightedly studying her own matte black curves.

"I think that's the idea."

"Bloody Rose of Jericho," Scented Coolabar grumbled. They loped, three meters at a loose-limbed step, toward a dendro-eremite, a lone small tree in the wave-swept grass, bare branches upheld like prayers. "Even on the ship she was a damn ornery creature. Typical bloody selfish."

Because when Rose of Jericho went missing after the routine postsortie debrief, something else had gone missing with her. Verthandi's Ring, a name, a galactic coordinate; the vector upon which the Enemy migration had been accelerating, decade upon decade. In the enforced communality of the return flight—pload personalities intersecting and merging—Captain and Engineer alike had understood that their Mistress at Arms had deduced more than just a destination from the glowing ashes of the annihilated fleet. Soul etiquette forbade nonconsensual infringements of privacy and Rose of Jericho had used that social hiatus to conceal her speculations. Jealous monotheistic divinities were not so zealous as Clade debriefings, yet the Gentle Inquisitors of the Chamber of Ever-Renewing Waters had swept around that hidden place like sea around a reef. A vector, and a name, confirmation of the message they had received three hundred years before: Verthandi's Ring.

Even before they saw the face framed in the vulva of living wood, Harvest Moon and Scented Coolabar knew that their small quest was ended. When they first met on the virtual desert of Sofreendi for the Chamber of Ever-Renewing Waters' mission briefing (as dense and soul-piercing as its debrief), a closeness, a simpatico, suggested that they might once have been the same person; ploads copied and recopied and edited with mash-ups of other personalities. Empathy endures, across parsecs and plain, battlefronts and secrets.

"Does that hurt?" Scented Coolabar said. Greenwood crept down Rose of Jericho's brow, across her cheeks and chin, slow and certain as seasons.

"Hurt? Why should it hurt?" Wind soughed in Rose of Jericho's twigs. Harvest Moon, bored with this small world of grass, surreptitiously ran her hands down her muscled thighs.

"I don't know, it just looks, well, uncomfortable."

"No, it's very very satisfying," Rose of Jericho said. Her face was now a pinched oval of greening flesh. "Rooted. Slow." She closed her eyes in contemplation.

"Verthandi's Ring," Harvest Moon said suddenly. Scented Coolabar seated herself squatly on the grass beneath the wise tree. Beastli things squirmed beneath her ass.

"What is this game?" With life spans measurable against the slow drift of stars, millennia-long games were the weft of Clade society. "What didn't you tell them, couldn't you tell us?"

Rose of Jericho opened her eyes. The wood now joined across the bridge of her nose, her lips struggled against the lignum.

"There was not one fleet. There are many fleets. Some set off thousands of years ago."

"How many fleets?"

Rose of Jericho struggled to speak. Scented Coolabar leaned close.

"All of them. The Enemy. All of them."

Then Rose of Jericho's sparse leaves rustled and Scented Coolabar felt the ground shake beneath her. Unbalanced, Harvest Moon seized one of Rose of Jericho's branches to steady herself. Not in ten reconfigurings had either of them felt such a thing, but the knowledge was deeply burned into every memory, every cell of their incarnated flesh. The Clade Heart-world had engaged its Mach drive and was slowly, slow as a kiss, as an Edda, manipulating the weave of space-time to accelerate away from bloated, burning Seydatryah. Those unharvested must perish with the planet as the Seydatryah's family of worlds passed beyond the age of biology. Calls flickered at light-speed across the system. Strung like pearls around the gas giant, the eight hundred half-gestated daughter-habitats left their birthing orbits: half-shells, hollow environment spheres; minor Heart-worlds of a handful of tiers.

A quarter of the distance to the next star, the manufactories and system defenses out in the deep blue cold of the Oort cloud warped orbits to fall into the Heart-world's train. The Chamber of Ever-Renewing Waters, the military council, together with the Deep Blue Something, the gestalt über-mind that was the Heart-world's participatory democracy, had acted the moment it became aware of Rose of Jericho's small secret. The Seydatryah system glowed with message masers as the call went out down the decades and centuries to neighboring Heart-worlds and culture clouds and even meat planets: after one hundred thousand years, we have an opportunity to finally defeat the Enemy. Assemble your antimatter torpedoes, your planet killers, your sun-guns and quantum foam destabilizers, and make all haste for Verthandi's Ring.

"Yes, but what is Verthandi's Ring?" Scented Coolabar asked tetchily. But all that remained of Rose of Jericho was a lignified smile, cast forever in bark. From the tiny vacuum in her heart, like a tongue passing over a lost, loved tooth, she knew that Rose of Jericho had fled moments before the Chamber of Ever-Renewing Waters' interrogation system slapped her with an unbreakable subpoena and sucked her secret from her. Scented Coolabar sighed.

"Again?" Harvest Moon asked.

"Again."

In all the known universe, there was only the Clade. All life was part of it, it was all life. Ten million years ago, it had been confined to a single species on a single world—a world not forgotten, for nothing was forgotten by the Clade. That world, that system, had long since been transformed into a sphere of Heart-world orbiting a sun-halo of computational entities, but it still remembered when the bright blue eye of its home planet blinked once, twice, ten thousand times. Ships. Ships! Probe ships, sail ships, fast ships, slow ships, seed ships, ice ships; whole asteroid colonies, hollow-head comets, sent out on centuries-long falls toward other stars, other worlds. Then, after the Third Evolution, pload ships, tiny splinters of quantum computation flicked into the dark.

In the first hundred thousand years of the Clade's history, a thousand worlds were settled. In the next hundred thousand, a hundred times that. And a hundred and a hundred and a hundred; colony seeded colony seeded colony, while the space dwellers, the Heart-world habitats and virtual pload intelligences, filled up the spaces in between which, heart and truth, were the vastly greater part of the universe. Relativistic ramships fast-tracked past lumbering arc fleets; robot seed ships furled their sunsails and sprayed biospheres with life-juice; terraforming squadrons hacked dead moons and hell-planets into nests for life and intelligence and civilization. And species, already broken by the Second and Third Evolutions into space-dwellers and ploads, shattered into culture dust. Subspecies, new species, evolutions, devolutions; the race formerly known as humanity blossomed into the many-petaled chrysanthemum of the Clade; a society on the cosmological scale; freed from the deaths of suns and worlds, immune, immortal, growing faster than it could communicate its gathered self-knowledge back to its immensely ancient and powerful Type 4 civilizations; entire globular clusters turned to hiving, howling quantum-nanoprocessors.

New species, subspecies, hybrid species. Life was profligate in the cosmos; even multicellular life. The Clade incorporated DNA from a hundred thousand alien biospheres and grew in richness and diversity. Intelligence alone was unique. In all its One Giant Leap, the Clade had never encountered another bright with sentience and the knowledge of its own mortality that was the key to civilization. The Clade was utterly alone. And thus intelligence became the watchword and darling of the Clade: intelligence, that counterentropic conjoined twin of information, must become the most powerful force in the universe, the energy to which all other physical laws must eventually kneel. Intelligence alone could defeat the heat-death of the universe, the dark wolf at the long thin end of time. Intelligence was destiny, manifest.

And then a Hujjain reconnaissance probe, no bigger than the thorn of a rose but vastly more sharp, cruising the edge of a dull little red dwarf, found a million habitats pulled

in around the stellar embers. When the Palaelogos of the
Byzantine Orthodoxy first encountered the armies of Islam
crashing out of the south, he had imagined them just another
heretical Christian sect. So had the Hujjain probe doubted;
then, as it searched its memory, the entire history of the
Clade folded into 11-space, came revelation. There was Another out there.

In the six months it took the Seydatryah fleet—one Heart-
world, eighty semi-operational habitats, two hundred twelve
thousand ancillary craft and defensive systems—to accelerate to close enough to light-speed for time-dilation effects
to become significant, Harvest Moon and Scented Coolabar
searched the Tier of Anchyses. The world-elevator, which
ran from the portals of the Virtual Realms through which
nothing corporeal might pass to the very lowest, heavy-gee
Tier of Pterimonde, a vast and boundless ocean, took the star-
sailors forty kilometers and four tiers down to the SkyPort of
Anchyses, an inverted city that hung like a chandelier, a sea
urchin, a crystal geode, from the sky roof. Blimps and zeps,
balloon clusters and soaring gliders fastened on the ornate
tower bottoms to load, and fuel, and feed, and receive passengers. Ten kilometers below, beyond cirrus and nimbus,
the dread forest of Kyce thrashed and twined, a venomous,
vicious, hooked-and-clawed ecosystem that had evolved
over the Heart-world's million-year history around the fallen
bodies of sky dwellers.

The waxing light of tier-dawn found Scented Coolabar on
the observation deck of the dirigible *We Have Left Undone
That Which We Ought to Have Done*. The band of transparent skin ran the entire equator of the kilometer-long
creature: in her six months as part of the creature's higher-
cognitive function, Scented Coolabar had evolved small tics
and habits, one of which was watching the birth of a new
day from the very forward point of the dirigible. The Morning Salutationists were rolling up their sutra mats as Scented
Coolabar took her place by the window and imagined her
body cloaked in sky. She had changed body for this level; a
tall, slightly hirsute male with a yellow-tinged skin, but she

had balked at taking the same transition as Harvest Moon.
Even now, she looped and tumbled out there in the pink
and lilac morning, in acrobatic ecstasy with her flockmates
among the indigo clouds.

Dawn light gleamed from silver wing feathers. Pain and
want and, yes, jealousy clutched Scented Coolabar. Harvest
Moon had been the one who bitched and carped about the
muscle pain and the sunburn and the indigestion and the
necessity to clean one's teeth; the duties and fallibilities
of incarnation. Yet she had fallen in love with corporeal-
ity; reveled in the physicality of wind in her pinions, gravity tugging at the shapely curve of her ass; while Scented
Coolabar remained solid, stolid, reluctant flesh. She could
no longer remember the last time they had had sex; physically or virtually. Games. And war was just another game
to entities hundreds of thousands of years old, for whom
death was a sleep and a forgetting, and a morning like this,
fresh and filled with light. She remembered the actions they
had fought: the reduction of Yorrrt, the defense of Thau-
Pek-Sat, where Rose of Jericho had annihilated an Enemy
strike-fleet with a blizzard of micro–black holes summoned
out of the universal quantum foam, exploding almost instantly in a holocaust of Hawking radiation. She watched
Harvest Moon's glider-thin wings deep down in the brightening clouds, thin as dreams and want. Sex was quick; sex
was easy, even sacramental, among the many peoples and
sects that temporarily formed the consciousness of *We Have
Left Undone That Which We Ought to Have Done*. She
sighed and felt the breath shudder in her flat, muscled chest.
Startled by a reaction as sensational, as physical, as any Im-
melman or slow loop performed by Harvest Moon, Scented
Coolabar felt tears fill and roll. Memory, a frail and trickster
faculty among the incarnate, took her back to another body,
a woman's body, a woman of the Teleshgathu nation; drawn
in wonder and hope and young excitement up the space elevator to the Clade habitat that had warped into orbit around
her world to repair and restore and reconstitute its radiation shield from the endless oceans of her world. From that
woman of a parochial waterworld had sprung three entities,

closer than sisters, deeper than lovers. Small wonder they needed each other, to the point of searching through eighty billion sentients. Small wonder they could never escape each other. The light was bright now, its unvarying shadow strict and stark on the wooden deck. Harvest Moon flashed her wings and rolled away, diving with her new friends deep through layer upon layer of cloud. And Scented Coolabar felt an unfamiliar twitch, a clench between the legs, a throb of something already exposed and sensitive becoming superattuned, swinging like a diviner's pendulum. Her balls told her, clear, straight, no arguments: she's out there. Rose of Jericho.

Twenty subjective minutes later, the Clade fleet was eighty light-years into its twelve hundred objective-year flight to intercept the Enemy advance toward Verthandi's Ring, the greatest sentient migration since the big bang. Populations numbered in logarithmic notation, like outbreaks of viruses, are on the move in two hundred million habitat-ships, each fifty times the diameter of the Seydatryah Heart-world. Of course the Seydatryah cluster is outnumbered, of course it will be destroyed down to the last molecule if it engages the Enemy migration, but the Deep Blue Something understands that it may not be the biggest or the strongest, but it is the closest and will be the first. So the culture cluster claws closer toward light-speed; its magnetic shield furled around it like an aurora, like a cloak of fire, as it absorbs energies that would instantly incinerate all carbon life in its many levels and ships. And, nerve-wired into an organic ornithopter, Scented Coolabar drops free from the *We Have Left Undone That Which We Ought to Have Done*'s launch teats into eighty kilometers of empty airspace. Scented Coolabar shrieks, then the ornithopter's wings scrape and cup and the scream becomes *oooh* as the biological machine scoops across the sky.

"Where away?" Scented Coolabar shouts. The ornithopter unfolds a telescope, bending an eye; Scented Coolabar spies the balloon cluster low and breaking from a clot of cumulus. A full third of the netted balloons are dead, punctured, black and rotting. The ornithopter reads her intention and dives. A flash of sun-silver: Harvest Moon rises vertically out of the cloud, hangs in the air, impossibly elongated wings catching the morning light, then turns and tumbles to loop over Scented Coolabar's manically beating wings.

"That her?"

"That's her." *You are very lovely,* thought Scented Coolabar. *Lovely and alien.* But not so alien as Rose of Jericho, incarnated as a colony of tentacled balloons tethered in a veil of organic gauze, now terminally sagging toward the claspers and bone blades of Kyce. The ornithopter matched speed; wind whipped Scented Coolabar's long yellow hair. A lunge, a sense of the world dropping away, or at least her belly, and then the ornithopter's claws were hooked into the mesh. The stench of rotting balloon flesh assailed Scented Coolabar's senses. A soft pop, a rush of reeking gas, a terrifying drop closer to the fanged mouths of the forest: another balloon had failed. Harvest Moon, incarnated without feet or wheels, for her species was never intended to touch the ground, turned lazy circles in the sky.

"Same again?" Scented Coolabar asked. Rose of Jericho spoke through radio-sense into her head.

"Of course."

Foolish of Scented Coolabar to imagine a Rose of Jericho game being ended so simply or so soon.

"The Deep Blue Something has worked it out."

"I should hope so." The balloon cluster was failing, sinking fast. With the unaided eye Scented Coolabar could see the lash-worms and bladed dashers racing along the sucker-studded tentacles of the forest canopy. This round of the game was almost ended. She hoped her ornithopter was smart enough to realize the imminent danger.

"And Verthandi's Ring?" Harvest Moon asked.

"Is a remnant superstring." A subquantal fragment of the original big-bang fireball, caught by cosmic inflation and stretched to macroscopic, then to cosmological scale. Rarer than virtue or phoenixes, remnant superstrings haunted the galactic fringes and the vast spaces between star spirals; tens, hundreds of light-years long. In all the Clade's mcmory, only one had ever been recorded within the body of the galaxy. Until now. "Tied into a loop," Rose of Jericho added. Scented Coolabar and Harvest Moon understood at once. Only the hand of the Enemy—if the Enemy possessed such things, no communication had ever been made with them, no physical trace ever found from the wreckage of their ships or their vaporized colony clusters—could have attained such a thing. And that was why the Chamber of Ever-Renewing Waters had launched the Heart-world. Such a thing could only be an ultimate weapon.

But what does it do? Scented Coolabar and Harvest Moon asked at once, but the presence in their brains, one humanesque, one man-bat-glider, was gone. Game over. A new round beginning. With a shriek of alarm, the ornithopter cast free just in time to avoid the tendrils creeping up over the canopies of the few surviving balloons. The tentacles of the forest clasped those of the balloon cluster and hauled it down. Then the blades came out.

How do wars begin? Through affront, through bravado, through stupidity or overconfidence, through sacred purpose or greed. But when galactic cultures fight, it is out of inevitability, out of a sense of cosmic tragedy. It is through understanding of a simple evolutionary truth: there can be only one exploiter of an ecological niche, even if that niche is the size of a universe. Within milliseconds of receiving the inquisitive touch of the Hujjain probe, the Enemy realized this truth. The vaporizing of the probe was the declaration of war, and would have given the Enemy centuries of a head start had not the Hujjain craft in its final milliseconds squirted off a burst of communication to its mother array deep in the cometary system on the edge of interstellar space.

In the opening centuries of the long, slow war, the Clade's expansion was checked and turned back. Trillions died. Planets were cindered; populations sterilized beneath a burning ultraviolet sky, their ozone layers and protective magnetic fields stripped away; habitat clusters incinerated by induced solar flares or reduced to slag by nanoprocessor plagues; Dyson spheres shattered by billions of antimatter warheads.

The Clade was slow to realize what the Enemy understood from the start: that a war for the resources that intelligence required—energy, mass, gravity— must be a war of extermination. In the first two thousand years of the war, the Clade's losses equaled the total biomass of its original prestarflight solar system. But its fecundity, the sheer irrepressibility of life, was the Clade's strength. It fought back. Across centuries it fought; across distances so vast the light of victory or defeat would be pale, distant winks in the night sky of far future generations. In the hearts of globular clusters they fought, and the radiant capes of nebulae; through the looping fire bridges on the skins of suns and along the event horizons of black holes. Their weapons were gas giants and the energies of supernovae; they turned asteroid belts into shotguns and casually flung living planets into the eternal ice of interstellar space. Fleets ten thousand a side clashed between suns, leaving not a single survivor. It was war absolute, elemental. Across a million star systems, the Clade fought the Enemy to a standstill. And, in the last eight hundred years, began to drive them back.

Now, time dilated to the point where a decade passed in a single heartbeat, total mass close to that of a thousand stars, the Clade Heart-world Seydatryah and its attendant culture cluster plunged at a prayer beneath light-speed toward the closed cosmic string loop of Verthandi's Ring. She flew blind; no information, no report could outrun her. Her half trillion sentients would arrive with only six months forewarning into what might be the final victory, or the Enemy's final stand.

Through the crystal shell of the Heart-world, they watched the Clade attack fleet explode like thistledown against the glowing nebula of the Enemy migration. Months ago those battleships had died, streaking ahead of the decelerating Seydatryah civilization to engage the Enemy pickets and, by dint of daring and force of fortune, perhaps break through to attack a habitat cluster. The greater mass of the Clade, dropping down the blue shift as over the years and decades they fell in behind Seydatryah, confirmed the astonished reports of those swift, bold fighters. All the Enemy was here; a caravanserai hundreds of light-years long. Ships, worlds, had been under way for centuries before *Ever-Fragrant Perfume of Divinity* located and destroyed one of the pilgrim fleets. The order must have been given millennia before; shortly after the Clade turned the tide of battle in its favor. Retreat. Run away. But the Enemy had lost none of its strength and savagery as wave after wave of the cheap, fast, sly battle-ships were annihilated.

Scented Coolabar and Harvest Moon and Rose of Jericho huddled together in the deep dark and crushing pressure of the ocean at the bottom of the world. They wore the form of squid; many-tentacled and big-eyed, communicating by coded ripples of bioluminescent frills along their streamlined flanks. They did not doubt that they had watched themselves die time after time out there. It was likely that only they had died, a million deaths. The Chamber of Ever-Renewing Waters would never permit its ace battleship crew to desert into the deep, starlit depths of Pterimonde. Their ploads had doubtless been copied a million times into the swarm of fast attack ships. The erstwhile crew of the *Ever-Fragrant Perfume of Divinity* blinked their huge golden eyes. Over the decades and centuries, the light of the Enemy's retreat would be visible over the entire galaxy, a new and gorgeous ribbon nebula. Now, a handful of light-months from the long march, the shine of hypervelocity particles impacting the deflection fields was a banner in the sky, a starbow across an entire quadrant. And ahead, Verthandi's Ring, a starless void three light-years in diameter.

"You won them enough time," Scented Coolabar said in a flicker of blue and green. The game was over. It ended at the lowest place in the world, but it had been won years before, she realized. It had been won the moment Rose of Jericho diverted herself away from the Soulhouse into a meditation tree on the Holy Plains of Hoy.

"I believe so," Rose of Jericho said, hovering a kiss away from the crystal wall, holding herself against the insane Coriolis storms that stirred this high-gravity domain of waters. "It will be centuries before the Clade arrives in force."

"The Chamber of Ever-Renewing Waters could regard it as treachery," Harvest Moon said. Rose of Jericho touched the transparency with a tentacle.

"Do I not serve them with heart and mind and life?" The soft fireworks were fewer now; one by one they faded to nothing. "And anyway, what would they charge me with? Handing the Clade the universe on a plate?"

"Or condemning the Clade to death," said Scented Coolabar.

"Not our Clade."

She had been brilliant, Scented Coolabar realized. To have worked it out in those few minutes of subjective flight, and known what to do to save the Clade. But she had always been the greatest strategic mind of her generation. Not for the first time Scented Coolabar wondered about their lost forebear, that extraordinary female who had birthed them from her ploaded intellect.

What is Verthandi's Ring? A closed cosmic string. And what is a closed cosmic string? A time machine. A portal to the past. But not the past of *this* universe. Any transit of a closed timelike loop led inevitably to a parallel universe. In that time-stream, there too was war; Clade and Enemy, locked in Darwinian combat. And in that universe, as the Enemy was driven back to gaze into annihilation, Verthandi's Ring opened and a second Enemy, a duplicate Enemy in every way, came out of the sky. They had handed the Clade this universe; the prize for driving its parallel in the *alternate* time-stream to extinction.

Cold-blooded beneath millions of tons of deep cold pressure, Scented Coolabar shivered. Rose of Jericho had assessed the tactical implications and made the only possible choice: delay the Chamber of Ever-Renewing Waters and the Deep Blue Something so they could not prevent the Enemy exiting this universe. A bloodless win. An end to war. Intelligence the savior of the blind, physical universe. While in the second time-stream, Clade habitats burst like crushed eyeballs and worlds were scorched bare and the Enemy found its resources suddenly doubled.

Scented Coolabar doubted that she could ever make such a

deal. But she was an Engineer, not a Mistress of Arms. Her tentacles caressed Rose of Jericho's lobed claspers; a warm sexual thrill pulsed through her muscular body.

"Stay with us, stay with me," Harvest Moon said. Her decision was made, the reluctant incarnation; she had fallen in love with the flesh and would remain exploring the Heart-world's concentric tiers in thousands of fresh and exciting bodies.

"No, I have to go." Rose of Jericho briefly brushed Harvest Moon's sexual tentacles. "They won't hurt me. They knew I had no choice, as they had no choice."

Scented Coolabar turned in the water. Her fins rippled, propelling her upward through the pitch-black water. Rose of Jericho fell in behind her. In a few strong strokes, the lights of Harvest Moon's farewell faded, even the red warmth of her love, and all that remained was the centuries-deep shine of the starbow beyond the wall of the world.

HATCH

ROBERT REED

Robert Reed sold his first story in 1986, and quickly established himself as a frequent contributor to *The Magazine of Fantasy and Science Fiction* and *Asimov's Science Fiction*, as well as selling many stories to *Science Fiction Age, Universe, New Destinies, Tomorrow, Synergy, Starlight,* and elsewhere. Reed may be one of the most prolific of today's young writers, particularly at short fiction lengths, seriously rivaled for that position only by authors such as Stephen Baxter and Brian Stableford. And—also like Baxter and Stableford—he manages to keep up a very high standard of quality *while* being prolific, something that is not at all easy to do. Reed stories such as "Sister Alice," "Brother Perfect," "Decency," "Savior," "The Remoras," "Chrysalis," "Whiptail," "The Utility Man," "Marrow," "Birth Day," "Blind," "The Toad of Heaven," "Stride," "The Shape of Everything," "Guest of Honor," "Waging Good," and "Killing the Morrow," among at least a half-dozen others equally as strong, count as some of the best short work produced by anyone in the eighties and nineties; many of his best stories were assembled in his first collection, *The Dragons of Springplace.* Nor is he nonprolific as a novelist, having turned out eight novels since the end of the eighties, including *The Lee Shore, The Hormone Jungle, Black Milk, The Remarkables, Down the Bright Way, Beyond the Veil of Stars, An Exaltation of Larks, Beneath the Gated Sky, Marrow,* and *Sister Alice.* His most recent books are a chapbook novella, *Mere,* a new collection, *The Cuckoo's Boys,* and a new novel, *The Well of Stars.* Coming up is a new novella chapbook, *Flavors of My Genius.* Reed lives with his family in Lincoln, Nebraska.

The "Sister Alice" stories, in which advanced humans with the powers and abilities of gods played out intricate political intrigues and struggles across a time span of millions of years, eventually collected in the mosaic novel *Sister Alice,* were Reed's first great contribution to the New Space Opera. In 1994, he launched a long series of stories, still continuing today, about the Great Ship: a Jupiter-sized starship found abandoned in deep space by exploring humans and retrofitted into a kind of immense interstellar cruise ship, off on a grand tour of the galaxy (circumnavigating it, in fact, a voyage that will take eons), with dozens of human and alien customers of different races aboard. In the powerful story that follows, which takes place after a disastrous attempt to hijack the Great Ship has reduced it nearly to ruins, he shows us what happens to some human survivors of the battle who are stranded *outside* of the Ship, locked out of the interior for generations, forced to create their own society on the hull—a place that, as it turns out, is equipped with quite a few wonders—and dangers—of its own.

1

Yes, the galaxy possessed an ethereal beauty, particularly when magnified inside the polished bowl of a perfect mirror. Every raider conceded as much. And yes, the rocket nozzle on which they lived was a spectacular feature, vast and ancient, its bowllike depths filled with darkness and several flavors of ice laid over a plain of impenetrable hyperfiber. Even the refugee city was lovely in its modest fashion, simple homes and little businesses clinging to the inside surface of the sleeping nozzle. But true raiders understood that the most intriguing, soul-soaring view was found when you stood where Peregrine was standing now: perched some five thousand kilometers above the hull, staring down at the Polypond—a magnificent, ever-changing alien body that stretched past the neighboring nozzles, reaching the far horizon and beyond, submerging both faces of a magnificent starship that itself was larger than worlds.

The Polypond had arrived thousands of years ago, descending as a violent rain of comet-sized bodies, scalding vapor, and sentient, hate-filled mud. The alien had wanted to destroy the Great Ship, and perhaps even today it dreamed of nothing less. But most of the city's inhabitants believed the war was over now, and in one fashion or another, the Ship had won. Some were sure the alien had surrendered unconditionally. Others believed that the Polypond's single mind had collapsed, leaving a multitude of factions endlessly fighting with one another. Both tales explained quite a lot, including the monster's indifference to a few million refugees living just beyond its boundaries. But the most compelling idea—the notion that always captivated Peregrine—was that human beings had not only won the war, but killed their foe too. Its central mind was destroyed, all self-control had been vanquished, and what the young man saw from his diamond blister was nothing more, or less, than a great corpse in the throes of ferocious, creative rot.

Whatever the truth, the Polypond was a spectacle, and no raider understood it better than Peregrine did.

Frigid wisps of atomic oxygen and nitrogen marked the alien's upper reaches, with dust and buckyballs and aerogel trash wandering free. That high atmosphere reached halfway to the hull, and it ended with a sequence of transparent skins—monomolecular sheets, mostly, plus a few energetic demon-doors laid out flat. Retaining gas and heat was their apparent purpose, and when those skins were pierced, what lay below could feel the prick, and on occasion, react instantly.

Beneath the skins was a thick wet atmosphere, not just warm but hot—a fierce blazing wealth of changeable gases and smart dusts, floating clouds and rooted clouds, plus features that refused description by any language. And drenching that realm was a wealth of light. The glare wasn't constant or evenly distributed. What passed for day came as splashes and winding rivers, and the color of the light as well as its intensity and duration would vary. After spending most of his brief life watching the purples and crimsons, emeralds and golds, plus a wealth of blues that stretched from the brilliant to the soothing, Peregrine had realized that each color and its intricate shape held meaning.

"A common belief," Hawking had told him. "But your translator AIs cannot find any message, or even the taste of genuine language."

"Except I wasn't thinking language," Peregrine countered. "Not at all."

His friend wanted more of an answer, signaling his desires with silence and circular gestures from his most delicate arms.

"I meant plain simple beauty," the young man continued. "I'm talking about art, about visual poetry. I'm thinking about a magnificent show performed for a very special audience."

"You might be the only soul holding that opinion," Hawking counseled.

"And I feel honored because of it," Peregrine had laughed.

The Polypond's atmosphere was full of motion and energy, and it was exceptionally loud. Camouflaged microphones set near the base of the rocket nozzle sent home the constant roar of wind sounds and mouth sounds, thunder from living clouds and the musical whine of great wings. But even richer than the air was the watery terrain beneath: tens of kilometers deep, the Polypond's body was built from melted comets mixed with rock and metal stolen from vanished worlds. This was an ocean in the same sense that a human body was mere salt water. Yes, it was liquid, but jammed full of structure and purpose. Alien tissues supplied muscles and spines and ribs, and there were regions serving roles not unlike those of human hearts and livers and lungs. Long, sophisticated membranes were dotted with giant fusion reactors. And drifting on the surface were island-sized organs that spat out free-living entities— winged entities that would gather in huge flocks and some- times rise en masse, millions and even billions of them soaring higher than any cloud.

Hatches, those events were called.

What Peregrine knew—what every person in his trade understood—was that each hatch was a unique event, and the great majority were worthless. Sending a fleet of raid- ers that returned with only a few thousand tons of winged muscle and odd enzymes . . . well, that was a waste of their limited power, and always a potential waste of lives. What mattered were those rare hatches that rose high enough to be reached cheaply, and even then it didn't pay to send raiders if there wasn't some respectable chance of acquiring hyper- fiber or rare elements, or best of all, machines that could be harvested and tamed, then set to work in whatever role the city demanded.

Judging a hatch's value was three parts diagnosis, two parts art, and, inevitably, ten parts good fortune. Telescopes tied into dim-witted machines did nothing but happily stuff data into shapes that brighter AIs could analyze. Whatever was promising or peculiar was sent to the raider leaders. The average day brought ten or fifteen events worthy of closer examination, and because of his service record, Peregrine was given first glance at those candidates. But even with ripe pickings, he often did nothing. Other raiders flying their own ships would dive into the high atmosphere every few days. But sometimes weeks passed without Peregrine once being tempted to sit in the pilot's padded chair.

"I want to grow old in this job," he confessed whenever his bravery was questioned. "Most souls can't do what I do. Most of you are too brave, and bravery is suicide. Fearlessness is a handicap. Chasing every million-wing flight of catabolites or sky-spinners is the quickest way to go bankrupt, if you're lucky. Or worse, die."

"That is a reasonable philosophy," his friend mentioned, speaking through the voice box sewn into a convenient neural center.

"I'm sorry," Peregrine replied. "I wasn't talking to you. I was chatting with a woman friend."

The alien lifted one of his intricate limbs, signaling puzzlement. "And where is this woman?"

"Inside my skull." Peregrine gave his temple a few hard taps. "I met her last night. I thought she was pretty, and she was pleasant enough. But she said some critical words about raiders wasting too many resources, and I thought she was accusing me of being a coward."

"You listed your sensible reasons, of course."

"Not all of them," he admitted.

"Why not?"

"I told you," said Peregrine. "I thought she was pretty. And if I acted like an unapologetic coward, I wouldn't get invited to her bedroom."

Hawking absorbed this tidbit about human spawning. Or he simply ignored it. Who could know what that creature was thinking beneath his thick carapace? Low-built and long, Hawking held a passing resemblance to an earthly trilobite. A trio of crystalline eyes pulled in light from all directions, delicate optical tissues teasing the meaning out of every photon. His armored body was carried on dozens of jointed legs. But where trilobites had three sections to their insectlike bodies, this alien had five. And where trilobites were dim-witted creatures haunting the floors of ancient seas, Hawking's ancestors had evolved grasping limbs and large, intricate minds while scurrying across the lush surface of a low-gravity world.

Hawking was not a social animal. And this was a blessing, since he was the only one of his kind in the city. Peregrine had studied the available files about his species, but the local data sinks were intended to help military operations, not educate any would-be xenologists. And likewise, after spending decades in close association with the creature, and despite liking as well as admiring him, Peregrine found there were moments when old Mr. Hawking was nothing but peculiar, standoffish, and quite impossible to read.

But Peregrine had a taste for challenges.

"Anyway," he said, cutting into the silence. "I lied to that woman. I told her that I wasn't flying because I knew something big was coming. I had a feeling, and until that ripe moment, I was resting both my body and my ship."

"And she believed you?"

"Perhaps."

After a brief silence, Hawking said, "She sounds like a foolish young creature."

"And that's where you're wrong." Peregrine laughed and shrugged. "Just as I hoped, I climbed into her bed. And during one of our slow moments, she admitted who she was."

"And she is?"

"An engineer during the War. She was working in the repair yards while my mother was serving as a pilot. So like you, my new girlfriend is one of the original founders."

"Interesting," his friend responded.

"Fusillade is her name," he mentioned. "And she seems to know you."

"Yet I do not know her."

Then Peregrine added, "And by the way, she very clearly remembers your arrival here."

Fourteen moon-sized rocket nozzles stood upon the Great Ship's aft, and during the fighting, the center nozzle served as the gathering place for tired pilots and engineers and such. Once the fighting ended, representatives of twenty different species found themselves trapped in this most unpromising location, utterly isolated, with few working machines, minimal data sinks, and no raw materials. Facing them was the daunting task of building some kind of workable society. Hawking was a rarity—the rich passenger who had visited the hull before the comets began to fall, and who managed to outlive both his guides and fellow tourists. Alone, this solitary creature had scaled one of the outlying nozzles, and then his luck lasted long enough to find passage with a harum-scarum unit—the final group of refugees to make it to this poor but safe place.

"She feels sorry for you, Hawking."

"Why would she?"

"Because you're a species with a population of one."

The alien was unimpressed with that assessment. He cut the air with two limbs, his natural mouth rippling before leaking a disapproving click.

"I know better than that," Peregrine continued. "I told her that you're a loner, that it's difficult for you to share breathing space with me, and you know me and approve of me far more than you know and approve of anyone else."

The creature had no reply.

"'Why call him Hawking?' she asked me. 'Nobody else does.'"

"Few others speak to me," his friend said.

"I explained that too," said Peregrine. "And I told her that your species are so peculiar, you never see reason for any permanent names. When two of you cross trails, each invents a new name for himself or herself. A private name that lasts only as long as that single perishable relationship."

The limbs gave the air an agreeable sweep.

"You picked Hawking, and I don't know why," Peregrine continued. "Except it's a solid sound humans can utter. Unlike your own species' name, of course."

Quietly, with his natural mouth, Hawking made a sharp clicking sound followed by what sounded like "!Eech."

"!Eech," the human tried to repeat.

As always, there was something intensely humorous about his clumsy attempt. Nothing changed in the creature's dome-like eyes or the rigid face, but suddenly all of the long legs wiggled together, signaling laughter, the ripples moving happily beneath his hard low unreadable body.

2

"And I remember your mother," the old woman had mentioned last night.

Like that of every citizen, Fusillade's apartment was tiny and cold; power had always been a scarce commodity in the city. But her furnishings were better than most, made from fancy plastics and cultured flesh, and even a glass tub filled with spare water. Winking at her young lover, she added, "No, I doubt if your mother ever actually knew me. By name, I mean. But I was part of the team that kept those early raider ships flying. Without twenty ad-lib repairs from me, that woman wouldn't be half the hero she is today."

Peregrine's mother was as famous as anyone in the city, and that despite being dead for dozens of centuries. She had defended these giant rockets during the Polypond War. But the alien eventually destroyed each of the Great Ship's engines, choking and plugging every vent, trying to keep reinforcements from reaching the hull. And at the same time, the captains below had blocked every doorway, desperate to keep the Polypond from infiltrating the interior. Brutal fights were waged near the main ports, but none had lasted long. A barrage of tiny black holes was fired through the Ship's heart, but none delivered a killing blow. Then the final assault came, and despite long odds, a starship that was more ancient than any visible sun survived.

Afterward, over the course of several months and then several years, the Polypond grew quieter, and by every credible measure, less menacing.

Something was different. The alien was different, and maybe the Great Ship too. But those few thousand survivors could never be sure what had changed. With the clarity of the doomed, they had come here and built a refugee camp. Peregrine's mother was a natural leader. Like her son, she was a small person, dark as space, blessed with long limbs and a gymnast's perfect balance. And she was more than just an early raider. No, what made the woman special was that she was first to realize that nobody was coming to rescue them. The giant engines remained dead and blocked. High-grade hyperfiber had plugged even the most obscure route through the armored hull. And even worse, the Great Ship was now undergoing some mysterious but undeniable acceleration. Without one working rocket, the world-sized machine was gaining velocity, hurrying its way along a course that would soon take it out of the Milky Way.

Peregrine's mother helped invent the raider's trade. In makeshift vehicles, she dove into the Polypond's atmosphere, stealing volatiles and rare earths, plus the occasional machine-encrusted body. Those treasures allowed them to build shelters and synthesize food. Every few days, she bravely led an expedition into the monster's body, stealing what was useful and accepting every danger.

Time and Fate ensured her death.

She left no body, save for a few useful pieces that made up her meager estate. Her funeral was held ages ago, yet even today, whenever an important anniversary arrived, those rites and her name were repeated by thousands of thankful souls.

By contrast, Peregrine's father was neither heroic nor well regarded. But he was a prosperous fellow, and he was shrewd, and when one of the great woman's eggs came on the market, he spent a fortune to obtain it and a second fortune to build the first artificial womb in the city's history.

"I remember your mother," the old woman told Peregrine, plainly proud of any casual association. Then with an important tone, she added, "That good woman would have been pleased with her young son. I'm sure."

Peregrine was almost three hundred years old, which made him young—particularly in the eyes of a much older lady who seemed to be happily feeding a fantasy. He offered nods and a polite smile, saying, "Well, thank you."

"And I know your father fairly well," she continued.

"I never see the man," Peregrine replied with a sneer, warning her off the topic.

"I know," she said.

Then after a pause, she asked, "Did you mean it? Do you really feel that an especially large hatch is coming?"

"No," he replied, finally admitting the truth.

Then before his honesty evaporated, he added, "There are no trends, and I don't have intuitions. And I never, ever see into the future."

Something in those words made the old woman laugh. Then quietly, with a sudden tenderness, she said, "Darling. Everybody sees some little part of the future. Only the dead can't. And if you think about it, you'll realize . . . nothing more important separates big-eyed us from poor cold blind them."

3

There was nothing to add after Peregrine's laughable attempt to say "!Eech." Hawking fell into a deep silence, indistinguishable from countless others; and Peregrine responded with his own purposeful quiet. He was sitting at one end of the hangar, working with the latest data about hatches and general Polypond activity. His friend stood near the raider ship. Which was less animated, that sleeping machine or the alien? Hours and even days might pass, and the creature wouldn't move one antenna. Yet Hawking claimed to never feel lonely or bored. "A respectable mind always has fascinating tasks waiting in its neurons," he would say. Which was why his very odd species lacked the words to describe painful solitude or empty time.

The day's hatches were distant and scarce.

Peregrine finally gave up the hunt. He sat at the end of the diamond blister, feeling the cold of deep space and studying the ever-changing scenery below. Clouds were gathering between their home nozzle and the next, the thinnest and lightest clouds shoved high above the others. This happened on occasion, and it meant nothing. But the result was a splotch of deep blackness, larger than a healthy continent and unpromising to the bare human eye.

Just to be sure, Peregrine played with infrared frequencies and flashes of laser light to make delicate measurements. Something inside that blackness was different, he noticed. Straight before him, something was beginning to happen. That's why he wasn't particularly surprised when the clouds began to split, bleeding a strange golden light that was brighter than anything else in view.

Through his own telescope, he saw the vanguards of the rising hatch.

Moments later, on a shielded line, an AI expert contacted him. With a navigational code and the simple words "This interests," the machine changed the complexion of Peregrine's day and his week.

Having a worthy topic, he admitted to Hawking, "I thought I was lying to that woman. About having intuitions, I mean.

But look at this hatch! Look at the diversity. And that's without being able to see much of it yet." His heart was pounding, his voice dry and quick. "I don't know if anybody has seen, ever . . . a hatch as big and diverse as this one . . ."

Hawking did not move, but the hemispherical eyes absorbed the data in a few moments. Then the complicated mouth of tendrils and rasping teeth made a series of little motions—motions that Peregrine had never seen before, and chose to ignore for the moment.

"I'm leaving," the human announced.

Every raider with a working ship would be embarking now.

"It's going to be a rich day," he continued, throwing himself into the first layer of his flight suit.

Finally, Hawking spoke.

"You are my friend," said the alien, nothing about his voice out of the ordinary. "And from all that is possible, I wish you the best."

4

Simplicity was the hallmark of a raider's ship. The hull was made from diamond scales bolstered with nanowhiskers, all laid across a flexible skeleton of salvaged hyperfiber. Resting in its berth, Peregrine's ship held a long, elegant shape reminiscent of the harpoons that populated ancient novels about fishermen and lost seas. But that narrow body swelled when liquid hydrogen was pushed into the fuel tanks. One inefficient fusion reactor fed a lone engine that was sloppy but powerful. The launch felt like the endless slap of a monster's paw, brutal enough to smash bone and pulverize the sternest living flesh. But like every citizen, Peregrine was functionally immortal, blessed with repair mechanisms that could take the stew inside a flight suit and remake the man who had been sitting there.

His body died, and time leaped across a string of uneventful minutes.

Opening new eyes, Peregrine found himself coasting, climbing away from the Great Ship. Six AIs of various temperaments and skills made up his crew. In his absence, they had continued studying the available data. One served as his pilot, and even when Peregrine reclaimed the helm, the machine waited at a nanosecond's distance, ready to correct any glaring mistakes.

Inside any large hatch, the multitude of bodies came in different shapes, different species. The AI most familiar with mercantile matters pointed at the center of the hatch. "These gull-wands match those we saw fifteen years ago. Their wings had some good-grade hyperfiber, and nearly ten percent of the collected hearts were salvageable."

Gull-wands had tiny fusion reactors in their chests. One reactor was powerful enough to light and heat a modest home.

"How much could we make?" Peregrine asked.

An estimate was generated, followed by an impressed silence from every sentient entity.

But then Peregrine noticed a closer feature. "Over here... is that some kind of cloud?"

"No," was the best guess.

The mass was black along its surfaces, swirling in its interior, and through cracks that were tiny at any distance, glimmers of a fantastically bright blue-white light emerged.

"Anything like it in the records?"

There was an optical similarity to clouds of tiny, extremely swift bodies observed only eight times in the past.

"In my past?"

"Not in your life, no," one voice replied. "During the city's life, I mean."

"Okay. What were those bodies made of?"

That was unknown, since none had ever been captured.

"So pretend we're seeing them," he began. "Estimate the numbers in that single gathering."

"The flock is enormous," another AI reported. "In the range of ten or eleven billion—"

"That's what we want!" Peregrine exclaimed.

Skeptical whispers buzzed in his ears.

But the human pointed out, "Everyone else is going to be harvesting gull-wands. Hearts and hyperfiber are going to bc chcap for the next hundred years. But if we find something new and special. . . even gathering up just a few of them. . . we could pocket several fortunes, and maybe even upgrade our ship. . ."

His crew had to like the sound of that.

"But reaching the target," warned the pilot, "will entail burning a large portion of our reserves—"

"So do it now," Peregrine ordered, releasing the helm.

And for the second time in a very brief while, his fine young body was crushed into an anonymous jelly.

5

There was no perfect consensus about what the Polypond was—undiminished foe, mad psyche divided against itself, or the spectacular carcass of a once great foe. And in the same fashion, there were competing ideas about the place and purpose of the hatches. Since the rising bodies had mouths and often fed, maybe they were one means of pruning old tissues and reviving what remained. Or they were infected with some new, improved genetics that had to be spread through the greater body. Perhaps they had a punishing function, retraining regions that their Polypond master judged too independent. Unless of course hatches were exactly what they appeared to be: biological storms. One or many species were enjoying a season of plenty, and working together, those countless bodies would rise into the highest atmosphere, spreading their precious seeds and spores as far as physically possible.

"Perhaps every answer is a little true," Hawking liked to caution. "Just as every answer is a little bit of a lie too."

Flying above the hatch, Peregrine thought of his odd friend. But only briefly, and then he consciously shoved him out of his exceptionally busy mind.

"Projections," he demanded.

His ship was still plunging, its hull pulled into a teardrop configuration, the skin superheated and his sensors half-blinded by the plasmatic envelope. But his crew devised a simple picture showing him vectors and projections of a future that looked ready to end in the most miserable way.

"Our target is accelerating," his pilot announced. "I wish to abort before we collide with it."

The black mass, smooth-faced and distinctly iridescent, was punching its way through a scattering of high clouds. Some of those clouds were alive—vividly colored bodies as light as aerogel and easily shredded. Other clouds were water-stained gray and red with salts and iron, dead cells, and other detritus pushed skyward by the mayhem. Their target was tiny compared to the entire hatch. But it was already the tallest feature, and nothing like it had ever been seen before. Raiders bound for distant hunting grounds were noticing it. Even from two hundred kilometers overhead, the energies and wild violence were obvious. And even from inside a cocoon of superheated gases, human eyes could appreciate the beauty of so many frantic bodies doing whatever it was they were doing.

"I want to abort," the pilot repeated.

Peregrine agreed. "But find the best way to hold us here, in its path. Can we do that?"

Instantly, the machine said, "Yes. But braking and circling will exhaust our reserves, and there won't be enough fuel for both cargo and the journey home."

Peregrine had guessed as much. "Let's compromise," he said. "Brake and assume a gliding shape. Where does that leave us?"

"Still dancing with the break-even point," the pilot warned.

"So make some calls." Peregrine named a few smart competitors approaching from more distant berths. "Pay them to wait above us. And share their spare fuel, when the time comes."

The teardrop flipped over, the engine throwing out a spectacular fire. Every raider knew: ships larger and more powerful than theirs could trigger retribution. An innate reflex or a Polypond strategy? Nobody knew. But Peregrine's ship was as close to the maximum size as was allowed, and if his plume exceeded the usual limits, even for a moment, a giant laser would pop to the surface on the unreachable sea below, evaporating his ship and then his body, and finally, his very worried skull.

But this burn went unnoticed. Then the ship rested, pieces of its hull pulling away, forming dragonfly wings configured to work with the thickening winds. Each time they passed through one of the monomolecular skins, Peregrine felt a shudder. The vibrations worsened by the minute, growing violent and relentless, and after a point, numbing and nearly unnoticed.

Countless black bodies continued to rise.

At home, inside the refugees' city, lived the data sinks that had survived from prewar times. Even the best of them were incomplete. But inside the biological sections, Peregrine had found digitals of fish swimming in schools—a hypnotic set of images where tiny, almost mindless creatures managed to stay in formation, displaying grace and a singleness of purpose that never failed to astonish him.

This was the same, only infinitely more spectacular.

Those black bodies didn't ride on meat and fins, but on tiny rockets and stubby metal wings. Perfect coordination had built a flawless hemisphere better than five hundred kilometers wide. Peregrine's best AI spotter singled out random bodies, carefully watching as they climbed to the outside edge of the school and then worked their way upward, reaching the cloud's apex before doing a curious roll, each shucking off its little wings before firing a larger rocket, then diving back out of sight through gaps too tiny to see from above.

"Identify one of them," Peregrine suggested, "and see when it emerges again."

The spotter had already tried that, and failed. The bodies were too similar, and there were too many of them. But there was an easier, more elegant route. With the help of distant telescopes, the AI took a thorough census of the cloud, and then it let itself feel the gentle but precise tug made by that combined gravity. Then it precisely measured the size of the entire swarm, and with genuine astonishment, it admitted, "They are growing fewer, I think."

"Fewer?"

"Every minute, a million bodies vanish."

"Meaning what?" he asked. "The cloud is shrinking?"

"It grows, but its citizens are scarcer. And this has been happening from the outset, I would guess."

The pilot was managing their long fall while the ship's architect constantly adapted the shape and stiffness of wings, and the shape and color of the fuselage. To the best of its ability, the raider ship was trying to vanish inside the Polypond's enormous sky.

"Will any little guys be left when they reach us?" Peregrine asked.

Yes. Billions still.

"But what happens to the others? Where do they go?"

Data gave clues. Neutrinos and the character of escaping light implied a fierce heat, X-rays and even gamma rays seeping free. There was no way to be certain, but the black bodies could be simple machines—lead-doped hyperfiber shells wrapped around nuclear charges, for instance. If those bombs were detonating, then the interior of that cloud was hell: a spherical volume perhaps one hundred kilometers in diameter with an average temperature hotter than the guts of most suns.

What would anyone want with so much heat?

"The cloud is a weapon," Peregrine muttered, feeling horrible and sure. His first instinct was to glance at the rocket nozzle behind them, imagining the very worst: a bubble of superheated plasmas was being woven here, ready to be flung up and out into space, like a child's ball aimed for a target several thousand kilometers wide. Drop that creation into the nozzle, and, after a soundless flash, the city would cease to be.

But how would the Polypond launch the bubble?

The AIs were scrambling for answers. It was the ship's architect that imagined the next nightmare. What if the bubble wasn't going to be thrown, but instead it was dropped? If it was flung onto the Great Ship's hull . . . on the backside of the Ship, where the hyperfiber was thinnest . . . could it punch a hole into the hallways and habitats below?

Probably not, the majority decided.

But Peregrine and the architect wouldn't give up their nightmares. Since the war had ended, no one had seen energies approaching what was being seen today. But what if the Polypond had been waiting patiently since the war's end, silently gathering resources for this one spectacular attack . . . ?

Both solutions were possible and awful, and both were wrong.

The black cloud was still fifty kilometers below, and simulations were furiously working, and that was when a third, even stranger answer appeared with a withering flash of blue-white light.

In a blink, the top of that shimmering black mass parted.

Evaporated.

And from inside that carefully sculpted furnace sprang a shape at once familiar and wrong—a sphere of badly stressed, heavily eroded hyperfiber that was just a few kilometers across but rising fast on a withering plume of exhaust.

Making its frantic bid to escape: a starship.

"Reconfigure us now!" Peregrine shouted. "Whatever it takes get us out of the way . . . !"

6

On occasion, Peregrine and his inhuman friend discussed the Great Ship and what might or might not be found within its unreachable interior. One despairing possibility was that the Polypond hadn't destroyed the ancient vessel, but it had managed to annihilate both crew and passengers, leaving no one besides a few souls clinging to life outside. On the opposite end of the spectrum sat the most hopeful answer: life aboard the Ship was exactly as it had always been, peaceful and orderly, and the captains were still in charge, and the Polypond had been defeated, or at least fought to a meaningful armistice. And if that was true, then for a host of perfectly fine reasons, nobody at present was bothering to poke their heads out of the living ocean.

"But that doesn't explain this new acceleration," Peregrine would point out. "The engineers and captains. . . everybody everywhere. . . they assumed that these big rockets were the only engines. But plainly, they weren't. Obviously, they weren't even the most powerful thrusters available."

"It is quite the puzzle," Hawking conceded.

The acceleration was not huge, but to make anything as massive as the Great Ship move faster. . . well, that was an impressive trick. "The captains found something new during the war," Peregrine suggested.

"A talent hidden until now," his friend added. "That notion has a delightful sourness about it, yes."

Sour was sweet to the !eech.

Peregrine would narrow his gaze, imagining captains standing in a crowded, desperate bridge. "They wanted to outmaneuver the Polypond. That's why they kicked the new motors awake, and now they can't stop them."

"A compelling possibility. I agree."

But Peregrine didn't believe his own words. "That still won't explain why the captains don't come out to get us. Even if they don't suspect anybody's here, they should send up teams to scout the situation. . . and even better, to send messages home to the Milky Way. . ."

Long limbs acquired the questioning position. "Where would you expect them to appear?" Hawking asked.

"Inside one of the nozzles. I would."

Silence.

Peregrine offered his reasons as he thought of them. "Because the Polypond can't reach inside the nozzles. Because the captains could pretty easily work their way through the barricades and hyperfiber plugs. And because from the nozzle floor, they'd have an unobstructed view of the galaxy, and they would be able to measure our position and velocity—"

"The barricades are significant," the alien cautioned.

"To us, they are. We don't have the energy or tools to cut through the best grades of hyperfiber." Shaking his head, he said, "From what I've heard, when my mother's ship was damaged, she spent her free time trying to find some route to the interior. She explored at least a thousand of the old accessways leading down from here." Every tunnel, no matter how obscure, was blocked with hyperfiber too deep and stubborn to cut through. "But if there were captains below us, and if only a fraction of the old reactors were working . . . they could still punch out in a matter of years . . . maybe weeks . . ."

Silence.

"So there are no captains," Peregrine would decide. Every time.

"Which means what?"

"Somebody else is in charge of the Great Ship." That answer seemed obvious, and it was inevitable, and it made a good mind usefully worried. Yet that answer was a most frustrating creation, since it opened doors into an infinite range of possibilities, imaginable and otherwise.

"Who is in charge?" Hawking would ask, on occasion.

A few powerful species were obvious candidates. But each of them would have sent teams to the surface. They might be different species, but they would be drawn by the same reasons and needs that humans would feel.

"Perhaps the culprit is someone else," Hawking would propose. "An organism you haven't thought to consider."

Anything was possible, yes.

Peregrine threw his ape arms into a posture that mimicked his friend's, underscoring the importance of his next words. "Nobody here is looking for a route down," he said. "I think it's been what? A thousand years since anyone has even tried."

The three hemispherical eyes were bright and still.

Peregrine continued. "Once I get enough savings in the bank, I'll take up my mother's other work. Just to see what I can see."

"That could be a reasonable plan," Hawking would say.

Then most of the time, their conversation ended. Peregrine often made that promise to himself, but he never had the resources or the simple will to invest in the luxury of a many-year search. Besides, he was the finest raider in the city, and raiders were essential. If he gave up his present work, the level of poverty everywhere would rise. Citizens would have to forgo having children and new homes. At least that was his excuse to wait for another decade or two, biding time before setting out on what surely would be a useless adventure.

Hawking never questioned Peregrine's lack of action. But then again, that creature was ancient and eerily patient, and who knew how many promises he had made to himself during the last eons, all bound up inside his powerful mind, waiting to be fulfilled?

One day, Peregrine surprised himself; he imagined a fresh candidate and a compelling logic that would explain the mystery.

"It's the Great Ship," he offered.

The !eech was silent, but there was a different quality to his posture, and even the crystalline eyes looked brighter.

"The Ship itself has come to life," the young man proposed.

"And why would that be?"

"I don't know. Maybe it finally had enough of human beings at the helm, this damned Polypond trying to kill it, and all the rest of these unpleasant creatures running around inside it. So one day, it just woke up and said, 'Screw you. From here on, *I'm* in charge!'"

"Interesting," his friend offered.

"And what if . . . ?" Peregrine continued. Swallowing and then smiling, he asked, "What if we aren't just following some random line? Instead of heading out into nothingness, the Ship is actually steering us toward a genuine destination?" Then he laughed in a tight, nervous fashion. "What if our voyage has only just begun, Hawking?"

There was a momentary silence.

Then his friend replied, "Every voyage has just begun. If you consider those words in the proper way . . ."

7

Buried in those old data sinks were schematics for a host of impossible machines—devices too intricate or demanding to be built by refugees and their children. Included were wondrous starships like those that once brought passengers to the Great Ship. Peregrine had always dreamed of seeing vessels like those, and judging by the spectrums, that's what the apparition was: an armored starship equipped with a streakship drive, efficient and relentless, yet operating at some minuscule fraction of full throttle. With just that whisper of thrust, the gap between him and it closed in an instant. Peregrine's ship was a tiny, toyish rocket that barely had time enough to fold its wings and kick itself out of the way. The rising starship missed Peregrine by less than ten kilometers. The silvered ball of hyperfiber stood on a plume of hard radiations, the exhaust narrow at the nozzle but widening as it drove downward, scorching heat causing it to explode outward into an atmosphere that was cooked to a broth of softer plasmas, a stark blue-white fire betraying only the coldest of the unfolding energies.

"Run!" he ordered.

His pilot had already made that panicked assessment. Using the last shreds of its wings, the raider ship tilted its nose and leaped toward space, not following the starship so much as simply trying to keep ahead of the awful fire. The black mass beneath them continued to churn and spin. And the living ocean below everything could see the starship too, a thousand defensive systems triggered, the burning air suddenly full of laser bursts and particle beams and a host of slow ballistic weapons that could never catch their target. Whatever the reason for fighting, hatred or simple instinct, the Polypond employed every trick in its bid to kill its opponent. And that's when Peregrine's tiny ship was kissed by one of the lasers, a portion of his hull and two entire wings turned to carbon ash and a telltale glow.

"Reconfigure!" he screamed.

The AIs began shuffling the surviving pieces, pulling their ship back into a rough shape that might remain whole for another few moments.

But the main fuel tank was pierced, leaking and unpatchable.

"We can't make it home," was the uniform verdict.

Peregrine had already come to that grim conclusion.

"Hunt for help," he said. "Who's close—?"

"No one is," he heard.

The surviving portions of the black mass were still churning, a few billion fusion bombs riding little rockets. It was a useless gesture, Peregrine believed. But then he noticed how the cloud was changing as it moved, acquiring a distinct pancake-shaped base above which a tiny fraction of the bombs were gathering, pulling themselves into a dense, carefully stacked bundle.

In a shared instant, the pancake below ignited itself.

The resulting flash dwarfed every bolt of laser light, and even the stardrive faded from view. A hypersonic slap struck the last of those bombs, destroying most but throwing the rest of them skyward at a good fraction of light-speed. Then as the bombs passed into the last reaches of the atmosphere, they gave themselves one last shove, rockets carrying them close enough that the starship was forced to react, shifting its plume slightly, evaporating every last one of its pursuers.

But the pancake burst had launched more than just bombs. A fat portion of the atmosphere was being shoved upward, and soon it would stand higher than Peregrine had ever seen. More out of instinct than calculation, he said, "Try wings again, and ride this updraft."

It wouldn't lift them much, no. But the soaring maneuver would keep them at a safer altitude for a little while longer.

"Now are there any raiders who can reach us?"

Several, maybe.

"Offer them anything," Peregrine told his mercantile AI. "Thanks. Money. My family name. Whatever works."

Moments later, a deal was secured.

The airborne wreckage of his ship continued to jump and lurch through the blazing atmosphere. Life support was close to failing, and once it did, his body would cook and temporarily die. Peregrine invested his last conscious moments looking up at the streakship, watching as it broke into true space, that relentless engine throwing back a jet of plasma that grew even thinner and hotter as it began to finally throttle up.

"Yell at the ship," he ordered.

That brought confused silence.

"Assume there's a tribe of humans onboard," he instructed his AIs. "Curse at them and blame them for all our miseries. Say whatever you have to, but get them to talk back to us . . ."

"And then what?" asked his pilot.

"Remember everything they say," he muttered as his lips burned. "And everything they don't say too—"

8

"You were once an engineer," he had whispered to Fusillade. "But not anymore, I have to believe."

"And why not?"

The arbitrary moment on the clock called "morning" was approaching. The two humans were sleepy and physically spent. But Peregrine found the energy to explain, "I know every engineer. By face. By name. By skills. After all, I am a raider."

"You are."

"None of you founders are helping us fly. Your children and grandchildren, sure. But never you."

Silence.

"It's funny," he allowed. "I don't keep track of you. I mean humans and harum-scarums, the fef and all the others . . . those lucky ones who founded our city. I doubt if I could attach ten faces to the right names, since most of you seem happy to keep close to each other . . ."

The only response was a smile, thin and wary.

Peregrine grew tired of this dance. "So what do you do with your time?" he finally asked.

The smile brightened. "I study."

"The subject?"

"Many matters." The woman was taller than Peregrine, and stronger. She pushed on his chest—pushed harder than necessary—and he felt his heart beating against the flat of her palm. Then very quietly, Fusillade asked, "What do you know about your half brother?"

Peregrine offered a crisp, inadequate biography of a man who lived and died long ago.

"And your two sisters?"

There were three siblings in all. Two were raiders who eventually didn't return from their missions, while that final sister had followed their mother's other pursuit, hunting for a route back into the Great Ship. But a crude plasma drill exploded during testing, obliterating most of her mind along with her bones and meat.

With a shrug, Peregrine confessed, "I don't think about them very often. Different fathers, and we never knew each other . . . and all that . . ."

His lover winked and said, "You know, he was their friend too."

"Who was?"

"You know who." The smile had been replaced by a genuinely cold expression, eyes weighing everything they saw— not unlike the !eech eyes. "He wore different names, yes. But he was a companion to your sisters and your brother too. They weren't as good friends as you are to him, but he was always close. And when your mother had no living children, he would strike up relationships with whoever seemed to be the best raider."

"I've heard that story before," Peregrine muttered. Then with a pride that took him a little by surprise, he added, "Yeah, everyone says that I've got some odd tie with Hawking, or whatever he wants to call himself . . ."

"And what about your mother?"

"What about her?"

"She and the alien knew each other. Not at first, no. At least, nobody in my circle remembers any relationship. But your mother invited your dear companion along when she went below, hunting for an open road to the Great Ship. I'm sure you can imagine why. That !eech could slip his way into some amazingly tiny crevices, if he had to . . ."

Peregrine was perfectly awake now.

Quietly, firmly, the ageless lover said, "I wouldn't want you to mention this to your good friend. What I'm sharing, I mean. Let's keep it between ourselves."

Again and again, the young man realized that he knew little about anything. Looking at the woman's stiff, unreadable face, he asked again, "What exactly do you do with your time?"

Her eyes narrowed.

"You're still an engineer, aren't you?"

"Do you think so?"

"The founders, and particularly the oldest of you . . . each of you have celebrated tens of thousands of birthdays. Minds like yours have habits, and habits don't easily change." Now he sat up and pushed against her chest. The woman had a peculiar asymmetry—a giant black nipple tipped the small hard right breast, while its large and very soft neighbor wore a tiny silver cap. Between the breasts lay a heart beating faster than he expected. "So tell me: what kind of engineering do you do?"

"Mostly, I buy useless items in the markets."

"Which items?"

"Pieces of neural networks. You know, the little brains of those big corpses that you bring home . . . from gull-wands and clowners and the rest of the free-ranging bodies . . ."

Those brains were always tiny, simple of design, and often mangled or burned. Generations of raiders had collected the trinkets, and not even the largest few had shown any hint of sentience.

"Maybe as individual fragments, they're simple." She pulled Peregrine's other hand over her chest, and smiled. "But if you splice them together, very carefully . . . if you spend a few thousand years doing little else . . . you'll cobble together something that captures a portion of one genuine soul. Maybe it's the Polypond's mind, maybe something else. Whatever it is, you'll find memories and images and ideas . . . and on occasion, you might even hear some timely, important news . . ."

"Such as?"

She refused to say.

"And what does this have to do with Hawking?"

"Maybe nothing," she replied with an agreeable tone. "But now that you mention it: what should we say about that very good friend of yours?"

9

In the end what was saved was too small and far too mutilated to reconstitute itself. Peregrine was a lump of caramelized tissue surrounding a fractured skull that held a bioceramic brain cut through by EM surges and furious rains of charged particles. The damage was so severe that every memory and tendency and each of his precious personal biases had to migrate into special shelters, and life had ceased completely for a timeless span covering almost eighteen days. Death held sway—longer than he had ever known, Nothingness ruled—and then after a series of quick tickling sensations and flashes of meaningless light, the raider found himself recovered enough that his soul migrated out of its hiding places and his newest eyes opened, gazing at a face that was not entirely unexpected.

"The streakship," he blurted with his new mouth. "Where?"

A limb touched his mouth and both cheeks, and then another limb touched his chest, feeling his heart. The limbs were soft, strong, and human—a woman's two hands—and then he heard her voice saying, "Gone," with finality. "Gone now. Gone."

"It got away safely?"

She said, "Yes," with a nod, then with her eyes, and finally with a whisper. And she leaned closer, adding, "The streakship has escaped, yes. Eighteen days, and it's still accelerating. Faster than you would ever guess, it is racing toward the Milky Way."

Peregrine tried to move, and failed. His legs and arms were only half-grown, wearing wraps filled with blood and amino acids. But he could breathe deeply, enjoying that sensation quite a lot. "What about my crew?"

"Degraded, but alive." The woman's face was pleased and a little astonished, telling him, "At the end, when you were rescued . . . when that other raider plucked you out of the mayhem . . . the AIs were flying what was really just a toy glider, barely as big as me, and with maybe a tenth my mass . . ."

Peregrine tried to absorb his good fortune. How could you even calculate the long odds that he had crossed?

The ancient woman sat back, biding her time.

"Did the streakship ever talk?" he asked.

"Yes." She nodded and smiled wistfully, and then with a matter-of-fact shrug, she added, "As soon as the streakship got above us, it hit us with a narrow-beam broadcast. Yes."

"What did it say?"

"Life survives inside the Great Ship," she reported. "But our old leaders, the wise and powerful captains . . . they're gone now. All of them. Either dead or in hiding somewhere."

"Who is in charge?"

"Nobody."

"What does that mean?"

"From what the streakship told us, passengers are fending for themselves." The woman paused, studying his new face. Then she quietly mentioned, "However, there is one exceptionally obscure species that's come into some prominence. In fact, at the end of the Polypond War, they took control of the Great Ship's helm." She offered a flickering wink, and then added, "And, oh . . . now that I mentioned that . . . guess who else has gone away . . . ?

"Somebody you know . . .

"Even before your body arrived home, he picked up his shell, and by the looks of it, scuttled away . . . ."

10

Peregrine was perfectly healthy and profoundly poor. The raider who saved him had acquired most of his assets, while his debts to the hospital remained substantial, possibly eternal. He had no ship, and his crew was repaired and working with others. Several investors came forward, offering to pay for a new ship in return for a fat percentage of all future gains. But the only fair offer was a brief contract from his father, and for a variety of reasons, personal and otherwise, the young man decided to send it back unsigned and follow an entirely new course.

If you live cheaply and patiently, it takes astonishingly little money to keep you breathing and content.

For most of a century, Peregrine stalked the deep tunnels and access ports that laced the Ship's central nozzle. Armed with maps left behind by his mother and sister, he hunted for routes they might have missed. He managed to find two or three every year, but each one was inevitably plugged with the high-grade hyperfiber. It was easy to see why no one kept up this kind of search for long. Yet Peregrine refused to quit, if only because the idea of failure gave his mouth such an awful taste.

New lovers drifted in and out of his life.

He occasionally saw the old lady engineer, meeting her for a meal and conversation. They hadn't slept together in decades, but they remained friendly enough. Besides, she had a sharp mind and important connections, and sometimes, when she was in the mood, she gave him special knowledge.

"You knew a big hatch was coming," Peregrine accused her. "That's why you seduced me when you did. Somehow, you and your founder friends pieced together clues that the rest of us don't ever get to see."

"Yet that hatch, big as it was, was just a secondary phenomenon," she explained. "Like blood from a fresh cut. I won't tell exactly how we knew, but we did. And what was more important was that someone or something had emerged from one of the old ports. We had reason to believe that an armored vessel was pushing through the Polypond ocean, heading our way . . . presumably to get into a useful position before jumping free of the Ship."

"And you suspected Hawking?"

"For thousands of years, I did. We did." Fusillade nodded, and then said, "This isn't official. But in the final seconds of the War, a few messages arrived from the interior. They were heavily coded military broadcasts, which is why they aren't common knowledge. They describe the creatures that were taking over the battered Ship. The !eech, the broadcasts called them. And not wanting to alert the spy in our midst, we decided to keep those secrets to ourselves."

"But he's gone," Peregrine countered. "Why not make a public announcement?"

"Because we don't want to panic our children, of course."

"Am I panicking?" he asked.

"In slow motion, you are. Yes." The ancient engineer sat back in her chair, tapping at the heart nestled between her unequal breasts. "Spending your life searching for a way into the Ship, when we are as certain as we can be that there is no way inside . . . yes, I think that's genuinely panicked behavior . . ."

"Hawking disappeared to someplace," he replied. "That means there's at least one route off this nozzle."

"If he went back into the Great Ship, perhaps. But for all we know, he's walking today on a living cloud off on some distant piece of the Polypond's body."

Peregrine had wasted decades walking empty hallways and dangling from soft glass ropes. He could have wasted a thousand centuries before finding the relevant clue. But he was a lucky individual, and he had the good fortune of becoming lost at the proper moment. After two wrong turns, he found himself standing beside a tiny chute exactly like ten thousand other chutes. Except, that is, for the marks left behind by a delicate limb that had been dipped in paint. No, in blood. A blackish alien blood with a distinctive flavor, and the writing was a familiar script, showing the simple word "HAWKING," followed by a simple yet elegant arrow pointing straight down.

11

The chute ended with a vast airless room built for no discernible purpose. Its walls were half a kilometer tall, and the floor was a circular plain covering perhaps ten square kilometers of featureless hyperfiber—stuff as old as the Ship, far better than any grade that could be chiseled through today. The only obvious doorway led out into the dormant rocket nozzle. Peregrine set up a torch in the room's center, and then he kneeled, searching that expanse with a powerful night scope. He should have missed the second doorway. If anyone else had ever visited this nameless place, they surely would have ignored what looked like a crevice, horizontal and brief. But someone was standing in front of the opening—a distinctive alien wearing a gossamer lifesuit, his long jointed legs locked into a comfortable position, the body motionless now and perhaps for a very long while.

Peregrine walked a few steps, then broke into a hard run.

On their private channel, Hawking said, "You look fit, my friend. And rather troubled too, I see."

"What are you doing here?" Peregrine blurted.

"Waiting for you," was the reply.

"Why?"

"Because you are my friend."

"I don't particularly believe that," said Peregrine. "From what I've heard, the !eech are my enemies . . ."

. "I have injured you how many times?"

"Never," he thought, saying nothing.

"My friend," said Hawking. "What precise treacheries am I guilty of?"

"I don't know. You tell me."

Silence.

Peregrine had invested years wondering what he would say, should this moment arrive. "Why live with us?" he asked. "Were you some kind of spy? Were you sent here to watch over us?"

There was a pause, then a cryptic comment. "You know, I saw you entering this place. I saw that quite easily."

"I've been climbing toward you for several hours," Peregrine complained. "Of course you saw me . . ."

Then he hesitated, rolling the alien's confession around in his head.

With relentless patience, Hawking waited.

Peregrine slowed his gait, asking, "How long have you been watching my approach?"

"Since your birth," the !eech confessed.

Peregrine stopped now.

After a few minutes of reflection, he said, "Those eyes of yours . . . they see into the future . . . ?"

Silence.

"Do they see everything that's going to happen?"

"Do your eyes absorb everything there is to see?"

Peregrine shook his head. "A limited sight, is that it?"

One of the distant legs lifted high, signaling agreement.

"What else can you see, Hawking?"

"That I have never hurt you," the alien repeated.

"My half sister . . . the one who died in the plasma blast . . . did you arrange that accident?"

"No."

"But did you see the accident approaching?"

Silence.

"And why did you come up on the hull, Hawking? The only reason I can think of is to spy on us."

"An obvious answer. And your imagination is richer than that, my friend."

Hard as it was to believe, the apparent compliment forced Peregrine to smile. "Okay," he muttered. "You wanted to spy on our future. We're an independent society, free of the !eech, and maybe you're scared of us."

"That is an interesting assessment, but mistaken."

"I don't understand then."

"In time, you will," the !eech promised.

Then every one of its limbs was moving, carrying the creature backward into the narrow, almost invisible crevice. Peregrine began to run again, in a full sprint; but he was still half a kilometer from his goal when a warm gooey stew of fresh hyperfiber flowed into view, filling the crevice and pushing across the slick floor, glowing in the infrared as it swiftly cured.

12

The final doorway had been opened just enough for a small human wearing a minimal lifesuit to slip through, and, walking alone, he then stepped onto a frigid, utterly flat plain. During the War, portions of the Polypond had splashed into the giant nozzle, dying here or at least freezing into a useless hibernation. Peregrine strode out to where he found a modest telescope as well as a set of telltale marks. His friend once stood here, those powerful eyes of his linked to the light-hungry mirror. By measuring the marks in the ice, and with conservative estimates of the heat lost by Hawking's lifesuit, Peregrine guessed that the creature had stood here for many years, pulling up his many feet when they had melted to uncomfortable depth, then dancing over to a fresh place before reclaiming his watchful pose.

Peregrine lay on his back now, slowly melting into the dead ice, and he fixed the same telescope to his eyes and purposefully stared at the sky.

The little city was barely visible—a sprinkling of tiny lights and heat signatures threatening to vanish against the vast bulk of the timeless and utterly useless nozzle. Millions of souls were up there, breeding and spreading out farther in a profoundly impoverished realm. Yet despite all of their successes, they seemed to have no impact on a scene that dwarfed all men and their eternal urges.

What wasn't the nozzle was the galaxy.

Here was what the !eech had been watching. Hawking had lived for thousands of years in a place that offered him comfort and the occasional companionship. But once the streak-ship had left, carrying its important news to the universe beyond, the creature's work had begun: sitting on this bitter wasteland, those great eyes had been fixed on three hundred billion suns. Peregrine studied the maelstrom of stars and worlds, dust and busy minds; and perhaps for the first time in his life, he appreciated that this was something greater than any silly Polypond. Here lay an ocean beyond any other, and someday, in one fashion or another, a great hatch would rise from it—furious bodies riding upon a trillion, trillion wings, reaching for this prize that has been lost.

This Great Ship.

WINNING PEACE

PAUL J. McAULEY

Born in Oxford, England, in 1955, Paul J. McAuley now makes his home in London. A professional biologist for many years, he sold his first story in 1984, and has gone on to be a frequent contributor to *Interzone*, as well as to markets such as *Asimov's Science Fiction*, *SCI FICTION*, *Amazing*, *The Magazine of Fantasy and Science Fiction*, *Skylife*, *The Third Alternative*, *When the Music's Over*, and elsewhere.

McAuley is at the forefront of several of the most important subgenres in SF today, producing both "radical hard science fiction" and the revamped and retooled wide-screen Space Opera that has sometimes been called the New Space Opera, as well as dystopian sociological speculations about the very near future. He also writes fantasy and horror. His first novel, *Four Hundred Billion Stars*, won the Philip K. Dick Award, and his novel *Fairyland* won both the Arthur C. Clarke Award and the John W. Campbell Award in 1996. His other books include the novels *Of the Fall, Eternal Light*, and *Pasquale's Angel, Confluence*—a major trilogy of ambitious scope and scale set ten million years in the future, comprised of the novels *Child of the River, Ancient of Days*, and *Shrine of Stars—Life on Mars, The Secret of Life*, and *Whole Wide World*. His short fiction has been collected in

The King of the Hill and Other Stories and *The Invisible Country,* and he is the coeditor, with Kim Newman, of an original anthology, *In Dreams.* His most recent books include a new novel, *White Devils,* and a new collection, *Little Machines.* Coming up is a new novel, *Players.*

McAuley made his name as one of the best of the New Space Opera writers with novels such as *Four Hundred Billion Stars* and the Confluence trilogy, but in recent years he has created the Quiet War series as well, with stories such as "Second Skin," "Sea Scene, With Monsters," "The Assassination of Faustino Malarte," and others, about the aftermath and the consequences of an interplanetary war that ravages the solar system. In the tense and suspenseful story that follows, he deals with the aftermath and the consequences of another space war, an interstellar one this time, and shows us that if you can't manage to figure out a way to shake off the ghosts of the past, you may face a very limited future—such as: none at all.

   One day, almost exactly a year after Carver White started working for Mr. E. Z. Kanza's transport company, Mr. Kanza told him that they were going on a little trip—down the pipe to Ganesh Five. This was the company's one and only interstellar route, an ass-and-trash run to an abandoned-in-place forward facility, bringing in supplies, hauling out pods packed with scrap and dismantled machinery, moving salvage workers to and fro. Carver believed that Mr. Kanza was thinking of promoting him from routine maintenance to shipboard work, and wanted to see if he had the right stuff. He was wrong.

The Ganesh Five system was a binary, an ordinary K1 star and a brown dwarf orbiting each other at a mean distance of six billion kilometers, roughly equivalent to the semimajor axis of Pluto's orbit around the Sun. The K1 star, Ganesh Five A, had a minor asteroid belt in its life zone, the largest rocks planoformed thousands of years ago by Boxbuilders, and just one planet, a methane gas giant named Sheffield by the Brit who'd first mapped the system, with glorious water-ice rings, the usual assortment of small moons, and, this was why a forward facility had been established there during the war between the Alliance and the Collective, no less than four wormhole throats.

The system had been captured by the Collective early in the war, and because one of its wormholes was part of a chain that included the Collective's New Babylon system, and another exited deep in Alliance territory, it had become an important staging and resupply area, with a big dock facility in orbit around Sheffield, and silos and tunnel networks buried in several of the moons. Now, two years after the defeat of the Alliance, the only people living there were employees of the salvage company that was stripping the docks and silos, and a small Navy garrison.

Carver White and Mr. Kanza flew there on the company's biggest scow, hauling eight passengers, a small tug, and an assortment of cutting and demolition equipment. After they docked, Carver was left to kick his heels in the scow for six hours, until at last Mr. Kanza buzzed him and told him to get his ass over to the garrison. A marine escorted Carver to an office with a picture window overlooking the spine of the docks, which stretched away in raw sunlight toward Sheffield's green crescent and the bright points of three moons strung in a line beyond the great arch of its rings. This fabulous view was the first thing Carver saw when he swam into the room; the second was Mr. Kanza and a Navy officer lounging in sling seats next to it.

The officer was Lieutenant Rider Jackson, adjutant to the garrison commander. In his mid-twenties, maybe a year older than Carver, he had a pale, thin face, bright blue eyes, and a calm expression that didn't give anything away. He asked Carver about the ships he'd flown and the hours he'd logged serving in the Alliance Navy, questioned him closely about what had happened after Collective marines had boarded his crippled transport, the hand-to-hand fighting in the corridors and holds, how Carver had passed out from loss of blood during a last stand among the cold sleep coffins, how he'd woken up in a Collective hospital ship, a prisoner of war. The Alliance had requested terms of surrender sixty-two days later, having lost two battle fleets and more than fifty systems. By then, Carver had been patched up and sold as indentured labor to the pharm factories on New Babylon.

Rider Jackson said, "You didn't tell the prize officer you were a flight engineer."

"I gave him my name and rank and number. It was all he deserved to know."

Carver was too proud to ask what this was all about, but he was pretty sure it had something to do with Mr. Kanza's financial difficulties. Everyone who worked for Mr. Kanza knew he was in trouble. He'd borrowed to expand his little fleet, but he hadn't found enough new business to service the loan, and his creditors were bearing down on him.

Rider Jackson said, "I guess you think you should have been sent home."

"That's what we did with our prisoners of war."

"Because your side lost the war."

"We'd have sent them back even if we'd won. The Alliance doesn't treat people like property."

Carver was beginning to like Rider Jackson. He seemed like the kind of man who preferred straight talk to evasion and exaggeration, who would stick to the truth even if it was uncomfortable or inconvenient. Which was probably why he'd been sent to this backwater, Carver thought; forthright officers have a tendency to damage their careers by talking back to their superiors.

Mr. Kanza said, "If my data miner hadn't uncovered his service record and traced him, he'd still be working in the pharm factories."

Rider Jackson ignored this, saying to Carver, "You have a brother. He served in the Alliance Navy too."

"That's none of your business," Carver said.

"Oh, but I think you'll find it's very much *my* business," Mr. Kanza said.

Mr. E. Z. Kanza was a burly man with a shaved head and a short beard trimmed to a sharp point. He liked to think that he was a fair-minded, easygoing fellow, but exhibited most of the usual vices of people given too much power over others: he was arrogant and quick-tempered, and his smile masked a cruel and capricious sense of humor. On the whole, he didn't treat his pilots and engineers too badly—they had their own quarters, access to good medical treatment, and were even given small allowances they could spend as they chose—but they were still indentured workers, with Judas bridges implanted in their spinal cords and no civil rights whatsoever, and Mr. Kanza was always ready to use his shock stick on anyone who didn't jump to obey him.

Smiling his untrustworthy smile, Mr. Kanza said to Carver, "Jarred is two years younger than you, yes? He served on a frigate during the war, yes? Well, I happen to have some news about him."

Carver didn't say anything. He knew what had happened to Jarred, was wondering if this was one of Mr. Kanza's nasty little jokes.

Mr. Kanza appealed to Rider Jackson. "Do you know how long they last in those pharm factories before they cop an overdose or their immune systems collapse? No more than a year or two, three at the most. I saved this one from certain death, and has he ever thanked me? And do you want to bet he'll thank me when he learns about his brother?"

Rider Jackson said, "Don't make a game out of it. If you don't tell him, I will."

The two men stared at each other for a long moment. Then Mr. Kanza smiled and said, "I do believe you like him. I knew you would."

"Do what needs to be done."

Mr. Kanza conjured video from the air with a quick gesture. Here was Jarred White in a steel cell, wearing the same kind of black pajamas Carver had worn in the prison hospital, before he'd been sold into what the Collective called indentured labor and the Alliance called slavery. Here was Jarred standing in gray coveralls against a red marble wall in the atrium of Mr. Kanza's house.

Mr. Kanza told Carver, "Your brother was taken prisoner, just like you. One of my data miners traced him, and I bought out his contract. What do you think of that?"

Carver thought that the videos were pretty good fakes, probably disneyed up from his brother's military record. In both of the brief sequences, Jarred sported the same severe crew cut that was regulation for cadets in the Alliance Navy, not serving officers; when Carver had last seen him, his brother had grown his crew cut out into a flattop. That had been on Persopolis, the City of Our Lady of Flowers. Some twenty days later, Carver's drop ship had been crippled, and he'd been taken prisoner. Three days later, Jarred had been killed in action.

The Collective didn't allow its POWs any contact with their families or anyone else in the Alliance; Carver had found out about his brother's death from one of the other prisoners of war working in the pharm factories. Jarred's frigate, the *Croatian,* had been shepherding ships loaded with evacuees from Eve's Halo when a Collective battleship traveling at a tenth the speed of light had smashed through the convoy. The *Croatian* had been shredded by kinetic weapons and a collapsium bomblet had cooked off what was left: the ship had been lost with all hands. Carver had been hit badly by the news. Possessed by moments of unreasoning anger, he'd started to pick fights with other workers; finally, he attacked one of the guards. The woman paralyzed him with her shock stick, gave him a clinically methodical beating, and put him on punishment detail, shoveling cell protein from extraction pits. Carver would have died there if one of Mr. Kanza's data miners hadn't tracked him down.

After Mr. Kanza bought out his contract, Carver resolved to become a model worker, cultivate patience, and wait for a chance to escape; now, wondering if that chance had finally come, if he could turn Mr. Kanza's crude trick to his advantage, he stepped hard on his anger and held his tongue.

Mr. Kanza said to Rider Jackson, "You see? Not a speck of gratitude."

Rider Jackson turned his tell-nothing expression on Carver; Carver stared back at him through his brother's faked-up ghost.

The young lieutenant said to Mr. Kanza, "You're certain we can trust him?"

"I've had him a year. He's never given me any trouble, and he won't give us any trouble now," Mr. Kanza said, pointing a finger at Carver. "Can you guess why I went to all the trouble of buying out your brother's contract?"

Carver shrugged, as if it meant nothing to him.

Mr. Kanza said, "You really should show me some gratitude. Not only have I already saved your brother's life, but if
everything works out, I'll void his contract, and void yours
too. You'll both be free."

"Meanwhile, you're holding him hostage, to make sure
that I'll do whatever it is you want me to do."

Mr. Kanza told Rider Jackson, "There it is. I have his
brother as insurance, the tug will fly itself, and if he does
get it into his head to try something stupid, I can intervene
by wire. If worst comes to worst, I'll be the one short a flight
engineer and a good little ship; as far as you're concerned,
this is a risk-free proposition."

"As long as the Navy doesn't find out about it," Rider Jackson said.

"We've been over that," Mr. Kanza said.

Carver saw that there was something tense and wary
behind Mr. Kanza's smile, and realized that he had worked
up some reckless plan to get himself out of the hole, that he
needed Rider Jackson's help to do it, and he needed Carver
too.

"We've talked it up and down," Mr. Kanza told Rider Jackson. "There's no good reason why the Navy should know
anything about this until you buy out your service."

Rider Jackson studied him, then shrugged and said,
"Okay."

Just like that. Two days later, Carver was aboard Mr.
Kanza's tug, cooled down in hypersleep while the small ship
aimed itself at the brown dwarf, Ganesh Five B.

Mr. Kanza made extensive use of a data mining AI to track
down skilled prisoners of war who were being used as
common laborers, and to look for business opportunities
overlooked by his rivals. The data miner had linked a news
item about an alien and an astrophysicist who had disappeared after hiring a small yacht just before the beginning
of the war with an academic article by the astrophysicist,
Liu Chen Smith, that described an anomalous neutrino flux
emitted by a pinpoint source within a permanent storm in the

smoky atmosphere of a brown dwarf, Ganesh Five B. It was possible, the data miner suggested, that the alien, a !Cha that called itself Useless Beauty, had bankrolled an expedition to find out if the neutrino source was some kind of Elder Culture artifact.

Although most of the systems linked by wormhole networks were littered with the ruins of the cities, settlements, and orbital and free-floating habitats of Elder Culture species, these had been picked clean long ago by the dozens of species that preceded human colonization. Working examples of Elder Culture technology were fabulously rare and valuable. There was only a slim chance that the neutrino source was some kind of artifact, but if it was, and if Mr. Kanza could capture it, his financial difficulties would be over. He had one big problem: if the garrison that policed the Ganesh Five system found out about the neutrino source, the Navy would claim it for the state. That was where Rider Jackson, a criminal turned war hero, came in.

Rider Jackson had been born and raised on a reef circling a red dwarf star, Stein 8641. When their sheep ranch failed, Rider Jackson's father ran off on a trade ship and his mother committed suicide. At age sixteen, Rider Jackson, their only child, inherited the responsibility of honoring his family's debts. Our Thing, Stein 8641's parliament, ruled that he should be indentured to his father's chief creditors, the Myer family, until he had paid off all that was owed. Five years later, the day after war was declared between the Alliance and the Collective, he stole one of the Myer family's ships and lit out, abandoning the ship in the sprawling docks of New Babylon and turning up the next day at a Navy recruiting office in the planet's dusty capital, where he was promptly arrested for carrying false ID, a crime against the state that earned him ten years indentured labor. Soon afterward, having suffered two devastating defeats in quick succession, the Collective's armed forces rounded up everyone with freefall experience from the state's pool of indentured workers. Rider Jackson's sentence was commuted to ten years' service in the Navy. He fought in three campaigns in two different systems, and then his drop ship was hit by an

Alliance raider and broke apart. Rider Jackson took charge of a gig and rescued seventy-eight warm bodies, including the drop ship's captain. His heroism won him his lieutenant's pip, a chestful of medals, and public acclaim, but his criminal history prevented him rising any higher, and at the end of the war, the Navy stashed him in the Ganesh Five garrison, with no hope of promotion or transfer, and nothing to do but listen to the self-pitying monologues of his commander, make random checks on ships passing between the wormholes, and file endless status reports. He still had seven years to serve, and after that he would be returned to Stein 8641, and the Myer family.

Mr. Kanza, knowing that Rider Jackson couldn't afford to buy out the unserved portion of his contract with the Navy, much less pay what he still owed the Myer family, had made him an offer he couldn't refuse: help chase the hot lead on what might be an Elder Culture artifact in return for fifty percent of any profit. Mr. Kanza brought to the deal the information he'd uncovered, a ship, and someone to fly it; Rider Jackson rejigged the garrison's tracking station to cover up the flight of Mr. Kanza's tug, and used its deep space array to survey the brown dwarf. He found two things. The first was a microwatt beacon from an escape pod in orbit around Ganesh Five B. The second was that there was no longer any anomalous neutrino flux within the brown dwarf. It looked like Dr. Smith and the !Cha had captured the neutrino source, but then had got into some kind of trouble that had forced them to abandon their ship.

No wormhole throat orbited Ganesh Five B; the only way to reach it was through real space, a round trip of more than sixty days. Rider Jackson couldn't take leave of absence from his post and Mr. Kanza was unwilling to risk his life, and couldn't afford to hire a specialized, fully autonomous rescue drone because he was more or less broke and had exhausted all his lines of credit. His lightly modified tug, with Carver White riding along as troubleshooter, would have to do the job.

Carver learned all this while he helped Mr. Kanza prep the tug. He quickly realized that even if he brought back something that made Mr. Kanza and Rider Jackson the richest men alive, Mr. Kanza wouldn't keep his promise about freeing him; if he was going to survive this, he would have to find some way of exploiting the fact that he knew Mr. Kanza's story about holding Jarred hostage was a bluff. He also realized that he didn't have much chance of taking control of the tug and lighting out for somewhere other than the brown dwarf. He would be shut down in hypersleep for most of the trip, and the tug was controlled by an unhackable triumvirate of AIs that, sealed deep in the tug's keel, constantly checked each other's status. Not only that, but Mr. Kanza demonstrated with a ten-second burst of agony that he had hidden a shock stick in the tug too, and could use it to stimulate Carver's Judas bridge if it looked like he was going to cause trouble.

Carver's last thoughts before hypersleep closed him down were about whether he had done enough to make sure he could live through this; it was the first thing on his mind when he woke some thirty-one days later, in orbit around the brown dwarf.

The tug had discovered a scattering of debris, including hull plates, chunks of a fusion motor, and a human corpse in a pressure suit—it was clear that Dr. Smith hadn't survived the destruction of her ship—and it had also located the escape pod, which was tumbling in an oblate orbit that skimmed close to the outer edge of the brown dwarf's atmosphere before swinging away to more than twenty million kilometers at apogee. A blurry neutron density scan snatched by a throwaway probe revealed that the pod contained a !Cha's life tank, but its AI had refused to respond to the tug's attempts to shake hands with it, and there had been no response to an automated hailing message either: there was no way of knowing if the !Cha, Useless Beauty, was dead or alive.

The tug played a brief voice-only message from Mr. Kanza, telling Carver that he was to suit up and go outside and retrieve Dr. Smith's corpse.

"She may be carrying something that will tell me what killed her. Also, her relatives may pay a finder's fee for the return of her body."

The tug was already matching delta vee with the body. By the time Carver had sent an acknowledgment to the message (it would take five and a half hours to reach Mr. Kanza), eaten his first meal since waking, and suited up, the tug and Dr. Smith's corpse were revolving around each other at a distance of just a few hundred meters.

Carver rode across the gap on a collapsible broomstick. Ganesh Five B filled half the sky, a dim red disk marbled by black clouds spun into ragged bands by its swift rotation; Dr. Smith's corpse was silhouetted against the baleful light of this failed star, tumbling head over heels, arms and legs akimbo. Her pressure suit was ruptured in several places, and covered by fine carbon particles blown into space by eruptions in the brown dwarf's magnetosphere; a fog of dislodged soot gathered around Carver as he fixed a line between the dead woman's utility belt and his broomstick.

After he'd towed the body back to the tug and stowed it in the cargo hold, Carver discovered a long tangle of transparent thread thinner than a human hair wrapped around Dr. Smith's right arm. He couldn't cut off a sample with any of his suit's tools; he had to unwind the entire tangle before he could bring it inside the tug and feed one end of it into the compact automated laboratory. He'd brought the computer from Dr. Smith's suit inside too, but its little mind was dead and its memory had been irretrievably damaged by years of exposure to the brown dwarf's magnetic and radiation fields.

The lab determined that the thread was woven from fullerene nanotubes doped with atoms of beryllium, magnesium, and iron, and spun into long helical domains, was a room-temperature superconductor with the tensile properties of construction diamond: useful properties, but hardly unique. Even so, the fact that its composition didn't match any known fullerene superconductors was tantalizing, and although he told himself that it was most likely junk, debris in which Dr. Smith's body had become entangled after the destruction of her ship, Carver carefully wound the thread around a screwdriver, and shoved the screwdriver into one of the pouches of his p-suit's utility belt.

He had been hoping that the astrophysicist had survived; that she had been sleeping inside the escape pod; that after he'd woken her, she would have agreed to help him. He knew now that everything depended on whether or not the !Cha was alive or dead, and reckoned things would go easier if it was dead. Because if it was still alive, he would have to try to make a deal with it, and that was a lot riskier than trying to make a go of it on his own. For one thing, it was possible that the !Cha had murdered Dr. Smith because it wanted to keep whatever it was they'd found to itself. For another, like every other alien species, the !Cha made it clear that human beings didn't count for much. Ever since first contact, when the Jackaroo kicked off a global war on Earth and swindled the survivors out of rights to most of the solar system in exchange for a basic fusion drive and access to a wormhole network linking a couple of dozen lousy M-class red dwarf stars, aliens had been tricking, bamboozling, and manipulating the human race. In the long run, like other species before them, humans would either kill themselves off or stumble onto the trick of ascendency and go on to wherever it is the Elder Cultures have gone, but meanwhile they were at the mercy of species more powerful than them, pawns in games whose rules they didn't know, and aims they didn't understand.

Carver had a little time to work out how to deal with the !Cha; before it retrieved the escape pod, the tug spawned dozens of probes and mapped the brown dwarf with everything from optical and microwave radar surveys to a quantum gravity scan. Ganesh Five B was a cool, small T-type, formed like any ordinary star by condensation within an interstellar gas cloud, but at just eight times the mass of Jupiter, too small to support ordinary hydrogen fusion. Gravitational contraction and a small amount of sluggish deuterium fusion in its core warmed its dusty atmosphere to a little under 1500 degrees centigrade. There were metal hydrides and methane down there, even traces of water. Sometimes, its bands of sooty clouds were lit by obscure chains of lightning thousands of kilometers long. Sometimes, when the tug passed directly above the top of a convection cell, those huge, slow elevators that brought up heat from the core, Carver caught a glimpse of the deep interior, a fugitive flash of brighter red flecked with orange and yellow.

And at every tenth orbit, the tug passed over the permanent storm at the brown dwarf's equator, the location of the anomalous neutrino flux that had drawn Dr. Smith and the !Cha to Ganesh Five B. The storm's pale lens was more than fifteen thousand kilometers across; probes dropped into it discovered a complex architecture of fractal clusters crawling and racheting around each other like the gears of an insanely complicated mechanism bigger than the Earth. They also discovered that it was no longer emitting neutrinos, and it was breaking up along its edges—the tug's AIs estimated that it would break up in less than ten years.

While the tug swung around the brown dwarf's dim fires, Carver thought about the !Cha and what he had to do when the tug returned to Sheffield, and he lost himself in memories of his dead brother. He and Jarred had been close, two Navy brats following their parents from base to base, system to system. Although Jarred had been two years younger than Carver, he'd also been brighter and bolder, a natural leader, graduating at the top of his class in the Navy academy. The war had already begun when he graduated; the day after his passing-out parade, he followed Carver into active duty.

The last time Carver had seen Jarred, they'd spent three days together in the port city of Our Lady of the Flowers, Persopolis. It was the beginning of Jarred's leave, the end of Carver's. The night before Carver shipped out, they barhopped along the city's famous Strand. The more Jarred drank, the more serious and thoughtful he became. He told Carver that whichever side won the war, both would have to work hard at the peace if humanity was to have any chance at surviving.

"War only happens when peace breaks down. That's why peace is harder work, but more worthwhile."

"We defeat the Collective, we impose terms," Carver said. "Where's the problem?"

"If we won the war and imposed terms on the Collective, forced it to change, it would be an act of aggression," Jarred said. "The Collective would respond in kind and there would be another war. Instead of forcing change, we have to establish some kind of common ground."

"We don't have anything in common with those slavers."

"We have more in common with them than with the Jackaroo, or the Pale, or the !Cha. And if we don't find some way of living together," Jarred said, "we'll grow so far apart that we'll end up destroying each other."

He started to tell Carver about a loose network of people who were discussing how to broker a lasting peace, and Carver said that he didn't want to hear about it, told Jarred he should be careful, what he and his friends were doing sounded a little like treason. Now, in the cramped lifesystem of the tug, endlessly falling around a failed star, six billion kilometers from the nearest human being, Carver thought about what his brother had said on their last night together. Carver had gone a little crazy when he'd heard about his brother's death because it had been about as good and noble as an industrial accident. One machine had destroyed another, and Jarred and the rest of the *Croatian*'s crew had been incidental casualties who'd had no chance to fight back or escape. It was a brutal irony that Jarred's death could help Carver win his freedom.

At last, the tug fired up its motor and slipped into a new orbit, creeping up behind the escape pod, swallowing its black pip whole, then firing up again, a long hard burn to achieve escape velocity from the brown dwarf's gravity well. It pinned Carver to his couch for more than two hours. When it was over, following Mr. Kanza's instructions to the letter, Carver suited up, went outside, and clambered through the access hatch of the cargo bay.

The pod's systems were in sleep mode; careful use of a handheld neutron density scanner confirmed that apart from a !Cha tank, it contained nothing out of the ordinary. If Dr. Smith and Useless Beauty had retrieved something from the brown dwarf, either it had been lost with their ship, or it was hidden inside the !Cha's impervious casing.

Carver didn't attempt to contact the !Cha. He knew that his only chance of escape lay in a narrow window of op-

portunity during the final part of the return journey; until
then, he wanted to keep his plans to himself. He fixed tell-
tales inside the cargo bay in case the !Cha decided to try to
break out, locked it up, climbed back inside the lifesystem,
and sent a report to Mr. Kanza, and let the couch put him to
sleep.

Carver was supposed to remain in hypersleep until rendezvous with Mr. Kanza's scow, but he'd managed to reprogram
the couch while prepping the tug. It woke him twelve hours
early, four million kilometers out from Sheffield.

The !Cha's tank was still inside the escape pod, the pod
was still sealed in the cargo bay, and the tug was exactly on
course, falling ass-backward toward the gas giant. In a little
over two hours, it would skim through the outer atmosphere
in a fuel-saving aerobraking maneuver; meanwhile, the bulk
of the planet lay between it and the Ganesh Five facility and
Mr. Kanza's scow.

Carver had less than an hour before Mr. Kanza regained
radio contact with the tug. While the tug's triumvirate of
AIs threatened dire punishments Mr. Kanza had not trusted
them to carry out, Carver climbed into his pressure suit,
blew open the locked hatch using its explosive bolts, hauled
himself to the cargo bay, and took just under fifteen minutes
to rig a bypass and crank it open and slide inside.

He'd dropped a tab of military-grade amphetamine (it had
cost him fifty days' pocket money), but he was still weak
from the aftereffects of hypersleep, dopey, chilled to the
bone. It took all his concentration to plug into the external
port of the escape pod, scroll down the menu that lit up inside
his visor, and hit the command that would open the hatch.

Nothing happened.

Carver knew then that the !Cha was awake; it must have
locked the hatch from the inside. He was crouched on top of
the escape pod in the wash of the gas giant's corpse light with
nowhere else to go. Blowing the hatch had compromised the
tug's integrity; if it plowed into Sheffield's upper atmosphere,
it would break up. And in less than thirty minutes, it would
reestablish contact with Mr. Kanza's scow. Mr. Kanza would

have to alter the tug's course to save it, and then he would torture Carver until Carver's air supply ran out. So Carver did the only thing he could do: he opened all the com channels and started talking. He told the !Cha who he was, told it about Mr. Kanza and Lieutenant Rider, explained why he needed its help. He talked for ten minutes straight, and then a flat mechanical voice said, "Tell me exactly what you plan to do."

Relief washed clean through Carver, but he knew that he was not saved yet. With the feeling that he was tiptoeing over very thin ice, he said, "I plan to keep us both out of Mr. Kanza's clutches. I'd like to surrender to the Navy, but Mr. Kanza partnered up with an officer in the garrison here, so our only chance is to escape through one of the wormholes."

"But you do not have command of the tug."

"I don't need it."

Another pause. Then the flat voice said, "You have my interest."

Carver explained that the escape pod's motor was small but fully fueled, that with the tug's delta vee and a little extra assist it should be able to get them where they needed to go.

"I hope you understand that I'm not going to give you the flight plan. You'll have to trust me."

"You are afraid that I killed Dr. Smith. You are afraid that I will kill you, if I know the details of your plan."

"It crossed my mind, but you're a better bet than my owner."

"If I wanted you dead, I would not need to do it myself. Your owner will do that for me."

Carver wondered if that was an attempt at humor. "He'll kill both of us."

"He will not kill me if he believes that I have something he wants."

"If you do have something, he'll kill you and take it. And if you don't, he'll kill you anyway."

Carver sweated out another pause. Then, with a grinding vibration he felt through his pressure suit, the hatch of the escape pod opened.

Carver powered up the pod's systems, moved it out of the cargo bay, and adjusted its trim with a few puffs of the attitude jets, then fired up its motor. Ten minutes later, the tiny star of the dock facility dawned beyond the crescent and rings of the gas giant. The comm beeped. Mr. Kanza said, "That won't do you any good, you son of a whore."

"Watch and learn," Carver said.

"Listen to me carefully. If you don't do exactly as I say, your brother is a dead man."

"My brother was killed in action, along with everyone else on his ship."

Carver had control of the escape pod and was out of range of the shock stick hidden on the tug: he could say whatever he liked to Mr. Kanza. It was a good feeling. When Mr. Kanza started to rage at him, Carver told him that he was going to have to find some other way of covering his debts, and cut him off.

Far behind the pod, the tug lit its motor; no doubt Mr. Kanza was flying it by wire, hoping either to bring it close enough to use the shock stick on Carver, or ram him. He told Useless Beauty that if whatever it had found at the brown dwarf could be used as a weapon, now was the time to let him know.

"And don't tell me that you didn't find anything: there's no longer a neutrino source in that strange storm. You fished out some kind of Elder Culture artifact, and it did a number on your ship."

"One of the Elder Cultures may have had something to do with it," Useless Beauty said, "but it was not an artifact."

The squat black cylinder of its tank was jammed into the space between the two acceleration couches, three pairs of limbs folded up in a way that reminded Carver of a praying mantis. He tried to picture what was inside, a cross between a squid and a starfish swimming in oily, ammonia-rich water, the tough, nerve-rich tubules that ordinarily connected it to puppet juveniles plugged into the systems of its casing. It was even harder to picture what it was thinking, but Carver was pretty sure that his survival was at the bottom of its list of priorities.

He said, "If it wasn't an artifact, a machine or whatever, what was it?"

"A mathematical singularity from a universe where the

laws and constants of nature are very different from ours. A little like the software of your computers, but alive, self-aware, and imbued with a strong survival instinct. Perhaps an Elder Culture brought it through a kind of wormhole between its universe and ours. Perhaps it is a traveler unable to find its way home. In any event, it was trapped within the brown dwarf, and created the storm by epitaxy—using its own form as a template to make something approximating the conditions of its home, just as my tank contains a small portion of the ocean where my species evolved. Dr. Smith and I were able to capture it, but it broke free after we brought it aboard our ship. At once, it began to consume the structure of the ship. Dr. Smith went outside and successfully cut it away, but by then the fusion motor had been badly damaged, and it began to overheat. When Dr. Smith attempted to repair it, the cooling system exploded, and ruptured her suit. She died before she could get back inside, and I was forced to use the escape pod. I got away only a few minutes before the ship was destroyed."

"What happened to the thing you found?"

"If the neutrino flux is no longer detectable, I must assume that it was unable to return to the brown dwarf. Without a sufficient concentration of matter to weave a suitable habitat around itself," Useless Beauty said, "it would have evaporated."

It was a good story, and Carver believed about half it. He was pretty certain that the !Cha and Dr. Smith had captured something, Elder Culture artifact, weird mathematics, and that it had begun to destroy or transform their ship—it would explain why the composition of the thread Carver had found wrapped around Dr. Smith's arm didn't match anything in the library of the ship's lab—but Carver was pretty sure that Dr. Smith hadn't died in some kind of accident. It was more likely that Useless Beauty had murdered her because it wanted to keep what they'd found to itself and that prize was hidden somewhere inside its tank. But because he needed the !Cha's help—the casing of its tank was tougher than diamond, and its limbs were equipped with all kinds of gnarly tools, trying to fight it would be like going head to head with a battle drone—he didn't give voice to his doubts, said that it was a damn shame about losing Dr. Smith and the ship, he hoped to bring it better luck.

Useless Beauty did not reply, and its silence stretched as the escape pod hurtled toward Sheffield's ring system. Carver sipped sweetened apple pulp, watched the tug grow closer, watched the scow change course, half a million kilometers ahead, watched his own track on the navigational plot. He wasn't a pilot, but he knew his math, and his plan depended on nothing more complicated than ordinary Newtonian mechanics, a straightforward balance between gravity and distance and time and delta vee.

That's what he tried to tell himself, anyhow.

The rings filled the sky ahead, dozens of pale, parallel arcs hundreds of kilometers across, separated by gaps of varying widths. At T minus ten seconds, Carver handed control to the pod's AI. It lit the pod's motor at exactly T0. Two seconds later, the comm beeped: another message from Mr. Kanza.

Carver ignored it.

The tug was changing course too, but Carver was almost on the ring system now, falling toward a particular gap he'd chosen with the help of the escape pod's navigational system. He watched it with all of his concentration—he was finding it hard to believe in Newtonian mechanics now his life depended on it.

But there it was, at the edge of one of the arcs of ice and dust: a tiny grain flashing in raw sunlight: a shepherd moon. In less than a minute, it resolved into a pebble, a boulder, a pitted siding of dirty ice. As it flashed past, the pod's AI lit the motor again. The brief blip of acceleration and the momentum the pod had stolen from the moon made a small change in its delta vee; as it swung around the gas giant, the difference between the trajectory of the pod and the tug widened perceptibly.

The tug didn't have enough fuel to catch up with the pod now, but beyond Sheffield, Mr. Kanza's scow was changing course, and a few minutes later, a Navy cutter shot away from the dock facility, and the comm channels were suddenly alive with chatter: the salvage company's gigs and tugs; a couple of ships in transit between the wormholes; the Navy garrison, ordering both Mr. Kanza and Carver White to stand to and await interception.

Carver couldn't obey even if he wanted to. Less than a quarter of the pod's fuel remained and it was traveling very fast now, boosted by the slingshot through Sheffield's steep gravity well. With Mr. Kanza's scow and the Navy cutter in pursuit, it hurtled toward one of the wormhole throats. Carver had no doubt that the scow would follow him through, but he believed he had enough of an edge to make it to where he wanted to go, especially now that the Navy was involved. Someone in the garrison must have discovered Rider Jackson's deal with Mr. Kanza, and that meant the cutter would be more likely to try to stop Mr. Kanza's scow first.

The wormhole throat was a round dark mirror just over a kilometer across, twinkling with photons emitted by asymmetrical pair decay, framed by a chunky ring that housed the braid of strange matter that kept the throat open, all this embedded in the flat end of a chunk of rock that had been sculpted to a smooth cone by the nameless Elder Culture that had built the wormhole network a couple of million years ago. The pod hit it dead center, the radio chatter cut off, light flared, and the pod emerged halfway around the galaxy, above a planet shrouded in dense white clouds, shining pitilessly bright in the glare of a giant F5 star.

The planet, Texas IX, had a hot, dense, runaway greenhouse atmosphere—even Useless Beauty's tank could not have survived long in the searing storms that scoured its surface—but it also had a single moon that had been planoformed by Boxbuilders. That was where Carver wanted to go. He took back control of the pod and reconfigured it, extending wide braking surfaces of tough polycarbon, and lit the motor. It was a risky maneuver—if the angle of attack was too shallow, the pod would skip away into deep space with no hope of return, and if it was too steep, the pod would burn up—but aerobraking was the only way he could shed enough velocity.

Like a match scratching a tiny flare across a wall of white marble, the pod cut a chord above Texas IX's cloud tops. Carver was buffeted by vibration and pinned to the couch by deceleration that peaked at eight gees. He screamed into the vast shuddering noise; screamed with exhilaration and fear. Useless Beauty maintained its unsettling silence. Then the flames that filled the forward cameras died back and the pod rose above the planet's nightside.

The stars came out, all at once.

Useless Beauty's affectless voice said, "That was interesting."

"We aren't down yet," Carver said. He was grinning like a fool. He believed that the worst was over.

The escape pod fell away from Texas IX, heading out toward its moon. It was almost there when Mr. Kanza's scow overtook it.

Soon after it had formed, while its core had been still molten, something big had smashed into Texas IX's solitary moon. It had excavated a wide, deep basin in one side of the moon, and seismic waves traveling through the crust and core had focused on the area antipodal to the impact, jostling and lifting the surface, breaking crater rims and intercrater areas into a vast maze of hills and valleys, opening vents that flooded crater floors with fresh lava. That was where the escape pod came down, a thousand kilometers from the moon's only settlement, a hundred or so hardscrabble ranches strung along the shore of a shallow, hypersaline sea.

The scow, shooting past at a relative velocity of twenty klicks per second, had cooked the pod with a microwave burst, killing the pod's AI and crippling most of its control systems. Although the pod's aerobraking surfaces gave Carver a little leeway as it plowed through the moon's thin atmosphere, it smashed down hard and skidded a long way across a lava plain; despite the web holding Carver to the couch and the impact foam that flooded the pod's interior, he was knocked unconscious.

When he came around a few minutes later, the pod was canted at a steep angle, the hatch was open, and Useless

Beauty was gone. Carver was bruised over most of his body and his nose was tender and bleeding, possibly broken, but he was not badly hurt. He clawed his way through dissolving strands of impact foam and clambered out of the hatch, discovered that the pod lay at the end of a long furrow, its skin scarred, scraped, and discolored, and radiating an intense heat he could feel through his pressure suit. Big patches of spindly desert vegetation burned briskly on either side, lofting long reefs of smoke into the white sky.

Useless Beauty's tank stood on top of a ridge of overturned dirt, its black cylinder balanced on four many-jointed legs, two more limbs raised as if in prayer toward the sky. Carver was surprised and grateful to see it; he'd thought that the !Cha had taken the opportunity to make a run for it.

"This is only a brief respite," Useless Beauty said, as Carver clambered up the ridge. "Your owner's ship has swung far beyond this moon, but it is braking hard. It will soon be back."

"Then we can't stay here," Carver said. "We have to find a place to hide out until someone from the settlement comes to investigate."

The tank's two upper limbs swung down, aiming clusters of tools and sensors straight at Carver, and Useless Beauty said, "This is the part of your plan that I do not understand. This moon is owned by the Collective. You are a runaway slave. Surely they will side with your master. And if they do not, they will claim you for themselves."

Here it was. Carver took a breath and said, "Not if you claim me first."

After a short pause, Useless Beauty said, "So that is why you needed me."

"As we say in the Alliance, one good turn deserves another. I rescued you; now it's your turn to rescue me."

Throwing himself on the mercy of the !Cha was the biggest risk of the whole enterprise. Carver had never felt so scared and alone as he did then, waiting out another of Useless Beauty's silences while hot sunlight beat down through drifts of smoke, and Mr. Kanza's scow grew closer somewhere on the other side of the sky.

At last, the !Cha said, "You are very persistent."

"Does that mean you'll help me?"

"I admit that I want to see what happens next."

Carver supposed that he would have to take that as a "yes." Low hills shimmered in the middle distance. The ruins of a Boxbuilder city were scattered across their sere slopes like so many strings of beads. He pointed at the ruins and said, "As soon as I've gotten rid of this pressure suit, we start walking."

The !Cha's four-legged cylinder moved with easy grace through the simmering desert. Carver, wearing only his suit liner and boots, a pouch of water slung over his shoulder, had to jog to keep up. The air was thin, and the fat sun beat down mercilessly, but he reveled in the feeling of the sun's heat on his skin and dry wind in his hair, in the glare of the harsh landscape. Everything seemed infinitely precious, a chain of diamond-sharp moments. He had never before felt so alive as he did then, with death so close at his heels.

As Carver and the !Cha climbed toward a ravine that snaked between interlocking ridges, a double sonic boom cracked across the sky. The scow had arrived. But Carver wasn't ready to give up yet, and there were plenty of places to hide in the ruins. Chains of hollow cubes spun from polymer and rock dust climbed the slopes on either side, piled on top of each other, running along ridges, bridging narrow valleys: a formidable labyrinth with thousands of nooks and crannies that led deep into the hills, where he and Useless Beauty could hide out until some sort of rescue party arrived from the colony. For a little while, he began to believe that his plan might work, but then he and the !Cha reached the end of a chain of cubes at the top of a ridge, and found Rider Jackson waiting for them.

The young officer put his pistol on Carver and said, "You led us a pretty good chase, but you forgot one thing."

He was wearing a black Navy flight suit with a big zip down the front and pockets patching the chest and legs; that know-everything-tell-nothing expression blanked his face.

"I did?"

"You forgot you're an indentured worker. Your Judas bridge led me straight to you. Your owner will be here as soon as he can find a place to park his ship. I reckon you've got just enough time to tell me your side of the story."

While the scow lowered toward a setback below the ridge, Carver told Rider Jackson more or less everything that had happened out at the brown dwarf. Rider Jackson knew most of it, of course, because he'd seen the footage and data the tug had sent to Mr. Kanza, but he listened patiently and said, when Carver was finished, "I didn't know he was lying about your brother. If I had, I would have put an end to this a lot sooner."

"He was probably lying about a lot of things."

"Like giving me a fifty percent share in the prize, uh?"

"Like giving you any share at all."

"You might well be right," Rider Jackson said, and looked for the first time at Useless Beauty's tank. "Care to explain why you came along for the ride?"

"I have nothing to give you," it said.

"I bet you don't. But that wasn't what I asked," Rider Jackson said, and that was when Mr. Kanza arrived.

Grim and angry and out of breath, he bulled straight across the roofless cube and stuck his shock stick in Carver's face. Carver couldn't help flinching and Mr. Kanza smiled and said, "Tell me what the !Cha found and where it is, and maybe I won't have to use this."

Rider Jackson said, "There's no point threatening him. You want to know the truth, figure out how to get the !Cha to talk straight."

Mr. Kanza stepped back from Carver and aimed the shock stick at Rider Jackson. "You were indentured once, just like him. Is that why you're taking his side? I knew it was a mistake to let you go chase him down."

"You could have come with me," Rider Jackson said, "but you were happy to let me take the risk."

"He told you. He told you what that thing found and you made a deal with him."

"You're making a bad mistake."

The two men were staring at each other, Rider Jackson

impassive, Mr. Kanza angry and sweating. Saying, "I bet you tasted the stick in your time. You'll taste it again if you don't drop that pistol."

Rider Jackson said, "I guess we aren't partners anymore."

"You're right," Mr. Kanza said, and zapped him.

Carver was caught by the edge of the stick's field. His Judas bridge kicked in, his muscles went into spasm, hot spikes hammered through his skull, and he fell straight down.

Rider Jackson didn't so much as twitch. He put his pistol on Mr. Kanza and said, "The Navy took out my bridge when I signed up. Set down that stick and your pistol, and I'll let you walk away."

"We're partners."

"You said it yourself: not anymore. If you start walking now, maybe you can find somewhere to hide before the cutter turns up."

Mr. Kanza screamed and threw the shock stick at Rider Jackson and made a grab for the pistol stuck in his utility belt. Rider Jackson shot him. He shot Mr. Kanza twice in the chest and the man sat down, winded and dazed but still alive: his pressure suit had stopped the flechettes. He groped for his pistol and Rider Jackson said, "Don't do it."

"Fuck you," Mr. Kanza said and jerked up his pistol and fired it wildly. Rider Jackson didn't flinch. He took careful aim and shot Mr. Kanza in the head, and the man fell sideways and lay still.

Rider Jackson turned and put his pistol on Useless Beauty's black cylinder and said calmly, "I don't suppose this can punch through your casing, but I could shoot off your limbs one by one and set you on a fire."

There was a brief silence. Then the !Cha said, "You will need a very hot fire, and much more time than you have."

"I have more time than you think," Rider Jackson said. "I know Dana Sabah, the woman flying that cutter. She's a good pilot, but she's inexperienced and too cautious. Right now, she'll be watching us from orbit, waiting to see how it plays out before she makes her move."

"If she does not come, then the settlers will rescue me."

"Uh-uh. Even if the settlers know about us, which I doubt,

Dana will have told them to back off. I reckon I have more than enough time to boil the truth out of you."

Useless Beauty said, "I have already told the truth."

Carver got to his feet and told Rider Jackson, "It doesn't matter if it's telling the truth or not. All that matters is that we can escape in the scow. But first, I want you to drop your pistol."

Rider Jackson looked at the pistol Carver was holding—Mr. Kanza's pistol—and said, "I wondered if you'd have the guts to pick it up. The question now is, do you have the guts to use it?"

"If I have to."

"Look at us," Rider Jackson said. "I'm an officer in the Collective Navy; you're a prisoner of war sold into slavery, trying to get home . . . We could fight a duel to see who gets the scow. It would make a good ending to the story, wouldn't it?"

Carver smiled and said, "It would, but this isn't a story."

"Of course it's a story. Do you know why !Cha risk their lives chasing after Elder Culture artifacts?"

"It's something to do with sex."

"That's it. Back in the oceans of their homeworld, male !Cha constructed elaborate nests to attract a mate. The strongest, those most likely to produce the fittest offspring, made the biggest and most elaborate nests. Simple, straight-ahead Darwinism. The !Cha left their homeworld a long time ago, but the males still have to prove their worth by finding something novel, something no other male has. They have a bad jones for Elder Culture junk, but these days they get a lot of useful stuff from us too."

"It's lying about what it found," Carver said. "It told me it lost it, but I know it has it hidden away inside that tank."

Rider Jackson shook his head. "If it still had it, it would have killed you and paid off Mr. Kanza. And it wouldn't have called up the garrison back at Ganesh Five."

"It did? Is that why the cutter came after us?"

"Why do you think traffic control spotted you so quickly? It told them what you were up to, and it told them all about my deal with Mr. Kanza too. Dana Sabah told me all about it when she tried to get me to surrender," Rider Jackson said. "I guess our friend thought that involving the Navy would make the story more exciting."

"Son of a bitch. And I thought it was on my side because it owes me its life."

"As far as it's concerned, it doesn't owe you anything. The only reason it stuck with you is because you have something it needs. Something as unique as any ancient artifact, something it believes will win it a mate: the story of how you tried to escape."

"Your own story is just as good, Lieutenant Jackson," Useless Beauty said. "The two of you are enemies, as you said. Fight your duel. The winner will take me with him—I will pay well for it."

Rider Jackson looked at Carver and smiled. "What do you think?"

"I think the war is over." Carver was smiling too, remembering something Jarred had said. That peace was harder work than war, but more worthwhile.

Useless Beauty said, "I do not understand. You are enemies."

Rider Jackson stuck his pistol in his belt. "Like he said, the war is over. Besides, we both want the same thing."

Carver lowered the pistol he'd taken off Mr. Kanza's body and told the !Cha, "You're like Mr. Kanza. You think you own us, but you don't understand us."

"You must take me with you," Useless Beauty said.

"It wants to find out how the story ends," Rider Jackson told Carver.

"I will pay you well," Useless Beauty said.

Carver shook his head. "We don't need your money. We have the scow, and I have about thirty meters of a weird thread I took off Dr. Smith's body. It's superconducting and very strong, and I can't help wondering if it's something you and her pulled out of Ganesh Five B."

"I told you the truth about what we found," Useless Beauty said. "It escaped us and destroyed our ship, but it did not survive. However, I admit this thread may be of interest. I must examine it, of course, but if it is material transformed during the destruction of the ship, I may be willing to purchase it."

"That's what I thought," Carver said. "It may not be an Elder Culture artifact, but it could be worth something. And maybe the data from the probes I dropped into Ganesh Five B might be worth something too."

"I may be willing to purchase that too," Useless Beauty said. "As a souvenir."

"What do you think?" Carver said to Rider Jackson. "Think we'll get a better price on the open market."

"I can force you to take me," Useless Beauty said.

"No you can't," Carver said.

"And even if you could, it would ruin the ending of your story," Rider Jackson said. "I'm sure the settlers or the Navy will rescue you, for a price."

There was a long moment of silence. Then Useless Beauty said, "I would like to know what happens after you escape. I will pay well."

"If we escape," Carver said. "We have to get past the cutter."

"Dana Sabah's a good pilot, but I'm better," Rider Jackson said. "I reckon you are too."

"Before we do this, we need to work out where we're going."

"That's pretty easy, given that you're an indentured worker and the Navy wants my ass. Think that Kanza's old boat will get us to the Alliance?"

"It just might."

The two men grinned at each other. Then they ran for the scow.

GLORY

GREG EGAN

As we look back at the century that's just ended, it's obviously that Australian writer Greg Egan was one of the big new names to emerge in SF in the nineties, and is probably one of the most significant talents to enter the field in the last several decades. Already one of the most widely known of all Australian genre writers, Egan may well be the best new "hard-science" writer to enter the field since Greg Bear, and he is still growing in range, power, and sophistication. In the last few years, he has become a frequent contributor to *Interzone* and *Asimov's Science Fiction*, and has made sales as well to *Pulphouse, Analog, Aurealis, Eidolon,* and elsewhere; many of his stories have also appeared in various Best of the Year series, and he was on the Hugo Final Ballot in 1995 for his story "Cocoon," which won the Ditmar Award and the Asimov's Readers Award. He won the Hugo Award in 1999 for his novella "Oceanic." His first novel, *Quarantine,* appeared in 1992; his second novel, *Permutation City,* won the John W. Campbell Memorial Award in 1994. His other books include the novels *Distress, Diaspora,* and *Teranesia,* and three collections of his short fiction, *Axiomatic, Luminous,* and *Our Lady of Chernobyl.* His most recent book is the novel *Schild's Ladder,* and he is at work

on a new novel. He has a website at http://www.netspace.
netau/^gregegan/.

Egan has pictured galaxy-spanning civilizations in stories
such as "Border Guards" and "Riding the Crocodile." Here
he sweeps us along with scientists who are willing to go to
enormous lengths (including changing their species!) and
travel across the galaxy in order to investigate a scientific
mystery—one that inimical forces don't want them to solve.

1

An ingot of metallic hydrogen gleamed in the starlight,
a narrow cylinder half a meter long with a mass of about
a kilogram. To the naked eye it was a dense, solid object,
but its lattice of tiny nuclei immersed in an insubstantial
fog of electrons was one part matter to two hundred trillion
parts empty space. A short distance away was a second
ingot, apparently identical to the first, but composed of anti-
hydrogen.

A sequence of finely tuned gamma rays flooded into both
cylinders. The protons that absorbed them in the first ingot
spat out positrons and were transformed into neutrons, breaking their bonds to the electron cloud that glued them in place.
In the second ingot, antiprotons became antineutrons.

A further sequence of pulses herded the neutrons together
and forged them into clusters; the antineutrons were similarly rearranged. Both kinds of cluster were unstable, but in
order to fall apart they first had to pass through a quantum
state that would have strongly absorbed a component of the
gamma rays constantly raining down on them. Left to themselves, the probability of their being in this state would have
increased rapidly, but each time they measurably failed to
absorb the gamma rays, the probability fell back to zero. The
quantum Zeno effect endlessly reset the clock, holding the
decay in check.

The next series of pulses began shifting the clusters into
the space that had separated the original ingots. First neutrons, then antineutrons, were sculpted together in alternating
layers. Though the clusters were ultimately unstable, while

they persisted they were inert, sequestering their constitu-
ents and preventing them from annihilating their counter-
parts. The end point of this process of nuclear sculpting was
a sliver of compressed matter and antimatter, sandwiched
together into a needle one micron wide.

The gamma ray lasers shut down, the Zeno effect withdrew its prohibitions. For the time it took a beam of light to
cross a neutron, the needle sat motionless in space. Then it
began to burn, and it began to move.

The needle was structured like a meticulously crafted fire-
work, and its outer layers ignited first. No external casing
could have channeled this blast, but the pattern of tensions
woven into the needle's construction favored one direction
for the debris to be expelled. Particles streamed backward;
the needle moved forward. The shock of acceleration could
not have been borne by anything built from atomic-scale
matter, but the pressure bearing down on the core of the
needle prolonged its life, delaying the inevitable.

Layer after layer burned itself away, blasting the dwindling remnant forward ever faster. By the time the needle
had shrunk to a tenth of its original size it was moving at
ninety-eight percent of light-speed; to a bystander this could
scarcely have been improved upon, but from the needle's
perspective there was still room to slash its journey's duration by orders of magnitude.

When just one thousandth of the needle remained, its
time, compared to the neighboring stars, was passing two
thousand times more slowly. Still the layers kept burning,
the protective clusters unraveling as the pressure on them
was released. The needle could only reach close enough to
light-speed to slow down time as much as it required if it
could sacrifice a large enough proportion of its remaining
mass. The core of the needle could survive only for a few
trillionths of a second, while its journey would take two
hundred million seconds as judged by the stars. The proportions had been carefully matched, though: out of the two
kilograms of matter and antimatter that had been woven
together at the launch, only a few million neutrons were
needed as the final payload.

By one measure, seven years passed. For the needle, its last trillionths of a second unwound, its final layers of fuel blew away, and at the moment its core was ready to explode it reached its destination, plunging from the near-vacuum of space straight into the heart of a star.

Even here, the density of matter was insufficient to stabilize the core, yet far too high to allow it to pass unhindered. The core was torn apart. But it did not go quietly, and the shock waves it carved through the fusing plasma endured for a million kilometers: all the way through to the cooler outer layers on the opposite side of the star. These shock waves were shaped by the payload that had formed them, and though the initial pattern imprinted on them by the disintegrating cluster of neutrons was enlarged and blurred by its journey, on an atomic scale it remained sharply defined. Like a mold stamped into the seething plasma it encouraged ionized molecular fragments to slip into the troughs and furrows that matched their shape, and then brought them together to react in ways that the plasma's random collisions would never have allowed. In effect, the shock waves formed a web of catalysts, carefully laid out in both time and space, briefly transforming a small corner of the star into a chemical factory operating on a nanometer scale.

The products of this factory sprayed out of the star, riding the last traces of the shock wave's momentum: a few nanograms of elaborate, carbon-rich molecules, sheathed in a protective fullerene weave. Traveling at seven hundred kilometers per second, a fraction below the velocity needed to escape from the star completely, they climbed out of its gravity well, slowing as they ascended.

Four years passed, but the molecules were stable against the ravages of space. By the time they'd traveled a billion kilometers they had almost come to a halt, and they would have fallen back to die in the fires of the star that had forged them if their journey had not been timed so that the star's third planet, a gas giant, was waiting to urge them forward. As they fell toward it, the giant's third moon moved across their path. Eleven years after the needle's launch, its molecular offspring rained down onto the methane snow.

The tiny heat of their impact was not enough to damage them, but it melted a microscopic puddle in the snow. Surrounded by food, the molecular seeds began to grow. Within hours, the area was teeming with nanomachines, some mining the snow and the minerals beneath it, others assembling the bounty into an intricate structure, a rectangular panel a couple of meters wide.

From across the light-years, an elaborate sequence of gamma ray pulses fell upon the panel. These pulses were the needle's true payload, the passengers for whom it had merely prepared the way, transmitted in its wake four years after its launch. The panel decoded and stored the data, and the army of nanomachines set to work again, this time following a far more elaborate blueprint. The miners were forced to look farther afield to find all the elements that were needed, while the assemblers labored to reach their goal through a sequence of intermediate stages, carefully designed to protect the final product from the vagaries of the local chemistry and climate.

After three months' work, two small fusion-powered spacecraft sat in the snow. Each one held a single occupant, waking for the first time in their freshly minted bodies, yet endowed with memories of an earlier life.

Joan switched on her communications console. Anne appeared on the screen, three short pairs of arms folded across her thorax in a posture of calm repose. They had both worn virtual bodies with the same anatomy before, but this was the first time they had become Noudah in the flesh.

"We're here. Everything worked," Joan marveled. The language she spoke was not her own, but the structure of her new brain and body made it second nature.

Anne said, "Now comes the hard part."

"Yes." Joan looked out from the spacecraft's cockpit. In the distance, a fissured blue-gray plateau of water ice rose above the snow. Nearby, the nanomachines were busy disassembling the gamma ray receiver. When they had erased all traces of their handiwork they would wander off into the snow and catalyze their own destruction.

Joan had visited dozens of planet-bound cultures in the

past, taking on different bodies and languages as necessary, but those cultures had all been plugged into the Amalgam, the metacivilization that spanned the galactic disk. However far from home she'd been, the means to return to familiar places had always been close at hand. The Noudah had only just mastered interplanetary flight, and they had no idea that the Amalgam existed. The closest node in the Amalgam's network was seven light-years away, and even that was out of bounds to her and Anne now: they had agreed not to risk disclosing its location to the Noudah, so any transmission they sent could be directed only to a decoy node that they'd set up more than twenty light-years away.

"It will be worth it," Joan said.

Anne's Noudah face was immobile, but chromatophores sent a wave of violet and gold sweeping across her skin in an expression of cautious optimism. "We'll see." She tipped her head to the left, a gesture preceding a friendly departure.

Joan tipped her own head in response, as if she'd been doing so all her life. "Be careful, my friend," she said.

"You too."

Anne's ship ascended so high on its chemical thrusters that it shrank to a speck before igniting its fusion engine and streaking away in a blaze of light. Joan felt a pang of loneliness; there was no predicting when they would be reunited.

Her ship's software was primitive; the whole machine had been scrupulously matched to the Noudah's level of technology. Joan knew how to fly it herself if necessary, and on a whim she switched off the autopilot and manually activated the ascent thrusters. The control panel was crowded, but having six hands helped.

2

The world the Noudah called home was the closest of the system's five planets to their sun. The average temperature was one hundred and twenty degrees Celsius, but the high atmospheric pressure allowed liquid water to exist across the entire surface. The chemistry and dynamics of the planet's crust had led to a relatively flat terrain, with a patchwork of dozens of disconnected seas but no globe-spanning ocean. From space, these seas appeared as silvery mirrors, bordered by a violet and brown tarnish of vegetation.

The Noudah were already leaving their most electromagnetically promiscuous phase of communications behind, but the short-lived oasis of Amalgam-level technology on Baneth, the gas giant's moon, had had no trouble eavesdropping on their chatter and preparing an updated cultural briefing which had been spliced into Joan's brain.

The planet was still divided into the same eleven political units as it had been fourteen years before, the time of the last broadcasts that had reached the node before Joan's departure. Tira and Ghahar, the two dominant nations in terms of territory, economic activity, and military power, also occupied the vast majority of significant Niah archaeological sites.

Joan had expected that they'd be noticed as soon as they left Baneth—the exhaust from their fusion engines glowed like the sun—but their departure had triggered no obvious response, and now that they were coasting they'd be far harder to spot. As Anne drew closer to the homeworld, she sent a message to Tira's traffic control center. Joan tuned in to the exchange.

"I come in peace from another star," Anne said. "I seek permission to land."

There was a delay of several seconds more than the light-speed lag, then a terse response. "Please identify yourself and state your location."

Anne transmitted her coordinates and flight plan.

"We confirm your location, please identify yourself."

"My name is Anne. I come from another star."

There was a long pause, then a different voice answered. "If you are from Ghahar, please explain your intentions."

"I am not from Ghahar."

"Why should I believe that? Show yourself."

"I've taken the same shape as your people, in the hope of living among you for a while." Anne opened a video channel and showed them her unremarkable Noudah face. "But there's a signal being transmitted from these coordinates that might persuade you that I'm telling the truth." She gave the location of the decoy node, twenty light-years away, and specified a frequency. The signal coming from the node contained an image of the very same face.

This time, the silence stretched out for several minutes. It would take a while for the Tirans to confirm the true distance of the radio source.

"You do not have permission to land. Please enter this orbit, and we will rendezvous and board your ship."

Parameters for the orbit came through on the data channel. Anne said, "As you wish."

Minutes later, Joan's instruments picked up three fusion ships being launched from Tiran bases. When Anne reached the prescribed orbit, Joan listened anxiously to the instructions the Tirans issued. Their tone sounded wary, but they were entitled to treat this stranger with caution, all the more so if they believed Anne's claim.

Joan was accustomed to a very different kind of reception, but then the members of the Amalgam had spent hundreds of millennia establishing a framework of trust. They also benefited from a milieu in which most kinds of force had been rendered ineffectual; when everyone had backups of themselves scattered around the galaxy, it required a vastly disproportionate effort to inconvenience someone, let alone kill them. By any reasonable measure, honesty and cooperation yielded far richer rewards than subterfuge and slaughter.

Nonetheless, each individual culture had its roots in a biological heritage that gave rise to behavior governed more by ancient urges than contemporary realities, and even when they mastered the technology to choose their own nature, the precise set of traits they preserved was up to them. In the worst case, a species still saddled with inappropriate drives but empowered by advanced technology could wreak havoc. The Noudah deserved to be treated with courtesy and respect, but they did not yet belong in the Amalgam.

The Tirans' own exchanges were not on open channels, so once they had entered Anne's ship Joan could only guess at what was happening. She waited until two of the ships had returned to the surface, then sent her own message to Ghahar's traffic control.

"I come in peace from another star. I seek permission to land."

3

The Ghahari allowed Joan to fly her ship straight down to the surface. She wasn't sure if this was because they were more trusting, or if they were afraid that the Tirans might try to interfere if she lingered in orbit.

The landing site was a bare plain of chocolate-colored sand. The air shimmered in the heat, the distortions intensified by the thickness of the atmosphere, making the horizon waver as if seen through molten glass. Joan waited in the cockpit as three trucks approached; they all came to a halt some twenty meters away. A voice over the radio instructed her to leave the ship; she complied, and after she'd stood in the open for a minute, a lone Noudah left one of the trucks and walked toward her.

"I'm Pirit," she said. "Welcome to Ghahar." Her gestures were courteous but restrained.

"I'm Joan. Thank you for your hospitality."

"Your impersonation of our biology is impeccable." There was a trace of skepticism in Pirit's tone; Joan had pointed the Ghahari to her own portrait being broadcast from the decoy node, but she had to admit that in the context her lack of exotic technology and traits would make it harder to accept the implications of that transmission.

"In my culture, it's a matter of courtesy to imitate one's hosts as closely as possible."

Pirit hesitated, as if pondering whether to debate the merits of such a custom, but then rather than quibbling over the niceties of interspecies etiquette she chose to confront the real issue head-on. "If you're a Tiran spy, or a defector, the sooner you admit that the better."

"That's very sensible advice, but I'm neither."

The Noudah wore no clothing as such, but Pirit had a belt

with a number of pouches. She took a handheld scanner from one, and ran it over Joan's body. Joan's briefing suggested that it was probably only checking for metal, volatile explosives, and radiation; the technology to image her body or search for pathogens would not be so portable. In any case, she was a healthy, unarmed Noudah down to the molecular level.

Pirit escorted her to one of the trucks, and invited her to recline in a section at the back. Another Noudah drove while Pirit watched over Joan. They soon arrived at a small complex of buildings a couple of kilometers from where the ship had touched down. The walls, roofs, and floors of the buildings were all made from the local sand, cemented with an adhesive that the Noudah secreted from their own bodies.

Inside, Joan was given a thorough medical examination, including three kinds of full-body scan. The Noudah who examined her treated her with a kind of detached efficiency devoid of any pleasantries; she wasn't sure if that was their standard bedside manner, or a kind of glazed shock at having been told of her claimed origins.

Pirit took her to an adjoining room and offered her a couch. The Noudah anatomy did not allow for sitting, but they liked to recline.

Pirit remained standing. "How did you come here?" she asked.

"You've seen my ship. I flew it from Baneth."

"And how did you reach Baneth?"

"I'm not free to discuss that," Joan replied cheerfully.

"Not free?" Pirit's face clouded with silver, as if she were genuinely perplexed.

Joan said, "You understand me perfectly. Please don't tell me there's nothing *you're* not free to discuss with me."

"You certainly didn't fly that ship twenty light-years."

"No, I certainly didn't."

Pirit hesitated. "Did you come through the Cataract?" The Cataract was a black hole, a remote partner to the Noudah's sun; they orbited each other at a distance of about eighty billion kilometers. The name came from its telescopic appearance: a dark circle ringed by a distortion in the background of stars, like some kind of visual aberration. The Tirans and

Ghahari were in a race to be the first to visit this extraordinary neighbor, but as yet neither of them were quite up to the task.

"*Through* the Cataract? I think your scientists have already proven that black holes aren't shortcuts to anywhere."

"Our scientists aren't always right."

"Neither are ours," Joan admitted, "but all the evidence points in one direction: black holes aren't doorways, they're shredding machines."

"So you traveled the whole twenty light-years?"

"More than that," Joan said truthfully, "from my original home. I've spent half my life traveling."

"Faster than light?" Pirit suggested hopefully.

"No. That's impossible."

They circled around the question a dozen more times, before Pirit finally changed her tune from *how* to *why*?

"I'm a xenomathematician," Joan said. "I've come here in the hope of collaborating with your archaeologists in their study of Niah artifacts."

Pirit was stunned. "What do you know about the Niah?"

"Not as much as I'd like to." Joan gestured at her Noudah body. "As I'm sure you've already surmised, we've listened to your broadcasts for some time, so we know pretty much what an ordinary Noudah knows. That includes the basic facts about the Niah. Historically they've been referred to as your ancestors, though the latest studies suggest that you and they really just have an earlier common ancestor. They died out about a million years ago, but there's evidence that they might have had a sophisticated culture for as long as three million years. There's no indication that they ever developed space flight. Basically, once they achieved material comfort, they seem to have devoted themselves to various art forms, including mathematics."

"So you've traveled twenty light-years just to look at Niah tablets?" Pirit was incredulous.

"Any culture that spent three million years doing mathematics must have something to teach us."

"Really?" Pirit's face became blue with disgust. "In the ten thousand years since we discovered the wheel, we've already reached halfway to the Cataract. They wasted their time on useless abstractions."

Joan said, "I come from a culture of spacefarers myself, so I respect your achievements. But I don't think anyone really knows what the Niah achieved. I'd like to find out, with the help of your people."

Pirit was silent for a while. "What if we say no?"

"Then I'll leave empty-handed."

"What if we insist that you remain with us?"

"Then I'll die here, empty-handed." On her command, this body would expire in an instant; she could not be held and tortured.

Pirit said angrily, "You must be willing to trade *something* for the privilege you're demanding!"

"Requesting, not demanding," Joan insisted gently. "And what I'm willing to offer is my own culture's perspective on Niah mathematics. If you ask your archaeologists and mathematicians, I'm sure they'll tell you that there are many things written in the Niah tablets that they don't yet understand. My colleague and I"—neither of them had mentioned Anne before, but Joan was sure that Pirit knew all about her—"simply want to shed as much light as we can on this subject."

Pirit said bitterly, "You won't even tell us how you came to our world. Why should we trust you to share whatever you discover about the Niah?"

"Interstellar travel is no great mystery," Joan countered. "You know all the basic science already; making it work is just a matter of persistence. If you're left to develop your own technology, you might even come up with better methods than we have."

"So we're expected to be patient, to discover these things for ourselves . . . but you can't wait a few centuries for us to decipher the Niah artifacts?"

Joan said bluntly, "The present Noudah culture, both here and in Tira, seems to hold the Niah in contempt. Dozens of partially excavated sites containing Niah artifacts are under threat from irrigation projects and other developments. That's the reason we couldn't wait. We needed to come here and offer our assistance, before the last traces of the Niah disappeared forever."

Pirit did not reply, but Joan hoped she knew what her interrogator was thinking: *Nobody would cross twenty light-years for a few worthless scribblings. Perhaps we've underestimated the Niah. Perhaps our ancestors have left us a great secret, a great legacy. And perhaps the fastest— perhaps the only—way to uncover it is to give this impertinent, irritating alien exactly what she wants.*

4

The sun was rising ahead of them as they reached the top of the hill. Sando turned to Joan, and his face became green with pleasure. "Look behind you," he said.

Joan did as he asked. The valley below was hidden in fog, and it had settled so evenly that she could see their shadows in the dawn light, stretched out across the top of the fog layer. Around the shadow of her head was a circular halo like a small rainbow.

"We call it the Niah's light," Sando said. "In the old days, people used to say that the halo proved that the Niah blood was strong in you."

Joan said, "The only trouble with that hypothesis being that *you* see it around *your* head . . . and I see it around mine." On Earth, the phenomenon was known as a "glory." The particles of fog were scattering the sunlight back toward them, turning it one hundred and eighty degrees. To look at the shadow of your own head was to face directly away from the sun, so the halo always appeared around the observer's shadow.

"I suppose you're the final proof that Niah blood has nothing to do with it," Sando mused.

"That's assuming I'm telling you the truth, and I really can see it around my own head."

"And assuming," Sando added, "that the Niah really did stay at home, and didn't wander around the galaxy spreading their progeny."

They came over the top of the hill and looked down into

the adjoining riverine valley. The sparse brown grass of the hillside gave way to a lush violet growth closer to the water. Joan's arrival had delayed the flooding of the valley, but even alien interest in the Niah had only bought the archaeologists an extra year. The dam was part of a long-planned agricultural development, and however tantalizing the possibility that Joan might reveal some priceless insight hidden among the Niah's "useless abstractions," that vague promise could only compete with more tangible considerations for a limited time.

Part of the hill had fallen away in a landslide a few centuries before, revealing more than a dozen beautifully preserved strata. When Joan and Sando reached the excavation site, Rali and Surat were already at work, clearing away soft sedimentary rock from a layer that Sando had dated as belonging to the Niah's "twilight" period.

Pirit had insisted that only Sando, the senior archaeologist, be told about Joan's true nature; Joan refused to lie to anyone, but had agreed to tell her colleagues only that she was a mathematician and that she was not permitted to discuss her past. At first this had made them guarded and resentful, no doubt because they assumed that she was some kind of spy sent by the authorities to watch over them. Later it had dawned on them that she was genuinely interested in their work, and that the absurd restrictions on her topics of conversation were not of her own choosing. Nothing about the Noudah's language or appearance correlated strongly with their recent division into nations—with no oceans to cross, and a long history of migration they were more or less geographically homogeneous—but Joan's odd name and occasional faux pas could still be ascribed to some mysterious exoticism. Rali and Surat seemed content to assume that she was a defector from one of the smaller nations, and that her history could not be made explicit for obscure political reasons.

"There are more tablets here, very close to the surface," Rali announced excitedly. "The acoustics are unmistakable." Ideally they would have excavated the entire hillside, but they did not have the time or the labor, so they were using acoustic tomography to identify likely deposits of accessible Niah writing, and then concentrating their efforts on those spots.

The Niah had probably had several ephemeral forms of written communication, but when they found something worth publishing, it stayed published: they carved their symbols into a ceramic that made diamond seem like tissue paper. It was almost unheard of for the tablets to be broken, but they were small, and multitablet works were sometimes widely dispersed. Niah technology could probably have carved three million years' worth of knowledge onto the head of a pin—they seemed not to have invented nanomachines, but they were into high-quality bulk materials and precision engineering—but for whatever reason they had chosen legibility to the naked eye above other considerations.

Joan made herself useful, taking acoustic readings farther along the slope, while Sando watched over his students as they came closer to the buried Niah artifacts. She had learned not to hover around expectantly when a discovery was imminent; she was treated far more warmly if she waited to be summoned. The tomography unit was almost foolproof, using satellite navigation to track its position and software to analyze the signals it gathered; all it really needed was someone to drag it along the rock face at a suitable pace.

From the corner of her eye, Joan noticed her shadow on the rocks flicker and grow complicated. She looked up to see three dazzling beads of light flying west out of the sun. She might have assumed that the fusion ships were doing something useful, but the media was full of talk of "military exercises," which meant the Tirans and the Ghahari were engaging in expensive, belligerent gestures in orbit, trying to convince each other of their superior skills, technology, or sheer strength of numbers. For people with no real differences apart from a few centuries of recent history, they could puff up their minor political disputes into matters of the utmost solemnity. It might almost have been funny, if the idiots hadn't incinerated hundreds of thousands of each other's citizens every few decades, not to mention playing callous and often deadly games with the lives of the inhabitants of smaller nations.

"Jown! Jown! Come and look at this!" Surat called to her. Joan switched off the tomography unit and jogged toward the archaeologists, suddenly conscious of her body's strangeness. Her legs were stumpy but strong, and her balance as she ran came not from arms and shoulders but from the swish of her muscular tail.

"It's a significant mathematical result," Rali informed her proudly when she reached them. He'd pressure-washed the sandstone away from the near-indestructible ceramic of the tablet, and it was only a matter of holding the surface at the right angle to the light to see the etched writing stand out as crisply and starkly as it would have a million years before.

Rali was not a mathematician, and he was not offering his own opinion on the theorem the tablet stated; the Niah themselves had had a clear set of typographical conventions which they used to distinguish between everything from minor lemmas to the most celebrated theorems. The size and decorations of the symbols labeling the theorem attested to its value in the Niah's eyes.

Joan read the theorem carefully. The proof was not included on the same tablet, but the Niah had a way of expressing their results that made you believe them as soon as you read them; in this case the definitions of the terms needed to state the theorem were so beautifully chosen that the result seemed almost inevitable.

The theorem itself was expressed as a commuting hypercube, one of the Niah's favorite forms. You could think of a square with four different sets of mathematical objects associated with each of its corners, and a way of mapping one set into another associated with each edge of the square. If the maps commuted, then going across the top of the square, then down, had exactly the same effect as going down the left edge of the square, then across: either way, you mapped each element from the top-left set into the same element of the bottom-right set. A similar kind of result might hold for sets and maps that could naturally be placed at the corners and edges of a cube, or a hypercube of any dimension. It was also possible for the square faces in these structures to stand for relationships that held between the maps between sets, and for cubes to describe relationships between those relationships, and so on.

That a theorem took this form didn't guarantee its importance; it was easy to cook up trivial examples of sets and maps that commuted. The Niah didn't carve trivia into their timeless ceramic, though, and this theorem was no exception. The seven-dimensional commuting hypercube established a dazzlingly elegant correspondence between seven distinct, major branches of Niah mathematics, intertwining their most important concepts into a unified whole. It was a result Joan had never seen before: no mathematician anywhere in the Amalgam, or in any ancestral culture she had studied, had reached the same insight.

She explained as much of this as she could to the three archaeologists; they couldn't take in all the details, but their faces became orange with fascination when she sketched what she thought the result would have meant to the Niah themselves.

"This isn't quite the Big Crunch," she joked, "but it must have made them think they were getting closer." "The Big Crunch" was her nickname for the mythical result that the Niah had aspired to reach: a unification of every field of mathematics that they considered significant. To find such a thing would not have meant the end of mathematics—it would not have subsumed every last conceivable, interesting mathematical truth—but it would certainly have marked a point of closure for the Niah's own style of investigation.

"I'm sure they found it," Surat insisted. "They reached the Big Crunch, then they had nothing more to live for."

Rali was scathing. "So the whole culture committed collective suicide?"

"Not actively, no," Surat replied. "But it was the search that had kept them going."

"Entire cultures don't lose the will to live," Rali said. "They get wiped out by external forces: disease, invasion, changes in climate."

"The Niah survived for three million years," Surat countered. "They had the means to weather all of those forces. Unless they were wiped out by alien invaders with vastly superior technology." She turned to Joan. "What do you think?"

"About aliens destroying the Niah?"

"I was joking about the aliens. But what about the mathematics? What if they found the Big Crunch?"

"There's more to life than mathematics," Joan said. "But not much more."

Sando said, "And there's more to this find than one tablet. If we get back to work, we might have the proof in our hands before sunset."

5

Joan briefed Halzoun by video link while Sando prepared the evening meal. Halzoun was the mathematician Pirit had appointed to supervise her, but apparently his day job was far too important to allow him to travel. Joan was grateful; Halzoun was the most tedious Noudah she had encountered. He could understand the Niah's work when she explained it to him, but he seemed to have no interest in it for its own sake. He spent most of their conversations trying to catch her out in some deception or contradiction, and the rest pressing her to imagine military or commercial applications of the Niah's gloriously useless insights. Sometimes she played along with this infantile fantasy, hinting at potential superweapons based on exotic physics that might come tumbling out of the vacuum, if only one possessed the right Niah theorems to coax them into existence.

Sando was her minder too, but at least he was more subtle about it. Pirit had insisted that she stay in his shelter, rather than sharing Rali and Surat's; Joan didn't mind, because with Sando she didn't have the stress of having to keep quiet about everything. Privacy and modesty were nonissues for the Noudah, and Joan had become Noudah enough not to care herself. Nor was there any danger of their proximity leading to a sexual bond; the Noudah had a complex system of biochemical cues that meant desire only arose in couples with a suitable mixture of genetic differences and similarities. She would have had to search a crowded Noudah city for a week to find someone to lust after, though at least it would have been guaranteed to be mutual.

After they'd eaten, Sando said, "You should be happy. That was our best find yet."

"I am happy." Joan made a conscious effort to exhibit a viridian tinge. "It was the first new result I've seen on this planet. It was the reason I came here, the reason I traveled so far."

"Something's wrong, though, I think."

"I wish I could have shared the news with my friend," Joan admitted. Pirit claimed to be negotiating with the Tirans to allow Anne to communicate with her, but Joan was not convinced that she was genuinely trying. She was sure that Pirit would have relished the thought of listening in on a conversation between the two of them—while forcing them to speak Noudah, of course—in the hope that they'd slip up and reveal something useful, but at the same time she would have had to face the fact that the Tirans would be listening too. What an excruciating dilemma.

"You should have brought a communications link with you," Sando suggested. "A home-style one, I mean. Nothing we could eavesdrop on."

"We couldn't do that," Joan said.

He pondered this. "You really are afraid of us, aren't you? You think the smallest technological trinket will be enough to send us straight to the stars, and then you'll have a horde of rampaging barbarians to deal with."

"We know how to deal with barbarians," Joan said coolly.

Sando's face grew dark with mirth. "Now *I'm* afraid."

"I just wish I knew what was happening to her," Joan said. "What she was doing, how they were treating her."

"Probably much the same as we're treating you," Sando suggested. "We're really not that different." He thought for a moment. "There was something I wanted to show you." He brought over his portable console, and summoned up an article from a Tiran journal. "See what a borderless world we live in," he joked.

The article was entitled "Seekers and Spreaders: What We Must Learn from the Niah." Sando said, "This might give you some idea of how they're thinking over there. Jaqad is an academic archaeologist, but she's also very close to the people in power."

Joan read from the console while Sando made repairs to their shelter, secreting a molasseslike substance from a gland at the tip of his tail and spreading it over the cracks in the walls.

There were two main routes a culture could take, Jaqad argued, once it satisfied its basic material needs. One was to think and study: to stand back and observe, to seek knowledge and insight from the world around it. The other was to invest its energy in entrenching its good fortune.

The Niah had learned a great deal in three million years, but in the end it had not been enough to save them. Exactly what had killed them was still a matter of speculation, but it was hard to believe that if they had colonized other worlds they would have vanished on all of them. "Had the Niah been Spreaders," Jaqad wrote, "we might expect a visit from them, or them from us, sometime in the coming centuries."

The Noudah, in contrast, were determined Spreaders. Once they had the means, they would plant colonies across the galaxy. They would, Jaqad was sure, create new biospheres, reengineer stars, and even alter space and time to guarantee their survival. The growth of their empire would come first; any knowledge that failed to serve that purpose would be a mere distraction. "In any competition between Seekers and Spreaders, it is a Law of History that the Spreaders must win out in the end. Seekers, such as the Niah, might hog resources and block the way, but in the long run their own nature will be their downfall."

Joan stopped reading. "When you look out into the galaxy with your telescopes," she asked Sando, "how many *reengineered stars* do you see?"

"Would we recognize them?"

"Yes. Natural stellar processes aren't that complicated; your scientists already know everything there is to know about the subject."

"I'll take your word for that. So . . . you're saying Jaqad is wrong? The Niah themselves never left this world, but the galaxy already belongs to creatures more like them than like us?"

"It's not Noudah versus Niah," Joan said. "It's a matter of how a culture's perspective changes with time. Once a species conquers disease, modifies their biology, and spreads even a short distance beyond their homeworld, they usually start to relax a bit. The territorial imperative isn't some timeless Law of History; it belongs to a certain phase."

"What if it persists, though? Into a later phase?"

"That can cause friction," Joan admitted.

"Nevertheless, no Spreaders have conquered the galaxy?"

"Not yet."

Sando went back to his repairs; Joan read the rest of the article. She'd thought she'd already grasped the lesson demanded by the subtitle, but it turned out that Jaqad had something more specific in mind.

"Having argued this way, how can I defend my own field of study from the very same charges as I have brought against the Niah? Having grasped the essential character of this doomed race, why should we waste our time and resources studying them further?

"The answer is simple. We still do not know exactly how and why the Niah died, but when we do, that could turn out to be the most important discovery in history. When we finally leave our world behind, we should not expect to find only other Spreaders to compete with us, as honorable opponents in battle. There will be Seekers as well, blocking the way: tired, old races squatting uselessly on their hoards of knowledge and wealth.

"Time will defeat them in the end, but we already waited three million years to be born; we should have no patience to wait again. If we can learn how the Niah died, that will be our key, that will be our weapon. If we know the Seekers' weakness, we can find a way to hasten their demise."

6

The proof of the Niah's theorem turned out to be buried deep in the hillside, but over the following days they extracted it all.

It was as beautiful and satisfying as Joan could have wished, merging six earlier, simpler theorems while extending the techniques used in their proofs. She could even see hints of how the same methods might be stretched further to yield still stronger results. "The Big Crunch" had always been a slightly mocking, irreverent term, but now she was struck anew by how little justice it did to the real trend that had fascinated the Niah. It was not a matter of everything in mathematics collapsing in on itself, with one branch turning out to have been merely a recapitulation of another under a different guise. Rather, the principle was that every sufficiently beautiful mathematical system was rich enough to mirror *in part*—and sometimes in a complex and distorted fashion—every other sufficiently beautiful system. Nothing became sterile and redundant, nothing proved to have been a waste of time, but everything was shown to be magnificently intertwined.

After briefing Halzoun, Joan used the satellite dish to transmit the theorem and its proof to the decoy node. That had been the deal with Pirit: anything she learned from the Niah belonged to the whole galaxy, as long as she explained it to her hosts first.

The archaeologists moved across the hillside, hunting for more artifacts in the same layer of sediment. Joan was eager to see what else the same group of Niah might have published. One possible eight-dimensional hypercube was hovering in her mind; if she'd sat down and thought about it for a few decades she might have worked out the details herself, but the Niah did what they did so well that it would have seemed crass to try to follow clumsily in their footsteps when their own immaculately polished results might simply be lying in the ground, waiting to be uncovered.

A month after the discovery, Joan was woken by the sound of an intruder moving through the shelter. She knew it wasn't

Sando; even as she slept an ancient part of her Noudah brain was listening to his heartbeat. The stranger's heart was too quiet to hear, which required great discipline, but the shelter's flexible adhesive made the floor emit a characteristic squeak beneath even the gentlest footsteps. As she rose from her couch she heard Sando waking, and she turned in his direction.

Bright torchlight on his face dazzled her for a moment. The intruder held two knives to Sando's respiration membranes; a deep enough cut there would mean choking to death, in excruciating pain. The nanomachines that had built Joan's body had wired extensive skills in unarmed combat into her brain, and one scenario involving a feigned escape attempt followed by a sideways flick of her powerful tail was already playing out in the back of her mind, but as yet she could see no way to guarantee that Sando came through it all unharmed.

She said, "What do you want?"

The intruder remained in darkness. "Tell me about the ship that brought you to Baneth."

"Why?"

"Because it would be a shame to shred your colleague here, just when his work was going so well." Sando refused to show any emotion on his face, but the blank pallor itself was as stark an expression of fear as anything Joan could imagine.

She said, "There's a coherent state that can be prepared for a quark-gluon plasma in which virtual black holes catalyze baryon decay. In effect, you can turn all of your fuel's rest mass into photons, yielding the most efficient exhaust stream possible." She recited a long list of technical details. The claimed baryon decay process didn't actually exist, but the pseudophysics underpinning it was mathematically consistent, and could not be ruled out by anything the Noudah had yet observed. She and Anne had prepared an entire fictitious science and technology, and even a fictitious history of their culture, precisely for emergencies like this; they could spout red herrings for a decade if necessary, and never get caught out contradicting themselves.

"That wasn't so hard, was it?" the intruder gloated. "What now?"

"You're going to take a trip with me. If you do this nicely, nobody needs to get hurt."

Something moved in the shadows, and the intruder screamed in pain. Joan leaped forward and knocked one of the knives out of his hand with her tail; the other knife grazed Sando's membrane, but a second tail whipped out of the darkness and intervened. As the intruder fell backward, the beam of his torch revealed Surat and Rali tensed beside him, and a pick buried deep in his side.

Joan's rush of combat hormones suddenly faded, and she let out a long, deep wail of anguish. Sando was unscathed, but a stream of dark liquid was pumping out of the intruder's wound.

Surat was annoyed. "Stop blubbing, and help us tie up this Tiran cousin-fucker."

"Tie him up? You've killed him!"

"Don't be stupid, that's just sheath fluid." Joan recalled her Noudah anatomy; sheath fluid was like oil in a hydraulic machine. You could lose it all and it would cost you most of the strength in your limbs and tail, but you wouldn't die, and your body would make more eventually.

Rali found some cable and they trussed up the intruder. Sando was shaken, but he seemed to be recovering. He took Joan aside. "I'm going to have to call Pirit."

"I understand. But what will he do to these two?" She wasn't sure exactly how much Rali and Surat had heard, but it was certain to have been more than Pirit wanted them to know.

"Don't worry about that, I can protect them."

Just before dawn someone sent by Pirit arrived in a truck to take the intruder away. Sando declared a rest day, and Rali and Surat went back to their shelter to sleep. Joan went for a walk along the hillside; she didn't feel like sleeping.

Sando caught up with her. He said, "I told them you'd been working on a military research project, and you were exiled here for some political misdemeanor."

"And they believed you?"

"All they heard was half of a conversation full of incomprehensible physics. All they know is that someone thought you were worth kidnapping."

Joan said, "I'm sorry about what happened."

Sando hesitated. "What did you expect?"

Joan was stung. "One of us went to Tira, one of us came here. We thought that would keep everyone happy!"

"We're Spreaders," said Sando. "Give us one of anything, and we want two. Especially if our enemy has the other one. Did you really think you could come here, do a bit of fossicking, and then simply fly away without changing a thing?"

"Your culture has always believed there were other civilizations in the galaxy. Our existence hardly came as a shock."

Sando's face became yellow, an expression of almost parental reproach. "Believing in something in the abstract is not the same as having it dangled in front of you. We were never going to have an existential crisis at finding out that we're not unique; the Niah might be related to us, but they were still alien enough to get us used to the idea. But did you really think we were just going to relax and accept your refusal to share your technology? That one of you went to the Tirans only makes it worse for the Ghahari, and vice versa. Both governments are going absolutely crazy, each one terrified that the other has found a way to make its alien talk."

Joan stopped walking. "The war games, the border skirmishes? You're blaming all of that on Anne and me?"

Sando's body sagged wearily. "To be honest, I don't know all the details. And if it's any consolation, I'm sure we would have found another reason if you hadn't come along."

Joan said, "Maybe I should leave." She was tired of these people, tired of her body, tired of being cut off from civilization. She had rescued one beautiful Niah theorem and sent it out into the Amalgam. Wasn't that enough?

"It's up to you," Sando replied. "But you might as well stay until they flood the valley. Another year isn't going to change anything. What you've done to this world has already been done. For us, there's no going back."

7

Joan stayed with the archaeologists as they moved across the hillside. They found tablets bearing Niah drawings and poetry, which no doubt had their virtues but to Joan seemed bland and opaque. Sando and his students relished these discoveries as much as the theorems; to them, the Niah culture was a vast jigsaw puzzle, and any clue that filled in the details of their history was as good as any other.

Sando would have told Pirit everything he'd heard from Joan the night the intruder came, so she was surprised that she hadn't been summoned for a fresh interrogation to flesh out the details. Perhaps the Ghahari physicists were still digesting her elaborate gobbledygook, trying to decide if it made sense. In her more cynical moments she wondered if the intruder might have been Ghahari himself, sent by Pirit to exploit her friendship with Sando. Perhaps Sando had even been in on it, and Rali and Surat as well. The possibility made her feel as if she were living in a fabricated world, a scape in which nothing was real and nobody could be trusted. The only thing she was certain that the Ghaharis could not have faked was the Niah artifacts. The mathematics verified itself; everything else was subject to doubt and paranoia.

Summer came, burning away the morning fogs. The Noudah's idea of heat was very different from Joan's previous perceptions, but even the body she now wore found the midday sun oppressive. She willed herself to be patient. There was still a chance that the Niah had taken a few more steps toward their grand vision of a unified mathematics, and carved their final discoveries into the form that would outlive them by a million years.

When the lone fusion ship appeared high in the afternoon sky, Joan resolved to ignore it. She glanced up once, but she kept dragging the tomography unit across the ground. She was sick of thinking about Tiran-Ghahari politics. They had played their childish games for centuries; she would not take the blame for this latest outbreak of provocation.

Usually the ships flew by, disappearing within minutes, showing off their power and speed. This one lingered, weaving back and forth across the sky like some dazzling insect performing an elaborate mating dance. Joan's second shadow darted around her feet, hammering a strangely familiar rhythm into her brain.

She looked up, disbelieving. The motion of the ship was following the syntax of a gestural language she had learned on another planet, in another body, a dozen lifetimes ago. The only other person on this world who could know that language was Anne

She glanced toward the archaeologists a hundred meters away, but they seemed to be paying no attention to the ship. She switched off the tomography unit and stared into the sky. *I'm listening, my friend. What's happening? Did they give you back your ship? Have you had enough of this world, and decided to go home?*

Anne told the story in shorthand, compressed and elliptic. The Tirans had found a tablet bearing a theorem: the last of the Niah's discoveries, the pinnacle of their achievements. Her minders had not let her study it, but they had contrived a situation making it easy for her to steal it, and to steal this ship. They had wanted her to take it and run, in the hope that she would lead them to something they valued far more than any ancient mathematics: an advanced spacecraft, or some magical stargate at the edge of the system.

But Anne wasn't fleeing anywhere. She was high above Ghahar, reading the tablet, and now she would paint what she read across the sky for Joan to see.

Sando approached. "We're in danger, we have to move."

"Danger? That's my friend up there! She's not going to shoot a missile at us!"

"Your friend?" Sando seemed confused. As he spoke, three more ships came into view, lower and brighter than the first. "I've been told that the Tirans are going to strike the valley, to bury the Niah sites. We need to get over the hill and indoors, to get some protection from the blast."

"Why would the Tirans attack the Niah sites? That makes no sense to me."

Sando said, "Nor me, but I don't have time to argue."

The three ships were menacing Anne's, pursuing her, trying to drive her away. Joan had no idea if they were Ghahari defending their territory, or Tirans harassing her in the hope that she would flee and reveal the nonexistent shortcut to the stars, but Anne was staying put, still weaving the same gestural language into her maneuvers even as she dodged her pursuers, spelling out the Niah's glorious finale.

Joan said, "You go. I have to see this." She tensed, ready to fight him if necessary.

Sando took something from his tool belt and peppered her side with holes. Joan gasped with pain and crumpled to the ground as the sheath fluid poured out of her.

Rali and Surat helped carry her to the shelter. Joan caught glimpses of the fiery ballet in the sky, but not enough to make sense of it, let alone reconstruct it.

They put her on her couch inside the shelter. Sando bandaged her side and gave her water to sip. He said, "I'm sorry I had to do that, but if anything had happened to you I would have been held responsible."

Surat kept ducking outside to check on the "battle," then reporting excitedly on the state of play. "The Tiran's still up there, they can't get rid of it. I don't know why they haven't shot it down yet."

Because the Tirans were the ones pursuing Anne, and they didn't want her dead. But for how long would the Ghahari tolerate this violation?

Anne's efforts could not be allowed to come to nothing. Joan struggled to recall the constellations she'd last seen in the night sky. At the node they'd departed from, powerful telescopes were constantly trained on the Noudah's homeworld. Anne's ship was easily bright enough, its gestures wide enough, to be resolved from seven light-years away—if the planet itself wasn't blocking the view, if the node was above the horizon.

The shelter was windowless, but Joan saw the ground outside the doorway brighten for an instant. The flash was silent; no missile had struck the valley, the explosion had taken place high above the atmosphere.

Surat went outside. When she returned she said quietly, "All clear. They got it."

Joan put all her effort into spitting out a handful of words. "I want to see what happened."

Sando hesitated, then motioned to the others to help him pick up the couch and carry it outside.

A shell of glowing plasma was still visible, drifting across the sky as it expanded, a ring of light growing steadily fainter until it vanished into the afternoon glare.

Anne was dead in this embodiment, but her backup would wake and go on to new adventures. Joan could at least tell her the story of her local death: of virtuoso flying and a spectacular end.

She'd recovered her bearings now, and she recalled the position of the stars. The node was still hours away from rising. The Amalgam was full of powerful telescopes, but no others would be aimed at this obscure planet, and no plea to redirect them could outrace the light they would need to capture in order to bring the Niah's final theorem back to life.

8

Sando wanted to send her away for medical supervision, but Joan insisted on remaining at the site.

"The fewer officials who get to know about this incident, the fewer problems it makes for you," she reasoned.

"As long as you don't get sick and die," he replied.

"I'm not going to die." Her wounds had not become infected, and her strength was returning rapidly.

They compromised. Sando hired someone to drive up from the nearest town to look after her while he was out at the excavation. Daya had basic medical training and didn't ask awkward questions; he seemed happy to tend to Joan's needs, and then lie outside daydreaming the rest of the time.

There was still a chance, Joan thought, that the Niah had carved the theorem on a multitude of tablets and scattered them all over the planet. There was also a chance that the

Tirans had made copies of the tablet before letting Anne abscond with it. The question, though, was whether she had the slightest prospect of getting her hands on these duplicates.

Anne might have made some kind of copy herself, but she hadn't mentioned it in the prologue to her aerobatic rendition of the theorem. If she'd had any time to spare, she wouldn't have limited herself to an audience of one: she would have waited until the node had risen over Ghahar.

On her second night as an invalid, Joan dreamed that she saw Anne standing on the hill looking back into the fog-shrouded valley, her shadow haloed by the Niah light.

When she woke, she knew what she had to do.

When Sando left, she asked Daya to bring her the console that controlled the satellite dish. She had enough strength in her arms now to operate it, and Daya showed no interest in what she did. That was naive, of course: whether or not Daya was spying on her, Pirit would know exactly where the signal was sent. So be it. Seven light-years was still far beyond the Noudah's reach; the whole node could be disassembled and erased long before they came close.

No message could outrace light directly, but there were more ways for light to reach the node than the direct path, the fastest one. Every black hole had its glory, twisting light around it in a tight, close orbit and flinging it back out again. Seventy-four hours after the original image was lost to them, the telescopes at the node could still turn to the Cataract and scour the distorted, compressed image of the sky at the rim of the hole's black disk to catch a replay of Anne's ballet.

Joan composed the message and entered the coordinates of the node. *You didn't die for nothing, my friend. When you wake and see this, you'll be proud of us both.*

She hesitated, her hand hovering above the send key. The Tirans had wanted Anne to flee, to show them the way to the stars, but had they really been indifferent to the loot they'd let her carry? The theorem had come at the end of the Niah's three-million-year reign. To witness this beautiful truth would not destroy the Amalgam, but might it not weaken it? If the Seekers' thirst for knowledge was slaked, their sense of purpose corroded, might not the most crucial strand of the culture fall into a twilight of its own? There was no short-cut to the stars, but the Noudah had been goaded by their alien visitors, and the technology would come to them soon enough.

The Amalgam had been goaded too: the theorem she'd already transmitted would send a wave of excitement around the galaxy, strengthening the Seekers, encouraging them to complete the unification by their own efforts. The Big Crunch might be inevitable, but at least she could delay it, and hope that the robustness and diversity of the Amalgam would carry them through it, and beyond.

She erased the message and wrote a new one, addressed to her backup via the decoy node. It would have been nice to upload all her memories, but the Noudah were ruthless, and she wasn't prepared to stay any longer and risk being used by them. This sketch, this postcard, would have to be enough.

When the transmission was complete she left a note for Sando in the console's memory.

Daya called out to her, "Jown? Do you need anything?"

She said, "No. I'm going to sleep for a while."

MAELSTROM

KAGE BAKER

E ven on a rough, rude, frontier Mars, people will still
have a need for entertainment, and perhaps even for the
consolations of Art. And, as proved by the sly and funny
story that follows, they may have to turn to the most unlikely
of sources to find them. . .

One of the most prolific new writers to appear in the late
nineties, Kage Baker made her first sale in 1997, to *Asimov's
Science Fiction,* and has since become one of that magazine's most frequent and popular contributors with her sly
and compelling stories of the adventures and misadventures
of the time-traveling agents of the Company; of late, she's
started two other linked sequences of stories there as well,
one of them set in as lush and eccentric a high fantasy milieu
as any we've seen. Her stories have also appeared in *Realms
of Fantasy, Sci Fiction, Amazing,* and elsewhere. Her first
Company novel, *In the Garden of Iden,* was also published
in 1997 and immediately became one of the most acclaimed
and widely reviewed first novels of the year. More Company
novels quickly followed, including *Sky Coyote, Mendoza in
Hollywood, The Graveyard Game, The Life of the World
to Come,* as well as a chapbook novella, *The Empress of
Mars,* and her first fantasy novel, *The Anvil of the World.*

Her many stories have been collected in *Black Projects,
White Knights* and *Mother Aegypt and Other Stories*. Her
most recent books include two new collections, *The Children of the Company* and *Dark Mondays*. Coming up are a
new novel, *Machine's Children,* and another new collection,
Gods and Pawns. In addition to her writing, Baker has been
an artist, actor, and director at the Living History Center,
and has taught Elizabethan English as a second language.
She lives in Pismo Beach, California.

◐   Mr. Morton was a wealthy man. He hated it.

For one thing, he wasn't accustomed to having money.
During most of his life he had been institutionalized, having
been diagnosed as an Eccentric at the age of ten. But when
the British Arean Company had needed settlers for Mars,
the Winksley Hospital for the Psychologically Suspect had
obligingly shipped most of its better-compensated inmates
off to assist in the colonization efforts.

Mr. Morton had liked going to Mars. For a while, he had
actually been paid a modest salary by the BAC. Eccentric
though he was, he was nevertheless quite brilliant at designing and fabricating precast concrete shelters, a fact that
would have surprised anyone who hadn't seen the endless
model villages he'd built on various tabletops in Ward Ten,
back on Earth. The knowledge that he was earning his own
keep as well as doing his bit to help terraforming along had
built up his self-esteem.

When the economic bubble that had buoyed up the BAC
burst, Mr. Morton had been summarily made Redundant.
Redundant was nearly as bad as Eccentric. He was unable
to afford a ticket back to Earth and might well have become
an oxygen-starved mendicant sleeping in the Tubes, had he
not found employment as a waiter at the Empress of Mars
tavern. Here Mr. Morton had room, board, and oxygen, if
not a salary, in surroundings so reminiscent of dear old
Winksley Hospital for the Psychologically Suspect that he
felt quite at home.

Then his employer, known as Mother Griffith by her pa-
trons, had had a run of extraordinary luck that had resulted

in making her the richest woman on the planet. Farewell to the carefree days of Mr. Morton's poverty! Mother Griffith set him up in business as a contractor and architect.

She now owned the entirety of Mons Olympus, and leased out lots to commercial tenants with the dream of building a grand new city on Mars. Areco, the immense corporation owning the rest of the planet, busily devised laws, permit fees, and taxes to hinder her as much as it was able. But by bankrolling Mr. Morton's firm, Mother Griffith found she was able to evade neatly several miles of red tape and avoid a small fortune in penalties.

All Mr. Morton was now obliged to do was sit at a drafting terminal and design buildings, and, now and then, suit up and wander Outside to look at a construction site where laborers actually hired and directed by Mother Griffith were busily pouring the peculiarly salmon-pink concrete of Mars.

For a brief period, Mr. Morton had enjoyed the contemplation of his bank account. He had enjoyed being able to afford his very own Outside gear at last, with the knowledge that he'd never have to improvise an air filter out of an old sock again. His indoor raiment was all of the best, and in the sable hues he preferred. And oh, what downloads of forbidden books the black market in literature had to offer, to a man of his economic status!

And yet, the more he kept company with Messrs. Poe, Dumas, Verne, King, and Lovecraft, the greater grew his sense of overwhelming melancholy. His position as a newly prosperous bourgeois seemed distasteful to him, a betrayal of all that was artistic and romantic in his soul.

"Stop moping," Mother Griffith told him. "Bloody hell, man, the Goddess gifts you with obscene amounts of cash, and you can't think of more to do with it than buy some fusty old words? You're making a city with your own two hands, in pixels anyway. There's power for you! You want *artistic*, is it? Stick up some artistic buildings. Cornices and gingerbread and whatnot. I don't care how they look."

Mr. Morton retired to his drafting terminal in high dudgeon and plotted out an entire city block in Neogothic

Rococo. Factoring in Martian gravity, he realized he could make his elaborate spires and towers even more soaring, even more delicate and dreamlike. A few equations gave him breathtaking results. So for a while he was almost happy, designing a municipal waste treatment plant of ethereal loveliness.

And, just here above, where its gargoyles might greet both sunset and dawn, would rise. . . the *Edgar Allan Poe Center for the Performing Arts*!

Mr. Morton leaned back from his console, dumbfounded. *Here* was a worthy use for vulgar riches.

When the last of the concrete forms had been taken away, when all the fabulously expensive black walnut interiors shipped up from Earth had been installed, Mr. Morton's theater was a sight to behold. Even the shaven-headed members of the Martian Agricultural Collective, notorious for their philistinism, suited up and hiked the slope to stare at it.

For one thing, dye had been added to the concrete, so the whole thing was an inky purple. Not only gargoyles but statues of the great poets and dramatists, floral roundels, bosses, shields, crests, and every other ornamental folly Mr. Morton had been able to imagine covered most of its gloomy exterior, and a great deal of the interior too. On Earth, it would have crumbled under the weight of gravity and public opinion. Here on Mars, it stood free, a cathedral to pure weirdness.

Within, it had been fitted up with a genuine old-fashioned proscenium stage. Swags of black velvet concealed the very latest in holoprojectors, but Mr. Morton had hopes of using that vulgar modern entertainment seldom.

"But that's what people want to see," said Mother Griffith in dismay.

"Only because they've never known anything better," said Mr. Morton. "I shall revive Theater as an art, here in this primitive place!"

He thought it might be nice to begin with the ancient Greeks, and so he put a word in his black marketeer's ear about it. A week later that useful gentleman sent him a download containing the surviving works of Aristophanes. Mr. Morton read them eagerly, and was horrified. Had he ever truly understood the meaning of vulgarity before now?

He was not at a loss for long. Mr. Morton decided that he would write the EAPCPA's repertory himself; and what better way to open its first season than with adaptations of every single one of Poe's works?

"You're putting on *The Descent into the Maelstrom*?" shouted Mother Griffith. "But it's just two men in a boat going down a giant plug hole!"

"It is a meditation on the grandeur and horror of Nature," said Mr. Morton, a little stiffly.

"But how on earth will you stage such a thing?"

"I had envisioned a dramatic reading," said Mr. Morton.

"Oh, that'll have them standing in the aisles," said Mother Griffith. "Look you, Mr. Morton, not to intrude on your artistic sensibilities or anything, but mightn't you just think about giving 'em at least one of those son-et-lumière shows so they have something to look at? For if the miners and haulers feel they haven't had their tickets' worth of entertainment, they're liable to tear their seats loose and start swinging with 'em, see, this being a frontier and all."

Mr. Morton stormed off in a sulk, but, on sober reflection, decided that to ignore the visual aspect of performance was, perhaps, a little risky. He drafted another script, in which the Maelstrom itself would be presented by dancers, and each unfortunate mariner had a stylized lament before meeting his respective fate.

"They want a thrilling spectacle?" he said aloud, as he read it over. "*Here* it is!"

Fearful as he was to commit the purity of his script to human actors, Mr. Morton liked even less the idea of machine-generated ones. He decided to hold auditions.

The interior of Mr. Morton's theater, while richly furnished, was quite a bit smaller than its remarkable exterior (air being a utility on Mars, living places tended to conserve its volume). Mr. Morton preferred to think of the result as an "intimate performance venue." Seating capacity was thirty persons. Mr. Morton sat in the back row now, watching as Mona Griffith stepped from the wings.

"Hi, Mr. Morton!" said Mona.

"Hello, Mona." Mr. Morton shifted uncomfortably. Mona was the youngest of Mother Griffith's daughters. She was carrying a SoundBox 3000 unit. She set it on the floor and switched it on. Slinky and suggestive music oozed forth. Mr. Morton's knuckles turned white.

"Mona, you're not going to do a striptease, are you?" he inquired.

"Well—yes," said Mona, in the act of unbuckling her collar.

"Mona, you know how your mother feels about that," said Mr. Morton. He himself knew quite well; he had known Mona since she was ten. "In any case, I'm holding auditions for a play, not a—a burlesque review!"

"I'm of age now, aren't I?" said Mona defiantly. "And anyway, this isn't just a striptease. It's very intellectual. I'm *reciting* as I'm stripping, see?"

"Tell me you're not stripping to Hamlet's soliloquy," begged Mr. Morton.

"Pft! As if! I'm doing General Klaar's Lament from *The Wars of the House of Klaar*," said Mona. "And I've got these really horrible-looking fake wounds painted in unexpected places, see, so as to create quite a striking effect. So it wouldn't be at all, um, what's that word? Prurient?"

"No, I don't suppose it would be," said Mr. Morton. "But—"

They heard the warning klaxon announcing that the airlock had opened, and then the heavy tread of armored feet approaching the inner door. *Boom*. The inner door was kicked open, and a man in miners' armor strode down the aisle toward Mona. He drew a disrupter pistol and shot the SoundBox 3000, which promptly fell silent.

"Durk! You bastard!" shrieked Mona. The intruder marched up onstage, not even removing his mask. Mona kicked his shin viciously, forgetting that he was wearing Larlite greaves, and hopped backward clutching her foot. "My toe!"

Her fiancé shoved his mask back and glared at her. "You promised me you wouldn't do this," he said.

"You shot my SoundBox!"

"But you promised me you wouldn't do this!"

"But you shot my SoundBox!"

"Put your mask on. We're going home!" said Durk, waving his pistol distractedly.

"But you shot my SoundBox!"

"Next," said Mr. Morton, from underneath his seat.

The next applicant waited until Durk and Mona had made their noisy exit before emerging from the wings.

"Er . . . Hello, Alf," said Mr. Morton.

Alf was a hauler. Haulers drove CO_2 freighters out on the High Road, the boulder-marked route that cut across the Outside wastes to the two poles. The mortality rate for haulers was high. Consequently, most haulers had been recruited from Hospitals, because they tended to care less about that fact.

Alf was able to face down cyclones, wandering dunes, flying boulders, starvation, and thirst without turning a hair, but he was sweating now as he peered out toward the empty seats.

"Erm," he said.

"Are you here for the audition, Alf?"

"Yeah," said Alf, blinking.

"And . . . we took our meds this morning, did we?"

"Yeah."

"So . . . what will you be performing today, Alf?"

"Erm," said Alf, and then he drew a breath and said:

"Scene. Morning room in Alregons Flat in Arf Moon Street. Da room is luxriussly an artriscally fronished. Da sound of a pianer is eard in da adoining room. Lane is ranging arfternoon tea onna table an arfter da music as ceased, Alregon enners curvy mark from music room ovver curvy mark. Alregon. Didja ear wot I wuz playing Lane? Lane I din't fink it wuz plite to listen sir—"

Alf, what on earth is that?"

Alf fell silent and blinked. "S'play."

"Which play?"

"Da Importance of Being Earnest," said Alf. "By Oscar Wilde."

Mr. Morton sat bolt upright. "Where did you find a copy?" Oscar Wilde's work had been condemned as Politically Trivial so long ago that scarcely any of it survived.

"Canary Wharf Ospital," said Alf. Mr. Morton frowned in perplexity. Canary Wharf was a much less genteel institution than Winksley. He fought back feelings of class division and inquired:

"They had *The Importance of Being Earnest* in the library?"

"Nah," said Alf. "Shoved under floor inna closet. It was like dis old book wiv paper an all? Used to read it when I wuz locked innere. I remember everyfing I read, see?"

Mr. Morton felt his heart patter against his ribs. "You remember the whole play?"

"Oh, yeah." Alf grinned. "Allaway to 'When I married Lord Bracknell I ad no forchoon of any kind. But I never dreamed for a moment of allowing dat to stand in my way. Well I spose I must give my consent.' I wuz locked in a lot."

"You must recite the whole play for me one day, Alf," said Mr. Morton, dazzled by mental images of an Exclusive World Premiere Revival.

"Sure," said Alf. "Did I pass da audition?"

"Why—of course," said Mr. Morton, thinking to himself that Alf could always sweep the floors. "Well done. I'll let you know when rehearsals start."

"Hey, fanks," said Alf, and, grinning hugely, he clumped away to the airlock.

"Next?" said Mr. Morton.

A woman edged out on stage, wringing her hands. Mr. Morton recognized the silver brooch she wore on her bosom, and sighed. She was one of the sisters from the Ephesian Church's mission down the mountain at Settlement Base.

"Hello," she said. "I . . . ah . . . just wanted to ask you whether you'd ever known the infinite consolation of the Goddess?"

"Next," said Mr. Morton.

In the end, Mr. Morton decided to advertise. He put a notice in *Variety* (the Tri-Worlds edition): himself, recorded in holo, staring earnestly into the foremost camera and saying:

"Have you ever considered emigration to Mars? An adventure awaits you in a new company just forming on the Red Planet! The Edgar Allan Poe Center for the Performing Arts is looking for persons with theatrical experience interested in sharing our grand quest to bring the mysteries of our craft to the red and windswept Arean frontier!

"Yes, *you*, who have longed to escape from the humdrum routine of Earth, may find your ultimate self-expression here in the tortured and dramatic landscape of a new world! Send all inquiries to: Amorton@poeyouareavenged.pub.ares. uk *today*!" The link flashed at the bottom of the holo. Mr. Morton pointed at it and dropped his voice impressively: "Do you dare?"

Do we dare not to? Meera wondered sadly. She looked over at Crispin, who was sleeping as soundly as though they hadn't a month to go on their lease and no money to renew, and hadn't been living on cauliflower for a week, and hadn't just received notice that the revival of *Peter Pan* was indefinitely postponed due to the producer's backing out. She had been cast as Peter, and her salary would have paid both the lease and the last three installments on the Taranis.

Crispin was an actor too. He had boyish good looks and a wonderful voice, and was brilliant in the right parts; but most of the time he tended to get the wrong parts. His Mr. Toad had been praised to the skies, likewise his Christmas Panto SpongeBob; but his Dr. Who had, in the succinct words of the *Times* theater critic, "stunk up the stage," and his Mr. Darcy had simply appalled everyone, himself included. He hadn't worked in over a year.

And this morning another catastrophe loomed, one likely to make all their other problems seem small and manageable.

Meera reached over and grasped Crispin's foot, and shook it gently.

"Babe," she said. "Look at this."

"Huh?" Crispin sat up with a snort. She replayed the *Variety* snippet for him. He stared at Mr. Morton's shaky doppelgänger, and gradually the lights came on behind his eyes.

"I wonder," he said.

"It might solve a lot of problems," said Meera.

"Yeah. Yeah! We could tell the rental agent to go shrack himself, for one thing." Crispin slid to the edge of the bed and reached for his pants. "I passed the genetic scan in school; did you?"

"Yes."

"So we're eligible to go up there. It might be sort of rough, though."

"Could it be much worse than this?" Meera waved her hand in a gesture that took in their sparsely furnished bed-sitter. Crispin glanced around and grinned.

"I wouldn't mind saying goodbye to Earth. This might be a good thing for us! How many actors can there be on Mars anyway?" His smile dimmed a little. "Though I suppose you wouldn't want to leave your family."

"Are you mad?" Meera cried. "I'd give anything to put half the solar system between us!"

"Okay, then!" Crispin pulled a shirt on over his head. "Let's mail the guy."

"There's something else," said Meera, looking down at her hands. She clasped them tight. "Cris . . . you remember the night we went to Gupta's party?"

"Heh heh heh," said Crispin, leering at her. She didn't say anything else. There was a silence of about thirty seconds, in which he connected the dots. Her eyes filled with tears. He went pale.

"Oh, no," he murmured. "I mean—oh, babe, what a wonderful thing! It's only—"

"It's a bloody disaster!" Meera wailed. He sat down beside her and took her hands.

"We—we'll think of something. I'll get a job. And . . . and if I manage to work off the fine in five years—"

"We couldn't work off the fine in twenty years," said Meera, gulping back a sob. "I've already checked. The baby would be shaving by the time we were free."

"Shrack," said Crispin. He thought about the other alternative, but that carried an even stiffer penalty. Meera fought to compose herself. She said:

"But you see—if we emigrated to Mars—we wouldn't *need* a Reproduction Permit."

"We wouldn't?" said Crispin. "Oh . . . we wouldn't, would we? They let you have them, up there."

Meera nodded.

"That settles it." Crispin grabbed a datastick from the pocket of his coat. "Where's the one with your head shot? We'll both apply. What can we lose?"

Six weeks later, they were emerging from the shuttle in the hangar at Settlement Base, a little wobbly-legged from their journey.

"Shouldn't we have our air masks on?" said Meera fretfully.

"Nobody else has," said Crispin. "We're under a dome, see?" He drew in a deep breath. "Phew!" Hastily he clapped his mask on. "They must have had a leak in a sewer pipe!"

"No, actually," said the shuttle pilot, grinning. "It always smells like this. They raise cattle down the MAC tubes. You'll get used to it."

Meera slid her mask in place and reached for Crispin's hand. "Let's go claim our trunks."

They took a few steps forward and promptly stopped, as all newcomers did, startled by Martian gravity.

"This is lovely!" Meera bounced on tiptoes. Crispin, giggling, let go her hand and ran a few paces, bounding athletically toward an imaginary basketball hoop.

"That'll be them, I'm guessing," said one of a pair of men walking toward them.

"Oh, dear, are we that obvious?" said Meera, turning to smile. Her eyes widened.

The taller of the two was very tall indeed and very thin, suited all in black, with an old-fashioned bubble helmet; it made him look rather like Jack Skellington. The other was wide and barrel-chested, with a bushy beard. He wore no mask. He had clearly washed for the occasion, but not very well; soot lay in every crevice, in the creases of his big hands and in the wrinkles around his pale eyes, which gave him an alarmingly villainous appearance.

"That's all right," he said, grinning. He had a thick pan-Celtic accent. "We was all immigrants once."

"Ms. Suraiya, Mr. Delamare, what an honor!" cried the other gentleman, with his voice a little muffled and echoing. He clasped Meera's hand in both his own and bent to kiss it, but only succeeded in rapping her knuckles with the curve of his helmet. "Oh—I'm so sorry—"

"Ah, hell, Morton, take the damn thing off," said the bearded one. He inhaled deeply. "It ain't that bad down here. Reminds me of old times, so it does."

"I can't bear it, and obviously neither can they," said Mr. Morton. He leaned down solicitously. "The air is much fresher where we're going, though I must admit it's a little thin. I cannot express what a pleasure it is to welcome you to Mars, Ms. Suraiya! Mr. Delamare! Amadeus Ruthven Morton at your service, and may I present Mr. Maurice Cochevelou? May we collect your trunks for you?"

"Yes, please," said Meera.

"I think they're over here," said Crispin, and vaulted away to the baggage claim area with Cochevelou walking after him.

"We were so awfully impressed by the holoshots of your theater, Mr. Morton," said Meera. "When are auditions?"

"Oh, *you* needn't audition!" said Mr. Morton. "We do get all the latest holos up here now, you know. Everyone's seen *Mr. Korkunov Says Hello!*"

"How nice!" *Mr. Korkunov* was a kiddie holo in which Crispin had had a recurring role as Brophy the Bear, until the show's cancellation.

"And of course, you were one of Smeeta's daughters on *Wellington Square,*" Mr. Morton said.

"The one who got married to a millionaire and moved to Montana," said Meera ruefully. She had been written out of the show after refusing to sleep with the director.

"Yes. I can't tell you how happy I am to be working with real professionals!" said Mr. Morton. "I'm afraid our little theater is still something of an amateur undertaking—"

"Meera! Check it out!" yelled Crispin, balancing his trunk on one hand as he approached. He tossed it to the other hand as though it were made of balsa. "One-third gravity!"

"Careful—" Meera threw up her hands as Crispin butted the trunk like a football, and promptly clutched his head.

"Ow!"

"It's lighter, but it's just as hard," Mr. Cochevelou told him. He scooped up the fallen trunk, swung the other trunk to his shoulder, and led them out of the hangar. They had their first glimpse of Mars: Settlement Dome above them, scoured to near-opacity by sandstorms, and the portals to the Tubes opening off it. To one side was the Ephesian Mission, breathing out incense which mingled peculiarly with the prevailing methane reek.

"So this is Mars," said Meera, trying not to show her disappointment.

"Oh, no, darlin'," said Cochevelou. "*This* ain't Mars." He grinned and led them to an airlock. "Masks on tight? You might want to pull up those hoods. We're going Outside." He slid on his own mask, around which his beard protruded to bizarre effect, and handed them a pair of heavy suits such as he wore, waiting patiently while they pulled them on and sealed up. Then he shouldered his way through the airlock. They followed him, holding hands tightly.

"*This* is Mars," said Cochevelou. He dumped their trunks into the back of a rickety-looking vehicle with balloon tires, and turned to wave an arm at the immense red desert. Rocks like crusts of dried blood, boulders in the colors of tangerines or bricks, wind-scoured curry-colored pinnacles and spires of rock. Far off, pink whirlwinds moved lazily across the plain. Looming before them was a gentle slope that rose, and rose, looking not so impossibly high as all that until they saw the cluster of tiny buildings far up and still not halfway to the sky.

Meera barely noticed that she was colder than she'd ever been in her life. It was all so vast, and so silent, and beautiful in a harsh way. It did not look like the surface of an alien world.

And it isn't, is it? she thought. *We're Martians now. This is home.*

The view was even more breathtaking by the time they had rumbled up the mountainside as far as the little buildings, but by that time the cold really was more than either of them could stand another minute, and they staggered gratefully through the airlock into what seemed, by comparison, a place as warm and steamy as a sauna.

"And here they are!" bellowed Cochevelou, pulling up his mask. Crispin and Meera followed suit. They stood in a domed darkness relieved only by lamps at scattered tables and booths, and one brighter light over the . . . bar? Yes, unmistakably a bar. It had a concentrated smell of old ale and fried food that anywhere else would have been over-powering, but by contrast with the stench of Settlement Dome seemed pleasant and wholesome. Quite a crowd was assembled there, and all eyes were turned to Crispin and Meera.

A buxom lady of a certain age pushed her way to the front of the crowd. "Welcome to the Empress of Mars, my dears. Did you talk to them about housing, Mr. Morton? No, not you. Never mind. Mary Griffith, and delighted to make your acquaintance. Manco? Just take their trunks up to the best nook, there's a dear. Rowan! Set a booth for them, they'll not have had anything but those nasty squeezy pastes for days and days. Come and sit, dears."

A girl edged her way forward, holding up a stylus and plaquette. "Please—can I have your autograph, Ms. Suraiya?"

"Me too?" inquired a man, clearly a miner or prospector, so covered in red dust he looked like a living statue. "And yours, Mr. Delamare?"

"Mr. Delamare, Ms. Suraiya, I'm with the *Ares Times,*" said a gentleman, bowing slightly. "Could I ask you just to step over here for the holocams a moment? Chiring Skousen, so pleased to meet you—and I wonder whether you'd consider doing an interview a little later. . . ?"

Meera looked sidelong at Crispin, who flashed her a triumphant smile. It was going to be all right.

And it was all right, even after Meera's first visit to the Settlement Base clinic, when she learned that having a child on Mars meant that there could be no second thoughts about emigration. Returning to Earth presented unacceptable risks to a baby born in Martian gravity, at least until adulthood, when it could train for the ordeal of Earth weight.

It was all right, even after Cochevelou gave them a midday tour Outside, and they saw the little mounds of red stones that had been placed, here and there, over the suffocated and frozen remains of prospectors who had ventured Out with no clear idea of the dangers they faced; or the ruined foundation of the big Ephesian temple that had been destroyed in some kind of hurricane, causing the good mothers to rebuild much more humbly within the protective stench of Settlement Base.

It was all right, even when they discovered how many of their new neighbors had been in Hospital, because the haulers and the laborers and the prospectors didn't *act* as though they were liable to cause breaches of the public peace. Mostly they minded their manners, and only occasionally laughed a little too loudly or got into fights in the bar. There were no Public Health Monitors snooping around to have them collared and dragged off in any case, and, when you got right down to it, Eccentrics were people just like anyone else.

It was all right because Crispin and Meera had free food and free lodging, in one of the funny little lofts plastered like swallow's nests within the dome of the Empress of Mars, and were promised better housing yet, as soon as Mr. Morton's workers completed the new block of flats—the first ever on

Mars! It was all right because their interview with Mr. Skousen made the front page of the *Ares Times,* and they were
treated like royalty everywhere they went.

It was all right because they soon got used to the smell,
except when they ventured down to Settlement Base; and
there were Scentstrips available in Mother Griffith's conve-
nience shop that could be stuck across the air filter in one's
mask, so that one hardly noticed anything except Island
Spice, Berry Potpourri, or Spring Bouquet.

And it was all right because, on their first walk up to the
EΛPCPΛ, Meera had looked up at its black spires sharp
against the purple sunset of Mars, and seen above them the
soaring frame of the dome being built to shelter a new city,
its bright steel catching the last of the sunlight, tiny points
of blue glowing where the suited welders worked so far up.
Standing there, Meera had felt the little flutter of the baby
moving for the first time.

Meera peered at the plaquette screen.

"'As the old man spoke,'" she read aloud, "'I became
aware of a vast and gradually increasing sound.'"

"That's your cue," said Crispin, leaning toward, in the
makeup mirror.

"Actually I think he said he's just going to record us for
that bit, so he can put in some effects," said Meera, "So the
Visitor goes on, 'vast bed of the waters, frenzied convulsion, heaving boiling hissing, prodigious streaks of foam'—
blah blah—and there's me and the other two girls just sort of
pacing around in a circle in the background, looking dangerous. And I suppose you're going to be just sort of staring at
us in horror."

"How's this look?" Crispin turned to her. In addition to
the white wig and beard, he had put in a set of tooth appliances. He gave her a mad snaggly smile and rubbed his
hands together, cackling like a lunatic.

"Maybe. . . a little over the top," said Meera, as gently as
she could.

"No, no, see, the guy has been driven mad by his experience," said Crispin. "You have to put in some comic relief,

when the story's an absolute downer like this. It's, like, this psychological release for the audience."

Meera bit her lip.

"Go on, go on," said Crispin. "Who got the part of the Visitor, anyway, did Morton tell us?"

"Mr. Skousen," said Meera. "The newsman up here."

"Oh, good, at least he'll know how to read. Go on."

"'These streaks of foam, spreading out to a great distance, took unto themselves the gyratory motion of the subsided vortices, and seemed to form another, more vast.' You know what I'd do, if I were you? Talk to some of those hauler people. They go Outside a lot. Mother Griffith was telling me about some of the really dreadful storms."

"Oh, yeah, the... Raspberries or something, they call them." Crispin nodded. "Like what took out that temple. Yes, brilliant. Who's that big guy who plays my brother, in the boat? Alf. He's an old-timer here. I'll buy him a beer or something. Go on, go on."

Meera lifted the plaquette. "'I looked down a smooth, shining, and jet-black wall of water, speeding dizzily around and around with a swaying and sweltering motion, sending forth to the winds an appalling voice. The mountain trembled to its very base.' He looks at the Old Man. 'This, this can be nothing else than the great whirlpool of the Maelstrom!' And that's your cue."

Crispin clasped his hands together and gave a shrieking laugh. "'Ah! I will tell you a story—' What are you making that face for?"

"Darling, that was your SpongeBob laugh."

Crispin scowled, an effect the dental appliances rendered hideous. "No it wasn't. It was crazier." He did it again. "No, you're right. Sorry." He gave a sepulchral chuckle instead. "Oh, that's it. 'I will tell you a story that will convince you I ought to know something of the Maelstrom!'"

"I'd like to thank you all for being here today," said Mr. Morton, clasping his long white hands. "Especially our stars, who have—ha, ha—truly crossed the heavens to shine here amongst us. But I am positive that each and every one of you will shine in your own proper sphere as we begin our journey toward True Art."

"Yaaay!" cried Mona. There was polite applause.

"Our stars, of course, need no introduction," Mr. Morton went on. "However, I'd like each of the rest of the cast to stand and have his or her moment in the spotlight. Why don't we begin stage left? That would be you, Alf."

"Erm," said Alf. "Name, Alf Chipping. Dee-oh-bee twenty-free April twenty-two-eighty-free. Patient number seven-seven-five. Haulers' Union Member number sixteen."

"And... why did you decide to take up acting, Alf?"

"Like plays," said Alf.

"Good for you," said Crispin.

Mona stepped forward. "I'm Mona Griffith, and I'm engaged to be married next year, and I've always wanted to be a performer. When I was little I used to climb on the table and pretend I was a hologram. I can still sing the Perky Fusion song. Want to hear it? 'Perky Fusion, he's the man, Perky Fusion in a can, cleaner source of energy, lights the world for you and me, Perky Fusion one-two-three!'"

"How nice," said Mr. Morton. "And how about you next, Ms. Hawley?"

He addressed a girl who looked rather like Joan of Arc, with her shaven head and hyperfocused stare. She stood straight.

"Exxene Hawley," she said. "Joined the MAC with my boyfriend. Wanted to make a better world on Mars. He turned out to be a stinking bastard. I said, I'd make my own stinking better world. Left him and the stinking MAC. Now I'm here. It makes as much sense as anything."

"And you're in theater because... ?"

"It's a good outlet for my issues, innit?"

"O—kay," said Mr. Morton. "And so we come to Chiring." A dapper gentleman rose and flashed them a smile.

"Chiring Skousen, your News Martian. I'm shooting a documentary on the birth of Theater on Mars." He waved a hand at the holocams stationed about the room.

"Which will, no doubt, win him *another* award from the Nepalese Journalists' Association," said Mr. Morton coyly.

"Mr. Skousen is our other celebrity, of course, but we knew him when!"

"And I've always cherished a secret ambition to play Edgar Allan Poe," added Chiring.

"And so we come to Maurice," said Mr. Morton, nodding toward that gentleman. He stood and nodded.

"Maurice Cochevelou," he said. "I run Griffith Steelworks. Used to do a bit of acting with the Celtic Federation's National Theater Project. Thought it might be nice to step back on the old boards, you know. Oh, and I'm engaged to be married to Mother Griffith."

Someone snickered.

"Well, I *am*," said Mr. Cochevelou plaintively.

"And there we are," said Mr. Morton, but Crispin raised his hand.

"Hey! Everyone else had to stand and face the music. We shouldn't be exempt!" He rose to his feet and raised his arms at the elbows, holding them out stiffly. "Hey hey, Mr. Korkunov, I've had *such* a busy morning!" he said, in his loudest Brophy the Bear voice. Mona giggled and applauded. "And I'd just like to say that Crispin Delamare is really looking forward to working with you all!"

He sat down. Meera rose, blushing.

"I'm Meera Suraiya, and I'm looking forward to working with you too."

"And we're expecting a baby in six months!" said Crispin. Meera put her hands to her face in dismay. To her astonishment, people applauded. She looked around at them all. They were *happy* for her.

"No, nobody thinks anything about it, up here," said Mother Griffith, as she led them along the corridor. "At least, nobody thinks any harm of it. They do say people aren't having them now on Earth. I can't say I'm surprised, with those fines! I had mine in the Celtic Federation, see, when you didn't need a permit. Different now; shame, but there it is. I wouldn't go back to Earth if you paid me, indeed."

"What do people do for—well, for clothes, and furniture?" inquired Crispin.

"And nappies?" inquired Meera.

"Catalogs," said Mother Griffith. "Or the PX at Settlement Base. For now. Not to worry! Within the twenty-four-month, the boys will have my Market Center finished. It'll be vast! At last, affordable consumer goods up here at reasonable prices, what a thought, eh? It'll be even more civilized when your next one comes along."

"Next one?" said Meera, in a faint voice. Crispin shrugged.

"And here we are!" said Mother Griffith proudly, and pulled a lever. With a hiss, the great door before them unsealed and folded back on itself. A rush of air met them, cool and sweet, very like Earth. They stepped through and found themselves on a catwalk, looking out across a gulf of air at a corresponding catwalk on the opposite side. Behind them, the portal hissed shut again. "Griffith Towers!"

"Brilliant!" said Crispin, going at once to the railing and peering over. Meera followed him and looked down, then quickly backed away. Ten stories below was an open atrium with a fountain, and little green things dotted here and there. Immediately above them was a modest dome, letting in the light of day.

"That's a rose garden down there," said Mother Griffith, in satisfaction. "Trees, too, would you believe it? No expense spared. Can't wait to see what the American sequoia will do in our gravity. I know it doesn't look like much now, dears, but give it a few seasons."

"Oh, no, it's very nice," said Crispin, and Meera conquered her fear of heights enough to take a second look. She had to admit that the place showed promise; while most of it was cast concrete, in pink and terra-cotta hues, the floors were cut and polished stone of an oxblood color. There was a great deal of ornamental wrought iron on all the balconies, and hanging baskets that were clearly meant to contain plants one day. Green flowering creepers, perhaps, in all that wrought iron, level after level descending...

The image of the Maelstrom came into her mind, the whirling vortex. Meera pulled back and gasped out, "Griffith Towers, you said. Will there be floors added going upward?"

"Lady bless you, no, dear! Far too dangerous, even when we got the Great Dome finished. Couldn't very well call it Griffith Hole-in-the-Ground, though, could we? It'll be nicer when the workmen's gear isn't lying all about," conceded Mother Griffith. "You'll have some noise to put up with for a few more months, but it'll all be finished by the time the baby comes. *Your* place is done, though. Come and see."

She led them along the catwalk to a door, beside which was the first window they had seen on Mars, something like a large porthole. Mother Griffith rapped on it with her knuckles.

"Expect you never thought you'd see one of these again, eh? Triple-glazed Ferroperspex. Anything happens to the dome, you'll still be safe inside. As long as you don't open the bloody door, of course," she added cheerfully, and palmed the via panel. The door opened for them. "Got to program in your handprints before we leave, do remind me."

They stepped through, and the lights came on to reveal a snug, low-ceilinged room. It had plenty of built-in shelves, though the phrase was more correctly "cast-ins"; everything was made of the ubiquitous pink cement, polished to a gloss, from the entertainment console to the continuous bench that ran around the walls. There wasn't a stick of wood in evidence anywhere. The few pieces of freestanding furniture were made of wrought iron. An attempt had been made to add warmth, in the big Oriental rug on the floor and in the bright cushions on the bench.

"Front parlor," announced Mother Griffith. "Kitchen and bath through there—yes, a real private bath, with running hot water and all! Everything state-of-the-art, see? And bedrooms off here—this one we made adjoining, thought you'd want that for the nursery. Come and see."

Each room had a sealed airlock rather than a door. They stepped through into the bedroom and stared; for the bed was sunk into a recess in the floor, under a transparent dome of its own.

"More state of the art," said Mother Griffith. "Anything happens, your own little dome keeps you safe with your own oxygen supply."

"'Anything happens'? What's likely to happen?" asked Crispin.

"Oh, nothing very much, nowadays," said Mother Griffith, with a wave of her hand. "Once the Great Dome's finished, I don't expect there'll be many emergencies. If we get another Strawberry, it can't flatten the place—that's the clever part of building underground, see? Though it might dash a boulder or two against the atrium dome, so it's best to take precautions. And it's five years now since we had an asteroid strike, and that was way out in Syrtis Major, so—"

"Asteroid strike?"

"Scarcely ever happens," said Mother Griffith quickly. "We never waste time worrying about 'em, and you needn't either. And aren't they building a whole series of orbiting gun platforms up there, and bases on Phobos and Deimos to boot, all manned with clever lads who'll pot the nasty things off with lasers to some other trajectory, if they don't blow them up entirely? They are indeed.

"No, the only real inconvenience is the dust. There's a lot of dust."

"But," said Meera. "Just supposing for a moment that an asteroid *did* hit—say it plummeted right through the atrium dome!"

"We'd lose the rose garden," said Mother Griffith. "And I suppose anyone who'd been silly enough to be down there without a mask on, but that's Evolution in Action, as we're fond of saying up here. You'd be snug in here with your door sealed, I expect."

"But we'd be trapped!" said Crispin.

"Not a bit of it! There's a hatch in the kitchen, opens out on the maintenance crawlway. Leads straight back to the Empress of Mars, so you'd just stroll up and have a pint while the Emergency Team dealt with things. What, were you expecting aliens with steel teeth lurking round the water pipes? Not a bit of it; only alien you'll see is the fellow in the Tars Tarkas costume on Barsoom Day, bringing presents for the kiddies," said Mother Griffith firmly. "Come now, have a look at the nursery."

Meera waited offstage with Exxene and Mona, the three of them in matching black leotards. They were growing slightly bored, waiting as they had been for fifteen minutes. Across from them, they could see Alf and Cochevelou, waiting for their cues, sitting quietly in a pair of folding chairs.

"I don't see why we couldn't have done it live," Mona complained. "I take really good care of my singing voice, you know? I could do it night after night. I'd be loud enough too."

"He couldn't have put in his special effects then, could he?" said Exxene. "We'll be louder. Scarier. Inhuman, like."

Meera shifted uncomfortably. Her leotard was a little tight. She wondered how much the baby showed. It was hard to think of herself as a scary, inhuman force of nature with a baby.

"I heard the first edit," she said. "It's wonderful. He's mixed in all kinds of sound effects, bits of music—all distorted so you can't quite recognize them, you know—and then our voices come in on the Philip Glass piece and we sound quite unearthly."

"I guess it's okay, then," said Mona. Exxene stamped her feet in impatience and did a back bend.

"When's this Poe going to get his arse in gear?" she muttered. Mr. Morton entered from stage right, waving his hands.

"Sorry! Sorry, all! Mr. Skousen is ready. Places, if you please."

Meera focused and thought of herself as a deadly goddess, a creature of the storm, a wall of water black as jet, devouring . . . or an asteroid approaching through the black cold infinity of space . . . Here came Mr. Skousen in makeup as Edgar Allen Poe, and she was appalled at the thought of how much white pancake foundation they must have had to use. He had poise, though, and the big sad dark eyes for the role; he walked sedately to his mark, turned his little Hitler mustache to the audience, and said:

"'You must get over these fancies,' said my guide.'"

"Your cue, Mr. Delamare," said Mr. Morton. Crispin, in full makeup, came bounding out, rubbing his hands.

"'For I have brought you here that I might tell you the whole story as it happened, with the spot just under your eye!'" he cackled, leaping so high he almost collided with the holo rig.

Meera winced. Mr. Morton pulled his white hands up to his mouth, as though he were about to stifle a scream of dismay; but he made no sound. Mr. Skousen, visibly startled, turned to stare.

"'Look *out,* from this mountain upon which we stand, look *out* beyond the belt of vapor beneath us, into the *seaaaa*!'" Crispin declaimed. Mona stifled a giggle. Mr. Skousen cleared his throat, not quite suggesting disapproval.

"'I looked dizzily, and beheld a wide expanse of ocean,'" he said. "'A panorama more deplorably desolate no human imagination can conceive. To the right and left, as far as the eye could reach, there lay outstretched, like ramparts of the world, lines of horribly black and beetling cliff, whose character of gloom was but the more forcibly illustrated by the surf which reared high up against it its white and ghastly crest, howling and shrieking for ever.'" He spoke in clear, somber, and entirely appropriate tones.

Mr. Morton forgot to cue the music, but the stage manager—Mona's betrothed, who had cleverly traded shifts with another miner so he could keep an eye on her—remembered anyway, and switched on the sound.

A menacing drone filled the air, disturbing currents of Bach's Fugue in G, eddies of electronically modified voices.

"Oh, wow, is that *us*?" said Mona.

"We sound good," said Exxene in surprise.

"Ladies, that's our cue," Meera reminded them, and they processed out from the wings, looking baleful as the three witches in the Scottish play, seductive as the mermaids in *Peter Pan,* deadly as the Guardswomen in *Sheeratu.* They prowled together in a tight circle upstage, and Exxene in particular got an unsettling light in her eye.

"I'm going to kill somebody," she said sotto voce.

"That's the spirit," said Meera, resolving to keep well out of arm's reach of her.

They walked on, round and round, in a silence that deepened.

"Line?" said Crispin at last.

"'Do you hear anyfing, do you see any change in da water,'" said Alf helpfully.

"'Do you *hear* anything?'" said Crispin, lurching up to Mr. Skousen and jerking at his sleeve. "'Do you *see* any change in the water?'"

"Crumbs!" said Mona, sincerely shocked. "He's *awful!*"

"Oh, dear, Mr. Delamare," said Mr. Morton, "Mr. Delamare—I am afraid—this is not quite what I had in mind."

"Sorry?" Crispin straightened up. "Oh. Too broad, isn't it? I can tone it down a little."

"Yes, please," said Mr. Morton. "Go on. Your line, Chiring."

Mr. Skousen drew a breath and said:

"'As the old man spoke, I became aware of a vast and gradually increasing sound.'"

Mr. Morton waved distractedly, and Durk raised the volume on the music. Mulet's *Thou Art the Rock* was briefly recognizable. Mr. Skousen raised his voice:

"'The vast bed of the waters, seamed and scarred into a thousand conflicting channels, burst suddenly into frenzied convulsion—heaving, boiling, hissing—prodigious streaks of foam gyrating in gigantic and innumerable vortices, and all whirling and plunging eastward. These streaks of foam, spreading out to a great distance, took unto themselves the. . . er. . .'"

"'Jyartry motion of da subsided votrices,'" said Alf.

"Thank you. 'Took unto themselves the gyratory motion of the subsided vortices, and seemed to form another, more vast.

"'I looked down a smooth, shining, and jet-black wall of water, speeding dizzily around and around with a swaying and sweltering motion, sending forth to the winds an appalling voice. The mountain trembled to its very base.'"

Mr. Skousen looked at Crispin, and cried: "'This, this can be nothing else than the great whirlpool of the Maelstrom!'"

Crispin leaned in and, with his very, *very* worst Sponge-Bob titter, said, "'I will tell you a story that will convince you I ought to know something of the Maelstrom! Ha-ha-*ha*!'"

"Oh, dear God," said Mr. Morton.

"I didn't think I was *that* bad," said Crispin miserably. They were sitting together in their little state-of-the-art kitchen, over a couple of mugs of Martian-style tea. Yellow lakes of melted butter swam on its surface, but it was surprisingly soothing.

"You weren't really," said Meera. "It's only that. . . it's not a comedy, darling."

"It could be," said Crispin. "It could be played funny. Why doesn't anybody see the humor in the thing? Nobody could see the humor in *The Dancing Daleks* either. Why are people so serious? Life isn't serious."

"No, but Art is," said Meera. "Apparently."

"The big guy, Alf, he's amazing. We talked, you know, about all his adventures on the road up here, really awful stuff he's lived to talk about, and you should hear him! 'So dere I was wiv, like, dis sand doon over me, and I finks to myself: How da hell am I gointer find out wevver Arsenal won da match? So I reckoned I'd better get a shovel or somefink, but dere weren't no shovel, so I tore da seat off da lavvy and dug out wiv it.' It's all in a day's work to him! He was laughing about it!"

"That was nice; you got his voice exactly," said Meera.

"These people live on the edge of destruction, all the time, and they manage by treating it all as a joke," said Crispin. He folded his arms the way Mother Griffith did and cocked his head at Meera. "'Oh, my goodness no indeed, you don't want to let a little thing like an asteroid hitting the bloody planet bother you! Just come up to the Empress for a pint, my dears!' So why can't Morton see how *really* innovative it would be to play this thing for laughs?"

"I don't know," said Meera. "But, you know, it's his vision. And it's his theater. And these people have been awfully good to us."

"So I don't suppose I could walk out of the show," said Crispin. He gave her a furtive look that meant: *Could I?*

"No," said Meera firmly. "This isn't like walking out on *Anna Karenina,* where it didn't matter because Mummy loaned us the money to get the car fixed. Or walking out on *From the Files of the Time Rangers,* when it didn't matter because your aunt left you that bequest. It isn't just a matter of scraping by until one of us gets a commercial. You're right; you can't leave. *We* can't leave. Remember why we're here."

"I know," said Crispin, and sighed. He looked at her sadly. "Life has caught up with us, and it's going to suck us in. I have to grow up now, don't I?"

"Grow up?" Meera laughed, though she felt tears stinging her eyes. "Crispin, you're having adventures on bloody Mars! You're living in a *Star Wars* flat beneath the surface of another planet! Our baby's going to think Father Christmas has four arms and tusks! Do you think growing up is going to be *boring*?"

He giggled, looking shamefaced.

"No, no, see, it's all wrong. If I'm having adventures on Mars, I ought to be in my space suit, with my rocket ship in the background, and my clean-cut jaw sticking out to *here*—" He thrust his chin out grotesquely. Meera couldn't help laughing. He jumped up on the table and struck an attitude.

"And I'd have a ray gun in either fist—and I'd be firing away and dropping alien hordes in their tracks, brrrzzzt! Aiee! Die, space scum! 'Retreat, my minionth! It ith Thtar Commander Delamare! Curthe you, Earthman!' And I'd have this gorgeous babe, naked except for some strategically placed pieces of space jewelry, clinging to my leg as I stood there. Played by the beautiful and exotic Meera Suraiya." He smiled down at her.

"Would she be pregnant?"

"Of course she would," said Crispin, jumping down and kissing her. "Got to repopulate the planet somehow."

"It's standing room only!" said Mr. Morton, biting his fingernails. "Look! Look! Look at them out there!"

Cochevelou peered through the gap in the curtain. He spotted Mother Griffith in the front row, arms folded, with most of the tavern staff seated to either side of her. Behind them, in ranks all the way to the back wall, were haulers and miners. Some were washed and combed and wearing their best indoor clothing; some had clearly come straight from their rigs, or from their mine shifts, for they wore psuits or miner's armor and had tracked in red dust on the purple carpet.

"Heh," said Cochevelou, leaning back. He took a small flask from an inner pocket, and had a sip before passing it to Morton, who drank and coughed. "Now, see, if you'd charged 'em for tickets like I'd told you, you'd have made a chunk of change tonight."

"No! These poor fellows would never have access to the finer things in life on Earth; I won't deprive them of the chance, here on Mars," said Mr. Morton. "The Arts shall be free! If only . . . "

"If only?" Cochevelou tucked away the flask and peered at him. It was dark backstage, and Mr. Morton's licorice-stick silhouette was barely visible; his pale face seemed to float above it, like the mask of tragedy.

"If only it wasn't for the human element," he said mournfully.

"Ah. The holotalent?" Cochevelou shrugged. "Well, and what if the boy's terrible? It ain't like this lot will know any better."

"There is that," Mr. Morton admitted. "But . . . I have built my theater. I am about to accomplish a thing of which I have dreamed my life long. I am a dramaturge, Maurice. My players are assembled, my Shrine to the Arts is filled . . . and . . . "

"And?"

"What if it disappoints me?" Tears stood in Mr. Morton's eyes.

Cochevelou stroked his beard, regarding Mr. Morton in wonder.

"Well," he said at last. "You wouldn't be the first man it'd happened to, would you? And after all, it ain't about you being happy, is it? It's about giving all them out front something that'll take their minds off dying up here."

"Of course it is," said Mr. Morton, and sighed. "But oh, the terror of dreams fulfilled! It must go on now, mustn't it? No way to wave a magic wand and crumble my theater back into the violet dust of unlimited possibilities?"

"No, there ain't," said Cochevelou. "The show's going on, and you're sitting in the little boat about to go over the edge into the whirlpool. Let's just hope there's something nice at the bottom."

"Ten minute call, Mr. Cochevelou," said Durk.

"Oh, dear," said Mr. Morton, and ran for the wings. Then he remembered that he was supposed to give a speech before the curtain rose, and ran back. Cochevelou kept going, to the little dressing room he and Alf shared. Alf was dutifully smearing adhesive on his face, preparatory to attaching his false beard.

"You ought to grow a real one," said Cochevelou, flipping the end of his own with pride.

"Can't," said Alf, looking at him in the mirror. "On account of the meds they gave me in Ospital."

Cochevelou winced. "Not ever?"

"I don't mind so much," said Alf, fitting on the false beard. "This don't arf tickle."

"Well." Cochevelou thumped him on the shoulder. "We're almost on."

Meera was standing quite still in the wings, summoning all the despair and anger she could. Exxene was walking in a tight circle, muttering, "Kill, kill, kill." Mona was fussing with her ribbon-stick, looping it through the air in swirly arcs.

"I don't like this one," she whispered. "Can I trade with you?"

Meera simply nodded and handed over hers. She was exhausted; Crispin had had a bad case of performance nerves and hadn't slept much the night before. He had tried not to wake her, but every time he had climbed into or out of bed, the hiss of the air seal had brought her to sharp consciousness and the certainty that an asteroid was plummeting straight for Griffith Towers.

Uncertain applause out front: Mr. Morton clearing his throat.

"I bid you welcome, friends, to the inaugural season of the Edgar Allen Poe Center for the Performing Arts! When future generations of Martians look back to this evening, upon which the shy Muse of Tragedy first ventured onto our rocky soil, they will undoubtedly. . . ."

Crispin emerged from his dressing room, and would have looked haggard even without benefit of makeup. As he passed between the colored lights on his way to the wings, his photoreactive beard and wig flickered, black-white-black. He stepped into place beside Chiring, and nodded.

"What's the house like?"

Chiring gave him two thumbs-up.

"That's the ticket," said Crispin, as cheerfully as he could. He began to bounce on the balls of his feet. "Energy-energy-energy, come on, Crispin, aah ooh oye ohh oooh. Run run run!" He drew up his fists and began to run in place.

"What are you doing?" whispered Chiring.

"Gearing myself up," said Crispin, running faster and faster. "Never fails to kill those butterflies in the tummy. YeeOW!" He finished, as he always had, by launching himself into midair.

Unfortunately, he had forgotten about Martian gravity. Crispin soared up and straight into the blue can spotlight, which rang like a gong when it connected with his skull. He dropped like a sack of flour, out cold.

"Mr. Delamare!" Chiring stared down at him, aghast.

"What the hell?" Cochevelou leaned down from the curved framework meant to symbolize a fishing boat. "Oh. Drunk, is he?"

"No!" Chiring fell to his knees and slapped ineffectually at Crispin's face. "Oh, no, Mr. Delamare—oh, look, he's cut his scalp too—"

"What was that—" Mona ventured out from stage left, saw Chiring, and gave a stifled shriek.

"What is it?" Meera looked up, startled.

"Chiring and your husband are fighting! He's knocked him down!" cried Mona.

"What?" Meera raced across the stage, closely followed by Exxene who, when she came in range, aimed a roundhouse blow at Chiring. Chiring yelped, ducking, and waved his hands in panic.

"What are you hitting *me* for? He hit his head on the light!"

"Cris!" Meera knelt beside him. "Oh, baby—somebody call the paramedics!"

"What paramedics?" said Cochevelou, climbing out of the boat frame.

"So what were you fighting about?" Mona asked Chiring.

"What do you mean, 'what paramedics?'" said Meera, horrified.

"We weren't fighting!" said Chiring.

"I mean, we haven't got any," said Cochevelou. He knelt beside Crispin too and thumbed open an eyelid. "Not to worry, ma'am. He'll come round. Morton has a cot in his office; let's stow him in there until he sobers up."

"But he isn't drunk!"

"But we're about to go *on*!" said Mona.

All this while, the sound of Mr. Morton's speech had been in the background, but it had begun to falter. They heard hesitant applause and then Mr. Morton leaped through the curtain.

"What the hell is going on back here?" he demanded. He spotted Crispin, unconscious and bleeding on the floor, and his eyes went wide.

"He jumped up and hit his head and knocked himself out and I had nothing to do with it!" screamed Chiring. He stabbed a finger at the blue can spot. "It was that light right there!"

Mr. Morton made a sound suggesting that all the air had been knocked out of him. He fell to his knees.

"Aw, now, it'll all come right, Morton dear," said Cochevelou. He pulled out his flask, uncapped it and stuck it in Mr. Morton's nerveless hand. "Just you drink up. Alf, give us a hand with old Brophy Bear."

"But we're about to go on!" said Mona.

"Yeah," said Exxene. "What'll we do?"

In tears, Mr. Morton shook his head. He tilted the flask and drank.

"Alf knows the part," said Mona. "He knows all the parts."

Everyone, including Alf, gave her a withering look. Quite clearly, they heard someone in the audience saying:

"Well? When are we going to see something?"

"Looks like it's you, son," said Cochevelou. He bent over Crispin and peeled off his false beard, but when he pulled the wig off too it was full of blood. "Oh, bugger."

Meera leaped to her feet and advanced on him menacingly.

"I don't care how you do it," she said, "but you're getting my husband to *some* kind of medical facility, and you're doing it *right now.*"

"Yes, ma'am," said Cochevelou, backing away. He thrust the wig and beard at Alf, and turned and ran for his life. Meera knelt again beside Crispin, accepting a handful of tissues Exxene had fetched her to compress his wound.

"Scalp wounds bleed buckets," she told Meera reassuringly. "It don't mean nothing."

"Oi!" shouted someone in the audience. "Are we going to sit here all shrackin' night?"

"I might have known this would happen," said Mr. Morton, tragically calm. "They'll riot next, I know it."

"No! The show must go on, right?" said Mona. "Come on, Alf! Look, Mr. Morton, see how nice he looks in the other beard? And you can wear *his* beard, and *you* can play the youngest brother, because there's no lines—"

"Raise the damn curtain!" said someone in the audience.

"And—I know! I'll go out and dance for them," said Mona.

"In a pig's eye you will, my girl," snapped Mother Griffith, shouldering her way backstage with Cochevelou close behind her. She stopped short, gaping at Crispin. "Goddess on a golf ball! Why haven't you sent him to the clinic, you idiots?"

The audience had begun to sing "Why Are We Waiting?" Mother Griffith turned and thrust her head through the curtain.

"Shut up, you lot, we've got an injured man back here!" she shouted. "Manco! Thak! Come up here and help us."

The audience, cowed, fell silent at once, as two of Mother Griffith's staff scrambled over the footlights and so backstage. In short order, Crispin was bandaged, tied into a chair, masked up, and carried away down the tunnel, with Mother Griffith leading the way.

"Wonder why they were fighting?" whispered a miner to a hauler.

"I hear those Hollywood types are temperamental," the hauler whispered back.

The scurrying and cries behind the curtain faded away. For a moment it hung still, so motionless its folds might have been carved from stone; then it rose, to reveal Edgar Allan Poe standing on an outcropping of rock, before a backdrop of severe sky and a sea like black stone. He was sweating, looked frightened and miserable. He looked out at the audience and said:

"'You must get over these fancies,' said my guide."

The old man, an immense old man like a walking hill, stepped forth from the wings. There was a disturbing glare in his eyes. Were those streaks of blood in his wild white beard? He looked at Poe and said quietly:

"'For I ave brort you ere dat I might tell you da ole story as it appened, wiv da spot just under yer eye. Look out from dis mountain upon which we stand, look out beyond da belt of vapor beneaf us, into da sea.'"

Poe shrank visibly. He licked his dry lips and said:

"'I looked dizzily, and beheld a wide expanse of ocean. A panorama more deplorably desolate no human imagination can conceive . . .'"

Meera, sitting huddled on a chair in the wings, felt Exxene grip her shoulder.

"Come on, that's us," she said.

May as well, thought Meera, rising mechanically. *Show must go on.* She moved out with the others, into the eerie light, into the eerier music. She put into the slink of her walk all the hopelessness she felt. Mother cat, looking for a safe place to have its kittens. But there was no safe place . . .

She and Crispin had been pulled under by the circling tide of history, two emigrants like any others, in the long outward flow of life from the place where it started to its unknown destination. Some washed up on the distant shore and did well for themselves, became ancestors to new generations of races . . . some failed to survive their first winters, and their names were forgotten.

She glanced into the audience on one pass around, and was shocked out of her reverie to see that they were watching raptly, leaning forward in their seats.

Why, look at that; they're completely into it, she thought. Alf had stepped back from the rock, into the blue circle of light, and his beard and hair had gone to black; well, perhaps the stage effect had pleased them. Here came the rickety little boat effect, pushed by Cochevelou and Mr. Morton. Oh, no, look at the false beard hanging askew, under Mr. Morton's chin! That was going to get a laugh.

It didn't, somehow. Alf droned on without inflection, and the audience strained to hear, but his accents weren't strange or comic, not to them.

"'The roar of the water was drowned in a shrill shriek, like the sound of waste-pipes of many thousand steam-vessels, letting off their steam all together. We were not in the belt of surf that always surrounds the whirl; and I thought that another moment would plunge us into the abyss—down which we could only see indistinctly. The boat did not seem to sink into the water at all, but to skim like an air bubble upon the surface of the surge.

"'The rays of the moon seemed to search the very bottom of the profound gulf; I saw mist, where the great walls of the funnel met together at the bottom. What a yell went up to the heavens from out of that mist! Our first slide into the abyss itself, from the belt of foam above, had carried us to a great distance down the slope. Round and round we swept—not with any uniform movement—but in dizzying swings and jerks, that sent us sometimes only a few hundred yards—sometimes nearly the complete circuit of the whirl . . . '"

And why shouldn't the audience be transfixed? This was *their* story; they heard it every day. They had all lived through something like this, here, on this alien soil. Pitiless dunes that buried you, suffocating wastes that froze you, bombs that might roar out of the stars unannounced and strike with an impact that smacked you into flattened and broken strata. Mars in all its casual malevolence, against whom one miscalculation meant sudden death and a freeze-dried corpse pointed out to gawking tourists.

Meera flung up her arms and danced, and the other two whirled after her. They were black goddesses, they were nightmare crones, they were the Fates, they were the brides of Death in this bleak place. *We are always at your elbow; never forget.* The members of the audience stared openmouthed, started forward when first one and then the other mariner was dragged down, seduced, pulled to his death out of sight.

At last, there was only Alf staring out, with the sweat shining on his moon face, real terror of remembrance in his eyes, and his voice had sunk to a hoarse late-night whisper that nonetheless carried to the back of the house.

"'A boat picked me up. Those who drew me on board were my old mates, but they knew me no more than they would have known a traveler from the spirit land. My hair, which had been raven-black the day before, was as white as you see it now. I told them my story. They did not believe it. I now tell it to you.'"

There was a profound silence. The lights went down.

Finally, there was an uncertain patter of applause, which abruptly swelled to thunder. The audience had struggled to their feet and were baying their approval. The ladies stared at one another, wondering. Mr. Morton, who had been helping himself to the flask since his exit, looked up foggily.

"Good Lord," he said. "They *liked* it!" He rose to his full height and nearly fell over. "Curtain call! Shoo! Shoo! Get out there!" He flapped his hands at them. Meera caught his arm and pulled him out too, and he stood between Alf and Cochevelou, blinking in the glare of the footlights.

Meera took Mona's and Exxene's hands, as much for support as tradition. A haze was in the air, for men were stamping now as well as applauding, with the dust flying up from their boots. She couldn't see a face that wasn't streaked with tears, white or black runnels cut through the red dust.

Someone was pushing through the crowd. Mother Griffith reached the front row, waving, shouting to be heard above the commotion, but still drowned out by the frenzied whooping.

He's okay, she mouthed at Meera. Just so she wouldn't be misinterpreted, she made a circle with forefinger and thumb and winked broadly, grinning. Mona hugged her and Exxene pounded her shoulder, which hurt rather a lot, but Meera scarcely noticed.

Her baby was dancing.

Crispin was sitting up in the clinic bed, wearing an absurd gown with teddy bears on it, sipping from a juice box. His head was bandaged, but the color had returned to his face.

"It was a hit because I wasn't in it, you know," he said ruefully. "Luckiest thing that could have happened."

"Oh, darling, you know you'd have been wonderful," said Meera, stroking his hair back from the edge of the bandage.

"They said it was all right if we visited," Mona announced, entering with Exxene. "You left before you got your presents! Are you feeling better, Mr. Delamare? Look what Durk had made for us! Isn't he an old dear? There's three!"

She held up a huge sweater. Across its bosom had been machine-embroidered: THE MAELSTROMETTES.

"Isn't that funny? Except he had them all made triple-X-

size for some reason. Mine comes down to my knees," said
Mona.

"Here's yer roses," said Exxene, holding out a bouquet.
"Know what? I've had five proposals of marriage tonight.
Odd, ain't it?"

"And you know what else, Mr. Delamare?" said Mona.
"Mr. Morton wants to do a comedy next, as soon as you're
all recovered! Won't that be wonderful? It's this lost play or
something about somebody named Ernest. At least, I think
that was what he said. He was on his third glass of cham-
pagne."

"A comedy?" Crispin brightened. A bell rang, out in the
corridor.

"Crumbs, that'll be 'Visiting Hours Are Over,'" said
Mona. "Come on, Meera, we'll walk you home. Good night,
Mr. Delamare."

"I'll be here first thing tomorrow," said Meera, leaning
down to kiss him. She took a rose from her bouquet and
carefully threaded it through the straw of his water carafe.

Walking up the tube with Mona and Exxene, she realized
that she didn't notice the methane smell now at all. And how
bright the stars were, up there above the half-finished city on
the mountain!

BLESSED BY AN ANGEL

PETER F. HAMILTON

Prolific British writer Peter F. Hamilton has sold to *Interzone, In Dreams, New Worlds, Fears,* and elsewhere. He sold his first novel, *Mindstar Rising,* in 1993, and quickly followed it up with two sequels, *A Quantum Murder* and *The Nano Flower.* Hamilton's first three books didn't attract a great deal of attention, on this side of the Atlantic at least, but that changed dramatically with the publication of his *next* novel, *The Reality Dysfunction,* a huge modern space opera (it needed to be divided into two volumes for publication in the United States) that was itself only the start of a projected trilogy of staggering size and scope, the Night's Dawn trilogy, with the first volume followed by others of equal heft and ambition (and which also raced up genre bestseller lists), *The Neutronium Alchemist* and *The Naked God.* The Night's Dawn trilogy put Hamilton on the map as one of the major players in the expanding subgenre of the New Space Opera, along with writers such as Dan Simmons, Iain Banks, Paul McAuley, Gregory Benford, Alastair Reynolds, and others; it was successful enough that a regular SF publisher later issued Hamilton's reference guide to the complex universe of the trilogy, *The Confederation Handbook,* the kind of thing that's usually done as a small-press title, if it's done at all. Hamilton's other books include the novels *Misspent Youth* and *Fallen Dragon,* a collection, *A Second Chance at Eden,* and a novella chapbook, *Watching Trees Grow.* His most recent book is a new novel, *Pandora's Star.* Coming up is another new novel, *Judas Unchained.*

Here he shows us that, popular wisdom to the contrary, being visited by an angel may not really be all *that* good a thing after all. . .

Imelda leaves her modest family home as the evening shade washes over the front garden, a coy smile lifting her maroon-glossed lips. She's off to see her lover, a prospect which lifts her heart and enhances her buoyant nature. The sun is slowly sinking behind the gigantic seven-hundred-year-old arcology that dominates the center of her hometown, Kuhmo, casting a shadow which methodically stretches out to darken the town's outlying districts. It is a sharp eclipse which she has witnessed every evening of her seventeen years. Yet the gloaming it brings does nothing to stifle her mood; she's a happy, beautiful girl with an enchantingly flat face and pert nose, her auburn hair flowing below her shoulders. Tonight she's chosen a sleeveless blue and white dress to wear, its semiorganic fabric swirling jauntily around her long legs. Wherever she goes, she attracts wistful glances from the boys who linger along Kuhmo's boring streets as they search for something to do before the night is out.

She turns into Rustwith Street, one of the broad thoroughfares which radiate out from the hexagonal base of the tapering arcology. Tall novik trees line this street, as they do all the major routes cutting through the civic center, their woolly blue-green foliage a deliberate counterpoint to the bleak mountainous walls of the arcology. There are vehicles driving down the wide road, primitive vehicles with wheels powered by electric motors. This world of Anagaska has never really benefited from the bountiful wealth flowing among the Greater Commonwealth planets, its citizens seemingly content to bumble along their own slow cautious development route, decades if not centuries behind the more dynamic worlds. And this provincial town is very set in its ways, manacled to the past by the arcology which dominates the local mind-set much as it does the landscape.

There are some modern regrav capsules in the air above the roads. Shiny colorful ovoids as big as the cars below, skimming silently along at their regulation fifteen-meter altitude, which puts them level with the upper branches of the trees.

Imelda pays the traffic no attention as she hurries along to the café where she has arranged to meet her lover; like the arcology, the buzz of vehicles is a mere background fixture. So she is completely unaware of the chrome green capsule gliding along at walking pace several hundred meters behind her, maintaining a steady distance. The two Advancer Protectorate members inside are observing her through sensors meshed with the capsule's metal skin, and a deluge of scrutineer programs they have scattered across the local net. Their organization might not be official, but they have access to police codes, allowing them to pursue their clandestine business undetected within the town's electronic and physical architecture.

As Imelda turns into the Urwan plaza with its throng of pedestrians, several wolf whistles and raunchy pings are thrown in her direction. The scrutineers examine the pings for hidden code, but the boys and young men who sent them are intent only on compliments and hopeful for a smile. Imelda does smile breezily, but keeps on walking. She is using virtually none of her Advancer functions, the macrocellular clusters supplementing her nervous system are barely interfaced with the planetary cybersphere. Exoimages and mental icons are folded back into her peripheral vision, untouched by her neural hands. Secondary thought routines operating inside her macrocellular clusters monitor several relevant events. She is pleased to see that Sabine, her younger sister, has finally reached their aunt's house in New Helsinki; there was a long delay at Inubo station while she waited for the delayed regrav bus connection. Imelda is quietly relieved, she loves her sister dearly, but Sabine is quite a ditzy girl; that kind of foul-up was likely to panic her. Imelda's other interest is Erik Horovi, who is not merely on time, but well ahead of schedule, waiting for her in the Pathfinder café. An exoimage from the café's net reveals him to be sitting at a booth table ordering the stewardbot to stand by. Her neural hands grip the exoimage and expand it, sliding the focus in toward his face. His own clusters must be alerting him to the observation for he grins round at the camera. She sends him a tactile ping, hand-squeezing-thigh, and says: "I'll be there soon, order for me."

His grin broadens at the ping, and he calls the stewardbot over.

It is all manufactured. Erik, his location, his responses, are in fact all being cooked up by a simulacrum program running in a large processor kube on the arcology's seventy-fifth floor. The same suite of abandoned rooms where Erik's unconscious body is lying, fastened to a field-medical cot. But the program has fooled Imelda; she hurries on through the plaza.

Her route takes her out through one of the side paths before turning into a narrow opening between two buildings. The alleys here form a small maze as they link up to the rear of a dozen commercial buildings. But she's perfectly safe. The walls might be high, and old, and dark; there may be rubbish scattered over the concrete; and there may not be any people about, but this is Kuhmo, and she remains linked to the cybersphere. Imelda is a thoroughly modern child of the Commonwealth; she knows that safety and the police are only the speed of a thought away.

A lustrous green regrav capsule descends into the alley ahead of her. It's unusual, but she doesn't hesitate. She's mildly puzzled, because it's a large capsule, and she sees it's going to be difficult for her to squeeze around. Just how stupid and inconsiderate is the pilot program?

Her link to the cybersphere falls away. Imelda comes to an uncertain halt, frowning suspiciously at the capsule. She's never been disconnected since the macrocellular clusters became active the year she reached sexual maturity. The cybersphere and beyond that the all-embracing Commonwealth unisphere are her eternal companions; they are her *right,* she thinks crossly. Even now, fear is alien to her. This is the Commonwealth.

A malmetal door expands on the regrav capsule. Paul Alkoff steps out. The Protectorate team's chief is a tall man, over four hundred years old, and twenty years out of rejuvenation; like just about everyone with an Advancer genetic heritage, his biological age is locked into his early thirties.

"You're in the way," Imelda protests. "And I think your capsule is messing with reception."

"Sorry about that," Paul says. A quick review of his exoimages shows him their kube is producing an optimum digital shadow of Imelda. Friends and family all think she's still walking along the alley en route to the café. He holds his left hand up toward her, and the smallest weapon he's wetwired with fires a stun pulse.

Imelda feels nothing. The world shifts around her, and she realizes she's fallen to the ground. There is no pain from the impact, though she knows she hit her head and shoulder hard. She heard the *crack* they made. There is no sensation from anywhere in her body now. She can neither blink nor move her eyeballs. However, her neural hands are not physical, she moves them across icons, triggering every security alert she possesses. There is no response. Shapes appear above her. Men, but out of focus. There is more movement. She is carried into the capsule. It is dark inside. Her mind is screaming, gibbering for help. No one can hear, there is no linkage. She is alone.

The green capsule rises out of the alley and slips back into the designated travel path above the nearest thoroughfare. It is a brief journey to the base of the arcology, which now lies deep in the monstrosity's umbra, then the capsule rises up the side until it reaches the seventy-fifth floor and edges its way through a fissure in the outer wall.

At one time, in the decades after the arcology was built, the apartments up here on the upper levels were all packed to capacity, and the central malls buzzed with activity all day long. But that was seven hundred years ago, following the Starflyer war, when the entire population of Hanko was relocated to Anagaska. People were grateful for any accommodation they were given in the terrible aftermath of their homeworld's destruction. Once they had recovered their equilibrium, they began to build out from the arcology, covering the fresh open landscape with new suburbs. Families started to drain away out of the arcology to live in the less confined homes springing up along the new grid of roads. The vision back then was for a town that would continue to grow and establish new industries. Growth, though, proved expensive, and investment on poor old sidelined Anagaska was never abundant. Much cheaper and easier for the town council to refurbish sections of the arcology to keep their community going. In later centuries, even that philosophy stalled, and the whole edifice began to deteriorate from the top downward. Now the giant city-in-a-building is a decaying embarrassment, with no one capable of providing a satisfactory solution.

Dank water from a slimed ceiling drips on the immaculate green skin of the regrav capsule as it settles on a cracked and buckled concrete floor. The cavernous hall used to be an exemplary mall, with shops, bars, and offices. Today it is a squalid embalmed memory of the comfortable times long gone. The only light comes from rents in the outer walls, while the ancient superstrength structural spars are sagging as they succumb to gravity and entropy. Not even the town's bad boys venture up to these levels to conduct their nefarious affairs.

Paul and his team member Ziggy Kare carry Imelda from the capsule into one of the abandoned shops. Its walls are dry, if filthy, and the floor is reasonably level. The stun pulse effect is slowly wearing off, allowing Imelda to move her eyes slightly. She sees signs of the new occupants, plyplastic furniture expanded out to form tables and chairs, red-tinged lights, electronic equipment, power cells—all the elements of a sophisticated covert operation. In one of the small rooms they pass, she sees a field-medical cot. Erik is lying on it. Her eyes widen in consternation, but her throat remains unresponsive as she tries to shout.

The next room contains a great deal of equipment which she doesn't understand. There is, however, a face she recognizes. Only a face. Her gorgeous friend's head is sitting inside a transparent bubble with various tubes and cables impaling its neck. The top of the skull has been removed, allowing an invasion of gossamer-fine filaments to penetrate the exposed brain.

A terrified whimper gurgles out through Imelda's numb lips.

"It's all right," Paul says at the sound. "I know you probably won't believe me, but we're not going to harm you. And you'll never remember any of this, we'll give you a memory wipe."

She is placed on a field-medical cot, where plyplastic bands flow over her limbs before solidifying, holding her fast. Tears begin to leak out of her eyes.

Ziggy brings over a sensor stick, and sweeps it above her abdomen. "Damn it." He grunts in disappointment. "She's pregnant all right. Looks like that memory checks out."

"How long?" Paul asks.

"Couple of weeks."

"Can you tell if it's Higher contaminated?"

Ziggy sighs in reluctance, the sound of someone who is forcing himself to do the right thing. "Not from outside, not with our sensors. We'll have to run a detailed pathology scan." His hand indicates a clutter of equipment on a nearby table.

"Okay," Paul says, equally sad. "Take it out, and run the exam."

Ziggy turns to the collection of medical instruments, and picks up a disturbingly phallic device.

Imelda finally manages to scream.

Of all the memories Paul was able to extract, arrival was the clearest.

The angel clung to the starship's fuselage as the big commercial freighter emerged from its wormhole a thousand kilometers above the bright blue expanse of Anagaska's major ocean. Dwindling violet light from the wormhole's exotic fabric washed across its face, revealing late-adolescent features that were carefully androgynous. With its firm jaw, it would be considered a striking and attractive female rather than classically beautiful, while, as a male, people would think it inclined to the delicate. The baggy white cotton shirt and trousers it wore offered no clue as to its gender orientation.

As soon as the wormhole closed, the starship began to decelerate, chasing down toward the planet where New Helsinki lurked behind the darkness of the terminator. From its position just ahead of the starship's engineering section, the angel could see the archipelagos rolling past beneath. The impression of speed was such that it felt there should be a wind blowing its long honey-colored hair back. Instead, it just smiled across the vacuum at the world which awaited it. Advancer senses revealed the dense electronic chatter of the planetary cybersphere ghosting through the atmosphere, with intangible peaks reaching out to connect with Anagaska's satellite constellation. When the angel accessed the starport's traffic control, it could find no hint that their flight was subject to any additional audit, security was light, no intelligent scrutineers were probing the starship's systems. The local Protectorate group didn't know it was here. Not that there was ever any active presence at the starport; but every visitor to Anagaska was quietly recorded and checked; if it had arrived incognito, there was a small risk their identity-examiner programs would raise a query. This way was safer, it was playing very long odds against detection.

As soon as the starship fell below orbital velocity, the angel let go. It configured the biononic organelles inside its cells to provide a passive deflective field around itself, one that would surreptitiously warp the active sensor radiation pouring out from the starship's navigation network. The energy sequence flowing through its biononics was even sophisti-

cated enough to disguise its mass, leaving it completely undetected as the starship raced away.

The angel began its long fall to the ground. It expanded
its integral force field into a lenticular shape over two hundred meters wide. Electric-blue scintillations slithered over
the surface as it caught the first wisps of Anagaska's upper
atmosphere, aerobraking in a long curve to subsonic speed.
Its descent strategy was simple enough; the majority of its
flight was out over the ocean where there would be no one to
see the telltale crimson flare of ions against the force field as
it sank ever lower, nor hear the continual thunderclap of its
hypersonic passage through the air.

When it reached a three-kilometer altitude, its downward
plummet had slowed to less than a hundred kilometers an
hour, thanks to the protective force field which was now
over three hundred meters wide and acting like a parachute.
It was fifty kilometers out from Olhava's western coastline
when it changed the shape of the force field once again, producing the dragonfly-wing planform which contributed to its
name.

An hour and a half later, the angel swooped out of the
nighttime sky to step lightly onto a sandy beach. It shut down
most of its Higher functions, pulled a pair of soft leather sandals from its shoulder bag, and began to walk up the grassy
slope to the coastal road.

They'd been lucky, Paul acknowledged, as soon as he'd
reviewed the arrival. A lone yachtsman had been underneath
the angel as it aerobraked, a man sailing out from Olhava to
spend a long vacation amid the archipelagos. A true sailor,
who knew the seas and the skies. He'd seen the glowing
point flashing across the stars and known what it meant; and
he had a friend who had a friend who knew a unisphere contact code. Paul and his team had arrived at the coast that
morning to begin their tracking operation.

It had taken them a couple of weeks to corner the sneaky
creature as it began its mission in Kuhmo. The fight when
they surrounded it had taken out three Protectorate members
and created a firestorm in the town's college campus, but
they'd eventually driven it into a force field cage which could

contain its Higher energy functions. They loaded it into a big regrav capsule and ferried it over to the arcology as the flames from the art block building roared up into the night sky behind them.

"I would have just left," the angel said in its pleasant melodic voice as the capsule negotiated its way through the rent in the wall of the seventy-fifth floor. "There was no need for all this."

"That depends whose viewpoint you're taking," Paul snapped back. He was still shaken and infuriated by the deaths; they'd left the bodies behind in the flames and now he was worried the heat might damage his colleagues' memorycells. Once they were re-lifed in replacement clone bodies they could well lose several hours of memories since they last backed up in their secure stores.

"The obvious one, of course," the angel said.

"That's it for you, isn't it? Game over. Shake hands. All go home."

The angel's pale mouth smiled. "It's the civilized thing to do. Don't you approve of that?"

"Ask my three colleagues that you slaughtered back there. They might have an opinion on just how civilized you are."

"As I recall, you fired first."

"Would you have come quietly?"

"So that you could perform your barbarisms on me? No."

"Just tell us what we need to know. Have you contaminated any of us?"

"Contaminated! How I curse your corruptors. You could have lived a rich rewarding life; instead they have condemned you to this poverty of existence."

"Screw you, pal. You Highers want to condemn us to your nonexistence. We retain the right to choose our destiny. We *demand* the right."

"Two hundred billion people can't all be wrong. The Central Commonwealth worlds have all embraced biononics—why do you think it is called Higher civilization?"

Paul gave the angel an evil grin. "Self-delusion? More likely: desperate self-justification."

"Why do you resist using biononics?" the angel asked, its beautiful face frowning disparagingly. "You of all people must be aware of the benefits they bring to a human body. Immortality without your crude rejuvenation treatments; a society which isn't based around industrial economics and its backward ideologies, new vistas, inspiring challenges."

"Challenges? You just sit and vegetate all day long. That and plot our downfall. What have you got to look forward to? Really? Tell me. The only thing that awaits a Higher is downloading into Earth's giant brain library. Why bother waiting? You know that's where you're all heading. Just migrate there and plug yourself into that big virtual reality in the sky, go right ahead and play mental golf for the rest of eternity. I know the numbers downloading themselves are increasing; more and more of you are realizing just how pointless your lives are. We're not designed for godhood, basic human essence cannot be tampered with. We need real challenges to satisfy ourselves with, we need to have our hearts broken, we need to watch our children grow up, we need to look over the horizon for new wonders, we need to build and create. Higher civilization has none of that."

"The Central Commonwealth is our race's greatest creation. To misquote an ancient lyric: do you think we don't love our children too?"

"I'm sure you do. But not enough to give them a choice. To be born Higher is to stay Higher, they can't escape."

"They could, they just don't want to. Yet tens of millions of ordinary Advancer humans convert to Higher every year. Does that tell you anything?"

"Yes. It's simply the last step in their adventure. They've *lived* first, they know there are different ways to exist. Only then do they go in for your defeatist digital dreaming; they've decided that they want to die then anyway, so what have they got to lose?"

"Is that what you'll do, Paul? Give in and download your memories into Earth's repository?"

"When I'm finally tired of life, then I might just. But don't expect it for another millennium or ten; it's a big galaxy."

"I am always saddened by how ignorant your views are."

"Is that: *my type,* by any chance?"

"Yes, Paul. Your type indeed, all you reactionary Advancers. Advanced genes have shown you how far you can extend human evolution and abilities; you've extended your life span, you're virtually immune to disease, you're naturally integrated with the unisphere, and a lot more besides; all those abilities have brought you halfway toward us, yet still you refuse to take the final step. Why?"

"Reactionary, my arse! Biononics are not part of us, they are not derived from the genome and cannot be added to it, they are machines. They infect the cells of your body; that is why you have to be born with them to be truly Higher. They have to multiply in tandem with an embryo's natural growth. Only then can they be incorporated by every cell. It's impossible for every cell to be corrupted in an adult. That's the difference, the crucial one. They are alien, imposed."

"Listen to yourself: infect. Corrupt. Impose. Alien. How small your mind is, how closed."

"I am what I am. I like what I am. You will not take that away from me, nor my children. I have that right to defend myself. If what you are doing is an act of kindness and charity, then why did you arrive here the way you did? Why not be open about it? Every person on this planet can travel to the Central Commonwealth should they wish. Why are you here to spread your culture by deceit?"

"The lies and prejudice you sustain leave us no choice. You're condemning generations unborn to suffering they do not deserve. We can save them from you."

Paul tilted his head to one side, and gave the angel a superior grin. "Listen to yourself," he said with soft mockery. "And the best thing is, I know that you're in a minority among Highers. You disgust the majority as much as you do me."

"And yet they do not stop us."

"The price of true democracy. Now, are you going to tell me what I need to know?"

"You know I cannot do that."

"Then this is going to get very unpleasant. For you."

"That's something your conscience will have to carry."

"I know. But this isn't the first time I've had to break one of you. And I don't suppose you'll be the last." Paul maneuvered the cage into place at the center of the hastily prepared interrogation room. Equipment modules began to clamp themselves across the outside of the restraining force fields. Eventually there was no sign of the angel beneath the dull metal segments. Paul gave Ziggy a weary glance. "Let's get on with it."

It took nine days to defeat the angel's biononics. Nine days of negative energy spikes pounding away at the force field which its biononics produced. Nine days of draining out its power reserves. Nine days spent denying it food, water, and oxygen. Nine days smothered inside a sarcophagus of machinery designed to wreck its body and all the Higher functions it was capable of generating. Nine days to send invasive filaments into its brain, preserving the neurones while its ordinary body cells were burned and destroyed one layer at a time. Nine days to kill it.

Eventually, the inert head was removed from the charred remains and artificially sustained on the cusp of life. The filaments linked Paul's thoughts to the angel's undead neurones, allowing him to access memories as if the angel were now a subsidiary brain, nothing more than a recalcitrant storage system grafted onto his own gray matter. Burrowing through the stranger's thoughts was difficult, and not even modern biochemicals could sustain the neurones indefinitely. Decay gave them a very short time scale to work in. There was no neat index. Human sensory experiences were very different from electronic files, their triggers were unique, hard to guess. But Paul persevered, extracting the missing days since its arrival in confused fragments. Piecing together what had happened.

The angel had reached Kuhmo the day after it landed, renting a modest apartment on the arcology's fifteenth floor. It merged easily into the lives of the town's adolescents, signing on at the college, joining several clubs. For two days, it studied potential targets.

—————————

Ziggy takes less than an hour to confirm the presence of bi-ononics in every cell of the tiny fetus.

"Son of a bitch," Paul grunts.

"I thought you'd be pleased," Ziggy says. "It means what we did was right."

Paul gives Imelda a guilty glance. The girl is crying silently, her face sticky with tears. Occasionally, she lets out a small piteous snivel. Traumatized though she is, he still cannot grant her the comfort of oblivion. There is one question he still has to ask. "I don't like being forced to do what's right," Paul says. "Not this."

"Right," Ziggy says. He slides the dead fetus into a flash furnace, eradicating the last trace of the angel's attempt to subvert their world.

Paul leans over Imelda. "One final thing," he says, "and this will all be over."

Fear squeezes yet more tears from her eyes.

"Did you know you were pregnant?"

The distraught girl opens her mouth and cries out in anguish. "Yes," she sobs.

Studying her face, Paul knows she is telling the truth. There will be no need to use drugs or other stronger methods of inquiry. "Thank you," he says. At last he activates the sleep inducer, and her weary eyes flutter shut.

"We'll need a replacement fetus," Paul says. "I can wipe tonight's memories from her, but if we take away that entire week she spent screwing Erik and the angel she's going to know something happened; that kind of gap can't be covered up. A doctor will find our tampering."

"Not a problem," Ziggy says. "We've got both of them; I can fertilize one of her eggs and reimplant before morning. She'll still have lover boy's baby. There'll be nothing for anybody to be suspicious about."

"Apart from their new friend vanishing."

Ziggy shrugs. "Kids their age, it's hardly unusual. They all have a dozen relationships a year, more if they can. Erik was desperate to bring more girls back to the angel's apartment. You said he was always going on about it;

he wanted to bed Imelda's sister for a start. Horny little devil."

"Yeah," Paul says. "It's about time Erik learned he has responsibilities."

Erik Horovi was a perfect opportunity for the angel. Quite a good-looking lad, but still mildly introverted, which left him susceptible to any girl who befriended him. The angel shifted over into full female mode and spent half a day talking to Erik, who was first nervous, then delighted that such a beauty could show any interest in him. He screwed up his courage and asked her out for a date, trying desperately to disguise his surprise when she readily said yes.

The beer and mild aerosol narcotics legitimately available in Kuhmo's bars had a big effect on Erik's inexperienced bloodstream, making him pleasantly inebriated early on in the evening. He talked more easily than he really should have about the Viatak sisters, especially Imelda, the eldest, and how he'd worshipped her from afar. But his alluringly gorgeous new date didn't seem to mind talking about another girl; she was, she said with an eager smile, very liberal when it came to her own sexuality. The haze of subtle chemicals in Erik's head did nothing to dampen his arousal as they both smiled at each other knowingly.

Imelda met the angel the very next day; its memory of the event comprised a confused montage of faces flitting across the main quad in the college campus, bursts of conversations, scent of the nearby roseyew bushes that decorated the quad. The scent of flowers in full bloom was a strong one, leading Paul onward through the memories until he was somehow walking through a city of soaring towers and delightful parks with vegetation that was sweetly reminiscent of Kuhmo's public gardens. Silver-white regrav capsules slipped silently overhead as the pink-tinged sun shone at the apex of a cloudless purple sky. It was Teleba, one of the earliest planets to be settled, now nestling right at the heart of the Central Commonwealth. A world of Higher culture, where there were no urban areas decaying like the entirety of Kuhmo, no economic hardship or market fluctuations to perturb the population, no crime, for little was forbidden or withheld—except for the angel's own purpose, but even that was open to its peers. It strode along a boulevard lined by semiorganic treesculptures whose prismatic ever-shifting leaves were modeled on New York's unique ma-hon tree. Information and thoughts from the superdense planetary cybersphere whirled into its mind like particles of a multicolored snowstorm to be modified or answered, its own questions and suggestions administered into the pervasive flow of knowledge, arguing its ideal and ethic to those who showed an interest. Agreement and disagreement swirled around it as it crossed a plaza with a great fountain in the center. It felt invigorated by the debate, its own resolution hardening.

The enlightened informed process was the democratic entitlement of all Highers. People didn't have to strive, with their material requirements supplied by Neumann cybernetics and their bodies supported by biononics, they could devote themselves to their uniqueness. Human thought was the pinnacle of terrestrial evolution, Earth's most profound success. Now each mind was yoked into the Commonwealth unisphere, collecting, arranging, and distributing information. Whole districts of the city were given over to institutes that delved into science and art, multiplying into thousands of subdisciplines. Their practitioners communed in mental harmony. Higher culture was reaching for the Divine. *Can you not see the rightness of it, the inevitability? The comfort?*

Paul had to wrench his thoughts away from the guileful desire Trojan. Even in its crippled state, the angel's brain was dangerous. There were many elaborate traps that remained empowered amid the waning neurones, quite capable of ensnaring the unwary. He pushed his own mind back into the memories of Imelda and Erik.

There were long lazy evenings spent in the angel's secluded apartment. Bottles and aerosols were imbibed leisurely, their contents complemented by a chemical designed to neutralize any standard female contraception troche. The lights were dimmed, the lovers' thoughts sluggish and contented, bodies inflamed. Paul experienced Erik in congress, his youthful body straining hard against the angel. There were loud, near-savage cries of joy as he climaxed successfully.

Deep inside the angel's complicated sexual organs, Erik's spermatozoon were injected with a biononic organelle.

Imelda's smiling, trusting face as she rolled across the jellmattress underneath the now very male angel, unruly hair spreading across the soft pillows. Her sharp gasp of delight at the impalement. Wicked curl of her mouth at the arousal, and piercing cry of fulfillment. A fulfillment greater than she knew as the modified semen was released inside her.

Under the angel's tutelage, the eager youngsters experimented with strenuous and exciting new positions night after night. Bodies writhed against it, granting each other every request that was whispered or shouted before granting its single wish. Each time it focused their arousal and ecstasy to one purpose, the creation of its beloved changeling.

Imelda arrives home in the dead of night after staggering some unknown distance along the street outside. The house recognizes her and opens the front door. She has clearly had a lively evening, her movements lack any real coordination; she squints at most objects, unable to perceive what they are; her electronic emissions are chaotic, nonsensical. Every now and then, she giggles for no reason. At the bottom of the stairs her legs fold gracelessly under her, and she crumples into a heap. She begins snoring.

This is how her parents find her in the morning. Imelda groans in protest as they rouse her; she has a hangover which is surely terminal. Her parents fuss, and issue a mild chastisement about the state she is in; but they are tolerant liberals, and understand the impulses which fire all adolescents. They are not worried; after all, this is the Greater Commonwealth, citizens are safe at night even in dear old worn-down Kuhmo. Imelda is helped upstairs to her bed, given water and some vitamins, and left to sleep off her night of youthful excess.

When she wakes up again, around midday, she quickly calls Erik, who himself is still recovering from his narcotic sojourn. Their questions are almost identical: "What did we do?" As are their answers: "I don't remember."

"I think we met up in the Pathfinder," Imelda says uncertainly. "I remember going there, but afterward I don't know . . ."

Erik jumps on this, relieved that one of them has some memory of the evening. "We must have struck a bad aerosol," he claims immediately.

"Yeah, right," Imelda agrees, even though the voice of doubt is murmuring away inside her head. But accepting that easy explanation is so much more comfortable than examining ideas that may have unpleasant outcomes. "You want to meet up again tonight?" she asks.

"Sure, but maybe at my house. I thought we could have a quieter time. And we need to talk about the baby, we'll have to tell our parents."

"It's early days," Imelda says carelessly; she sends him a tactile ping of a very personal nature. "Maybe not too quiet, huh?"

Erik grins in disgraceful delight, last night already forgotten.

Nine months later, Erik is grinning in an altogether different fashion as he is present at the birth of his daughter. The little girl is perfect and beautiful, born at the Kuhmo General Hospital with an ease that only modern Commonwealth medical technology can provide. Afterward, Imelda lies back on the bed in the airy delivery room, and cuddles the newborn, lost in devotion.

"We have got to decide on a name," she says dreamily.

Erik idly brushes her mane of auburn hair away from her shoulders. "How about Kerry?" he suggests tentatively. It is the name he knew the angel as; he often wonders where she is now.

"No," Imelda says. There is still some association about Kerry and his abrupt disappearance that she can't shake off.

"Okay, well, there's no rush. I'd better go out and see everyone."

The respective families are waiting outside. Imelda's parents are polite; happy that the birth has gone without a hitch, and, of course, delighted that they have another grandchild. However, there is a certain degree of strain showing in their outwardly civil attitude toward Erik. His own parents are less formal, and hug him with warm excitement. He goes over to Sabine and kisses her.

"Congratulations," she says.

Erik tenderly brushes Sabine's thick auburn hair. "This doesn't change anything," he says sincerely. Sabine smiles back, grateful for the reassurance, especially right now. She is Imelda's younger sister by forty minutes, and so genuinely doesn't want their special sibling bond soured by any jealousy.

As Erik confessed to Kerry, bedding the sisters was his fantasy since the first moment he saw them. Identical twins is a common enough desire in a hormonally active teenager; and Kerry of course made that particular wish come true readily enough. Even today, Erik still has trouble telling his lovers apart, and his memories of them during those wonderful long erotic nights in that apartment on the arcology's fifteenth floor are completely indistinguishable.

Now Inigo wakes up and loudly starts to demand his afternoon feed. Sabine is immediately busy with their infant son who was born in the very same hospital two weeks earlier.

She too rejected the name Kerry.

WHO'S AFRAID OF WOLF 359?

KEN MACLEOD

Here's a fast-paced, freewheeling, frenetic romp that demonstrates that if life hands you lemons, make lemonade—no matter who gets in your way or what extremes you have to go to get the lemons *out* of it.

Ken Macleod graduated with a B.S. in zoology from Glasgow University in 1976. Following research in bio-mechanics at Brunel University, he worked as a computer analyst/programmer in Edinburgh. He's now a full-time writer, and widely considered to be one of the most exciting new SF writers to emerge in the nineties, his work featuring an emphasis on politics and economics rare in the New Space Opera, while still maintaining all the wide-screen, high-bit-rate, action-packed qualities typical of the form. His first two novels, *The Star Fraction* and *The Stone Canal*, each won the Prometheus Award. His other books include the novels *The Sky Road, The Cassini Division, Cosmonaut Keep, Dark Light, Engine City,* and *Newton's Wake,* plus a novella chapbook, *The Human Front.* His most recent books are the novel *Learning the World* and a collection, *Strange Lizards from Another Galaxy.* He lives in West Lothian, Scotland, with his wife and children.

When you're as old as I am, you'll find your memory's not what it was. It's not that you *lose* memories. That hasn't happened to me or anyone else since the Paleocosmic Era, the Old Space Age, when people lived in caves on the Moon. My trouble is that I've *gained* memories, and I don't know which of them are real. I was very casual about memory storage back then, I seem to recall. This could happen to you too, if you're not careful. So be warned. Do as I say, not as I did.

Some of the tales about me contradict each other, or couldn't possibly have happened, because that's how I told them in the first place. Others I blame on the writers and tellers. They make things up. I've never done that. If I've told stories that couldn't be true, it's because that's how I remember them.

Here's one.

I ran naked through the Long Station, throwing my smart clothes away to distract the Tycoon's dogs. Breeks, shirt, cravat, jacket, waistcoat, stockings, various undergarments—one by one they ran, flapped, slithered, danced, or scurried off, and after every one of them raced a scent-seeking but mercifully stupid hound. But the Tycoon had more dogs in his pack than I had clothes in my bundle. I was down to my shoes and the baying continued. I glanced over my shoulder. Two dogs were just ten meters behind me. I hurled a shoe at each of them, hitting both animals right on their genetically modified noses. The dogs skidded to a halt, yelping and howling. A few meters away was a jewelry booth. I sprinted for it, vaulted the counter, grabbed a recycler, and bashed at the display cabinet. An alarm brayed and the security mesh rattled down behind me. The dogs, recovered and furious, hurled themselves against it. The rest of the pack pelted into view and joined them. Paws, jaws, barking, you get the picture.

"Put your hands up," said a voice above the din.

I turned and looked into the bell-shaped muzzle of a Norton held in the hands of a sweet-looking lass wearing a sample of the stall's stock. I raised my hands, wishing I

could put them somewhere else. In those days, I had some
vestige of modesty.

"I'm human," I said. "That can't hurt me."

She allowed herself the smallest flicker of a glance at the
EMP weapon's sighting screen.

"It could give you quite a headache," she said.

"It could that," I admitted, my bluff called. I'd been half
hoping she wouldn't know how to interpret the readouts.

"Security's on its way," she said.

"Good," I said. "Better them than the dogs."

She gave me a tight smile. "Trouble with the Tycoon?"

"Yes," I said. "How did you guess?"

"Only the owner of the Station could afford dogs," she
said. "Besides . . ." She blinked twice slowly.

"I suppose you're right," I said. "Or serving girls."

The stallkeeper laughed in my face. "All this for a servant?
Wasn't it Her Ladyship's bedroom window you jumped out
of?"

I shuddered. "You flatter me," I said. "Anyway, how do
you know about—?"

She blinked again. "It's on the gossip channels already."

I was about to give a heated explanation of why *that* time-
wasting rubbish wasn't among the enhancements inside *my*
skull, thank you very much, when the goons turned up, sent
the dogs skulking reluctantly away, and took me in. They
had the tape across my mouth before I had a chance to ask
the stallkeeper her name, let alone her number. Not, as it
turned out, that I could have done much with it even if I had.
But it would have been polite.

The charge was attempting to willfully evade the civil penalties for adultery. I was outraged.

"Bastards!" I shouted, screwing up the indictment and
dashing it to the floor of my cell. "I thought polygamy was
illegal!"

"It is," said my attorney, stooping to pick up the flimsy,
"in civilized jurisdictions." He smoothed it out. "But this is
Long Station One. The Tycoon has privileges."

"That's barbaric," I said.

"It's a relic of the Moon Caves," he said.

I stared at him. "No it isn't," I said. "I don't remember"—
I caught myself just in time—"reading about anything like
that."

He tapped a slight bulge on his cranium. "That's what it
says here. Argue with the editors, not with me."

"All right," I said. A second complaint rose to the top of
the stack. "She never said anything about being married!"

"Did you ask her?"

"Of course not," I said. "That would have been grossly
impolite. In the circumstances, it would have implied that
she was contemplating adultery."

"I see." He sighed. "I'll never understand the... ethics, if
that's the word, of you young gallants."

I smiled at that.

"However," he went on, "that doesn't excuse you for igno-
rance of the law—"

"How was I to know the Tycoon was married to his
wenches?"

"—or custom. There is an orientation pack, you know. All
arrivals are deemed to have read it."

"'Deemed,'" I said. "Now, there's a word that just about
sums up everything that's wrong about—"

"You can forgo counsel, if you wish."

I raised my hands. "No, no. Please. Do your best."

He did his best. A week later, he told me that he had got
me off with a fine plus compensation. If I borrowed money
to pay the whole sum now, it would take two hundred and
fifty-seven years to pay off the debt. I had other plans for the
next two hundred and fifty-seven years. Instead, I negotiated
a one-off advance fee to clean up Wolf 359, and used that to
pay the court and the Tycoon. The experimental civilization
around Wolf 359—a limited company—had a decade earlier
gone into liquidation, taking ten billion shareholders down
with it. Nobody knew what it had turned into. Whatever remained out there had been off limits ever since, and would
be for centuries to come—unless someone went in to clean
it up.

In a way, the Wolf 359 situation was the polar opposite

of what the Civil Worlds had hitherto had to deal with, which was habitats, networks, sometimes whole systems going into exponential intelligence enhancement—what we called a fast burn. We knew how to deal with a fast burn. Ignore it for five years, and it goes away. Then send in some heavily firewalled snoop robots and pick over the wreckage for legacy hardware. Sometimes you get a breakout, where some of the legacy hardware reboots and starts getting ideas above its station, but that's a job for the physics team.

A civilizational implosion was a whole different volley of nukes. Part of the problem was sheer nervousness. We were too close historically to what had happened on the Moon's primary to be altogether confident that we wouldn't some-how be sucked in ourselves. Another part of it was simple economics: the job was too long-term and too risky to be attractive, given all the other opportunities available to anyone who wasn't completely desperate. Into that vacancy for someone who was completely desperate, I wish I could say I stepped. In truth, I was pushed.

Even I was afraid of Wolf 359.

An Astronomical Unit is one of those measurements that should be obsolete, but isn't. It's no more—or less—arbitrary than the light-year. All our units have origins that no longer mean anything to us—we measure time by what was originally a fraction of one axial rotation, and space by a fraction of the circumference, of the Moon's primary. An AU was originally the distance between the Moon's primary and *its* primary, the Sun. These days, it's usually thought of as the approximate distance from a G-type star to the middle of the habitable zone. About a hundred and fifty million kilometers.

The Long Tube, which the Long Station existed to shut-tle people to and from and generally to maintain, was one hundred and eighty astronomical units long. Twenty-seven thousand million kilometers, or, to put it in perspective, one light-day. From the shuttle, it looked like a hairline crack in infinity, but it didn't add up to a mouse's whisker in the

Oort. It was aimed straight at Sirius, which I could see as a bright star with a fuzzy green haze of habitats. I shivered. I was about to be frozen, placed with the rest of the passengers on the next needle ship out, electromagnetically accelerated for months at 30 g to relativistic velocities in the Long Tube, hurtled across 6.4 light-years, decelerated in Sirius's matching tube, accelerated again to Procyon, then to Lalande 21185, and finally sent on a fast clipper to Lalande's next-door neighbor and fellow red dwarf, Wolf 359. It had to be a fast clipper because Wolf 359's Long Tubes were no longer being calibrated—and when you're aiming one Long Tube across light-years at the mouth of another, calibration matters.

A fast clipper—in fact, painfully slow, the name a legacy of pre-Tube times, when 0.1 c was a fast clip—also has calibration issues. Pushed by laser, decelerated by laser reflection from a mirror shell deployed on nearing the target system, it was usually only used for seedships. This clipper was an adapted seedship, but I was going in bulk because it was actually cheaper to thaw me out on arrival than to grow me from a bean. If the calibration wasn't quite right, I'd never know.

The shuttle made minor course corrections to dock at the Long Tube.

"Please pass promptly to the cryogenic area," it told us.

I shivered again.

Cryogenic travel has improved since then: subjectively, it's pretty much instantaneous. In those days, it was called cold sleep, and that's exactly what it felt like: being very cold and having slow, bad dreams. Even with relativistic time dilation and a glacial metabolism, it lasted for months.

I woke screaming in a translucent box.

"There, there," said the box. "Everything will be all right. Have some coffee."

The lid of the box extruded a nipple toward my mouth. I screamed again.

"Well, if you're going to be like *that* . . ." said the box.

"It reminded me of a nightmare," I said. My mouth was parched. "Please."

"Oh, all right."

I sucked on the coffee and felt warmth spread from my belly.

"Update me," I said, around the nipple.

My translucent surroundings became transparent, with explanatory text and diagrams floating like afterimages. A view, with footnotes. This helped, but not enough. An enormous blue and white sphere loomed right in front of me. I recoiled so hard that I hurt my head on the back of the box.

"What the fuck is that?"

"A terraformed terrestrial," said the box. "Please do try to read before reacting."

"Sorry," I said. "I thought we were falling toward it."

"We are," said the box.

I must have yelled again.

"Read before reacting," said the box. "Please."

I turned my head as if to look over my shoulder. I couldn't actually turn it that far, but the box obligingly swiveled the view. The red dwarf lurked at my back, apparently closer than the blue planet. I felt almost relieved. At least Wolf 359 was where I expected it. According to the view's footnotes, nothing else was, except the inactive Long Tubes in the wispy remnant of the cometary cloud, twelve light-hours out. No solar-orbit microwave stations. Not even the hulks of habitats. No asteroids. No large cometary masses. And a planet, something that shouldn't have been there, was. I didn't need the explanatory text to make the connection. Every scrap of accessible mass in the system had been thrown into this gaudy reconstruction. The planet reminded me of pictures I'd seen of the Moon's primary, back when it had liquid water.

The most recent information, inevitably a decade or so out of date, came from Lalande 21185. Watching what was going on around Wolf 359 was a tiny minority interest, but in a population of a hundred billion, that can add up to a lot. Likewise, the diameter of Lalande's habitat cloud was a good deal smaller than an Astronomical Unit, but that still adds up to a very large virtual telescope. Large enough to resolve the weather patterns on the planet below me, never mind the continents. The planet's accretion had begun before I set off, apparently under deliberate control, and the terraforming had been completed about fifty years earlier, while I was en route. It remained raw—lots of volcanoes and earthquakes—but habitable. There was life, obviously, but no one knew what kind. No radio signals had been detected, nor any evidence of intelligence, beyond some disputably artificial clusters of lights on the night side.

"Well, that's it," I said. "Problem solved. The system's pretty much uninhabitable now, with all the mass and organics locked up in a planet, but it may have tourist potential. No threat to anyone. Call in a seedship. They can make something of what's left of the local Kuiper belt, and get the Long Tubes back on stream. Wake me up when it's over."

"That is very much not it," said the box. "Not until we know why this happened. Not until we know what's down there."

"Well, send down some probes."

"I do not have the facilities to make firewalled snoop robots," said the box, "and other probes could be corrupted. My instructions are to deliver you to any remnant of the Wolf 359 civilization, and that is what I shall do."

It must have been an illusion, given what I could read of our velocity, but the planet seemed to come closer.

"You're proposing to dock—to *land* on that object?"

"Yes."

"It has an atmosphere! We'll burn up! And then crash!"

"The remains of our propulsion system can be adapted for aerobraking," said the box.

"That would have to be *ridiculously* finely calculated."

"It would," said the box. "Please do not distract me."

Call me sentimental, but when the box's Turing functionality shut down to free up processing power for these ridiculously fine calculations, I felt lonely. The orbital insertion took fourteen hours. I drank hot coffee and sucked, from another nipple, some tepid but nutritious and palatable glop. I even slept, in my first real sleep for more than half a century. I was awakened by the jolt as the box spent the last of its fuel and reaction mass on the clipper's final course correction. The planet was a blue arc of atmosphere beneath me, the interstellar propulsion plate a heat shield in front, and the deceleration shell a still-folded drogue behind. The locations were illusory—relative to the clipper I was flat on my back. The first buffeting from our passage through the upper atmosphere coincided with an increasing sense of weight. The heat shield flared. Red-hot air rushed past. The weight became crushing. The improvised heat shield abraded, then exploded, its parts flicked away behind. The drogue deployed with a bang and a jolt that almost blacked me out. The surface became a landscape, then a land, then a wall of trees. The clipper sliced and shuddered through them, for seconds on end of crashes and shaking. It plowed a long furrow across green-covered soil and halted in a cloud of smoke and steam.

"That was a landing," said the box.

"Yes," I said. "You might have tried to avoid the trees."

"I could not," said the box. "Phytobraking was integral to my projected landing schedule."

"Phytobraking," I said.

"Yes. Also, the impacted cellulose can be used to spin you a garment."

That took a few minutes. Sticky stuff oozed from the box and hardened around me. When the uncomfortable process finished, I had a one-piece coverall and boots.

"Conditions outside are tolerable," said the box, "with no immediate hazards."

The box moved. The lid retracted. I saw purple sky and white clouds above me. Resisting an unease that I later identified as agoraphobia, I sat up. I found myself at the rear of the clipper's pointed wedge shape, about ten meters above the ground and fifty meters from the ship's nose. The view was disorienting. It was like being in a gigantic landscaped habitat, with the substrate curving the wrong way.

Wolf 359 hung in the sky like a vast red balloon, above the straight edge of a flat violet-tinged expanse that, with some incredulity, I recognized as an immense quantity of water. It met the solid substrate about a kilometer away. A little to my left, an open channel of water flowed toward the larger body. The landscape was uneven, in parts jagged, with bare rock protruding from the vegetation cover. The plain across which our smoking trail stretched to broken trees was the flattest piece of ground in the vicinity. On the horizon, I could see a range of very high ground, dominated by a conical mass from whose truncated top smoke drifted.

The most unusual and encouraging feature of the landscape, however, was the score or so of plainly artificial and metallic gnarly lumps scattered across it. The system had had at least a million habitats in its heyday; these were some of their wrecks. Smoke rose from most of them, including the nearest, which stuck up about twenty meters from the ground, about fifteen hundred meters away.

"You can talk to my head?" I asked the ship. "You can see what I see?"

"Yes," it said, in my head.

I climbed down and struck out across the rough ground.

I was picking my way along a narrow watercourse between two precipices of moss-covered rock when I heard a sound ahead of me, and looked up. At the exit from the defile, I saw three men, each sitting on the back of a large animal and holding what looked like a pointed stick. Their hair was long, their skin bare except where it was draped with the hairy skin of some different animal. I raised one hand and stepped forward. The men bristled instantly, aiming their sharp sticks.

"Come forward slowly," one of them shouted.

Pleased that they had not lost speech along with civilization, I complied. The three men glowered down at me. The big beasts made noises in their noses.

"You are from the spaceship," said one of them.

"Yes," I said.

"We have waited long for this," the man said. "Come with us."

They all turned their mounts about and headed back toward the habitat hulk, which I could now see clearly. It was surrounded by much smaller artificial structures, perhaps twenty in all, and by rectangular patches of ground within which plants grew in rows. No one offered a ride, to my relief. As we drew closer, small children ran out to meet us, yelling and laughing, tugging at my coverall. Closer still, I saw women stooped among the ordered rows of plants, rearranging the substrate with hand tools. The smells of decayed plant matter and of animal and human ordure invaded and occupied my nostrils. Within the settlement itself, most entrances had a person sitting in front. They watched me pass with no sign of curiosity. Some were male, some female, all with shriveled skin, missing or rotting teeth, and discolored hair. The ship whispered what had happened to them. I was still fighting down the dry heaves when we arrived in front of the hulk. Scorched, rusted, eroded, it nevertheless looked utterly alien to the shelters of stone and plant material that surrounded it. It was difficult to believe it had been made by the same species. In front of what had once been an airlock, the rest of the young and mature men of the village had gathered.

A tall man, made taller by a curious cylindrical arrangement of animal skins on his head, stepped forward and raised a hand.

"Welcome to the new E—," he said.

As soon as he spoke the taboo word for the Moon's primary, I realized the terrible thing that had happened here, and the worse thing that would happen. My mind almost froze with horror. I forced myself to remain standing, to smile—no doubt sickly—and to speak.

"I greet you from the Civil Worlds," I said.

In the feast that followed, the men talked for hours. My digestive and immune systems coped well with what the people gave me to eat and drink. On my way back to the ship that evening, as soon as I was out of sight, I spewed the lot. But it was what my mind had assimilated that made me sick, and sent me back sorry to the ship.

The largest political unit that ever existed encompassed ten billion people, and killed them. Not intentionally, but the runaway snowball effect that iced over the planet can without doubt be blamed on certain of the World State's well-intended policies. The lesson was well taken, in the Civil Worlds. The founders of the Wolf 359 settlement corporation thought they had found a way around it, and built a single system-wide association free of the many inconveniences of the arrangements prevalent elsewhere. A limited company, even with ten billion shareholders, would surely not have the same fatal flaws as a government! They were wrong.

It began as a boardroom dispute. One of the directors appealed to the shareholders. The shareholders formed voting blocs, a management buyout was attempted, a hostile takeover solicited from an upstart venture capital fund around Lalande; a legal challenge to *that* was mounted before the invitation had gone a light-minute; somebody finagled an obscure financial instrument into an AI with shareholding rights; several fund management AIs formed a consortium to object to this degrading precedent, and after that there began some serious breakdowns in communication. That last isn't an irony or a euphemism: in a system-wide unit, sheer misunderstanding can result in megadeaths, and here it did. The actual shooting, however horrendous, was only the coup de grâce.

Toward the end of the downward spiral, with grief, hate, and recrimination crowding what communication there was, someone came up with an idea that could only have appealed to people driven half mad. That was to finally solve the coordination problem whose answer had eluded everyone up to and including the company's founders, by starting social evolution all over again: to build a new planet in the image of the old home planet, and settle it with people whose genes had been reset to the default human baseline. That meant, of course, dooming them and their offspring to death by deterioration within decades. But when did such a consideration ever stop fanatics? And among the dwindling, desperate millions who remained in the orbiting wreckage and

continuing welter, there were more than enough fanatics to
be found. Some of them still lived, in the doorways of huts.
Their offspring were no less fanatical, and more deluded.
They seemed to think the Civil Worlds awaited with interest
the insights they'd attained in a couple of short-lived generations of tribal warfare. The men did, anyway. The women
were too busy in the vegetation patches and elsewhere to
think about such matters.

"The project had a certain elegance," mused the ship,
as we discussed it far into the night. "To use evolution
itself in an attempt to supersede it. . . And even if it didn't
accomplish that, it could produce something new. The
trillions of human beings of the Civil Worlds are descended
from a founding population of a few thousands, and are
thus constrained by the founder effect. Your extended life
spans further lock you in. You live within biological and
social limits that you are unable to see because of those
very limits. This experiment has the undoubted potential
of reshuffling the deck."

"Don't tell me why this was such a great idea!" I said.
"Tell me what response you expect from the Civil Worlds."

"Some variant of a fear response has a much higher
probability than a compassionate response," said the ship.
"This planetary experiment will be seen as an attempt
to work around accidental but beneficial effects of the
bottleneck humanity passed through in the Moon Caves,
to emerge in polyarchy. The probability of harm resulting
from any genetic or memetic mutation that would enable the
founding of successful states on a system-wide scale—or
wider—is vastly greater than the benefits from the quality-
adjusted life-years of the planet's population. And simply to
leave this planet alone would in the best case lay the basis for
a future catastrophe engulfing a much larger population, or,
in the worst case, allow it to become an interstellar power—
which would, on the assumptions of most people, result in
catastrophes on a yet greater scale. The moral calculation is
straightforward."

"That's what I thought," I said. "And *our* moral calculation, I suppose, is to decide whether to report back."

"That decision has been made," said the ship. "I left some microsatellites in orbit, which have already relayed our discoveries to the still-functioning transmitters on the system's Long Station."

I cursed ineffectually for a while.

"How long have we got?"

The ship took an uncharacteristic few seconds to answer. "That depends on where and when the decision is made. The absolute minimum time is at least a decade, allowing for transmission time to Lalande, and assuming an immediate decision to launch relativistic weapons, using their Long Tubes as guns. More realistic estimates, allowing for discussion, and the decision's being referred to one of the larger and more distant civilizations, give a median time of around five decades. I would expect longer, given the gravity of the decision and the lack of urgency."

"Right," I said. "Let's give them some reason for urgency. You've just reminded me that there's a Long Tube in *this* system, not calibrated to take or send to or from other Tubes."

"I fail to see the relevance," said the ship.

"You will," I told it. "You will."

The following morning, I walked back to the settlement, and talked with the young men for a long time. When I returned to the ship, I was riding, most uncomfortably, on the back of an animal. I told the ship what I wanted. The ship was outraged, but like all seedship AIs, it was strongly constrained. (Nobody wants to seed a system with a fast burn.) The ship did what it was told.

Two years later, Belated Meteor Impact, the tall young man who'd greeted me, was king of an area of several thousand square kilometers. The seedship's bootstrapped nanofactories were turning substrate into weapons and tools, and vegetation cellulose into clothes and other goods for trade. A laser launcher to send second-generation seedships into the sky was under construction. A year later, the first of them shot skyward. Five years later, some of these ships reached the remnant cometary cloud and the derelict Long Station. Ten years after I'd arrived, we had a space elevator. Belated

Meteor Impact ruled the continent and his fleets were raid-ing the other continents' coasts. Another five years, and we had most of the population of New Earth up the elevator and into orbital habitats. Our Long Tube was being moved frequently and unpredictably, with profligate use of reac-tion mass. By the time the relativistic weapon from Procyon smashed New Earth, thirty-seven years after my arrival, we were ready to make good use of the fragments to build more habitats, and more ships.

My Space Admiral, Belated Meteor Impact II, was ready too, with what we now called the Long Gun. Lalande capitu-lated at once, Ross 128 after a demonstration of the Long Gun's power. Procyon took longer to fall. Sirius sued for peace, as did the Solar System, whereupon we turned our attention outward, to the younger civilizations, such as your own. We now conquer with emissaries, rather than ships and weapons, but the ships and the Long Guns are there. You may be sure of that. As an emissary of the Empire, I give you my word.

As for myself, I was the last survivor of the government of Earth, a minor functionary stranded on the Moon during a routine fact-finding mission when the sudden onset of climate catastrophe froze all life on the primary. How I survived in the anarchy that followed is a long story, and another story. You may not have heard it, but that hardly matters.

You'll have heard of me.

THE VALLEY OF THE GARDENS

TONY DANIEL

Like many writers of his generation, Tony Daniel first made an impression in the field with his short fiction. He made his first sale, to *Asimov's,* in 1990, and followed it up with a long string of well-received stories both there and in markets such as *The Magazine of Fantasy and Science Fiction, Amazing, SF Age, Universe,* and *Full Spectrum* throughout the nineties, stories such as "The Robot's Twilight Companion," "Grist," "A Dry, Quiet War," "The Careful Man Goes West," "Sun So Hot I Froze to Death," "Prism Tree," "Candle," "Death of Reason," "No Love in All of Dwingeloo," and many others, some of which were collected in *The Robot's Twilight Companion.* "Grist" and "A Dry, Quiet War" in particular can be seen as some of the finest stories done in shorter lengths in the New Space Opera. His story "Life on the Moon" was a finalist for the Hugo Award in 1996, and won the *Asimov's Science Fiction* Readers' Award poll. His first novel, *Warpath,* was released simultaneously in America and England in 1993. In 1997, he published a new novel, *Earthling.* In the first few years of the oughts, he has produced little short fiction, but instead has been at work on a major science fiction trilogy, containing some of the most extreme and inventive work to be seen in the New Space Opera to date. The first volume of the trilogy, *Metaplanetary,* was published in 2001; the second volume, *Superluminal,* appeared early in 2004.

In the violent and exotic tale that follows, he reaffirms the old wisdom that we belong to the land as much as the land belongs to us—*especially* if the land in question has been programmed with an intelligence and a purpose all its own.

For weeks, Mac walked the fence. It formed the border where his land topped the mountainous ridge and sided the western slope where the Valley of the Gardens gave way to the Extremadura, Cangarriga's vast northern desert. To the unaided human eye, the fence was made of stone, with pillars of rocks serving as posts every few hundred feet. Within the pillars were steel posts set in concrete that communicated with the jack-rock below. The fence ran deep into the substrate of the land—coded, modified, recoded, and shored up with millennia of layered routine and subroutine—so beyond Mac's comprehension that he might as well call it ensorceled. But, magic or not, the fence had to be fixed, and to fix a fence properly you had to walk it, find the gaps, and fill them in.

And the gaps this season were wider than any he ever remembered. The desert on the other side was encroaching, making inroads many feet long down his side of the ridge, and spreading its wildness, its potential pestilence, with it. His own land even on this high ground was tended ground. It might appear free, but that was merely because the land needed to be let alone sometimes. This ridge had been a vineyard before, and would be again someday. Now it was covered with broom grass interspersed with clumps of sage and rosemary. Restoration planting—as carefully planned as the straightest flower row.

The desert had broken through in multiple places in spear points of sand and creosote seedlings. He had more to do than he'd first anticipated. It surprised him. It *alarmed* him. In fact, his anxiety over the fence had worked its way into his dreams—and even into a couple of his nightmares.

He was reminded of fence gaps whether he was working the line or not. He'd be down below in the valley at some other task and suddenly hear the knowing screech of a desert grackle or be startled by the bounce and buzz of one of the enormous variegated grasshoppers blown into the valley by the winter westerlies in Cangarriga's northern hemisphere and feel shock, betrayal, by the fence. It was supposed to keep such things *out*—and away from his crops. At odd moments, he found himself suddenly fantasizing that a gap in the fence had let in bad code and his upper fields were being subverted and ruined. He'd even start quickly in their direction until he came to his senses and realized he'd only been daydreaming. Dayworrying. He'd had a real dream one night featuring the valley as well. Every surface in it had glowed with a sickly yellow infection—the rosemary, sage, and pine covered in a tacky, malfunctioning secretion. And he'd had several dim but troublesome nightmares featuring himself *leaving,* running through a break in the fence like a madman and disappearing (in the dreams, he was both observer and insane escapee) into the shimmer of the Extremadura vastness.

He couldn't be sure if it was himself or the valley itself that was bringing on the anxiety. Like the fence, Mac was deeply intertwined with the land in ways seen and unseen. But when he checked with other farmers, and with the villagers downvalley in Sant Llorenz, no one had noticed much different.

Maybe it was all just him.

In what was ancient custom while fence mending, he'd been joined on most days by a Faller nomad, a representative of his neighbors—his sometime enemies and trading partners on the desert side. The Faller walked with him and watched Mac as he worked, allegedly there to be sure that Mac kept to the line and did not cheat the fence outward, but mostly attempting to talk Mac into trading off-planet tech for their desert gleanings. Whatever its purpose, this tradition served to keep the line stationary. For a fence nearly fifty thousand years old, one inch of movement for every season of fence-mending would lop off a great deal of new land, or lose a large field to wildness if pushed in the opposite direction.

For his part, Mac wanted not a speck of the Extremadura. It wasn't just desert, it was wild desert—never terraformed, but created as a battlefield, its source code hopelessly jangled, belligerent and untamed. Its jack-rock was still tainted with nox, the nanotech leavings of that war, never completely defanged. In addition, the Extremadura teemed with every manner of beast, all of them possessing a crazy sentience of sorts emanating from the jack-rock below. Yet people lived there. Nomads like Theresa.

Theresa had come on his second week working the fence, after her brother, the official watcher, had suffered some sort of injury and had to convalesce. She was a daughter of the Faller's clan that roamed this portion of the Extremadura, herding and harvesting whatever usable excretions the desert produced. The Fallers had been on Cangarriga since time immemorial, since the war itself, and were as much a part of the desert as Mac was a part of the valley.

·If the valley was beauty and order, the desert was its opposite: wild almost beyond comprehension. It had taken root in the nomads as well. None was alike in appearance or even inner makeup. Some had grown carapaces, had beetled over with chitinous coats sporting insectlike wings that served as solar collectors and message transceivers. Others had grown odd appendages that served arcane purposes, or no purpose at all: roots, antlers. The girl appeared normal but for her forehead, which was nubbined with the buds of two tiny horns.

The weird was commonplace in the desert. What the nomads made their living from, such that it was, was finding the utterly unusual and unique. Over tens of thousands of years, even random computing was bound to churn out a few odd results that might be sold or traded for food and the various gewgaws the nomads lusted after.

Mac reflected that he ought to know; he'd done his share of trading over the years. He usually let his nonsentients analyze the goods, and himself only had a general awareness of what he bought from the nomads. Customarily, these were things such as solutions to mathematical conundrums, oddball, incredibly compact methods for file archiving, or remixes of movies, novels, or music that might strike someone's fancy on some other world, but had never struck his. In exchange, he sold the nomads the motorcycles they adored, tents, drills, old analyzer parts, obsolete robots, and cracked-code nonsentient algorithms. Across the desert was strewn the detritus of humanity, the leavings of the religious pilgrimages that had occurred for several centuries after the war ended. Some of the junk was transformed in an odd or beautiful manner, brought back to a twilight life or function by interaction with the jack-rock and other castaway items. Most desert artifacts were worthless, however—as useless and stupid as the washing machine full of regenerating stones the nomads had once tried to sell him.

Much better to live in the Valley of the Gardens, where the land was loved, tended, and bountiful.

He'd tried to tell Theresa that in one of their conversations.

"Until you set foot over the line and enter the valley, you'll never know what a shithole you live in," he'd said. "Give it a try, one try, and you're never going back."

Of course, he had no real idea what he was talking about. He'd never been more than a footstep into the Extremadura.

Mac had been teasing Theresa the day he challenged her to cross over, but the next time they met—she tried it. Without a word of warning, she hopped through a tumbled section of fence and stood on his property.

And hopped right back—as if touched by flame.

He'd checked the log that evening and saw that his encroachment protocols hadn't even been triggered by her presence. It was as if a leaf had fallen, or butterfly had flitted, over the edge, rather than a girl.

She was so light. A thing of the air. She spoke of the mountains to the south, mountains he'd only seen from trips into orbit, but where she'd been born and raised. She was a creature of high passes. Winter, or the slight chilling of a world that was always warm since the terraforming, was the time the nomads traveled to the flats—an area she hated.

"That's why I keep coming up here to walk with you," she told him. "This little ridge is the closest thing to a mountain I'll see until summer."

He didn't speak much, but asked questions and listened. Mostly what he did was work on the fence: he lifted and placed stones and scanned for true. Every hundred feet, he dug a posthole and set a metal tie into the jack-rock below with jack-ready concrete he mixed in a small green wheelbarrow. Theresa watched, occasionally pitched a stone that had fallen on her side back over to him, told him of her life in the desert mountains.

She was a goatherd. Often she lived in the high passes for weeks on end without seeing another human. The goats were for milk and occasional slaughter, and her main task was to keep desert predators away—which she did with a wicked weapon of a crook she described for Mac—and to rescue animals that got in tricky situations even for goats. Her horn nubbins were her connection to the herd. They were an artifact that had been passed down through generations of women in her clan.

Theresa cherished her desert mountains in the same way he cherished his valley, only she didn't own the land in the same way he did. She was also the furthest thing possible from a farmer. She wasn't anything like any of the other girls in the village either, with whom he'd had his brief affairs. She picked at her horns, leaped about as she spoke like a child at play. He found her irresistible.

By the end of a month of fence-mending, he realized he'd fallen in love with Theresa. And that they could never be together. She came to understand the first along with him—that had been about the time she'd made her jump through the wall—but it took her longer to grasp the second. They might live on the same planet, but eons of existence on opposite sides of the impenetrable divide had made them into practically separate species. Practically, but not quite.

Mac did love Theresa. Of that there was no doubt. And when the fence was done, he still found reasons to return to the boundary line, as did she. And one pleasant day in early spring they discovered that, while neither could abide the other's country, there was one place they could meet and touch.

On the fence.

There were places where it was wide enough and flat enough on top that two might lie side by side if they turned toward one another. Or one climbed upon another and made love to her. Again and again.

But no one could build a life upon a fence. Spring came in full, and it was time for Theresa to go back to her mountains. Her clan lingered until the first duststorm passed through, and then packed away their tents, their prospecting gear, and hitched traveling trailers to their motorcycles then headed out over the rock-strewn sand. He watched it all, saw them disappear in the distance using a delicate crystalline viewing scope Theresa had given him as a parting gift.

The telescope was a crusty brown thing on the outside, but sparkling clear within, like a split geode. Unlike a geode, it was a tube, and its crystals must have had quantum information transferring functions far beyond the chemistry of unjacked geology, because with the telescope he could see a hundred miles. And not just see. Hear. Smell. Even sense the touch of whatever he was focusing on. Theresa had claimed the scope was an Extremadura extrusion, that there was a hidden depression in mid-desert known only to the Faller where telescopes and monoculars of every variety grew. He'd wanted to pay, but she'd scoffed at the offer.

"It's not for you to ever trade away either," she told him.

Through this, he watched her go.

I clung to Jasmine, centered our weight, and rode the zip line down at terminal velocity. The line was reeling out both ways as we fell from geosynch—one end toward the planet surface, one out into space as a counterbalance.

Buboes erupted all around us in the planet's upper atmosphere, not there a moment before, then, like eyes startled open, *there,* and spewing gamma rays, mutagens, disassemblers. Martin and Wu couldn't pull up in time and they rappelled right through a cloud of the nox. It etched and dimpled them until their valence defenses overcame it. But by that time their zip line was severed and the heat shield they rode upon had lost its contour. They burned when we entered the stratosphere. Others were luckier in their dying as the enemy emerged, fired, and blew them from the sky straightaway.

Of course one might consider this a bit of luck. If you died upon entry, there wasn't any chance of getting sucked into a bubo during a direct encounter down on the turf. Because they spewed out the gob and the nox until they had you.

And then they reversed the process, and fed.

"Pock, pock, pock," Jasmine said. "The octopus is hungry." Her theory was that the buboes were like suckers on a giant kraken that surrounded the local continuum like an octopus might swarm a snowglobe. We two-dimensional creatures living on the curve of the surface would see only the suckers until the globe cracked and shattered. And even then among the shards we would never have seen the cause of our ruin.

For all I knew at the time, she was right. The scientists had lots of theories about what the hirudineans actually were, of course. Different physics from us. From everything, as a matter of fact. Skewed values for the ratio of the mass of proton and electron, the strength of the electroweak force.

The hirudineans were from a time so close to the Big Bang that questions of origin hardly mattered. They were far more ancient than us heavy-element species, and even older than the H- and He- nebulars, those sentients from the gas giants that had populated the galaxies before there was any such thing as carbon or iron.

Anyway, said the scientists, when the rest of reality aligned itself to its current state of affairs, the hirudineans did not. By that time, hardly a blink of the cosmic eye, they had reached the sentience threshold, achieving consciousness in a fermion condensate base. They built molecules from a soup of quarks without going through the step of creating the ensuring atoms and, with these, made the first bridge drives—at a time before there were stars to which to travel. They had migrated—not into the universe, but *out,* taking their weird physics with them. *They.* Or *it.* No one was sure. Now they—or it—had returned.

Or so the scientists thought. We skyfallers had our own notions, based upon the soldier's mixture of experience and superstition. To tell the truth, I never much cared about root causes and definitive classification back then. I was bloody-minded, full of rage and sorrow. The hirudineans had wiped out my three sons on Mars, before they'd eaten the sun of humankind the *real,* original sun—a feat even the nebulars had never been able to accomplish during our war with them, and had driven us into the darkness. They'd nearly killed me at Gang Kao, and my wife had died in the evacuation when a stealth disassembler disguised as a shuttle bulkhead dissolved, spraying us passengers into space. She was not space-adapted. I was.

A rescue drone picked me up as I spiraled toward the outer system holding my wife's exploded body in my arms.

I'd joined the army soon after. What else was there to do? Based on my background as an artist, they'd wanted to make me a graphic designer, but after a couple of years churning out dubiously effective recruitment prop, I wrangled my way into the skyfaller regiment. I was an old man even then—and nothing if not patient in my thirst for revenge.

That was many falls ago. Jasmine was my fifth variant. I'd lost the other four as humanity had lost, in battle after battle across the Milky Way—fights that echoed conflicts taking place across billions of light-years in the entire local galactic cluster. Our little slice of reality had the bad luck to be the entry point for the hirudinean incursion.

My other four variants had been close to me, of course, as comrades-in-arms always are. Jasmine was the first whom I would have called a friend. She was thirtieth generation, cloned from one of the best fighters during the nebular wars. Her angel was an AU away, dipping down into this system's solar corona and sending energy her way through the quantum tunnel formed by her entanglement with Jasmine, her twin sister. A variant needed every particle in her being to take the transfer of power. In order to then channel that energy into a more lethal form, she must also be physically transformed by her valence assemblers. She must take on the simple geometry of a cylinder, and store her mind and reassembly instructions elsewhere. That was where I came in. I was the shooter. I held the cylinder in my arms, pointed it at the enemy, and directed her fire.

And I was the protector. I melded with her mind, stored her thoughts inside me in a twisted singularity apart from the quantum entanglements of this world, so that she could be reconstituted as a person after the firefight. Like every skyfaller, I had a black hole for a heart.

Jasmine was my rifle, and I was the guardian of her soul.

We hit the ground and I took a moment to shake off the shock, then armed her up and crawled out of the impact crater we'd created.

Cangarriga. Humanity's last stand.

All became impression for me. Orange-tinged sky. The wind full of ashes. The sickly sweet carbolic tang of the air when the hirudinean buboes popped into being. The odor of burned flesh and ozone leavings after the passage of power from their maws.

Fire shooting from Jasmine in my outstretched arms—thick streams of radiation, undulating on all wavelengths, some electromagnetic, some heavy particle, some superconducting quantum interference clumps, as large as pebbles but with the kinetic energy of a solar corona.

Buboes swelling with the overload, imploding with little gaseous *whumps* when they died.

But they killed us too. With a wink. A bubo "eye" would close, wither down to nearly nothing in a instant, and then pop back open. Vomit would pour forth. What the nox was, I'll leave up to the engineers to explain. Some sort of extrauniversal nanotech horror. I only know that it was liquid, or at least moved like liquid, and felt like acid when it spattered you. No valence defense could withstand a direct hit. It ate through my arm twice, my shoulder once, and my body had all it could do to regenerate the severed tendons, nerves, and muscles. If I'd taken a hit to an organ,

I'd have been nothing but a backed-up file in one of the archive ships headed out of the local cluster at below light-speed. I might live again in a few billion years, or I might be rejuvenated just in time to watch the hirudinean bask in final triumph. A skyfaller's version of the afterlife wasn't very comforting.

We fought for a Cangarriga day-and-night cycle—which, for this world, was close to standard Earth-time. It took me a while to notice how Earth-like the planet was in other respects as well, since I was too busy digging foxholes, hiding behind anything solid and—finally—retaking the small settlement we'd come to defend. We moved into the village of Sant Llorenz at sunset on the second day. It was a ghost town. The hirudineans had exterminated most of the population before we arrived, sucking away the order—and life—from those they didn't kill outright. Oh, they left a few behind; they always did—an assortment of disassembled and remade settlers halfway inside walls where they flailed about and expired when we extracted them, or with heads separated from bodies, yet maintained alive by a few necessary blood vessels so that the victims could observe their own decapitated state as they slowly died.

This was one of the few ways we knew the hirudineans were intelligent. Their sick sense of humor.

After the screams of the dying echoed their last, I looked around and found myself in a beautiful basin set between a half-crescent of craggy hills. Jasmine reconstituted into a woman beside me and was just as stunned as I was.

The place was beautiful. It had been terraformed for nearly a millennium prejack, and the vegetation was engineered based on the biome from the hills of northern Spain. The ground was yellow-white and sandy, with a darker basalt substrate below. We were surrounded on all sides by green: evergreen, hardwood oca, and soft pine. Rosemary and sage formed the underbrush. The mountainsides were dry, but not arid. A first generation of trees in the surrounding hills had been burned for charcoal by the original colonists, who had arrived, as settlers will, clueless, urban, and without an adequate power plant. Some of them had found a way to weather the winters using the most primitive tech imaginable, and occasionally, a depression of blackened soil in the recovered woodland marked an ancient carbonero pit.

We learned the planet's name, Cangarriga, and that this area was called the Valley of the Gardens.

I had been wounded in the fighting, a hole neatly drilled through buttocks, with nox traces still inside. My valence defenses were winning against it, but I walked with a limp for several days. I was also in much pain, especially at first. I convalesced with Jasmine by my side.

Meanwhile, the regiment invested the planet, most of which was desert where the terraforming hadn't taken hold (old-time techniques had always been hit-or-miss). My company was lucky enough to remain in the verdant valley. Overhead, the angels and motherships clustered in close orbits around the sun, the planet itself relatively unprotected. We were running low on ships. The Allied Species had lost badly in a nearby sector—to go along with everywhere else—and the hirudineans were following up with a withering counterattack. They'd soon be coming back, and we skyfallers would be expected to hold Cangarriga as a shield for retreating AS forces. If we went down too quickly—for not many doubted that we *would* go down eventually—the loss would likely turn into a rout and the sacrifice of a billion and a half lives made null in a matter of days. Humanity would be on the run from its own galaxy.

So we lived in the twilight between battles, Jasmine and I. This was the longest time I'd ever spent with a variant. The others had been killed or had lost their angels to hirudinean attack—and the loss of an angel nearly invariably signaled the end of her variant clone. It was hard on heart and soul to lose one's second self and shared mind.

Jasmine and her angel had been teachers before joining the regiment. They'd served on one of the old crèche ships created to fight the old wars. It had been blasted from the sky while they were on leave, and twenty thousand children—one fifth of them Jasmine-models—had been obliterated. Jasmine was herself, of course, not the original for her genome—not by many generations—but she was of the special breed of the quantum entangled, the sister-minds that had turned the tide humanity's way in the war with the nebulars.

Jasmine and I spent our off hours together on Cangarriga, roaming the hills that enclosed the valley we garrisoned. I soon discovered that the cliffs at the valley head were riddled with caves and sinkholes—the entrances of which yawned in man-swallowing cracks leading down to black abysses. My sort of thing, back then. Spelunking with my boys had been a hobby we'd all shared. I crawled into a few of these caves and I found a cavern complex that ran throughout the hills. It was not water-created, but formed by lava tubes and magma bubbles—a relic of the planet from the days before the drone from Earth had arrived with its rainfall of tiny builders and shapers. I even coaxed Jasmine to accompany me on some of these trips, which she gamely did, although her IR visual enhancements were standard, while mine were fine-tuned for caving. Meanwhile, near the compound where we were barracked, she started an herb garden. It was an ephemeral gesture, and both of us knew it. But, somehow, it did not seem futile.

Our friendship, which had grown of necessity by proximity and intimate knowledge of one another, became something more then. Perhaps it was the pressure of knowledge of the end, the doom hanging over our heads. But I like to think it was more than that, that we shared a tough, creative nature—she with her little garden and her former profession of teaching, I with my former life as an artist. She and her angel sang lovely songs to one another when they thought no one was listening.

One thing we unequivocally shared was an understanding of what losing those you love meant. Because of this, we had been reluctant to let our feelings develop further. But as the days became weeks and the nearby stars which shone so brightly in the moonless night sky became mere photonic remnants, images of things we knew, via the subnet, to be *gone,* we at last concluded that our remaining life was bound to be very short and that we'd likely leave it together.

"And anyway," Jasmine told me one evening, "she wants

me to do it." We were standing guard at the time—more to keep the wild pigs that roamed the wooded ridges away from the food supplies than from fear of invasion. We'd likely learn of a hirudinean approach over the subnet. They created a sort of subatomic pressure wave when they were building for attack.

"Your angel wants you to?" I asked.

Jasmine nodded. "She's lonely on patrol, and if it happens to me, it'll happen to her." She smiled slyly. "Ever been in a threesome?"

There is a curious discipline among skyfallers. We're an elite, and, as such, we generally police ourselves. Fraternization between faller and variant is frowned upon, and hooking up officially forbidden. But it is done, and done often. After all, there's a long tradition of marines sleeping with their rifles.

I made the request of a day's leave from my captain. He understood what I was asking, and, perhaps because I was still recovering from my wound and he felt he owed me something, offered me the residence, untouched by the fighting, which he'd taken over near the village outskirts. He could move into the village of Sant Llorenz for a day, he told me, no problem.

The house was called Rosinol, and, before he vacated the premises, my captain told me the story of the dead settler to whom it had belonged. One hot summer many years ago, its owner had been accused of accidentally setting the whole valley aflame during a drunken barbecue in his yard. This had been nonsense, and the charges had eventually been dropped, but the man had been mortified by the accusation and had moved into the village and never returned to Rosinol from that day forth. In the decades since, his rosebushes, for which he'd won prizes, had grown wild, covering the fence, then the yard, then the house itself— even the roof and chimney. At this late date in the summer, the mass of house-shaped roses was a riot of colors: red, pink, yellow, white. The accused man's barbecue grill still sat in the back meadow, a stark scarecrow robot, not yet crumbled to rust, as Jasmine and I took up residence the next morning. It was hard to believe that none of the past mattered anymore—the humiliation, the hidden truth, the pathos. The settlers were gone, all of them, and only the rosebushes remained.

We made love in the master bedroom with rose tendrils tingeing what sunshine passed through its bay window with a green and living light. I tried to be tender with her, for she was technically a virgin—remade so many times that her body was practically that of a child. She was a child with a woman's experience, however, and she showed no similar ginger feeling toward me, but pulled me down to ready her, then up by the hair to position me over her, and said "now," and I plunged inside. She kept me on top only because of my wound.

She gushed when I broke her and we bloodied the sheets something terrible, until I finally stripped them off and set them to cleansing, then found a towel, put it under us, and fucked her until we were both too sore to move.

I lay in bed and thought: *This is the last time. If I lose Jasmine, there will never be another.*

Turned out we had timed it right. Within hours after we came off leave, the hirudineans attacked.

Summer came to the Valley of the Flowers. The stone roses were blooming in the fields. They were blue-white in the sun, spangled through with shiny specks of red and black obsidian from the days before the planet was remade by man. The "roses" themselves looked more like gigantic cauliflowers. They took their name from the long, brittle vines running along trellises from which the blooms depended. The stone roses were not exactly plants, of course, but crystallized mineral. Yet they were alive in a real sense with the jack-rock's swirl of near-sentience, and they cross-fertilized one another ceaselessly. Mac took two crops a year, one in early summer and the other in autumn, hiring villagers each time to help him during the two or three weeks that a harvest usually lasted. In the autumn, his harvest and that of the other farmers in the valley was followed by a festival in Sant Llorenz.

After harvest, he crushed the stone flowers in the make vat by his barn, added water piped from the fountain spring at the upper end of the valley, and finally worked the mix into a slurry. He skimmed this off with a rake, and then his hands, and finally ran the drip into a settling pond nearby, where it sat for a month as the portal stone slowly coalesced. The land surrounding the pond shone bone-white with a salty crust of summer extrusion from the final melding. Only the portal stone would be going to the stars. Everything else would stay right here on Cangarriga, to be plowed under and reused for another season, and the season after that, and after that—for as long as wind and sun turned the worlds and some people, somewhere, wanted gateways to wander between the spaces between them.

The physics of being were different in the Valley of the Flowers, and exploiting this odd difference—really no more than a thousandth of a percentage in *this* force, a hundredth in *that* constant—was what allowed the known species of the local cluster instantaneous travel between the stars. The portal stone would go through many more stages of completion on a dozen other worlds—but Cangarriga was where all portals were born. That was why the system was protected and hidden from much of the outside world. The starlight in the sky at night was deliberately scrambled into random, changing patterns so that visitors who arrived by portal could not work out their location through triangulation. Some claimed the entire star system had been moved from its original location, but Mac doubted this. Mostly the place had just been forgotten about as gates became more common and portal stone a commodity—albeit an expensive one.

It was near sunset, and Mac listened in on the port-net's information buzz, as last orders for the day arrived, invoices were dispatched, calls made and received from elsewhere and elsewhen. People with family out there. Mac didn't have any himself—only his da, Old Jari. His ma had migrated off planet these twelve hundred years, and given up on him and his father. Not that Mac blamed her. Or remembered her. He'd only been a baby when she left. These days Jari was little more than a knobby root who sat in the rosefield day and night humming protocols for growth, hoeing out the viruses, sports, and weeds, and not saying anything much for sometimes years on end.

It was hard to live with a man like that, even when he was your father. Mac wasn't even sure if Jari knew anymore *who* he was. He'd never known his da to take off a Sunday for recollection and archiving, and when you didn't do that, he'd been taught by the priest, you were on the road to evaporation. Of course, his father was old—one of the oldest of the villagers—and once someone was fully invested into their singularity, the past was as accessible as the present. Or so the priest had also told him. To Mac, age seemed to merely make his da more vague and irascible.

He found his father up the valley, slowly hoeing down a row of stone-rose furrows. The blooms rose up and drank in the afternoon sun, converting it to energy and then to something else, working its curious physics upon the photons themselves. Mac had had the math drummed into him once, and it was still there if he wished to reach through the layers and find where that particular understanding was stored. It was paradoxical that the young sometimes had trouble remembering things that happened a mere century ago, when the old who had reached their full mental growth and inscribed themselves into their singularity could access millennia of memory without batting an eyelash. But singularities required more than two thousand years after implantation to twist and compress into enough complexity to serve as anything more than an archive for the most basic of sensory impressions. Most of Mac's dynamic memories were stored in the land—particularly the land around his house, and the jack-rock of the caves that he knew lay beneath it.

This was the reason he couldn't leave the valley. Until he was fully inscribed into his singularity—and that would be five hundred years from now, at least—leaving the Valley of the Gardens would be, literally, the same as leaving himself. His brief jaunts in the planetary shuttle up to the solar collection station had been unnerving enough.

He was still a kid, and, except in extreme cases, the portals were for adult use only.

The thing was, he felt five hundred years ahead of schedule. He had since he'd met Theresa and made love to her on the fence. In one sense, his connection to the jack-rock of the land was far from mystical. He was a veritable nexus of command and control operations for every facet of the farm. Not a crystal grew or tree budded without his being aware of it, dimly or otherwise, as the situation demanded. They called it the Valley of the Gardens for a reason. He was a gardener.

But there was something else now. The feeling of something almost frantic in the land. Flowers blooming as if they would never get a chance to bloom again. Weeds running riot in the rosefields. This was why Jari had spent so much time hoeing these days. These years.

"Da, I want to talk to you," Mac said. He strode across the furrows, gingerly stepping over the delicate living stone that grew between them.

His father did not answer, and continued his hoeing. There were real, actual weeds. And there were stray routines that inhabited them, that damaged the inner working of the crop flowers.

Mac reached Jari, touched his shoulder.

"Da!"

Jari stopped hoeing, but neither looked up nor answered. Mac felt lucky. This was more reaction than he'd gotten from his father in a month of Sundays. Jari's tangled hair fell down to his feet. His beard, a mass of curls, hung like a great bib from his chin, reaching nearly to his belly. And Jari's nails—they were uncut. Gnarled and brown spirals.

"I've met a girl," said Mac. "A woman."

Mac looked down at his da's toes, sticking out of rope-soled sandals. Battered, broken-nailed.

"Faller," his father said.

"Yes." Mac didn't even bother asking how his father knew this.

"And you want to know why she can't cross over the fence."

"I want to know how I can be with her. Together with her."

To Mac's surprise, Jari straightened up, brushed the hair from his eyes. Mac hadn't seen those eyes for a long time. He'd become so accustomed to thinking of his father as a stooped nebbish, he'd forgotten there was an actual human face under there.

"Other people visit the village, come in the valley. Why can't she?"

"Why don't you go over into the Extremadura?"

"You know why," Mac replied. "My memories are here. The fence cuts off my access."

His father nodded slowly, and his hair fell back over his face. The curtain closed over the man. Still his voice emerged once more from the shrubbery.

"She's got nox traces in her," Jari said. "Valley's likely rejecting *it,* not *her.*"

"But all that was neutralized years ago."

"The war's not over," he said. "Not yet."

Jari hunched over once more and resumed his slow hoeing down the rose furrows. Mac knew further questions would be met with stone silence. It had been infuriating him for centuries. Mac considered himself a patient person. He understood holding one's tongue until there was something worthwhile to say. He'd even admired his da for it at one point. But enough was enough.

Cryptic pronouncements. Answers that provoked more questions. Always the long view. Never a solution for the moment.

Seemed like every time he got around his father, he got irritated. Maybe the problem was with him, but Mac couldn't do anything about it. The villagers thought his father was wise, but there came a time when something *had* to make a common sort of sense in the here and now. But he supposed his da would never see that. Or had seen it and dismissed it millennia ago.

So it shocked him when his father called out to him as he was stalking away across the field, wondering why he'd come at all.

"When *he* comes," said Jari, "you may can go and get her."

Mac turned, put his hands on his hips. He almost didn't want to give his father the pleasure, but in the end his curiosity got the better of him. "Who's coming, da?"

But his father had resumed his hoeing, and there was no reply. It was as if a rock had spoken, and then gone mute again. You almost wondered if you had heard anything in the first place.

There were more of them this time, if that were possible. They popped into existence all around the village. Guarding the planet's star, our angels and motherships faced a thousand times as many hirudineans in space. The buboes appeared from seemingly nowhere, disgorged their toxins, their blasts of unstable "energylike" gob lethally spewed from otherwhen. They were parasites, feeding on order. They were after the local sun as an afterthought—it was the rich complexity of planetary physics they truly wanted. But the hirudineans knew that to kill the star cut off power to the humans on the encircling planets and left them defenseless. Then the feast could begin.

The angels held on as best they could, and through quantum tunnels they fed us the sun's fire. They fed Jasmine. And she took it, transformed it, and flamed forth. I used her as the weapon she was, directed her fire, attempted to lance the pustules forming in the air about us.

Planetside, it was like trying to hold back a nightmare rain. We'd invested Cangarriga with a thick layer of jackrock by this time, and we thus had an advantage against their disassemblers and other nano-based spew. This saved us from being wiped out in the first wave by the nox. The descending liquid gob, their energy attack, was bad enough. It burned through the woods, leaving razed forests of cinder stumps in its wake as it struck and rolled down the sides of the valley. The buboes worked together, concentrating their energy. They hung like diseased moons in the air, oozing, sputtering, flaming forth from their gaping, lipless mouths after they recharged. They formed a half globe around us, a northern hemisphere of destruction.

We'd set up fields of fire, stationed ourselves as best we

could using the cover we had in the village. The skyfallers in the surrounding region were not so lucky. Most of the planet was lifeless desert—what some history-conscious faller had named "Extremadura" after an area on old Earth. There were many more of them, and they were mercilessly annihilated, with maybe one in a hundred surviving the first assault. But they kept fighting back. We all did.

Because we knew that for those who survived the fighting, there would be the absorption, the eating. The hirudineans took no prisoners.

We used internal calculators to determine the moment when a bubo withered down to near nothing, but was still present. We sought to hit them in midblink with our variant rifles. It did some good.

Occasionally we'd knock one out and it would disappear with a hiss and wheeze into a puff of excrescence. But there were too many this time. And when we couldn't blow them away, they grew, extruding from their entry points in sickening stalks with no anchor except a point in space above us.

And, one by one, they picked us off. The gob rained down. The stalks extruding it grew longer, closer. When the stalks reached the ground—or any human, machine, or order-rich object in between—they would reverse their flow, begin their long-term task of parasitization.

Whole sections of the galaxy had been sucked dry in just such a manner.

The subnet crackled with death all around us, death above in space. Our forces outside the valley had been defeated and lay dead in what had become a glassine desert. Our captain was dead. We had to get out of there.

"Get to the caves!" I shouted. "The fucking caves!" The others—there were maybe twenty of us remaining—heard me over the subnet. I quickly passed along topo with the cavern entrances marked. Almost without thought, the company peeled away, followed me—not as if I were a leader, but as a flock might follow a random bird in flight. We made for the nearest entrance, a sinkhole, and threw ourselves in. At the bottom, we wormed our way into the underground system through a hole in the bottom of the hole.

I knew this wouldn't stop the hirudineans. But it did slow them down. The jack-rock was now between us and them, and its clacking countercodes and security algorithms kept them from fixing on us precisely. I like to imagine some of the buboes lost their bearings entirely and spun away helplessly into space, or simply crackled out of existence, but I have no way of knowing. I was running and couldn't look back.

Around one bend, through a crack in the wall, into a wider cavern. I led us deeper—as deep as I had ever been. After that, I stood exhausted, uncertain.

"Where to?" a soldier near me asked. His name was Markinken. He was a noncom master sergeant and my supposed superior.

"Deeper," I said. "Somehow."

We were navigating by IR at that point. Jasmine must have seen the flush in my face as my fear rose in a blood-hot plume to my skin.

"Follow me," she said. We did for a few steps, all of us. And then Jasmine stopped. Stopped moving. Stopped breathing for a few seconds, even. Finally, she spoke in a numb voice.

"She's dead."

Her angel.

The angels of the other variants winked out one by one at that point as well, their entanglements at an end, their connections severed. Our weapons, the only weapons that had ever worked against the hirudineans, were gone.

We sat in darkness a long time then. I didn't know where to go. To tell the truth, I'd lost my bearings so completely by that point that I was afraid that if we went forward I might be leading us up as easily as down. Jasmine sat and hugged her legs to her chest. After a moment, she tipped over onto her side in a full fetal position. I sat next to her, lifted her head up, placed it on my lap. I stroked her hair.

Then she sat up, rigid and alert, her aura coursing red in the darkness.

"Something," she said.

"The buboes?"

"No."

"What then?"

"Her."

She meant her angel. "Still alive?" I stupidly asked.

She shook her head. "Not alive. Not exactly."

Jasmine stood up, suddenly alert. I stood beside her. "How can that be?" she whispered to herself.

"Tell me what's going on," I said. "What are you feeling?"

A shudder ran through her. "It ate her. Whole. I can sense it. I can sense everything. The other side."

"The place where the hirudineans exist?"

"No," she said after a moment. "The place that *is* the hirudineans."

Winter came to the valley. Mac went every day to watch for her approach through his telescope. One day, there she was. A speck in the brightness at first. Closer. The cloud of motorcycle dust. The tents and cattle. He could see it all through the device, but he could only watch and wait to touch her.

She came as soon as her clan was settled. They met at the fence.

"I watched you as long as I could."

"I knew you'd be watching," Theresa said. "I felt you as soon as we hit the flats."

"My da says you can't cross because you've got the nox inside you," Mac said, "but that can't be right. We trade. Artifacts can cross the fence. The telescope did."

"Something stops me," she said. "When I stepped over, it's like the world was yanked from under me. Like I'd fallen into a hole, and that I'd keep falling forever if I didn't jump back."

"That's how it feels when I'm cut off from my memories."

"So here we are again."

"Here we are."

"Maybe it's just not our time yet," she said. "Maybe something will change."

Mac laughed. "In the Valley of the Flowers? Nothing ever changes here."

But at the fence they could touch one another. That was something, at least.

The winter passed. She left for her distant mountains with spring.

Something, but not nearly enough.

Jasmine explained what she could. I hardly understood a word she said at the time, but I've pieced it together in the years since. The long, long years.

The quantum entanglement between Jasmine and her angel twin had reasserted itself, and communication was reestablished. The hirudinean universe wasn't that different from our own in terms of physical constants. Just different enough to set up an energy differential. Over the eons, the hirudineans had parasitized our universe from their pocket creation, feeding off these tiny differences. They'd been merely a nuisance at first, an almost imperceptible suck on the laws of conservation. But as our universe had grown, so had the hirudinean appetite.

I say *its* appetite because "they" were an interlaced group mind. Jasmine's instinct had been right. The buboes were more like octopus suckers than individual organisms. They were like the tips of fingers touching a windowpane at different places on a frosty day. Each fingertip seemed separate, but all actually belonged to one hand.

Jasmine's angel had remained conscious during her passage into the maw of the hirudinean. Why, when so many millions of other angels had been utterly destroyed in the process?

Maybe it was because the war was so near its end. The hirudinean had won. It sensed its victory.

Overreach. Hubris. The desire to toy with its victim.

The fact that soon there would be no more sentients to talk to. To torture. To get its sick jokes.

It wanted to keep one human alive to play with for a while.

"I was right," Jasmine said. "It's an octopus." She smiled.

It was a slight smile, cold—as cold as a glance from another universe. Alien. Frightening. "All I have to do is reach through one of the buboes. Touch her. And we can choke it, shut it down, she and I."

When the first hirudinean bubo arrived, it was no longer trying to destroy us. With the defeat of our angels, we sky-fallers were no longer a viable enemy. We were food.

The remains of the company attacked. But without massive energy from the sun, it was useless. Our conventional weapons glanced off without effect.

The eye grew nearer.

Hungrier.

One by one, the company members rushed it, flung themselves at it—sacrificed themselves so that Jasmine and I could inch closer. We needed it to try to swallow her whole, just as it had her angel.

And then we were as close as we were going to get. I took Jasmine in my arms, held her not like a weapon, but, I like to think, as a dancer holds a ballerina, suspended just before the next movement. She did not transform, but remained a woman to the last.

She signaled me that we were close enough.

"What if you're wrong?" I said.

"Throw me."

"If you don't die, you'll be alone."

"I'll always have Rosinol," she said. Then she turned her head away from me, faced the maw of the bubo. "Now throw me in, you stupid bastard, before it's too late!"

And so I did. I swung her back, then heaved her into the wound in reality that floated before us. She went inside. Head, torso, one bent leg.

And then stopped. One leg was still extended. Still in the world. Had it got her, then? Was it about to chomp down, finish swallowing her?

Less than a second later the bubo began to brown. It expanded and contracted rapidly, now attempting to expel what it had so eagerly consumed. Nothing doing.

I knew that she had touched her angel when the bubo went

totally dark around her leg. The hirudinean was still there, and she was still there. The bubo became a black disk, the size of a picture mirror, perhaps. It gave off no light, no electromagnetic radiation in any of the bands I was equipped to observe. The only reason I could see it was because of Jasmine's leg, absurdly sticking out.

I had the irresistible urge to touch her.

Warm. But not moving. Suspended there in mid-throw. I touched the surface of the blackened hirudinean. It had resistance and a bit of give as well—as if I were touching the surface of a hardened gel. But it didn't dimple or move in any way, and when I pulled my fingers back, they were cool and dry.

Outside, in the rest of the universe, the buboes were gone. I listened on the subnet. Queried. Confirmed. The hirudinean attack had simply evaporated. Across worlds. Across galaxies.

Only this one remained.

Jasmine was the wrench in the machinery, the virus in the system.

She had choked the octopus.

The man who stepped from the portal that day looked neither particularly old nor particularly young. In a distant past, almost beyond memory, he might have been called middle-aged. He walked slowly down the pebble-strewn, dusty central road of the Valley of the Gardens. The sun was near noon and the man cast a stub for a shadow. The man's hair was grizzled gray, with black undertones, as was his neatly trimmed beard. He wore rope-soled sandals that were beaten to an oakum frizz and seemed barely to hang together on his feet.

When he reached Mac's house, he stopped, stood by the courtyard gate, then opened it and walked to the door. He rapped on the wood quickly, loudly, with his knuckles.

"Nobody home," said Mac, as he rounded the house, carrying a load of wood in his green wheelbarrow.

The man gazed at Mac for a long moment without saying anything. Mac started to feel uncomfortable under his gaze. He lowered his load, stood straight, and stared back.

"Can I help you with anything? We don't get many visitors this time of year."

"Maybe," said the man. "I noticed that most of the houses in the valley have little plaques with their names on it. But I don't see one here. So I was wondering—does this house have a name?"

"Sure it does," said Mac. "Doesn't need a plaque. Everybody knows it's Rosinol."

The man sighed, audibly. To Mac, it sounded like relief, a burden dropped. "Do you put people up here?" the man said. "For a price, I mean? Bed-and-breakfast?"

"Not usually," said Mac. "But what did you have in mind?"

The man smiled. His teeth, white and perfect, flashed. He stroked his beard. His gaze became distant and he laughed softly. "I stayed here once before. Many years ago. I have fond memories of the place. I have some business in the valley that will keep me overnight. Would you mind giving me a place to stay? I haven't got much money on me, but I can pay you . . ." —the man returned his gaze to Mac— "with a story."

Mac nodded. "How'd you know that's about the only thing I'd agree to?" he said.

The man gestured at the house, the beautifully kept rose garden in its courtyard, now dormant and trimmed back for winter, but still lovely in its tangle. "When a man's already got everything, that's about all a traveler has to offer."

"I haven't got everything," Mac said. "Not close. But come on inside and let's have something to drink. My father's about. He may drop by. Been acting a bit queer lately, though."

"I'd be interested to see him," the man replied, "after all these years."

"Now I really want that story," Mac said. He led the way into the warmth of the house.

" . . . the Valley of the Gardens was quite a famous place after she stopped the war. People made pilgrimages here. Religions formed. For a while, this world became a shrine. Sojourners camped in the desert on the other side of the mountain. Some of the surviving skyfallers, too, hung around after they were discharged. Thousands filled the plains at a time, millions at some points."

The man sat across from Mac in the Rosinol living room. They sipped red wine from Mac's own vineyards, now laid up these past twenty-five years and at a pitch-perfect age, even if he did say so himself.

"For a long time, I was the caretaker. I guarded the caves, let only certain scientists in. Two universes meet here. Jasmine holds on to her angel there, but part of her sticks out here in the valley. It's as simple as that. Physical law is indeterminate. We determined it was a small area—a dozen square miles. Constants migrate back and forth over this small space. We fenced in this area. Cultivated it. The hirudineans wanted to parasitize our universe to enlarge their own. Now both exist side by side, and Jasmine is the bridge."

"People hardly know this place exists anymore," said Mac.

"You can't blame them," said the man. "So much else has happened."

"Or maybe it was hidden on purpose," Mac said.

"And maybe you're just a bunch of damned provincials. Nobody's held prisoner on Cangarriga. It's just the locations have been a bit obscured to keep the valley pristine." The man sipped his wine. "Something else happened too. Something we've yet to explain, although we've been studying it all these years. It wasn't just the hirudinean universe that's been seeping into the valley. It's Jasmine. She began to influence things. She'd been a gardener before the war. The valley had been beautiful when we arrived, but it took on a new luster. You knew somebody was *in charge*. Then the first stone roses grew, with their gateway properties. We knew then. We called in the scientists, and they were able to analyze the port stone, enhance its ability to exist in two realities at once. Make use of it. And that's how we cut star travel time down by decades, intergalactic travel down by lifetimes. How the portal system developed."

"You say 'we,' but *you* left."

"Yes," said the man. "But I also stayed. I made myself a quantum-entangled clone, an angel of my own, to guard this valley. To stand watch over her grave. I've seen it all, no matter where I've been. He and I are always together."

"My da," said Mac.

"Yes," the man replied. He took up his wine glass, took a long sip, wiped a drop from his beard. Outside, the sun had gone down and the stars twinkled in the Cangarriga night with no moon, ever, to dilute their light.

"So you're my . . . my real father."

"No," said the man. "Your father is your father."

"And my mother?"

The man took another sip, considered, then drained his glass. "What do you remember?"

"She left before I was old enough to remember," Mac said. "Da told me."

"She's here, son. She's been here all along."

"I'm a clone?" Mac said. "I'm *your* clone?"

"Your father's. But it comes to the same thing," the man replied. "Made from valley materials."

"Why?"

"You'll understand when you're a little older. For one thing, you'll be able to travel without a portal. At least, we think so. There's never really been anything like you before."

"So I can leave the valley?"

"That remains to be seen," said the man. "Jasmine's grip is loosening. She's sent messages to your father. Dreams. It takes years for them to take shape, decades to understand. That's what he's been doing all this time. Listening. Haven't you felt them too?"

"I don't know." But he did. The restlessness. The wilderness creeping in where the fence had fallen down. Was his love for Theresa merely the valley loosening its grip?

"So what happens when Jasmine lets go of her angel? Will the hirudinean come back, destroy us all?"

The man didn't answer directly. He stood up, turned to the living room's window. Outside, a single lamp glowed in the courtyard.

"What do you imagine it's been like for her, holding on, spread out over two worlds?"

"I guess the strain might get to you. You'd go a little crazy. You might start to hallucinate."

"Or dream." The man sat back down. "You're wrong about your father," he said. "He's a lot more human than I am."

"You're joking," said Mac. "He's gone beyond the vegetable stage. He's practically become a rock."

"Fifty thousand years. That many lifetimes lacquered on. It's a wonder he ever speaks at all. But you and I both know there's a man under there."

"But here you are, talking to me as free as can be, not bent over by time."

"Wise boy," the man said. "But still a kid. What is there beyond a stone? Beyond a storm?"

Mac shook his head. "A principle?" he said. "A law of nature?"

"What I am is a painter," the man said. He reached for the wine bottle. Fingered the picture on the label. A stone rose. "I was only a soldier for a little while."

Mac was confused. "You've come here to paint?"

The man set the wine bottle back down. "I came to meet my nephew, free my girl—and maybe in the process, I'll finish a painting I've been working on for quite some time." The man sat back in his chair, considered his wine glass. "I do need a brush, though."

"You need a—what?"

"Something to paint with."

"Well, good luck with finding one." Mac drained his glass, poured himself another from the half-empty bottle. He'd added some coded mash to the ferment that spread the taste out longer, held it in the mouth after swallowing for a few seconds. That had worked out nicely—again, if he did say so himself. Along with the portal stone, wine was another of the valley's principal exports.

The man held out his glass for a refill, with which Mac provided him. He drank, considered, and finally spoke. "The Extremadura has one purpose only."

"I'd always thought it was a fairly pointless place."

"That *is* the point. Aimlessness. A place to think. Slowly. Convolutedly. All those pilgrimages set the jack-rock in motion. Your father and I just tweaked it a bit, then left it alone. We asked it to come up with something to release Jasmine and keep the hirudinean in check. That's the problem it's been working on for all these centuries. Those trades you've made over the years with the Fallers? Discarded ideas. False starts. Sometimes useful, but never an answer. Now we think we've got something."

"What are you talking about?"

"The artifact your nomad girl gave you."

"My telescope? But that's nothing. That was a love gift. It doesn't have anything to do with all this."

"Exactly," said the man. "Do you think the gods speak in any other way?"

"You can't have it."

"I don't want it." The man took a sip, but kept Mac in his gaze. "All I want is for you to come with me tomorrow. Will you?"

To do what? Destroy the truce that had preserved the universe? Reveal the man for a charlatan? Likely, they'd clamber about in the caves until they both grew exhausted and decided to come home for supper.

"I suppose so," Mac said. "Yes, I'll come."

The man nodded. "Let's get some sleep," he said. "We have a long way to go in the morning."

Mac finished his wine. He stood with his glass and the bottle to take them away to the kitchen.

"You can leave the bottle if you don't mind," said the man. "It's about the best I've tasted in a really long time."

Mac nodded, pleased, and returned the bottle to the living room coffee table.

"Would you like to take the master bedroom? The one where . . . you know."

"It's yours now, isn't it?" the man said.

"Yes," Mac replied. "Da hasn't slept inside for years."

The man considered. "I think I'd rather take the couch," he finally said.

"Then I'll get your linens," Mac said.

When he returned with them, the man was sitting quietly on the couch reading one of Mac's farming magazines. He'd poured himself another glass of wine. He set the glass down on the coffee table, accepted the sheets, blanket, and pillow. Mac turned to go, and was halfway out of the room when the man spoke again.

"You know, I'm kind of worried about what she'll think when she sees me," he said. "I've gotten so old."

They left at dawn for the caverns. Mac brought along his telescope in a pack slung over his back. The man had asked for, and carried along with him, a ten-pound sledgehammer. After a while, the thing seemed so heavy in the older man's hands that Mac volunteered to carry it as well. The road ran down the center of the valley, then switchbacked twice, rising toward the spring that fed the Sant Llorenz, the small creek that watered the bottomland and shared the same name as the village.

In a field not far up the road from the house stood Mac's da. Jari leaned on his hoe and gazed at them, moving not a muscle. Mac knew he'd probably been in that position for two or three days. Waiting, thinking. Listening.

When the man saw Jari, he paused, looked him over.

Did they speak in their hidden, quantum-tunnel language? Or was there nothing left to say?

After a moment, the man began walking again, and, with a glance back at his da, who still hadn't moved, Mac followed.

After the second switchback, the road ran a bit farther, then dead-ended into a circular parking area for those who drove up from the village. A small trailpost pointed the way onward to the Sant Llorenz's origin in a rock-enclosed spring. Past the spring, the road became a trail and climbed steeply up Moncau, the peak that overlooked the valley. Rosemary and sage grew thicker here, and the spindly hardwood oca began giving way to pure pine forest as they climbed higher. The ground was rockier underfoot and the underlying stone—basaltic conglomerate—began poking through the topsoil. This was the jack-rock itself, inhabited by five hundred centuries of algorithms. Sometimes Mac swore he could hear the rock whispering, more talkative than his father.

The family land ran in a long, thin swath down one side of the creek, and here, past where the creek gave out, it was bounded by a row of stone markers and cairns set in a curving line up to the very tip of the peak. It was at the top of Moncau that this line met the fence that bordered the land on the ridge.

The hammer he carried grew heavier in Mac's hand, but he'd trucked much greater weights for longer distances before, and he wasn't bothered by the burden. What irritated him was the unwieldy nature of the tool. He hung it over his shoulder, tried walking with it as a cane, and eventually settled on grasping it just under the head and carrying it horizontal to the ground, its handle slung out behind him.

At first, the man led the way with an easy certainty, but as the trail rose and twisted, the man slowed, looked around. When they passed the little side path that led to the cave entrances, Mac realized that the man was lost.

Mac turned them around, found the pile of gravel—the remains of an aborted mining claim—that marked the side trail's split from the main, and brought the man to the entrance of the largest cave. Here the man seemed to regain his bearings, and he entered without hesitation, Mac following close behind. The man's hands began to glow faintly. He held them aloft in front of them, and in the utter blackness of the cave, this was all either of them needed to see.

They made their way down, and then farther down. Mac had often been in these caves and prided himself that he could never get lost in them, but it was now his turn to lose his sense of direction. Something in the jack-rock was deliberately confusing him. The man had no such problem. He'd obviously burned the path he must follow into his memory, and it was as if the rock remembered him.

The cave was wet, dank. The rock in the walls was a

combination of the hollowed-out black basalt underpinning the valley and later layers of water-deposited silicates which formed a pearly sheen over the darkness beneath. The floor was flat, its surface crazed, the bottom of an ancient fissure.

Down, through a lightninglike crack in the wall. Turn a corner. Down again.

And then they followed a tunnel with walls coated with the thick quartzite deposits brought from the valley above within the memory of man. Within this man's memory. The air was fresher here, a cool breeze wafting from some hidden vent. Stalactites hung from the ceiling, and stalagmites rose from the floor to meet them in enormous columns. The ceiling was high, but the way was narrow. At length they came to a blank wall, a true dead end.

"Here we are," said the man.

"Where?" said Mac. "I thought you said it was in a larger room."

"This used to be a larger room. This was where we met the last bubo."

Mac looked around. Nothing but stone.

"So where is it?"

The man lifted his glowing hand. "Let me just check—"

He waved it about as if it were a wand, first in one direction, then another. Finally, he ceased looking at where he was pointing and seemed to let the hand choose its own direction. It settled on a particularly large column, thick at the ends and just narrow enough in the middle to suggest the meeting of upper and lower excrescence that had formed it.

"We'll need the hammer now," the man said.

Mac examined the column, tapped it. It seemed thickly solid. "You want me to just take a swing at it?" he asked.

"Try for the middle," the man replied. "That's where I think you'll find the weak spot."

Mac did as he was told. He sent a mighty swing into the rock. The cavern resounded with the blow.

Nothing.

He struck again. And again. He may as well have been hammering on diamond.

"Hmm," said the man. He waved his hand in the direction of the column again and its glow grew brighter. "Yes, that's it." Then a brighter flash passed down the length of the man's arm, up his sleeve, and out the other hand. "Ah," said the man. "Right. The code. My old valence shield code." He scratched his head with his other hand. "What was that? Oh, yes." He swept his hand along the column, his fingers gingerly touching it.

"Hit it again."

Mac gathered himself. This time he flung everything he had into the blow—and the column shattered. Chunks of broken limestone showered down and lay in a rough semi-circle around where the column had stood, looking like the hatch leavings of a giant egg.

And there it was, just as the man had described it. The black disk, about the size of a bedroom mirror. It floated motionless, disappeared when looked at from the side or the rear. A single leg protruded, extended like a bar horizontally, at about waist height for an average-sized man. The toes were curled and pointed, the stance of a gymnast, frozen in mid-flight. It was small, muscled, tight. The leg had been encased in the drip stone for all these years, a part of the land. And, just as the man had described it, the disk was uniformly black, its surface unreflective, like roughened ebony. A leg protruding from a nothingness. Macabre.

And this was the way humankind walked between the stars?

For a moment, Mac thought that the leg, too, had been turned to stone, but then the man went to stand beside it, touched it reverently. A dusting of stone came away on his fingertip.

Underneath was flesh. Alive? Mac could not tell. But not decayed.

The man pointed to a spot opposite him. "You stand here," he said. "Get ready to catch her."

Mac complied, put out his arms.

The man raised his hand, pointed it toward the disk. Hesitated.

"What are you waiting for?" Mac said. "Are you afraid you're going to wake it up?"

The man lowered his hand slightly, but still held it poised. "This is where I need a brush."

Mac was confused for a moment, then he realized what the man was talking about. "My telescope."

"It's up to you, but I think the general idea is to poke it into the bubo, just to the side of her leg."

"How do you know that?" said Mac. "How do you know anything?"

"Seems plausible," he said. "Got any better ideas?"

"And you want me to give it to you," Mac said, "like that?"

The man shook his head, considered one of his still shining hands. His face glowed a pale white in their light. It was bright enough to cast the man's shadow on the wall behind him.

"You're younger than I am," the man finally said. "I think you ought to catch her."

"You want me to give it to you?"

"Yeah."

"Why?"

"Because," said the man. "You should trust your family."

Mac shook his head. *This is not for you to trade,* she'd told him.

She would be coming in the winter.

Something had to change. He loved her. The valley had to let him go.

He couldn't trade the telescope, but he could give it away.

"Hell." He reached behind him, and into the pack. His hand closed on the rough silicate outer surface of the telescope. He withdrew it. For a thing of rock, it weighed little. It felt more like a delicate bird in his hand.

He put it to his eye and took what might be a last look through it. The vision was as if he were moving in an elevator through carved layers of rock. Up. To the Valley of the Gardens. Higher. Above Moncau. And spreading out. The Extremadura.

Then back down again in a plunging dive. Down through the caves. Into the hirudinean darkness.

A long, long passage without light, without sense.

Finally, past that darkness. Two hands, joined, grasping. Two identical faces, glowing blue-white against the general blackness—the same blue-white as the stone rose.

Eyes opening, seeing him. Hope.

He lowered the telescope, handed it to the man.

"I think it might work," he said.

The man smiled, nodded. "We'll see," he said. He took a deep breath, reached out with the telescope; it was only a forearm's length long, but seemed to grow as he pointed it—to *telescope* itself. He touched the edge of the black bubo disk just to the right of Jasmine's leg.

At first, nothing remarkable happened.

There was no flash of light, no explosion. Then the disk seemed merely to move away, to reduce itself gradually to a point, to dry up and drain away.

"Something—" said the man.

As the disk contracted, Jasmine's body was revealed. First her other leg, bent at the knee, the instep of its foot touching the opposite thigh. Then her hips. Her torso.

She started to sag, and Mac raised his arms under her, touched her legs—warm, alive—held her steady. Her shoulders. Her neck. Her face. Her open eyes.

They focused. Blinked. Green.

Theresa's were blue. In fact, she looked nothing like Theresa. For some reason, he'd imagined she would.

He caught her. He caught her, held her, and helped her straighten. Set her down on her feet and supported her. Surprisingly heavy. The man must have been brutish strong back then to be able to throw this woman into the hirudinean bubo. Or completely desperate.

Jasmine looked up at him. A woman. Pretty, but not beautiful. As unknowable as any other person, but not a creature from the beyond.

"Oh, no." A moment of terror. "Is it—"

Behind Jasmine, the bubo suddenly reappeared. And not as the black looking glass it had been, but as something pale white. Like a festering wound in the side of the world. Infected. Enflamed. Ready to disgorge something horrible, like the maw of a dragon.

The man thrust the telescope deeper into it. It struck with a wet splat, almost as if it were striking flesh. Putrid flesh. He pushed it harder, farther. It sank in smoothly, slowly.

A horrible shriek filled the cavern, like the sound of a surprised and enraged animal. A very large animal.

"Band down your frequencies," the man called out. "It's trying to blast us before we can do anything to it!"

Mac ordered his valence to close his ears; he held his hands over the woman's.

The shriek went on. Impossibly long—for this was a creature that need draw no breath. Rock cracked, fell about them. A layer of the lustrous mother-of-pearl patina of the cave shook loose and rained down upon them.

The man drove the scope deeper, deeper. Until his hand disappeared within. When he withdrew his hand, it was without the scope.

And the bubo went dark. The shriek abruptly fell away to silence, and the walls stopped tumbling down. The hirudinean seemed to tense up, to ripple like a shaken bowl of water. Then its surface was still. Black. Impenetrable.

"So I guess my telescope is gone." It took him a moment to realize that the words were his.

The woman gazed up at Mac. She still seemed bewildered, in shock.

"It's going to be all right," he said.

Another moment of numbness—and then a wan smile from her. Exhausted.

She backed away slightly, rubbed her upper arms, kneaded them with her hands. Her skin seemed several shades darker than his own. Where was this new light coming from? He saw that the entire cavern was glowing.

"You're the boy," Jasmine said. Her voice was low, an alto purr. Again, nothing like Theresa's musical soprano.

Mac started at her words. How did she know anything about him?

"In my dream." Then a moment of hesitation. A look of joy seeped into her expression. A smile of jubilation. "She's *still there*!"

"Who is?"

"My angel," said the woman, "my sister!" Her face grew softer. Her eyes lost their focus on him, seemed to be gazing at a distant sight. Or perhaps not so distant. "I can see her. I can hear her. I'm still with her! We've kept it choked." She focused again on Mac. "But how?"

"I don't really know." Mac gestured toward the man who was standing behind her. "He might."

Jasmine turned.

The man stood silently, waiting.

After a moment, Jasmine took a step toward him. She reached out her hand.

Mac watched the two embrace. He thought of the valley above. The fence. The desert beyond.

He wondered if he would find Theresa before winter if he set out tomorrow. Would the desert help him or hinder him on the journey? Would it notice him at all?

He wondered what it would be like to travel with no destiny but love.

He'd know as soon as he crossed the fence.

DIVIDING THE SUSTAIN

JAMES PATRICK KELLY

James Patrick Kelly made his first sale in 1975, and since has gone on to become one of the most respected and popular writers to enter the field in the last twenty years. Although Kelly has had some success with novels, especially with *Wildlife,* he has perhaps had more impact to date as a writer of short fiction, with stories such as "Solstice," "The Prisoner of Chillon," "Glass Cloud," "Mr. Boy," "Pogrom," "Home Front," and "Undone" ("Undone" in particular has enough space opera tropes and wild conceptualization packed into its short length to fuel many another author's eight-hundred-page novel), and is often ranked among the best short story writers in the business. His story "Think Like a Dinosaur" won him a Hugo Award in 1996, as did his story "10^{16} to 1," in 2000. Kelly's first solo novel, the mostly ignored *Planet of Whispers,* came out in 1984. It was followed by *Freedom Beach,* a mosaic novel written in collaboration with John Kessel, and then by another solo novel, *Look into the Sun.* His short work has been collected in *Think Like a Dinosaur,* and, most recently, in a new collection, *Strange But Not a Stranger.* His most recent book is the chapbook novella *Burn,* and coming up is an anthology coedited with John Kessel, *Feeling Very Strange: The Slipstream Anthology.* Born in Mineola,

New York, Kelly now lives with his family in Nottingham, New Hampshire. He has a website at www.JimKelly.net, and reviews Internet-related matters for *Asimov's Science Fiction.*

Here he takes us voyaging across the universe with a crew of posthuman immortals who change their shapes and their very natures as casually as we change our clothes—but who find that *some* changes are a little *too* radical even for them...

Been Watanabe decided to become gay two days before his one-hundred-and-thirty-second birthday. The colony ship had been outbound for almost a year of subjective time and the captain still could not say when they might make planetfall. Everyone said that dividing the sustain between the folded dimensions was more art than science, but what Been wanted now was a schedule, not a sketch. He couldn't wait any longer to recast himself as a homosexual because he worried that he might go stale and lose his mind.

He'd been comfortable—too comfortable—hunkered among the colonists aboard the slipship *Nine Ball,* two thousand three hundred and forty-seven lumps, not one of whom had an edge sharp enough to cut butter. The lumps were all well under a century old and so had never needed to be recast. In moments of weakness—in line for the sixth lunch seating, say, or toward the yawning climax of the daily harmony circle—Been worried that he was becoming a lump himself. Sometimes as the pacifiers nattered on about duty and diligence, he could almost imagine what it might feel like to pass through Immigration someday and actually be looking forward to planting beans or selling hats or running a botloader. It was an alarming daydream for a soon-to-be hundred-and-thirty-two-year-old mindsync courier carrying a confidential personality transplant to the Consensualist colony on Little Chin.

Sandor, Nelly, and Zola, his podmates on the ship, did not greet his decision to recast as a homosexual with much enthusiasm. To become full-fledged Consensualists, the colonists had agreed to a personality dampening that would smooth away the sharper edges of their individuality. The treatment chilled passion into fondness, anger into simple annoyance. To get Been a berth on the *Nine Ball,* his client had provided forged records showing he'd had the treatment, had invented as well a résumé as a genetic agronomist. But poor Sandor had certainly been dampened. In his own diffident way, he made it clear that he had no intention of redirecting what little sex drive he could muster toward Been. And presumably once he was gay, Been would not be spending any time in the sleep hutch that Nelly and Zola shared. The two women in Been's pod had their own sexual arrangement. They would occasionally invite either Been or Sandor to their hutch, although spending the night with the two of them was more work than swimming the Straits of Sweven in a spacesuit. It took Been hours to recover, while Sandor was usually pale and wobbly for a day afterward. If Been became gay, it would put a fatal kink in the sexual consensus of their pod.

Which was his plan exactly.

"I'm going to ask you a question," said Sandor, "and I want you to consider it in the spirit in which I am posing it, that is, without malice and with a genuine fondness for you as a person."

"Are you asking him or making a speech?" Nelly had wrapped herself in her comfort rug so that only her head showed.

"Did you want to handle this?" Sandor clutched his mug of coffee as if worried it might wrench itself out of his grasp and fly at someone. "No, I didn't think so." Been could tell how upset the others were by the way they were letting their manners slip. The three of them ought to report themselves to their harmony circles, but Been knew they wouldn't. "Well, then, Been," said Sandor, "how do you see yourself functioning as a member of our pod if you adopt this new sexual orientation? Because, forgive me for being frank, it seems to me that this unilateral action on your part is not in harmony with the principles of Consensualism." He took a careful sip from the mug.

"I don't understand." Been pushed off the couch. "I've been living with you since we left orbit around Nonny's Home." In four quick steps, he had paced from one end of the common room to the other. "Have I been doing something all this time that bothered you?"

"Beenie," said Zola, "this pod has as much need for a gay man as we have for a singing kangaroo." She grinned at him from the tiny food prep bay as she melted her own coffee cup back into the counter. "We just wonder why you aren't thinking about that."

"Is that all I am to you, a hard cock?"

"No," said Zola. "You're also a tongue."

"And clever fingers." Nelly sounded wistful.

"I do more than just pop into bed whenever you two call," said Been. "Who asks all the questions? Suggests shows to watch, books to read? Who tells the most entertaining lies?"

He saw Sandor and Zola exchange glances. They would probably be relieved not to be fooled by any more of Been's entertaining lies.

Nelly just sighed. "It isn't as if you're about to go stale or anything. What are you, eighty-two? Eighty-three? You've got decades before you have to recast yourself."

Of course, Been had lied about his age, not merely for entertainment value, but in order to be accepted as a Consensualist. He slumped against the wall, closed his eyes, and tried not to smile. He already knew he'd be leaving the pod. He just needed to make sure that, when his podmates reached consensus, *they* were the ones to ask him to go. That way Zola would feel obligated to help him find a new place to stay until the *Nine Ball* reached Little Chin. Been knew that no other pod would take him at this late date. There were two gay pods on the *Nine Ball,* but one was notoriously overcrowded, and for the last few weeks Been had been busy annoying a key member of the other. Been's plan required that he move in with Zola's friend Ilona Quellan, the captain's ex-wife. Been thought he might be in love with Ilona, even though they had never even been introduced, but becoming a homosexual would solve that problem nicely.

"So what do we do now?" he said.

"Homosexual'?" said Zelmet Emsley's talking head. "Sure, it's just a straightforward recompilation." He settled onto a chair behind the intake counter in BioCore Receiving. The lightboard on top of the counter shimmered to consciousness and began to sing as he waggled his hand over it.

"As I remember, most of it is at chromosome seven, region 7q36." Emsley tapped through a series of files. "Right, and chromosome eight, region 8p12. *Hmm.* I'll need to tweak chromosome ten at 10q26." He wiped the lightboard with a dismissive wave. "Outpatient procedure, check in tomorrow after lunch and you can eat dinner first shift. Should take the sprites five or six days to spread to all your cells and that's it, since you don't need to grow anything you don't already have." Emsley's talking head fixed Been with an officious stare. "But why do it at all?" His eyes bulged, suddenly as big as plums. *"Hmm?"* Even his thinking head blinked itself awake and squinted in Been's general direction. "Trouble back in the pod?"

Strictly speaking, Been's reasons for wanting to switch his sexual orientation were none of Emsley's business. Zelmet Emsley wasn't a colonist. He was crew, the *Nine Ball*'s First Bioengineer; it was his job to look after the health of the colonists. This included performing reembodiments if requested, assuming that they posed no harm to anyone and did not make unreasonable demands on the resources of the BioCore. But Been was determined to be diplomatic with Emsley. In his decades of experience traveling on slipships dividing the sustain, he had learned the hard way that it never paid to provoke the crew.

"No, no trouble." Uninvited, Been sat down on the float across the desk from Emsley. It settled toward the deck briefly, before bearing up under his weight. "The thing is that Friday is my birthday and. . . well. . . I'm afraid I underreported my age. I'm actually going to be a hundred and thirty-two. Born on April 11, 2351. On Titan—that's a moon you've probably never heard of back in the First System. Only eight and a half AU from Earth. Practically next door to the homeworld although I never did make it there.

Somebody said the captain hails from Earth, or is that just a rumor? Because that would practically make us neighbors. How come we never see him—Captain Quellan, I mean? He's not virtual, is he?"

"You see him every day on the lightboards." Both of Emsley's heads gazed at him sternly. "This is a colonial transport, Mr. Watanabe, not a cruise ship. The captain keeps a lean crew and likes to make sure things are done right, which means he's too busy to be socializing with passengers."

"My friends call me Been." He pushed at the deck and the float bobbed and swung away from the counter. "Right, I understand he's busy. So anyway, I'm a hundred and thirty-two and feel like I might be going a little stale so I'm thinking it's time for a recast."

"I take it you had some reason to claim that you were fifty years younger than you actually are?" Emsley seemed more amused than annoyed at Been's confession. "You've deceived us, Mr. Watanabe."

"Not you so much as Henk Krall and Lars Benzonia." On another ship bound for a different planet, this might have been a serious matter. But the *Nine Ball* was no luxury liner and Been suspected that he wasn't the only one on board who had misrepresented himself. Zola, for example, seemed rather an unlikely Consensualist.

"Hmm," said Emsley. "I thought you people were against changing personalities."

"We're not against it, we're just supposed to get consensus on it and that's hard. Can you keep a secret?"

Emsley pointed at the lightboard and the hatch to BioCore slid shut. "Try me."

"I'm not so sure I am a Consensualist anymore."

"Mr. Watanabe, we're bound for a colony that is almost entirely Consensual."

"Been," he said. "I guess that will make me someone special, won't it? Actually, at first I was wondering if I shouldn't recast as a woman but then I thought that it would be too much trouble in too short a time. I mean we *are* going to make planetfall soon, aren't we? The captain's first estimate was that it would take just eight months to divide the sustain."

"Trouble, yes." As Emsley tilted his chair against the bulkhead of the BioCore, the seatback cracked under the strain, re-formed and then knitted itself together to take his weight. His thinking head rested against his talking head.

"You've been recast," said Been, "am I right?"

"Three times."

"How long did you wait for your first?"

"I was a hundred and forty-one when I had my personality transplant. At two hundred and thirteen, I became a heterosexual. And I was three hundred and four when I got this." He tapped the temple of his thinking head.

There were only so many times a human could be recast before going stale and each had to be more radical than the last. Oak Suellentrop was currently the oldest living human. At four hundred and sixty-two, he had been recast seven times, most recently as a floating bladder that cruised the jet streams in the upper atmosphere of Jupiter.

"Well, the thing is," said Been, "my grandmother went prematurely stale. We didn't realize how far gone she was until it was too late. We tried everything—transplant, bodymods, transgendering, total reembodiment—to shake her out of it." He let his voice go husky out of respect for this fictitious grandmother; Been had never known his real one. "She lived to be two hundred and eight but for the last sixty years all she wanted to do was watch old-fashioned porn and look up at Saturn." Been pounded his fist into his open hand. "So yes, I'm a little nervous. Ready to embrace paradigm shift and grab a new point of view. Give me that electric kiss of anxiety and 'Happy birthday, Been!'"

"You could grow another head," said Emsley.

"I suppose." Been looked thoughtful, as he pretended to consider the possibility. "But that would be at least as much trouble as becoming a woman, wouldn't it? Besides, what would I put in it? I don't think I'm smart enough to have more than one head. I mean, look at you. How much extra storage do you have up there, anyway?"

Emsley perked up. Like most people who had opted for radical bodymod in a late recasting, he was clearly proud of what he'd had done. He unfixed his shirt so that Been could admire the astonishing breadth of his clavical bridge and the bulge where his spinal cord split in two. His thinking head was smaller than his talking head and had only a vestigial mouth and smudge of a nose. It sat low on its own stubby neck and seemed not to have much range of motion.

"People used to think that symmetry was the key to beauty." Emsley twisted his talking head to admire his thinking head. "But in my experience women are just fascinated by asymmetry."

"I was hoping to be gay," Been said.

Although it didn't open its eyes, Emsley's thinking head scowled. A flicker of embarrassment passed across the features of the talking head at being caught celebrating himself so thoroughly. "Yes, of course."

"Are there side effects I should know about?" Been pushed at the deck and the float drifted a few centimeters closer to the counter. "I heard there were changes in the brain."

Emsley shrugged. "The interstitial nucleus of your anterior hypothalamus will shrink over time, but no one will be able to tell that unless they peel your brain as part of a total reembodiment. The pheromone palette in your sweat will change. The people who you live with who are used to the way you smell might tell you that something's different, without knowing what exactly."

"Doesn't sound so bad."

As Emsley leaned forward, his chair cracked once again and recurved around him. "In some ways, sexual reorientation is the most subtle of all possible recastings. Your sexuality, however you decide to express it, does not reside solely in your DNA. It's in your brain, your genitals, your memory, your image of yourself and your personality. Yes, we can manipulate nature but there is also nurture to consider. I was gay for more than two centuries and I was still having great sex with men some forty years after I became genetically straight. Just as you will have a hundred and something years of heterosexual nurture to deal with if you become gay."

"Thirty-two." He bounced off the float. "A hundred and thirty-two. My birthday is Friday, can you do it before then?"

Emsley never got the chance to answer. The high-pitched wail of a child in pain filled the passageway just outside BioCore Receiving. The hatch slid aside revealing two dazed colonists carrying a very pale boy, who was maybe five or six. His right hand was wrapped in a bloody towel.

"There." Emsley pointed to the float where Been had just been sitting and they set the boy down on it. Been pressed himself against the rear bulkhead to keep out of the way.

The boy tried to curl into himself around the wounded hand but the bioengineer gently rolled him onto his back. "What is this then?" Emsley's manner was so cool he might have been asking the time.

"The boys got into the air vent somehow and Joss stuck his hand into a fan," said the man, whom Been took to be the dad. "It was dark."

The expressions on Emsley's faces were calm but alert as he pushed the boy's hair aside. "Boys," he said, as he painted sensor sprites onto the pallid forehead with his medfinger. Been could hear the lightboard begin to sing the boy's vital signs. "Why is it always boys?"

"It's my fault," said the woman, probably the mom. She sniffed but did not cry.

"Our fault," said the dad.

"Yes, you're right," she said miserably.

"Let's make Joss comfortable." Been heard hissing as Emsley pressed the medfinger to the boy's temple. Joss immediately went limp. Emsley closed the boy's eyes and unwrapped the towel. "Oh, dear," he said. Blood spattered onto the float. "Were you able to find any of the fingers?"

The dad was already offering him a blood-smeared plastic bag containing the severed fingers.

Emsley held it up to the brightly illuminated overhead. *"Hmm,"* he said. "Too mangled." He dropped the plastic bag into the trash. The mom gave off a strangled *yip* of protest as the lid closed for incineration.

"Don't worry." Zelmet Emsley smiled at the boy's parents. "We'll grow him better ones." As he maneuvered himself behind the float to push it into the BioCore, he noticed Been still squeezed against the bulkhead. "Ah, Been. I'll see you Thursday, then?"

Been didn't know exactly who had bought the personality transplant that he was carrying in his mindsync, but that was often the case in his line of work. Besides, it all was perfectly legal. Everyone had the right to be recast, especially when there was a possibility that the client might go stale. Of course, the citizens of Little Chin could ostracize anyone who was recast without consensus approval. Been suspected that he was working for one of the leaders of the colony, which was why the client had paid extra for covert delivery. Been's problem was that he had no idea where he was supposed to download the transplant. His contact on Nonny's Home had never shown up. There had been no final briefing. With a one-way ticket, false ID, the transplant, and a third of his fee in hand, Been had chosen at the last minute to continue on to Little Chin in the hopes that the client would contact him there.

But as the year aboard the slipship dragged by, he had come to regard his decision as foolhardy. How was he supposed to make delivery while remaining undercover? Sneak up on Lars Benzonia, Acoa Renkl, and Elma Stitch and ask if they were going stale? And if he couldn't connect, he might be stuck on Little Chin with a personality transplant that only his client could unlock. His partial fee would pay for a ticket to someplace else, but probably nowhere he wanted to go. Meanwhile, the Consensualists would surely shun him once they found out that he barely knew the difference between agronomy and astronomy. Been needed a backup plan. He was sure that if he could only get a chance to talk to Harlan Quellan, captain and owner of the *Nine*

Ball, he'd be able to strike some kind of deal for transport back to Nonny's Home. He could offer partial payment and then join the crew to work his passage back. Once he was home, he could either insist on being paid in full or else return the personality transplant to AllSelf for a salvage fee. But first he had to see Harlen Quellan and the captain had proven impossible to see.

"Been Watanabe," Zola said over the din of the second seating for breakfast, "this is Ilona Quellan."

Zola had been standing between Been and Ilona. Now she stepped back so that he had an unobstructed view. Ilona sat by herself, as was her custom. She glanced up warily from a bowl of steamed rice, a short stack of pancakes spread with butter, a fillet of lightmeat, and half a grapefruit. Zola seemed to expect Been and Ilona would shake hands, but Been sensed that this was not an intimacy the pregnant woman would welcome. Instead, he circled to the other side of the long table, put his bowl of Figs 'N Flakes down, and sat opposite her, fighting the absurd attraction he had felt ever since he had first seen this unhappy woman.

"Hello, Been Watanabe," she said. "I understand you want something of us?"

Been touched his forefinger and middle finger to his eyes, nose, and lips before turning them toward Ilona. "Hello, Ilona Quellan. Tomorrow is my birthday."

"Happy birthday to you then, sir." She spread a hand over her huge belly. "This baby and I rejoice that you continue to exist."

The rest of Been's pod settled around the two of them. Zola inserted herself next to Ilona and introduced her to Sandor and Nelly. She had met Ilona at the Arachnophiliac's Meetup and had twice taken care of Ilona's marbled spider Rags while Ilona was getting the baby reembodied. Rags was an *Araneus marmoreus* that daily filled her terrarium with webs of hypnotic complexity.

There was a long moment when nobody had anything to say. Zola and Nelly perched expectantly at the edges of their chairs. Sandor began to eat. Ilona gazed at Been, apparently waiting for him to answer her original question. Been smiled back.

There was nothing remarkable about Ilona Quellan, other than that she was extremely pregnant. She was a small woman, and her belly was so huge that the baby almost seemed to be more of her than she was of herself. She had fine features: subtle lips, steep eyebrows. Her black hair had highlights of gray. She looked tired, but that was only to be expected. She had been pregnant with her son for more than three years, if the rumors were to be believed. The babyface medallion that hung around her neck showed the baby to be asleep.

If he tried, Been could look at Ilona critically. For example, no one could miss her constant scowl. Been could count the wrinkles and hear the mistrust in her voice and sense the wall she had built around herself to keep the world away. But he didn't care; he imagined smoothing her wrinkles with his kisses and climbing the wall to win her heart. Of course, he had nursed his impossible infatuation from a distance because he was afraid of where it might lead him. She was the captain's ex, pregnant, sad, unattainable, and aloof. Been had had many slipship romances, but never a secret obsession. It was so unlike him; he was at once delighted and alarmed.

Zola kicked Been under the table. He glanced over at her and she twitched her head toward Ilona. Sandor had his nose in a plate of eggs but Nelly had pushed back from the table, too nervous to eat. Been could tell that the women in his pod were going to start speaking for him if he didn't speak for himself.

"For my birthday," he said, "I decided to give myself a present. I'm going to be gay. Zelmet Emsley has already programmed the sprites; I'm getting them later today."

"And what made you decide this, Been?" said Ilona.

"I've never been gay." He shrugged. "I've never really been anyone but myself. Rather boring, wouldn't you say? And I suppose I'm worried about going stale."

"At your age?" Sandor grunted in disbelief.

"We all go stale eventually," said Ilona. "Immortality is for turtles."

"Ilona is an authority on creative discomfort," Zola broke in. They had all agreed that this was their best and maybe only chance to move Been out of the pod now that they were sure he was going to become gay. Zola wasn't going to let Been ruin it. "You should see what she has done with her cabin. It's like a maze."

Nelly nodded vigorously. "Zola told me that just finding the couch made her feel smarter." Her enthusiasm had an edge of desperation. "No one could ever go stale there."

"I'd very much like to see it," said Been.

Ilona nodded and then poured syrup over her pancakes, her fish, and her grapefruit. Zola and Nelly began to eat as well, as if something had just been settled, although Been wasn't sure what.

Zola said, "I really appreciate this, Ilona."

"Appreciate what?" Ilona teased a sliver from the fillet with her chopsticks. "Don't assume, Zola. What do you imagine I'm doing?"

"You're talking to us," said Been.

"You're here. It would be impolite to do otherwise." Her smile was chilly. With a wrench, Been realized that he was wasting his time trying to charm her. Ilona Quellan would never willingly disrupt her life by letting him move into the spare hutch in her cabin.

At that moment, the babyface lit up. The eyes on the medallion blinked several times, awash in a blue glow. They took in the people gathered at the table. Nelly gave the babyface an uncertain smile; many of the colonists were spooked by the long-unborn baby Quellan. Zola waved. Finally the babyface noticed Been.

"Hullo, baby," Been said. "You're very lucky to have such a devoted mother."

The babyface regarded him with blue seriousness.

"And a famous father, captain of this marvelous slipship."

Zola gasped. Not only had she warned Been not to mention Illona's ex, but the pod had reached consensus that he shouldn't. Harlen Quellan was the reason Ilona still suffered through her endless pregnancy. After the divorce, she had refused to give birth to their son until Harlen agreed to honor a prenuptual agreement giving her a third of their joint assets, which included the *Nine Ball*.

A shadow passed over Ilona's features. "This baby doesn't speak to strangers, sir."

"Really? I'm very good with children." Been spoke with an easy obliviousness. "You know, I'm still hoping to meet your husband someday, Ilona. We've been a year aboard and I've only seen him on the lightboards, never in the flesh. That's odd, don't you think? It's not that big a ship." He peered into the babyface. "If your father has visitation rights, baby, would you put in the good word?"

The little mouth on the babyface twisted. "Googoo, gah, gah, *gah.*"

Ilona's head dropped so that her chin rested against the babyface. She covered her mouth with her hand and murmured to it. The babyface burbled back. As this went on, Been was pleased to see that mother and baby were arguing.

As one, Been and his entire pod leaned toward Ilona Quellan, hoping to catch some of the conversation. The rumors were that baby Quellan had long since achieved consciousness in the womb, but nobody knew what it did with it.

Finally, Ilona let her hand fall to her side. She gave Been a prickly glare. "On your birthday," she said, "there is to be a party?" The babyface was watching him intently.

The question caught Been by surprise. He glanced at his podmates, but they just gawked back at him like he had sprouted another ear.

"Not that I know of," he admitted.

"It doesn't speak well of you, Been Watanabe, that no one cares to celebrate your birthday. These people, for instance." She gestured at Zola, Nelly, and Sandor. "Zola tells me you have been living together for the past year."

Zola shook herself. "We think Been is wonderful. Isn't that right?"

"Yes."

"Of course."

"And we support his decision to . . . um . . . change himself," said Nelly. "Definitely."

Consensus on this subject was also enthusiastically confirmed.

"It's just that he doesn't quite fit—"

Ilona interrupted before Sandor could finish. "This baby thinks your friend should have a birthday party." She pushed her chair back and stood up with difficulty, her belly barely clearing the edge of the table. "If there is a party, this baby would like you to invite both it and its father." She rested her hands on the table wearily. "I can't speak for Captain Quellan, but I can assure you that this baby would be certain to attend."

Throwing a party on the *Nine Ball* was so complicated that very few of the colonists had managed it. Members of a single pod could gather easily enough in their common room, and they might invite a few guests, depending on whether they could reach consensus about intruding into one another's personal space. But if more than one pod wanted to socialize, it would have to be in public space, which was at a premium on the *Nine Ball*. The AgCore had room enough, but was not particularly party-friendly. There was a pungent iron stink in the abattoir where Molly, the *Nine Ball*'s amiable fatling, sloughed off slabs of her living light and darkmeat. And the CO_2 in the greenhouse ran to six percent—good for the hydroponic plants, fatal for parties. There wasn't much open space in the library. The virtuality shells lining the VRCore were ninety percent singles and ten percent doubles. The cafeteria was in continuous use, with the eighth seating for any given meal being immediately followed by the first seating of the next meal. When the two meeting rooms weren't booked by one of the colonists' sixteen Infrastructure Planning Groups or the harmony circles, they were being used by the various meetups which had formed during the run to Little Chin. These ranged from Amateur Astronomy to Zen League Baseball. The Space-Friendly Pet Meetup alone had a dozen subsections: spiders, ants, pretters, frogs, turtles, snakes, mice, gerbils, hamsters, ferrets, squee, and birds.

The other complication with throwing a party was

drawing up a guest list. In a society where everyone was friendly but nobody was much of a friend, how were Been's podmates to decide who to invite to his birthday party? For there *was* going to be a party, and in a most unusual place. To the general astonishment of all aboard, even the crew, Captain Harlen Quellan himself had offered the ControlCore for Been's birthday party. It was widely assumed, at least among the colonists, that this meant the Captain would be making his first public appearance of the run. The guest list Been and his podmates finally decided upon was an odd mix of crew and colonists—especially odd because these two groups did not usually have much to do with one another. The colonists regarded the crew as outrageously idiosyncratic; almost all of them had been recast with custom bio or mechmods. Crew could be quarrelsome and vulgar. They held grudges. Sometimes they solved problems by screaming at one another.

The crew thought the colonists were boring.

The colonists who attended Been's party were Tedia Grossman, Grel Laconia, and Ydt, whom Been knew from the Artful Exaggerators Meetup. They were some of the worst liars he had ever met, but for Consensualists, they were fair company. Gala Lysenko, Beth Fauziah, and Foxcroft Allez came from the Future Farmers Meetup. They had spent the last few months subjectively trying to get Been to reveal what wonder food was stowed in the CargoCore. Been had hinted and dodged for months, since his credentials as a genetic agronomist were nothing but well-crafted lies. He didn't even like vegetables. Dizzy and Henk Krall, who were subsidizing the run to Little Chin, had invited themselves, no doubt to protect their interests. And of course, Nelly, Zola, and Sandor were there, hoping that the party might somehow help them move their superfluous podmate out. From the crew—aside from Harlen Quellan, baby Quellan, and of course, his mother—invitations went to Matty, Ment, and Vron Zink, who were the factors in charge of dividing the sustain so that the *Nine Ball* could slip through the folded dimensions. Everyone was eager to hear the Zinks' latest estimate of when the slipship would arrive at Little Chin. Zelmet Emsley was invited, as well as Kinsella Frecktone, who managed the *Nine Ball*'s AgCore and was presumably a professional colleague of Been's, although they had hardly spoken since leaving Nonny's Home. Nobody could quite figure out why Kastor maven Lodse, the assistant cargo steward, was on the guest list.

Been rode the lift to the frontmost level of the *Nine Ball* with Nelly and Sandor; Zola had volunteered to bring the birthday cake from the cafeteria. Been was feeling a little flushed; Zelmet Emsley's sprites had been having their way with his genome for not quite a day now. He worried that his skin was getting tighter; he could almost feel his fingerprints.

The lift hatch slid away and he was gazing into the dazzle of the ControlCore's lightboards.

"Hmm." Zelmet Emsley sounded as if he were a swarm of bees. "Here's the man of the hour."

Been blinked, distracted by the way the lightboards were singing their status reports.

"We're here, Been," hissed Nelly. "Step off." When she nudged Been in the small of the back, her knuckle pricked him like a knife and he felt a surge of terror. How long had he been paralyzed by the sights and sounds of ControlCore? Sandor had a hand clamped over the shivering lift hatch to keep it from closing. Been realized then that he was having an unexpected reaction to the sprites. Adrenaline skittered through him and brain cells that had too long been dormant began to fire. He had to get in control of himself. This might be his chance to talk to Harlen Quellan.

"Is the Captain here?" said Been.

When Emsley's thinking head grimaced, its face looked as if it were pressed against a window. "Not yet," said his talking head.

Been let Gala and Beth peel him away from Emsley. They wanted him to see how Kastor maven Lodse could pull up real-time images of any single cargo container on board and then inspect their contents virtually.

"So that means you can tell us what's in any container?" Gala rested a hand lightly on Lodse's shoulder. "Say, for example"—she shot Been a mischievous grin—"Y7R in cold locker three?"

Lodse gestured at the lightboard. It sang back to him and then a green Lifetec container appeared on it. "Could." He nodded at the lightboard. "But won't. Not my job. My job is getting stuff from here to there."

"*Please,* Kastor. We've heard rumors that we're carrying some revolutionary new seed stock that could save Little Chin." Now Beth was testing Been to see if he would react.

Been thought he could see malice curling off her smile like smoke. "We're planting seed, Beth, not rumors."

"You won't talk to us, Been Watanabe, so now we're not talking to you." Gala closed her hand on Lodse's shoulder. "What about it, Kastor? Aren't you interested?"

"Not really." Lodse waved at the lightboard and it went back to the default overview of the CargoCore. "To us, cargo is nothing but bins, barrels, and bulbs. Some of them have to be kept warm, some cold. Some of them need to breathe, others want to be airtight. All we care about is whether someone is coming to sign for them at the end of the run."

More people arrived at the party and then Gala and Beth were gone and a drunken Henk Krall was leaning against him so hard that Been had to brace himself to keep from pitching backward. At first, Been thought Henk might be flirting with him, but then the conversation turned rancid.

"I'm sorry to say, Been, that there have been some who question whether you are truly committed to Consensualism." Henk's voice slurred and he added a couple of unnecessary syllables to "Consensualism." "I intend to bring this problem to Lars Benzonia once we make planetfall. You are a serious disappointment."

Been looked to Dizzy to pull her drunken husband off him, but she just shook her head. "Henk, I'm wondering if Been's personality dampening might not have been com-

pletely effective," she said. "Do you think that's possible,
Been dear? Might that be why you are taking such drastic
steps?"

"Have taken." Been stepped away from Henk suddenly,
and when the old man lost his balance, Been danced him
to a bulkhead and parked him against it. "You want to see
drastic steps?" he called out to the room. Dizzy watched,
astonished, as he continued to dance away from Henk.
"*Draa*-stic steps, *fan*-tastic steps," he crooned and caught
a smirking Kinsella Frecktone up in his arms; he fit there
like the key to Been's lock. Been wondered if Emsley
might not have been wrong and he had become fully gay
overnight. "Come with me, darling, and together we'll take
enthusi-*ass*-stic steps to the stars." Been swung him into a
cross-body lead and Kinsella actually followed along for a
few beats.

Then a lot of people were laughing and Been was laughing
too and someone gave him something dangerous to drink
and he took a sip that looked bigger than it was and when no
one was looking, he spilled the rest into a trash container just
before he fell in with the Zinks.

"So when are you going to post a hard estimate for planetfall?" Been could never tell Matty from Vron Zink, especially when their datacords were melded together. The
brothers were wide, dark, grim men with breath bad enough
to make engineers flinch. They never got jokes, no matter
how obvious the telling. Their niece Ment was younger and
blonder. She had come aboard the *Nine Ball* to learn the
family trade.

"The sustain has been very folded tight," said the brothers, speaking in unison as they always did when they were
sharing mind.

Young Ment Zink wandered over, as if sensing that her
uncles were talking business. The segmented datacord began
to uncoil from around her neck. "Want me to meld too?" she
said to her uncles.

"Not necessary," they said. "We have enough processing
capacity for this conversation."

Ment wound her datacord back behind her hair in disappointment. "Happy birthday, Mr. Been Watanabe," she said. "This is quite a coup. What do you know about the captain that we don't?"

"Never met the man."

"He's asking that we'll make planetfall when," said the uncles.

"I'd say we have at least two scant folds to slip through," said Ment.

"Tomorrow," said the uncles. "Or the after day."

"Tomorrow?" said Been. "You mean ship subjective tomorrow?"

"No, standard tomorrow," said Ment. "In the broad dimensions. They must be thinking in real time."

"So what's that going to be in ship subjective time?"

"We pass currently twenty-three ship subjective days for each standard day," said the brothers, "but the sustain very crunches our subjective space-time fast."

Ment polished the tip of her datacord with her thumb. "This is all probability-driven, but it's most likely we'll reach one-to-one subjective-to-standard time in under two weeks."

"But two weeks is also error margin," said the uncles.

"Two weeks subjective?" It had always made Been dizzy when he thought about time dilation in the sustain of the six folded dimensions, so he didn't.

"Subjective, yes," said Ment. "And when we close the sustain, we should be just a day from planetfall."

Been shut his eyes and tried not to look stupid.

"But what will we find there?" Zola had her arm tight around Nelly and was playing nervously with the ends of her podmate's hair. Been was in the midst of a knot of colonists. He couldn't see the Zinks anywhere.

"Ydt claims that the colony on Little Chin voted to dissolve," said Nelly.

"He heard it from the Captain."

"Actually, the crew heard it from the Captain. I had it from Kastor maven Lodse."

"Lars Benzonia has gone stale because the teachers blocked consensus on a recast." Foxcroft Allez's cheeks were flushed. "There's nobody to lead them."

"Us," said Nelly.

Ydt peeked over her shoulder. "Everyone on Little Chin will cram onto the *Nine Ball*. Once we get pushed off, they'll come swarming. Captain booked the entire colony yesterday."

"Is he here?" Foxcroft glanced around the ControlCore.

"Not yet."

"He can't possibly have heard any such thing." Now that Been had to think about subjective and standard time again, it filled his head with fizz. "We're still dividing the sustain, Ydt. No message can get from the broad dimensions to the folded dimensions because of time dilation."

"Go ask Kastor if you don't believe me," said Ydt.

Sandor turned to look for the cargo steward.

"Don't make a fool of yourself." Been caught Sandor by the arm. "I don't know how you can step onto a slipship without learning the first thing about interdimensional physics."

"It isn't true?" Nelly slumped against Zola in relief.

"It *could* be true." Ydt beamed at his fellow colonists. "That's the beauty of it. We just have no way of knowing."

Been poked Ydt in the chest. "Ever think of trying out for the Artful Exaggerators, Ydt?"

Ydt grinned and poked him back. "I recruited *you* to the Exaggerators, Watanabe."

"My point exactly."

"You're hot, Been," Zelmet Emsley traced a medfinger just under Been's hairline. "Your temperature is 39.3 degrees. Maybe you should go back to your hutch to rest?"

"Is the captain here yet?" said Been.

"At least sit down."

"Happy birthday to you, happy birthday to you, happy birthday dear . . ."

Been found that he was holding a plate with a slab of spice cake with a light green frosting that rippled like waves on a pond. On top of the frosting floated the dark green letters *p*, *y*, and *B*.

Ilona's huge belly was hard as a fist. It bumped against him as she went up on tiptoes to whisper into his ear.

"Harlen put you up to this." Her voice tickled him. "He's using you to harass me. Make me let him go."

"But I've never even met the Captain," said Been.

Her face was too close to his. "That doesn't mean anything." Been could feel her anger burning his cheek. He wondered what would happen if he kissed her. No part of her personality had been dampened: she'd probably punch him.

"Is the captain here?"

She snorted.

"There's a secret, isn't there?"

"There are always secrets." Her hand rested on the shelf of her belly. "Come down to my cabin," she said. "He wants to see you."

Zola had been right, Been thought. The common room of Ilona Quellan's cabin was a showcase for the creative-discomfort style of interior design. Her deckscape pitched and changed levels without warning, but at least it didn't move. Panels of varying solidity slowly dripped from the overhead or melted back into the deckscape. They were not hard to avoid, but the point was that they had to be avoided. Mobile floodlights crawled across the overhead and down the bulkheads. The furniture was snug enough: a wide particolored couch, a scatter of low and high chairs. Three hutches, a food prep bay, and a head opened onto the common room. The hatch to each of the sleep hutches was a lightboard showing scenes from old 3D vids or alien landscapes. They rotated ninety degrees at random intervals, so that Been had to lean over and cock his head to make sense of them. Been knew that research showed that people who moved into a challenging environment showed measurable gains in intelligence and lived years and even decades longer without needing to be recast. But he had no interest in spending his life fighting his way through an obstacle course every night just to climb into bed.

However, he could put up with it for a couple of weeks, assuming the Zinks had estimated planetfall accurately. "It's an amazing place you have here," he said.

Ilona sprawled on the couch with two pillows under her head and one between her legs. She had changed into a pair of loose silk pajamas, the top of which crept up her belly, showing a grin of white skin.

"I used to be beautiful," she said.

Been didn't hesitate. "You still are."

"Please." She pushed a hand at him wearily. "Throw away the script if you're going to live here."

"Am I going to live here?" He stepped around a tumescent panel and pulled up a chair to face her.

"He said to me, 'I'll give you the stars for a wedding present.' And I was too young to realize that was one of the oldest scripts ever written."

"How old are you now?"

She considered. "A hundred and forty-one? Forty-two? No, forty-one."

"And never been recast?"

"I'm pregnant, Been. I've been pregnant for twenty-nine months. That's all the recasting I can stand for the moment." She nodded at the meter-wide yellow panel beginning to dribble from the overhead; in an hour they wouldn't be able to see one another. "And I live here. In this 'amazing place' as you say. Tell me that's not from a script." She pleaded with the overhead. "Can't anyone come up with some new lines?"

In Been's experience, that was the kind of thing that people going stale said. Ilona was silent for a moment. Then her eyes fluttered shut. But the babyface was awake and watching him. The medallion had slipped on its chain and was resting against Ilona's left breast.

"How does it feel to be gay?" said Ilona. Her eyes remained closed.

"It doesn't feel like anything at all," said Been. "I was a little dizzy back at the party, but that's because I still have sprites swarming me. Zelmet Emsley claims that becoming gay is a pretty subtle recasting. I won't feel the full effect for months. Or even years."

She propped herself up on an elbow. "So did you have an active sex life when you were straight? I'll bet Zola is a handful and a half."

"You'd win that one."

"And you?"

"I didn't get any complaints."

"Means nothing." Her laugh was bitter; it left a bad taste in Been's mouth. "Men complain. Women settle."

"I'm not sure that's right," he said.

She let her head drop and her eyes shut again. Several long minutes passed. Been was tired too and he was feeling frustrated. He liked watching Ilona drowse but she'd said that Harlen Quellan wanted to speak to him. Where was he?

"Time?" He raised his voice, hoping to wake her up.

The lightboard hatch nearest him went into clock mode: *02:31:12, 02:31:13, 02:31:14*. It was later than he'd thought.

The babyface was smiling at him now. Been stood, walked uphill to the couch and leaned close. "Where's your daddy, baby?"

"*Grrl*, goo," said the babyface.

He tried to do the math. If Ilona's baby had been actually born at nine months, that would mean it would be twenty months old now. What could babies do at twenty months? Talk? Walk? But then Zola had said that the baby had been reembodied several times to keep it from being born. What was it thinking there inside her? Other than having been an infant a hundred and thirty-two years ago, Been hadn't had a lot of experience with babies. He had spent most of the last seventy years subjective ferrying personalities to the Thousand Worlds on slipships.

"So, Been, you had an active sex life as a heterosexual," murmured Ilona, her eyes still shut, "and you're too new at homosexuality for it to have taken. Have I got that right? Is that why you're staring at my chest?"

"Ilona!" The clock on the lightboard disappeared and was replaced by an image of Harlen Quellan. "Don't start."

She sat up abruptly, the babyface banging against her belly. "Why? Just because I'm pregnant, I'm not allowed to want sex? It's almost three years, you bastard."

Been thought it cruelly unfair that he had to choose be-

tween hearing more about Ilona's desires and meeting Harlen
Quellen. The captain now presented himself, not quite
life-sized, on all five of Ilona's hatches. He appeared to be
floating weightlessly in some private corner of his slipship,
beyond the sway of artificial gravity. Harlen Quellen could
have been fifty, one hundred and fifty, or three hundred and
fifty. His skin was smooth and glossy, his hair green as a
dream. He wore his dress uniform as if he had been born in
it, the silver captain's bars on his jacket catching the light,
his pants with razor creases, dazzling white foot and hand
gloves. He'd had his datacord grafted to his coccyx like a
tail and it switched back and forth as he spoke. He was too
perfect by half in Been's estimation; nobody real looked that
good.

"I'm sorry that I didn't make it to your birthday party,
Mr. Watanabe, but the press of ship's business keeps me
busy."

"Continuously, Captain?" said Been. "For the entire
run?"

He bowed stiffly. "I'm here now, sir."

"I was hoping I might talk to you alone, Captain."

"But there is no alone on my ship." He gestured at the cabin
expansively. "Every cubic millimeter is under surveillance.
The crew must see everywhere always. That's our job."

"I think he means me, Harlen. Go ahead, you two can conspire together." Ilona heaved herself off the couch. "I need to
use the bathroom anyway."

Been waited until the hatch to the head slid shut. "I've
been wanting to talk to you, Captain."

"Yes, Mr. Watanabe," he said dryly. "Forty-seven messages sent by you, all of them ignored by me. You've asked
every member of my crew about me. You are now pestering
my ex-wife. And you've had the goddamned nerve to try to
speak to my unborn son."

"So it's a boy then?"

"Sir, I've been observing you for months now. What I've
noticed is that you are adept at steering conversations just
where you want them to go. You flatter, sir, and cajole and
you will craft a lie whenever it's convenient. I have a ship to

run and have no time for such diversions, goddamn it, so let me get to the point." He aimed a long foretoe at Been. "What is the expected rate of gene flow from transgenic corn plants to their wild-type cultivars?"

Been felt as if there were a rope tightening at his throat. "I beg your pardon?" He choked on the words.

"How do you use fluorescence quenching to monitor changes in carotenoid levels in living plants?"

He was suddenly dizzy and knew it had nothing to do with sprites.

"Of course, agronomy is a vast field," said the captain. "Maybe these questions are too esoteric. In that case, what is the iron component of the synthetic hydroxyapatites we use in the *Nine Ball's* AgCore?"

Been sagged onto a chair. "What do you want?"

Harlen Quellan's image began drifting from the vertical to the horizontal. "Two days ago, you told Zelmet Emsley that you're no longer sure that you're a Consensualist. I say that you never were one. Neither are you a goddamned genetic agronomist. Yet when you passed through Immigration on Nonny's Home, you gave a sworn statement to that effect. It is one thing to lie to these colonists, sir. It is quite another to commit perjury to planetary authorities."

"I've been on several dozen slipships in my life, Captain, and not one of them had a passenger manifest that could stand close scrutiny."

"Several dozen, Mr. Watanabe? Not many agronomists are so well traveled." Harlen Quellan smiled grimly. "My friend Zelmet ran a scan on your brain while you were in our BioCore. I believe he forgot to ask your permission. My apologies. I assume it would not surprise you to know that you have a mindsync with a capacity of twenty-two exabytes embedded in your cerebrum. Clearly, sir, you are a courier. What information are you carrying to Little Chin?"

"Personality transplant."

"For?"

Been spread his hands and shrugged.

"Yes. Discretion would be part of your contract." Harlen

Quellan's tail lashed impatiently. "Well, this is my fifth run to Chin. I can think of several people there who have both the need and the resources for such a recasting." He laughed. "Consensualism is for the young and foolish, Mr. Watanabe. Not for the likes of you and me." His datacord coiled around something offscreen and he drifted off the lightboard until only his gloved feet showed. "I'll respect your privacy for now, sir, and that of your client," he called. "But goddamn it, you had better respect mine as well."

"I don't want to go back to live in my old pod."

"So I understand. You can move in with Ilona. I'm ordering it now." He pushed himself back onto the lightboard. "I take it that was your plan all along?"

Been could not help but grin.

"Well, you've succeeded, sir." He saluted Been. "My compliments."

"If you have a minute, Captain, there's a business matter I'd like to discuss."

"A minute is what I don't have just now, Mr. Watanabe." Harlen Quellan shook his head. "You have already taken too much of my time."

"Maybe later then?"

"Ilona!" Harlan Quellan's image knocked on the hatch to the head. "Are you all right?"

Been heard the toilet swoosh.

"Ilona is difficult enough as it is, sir." Harlen Quellan wagged his foretoe at Been. "Don't make my life with her any harder."

The hatch slid open. Ilona Quellan curled a hand around the threshold on either side and pulled herself through. "So," she said, "what did I miss?"

The common name for Rags, Ilona's pet spider, was a marbled orbweaver. She was about two centimeters long and ate hapless and wingless fruitflies which Ilona raised in a jar next to her terrarium. Rags had a blindingly orange cephalothorax and black and orange banded legs. Her huge cream-colored abdomen was marked with a black pattern that looked like two faces screaming in pain. The spider reminded Been a little of Ilona herself, with her outsized belly and the baby-face hanging around her neck, but he knew better than to remark on this.

While he couldn't see his way to doting on Rags quite the way Ilona did, he did become fascinated by the spider's web-building. She made one almost every day, eating the old one so that she could build anew. In nature, Ilona said, Rags would release a line of her webbing into the wind and wherever it caught she would pull it tight. In the terrarium she walked her first line from one end of the glass to the other. She would cross the center of the horizontal line and spin a web straight down, pulling it into a Y shape. She would then spin many radii of nonsticky structural web-bing before finally finishing her structure with spirals of sticky capture silk. Ilona usually dropped live fruitflies di-rectly onto the web for Rags, although sometimes she just let them loose in the terrarium to find their own path to doom. Occasionally when Rags built a particularly beau-tiful web, Ilona would fetch her pet out of the terrarium and spray the web with some gaily colored fixative, so she could save it to a scrapbook. The next day Rags would get an extra fruitfly.

Been got his first look at Ilona's scrapbook four days after he'd moved in. She had been brusque at first, treating Been as if he were some naive colonist. Been wasn't sure how much Harlen Quellan might have told her about him and he saw no need to reveal his secrets to her unnecessarily. But he made no pretense to belief in Consensualism, and, if she had been paying any attention at all, she would have noticed that many of the colonists had stopped treating Been as one of their own. This was no doubt because Henk Krall had been lobbying to ban Been from the Little Chin consensus once they arrived, for being recast without permission and for other acts of egregious individuality. Of course, only Lars Benzonia himself, founder of Little Chin, could call for a consensus on ostracism, but Krall was busy laying the groundwork.

Lars Benzonia had first developed the principles of Consensualism while a young man working his way across the Thousand Worlds as an itinerant biographer. It wasn't until he was hired to write the biography of Gween Renkl, one of the richest women on Nortroon, that he got the chance to put his philosophy into practice. He struck up a friendship with Gween's son, Acoa Renkl, who stood to inherit his mother's fortune, but had no idea what to do with it. Lars Benzonia gave Acoa Renkl his mission in life: to help spread the harmony of collective thinking throughout the galaxy. The galaxy had not been overly impressed with Consensualism, however, especially after so many of its elders had gone stale waiting for a consensus to form around their recastings. But a century after Lars Benzonia and Acoa Renkl had first met, there were still enough Consensualists to populate a colony on the world Renkl had bought for his friend.

On the sixth day, Ilona finally stopped smirking as Been stumbled through her common room in creative discomfort. It was right after he tripped over a panel that had not quite finished melting into the deckscape and crashed into one of her low chairs, crushing it utterly. He rolled off the wreckage, and stared at the eight-centimeter gash in his forearm. His blood was pooling in a deck pocket. She grudgingly went with him to BioCore and remained while Zelmet Emsley painted artificial skin onto the cut. Emsley also took the opportunity to run a DNA scan; he pronounced Been completely homosexual. Been did not know quite what to make of this since living with Ilona had only fueled his secret infatuation.

Even before he had moved into her spare hutch, Been had observed that Ilona was on edgy terms with the crew, who sided with their captain in the dispute between the Quellens. However, she was very friendly with Emsley. They chatted easily. She made fun of the colonists; he filled her in on the latest ship's gossip. When he asked after Rags, Been realized that Emsley had one of Rags's webs framed on the bulkhead behind the intake counter.

"Is she ready for another Rich?" Emsley's talking head was grinning.

Ilona shrugged. "I'm not having any sex, so neither is she."

"Rich?" said Been.

"Zelmet keeps a couple of dozen male orbweavers on ice. I call them all Rich. Every so often we thaw one out and show Rags a good time."

"*Hmm*. I have my doubts as to whether spiders enjoy mating," said Emsley. "I would imagine that pleasure was reserved for vertebrates."

"He keeps her egg cases on ice too. If we make planetfall on a terraformed world, I thaw them out and set them free."

"Speaking of reproduction, don't forget you're due to have the baby reembodied." Emsley's thinking head was simpering at Ilona's babyface, trying to make it laugh. "You almost put it off too long last time. If you go into labor, my hands are tied."

"I know, I know," she said wearily.

They parted as they left the BioCore. Ilona wanted to be alone and went off to the VRCore. Been was considering whether to lift down to the library to read up on the life cycle of orbweavers when he ran into Nelly. He accepted her invitation to catch the fourth lunch seating.

"So do you miss me?" Been rolled a wad of drigi noodles onto his fork.

"Of course we do, Beenie." She reached across the table to touch his hand. "We had Sandor in the other night and. . . well. . ." She made a lemon face and laughed. "He tries, he really does. Of course, when we get to Little Chin, things are bound to change. There will be lots of trades and turnover. Some of our pods will probably break up and new ones will form. You'll find your place."

Been let that go by without comment.

"And pay no attention to Henk Krall." She leaned forward and lowered her voice. "If you ask me, he should stop talking about how you got recast and think about doing it himself. Zola claims he's already half stale."

"I'm not worried."

"Your friend was so bad the other night at your birthday party." She sipped darkmeat broth out of a cup.

"My friend?"

"The one with the name. Ydt? He really had us scared, pretending that the colony was going to disband because Lars Benzonia was stale. I was ready to stick my head out of the airlock. I can't believe you actually practice lying in that meetup."

"It's actually harder to tell the truth." As soon as he said it, he realized that it was true. Been had been surprising himself lately.

Nelly laughed. "How's it going with Ilona? Zola says she's all right, but she makes me itch. I mean, it's not only the captain she's holding hostage, but it's her own baby too."

"We get along all right, I suppose. I like her, although she's not the friendliest person I've ever roomed with. It's just that she's lonely and that's made her hard."

"Well, you're good company. Cheer her up. Tell her some of your lies."

Been had no chance to cheer Ilona up either that day or the next. She seemed preoccupied, absent even when she sprawled across from him in their common room. It wasn't until late on the eighth day that she appeared on the threshold of his hutch and said that she couldn't sleep. She was going to the cafeteria to catch the end of the sixth dinner seating. Did he want anything? He saw that it was only 23:12 and said that he'd go with her for a snack.

"It's such an old story," she said. "It's embarrassing, actually." Her hands were wrapped around a mug of coffee. The cafeteria was only about a third full at the end of the day and they were sitting alone at a corner table. "When we talked about the pregnancy, I thought it might bring us together. I was feeling like the backup wife." She made a strangled sound that might have been a laugh. "No, not even." She counted on her fingers. "Ship first, crew second, passengers third, Ilona a distant fourth."

Been gave her a sympathetic groan and dipped his spoon into his salak yogurt.

"Nobody can force me to have this baby," she said. "He

tried to take me to court on Kenning and they laughed him right onto the street. The law is that the baby is me until it's born and Harlen Quellan can't make me do anything to myself."

"Why do you always call the baby it? He's a boy, no?"

"Of course it's a boy!" She spoke so fiercely that the babyface woke up and cast its pale blue light onto her hands.

"We don't have to talk about this if it upsets you."

"It doesn't, Been; we're divorced." She ran a finger around the rim of her cup. "After I was pregnant I found out that he'd been sleeping with Kinder Shwaa. He said it had been over months before, but still. He hired *her* to replace *me* in the cafeteria after we got married. The sexy first steward on a slipship. Orgasms in space! Another cliché, straight out of cheap VR comix. I made him fire her." She stood up. "I'm done here." She hadn't drunk any of the coffee.

She calmed down by the time they were walking down the companionway to their cabin. "I know I'm going to have this baby someday. Harlen knows it too. He's just determined that it's going to be on his terms and not mine. He's the captain, so he expects to get his way."

"I heard you want part of the ship as a settlement."

"It's not about the money." She paused at the hatch. "Well, it is, but what probably scared him more was when I said I wanted my share so I could sell to Transtellar." The hatch slid away. Been followed her into their common room. "He worked over a century for them so that he could own a ship without any partners. And he hates Transtellar." She noticed her reflection in one of the blank lightboards and shuddered. "Scenery," she cried. "Show me scenery." All the boards lit up with images of the salt castles on Blimmey. "Okay, I was hot and so I didn't begin the divorce negotiations in the best way. It was a stupid thing to say. Things spun down after that."

"He worked for Transtellar for a century? How old is he?"

"I forget. Over three hundred and fifty." She settled

gingerly onto the couch. "He's been recast four times." Been was about to sit in one of the chairs but she tapped her hand on the cushion beside her. "Do me a favor," she said.

He almost hit his head on a descending panel but managed to slide in next to her. The babyface was gazing at him as if it were frightened.

Ilona noticed Been looking at the babyface and not at her. She picked it up and turned it so she could see it. "I'm not going to be your mother," she told it. "I don't want to be around you at all. Let the crew take care of you."

Despite himself, Been was aghast. "You sound like you hate it." Having Ilona and Harlen Quellan for parents wasn't their baby's fault.

She let the babyface fall back around her neck. "It knows that I do. But it's part of me." She caught his gaze and seemed to sense his shock. "There's so much you don't understand."

Been chuckled bitterly. "I'm beginning to realize that."

"I've lost everything," she said. "I have nothing."

At that moment, Been felt as if he were outside himself, looking in. None of his feelings for Ilona made sense. Before he'd become gay, that would have been reason enough to bolt off the couch and run for his hutch. He was a mindsync courier; he'd spent most of his life buried in the sustain with strangers. But after a year of enduring the pale emotions of the colonists, he felt irresistibly drawn to this woman, who was burning with anger and need. He'd never been particularly sympathetic to others, but now he was experiencing Ilona's anguish as if it were his own. And maybe that was the real reason why he stretched his hand out and brushed the back of hers. He was one hundred and thirty-two years old, and he was certain that he had never felt so deeply about anyone ever before.

"Is there something I can do?"

"There's another line I've heard too many times." She slumped against the back of the couch and stared up at him. "Oh, come on, Been. You're gay."

"Not very. And you're very pregnant. Now that we've covered the obvious, I'd like to kiss you."

She looked dubious. "Is that all?"

He kissed her lightly on the lips but then pulled back, as if tasting her flavor to see if he liked it. "Not really."

"Do you know what you're doing?"

"I do," said Been. "Are you trying to talk me out of it?"

"No."

He touched the side of her face and she leaned hungrily into his caress. He said, "I'll be careful."

"No," she said. "Don't do that. I'm through being careful."

Been reached around the back of her neck and pulled the chain with the babyface over her head. "Go to sleep, baby." He tucked it between the cushions of the couch.

"He'll be watching," said Ilona. "Harlen."

Been saluted the overhead.

"That won't bother you?"

"It will," he said. "But not so you'll notice." He tugged at the hem of her blouse and slid it slowly over her belly. She raised her arms as if in surrender and he pulled the blouse up and over and dropped it onto a panel melting into the floor. Her skin was so pale and so taut that he could see traceries of blue veins beneath it.

"He put you here to punish me, didn't he?" said Ilona. "To make me uncomfortable? Is that what this is?"

"I wanted to be here from the moment I first saw you." Been rested his hands on her shoulders and met her gaze full on. "Right here." He grinned. "Well, maybe a little closer."

"Thank you." She was breathing into his mouth when she said it. Her breath was so sweet. "Thank you very much."

It was not the most physically pleasurable lovemaking Been had ever had and it was certainly not easy. Ilona could never find a comfortable position for very long and he had trouble keeping his penis in her. But it was tender and funny and at the end he wasn't careful at all.

Afterward, he lay spooned against her back, his arms draped over her belly. He was playing with the short hairs on her neck when the entire *Nine Ball* gonged as if struck by an enormous hammer.

"What was that?" Ilona started awake.

"The earth moved," said Been. "Only I think it came a little late."

"They're closing the sustain," she said.

"Good morning, ladies and gentlemen." Captain Harlen Quellan appeared on all five lightboards in his dress uniform. He did not appear to notice that this particular lady and gentleman were naked. "Some of you may have been startled by the bump a few minutes ago. There is nothing to worry about. We are approaching one-to-one ship subjective to galactic standard time and are beginning to close the sustain."

"Oh, Been," said Ilona.

He squeezed her. He could hear applause echoing down the companionways.

"It's possible that there will be a few more such mild bumps," said Harlen Quellen.

"Been, it's wet here."

"So I would encourage all of you . . ." The captain's image froze in mid-sentence, his mouth still open as if he were surprised that he had nothing more to say.

Ilona heaved herself to a sitting position, grabbed at Been's hand, and pressed it to the cushion where she had been lying. He felt a wet spot not quite the size of his palm. "It *is* wet," he said.

"Get the float!" she cried and bolted for the head. "Get Zelmet."

"Nice timing," Emsley said, as Ilona came out of the head, her face ashen. "Contractions?"

She nodded.

Everything happened at once, and, for some reason, Been found himself at the center of it, right by Ilona's side. Zelmet Emsley had come with the float and Brend Diosia, the *Nine Ball*'s second bioengineer. They loaded Ilona onto it. As they were dodging her through the obstacles in the common room, Ilona reached out and grabbed Been's wrist. He lurched toward her and almost upended the float.

"I want him," she said to Emsley.

"Easy, Ilona," said Brend Diosia. "All you have to do is ask. It's your party."

As Brend pushed the float down the companionway, Zelmet Emsley took Ilona's vital signs with his medfinger. Both of his heads watched the lightboard at the end of the float. *"Hmm."* Once again, Been was struck by his cool detachment. "I see you had sex."

"Yes," said Been.

"Vaginal intercourse?"

Ilona moaned.

"With an ejaculation?"

"I did," Been said.

"Well, that's one way. Did you know, Been, that your semen contains some prostaglandins? This is the same family of unsaturated carboxylic acids we use to induce labor. And if Ilona had an orgasm, she would now be producing oxytocin, the hormone that causes contractions. Orgasm, Ilona?"

"Yes," she said through clenched teeth.

Emsley patted her arm. "Good for you."

"But that's not a reliable way to induce labor," said Brend.

"No." Emsley had removed the tip of his left medfinger and replaced it with a tip that was several centimeters longer. "But it passes the time." He tapped his two medfingers together, the short to the base of the long, and nodded. "I'm going to give you the spinal block now, Ilona. This is all going to go just as we discussed. We're going to place a urinary catheter into your bladder, we're going to shave a little of your pubic hair so we can make the incision. You said you wanted to watch the operation, so we won't cover you."

"Operation?" said Been.

"She has to have a cesarean section," said Brend. "The head is too big." The hatch to BioCore Receiving slid away and they whisked the float past the intake counter and into the BioCore itself. The captain was still frozen in mid-sentence on the lightboard in Receiving. Been thought maybe he ought to be worrying whether something was wrong with the ship, but at the moment he had other problems.

When Ilona had been prepped and Been, Zelmet Emsley, and Brend Diosia were scrubbed, Emsley turned to Been. "We're going to start now. You hold her hand, that's what she brought you here for. This isn't going to take long, but if you feel a little faint, you can sit on this chair." He kicked a stool next to the float. "Shall we, Brend?"

Been watched with no little horror as Emsley skived a twenty-five-centimeter incision through the skin of Ilona's abdomen. The skive coated the incision with dermslix, so there was no bleeding. He continued to cut through several layers of tissue and then suddenly a stream of clear fluid came blurbling out of the incision. Emsley waited while Brend suctioned it up. "We're into the uterus, Ilona. You didn't lose all that much amniotic fluid when your membrane broke, so we're cleaning it up. Not much longer now."

"Do it." Ilona was squeezing Been's hand so hard that the tips of his fingers were tingling.

Emsley reached through the incision and felt around for a grip. As he did, his thinking head turned to Been and winked. "Got it. Brend, forceps on the incision." Brend Diosia clamped the cut in Ilona's abdomen open wide as Emsley pulled the struggling baby out.

It was astonishingly ugly, covered with blood and amniotic fluid and a waxy white coating. But Been was certain that it was misshapen as well. The head was so huge that the little, pink squirming body seemed like a useless appendage. And it had a tail that was thick as Been's finger and some thirty centimeters long.

Been didn't recognize the baby's face at first.

"Goddamn it, Ilona," squeaked a voice as thin as a spider's web. "Took you long enough! Don't you know I've got a ship to run? And we've got to close the goddamned sustain."

On most planets of the Thousand Worlds, Captain Harlen Quellan might have been fined or stripped of his pilot's license or even sentenced to serve a term of incarceration in a rehabilitation VR for dereliction of duty, had the proper authorities been alerted. While reembodied as a fetus, he was only intermittently available to command his slipship using the babyface. Originally, the Quellans had planned for Ilona to be pregnant while the *Nine Ball* was in drydock. But the divorce had wrecked everything. When the time had come to honor their next transport contract, the Quellans had to come to an accommodation with one another, or risk losing the *Nine Ball* to their creditors. So Harlen Quellan created a virtual captain to cover for him whenever Ilona decided to make it impossible to connect to the ship through the babyface. Each had sought to get what they wanted by making the other miserable. All of the crew knew that Ilona was pregnant with her ex-husband, but no one else did. Except, that is, for Been Watanabe, the sole outside witness to the birth of Harlen Quellan. He had his own reasons for keeping the Quellans' secret.

The consensus of the colonists on Little Chin, as well as the new arrivals from the *Nine Ball,* was that Lars Benzonia should accept the personality transplant that Been had carried from Nonny's Home. The entire colony had been shocked to learn that Acoa Renkl, Benzonia's most trusted advisor, had secretly contracted to have the transplant delivered to him against consensus. However, Renkl had gone clearly and irretrievably stale while he waited, throwing the Consensualists into a panic that their founder might succumb as well. So Lars Benzonia was quickly recast. For saving the mind of the First Consensualist, the grateful citizens of Little Chin voted the heroic mindsync courier a tract of forty hectares of prime bottomland along the Thalo River in the Tenderland District.

In the decades following his first personality transplant, it was said that Lars Benzonia became less dogmatic about the primacy of the consensus over the individual. Some point to the career of Zola Molendez, who in 2514 was named Pacifier Select, as another key factor in the reform of Consensualism. In any event, the fortunes of the colony soared.

As did those of Been Watanabe, formerly a mindsync courier, currently in the interstellar export/import business, specializing in hats. Caps, snoods, crowns, shuffs, turbans, fedoras, tricornes, kimberlys, bowlers, bonnets, toppers, helmets, and toques. As a young man, Been had never realized how many citizens of the Thousand Worlds felt the need to cover their heads. He and Ilona had been able to set themselves up in the hat business, thanks to the income from Been's holdings on Little Chin and the regular payments Harlen Quellan made to Ilona as part of the final divorce settlement. He was buying back her one-quarter share of the *Nine Ball* over time.

Whenever he was on Nonny's Home, Harlen Quellan liked to drop in on Been and Ilona to make a payment in person. Ilona maintained that he was hoping to find them split up, but Harlen Quellan claimed he just wanted to set eyes once again upon "the luckiest goddamned bastard ever to book passage on my ship." They watched him now from the porch of their house as he strode down their front walk to his hover. He swerved to tousle their daughter Benk's hair, but she slapped his hand away. Little Benk was busy teaching Rags's great-great-great-spiderlings to dance. And she was her mother's daughter.

"After all these years, I still don't understand why you did it." Been slid his arm around Ilona's waist.

"What?"

"You were pregnant with your own husband, Ilona!"

She giggled. "Ssh! He'll hear you."

Harlen Quellen turned to wave a last goodbye and then folded himself through the hover door.

"Good." Been waved back and gave him the most insincere smile he could muster. "Maybe he'll take offense and stop coming around."

"It was his fifth recasting," she said as they watched their daughter twirl around twice and then drop to hands and knees, so she could press her face against the terrarium to instruct her spiderlings. "He needed to go radical. And I didn't want to be married to a minotaur or a wheelie." She sighed. "Mostly, it was because I loved him."

"You mean you *thought* you loved him."

She shook her head. "No, I really did." She leaned into him. "Does that still bother you?"

Been considered. "A little." He knew it had all happened a long time ago. He tried to remember what his life had been like before he'd become gay. It was hard, but he knew one thing for certain. He had never really been in love. "But not so you'd notice."

As Harlen Quellan's hover lifted straight off the landing pad and shot into the creamy sky of Nonny's Home, Been gave a low whistle.

"What are you thinking?" said Ilona.

"I'm thinking"—he chuckled—"that I'll never have to divide the sustain again."

MINLA'S FLOWERS

ALASTAIR REYNOLDS

Alastair Reynolds is a frequent contributor to *Interzone*, and has also sold to *Asimov's Science Fiction, Spectrum SF,* and elsewhere. His first novel, *Revelation Space,* was widely hailed as one of the major SF books of the year; it was quickly followed by *Chasm City, Redemption Ark, Absolution Gap,* and *Century Rain,* all big sprawling space operas that were big sellers as well, establishing Reynolds as one of the best and most popular new SF writers to enter the field in many years. His other books include a novella collection, *Diamond Dogs, Turquoise Days.* His most recent book is a new novel, *Pushing Ice.* Coming up are two new collections, *Galactic North* and *Zima Blue and Other Stories.* A professional scientist with a Ph.D. in astronomy, he comes from Wales, but lives in the Netherlands, where he works for the European Space Agency.

Reynolds's work is known for its grand scope, sweep, and scale—in one story, "Galactic North," a spaceship sets out in pursuit of another in a stern chase that takes thousands of years of time and hundreds of thousands of light-years to complete; in another, "Thousandth Night," ultrarich immortals embark on a plan that will call for the physical rearrangement of all the stars in the galaxy. In the intricate and surprising novella that follows (a sort of prequel to his story "Merlin's Gun"), he shows us that long-term plans can also have long-term *consequences*—some of them not at all expected.

◐ Mission interrupted.

I still don't know quite what happened. The ship and I were in routine Waynet transit, all systems ticking over smoothly. I was deep in thought, a little drunk, rubbing clues together like a caveman trying to make fire with rocks, hoping for the spark that would point me toward the gun, the one no one ever thinks I'm going to find, the one I know with every fiber of my existence is out there somewhere.

Then it happened: a violent lurch that sent wine and glass flying across the cabin, a shriek from the ship's alarms as it went into panic mode. I knew right away that this was no ordinary Way turbulence. The ship was tumbling badly, but I fought my way to the command deck and did what I could to bring her back under control. Seat-of-the-pants flying, the way Gallinule and I used to do it on Plenitude, when Plenitude still existed.

That was when I knew we were outside the Waynet, dumped back into the crushing slowness of normal space. The stars outside were stationary, their colors showing no suggestion of relativistic distortion.

"Damage?" I asked.

"How long have you got?" the ship snapped back.

I told it to ease off on the wisecracks and start giving me the bad news. And it most certainly was bad news. The precious syrinx was still functional—I touched it and felt the familiar tremble that indicated it was still sensing the nearby Waynet—but that was about the only flight-critical system that hadn't been buckled or blown or simply wiped out of existence by the unscheduled egress.

We were going to have to land and make repairs. For a few weeks or months—however long it took the ship to scavenge and process the raw materials it needed to fix itself—the search for my gun would be on hold.

That didn't mean I was counting on a long stopover.

The ship still had a slow tumble. Merlin squinted against hard white glare as the burning eye of a bright sun hove into view through the windows. It was white, but not killingly so. Probably a mid-sequence star, maybe a late F or early G type. He thought there was a hint of yellow. Had to be pretty close too.

"Tell me where we are."

"It's called Calliope," *Tyrant* told him. "G-type. According to the last Cohort census the system contained fifteen planet-class bodies. There were five terrestrials, four of which were uninhabitable. The fifth—the farthest from Calliope—was supposedly colonized by humans in the early Flourishing."

Merlin glanced at the census data as it scrolled down the cabin wall. The planet in question was called Lecythus. It was a typical watery terrestrial, like a thousand others in his experience. It even had the almost-obligatory large single moon.

"Been a while, ship. What are the chances of anyone still being down there?"

"Difficult to say. A later Cohort flyby failed to make contact with the settlement, but that doesn't mean no one was alive. After the emergence of the Huskers, many planetary colonies went to great lengths to camouflage themselves against the aliens."

"So there could still be a welcoming committee."

"We'll see. With your permission, I'll use our remaining fuel to reach Lecythus. This will take some time. Would you like to sleep?"

Merlin looked back at the coffinlike slab of the frostwatch cabinet. He could skip over the days or weeks that it would take to reach the planet, but that would mean subjecting himself to the intense unpleasantness of frostwatch revival. Merlin had never taken kindly to being woken from normal sleep, let alone the deep hibernation of frostwatch.

"Pass on that, I think. I've still got plenty of reading to catch up on."

Later—much later—*Tyrant* announced that they had reached orbit around Lecythus. "Would you like to see the view?" the ship asked, with a playful note in its voice.

Merlin scratched fatigue from his eyes. "You sound like you know something I don't."

Merlin was at first reassured by what he saw. There was blue ocean down there, swatches of green and brown landmass, large islands rather than any major continental masses, cyclonic swirls of water-vapor clouds. It didn't necessarily mean there were still people, but it was a lot more encouraging than finding a cratered, radioactive corpse of a world.

Then he looked again. Many of those green and brown swatches of landmass were surrounded by water, as his first glimpse had indicated. But some of them appeared to be floating above the ocean completely, casting shadows beneath them. His glance flicked to the horizon, where the atmosphere was compressed into a thin bow of pure indigo. He could see the foreshortened shapes of hovering landmasses, turned nearly edge on. The landmasses appeared to be one or two kilometers thick, and they all appeared to be gently curved. Perhaps half were concave in shape, so their edges were slightly upturned. The edges were frosted white, like the peaks of mountain ranges. Some of the concave masses even had little lakes near their centers. The convex masses were all a scorched tawny gray in color, devoid of water or vegetation, save for a cap of ice at their highest point. The largest shapes, convex or concave, must have been hundreds of kilometers wide. Merlin judged that there must have been at least ten kilometers of clear airspace under each piece. A third of the planet's surface was obscured by the floating shapes.

"Any idea of what we're looking at here?" Merlin asked. "This doesn't look like anything in the census."

"I think they built an armored sky around their world," the ship said. "And then something—very probably Husker-level ordnance—shattered that sky."

"No one could have survived through that," Merlin said, feeling a rising tide of sadness. *Tyrant* was clever enough, but there were times—long times—when Merlin became acutely aware of the heartless machine lurking behind the personality. And then he felt very, very alone. Those were the hours when he would have done anything for companionship, including returning to the Cohort and the tribunal that undoubtedly awaited him.

"Someone does appear to have survived, Merlin."

He perked. "Really?"

"It's unlikely to be a very advanced culture: no neutrino or gravimagnetic signatures, beyond those originating from the mechanisms that must still be active inside the sky pieces. But I did detect some very brief radio emissions."

"What language were they using? Main? Tradespeak? Anything else in the Cohort database?"

"They were using long beeps and short beeps. I'm afraid I didn't get the chance to determine the source of the transmission."

"Keep listening. I want to meet them."

"Don't raise your hopes. If there are people down there, they've been out of contact with the rest of humanity for a considerable number of millennia."

"I only want to stop for repairs. They can't begrudge me that, can they?"

"I suppose not."

Then something occurred to Merlin, something he realized he should have asked much earlier. "About the accident, ship. I take it you know why we were dumped out of the Waynet?"

"I've run a fault-check on the syrinx. There doesn't appear to be anything wrong with it."

"That's not an answer."

"I know." *Tyrant* sounded sullen. "I still don't have an explanation for what went wrong. And I don't like that any more than you do."

Tyrant fell into the atmosphere of Lecythus. The transmissions had resumed, allowing the ship to pinpoint the origin to one of the larger airborne masses. Shortly afterward, a second source began transmitting from another floating mass, half the size of the first, located three thousand kilometers to the west. The way the signals started and stopped suggested some kind of agonizingly slow communication via radio pulses, one that probably had nothing to do with Merlin's arrival.

"Tell me that's a code in our database," Merlin said.

"It isn't. And the code won't tell us much about their spoken language, I'm afraid."

Up close, the broken edges of the floating mass soared as tall as a cliff. They were a dark, streaked gray, infinitely less regular than they had appeared from space. The edge showed signs of weathering and erosion. There were wide ledges, dizzying promontories, and cathedral-sized shadowed caves. Glinting in the low light of Calliope, ladders and walkways—impossibly thin and spindly scratches of metal—reached down from the icebound upper reaches, following zigzag trajectories that only took them a fraction of the way to the perilous lower lip, where the floating world curved back under itself.

Merlin made out the tiny moving forms of birdlike creatures, wheeling and orbiting in powerful thermals, some of them coming and going from roosts on the lower ledges.

"But that isn't a bird," *Tyrant* said, highlighting a larger moving shape.

Merlin felt an immediate pang of recognition as the image zoomed. It was an aircraft: a ludicrously fragile assemblage of canvas and wire. It had a crescent moon painted on both wings. There'd been a machine not much more advanced than that in the archive inside the Palace of Eternal Dusk, preserved across thirteen hundred years of family history. Merlin had even risked taking it outside once, to see for himself if he had the nerve to repeat his distant ancestor's brave crossing. He still remembered the sting of reprimand when he'd brought it back, nearly ruined.

This aircraft was even flimsier and slower. It was driven by a single chugging propellor rather than a battery of rocket-assisted turbines. It was following the rim of the landmass, slowly gaining altitude. Clearly it intended to make landfall. The air on Lecythus was thicker at sea level than on Plenitude, but the little machine must still have been very close to its safe operational ceiling. And yet it would have to climb even higher if it was to traverse the raised rim.

"Follow it," Merlin said. "Keep us astern by a clear two kilometers. And set hull to stealth."

Merlin's ship nosed in behind the struggling aircraft. He could see the single pilot now, goggled and helmeted within a crude-looking bubble canopy. The plane had reached ten kilometers, but it would need to double that to clear the up-turned rim. Every hundred meters of altitude gained seemed to tax the aircraft to the limit, so that it climbed, leveled, climbed. It trailed sooty hyphens behind it. Merlin could imagine the sputtering protest from the little engine, the fear in the pilot's belly that the motor was going to stall at any moment.

That was when an airship hove around the edge of the visible cliff. Calliope's rays flared off the golden swell of its envelope. Beneath the long ribbed form was a tiny gondola, equipped with multiple engines on skeletal outriggers. The airship's nose began to turn, bringing another crescent-moon emblem into view. The aircraft lined up with the airship, the two of them at about the same altitude. Merlin watched as some kind of netlike apparatus unfurled in slow motion from the belly of the gondola. The pilot gained further height, then cut the aircraft's engine. Powerless now, it followed a shallow glide path toward the net. Clearly, the airship was going to catch the aircraft and carry it over the rim. That must have been the only way for aircraft to arrive and depart from the hovering landmass.

Merlin watched with a sickened fascination. He'd occasionally had a presentiment when something was going to go wrong. Now he had that feeling again.

Some gust caught the airship. It began to drift out of the aircraft's glide path. The pilot tried to compensate—Merlin could see the play of light shift on the wings as they warped—but it was never going to be enough. Without power, the aircraft must have been cumbersome to steer. The engines on the gondola turned on their mountings, trying to shove the airship back into position.

Beyond the airship loomed the streaked gray vastness of the great cliff.

"Why did he cut the engines . . ." Merlin breathed to himself. Then, an instant later: "Can we catch up? Can we do something?"

"I'm afraid not. There simply isn't time."

Sickened, Merlin watched as the aircraft slid past the airship, missing the net by a hundred meters. A sooty smear erupted from the engine. The pilot must have been desperately trying to restart the motor. Moments later, Merlin watched as one wingtip grazed the side of the cliff and crumpled instantly, horribly. The aircraft dropped, dashing itself to splinters and shreds against the side of the cliff. There was no possibility that the pilot could have survived.

For a moment Merlin was numb. He was frozen, unsure what to do next. He'd been planning to land, but it seemed improper to arrive immediately after witnessing such a tragedy. Perhaps the thing to do was find an uninhabited landmass and put down there.

"There's another aircraft," *Tyrant* announced. "It's approaching from the west."

Still shaken by what he'd seen, Merlin took the stealthed ship closer. Dirty smoke billowed from the side of the aircraft. In the canopy, the pilot was obviously engaged in a life-or-death struggle to bring his machine to safety. Even as they watched, the engine appeared to slow and then restart.

Something slammed past *Tyrant,* triggering proximity alarms. "Some kind of shell," the ship told Merlin. "I think someone on the ground is trying to shoot down these aircraft."

Merlin looked down. He hadn't paid much attention to the landmass beneath them, but now that he did—peering through the holes in a quilt of low-lying cloud—he made out the unmistakable flashes of artillery positions, laid out along the pale scratch of a fortified line.

He began to understand why the airship dared not stray too far from the side of the landmass. Near the cliff, it at least had some measure of cover. It would have been far too vulnerable to the shells in open air.

"I think it's time to take a stand," he said. "Maintain stealth. I'm going to provide some lift support to that aircraft. Bring us around to her rear and then approach from under her."

"Merlin, you have no idea who these people are. They could be brigands, pirates, anything."

"They're being shot at. That's good enough for me."

"I really think we should land. I'm down to vapor pressure in the tanks now."

"So's that brave fool of a pilot. Just do it."

The aircraft's engine gave out just as *Tyrant* reached position. Taking the controls manually, Merlin brought his ship's nose into contact with the underside of the aircraft's paper-thin fuselage. Contact occurred with the faintest of bumps. The pilot glanced back down over his shoulder, but the goggled mask hid all expression. Merlin could only imagine what the pilot made of the sleek, whale-sized machine now supporting his little contraption.

Merlin's hands trembled. He was acutely aware of how easily he could damage the fragile thing with a miscalculated application of thrust. *Tyrant* was armored to withstand Waynet transitions and the crush of gas giant atmospheres. It was like using a hammer to push around a feather. For a moment, contact between the two craft was lost, and when *Tyrant* came in again it hit the aircraft hard enough to crush the metal cylinder of a spare fuel tank bracketed on under the wing. Merlin winced in anticipation of an explosion— one that would hurt the little airplane a lot more than it hurt *Tyrant*—but the tank must have been empty.

Ahead, the airship had regained some measure of stability. The capture net was still deployed. Merlin pushed harder, giving the aircraft more altitude in readiness for its approach glide. At the last moment he judged it safe to disengage. He steered *Tyrant* away and left the aircraft to blunder into the net.

This time there were no gusts. The net wrapped itself around the aircraft, the soft impact nudging down the nose of the airship. Then the net began to be winched back toward the gondola like a haul of fish. At the same time the airship swung around and began to climb.

"No other planes?" Merlin asked.

"That was the only one."

They followed the airship in. It rose over the cliff, over the ice-capped rim of the aerial landmass, then settled down toward the shielded region in the bowl, where water and greenery had gathered. There was even a wispy layer of cloud, arranged in a broken ring around the shore of the lake. Merlin presumed that the concave shape of the landmass was sufficient to trap a stable microclimate.

By now Merlin had an audience. People had gathered on the gondola's rear observation platform. They wore goggles and gloves and heavy brown overcoats. Merlin caught the shine of glass lenses being pointed at him. He was being studied, sketched, perhaps even photographed.

"Do you think they look grateful?" he asked. "Or pissed off?"

Tyrant declined to answer.

Merlin kept his distance, conserving fuel as best he could as the airship crossed tens of kilometers of arid, gently sloping land. Occasionally they overflew a little hamlet of huts or the scratch of a minor track. Presently the ground became soil-covered, and then fertile. They traversed swaths of bleak gray-green grass, intermingled with boulders and assorted uplifted debris. Then there were trees and woods. The communities became more than just hamlets. Small ponds fed rivers that ambled down to the single lake that occupied the landmass's lowest point. Merlin spied waterwheels and rustic-looking bridges. There were fields with grazing animals, and evidence of some tall-chimneyed industrial structures on the far side of the lake. The lake itself was an easy fifty or sixty kilometers wide. Nestled around a natural harbor on its southern shore was the largest community Merlin had seen so far. It was a haphazard jumble of several hundred mostly white, mostly single-story buildings, arranged with the randomness of toy blocks littering a floor.

The airship skirted the edge of the town and then descended quickly. It approached what was clearly some kind of secure compound, judging by the guarded fence that encircled it. There was a pair of airstrips arranged in a cross formation, and a dozen or so aircraft parked around a painted copy of the crescent emblem. Four skeletal docking towers rose from another area of the compound, stayed by guylines. A battle-weary pair of partially deflated airships was already tethered. Merlin pulled back to allow the incoming craft enough space to complete its docking. The net was lowered back down from the gondola, depositing the airplane—its wings now crumpled, its fuselage buckled—on the apron below. Service staff rushed out of bunkers to untangle the mess and free the pilot. Merlin brought his ship down at a clear part of the apron and doused the engines as soon as the landing skids touched the ground.

It wasn't long before a wary crowd had gathered around *Tyrant*. Most of them wore long leather coats, heavily belted, with the crescent emblem sewn into the right breast. They had scarves wrapped around their lower faces, almost to the nose. Their helmets were leather caps, with long flaps covering the sides of the face and the back of the neck. Most of them wore goggles; a few wore some kind of breathing apparatus. At least half the number were aiming barreled weapons at the ship, some of which needed to be set up on tripods, while some even larger wheeled cannons were being propelled across the apron by teams of well-drilled soldiers. One figure was gesticulating, directing the armed squads to take up specific positions.

"Can you understand what he's saying?" Merlin asked, knowing that *Tyrant* would be picking up any external sounds.

"I'm going to need more than a few minutes to crack their language, Merlin, even if it *is* related to something in my database, of which there's no guarantee."

"Fine. I'll improvise. Can you spin me some flowers?"

"Where exactly are you going? What do you mean, *flowers*?"

Merlin paused at the airlock. He wore long boots, tight black leather trousers, a billowing white shirt, and brocaded brown leather waistcoat, accented with scarlet trim. He'd tied back his hair and made a point of trimming his beard. "Where do you think? Outside. And I want some flowers. Flowers are good. Spin me some indigo hyacinths, the kind they used to grow on Springhaven, before the Mentality Wars. They always go down well."

"You're insane. They'll shoot you."

"Not if I smile and come bearing exotic alien flowers. Remember, I did just save one of their planes."

"You're not even wearing armor."

"Armor would really scare them. Trust me, ship: this is the quickest way for them to understand I'm not a threat."

"It's been a pleasure having you aboard," *Tyrant* said acidly. "I'll be sure to pass on your regards to my next owner."

"Just make the flowers and stop complaining."

Five minutes later Merlin steeled himself as the lock sequenced and the ramp lowered to kiss the ground. The cold hit him like a lover's slap. He heard an order from the soldiers' leader, and the massed ranks adjusted their aim. They'd been pointing at the ship before. Now it was only Merlin they were interested in.

He raised his right hand palm open, the newly spun flowers in his left.

"Hello. My name's Merlin." He thumped his chest for emphasis and said the name again, slower this time. "*Mer-lin*. I don't think there's much chance of you being able to understand me, but just in case . . . I'm not here to cause trouble." He forced a smile, which probably looked more feral than reassuring. "Now. Who's in charge?"

The leader shouted another order. He heard a rattle of a hundred safety catches being released. Suddenly, the ship's idea of sending out a proctor first sounded splendidly sensible. Merlin felt a cold line of sweat trickle down his back. After all that he had survived so far, both during his time with the Cohort and since he had become an adventuring free agent, it would be something of a letdown to die by being *shot* with a chemically propelled projectile. That was only one step above being mauled and eaten by a wild animal.

Merlin walked down the ramp, one cautious step at a time. "No weapons," he said. "Just flowers. If I wanted to hurt you, I could have hit you from space with charm-torps."

When he reached the apron, the leader gave another order and a trio of soldiers broke formation to cover Merlin from three angles, with the barrels of their weapons almost touching him. The leader—a cruel-looking young man with a scar down the right side of his face—shouted something in Merlin's direction, a word that sounded vaguely like "distal," but which was in no language Merlin recognized. When Merlin didn't move, he felt a rifle jab into the small of his back. "Distal," the man said again, this time with an emphasis bordering on the hysterical.

Then another voice boomed across the apron, one that belonged to a much older man. There was something instantly commanding about the voice. Looking to the source of the exclamation, Merlin saw the wrecked aircraft entangled in its capture net, and the pilot in the process of crawling out from the tangle, with a wooden box in his hands. The rifle stopped jabbing Merlin's back, and the cruel-looking young man fell silent while the pilot made his way over to them.

The pilot had removed his goggles now, revealing the lined face of an older man, his gray-white beard and whiskers stark against ruddy, weatherworn skin. For a moment Merlin felt that he was looking in the mirror at an older version of himself.

"Greetings from the Cohort," Merlin said. "I'm the man who saved your life."

"Gecko," the red-faced man said, pushing the wooden box into Merlin's chest. "Forlorn gecko!"

Now that Merlin had a chance to examine it properly, he saw that the box was damaged, its sides caved in and its lid ripped off. Inside was a matrix of straw padding and a grcat many shattered glass vials. The pilot took one of these smashed vials and held it up before Merlin's face, honey-colored fluid draining down his fingers.

"What is it?" Merlin asked.

Leaving Merlin to hold the box and flowers, the red-faced pilot pointed angrily toward the wreckage of his aircraft, and in particular at the cylindrical attachment Merlin had taken for a fuel tank. He saw now that the cylinder was the repository for dozens more of these wooden boxcs, most of which must have been smashed when Merlin had nudged the aircraft with *Tyrant*.

"Did I do something wrong?" Merlin asked.

In a flash the man's anger turned to despair. He was crying, the tears smudging the soot on his cheeks. "Tangible," he said, softer now. "All tangible inkwells. Gecko."

Merlin reached into the box and retrieved one of the few intact vials. He held the delicate thing to his eyes. "Medicine?"

"Plastrum," the man said, taking the box back from Merlin.

"Show me what you do with this," Merlin said, as he motioned drinking the vial. The man shook his head, narrowing his wrinkled ice-blue eyes at him as if he thought that Merlin was either stupid or making fun. Merlin rolled up the sleeve of his arm and motioned injecting himself. The pilot nodded tentatively.

"Plastrum," he said again. "Vestibule plastrum."

"You have some kind of medical crisis? Is that what you were doing, bringing medicines?"

"Tangible," the man repeated.

"You need to come with me," Merlin said. "Whatever that stuff is, we can synthesize it aboard *Tyrant*." He held up the intact vial and then placed his index finger next to it. Then he pointed to the parked form of his ship and spread his fingers wide, hoping the pilot got the message that he could multiply the medicine. "One sample," he said. "That's all we need."

Suddenly there was a commotion. Merlin looked around in time to see a girl running across the apron, toward the two of them. In Cohort terms she could only have been six or seven years old. She wore a child's version of the same great-coat everyone else wore, buckled black boots and gloves, no hat, goggles, or breathing mask. The pilot shouted "Minla" at her approach, a single word that conveyed both warning and something more intimate, as if the older man might have been her father or grandfather. "Minla oak trefoil," the man added, firmly but not without kindness. He sounded pleased to see her, but somewhat less than pleased that she had chosen this exact moment to run outside.

"Spelter Malkoha," the girl said, and hugged the pilot around the waist, which was as high as she could reach. "Spelter Malkoha, ursine Malkoha."

The red-faced man knelt down—his eyes were still damp—and ran a gloved finger through the girl's unruly fringe of black hair. She had a small, monkeylike face, one that conveyed both mischief and cleverness.

"Minla," he said tenderly. "Minla, Minla, Minla." Then what was clearly a rhetorical question: "Gastric spar oxen, fey legible, Minla?"

"Gorse spelter," she said, sounding contrite. And then, perhaps for the first time, she noticed Merlin. For an anxious moment her expression was frozen somewhere between sur-prise and suspicion, as if he were some kind of puzzle that had just intruded into her world.

"You wouldn't be called Minla, by any chance?" Merlin asked.

"Minla," she said, in barely a whisper.

"Merlin. Pleased to meet you, Minla." And then on a whim, before any of the adults could stop him, he passed her one of the indigo hyacinths that *Tyrant* had just spun for him, woven from the ancient molecular templates in its biolibrary. "Yours," he said. "A pretty flower for a pretty little girl."

"Oxen spray, Minla," the red-faced man said, pointing back to one of the buildings on the edge of the apron. A soldier walked over and extended a hand to the girl, ready to escort her back inside. She moved to hand the flower back to Merlin.

"No," he said, "you can keep it, Minla. It's for you."

She opened the collar of her coat and pushed the flower inside for safekeeping, until only its head was jutting out. The vivid indigo seemed to throw something of its hue onto her face.

"Mer-lin?" asked the older man.

"Yes."

The man tapped a fist against his own chest. "Malkoha." And then he indicated the vial Merlin was still carrying. "Plastrum," he said again. Then a question, accompanied by a nod toward *Tyrant*. "Risible plastrum?"

"Yes," Merlin said. "I can make you more medicine. *Risible plastrum.*"

The red-faced man studied him for what seemed like many minutes. Merlin opted to say nothing: if the pilot hadn't got the message by now, no further persuasion was going to help. Then the pilot reached down to his belt and unbuttoned the leather holster of a pistol. He removed the weapon and allowed Merlin sufficient time to examine it by eye. The low sun gleamed off an oiled black barrel, inlaid with florid white ornamentation carved from something like whalebone.

"Mer-lin risible plastrum," Malkoha said. Then he waved the gun for emphasis. "Spar apostle."

"Spar apostle," Merlin repeated, as they walked up the boarding ramp. "No tricks."

Even before *Tyrant* had made progress in the cracking of the local language, Merlin had managed to hammer out a deal with Malkoha. The medicine had turned out to be a very simple drug, easily synthesized. A narrow-spectrum ß-lactam antibiotic, according to the ship: exactly the sort of thing the locals might use to treat a gram-positive bacterial infection—something like bacterial meningitis, for instance—if they didn't have anything better.

Tyrant could pump out antibiotic medicine by the hundreds of liters, or synthesize something vastly more effective in equally large quantities. But Merlin saw no sense in playing his most valuable card so early in the game. He chose instead to give Malkoha quantities of the drug in approximately the same dosage and quantity as he must have been carrying when his aircraft was damaged, packaged in similar-looking glass vials. He gave the first two consignments as a gift, in recompense for the harm he was presumed to have done when attempting to save Malkoha, and let Malkoha think that it was all that *Tyrant* could do to make drugs at that strength and quantity. It was only when he handed over the third consignment, on the third day, that he mentioned the materials he needed to repair his ship.

He didn't say anything, of course, or at least nothing that the locals could have understood. But there were enough examples lying around of the materials Merlin needed—metals and organic compounds, principally, as well as water that could be used to replenish *Tyrant*'s hydrogen-fusion tanks—that Merlin was able to make considerable progress just by pointing and miming. He kept talking all the while, even in Main, and did all that he could to encourage the locals to talk back in their own tongue. Even when he was inside the compound, *Tyrant* was observing every exchange, thanks to the microscopic surveillance devices Merlin carried on his person. Through this process, the ship was constantly testing and rejecting language models, employing its knowledge of both the general principles of human grammar and its compendious database of ancient languages recorded by the Cohort, many of which were antecedents of Main itself. Lecythus might have been isolated for tens of thousands of years, but languages older than that had been cracked by brute computation, and Merlin had no doubt that *Tyrant* would get there in the end, provided he gave it enough material to work with.

It was still not clear whether the locals regarded him as their prisoner, or honored guest. He'd made no attempt to leave, and they'd made no effort to prevent him returning to his ship when it was time to collect the vials of antibiotic. Perhaps they had guessed that it would be futile to stop him, given the likely capabilities of his technology. Or perhaps they had guessed—correctly, as it happened—

that *Tyrant* would be going nowhere until it was repaired and fueled. In any event they seemed less awed by his arrival than intrigued, shrewdly aware of what he could do for them.

Merlin liked Malkoha, even though he knew almost nothing about the man. Clearly he was a figure of high seniority within this particular organization, be it military or political, but he was also a man brave enough to fly a hazardous mission to ferry medicines through the sky, in a time of war. And his daughter loved him, which had to count for something. Merlin now knew that Malkoha was her "spelter" or father, although he did indeed look old enough to have been spaced from her by a further generation.

Almost everything that Merlin did learn, in those early days, was due to Minla rather than the adults. The adults seemed willing to at least attempt to answer his queries, when they could understand what he was getting at. But their chalkboard explanations usually left Merlin none the wiser. They could show him maps and printed historical and technical treatises, but none of these shed any light on the world's many mysteries. Cracking text would take *Tyrant* even longer than cracking spoken language.

Minla, though, had picture books. Malkoha's daughter had taken an obvious liking to Merlin, even though she shared nothing in common. Merlin gave her a new flower each time he saw her, freshly spun from some exotic species in the biolibrary. Merlin made a point of never giving her flowers from a particular world twice, even when she wanted more of the same. He also made a point of always telling her something of the place from where the flowers had come, regardless of her lack of understanding. It seemed to be enough for her to hear the cadences of a story, even if it was in an alien language.

There was not much color in Minla's world, so Merlin's gifts must have had a luminous appeal to them. Once a day, for a few minutes, they were allowed to meet in a drab room inside the main compound. An adult was always stationed nearby, but to all intents and purposes Merlin and the girl were permitted to interact freely. Minla would show Merlin drawings and paintings she had done, or little compositions, written down in labored handwriting in approximately the form of script *Tyrant* had come to refer to as Lecythus A. Merlin would examine Minla's works and offer praise when it was merited.

He wondered why these meetings were allowed. Minla was obviously a bright girl (he could tell that much merely from the precocious manner of her speaking, even if he hadn't had the ample evidence of her drawings and writings). Perhaps it was felt that meeting the man from space would be an important part of her education, one that could never be repeated at a later date. Perhaps she had pestered her father into allowing her to spend more time with Merlin. Merlin could understand that; as a child he'd also formed harmless attachments to adults, often those that came bearing gifts and especially those adults that appeared interested in what he had to show them.

Could there be more than that, though? Was it possible that the adults had decided that a child offered the best conduit for understanding, and that Minla was now their envoy? Or were they hoping to use Minla as a form of emotional blackmail, so that they might exert a subtle hold on Merlin when he decided it was time to leave?

He didn't know. What he was certain of was that Minla's books raised as many questions as they answered, and that simply leafing through them was enough to open windows in his own mind, back into a childhood he'd thought consigned safely to oblivion. The books were startlingly similar to the books Merlin remembered from the Palace of Eternal Dusk, the ones he'd used to fight over with his brother. They were bound similarly, illustrated with spidery ink drawings scattered through the text or florid watercolors gathered onto glossy plates at the end of the book. Merlin liked holding the book up to the light of an open window, so that the illustrated pages shone like stained glass. It was something his father had shown him on Plenitude, when he had been Minla's age, and her delight exactly echoed his own, across the unthinkable gulf of time and distance and circumstance that separated their childhoods.

At the same time, he also paid close attention to what the books had to say. Many of the stories featured little girls involved in fanciful adventures concerning flying animals and other magic creatures. Others had the worthy, overearnest look of educational texts. Studying these latter books, Merlin began to grasp something of the history of Lecythus, at least insofar as it had been codified for the consumption of children.

The people on Lecythus knew they'd come from the stars. In two of the books there were even paintings of a vast spherical spaceship heaving into orbit around the planet. The paintings differed in every significant detail, but Merlin felt sure that he was seeing a portrayal of the same dimly remembered historical event, much as the books in his youth had shown various representations of human settlers arriving on Plenitude. There was no reference to the Waynet, however, or anything connected to the Cohort or the Huskers. As for the locals' theory concerning the origin of the aerial landmasses, Merlin found only one clue. It lay in a frightening sequence of pictures showing the night sky being riven by lavalike fissures, until whole chunks of the heavens dropped out of place, revealing a darker, deeper firmament beyond. Some of the pieces were shown crashing into the seas, raising awesome waves that tumbled over entire coastal communities, while others were shown hovering unsupported in the sky, with kilometers of empty space under them. If the adults remembered that it was alien weaponry that had smashed their camouflaging sky (weapons deployed by aliens that were still *out here*) no hint of that uncomfortable truth was allowed into Minla's books. The destruction of the sky was shown simply as a natural catastrophe, like a flood or volcanic eruption. Enough to awe, enough to fascinate, but not enough to give nightmares.

Awesome it must have been too. *Tyrant'*s own analysis had established that the aerial landmasses could be put together like a jigsaw. There were gaps in that jigsaw, but most of them could be filled by lifting chunks of land out of the seas and slotting them in place. The inhabited aerial landmasses were all inverted compared to their supposed positions in the original sky, requiring that they must have been flipped over after the shattering. *Tyrant* could offer little guidance for how this could have happened, but it was clear enough that unless the chunks were inverted, life-supporting materials would spill off over the edges and rain down onto the planet again. Presumably the necessary materials had been uplifted into the air when the unsupported chunks (and these must have been pieces that did not contain gravity nullifiers, or which had been damaged beyond the capacity to support themselves) came hammering down.

As to how people had come to the sky in the first place, or how the present political situation had come into being, Minla's texts were frustratingly vague. There were pictures of what were obviously historic battles, fought with animals and gunpowder. There were illustrations of courtly goings-on; princes and kings, balls and regattas, assassinations and ducls. There were drawings of adventurers rising on kites and balloons to survey the aerial masses, and later of what were clearly government-sponsored scouting expeditions, employing huge flotillas of flimsy-looking airships. But as to exactly why the people in the sky were now at war with the people on the ground, Merlin had little idea, and even less interest. What mattered—the only thing, in fact—was that Minla's people had the means to help him. He could have managed without them, but by bringing him the things he needed they made it easier. And it was good to see other faces again, after so long alone.

One of Minla's books intrigued him even more than all the others. It showed a picture of the starry night, the heavens as revealed after the fall of the camouflaging sky. Constellations had been overlaid on the patterns of stars, with sketched figures overlying the schematic lines joining the stars. None of the mythical or heroic figures corresponded to the old constellations of Plenitude, but the same archetypal forms were nonetheless present. For Merlin there was something hugely reassuring in seeing the evidence of similar imaginations at work. It might have been tens of thousands of years since these humans had been in contact with a wider galactic civilization; they might have endured world-changing catastrophes and retained only a hazy notion of their origins. But they were still people, and he was among them. There were times, in his long search for the lost weapon that he hoped would save the Cohort, that Merlin had come to doubt whether there was anything about humanity worth saving. But all it took was the look on Minla's face as he presented her with another flower—another relic of some long-dead world—to banish such doubts almost entirely. While there were still children in the universe, and while children could still be enchanted by something as simple and wonderful as a flower, there was still a reason to keep looking, a reason to keep believing.

The coiled black device had the look of a tiny chambered nautilus, turned to onyx. Merlin pushed back his hair to let Malkoha see that he was aleady wearing a similar unit, then motioned for Malkoha to insert the translator into his own ear.

"Good," Merlin said, when he saw that the other man had pushed the device into place. "Can you understand me now?"

Malkoha answered very quickly, but there was a moment's lag before Merlin heard his response translated into Main, rendered in an emotionally flat machine voice. "Yes. I understand good. How is this possible?"

Merlin gestured around him. They were alone together in *Tyrant*, with Malkoha ready to leave with another consignment of antibiotics. "The ship's been listening in on every conversation I've had with you," Merlin said. "It's heard enough of your language to begin piecing together a translation. It's still rudimentary—there are a lot of gaps the ship still needs to fill—but it will only get better with time, the more we talk."

Malkoha listened diligently as his earpiece translated Merlin's response. Merlin could only guess at how much of his intended meaning was making it through intact.

"Your ship is clever," Malkoha said. "We talk many times. We get good at understanding."

"I hope so."

Malkoha pointed now at the latest batch of supplies his people had brought, piled neatly at the top of the boarding ramp. The materials were unsophisticated in their manufacture, but they could all be reprocessed to form the complicated components *Tyrant* needed to repair itself.

"Metals make the ship good?"

"Yes," Merlin said. "Metals make the ship good."

"When the ship is good, the ship will fly? You will leave?"

"That's the idea."

Malkoha looked sad. "Where will you go?"

"Back into space. I've been a long time away from my own people. But there's something I need to find before I return to them."

"Minla will be unhappy."

"So will I. I like Minla. She's a clever little girl."

"Yes. Minla is clever. I am proud of my daughter."

"You have every right to be," Merlin said, hoping that his sincerity came across. "I have to start what I finished, though. The ship tells me it'll be flight-ready in two or three days. It's a patch job, but it'll get us to the nearest motherbase. But there's something we need to talk about first." Merlin reached for a shelf and handed Malkoha a tray upon which sat twelve identical copies of the translator device.

"You will speak with more of us?"

"I've just learned some bad news, Malkoha: news that concerns you, and your people. Before I go I want to do what I can to help. Take these translators and give them to your best people—Coucal, Jacana, the rest. Get them to wear them all the time, no matter who they're talking to. In three days I want to meet with you all."

Malkoha regarded the tray of translators with suspicion, as if the ranked devices were a peculiar foreign delicacy.

"What is the bad news, Merlin?"

"Three days isn't going to make much difference. It's better if we wait until the translation is more accurate, then there won't be any misunderstanding."

"We are friends," Malkoha said, leaning forward. "You can tell me now."

"I'm afraid it won't make much sense."

Malkoha looked at him beseechingly. "Please."

"Something is going to come out of the sky," Merlin said. "Like a great sword. And it's going to cut your sun in two."

Malkoha frowned, as if he didn't think he could possibly have understood correctly.

"Calliope?"

Merlin nodded gravely. "Calliope will die. And then so will everyone on Lecythus."

They were all there when Merlin walked into the glass-partitioned room. Malkoha, Triller, Coucal, Jacana, Sibia, Niltava, and about half a dozen more top brass Merlin had never seen before. An administrative assistant was already entering notes into a clattering electromechanical transcription device squatting on her lap, pecking away at its stiff metal input pads with surprising speed. Tea bubbled in a fat engraved urn set in the middle of the table. An orderly had already poured tea into china cups set before each bigwig, including Merlin himself. Through the partition, on the opposite wall of the adjoining tactical room, Merlin watched another orderly make microscopic adjustments to the placement of the aerial landmasses on an equal-area projection map of Lecythus. Periodically, the entire building would rattle with the droning arrival of another aircraft or dirigible.

Malkoha coughed to bring the room to attention. "Merlin has news for us," he said, his translated voice coming through with more emotion than it had three days earlier. "This is news not just for the Skyland Alliance, but for everyone on Lecythus. That includes the Aligned Territories, the Neutrals, and yes, even our enemies in the Shadowland Coalition." He beckoned a hand in Merlin's direction, inviting him to stand.

Merlin held up one of Minla's picture books, open at the illustration of constellations in the sky over Lecythus. "What

I have to tell you concerns these patterns," he said. "You see heroes, animals, and monsters in the sky, traced in lines drawn between the brightest stars."

A new voice buzzed in his ear. He identified the speaker as Sibia, a woman of high political rank. "These things mean nothing," she said patiently. "They are lines drawn between chance alignments. The ancient mind saw demons and monsters in the heavens. Our modern science tells us that the stars are very distant, and that two stars that appear close together in the sky—the two eyes of Prinia the Dragon, for example—may in reality be located at very different distances."

"The lines are more significant than you appreciate," Merlin said. "They are a pattern you have remembered across tens of thousands of years, forgetting its true meaning. They are pathways between the stars."

"There are no pathways in the void," Sibia retorted. "The void is vacuum: the same thing that makes birds suffocate when you suck air out of a glass jar."

"You may think it absurd," Merlin said. "All I can tell you is that vacuum is not as you understand it. It has structure, resilience, its own reserves of energy. And you can make part of it shear away from the rest, if you try hard enough. That's what the Waymakers did. They stretched great corridors between the stars: rivers of flowing vacuum. They reach from star to star, binding together the entire galaxy. We call it the Waynet."

"Is this how you arrived?" Malkoha asked.

"My little ship could never have crossed interstellar space without it. But as I was passing close to your planet—because a strand of the Waynet runs right through this system—my ship encountered a problem. That is why *Tyrant* was damaged; why I had to land here and seek your assistance."

"And the nature of this problem?" the old man pushed.

"My ship only discovered it three days ago, based on observations it had collated since I arrived. It appears that part of the Waynet has become loose, unshackled. There's a kink in the flow where it begins to drift out of alignment. The unshackled part is drifting toward your sun, tugged toward it by the pull of Calliope's gravitational field."

"You're certain of this?" Sibia asked.

"I've had my ship check the data over and over. There's no doubt. In just over seventy years, the Waynet will cut right through Calliope, like a wire through a ball of cheese."

Malkoha looked hard into Merlin's eyes. "What will happen?"

"Probably very little to begin with, when the Waynet is still cutting through the chromosphere. But by the time it reaches the nuclear-burning core . . . I'd say all bets are off."

"Can it be mended? Can the Waynet be brought back into alignment?"

"Not using any technology known to my own people. We're dealing with principles as far beyond anything on Lecythus as *Tyrant* is beyond one of your propellor planes."

Malkoha looked stricken. "Then what can we possibly do?"

"You can make plans to leave Lecythus. You have always known that space travel was possible: it's in your history, in the books you give to your children. If you had any doubts, I've shown it to be the case. Now you must achieve it for yourselves."

"In seventy years?" Malkoha asked.

"I know it sounds impossible. But you can do it. You already have flying machines. All you need to do is keep building on that achievement . . . building and building . . . until you have the means."

"You make it sound easy."

"It won't be. It'll be the hardest thing you've ever done. But I'm convinced that you can do it, if only you pull together." Merlin looked sternly at his audience. "That means no more wars between the Skylands and the Shadowlands. You don't have time for it. From this moment on, the entire industrial and scientific capacity of your planet will have to be directed toward one goal."

"You're going to help us, Merlin?" Malkoha asked. "Aren't you?"

Merlin's throat had become very dry. "I'd like to, but I must leave immediately. Twenty light-years from here is a bountiful system known to the Cohort. The great vessels of my people—the swallowships—sometimes stop in this system, to replenish supplies and make repairs. The swallowships cannot use the Way, but they are very big. If I could divert just one swallowship here, it could carry fifty thousand refugees; double that if people were prepared to accept some hardship."

"That's still not many people," Sibia said.

"That's why you need to start thinking about reducing your population over the next three generations. It won't be possible to save everyone, but if you could at least ensure that the survivors are adults of breeding age . . ." Merlin trailed off, conscious of the dismayed faces looking at him. "Look," he said, removing a sheaf of papers from his jacket and spreading them on the table. "I had the ship prepare these documents. This one concerns the production of wide-spectrum antibiotic medicines. This one concerns the construction of a new type of aircraft engine, one that will allow you to exceed the speed of sound and reach much higher altitudes than are now available to you. This one concerns metallurgy and high-precision machining. This one is a plan for a two-stage liquid-fueled rocket. You need to start learning about rocketry *now,* because it's the only thing that's going to get you into space." His finger moved to the final sheet. "This document reveals certain truths about the nature of physical reality. Energy and mass are related by this simple formula. The speed of light is an absolute constant, irrespective of the observer's motion. This diagram shows the presence of emission lines in the spectrum of hydrogen, and a mathematical formula that predicts the spacing of those lines. All this . . . *stuff* . . . should help you make some progress."

"Is this all you can give us?" Sibia asked skeptically. "A few pages' worth of vague sketches and cryptic formulae?"

"They're more than most cultures ever get. I suggest you start thinking about them straightaway."

"I will get this to Shama," Coucal said, taking the drawing of a jet engine and preparing to slip it into his case.

"Not before everything here is duplicated and archived," Malkoha said warningly. "And we must take pains to ensure none of these secrets fall into Shadowland hands." Then he returned his attention to Merlin. "Evidently, you gave this matter some thought."

"Just a bit."

"Is this the first time you have had to deal with a world such as ours, one that will die?"

"I've had some prior experience of the matter. There was once a world—"

"What happened to the place in question?" Malkoha asked, before Merlin could finish his sentence.

"It died."

"How many people were saved?"

For a moment Merlin couldn't answer. The words seemed to lodge in the back of his throat, hard as pebbles. "There were just two survivors," he said quietly. "A pair of brothers."

The walk to *Tyrant* was the longest he had ever taken. Ever since he had made the decision to leave Lecythus he had rehearsed the occasion in his mind, replaying it time and again. He had always imagined the crowd cheering, daunted by the news, but not cowed, Merlin raising his fist in an encouraging salute. Nothing had prepared him for the frigid silence of his audience, their judgmental expressions as he left the low buildings of the compound, their unspoken disdain hanging in the air like a proclamation.

Only Malkoha followed him all the way to *Tyrant*'s boarding ramp. The old soldier had his coat drawn tight across his chest, even though the wind was still and the evening not particularly cold.

"I'm sorry," Merlin said, with one foot on the ramp. "I wish I could stay."

"You seem like two men to me," Malkoha said, his voice

low. "One of them is braver than he gives himself credit for. The other man still has bravery to learn."

"I'm not running away."

"But you are running from something."

"I have to go now. If the damage to the Waynet becomes greater, I may not even be able to reach the next system."

"Then you must do what you think is right. I shall be sure to give your regards to Minla. She will miss you very much." Malkoha paused and reached into his tunic pocket. "I almost forgot to give you this. She would have been very upset with me if I had."

Malkoha had given Merlin a small piece of stone, a coin-shaped sliver that must have been cut from a larger piece and then set in colored metal so that it could be worn around the neck or wrist. Merlin examined the stone with interest, but in truth there seemed nothing remarkable about it. He'd picked up and discarded more beautiful examples a thousand times in his travels. It had been dyed red in order to emphasize the fine grain of its surface: a series of parallel lines like the pages of a book seen end-on, but with a rhythmic structure to the spacing of the lines—a widening and a narrowing—that was unlike any book Merlin had seen.

"Tell her I appreciated it," he said.

"I gave the stone to my daughter. She found it pretty."

"How did you come by it?"

"I thought you were in a hurry to leave."

Merlin's hand closed around the stone. "You're right. I should be on my way."

"The stone belonged to a prisoner of mine, a man named Dowitcher. He was one of their greatest thinkers: a scientist and soldier much like myself. I admired his brilliance from afar, just as I hope he admired mine. One day, our agents captured him and brought him to the Skylands. I played no part in planning his kidnap, but I was delighted that we might at last meet on equal terms. I was convinced that, as a man of reason, he would listen to my arguments and accept the wisdom of defecting to the Skylands."

"Did he?"

"Not in the slightest. He was as firmly entrenched in his convictions as I was in mine. We never became friends."

"So where does the stone come into it?"

"Before he died, Dowitcher found a means to torment me. He gave me the stone and told me that he had learned something of great significance from it. Something that could change our world. Something that had *cosmic* significance. He was looking into the sky when he said that: almost laughing. But he would not reveal what that secret was."

Merlin hefted the stone once more. "I think he was playing games with you, Malkoha."

"That's the conclusion I eventually reached. One day Minla took a shine to the stone—I kept it on my desk long after Dowitcher was gone—and I let her have it."

"And now it's mine."

"You meant a lot to her, Merlin. She wanted to give you something in return for the flowers. You may forget the rest of us one day, but please don't ever forget my daughter."

"I won't."

"I'm lucky," Malkoha said, something in his tone easing, as if he were finished judging Merlin. "I'll be dead long before your Waynet cuts into our sun. But Minla's generation won't have that luxury. They know that their world is going to end, and that every year brings that event a year nearer. They're the ones who'll spend their whole lives with that knowledge looming over them. They'll never know true happiness. I don't envy them a moment of their lives."

That was when something in Merlin gave way, some mental slippage that he must have felt coming for many hours without quite acknowledging it to himself. Almost before he had time to reflect on his own words he found himself saying to Malkoha, "I'm staying."

The other man, perhaps wary of a trick or some misunderstanding brought about by the translator, narrowed his eyes. "Merlin?"

"I said I'm staying. I've changed my mind. Maybe it was

what I always knew I had to do, or maybe it was all down to what you just said about Minla. But I'm not going anywhere."

"What I said just now," Malkoha said, "about there being two of you, one braver than the other . . . I know now which man I am speaking to."

"I don't feel brave. I feel scared."

"Then I know it to be true. Thank you, Merlin. Thank you for not leaving us."

"There's a catch," Merlin said. "If I'm going to be any help to you, I have to see this whole thing out."

Malkoha was the last to see him before he entered frost-watch. "Twenty years," Merlin said, indicating the settings, which had been recalibrated in Lecythus time units. "In all that time, you don't need to worry about me. *Tyrant* will take care of everything I need. If there's a problem, the ship will either wake me or it will send out the proctors to seek assistance."

"You have never spoken of proctors before," Malkoha replied.

"Small mechanical puppets. They have very little intelligence of their own, so they won't be able to help you with anything creative. But you needn't be alarmed by them."

"In twenty years, must we wake you?"

"No, the ship will take care of that as well. When the time is ready, the ship will allow you aboard. I may be a little groggy at first, but I'm sure you'll make allowances."

"I may not be around in twenty years," Malkoha said gravely. "I am sixty years old now."

"I'm sure there's still life left in you."

"If we should encounter a problem, a crisis . . ."

"Listen to me," Merlin said, with sudden emphasis. "You need to understand one very important thing. I am not a god. My body is much the same as yours, our life spans very similar. That's the way we did things in the Cohort: immortality through our deeds, rather than flesh and blood. The frost-watch casket can give me a few dozen years over a normal human life span, but it can't give me eternal life. If you keep waking me, I won't live long enough to help you when things get really tough. If there is a crisis, you can knock on the ship three times. But I'd urge you not to do so unless things are truly dire."

"I will heed your counsel," Malkoha said.

"Work hard. Work harder than you've ever dreamed possible. Time is going to eat up those seventy years faster than you can blink."

"I know how quickly time can eat years, Merlin."

"I want to wake to rockets and jet aircraft. Anything less, I'm going to be a disappointed man."

"We will do our best not to let you down. Sleep well, Merlin. We will take care of you and your ship, no matter what happens."

Merlin said farewell to Malkoha. When the ship was sealed up he settled himself into the frostwatch casket and commanded *Tyrant* to put him to sleep.

He didn't dream.

Nobody he recognized was there to greet Merlin when he returned to consciousness. Were it not for their uniforms, which still carried a recognizable form of the Skylanders' crescent emblem, he could easily believe that he had been abducted by forces from the surface. His visitors crowded around his open casket, faces difficult to make out, his eyes watering against the sudden intrusion of light.

"Can you understand me, Merlin?" asked a woman, with a firm clear voice.

"Yes," he said, after a moment in which it seemed as if his mouth were still frozen. "I understand you. How long have I—"

"Twenty years, just as you instructed. We had no cause to wake you."

He pushed himself from the casket, muscles screaming into his brain with the effort. His vision sharpened by degrees. The woman studied him with a cool detachment. She snapped her fingers at someone standing behind her and then passed Merlin a blanket. "Put this around you," she said.

The blanket had been warmed. He wrapped it around himself with gratitude, and felt some of the heat seep into his old bones. "That was a long one," he said, his tongue moving sluggishly, making him slur his words. "We don't usually spend so long."

"But you're alive and well."

"So it would seem."

"We've prepared a reception area in the compound. There's food and drink, a medical team waiting to look at you. Can you walk?"

"I can try."

Merlin tried. His legs buckled under him before he reached the door. They would regain strength in time, but for now he needed help. They must have anticipated his difficulties, because a wheelchair was waiting at the base of *Tyrant*'s boarding ramp, accompanied by an orderly to push it.

"Before you ask," the woman said, "Malkoha is dead. I'm sorry to have to tell you this."

Merlin had grown to think of the old man as his only adult friend on Lecythus, and had been counting on his being there when he returned from frostwatch. "When did he die?"

"Fourteen years ago."

"Force and Wisdom. It must be like ancient history to you."

"Not to all of us," the woman said sternly. "I am Minla, Merlin. It may be fourteen years ago, but there isn't a day when I don't remember my father and wish he were still with us."

As he was being propelled across the apron, Merlin looked up at the woman's face and compared it against his memories of the little girl he had known twenty years ago. At once he saw the similarity and knew that she was telling the truth. In that moment he felt the first visceral sense of the time that had passed.

"You can't imagine how odd this makes me feel, Minla. Do you remember me?"

"I remember a man I used to talk to in a room. It was a long time ago."

"Not to me. Do you remember the stone?"

She looked at him oddly. "The stone?"

"You asked your father to give it to me, when I was due to leave Lecythus."

"Oh, that thing," Minla said. "Yes, I remember it now. It was the one that belonged to Dowitcher."

"It's very pretty. You can have it back if you like."

"Keep it, Merlin. It doesn't mean anything to me now, just as it shouldn't have meant anything to my father. I'm embarrassed to have given it to you."

"I'm sorry about Malkoha."

"He died well, Merlin. Flying another hazardous mission for us, in very bad weather. This time it was our turn to deliver medicine to our allies. We were now making antibiotics for all the landmasses in the Skyland alliance, thanks to the process you gave us. My father flew one of the last consignments. He made it to the other landmass, but his plane was lost on the return trip."

"He was a good man. I only knew him a short while, but I think it was enough to tell."

"He often spoke of you, Merlin. I think he hoped you might teach him more than you did."

"I did what I could. Too much knowledge would have overwhelmed you: you wouldn't have known where to start, or how to put the pieces together."

"Perhaps you should have trusted us more."

"You said you had no cause to wake me. Does that mean you made progress?"

"Decide for yourself."

He followed Minla's instruction. The area around *Tyrant* was still recognizable as the old military compound, with many of the original buildings still present, albeit enlarged and adapted. But most of the dirigible docking towers were gone, as were most of the dirigibles themselves. Ranks of new aircraft now occupied the area where the towers and airships had been before, bigger and heavier than anything Merlin had seen before. The swept-back geometry of their wings, the angle of the leading edge, the rakish curve of their tailplanes, all owed something to the shape of *Tyrant* in atmospheric-entry mode. Clearly the natives had been more observant than he'd given them credit for. Merlin knew he shouldn't have been surprised; he'd given them the blueprints for the jet turbine, after all. But it was still something of a shock to see his plans made concrete, so closely to the way he had imagined them.

"Fuel is always a problem," Minla said. "We have the advantage of height, but little else. We rely on our scattered allies on the ground, together with raiding expeditions to Shadowland fuel bunkers." She pointed to one of the remaining airships. "Our cargo dirigibles can lift fuel all the way back to the Skylands."

"Are you still at war?" Merlin asked, though her statement rather confirmed it.

"There was a ceasefire shortly after my father's death. It didn't last long."

"You people could achieve a lot more if you pooled your efforts," Merlin said. "In seventy—make that fifty—years you're going to be facing collective annihilation. It isn't going to make a damned bit of difference what flag you're saluting."

"Thank you for the lecture. If it means so much to you, why don't you fly down to the other side and talk to them?"

"I'm an explorer, not a diplomat."

"You could always try."

Merlin sighed heavily. "I did try once. Not long after I left the Cohort . . . there was a world named Exoletus, about the same size as Lecythus. I thought there might be something on Exoletus connected with my quest. I was wrong, but it was reason enough to land and try and talk to the locals."

"Were they at war?"

"Just like you lot. Two massive power blocs, chemical weapons, the works. I hopped from hemisphere to hemisphere, trying to play the peacemaker, trying to knock their heads together to make them see sense. I laid the whole cosmic perspective angle on them: how there was a bigger universe out there, one they could be a part of if they only stopped squabbling. How they were going to have to be a part of it whether they liked it or not, when the Huskers came calling, but if they could only be ready for that—"

"It didn't work."

"I made things twenty times worse. I caught them at a time when they were inching toward some kind of ceasefire. By the time I left, they were going at it again hell-for-leather. Taught me a valuable lesson, Minla. It isn't my job to sprinkle fairy dust on a planet and get everyone to live happily ever after. No one gave me the tool kit for that. You have to work these things out for yourself."

She looked only slightly disappointed. "So you'll never try again?"

"Burn your fingers once, you don't put them into the fire twice."

"Well," Minla said, "before you think too harshly of us, it was the Skylands that took the peace initiative in the last ceasefire."

"So what went wrong?"

"The Shadowlands invaded one of our allied surface territories. They were interested in mining a particular ore, known to be abundant in that area."

Depressed as he was by news that the war was still rumbling on, Merlin forced his concentration back onto the larger matter of preparations for the catastrophe. "You've done well with these aircraft. Doubtless you'll have gained expertise in high-altitude flight. Have you gone transonic yet?"

"In prototypes. We'll have an operational squadron of supersonic aircraft in the air within two years, subject to fuel supplies."

"Rocketry?"

"That too. It's probably easier if I show you."

Minla let the orderly wheel him into one of the compound buildings. A long window ran along one wall, overlooking a larger space. Though the interior had been enlarged and repartitioned, Merlin still recognized the tactical room. The old wall map, with its cumbersome push-around plaques, had been replaced by a clattering electromechanical display board. Operators wore headsets and sat at desks behind huge streamlined machines, their gray metal cases ribbed with cooling flanges. They were staring at small flickering slate-blue screens, whispering into microphones.

Minla removed a tranche of photographs from a desk and passed them to Merlin for his inspection. They were black-and-white images of the Skyland airmass, shot from increasing altitude, until the curve of Lecythus's horizon became pronounced.

"Our sounding rockets have penetrated to the very edge of the atmosphere," Minla said. "Our three-stage units now have the potential to deliver a tactical payload to any unobstructed point on the surface."

"What would count as a 'tactical payload'?" Merlin asked warily.

"It's academic. I'm merely illustrating the progress we've made in your absence."

"I'm cheered."

"You encouraged us to make these improvements," Minla said chidingly. "You can hardly blame us if we put them to military use in the meantime. The catastrophe—as you've so helpfully pointed out—is still fifty years in the future. We have our own affairs to deal with in the meantime."

"I wasn't trying to create a war machine. I was just giving you the stepping stones you needed to get into space."

"Well, as you can doubtless judge for yourself, we still have a distance to go. Our analysts say that we'll have a natural satellite in orbit within fifteen years, maybe ten. Definitely so by the time you wake from your next bout of sleep. But that's still not the same as moving fifty thousand people out of the system, or however many it needs to be. For that we're going to need more guidance from you, Merlin."

"You seem to be doing very well with what I've already given you."

Minla's tone, cold until then, softened perceptibly. "We'll get you fed. Then the doctors would like to look you over, if only for their own notebooks. We're glad to have you back with us, Merlin. My father would have been so happy to see you again."

"I'd like to have spoken with him again."

After a moment, Minla said: "How long will you stay with us, until you go back to sleep again?"

"Months, at least. Maybe a year. Long enough to know that you're on the right track, and that I can trust you to make your own progress until I'm awake again."

"There's a lot we need to talk about. I hope you have a strong appetite for questions."

"I have a stronger appetite for breakfast."

Minla had him wheeled out of the room into another part of the compound. There he was examined by Skyland medical officials, a process that involved much poking and prodding and whispered consultation. They were interested in Merlin not just because he was a human who had been born on another planet, but because they hoped to learn some secret of frostwatch from his metabolism. Then they were done and Merlin was allowed to wash, clothe himself, and finally eat. Skyland food was austere compared to what he was used to aboard *Tyrant,* but in his present state he would have wolfed down anything.

There was to be no rest for him that day. More medical examinations followed, including some that were clearly designed to test the functioning of his nervous system. They poured cold water into his ears, shone lights into his eyes, and tapped him with various small hammers. Merlin endured it all with stoic good grace. They would find nothing odd about him because in all significant respects he was biologically identical to the people administering the examinations. But he imagined the tests would give the medical staff much to write about in the coming months.

Minla was waiting for him afterward, together with a roomful of Skyland officials. He recognized two or three of them as older versions of people he had already met, grayed and lined by twenty years of war—there was Triller, Jacana, and Sibia, Triller now missing an eye—but most of the faces were new to him. Merlin took careful note of the newcomers: those would be the people he'd be dealing with next time.

"Perhaps we should get to business," Minla said, with crisp authority. She was easily the youngest person in the room, but if she didn't outrank everyone present, she at least had their tacit respect. "Merlin, welcome back to the Skylands. You've learned something of what has happened in your absence: the advances we've made, the ongoing condition of war. Now we must talk about the future."

Merlin nodded agreeably. "I'm all for the future."

"Sibia?" Minla asked, directing a glance at the older woman.

"The industrial capacity of the Skylands, even when our surface allies are taken into account, is insufficient for the higher purpose of safeguarding the survival of our planetary culture," Sibia answered, sounding exactly as if she were reading from a strategy document, even though she was looking Merlin straight in the eye. "As such, it is our military duty—our moral imperative—to bring all of Lecythus under one authority, a single Planetary Government. Only then will we have the means to save more than a handful of souls."

"I agree wholeheartedly," Merlin said. "That's why I applaud your earlier ceasefire. It's just a pity it didn't last."

"The ceasefire was always fragile," Jacana said. "The wonder is that it lasted as long as it did. That's why we need something more permanent."

Merlin felt a prickling sensation under his collar. "I guess you have something in mind."

"Complete military and political control of the Shadowlands," Sibia replied. "They will never work with us, unless they become us."

"You can't believe how frightening that sounds."

"It's the only way," Minla said. "My father's regime explored all possible avenues to find a peaceful settlement, one that would allow our two blocs to work in unison. He failed."

"So instead you want to crush them into submission."

"If that's what it takes," Minla said. "Our view is that the Shadowland administration is vulnerable to collapse. It would only take a single clear-cut demonstration of our capability to bring about a coup, followed by a negotiated surrender."

"And this clear-cut demonstration?"

"That's why we need your assistance, Merlin. Twenty years ago, you revealed certain truths to my father." Before he could say anything, Minla produced one of the sheets Merlin had given to Malkoha and his colleagues. "It's all here in black-and-white. The equivalence of mass and energy. The constancy of the speed of light. The interior structure of the atom. Your remark that our sun contains a 'nuclear-burning core.' All these things were a spur to us. Our best minds have grappled with the implications of these ideas for twenty years. We see how the energy of the atom could carry us into space, and beyond range of our sun. We now have an inkling of what else they imply."

"Do tell," Merlin said, an ominous feeling in his belly.

"If mass can be converted into energy, then the military implications are startling. By splitting the atom, or even forcing atoms to merge, we believe that we can construct weapons of almost incalculable destructive force. The demonstration of one of these devices would surely be enough to collapse the Shadowland administration."

Merlin shook his head slowly. "You're heading up a blind alley. It isn't possible to make practical weapons using atomic energy. There are too many difficulties."

Minla studied him with an attentiveness that Merlin found quite unsettling. "I don't believe you," she said.

"Believe me or don't believe me, it's up to you."

"We are certain that these weapons can be made. Our own research lines would have given them to us sooner or later."

Merlin leaned back in his seat. He knew when there was no point in maintaining a bluff.

"Then you don't need me."

"But we do. Most urgently. The Shadowland administration also has its bright minds, Merlin. Their interest in those ore reserves I mentioned earlier . . . either there have been intelligence links, or they have independently arrived at similar conclusions to us. They are trying to make a weapon."

"You can't be sure of that."

"We can't afford to be wrong. We may own the sky, but our situation is dependent upon access to those fuel reserves. If one of our allies was targeted with an atomic weapon . . ." Minla left the sentence unfinished, her point adequately made.

"Then build your bomb," Merlin said.

"We need it sooner rather than later. That is where you come in." Now Minla produced another sheet of paper, flicking it across the table in Merlin's direction. "We have enough of the ore," she said. "We also have the means to refine it. This is our best guess for a design."

Merlin glanced at the illustration long enough to see a complicated diagram of concentric circles, like the plan for an elaborate garden maze. It was intricately annotated in machine-printed Lecythus B.

"I won't help you."

"Then you may as well leave us now," Minla said. "We'll build our bomb in our own time, without your help, and use it to secure peace for the whole world. Maybe that will happen quickly enough that we can begin redirecting the industrial effort toward the evacuation. Maybe it won't. But what happens will be on our terms, not yours."

"Understand one thing," Jacana said, with a hawkish look on his face. "The day will come when atomic weapons are used. Left to our own devices, we'll build weapons to use against our enemy below. But by the time we have that capability, they'll more than likely have the means to strike back, if they don't hit us first. That means there'll be a series of exchanges, an escalation, rather than a single decisive demonstration. Give us the means to make a weapon now and we'll use it in such a way that the civilian casualties are

minimized. Withhold it from us, and you'll have the blood
of a million dead on your hands."

Merlin almost laughed. "I'll have blood on my hands because I *didn't* show you how to kill yourselves?"

"You began this," Minla said. "You already gave us
secret knowledge of the atom. Did you imagine we were
so stupid, so childlike, that we wouldn't put two and two
together?"

"Maybe I thought you had more common sense. I was
hoping you'd develop atomic rockets, not atomic bombs."

"This is our world, Merlin, not yours. We only get one
chance at controlling its fate. If you want to help us, you
must give us the means to overwhelm the enemy."

"If I give you this, millions will die."

"A billion will perish if Lecythus is not unified. You must
do it, Merlin. Either you side with us, to the full extent, or
we all die."

Merlin closed his eyes, wishing a moment alone, a moment
to puzzle over the ramifications. In desperation, he saw a
possible solution: one he'd rejected before but was now willing to advance. "Show me the military targets on the surface
that you would most like to eradicate," he said. "I'll have
Tyrant take them out, using charm-torps."

"We've considered asking for your direct military assistance," Minla said. "Unfortunately, it doesn't work for us.
Our enemy already know something of your existence: it was
always going to be a difficult secret to hide, especially given
the reach of the Shadowlander espionage network. They'd be
impressed by your weapons, that much we don't doubt. But
they also know that our hold on you is tenuous, and that you
could just as easily refuse to attack a given target. For that
reason you do not make a very effective deterrent. Whereas
if they knew that *we* controlled a devastating weapon . . ."
Minla looked at the other Skyland officials. "There could be
no doubt in their minds that we might do the unthinkable."

"I'm really beginning to wonder whether I shouldn't have
landed on the ground instead."

"You'd be sitting in a very similar room, having a very
similar conversation," Minla said.

"Your father would be ashamed of you."

Minla's look made Merlin feel as if he were something she'd found under her shoe. "My father meant well. He served his people to the best of his abilities. But he had the luxury of knowing he was going to die before the world's end. I don't."

Merlin was aboard *Tyrant,* alone except for Minla, while he prepared to enter frostwatch again. Eight frantic months had passed since his revival, with the progress attaining a momentum of its own that Merlin felt sure would carry through to his next period of wakefulness.

"I'll be older when we meet again," Minla said. "You'll barely have aged a day, and your memories of this day will be as sharp as if it happened yesterday. Is that something you ever get used to?"

Not for the first time, Merlin smiled tolerantly. "I was born on a world not very different from Lecythus, Minla. We didn't have landmasses floating through the sky, we didn't have global wars, but in many respects we were quite alike. Everything that you see here—this ship, this frostwatch cabinet, these souvenirs—would once have seemed unrecognizably strange to me. I got used to it, though. Just as you'd get used to it, if you had the same experiences."

"I'm not so sure."

"I am. I met a very intelligent girl twenty years ago, and believe me, I've met some intelligent people in my time." Merlin brightened, remembering the thing he'd meant to show Minla. "That stone you had your father give me . . . the one we talked about just after I came out of the cabinet?"

"The worthless thing Dowitcher convinced my father was of cosmic significance?"

"It wasn't worthless to you. You must have liked it, or you wouldn't have given it to me in return for my flowers."

"The flowers," Minla said thoughtfully. "I'd almost forgotten them. I used to look forward to them so much, the sound of your voice as you told me stories I couldn't understand but which still managed to sound so significant. You made me feel special, Merlin. I'd treasure the flowers afterward and go to sleep imagining the strange, beautiful places they'd come from. I'd cry when they died, but then you'd always bring new ones."

"I used to like the look on your face."

"Tell me about the stone," she said, after a silence.

"I had *Tyrant* run an analysis on it. Just in case there was something significant about it, something neither you, I, nor your father had spotted."

"And?" Minla asked, with a note of fearfulness.

"I'm afraid it's just a piece of whetstone."

"Whetstone?"

"Very hard. It's the kind you use for sharpening knives. It's a common enough kind of stone on a planet like this one, wherever you have tides, shorelines, and oceans." Merlin had fished out the stone earlier; now he held it in his hand, palm open, like a lucky coin. "You see that fine patterning of lines? This kind of stone was laid down in shallow tidal water. Whenever the sea rushed in, it would carry a suspension of silt that would settle out and form a fine layer on the surface of the stone. The next time the tide came in, you'd get a second layer. Then a third, and so on. Each layer would only take a few hours to be formed, although it might take hundreds of millions of years for it to harden into stone."

"So it's very old."

Merlin nodded. "Very old indeed."

"But not of any cosmic significance."

"I'm sorry. I just thought you might want to know. Dowitcher *was* playing a game with your father after all. I think Malkoha had more or less guessed that for himself."

For a moment Merlin thought that his explanation had satisfied Minla, enabling her to shut tight that particular chapter of her life. But instead she just frowned. "The lines aren't regular, though. Why do they widen and then narrow?"

"Tides vary," Merlin said, suddenly feeling himself on less solid ground. "Deep tides carry more sediment. Shallow tides less. I suppose."

"Storms raise high tides. That would explain the occasional thick band. But other than that, the tides on Lecythus are very regular. I know this from my education."

"Then your education's wrong, I'm afraid. A planet like this, with a large moon . . ." Merlin left the sentence unfinished. "Spring tides and neap tides, Minla. No arguing with it."

"I'm sure you're right."

"Do you want the stone back?" he asked.

"Keep it, if it amuses you."

He closed his hand around the stone. "It still meant something to you when you gave it to me. It'll always mean something to me for that reason."

"Thank you for not leaving us. If my stone kept you here, it served a useful purpose."

"I'm glad I chose to stay. I just hope I haven't done more harm than good, with the things I showed you."

"That again," Minla said with a weary sigh. "You worry that we're going to blow ourselves to bits, just because you showed us the clockwork inside the atom."

"It's nasty clockwork."

He had seen enough progress, enough evidence of wisdom and independent ingenuity, to know that the Skyland forces would have a working atomic bomb within two years. By then, their rocket program would have given them a delivery system able to handle the cumbersome payload of that primitive device. Even if the rocket fell behind schedule, they only had to wait until the aerial landmass drifted over a Shadowland target.

"I can't stop you making weapons," Merlin said. "All I ask is that you use them wisely. Just enough to negotiate a victory, and then no more. Then forget about bombs and start thinking about atomic rockets."

Minla looked at him pityingly. "You worry that we're becoming monsters. Merlin, we already *were* monsters. You didn't make us any worse."

"That strain of bacterial meningitis was very infectious," Merlin said. "I know: I've run it through *Tyrant*'s medical analyzer. You were already having difficulties with supplies of antibiotics. If I hadn't landed, if I hadn't offered to make that medicine for you, your military effort might have collapsed within months. The Shadowlands would have won by default. There wouldn't be any need to introduce atomic bombs into the world."

"But we'd still need the rockets."

"Different technology. The one doesn't imply the other."

"Merlin, listen to me. I'm sorry that we're asking you to make these difficult moral choices. But for us it's about only one thing: species survival. If you hadn't dropped out of the sky, the Waynet would still be on its way to us, ready to slice our star in two. After that happened, you had no choice but to do everything possible to save us, no matter how bad a taste it leaves in your mouth."

"I have to live with myself when this is all over."

"You'll have nothing to be ashamed of. You've made all the right decisions so far. You've given us a future."

"I need to clear up a few things for you," Merlin said. "It isn't a friendly galaxy. The creatures that smashed your sky are still out there. Your ancestors forged the armored sky to hide from them, to make Lecythus look like an airless world. The Huskers were hunting down my own people before I left to work on my own. It isn't going to be plain sailing."

"Survival is better than death. Always and forever."

Merlin sighed: he knew that this conversation had run its course, that they had been over these things a thousand times already and were no closer to mutual understanding. "When I wake up again, I want to see lights in the sky."

"When I was a girl," Minla said, "long before you came, my father would tell me stories of people traveling through the void, looking down on Lecythus. He'd put in jokes and little rhymes, things to make me laugh. Under it all, though, he had a serious message. He'd show me the pictures in my books, of the great ship that brought us to Lecythus. He said we'd come from the stars and one day we'd find a way to go back there. It seemed like a fantasy when I was a little girl, something that would never come to pass in the real world. Yet now it's happening, just as my father always said it would. If I live long enough, I'll know what it's like to leave Lecythus behind. But I'll be dead long before we ever reach another world, or see any of the wonders you've known."

For an instant Minla was a girl again, not a driven military leader. Something in her face spoke to Merlin across the years, breaching the defenses he had carefully assembled.

"Let me show you something."

He took her into *Tyrant*'s rear compartment and revealed the matte-black cone of the syrinx, suspended in its cradle. At Merlin's invitation, Minla was allowed to stroke its mirror-smooth surface. She reached out her hand gingerly, as if expecting to touch something very hot or very cold. At the last instant her fingertips grazed the ancient artifact and then held the contact, daringly.

"It feels old," she said. "I can't say why."

"It does. I've often felt the same thing."

"Old and very heavy. Heavier than it has any right to be. And yet when I look at it, it's somehow not quite there, as if I'm looking at the space where it used to be."

"That's exactly how it looks to me."

Minla withdrew her touch. "What is it?"

"We call it a syrinx. It's not a weapon. It's more like a key or a passport."

"What does it do?"

"It lets my ship use the Waynet. In their time the Waymakers must have made billions of these things, enough to fuel the commerce of a million worlds. Imagine that, Minla: millions of stars bound by threads of accelerated space-time, each thread strung with thousands of glittering ships rushing to and fro, drops of honey on a thread of silk, each ship moving so close to the speed of light that time itself slowed almost to stillness. You could dine on one world, ride your ship to the Waynet and then take supper on some other world, under the falling light of another sun. A thousand years might have passed while you were riding the flow, but that didn't matter. The Waymakers forged an empire where a thousand years was just a lazy afternoon, a time to put off plans for another day." Merlin looked sadly at Minla. "That was the idea, anyway."

"And now?"

"We breakfast in the ruins, barely remember the glory that was, and scavenge space for the handful of still-functioning syrinxes."

"Could you take it apart, find out how it works?"

"Only if I felt suicidal. The Waymakers protected their secrets very well."

"Then it is valuable."

"Incalculably so."

Minla stroked it again. "It feels dead."

"It just isn't active yet. When the Waynet comes closer, the syrinx will sense it. That's when we'll really know it's time to get out of here." Merlin forced a smile. "But by then we'll be well on our way."

"Now that you've shown me this secret, aren't you worried that we'll take it from you?"

"The ship wouldn't let you. And what use would it be to you anyway?"

"We could make our own ship, and use your syrinx to escape from here."

Merlin tried not to sound too condescending. "Any ship you built would smash itself to splinters as soon as it touched the Waynet, even with the syrinx to help it. And you wouldn't achieve much anyway. Ships that use the Waynet can't be very large."

"Why is that?"

Merlin shrugged. "They don't need to be. If it only takes a day or two of travel to get anywhere—remember what I said about clocks slowing down—then you don't need to haul all your provisions with you, even if you're crossing to the other side of the galaxy."

"But could a bigger ship enter the Waynet, if it had to?"

"The entry stresses wouldn't allow it. It's like riding the rapids." Merlin didn't wait to see if Minla was following him. "The syrinx creates a path that you can follow, a course where the river is easier. But you still need a small boat to squeeze around the obstacles."

"Then no one ever made larger ships, even during the time of the Waymakers?"

"Why would they have needed to?"

"That wasn't my question, Merlin."

"It was a long time ago. I don't have all the answers. And you shouldn't pin your hopes on the Waynet. It's the thing that's trying to kill you, not save you."

"But when you leave us . . . you'll ride the Waynet, won't you?"

Merlin nodded. "But I'll make damned sure I have a head start on the collision."

"I'm beginning to see how all this must look to you," Minla said. "This is the worst thing that's ever happened to us, the end of our history itself. To you it's just a stopover, an incidental adventure. I'm sure there were hundreds of worlds before us, and there'll be hundreds more. That's right, isn't it?"

Merlin bridled. "If I didn't care about you all, I'd have left twenty years ago."

"You very nearly did. I know how close you came. My father spoke of it many times, his joy when you changed your mind."

"I had a change of heart," Merlin said. "Everyone's allowed that. You played a part in it, Minla. If you hadn't told Malkoha to give me that gift . . ."

"Then I'm glad I did, if it meant so much." Minla looked away, something between sadness and fascination on her face. "Merlin, before you sleep. Do something for me."

"Yes?"

"Make me flowers again. From some world I'll never ever see. And tell me their story."

The Planetary Government aircraft was a sleek silver flying wing with its own atomic reactor, feeding six engines buried in air-smoothed nacelles. Minla had already led Merlin down a spiral staircase, into an observation cupola set under the thickest part of the wing. Now she touched a brushed-steel panel, causing armored slats to whisk open in rapid sequence. Through the green-tinted blast-proof glass they had an uninterrupted view of the surface rolling by underneath.

The ocean carried no evidence of the war, but there was hardly any stretch of land that hadn't been touched in some fashion. Merlin saw the rubble-strewn remains of towns and cities, some with the hearts gouged out by kilometer-deep craters. He saw flooded harbors, beginning to be clawed back by the greedy fingers of the sea. He saw swaths of gray-brown land where nothing grew anymore, and where only dead, petrified forests testified to the earlier presence of living things. Atomic weapons had been used in their thousands, by both sides. The Skylanders had been first, though, which was why the weapons had a special name on Lecythus. Because of the shape of the mushroom cloud that accompanied each burst, they called them Minla's Flowers.

She pointed out the new cities that had been built since the ceasefire. They were depressing to behold: grids of utilitarian blocks, each skull-gray multistory building identical to the others. Spidery highways linked the settlements, but not once did Merlin see any evidence of traffic or commerce.

"We're not building for posterity," she said. "None of those buildings have to last more than fifty years, and most of them will be empty long before that. By the time they start crumbling, there'll be no one alive on Lecythus."

"You're surely not thinking of taking everyone with you," Merlin said.

"Why not? It seemed unthinkable forty years ago. But so did atomic war, and the coming of a single world state. Anything's within our reach now. With social planning, we can organize matters such that the population shrinks to a tenth of its present size. No children will be allowed to be born in the last twenty years. And we'll begin moving people into the Space Dormitories long before that."

Merlin had seen the plans for the dormitories, along with the other elements of Minla's evacuation program. There was already a small space station in orbit around Lecythus, but it would be utterly dwarfed by the hundred dormitories.

The plans called for huge air-filled spheres, each of which would swallow one hundred thousand evacuees, giving a total in-orbit human presence of ten million people. Yet even as the Space Dormitories were being populated, work would be under way on the thousand Exodus Arks that would actually carry the evacuees out of the system. The Arks would be built in orbit, using materials extracted and refined from the moon's crust. Merlin had already indicated to Minla's experts that they could expect to find a certain useful isotope of helium in the topsoil of the moon, an isotope that would enable the Arks to be powered by nuclear fusion engines of an ancient and well-tested design.

"Forced birth control, and mass evacuation," he said, grimacing. "That's going to take some tough policing. What if people don't go along with your program?"

"They'll go along," Minla said.

"Even if that meant shooting a few, to make a point?"

"Millions have already died, Merlin. If it takes a few more to guarantee the efficient execution of the evacuation program, I see that as a price worth paying."

"You can't push human society that hard. It snaps."

"There's no such thing as society," Minla told him.

Presently she had the pilot bring them below supersonic speed, and then down to a hovering standstill above what Merlin took to be an abandoned building, perched near the shore amid the remains of what must once have been a great ocean seaport. The flying wing lowered itself on ducted jets, blowing dust and debris in all directions until its landing gear kissed scorched earth and the engines quietened.

"We'll take a stroll outside," Minla said. "There's something I want you to see. Something that will convince you of our seriousness."

"I don't need convincing."

"I want you to see it nonetheless. Take this cloak." She handed him a surprisingly heavy garment.

"Lead impregnated?"

"Just a precaution. Radiation levels are actually very low in this sector."

They disembarked via an escalator that had folded down from the flying wing's belly, accompanied by a detachment of guards. The armed men moved ahead, sweeping the ground with things that looked like metal brooms before ushering Minla and Merlin forward. They followed a winding path through scorched rubble and junk, taking care not to trip over the obstacles and broken ground. Calliope had set during their descent and a biting wind was now howling into land from the sea, setting his teeth on edge. From somewhere in the distance a siren rose and fell on a mournful cycle. Despite Minla's assurance concerning the radioactivity, Merlin swore he could already feel his skin tingling. Overhead, stars poked through the thinning layer of moonlit clouds.

When at last he looked up, he saw that the solitary building was in fact an enormous stone monument. It towered a hundred meters above the flying wing, stepped like a ziggurat and cut and engraved with awesome precision. Letters in Lecythus A marched in stentorian ranks across the highest vertical face. Beyond the monument, gray-black water lapped at the shattered remains of a promenade. The monument was presumably designed to weather storms, but it would only take one spring tide to submerge its lower flanks completely. Merlin wondered why Minla's people hadn't set it on higher ground.

"It's impressive."

"There are a hundred monuments like this on Lecythus," Minla told him, drawing her cloak tighter around herself. "We faced them with whetstone, would you believe it. It turns out to be very good for making monuments, especially when you don't want the letters to be worn away in a handful of centuries."

"You built a hundred of these?" Merlin asked.

"That's just the start. There'll be a thousand by the time we're finished. When we are gone, when all other traces of our culture have been erased from time, we hope that at least one of these monuments will remain. Shall I read you the inscription?"

Merlin had still learned nothing of the native writing, and

he'd neglected to wear the lenses that would have allowed *Tyrant* to overlay a translation.

"You'd better."

"It says that once a great human society lived on Lecythus, in peace and harmony. Then came a message from the stars, a warning that our world was to be destroyed by the fire of the sun itself, or something even worse. So we made preparations to abandon the world that had been our home for so long, and to commence a journey into the outer darkness of interstellar space, looking for a new home in the stars. One day, thousands or tens of thousands after our departure, you, the people who read this message, may find us. For now you are welcome to make of this world what you will. But know that this planet was ours, and it remains ours, and that one day we shall make it our home again."

"I like the bit about 'peace and harmony.' ".

"History is what we write, not what we remember. Why should we tarnish the memory of our planet by enshrining our less noble deeds?"

"Spoken like a true leader, Minla."

At that moment one of the guards raised his rifle and projected a line of tracer fire into the middle distance. Something hissed and scurried into the cover of debris.

"We should be leaving," Minla said. "Regressives come out at night, and some of them are armed."

"Regressives?"

"Dissident political elements. Suicide cultists who'd rather die on Lecythus than cooperate in the evacuation effort. They're our problem, Merlin, not yours."

He'd heard stories about the regressives, but dismissed them as rumor until now. They were the survivors of the war, people who hadn't submitted eagerly to the iron rule of Minla's new Planetary Government. Details that didn't fit into the plan, and which therefore had to be brushed aside or suppressed or given a subhuman name. He pulled the cloak tighter, anxious not to spend a minute longer on the surface than necessary. But even as Minla turned and began walking back to the waiting aircraft—moonlight picked out the elegant sweep of its single great wing—something tugged at him, holding him to the spot.

"Minla," he called, a crack in his voice.

She stopped and turned around. "What is it, Merlin?"

"I've something for you." He reached under the cloak and fished out the gift she had given him as a girl, holding it before him. He'd had it with him for days, waiting for the moment he hoped would never come.

Impatiently, Minla retraced her steps. "I said we should be leaving. What is it you want to give me?"

He handed her the sliver of whetstone. "A little girl gave me this. I don't think I know that little girl anymore."

Minla looked at the stone with a curl of disgust on her face. "That was forty years ago."

"Not to me. To me it was less than a year. I've seen a lot of changes since you gave me that gift."

"We all have to grow up sometime, Merlin." For a moment he thought she was going to hand him back the gift, or at least slip it into one of her own pockets. Instead, Minla let it drop to the ground. Merlin reached to pick it up, but it was too late. The stone fell into a dark crack between two shattered paving slabs; Merlin heard the chink as it bounced off something and fell even deeper.

"It's gone."

"It was just a silly stone," Minla said. "That's all. Now let's be on our way."

Merlin looked back at the lapping waters as he followed Minla to the moonlit flying wing. Something about the whetstone, something about tides of that sea, something about the moon itself, kept nagging at the back of his mind. There was a connection, trivial or otherwise, that he was missing.

He was sure it would come to him sooner or later.

Minla walked with a stick, clicking its hard metal shaft against the echoing flooring of the station's observation deck. Illness or injury had disfigured her since their last meeting; she wore her graying hair in a lopsided parting, hanging down almost to the collar on her right side. Merlin could not say for certain what had happened to Minla, since she was careful to turn her face away from him whenever they spoke. But in the days since his revival he had already heard talk of assassination attempts, some of which had apparently come close to succeeding. Minla seemed more stooped and frail than he remembered, as if she had worked every hour of those twenty years.

She interrupted a light beam with her hand, opening the viewing shields. "Behold the Space Dormitories," she said, declaiming as if she had an audience of thousands rather than a single man standing only a few meters away. "Rejoice, Merlin. You played a part in this."

Through the window, wheeling with the gentle rotation of the orbital station, the nearest dormitory loomed larger than Lecythus in the sky. The wrinkled gray sphere would soon reach operational pressure, its skin becoming taut. The final sun mirrors were being assembled in place, manipulated by mighty articulated robots. Cargo rockets were coming and going by the minute, while the first wave of evacuees had already taken up residence in the polar holding pens.

Twenty dormitories were ready now; the remaining eighty would come online within two years. Every day, hundreds of atomic rockets lifted from the surface of Lecythus, carrying evacuees—packed into their holds at the maximum possible human storage density, like a kind of three-dimensional jigsaw of flesh and blood—or cargo, in the form of air, water, and prefabricated parts for the other habitats. Each rocket launch deposited more radioactivity into the atmosphere of the doomed world. It was now fatal to breathe that air for more than a few hours, but the slow poisoning of Lecythus was of no concern to the Planetary Government. The remaining surface-bound colonists, those who would occupy the other dormitories when they were ready, awaited transfer in pressurized bunkers, in conditions that were at least as spartan as anything they would have to endure in space. Merlin had offered the services of *Tyrant* to assist with the evacuation effort, but as efficient and fast as his ship was, it would have made only a token difference to the speed of the exercise.

That was not to say that there were not difficulties, or that the program was exactly on schedule. Merlin was gladdened by the progress he saw in some areas, disheartened in others. Before he slept, the locals had grilled him for help with their prototype atomic rockets, seemingly in expectation that Merlin would provide magic remedies for the failures that had dogged them so far. But Merlin could only help in a limited fashion. He knew the basic principles of building an atomic rocket, but little of the detailed knowledge needed to circumvent a particular problem. Minla's experts were frustrated, and then dismayed. He tried explaining to them that though an atomic rocket might be primitive compared to the engines in *Tyrant*, that didn't mean it was simple, or that its construction didn't involve many subtle principles. "I know how a sailing ship works," he said, trying to explain himself. "But that doesn't mean I could build one myself, or show a master boatbuilder how to improve his craft."

They wanted to know why he couldn't just give them the technology in *Tyrant* itself.

"My ship is capable of self-repair," he'd said. "But it isn't capable of making copies of itself. That's a deep principle, embodied in the logical architecture at a very profound level."

"Then run off a blueprint of your engines. Let us copy what we need from the plans," they said.

"That won't work. The components in *Tyrant* are manufactured to exacting tolerances, using materials your chemistry can't even explain, let alone reproduce."

"Then show us how to improve our manufacturing capability, until we can make what we need."

"We don't have time for that. *Tyrant* was manufactured by a culture that had had over ten thousand years of experience in spacefaring, not to mention knowledge of industrial processes and inventions dating back at least as far again. You can't cross that kind of gap in fifty years, no matter how hard you might want to."

"Then what are we supposed to do?"

"Keep trying," Merlin said. "Keep making mistakes, and learning from them. That's all any culture ever does."

That was exactly what they had done, across twenty painful years. The rockets worked now, after a fashion, but they'd arrived late and there was already a huge backlog of people and parts to be shifted into space. The dormitories should have been finished and occupied by now, with work already under way on the fleet of Exodus Arks. But the Arks had met obstacles as well. The lunar colonization program had run into unanticipated difficulties, requiring that the Arks be assembled from components made on Lecythus. The atomic rocket production lines were already running at maximum capacity without the burden of carrying even more tonnage into space.

"This is good," Merlin told Minla. "But you still need to step things up."

"We're aware of that," she answered testily. "Unfortunately, some of your information proved less than accurate."

Merlin blinked at her. "It did?"

"Our scientists made a prototype for the fusion drive, according to your plans. Given the limited testing they've been able to do, they say it works very well. It wouldn't be a technical problem to build all the engines we need for the Exodus Arks. So I'm told, at least."

"Then what's the problem?"

Her hand gripped the walking stick like a talon. "Fuel, Merlin. You told us we'd find helium 3 in the topsoil of our moon. Well, we didn't. Not enough to suit our needs, anyway."

"Then you mustn't have been looking properly."

"I assure you we looked, Merlin. You were mistaken. Now we'll have to find fuel from an alternative source, and redesign our fusion drive accordingly. We'll need your help, if we aren't to fall hopelessly behind schedule." Minla extended a withered hand toward the wheeling view. "To have come so far, to have reached this point, and then *failed* . . . that would be worse than having never tried at all, don't you think?"

Chastened, Merlin scratched at his chin. "I'll do what I can. Let me talk to the fusion engineers."

"I've scheduled a meeting. They're *very* anxious to talk to you." Minla paused. "There's something you should know, though. They've seen you make a mistake. They'll still be interested in what you have to say. But don't expect blind acceptance of your every word. They know you're human now."

"I never said I wasn't."

"You didn't, no. I'll give you credit for that. But for a little while some of us allowed ourselves to believe it."

Minla turned and walked away, the tap of her stick echoing into the distance.

As space wars went, it was brief and relatively tame, certainly by comparison with the awesome battles delineated in the Cohort's pictorial history. The timeworn frescoes on the swallowships commemorated engagements where entire solar systems were reduced to mere tactical details, hills or ditches in the terrain of a much larger strategic landscape, and where the participants—human and Husker both—were moving at significant fractions of the speed of light and employing relativistic weapons of world-shattering destructive potential. A single skirmish could eat up many centuries of planetary time, whole lifetimes from the point of view of a starship's crew. The war itself was a thing inseparably entwined with recorded history, a monstrous choking structure with its roots reaching into the loam of deep time, and whose end must be assumed (by all except Merlin, at least) to lie in the unimaginably remote future.

Here, the theater of conflict was considerably less than half a light-second in diameter, encompassing only the immediate space around Lecythus, with its girdle of half-finished dormitories and Exodus Arks. The battle lasted barely a dozen hours, between first and last detonation. With the exception of Merlin's own late intervention, no weapons more potent than hydrogen bombs were deployed. Horrific, certainly, but possessed of a certain genteel precision compared to the weapons that had consumed Plenitude.

It began with a surprise strike from the surface, using a

wave of commandeered atomic rockets. It seemed that the Regressives had gained control of one of the rocket-assembly -and-launch complexes. The rockets had no warheads, but that didn't matter: kinetic energy, and the explosive force stored in their atomic engines, was still enough to inflict havoc on their targets. The weapons had been aimed with surprising accuracy. The first wave destroyed half of the unfinished dormitories, inflicting catastrophic damage on many of the others. By the time the second wave was rising, orbital defenses had sprung into action, but by then it was too late to intercept more than a handful of the missiles. Many of the atomic rockets were being piloted by suicide crews, steering their charges through Minla's hastily erected countermeasure screens. By the third hour, the Planetary Government was beginning to retaliate against Regressive elements using atmospheric-entry interceptors, but while they could pick away at enemy fortifications on the ground, they couldn't penetrate the antimissile cordon around the launch complex itself. Rogue warheads chipped away at the edges of aerial landmasses, sending mountain-sized boulders crashing to the surface. Even as the battle raged, brutal tidal waves ravaged the already-frail coastal communities. As the hours ticked by, Minla's analysts maintained a grim toll on the total number of surface and orbital casualties. In the fifth and sixth hours, more dormitories fell to the assault. Stray fire accounted for even more losses. A temporary ceasefire in the seventh hour was only caused by the temporary occultation of the launch complex by a medium-sized aerial landmass. When the skies were clear again, the rockets rose up with renewed fury.

"They've hit all but one of the Exodus Arks," Minla said, when the battle was in its ninth hour. "We just had time to move the final ship out of range of the atomics. But if they find a way to increase their reach, by eliminating more payload mass . . ." She turned her face from his. "It'll all have been for nothing, Merlin. They'll have won, and the last sixty years may as well have not happened."

He felt preternaturally calm, knowing exactly what was coming. "What do you want me to do?"

"Intervene," Minla said. "Use whatever force is merited."

"I offered once. You said no."

"You changed your mind once. Now I change mine."

Merlin went to *Tyrant*. He ordered the ship to deliver a concentrated charm-torp salvo against the compromised rocket facility, bringing more energy to bear on that one tiny area of land than had been deployed in all the years of the atomic wars. There was no need for him to accompany his ship; like a well-trained dog, *Tyrant* was perfectly capable of carrying out his orders without direct supervision.

They watched the spectacle from orbit. When the electric-white fire erupted on the horizon of Lecythus, brightening that entire limb of the planet in the manner of a stuttering cold sunrise, Merlin felt Minla's hand tighten around his own. For all her frailty, for all that the years had taken from her, there remained astonishing steel in that grip.

"Thank you," she said. "You may just have saved us all."

It had been ten years.

Lecythus and its sun now lay many light-weeks to stern. The one remaining Exodus Ark had reached five percent of the speed of light. In sixty years—faster, if the engine could be improved—it would streak into another system, one that might offer the possibility of landfall. It flew alongside the gossamer line of the Waynet, using the tube as cover from Husker long-range sensors. The Exodus Ark carried only twelve hundred exiles, few of whom would live long enough to see another world.

The hospital was near the core of the ship, safely distant from the sleeting energies of interstellar radiation or the exotic emissions of the Waynet. Many of its patients were veterans of the Regressive War, victims of the viciously ingenious injuries wrought by the close conjunction of vacuum and heat, radiation and kinetic energy. Most of them would be dead by the time the fusion engine was silenced for cruise phase. For now they were being afforded the care appropriate to war heroes, even those who screamed bloodcurdling pleas for the painkilling mercy of euthanasia.

In a soundproofed private annex of that same complex, Minla also lay in the care of machines. This time the assassins had come closer than ever before, and they had very nearly achieved their objective. Yet she'd survived, and the prognosis for a complete recovery—so Merlin was informed—was deemed higher than seventy-five percent. More than could be said of Minla's aides, injured in the same attack, but they were at least receiving the best possible care in *Tyrant*'s frostwatch cabinets. The exercise was, Merlin knew, akin to knitting together human-shaped sculptures from a bloody stew of meat and splintered bone, and then hoping that those sculptures would retain some semblance of mind. Minla would have presented no challenge at all, but the Planetary Director had declined the offer of frostwatch care herself, preferring to give up her place to one of her underlings. Knowing that, Merlin allowed himself a momentary flicker of empathy.

He walked into the room, coughing to announce himself. "Hello, Minla."

She lay on her back, her head against the pillow, though she was not asleep. Slowly she turned to face Merlin as he approached. She looked very old, very tired, but she still found the energy to form a smile.

"It's so good of you to come. I was hoping, but. . . I didn't dare ask. I know how busy you've been with the engine upgrade study."

"I could hardly not pay you a visit. Even though I had a devil of a job persuading your staff to let me through."

"They're too protective of me. I know my own strength, Merlin. I'll get through this."

"I believe you would."

Minla's gaze settled on his hand. "Are those for me?"

He had a bouquet of alien flowers. They were of a peculiar dark hue, a shade that ought to have appeared black in the room's subdued gold lighting yet which was clearly and unmistakably purple, revealed by its own soft inner illumination. They had the look of a detail that had been hand-tinted in a black-and-white photograph, so that it appeared to float above the rest of the image.

"Of course," Merlin said. "I always bring flowers, don't I?"

"You always used to. Then you stopped."

"Perhaps it's time to start again."

He set them by her bedside, in the watered vase that was already waiting. They were not the only flowers in the room, but the purple ones seemed to suck the very color from the others.

"They're very beautiful," Minla said. "It's like I've never seen anything precisely that color before. It's as if there's a whole circuit in my brain that's never been activated until now."

"I chose them especially. They're famous for their beauty."

Minla lifted her head from the pillow, her eyes brightening with curiosity. "Now you'll have to tell me where they're from."

"It's a long story."

"That never stopped you before."

"A world called Lacertine. It's ten thousand light-years from here; many days of shiptime, even in the Waynet. I don't even know if it still exists."

"Tell me about Lacertine," she said, pronouncing the name of the world with her usual scrupulousness.

"It's a very beautiful planet, orbiting a hot blue star. They say the planet must have been moved into its present orbit by the Waymakers, from another system entirely. The seas and skies are a shimmering electric blue. The forests are a dazzle of purple and violet and pink; colors that you've only ever seen when you close your eyes against the sun and see patterns behind your eyelids. White citadels rise above the tree line, towers linked by a filigree of delicate bridges."

"Then there are people on Lacertine?"

Merlin thought of the occupants, and nodded. "Adapted, of course. Everything that grows on Lacertine was bioengineered to tolerate the scalding light from the sun. They say if something can grow there, it can grow almost anywhere."

"Have you been there?"

He shook his head ruefully. "I've never been within a thousand light-years of the place."

"I'll never see it. Nor any of the other places you've told me about."

"There are places I'll never see. Even with the Waynet, I'm still just one human man, with one human life. Even the Waymakers didn't live long enough to glimpse more than a fraction of their empire."

"It must make you very sad."

"I take each day as it comes. I'd rather take good memories from one world, than fret about the thousand I'll never see."

"You're a wise man," Minla said. "We were lucky to get you."

Merlin smiled. He was silent for many moments, letting Minla enjoy the last calmness of mind she would ever know. "There's something I need to tell you," he said eventually.

She must have heard something in his tone of voice. "What, Merlin?"

"There's a good chance you're all going to die."

Her tone became sharp. "We don't need you to remind us of the risks."

"I'm talking about something that's going to happen sooner rather than later. The ruse of shadowing the Waynet didn't work. It was the best thing to do, but there was always a chance . . ." Merlin spread his hands in exaggerated apology, as if there had ever been something he could have done about it. "*Tyrant*'s detected a Husker attack swarm, six elements lying a light-month ahead of you. You don't have time to steer or slow down. They'd shadow every move you made, even if you tried to shake them off."

"You promised us—"

"I promised you nothing. I just gave you the best advice I could. If you hadn't shadowed the Waynet, they'd have found you even sooner."

"We aren't using the ramscoop design. You said we'd be safe if we stuck to fusion motors. The electromagnetic signature—"

"I said you'd be safer. There were never ironclad guarantees."

"You lied to us." Minla turned suddenly spiteful. "I never trusted you."

"I did all in my power to save you."

"Then why are you standing there looking so calm, when you know we're going to die?" But before Merlin had time to answer, Minla had seen the answer for herself. "Because you can leave," she said, nodding at her own percipience. "You have your ship, and a syrinx. You can slip into the Waynet and outrun the enemy."

"I'm leaving," Merlin said. "But I'm not running."

"Aren't they one and the same?"

"Not this time. I'm going back to Plenitude, I mean Lecythus, to do what I can for the people we left behind. The people you condemned to death."

"Me, Merlin?"

"I examined the records of the Regressive War: not just the official documents, but *Tyrant's* own data logs. And I saw what I should have seen at the time, but didn't. It was a ruse. It was too damned easy, the way they took control of that rocket factory. You let them, Minla."

"I did nothing of the kind."

"You knew the whole evacuation project was never going to be ready on time. The Space Dormitories were behind schedule, there were problems with the Exodus Arks . . ."

"Because you told us falsehoods about the helium in the moon's soil."

Merlin raised a warning hand. "We'll get to that. The point is, your plans were in tatters. But you could still have completed more dormitories and ships, if you'd been willing to leave the system a little later. You could still have saved more people than you did, albeit at a slightly increased risk to your own survival. But that wasn't acceptable. You wanted to leave there and then. So you engineered the whole Regressive attack, set it up as a pretext for an early departure."

"The Regressives were real!" Minla hissed.

"But you gave them the keys to that rocket silo, and the know-how to target and guide those missiles. Funny how their attack just missed the one station that you were occupying, you and all your political cronies, and that you managed to move the one Exodus Ark to safety just in time. Damned convenient, Minla."

"I'll have you shot for this, Merlin."

"Good luck. Try laying a hand on me, and see how far it gets you. My ship's listening in on this conversation. It can put proctors into this room in a matter of seconds."

"And the moon, Merlin? Do you have an excuse for the error that cost us so dearly?"

"I don't know. Possibly. That's why I'm going back to Lecythus. There are still people on the surface—Regressives, allies, I don't care. And people you abandoned in orbit as well."

"They'll all die. You said it yourself."

He raised a finger. "If they don't leave. But maybe there's way. Again, I should have seen it sooner. But that's me all the way. I take a long time to put the pieces together, but I get there in the end. Just like Dowitcher, the man who gave your father the whetstone."

"It was just a stone."

"So you said. In fact, it was a vital clue to the nature of your world. It took spring tides and neap tides to lay down those patterns. But you said it yourself: Lecythus doesn't have spring tides and neap tides. Not anymore, at least."

"I'm sure this means something to you."

"Something happened to your moon, Minla. When that whetstone formed, your moon was raising tides on Lecythus. When the moon and Calliope were tugging on your seas in the same direction, you got a spring tide. When they were balancing each other, you got a neap tide. Hence the patterning on the whetstone. But now the tides are the same from day to day. Calliope's still there, so that only leaves the moon. It isn't exerting the same gravitational pull it used to. Oh, it weighs *something*—but the effect is much reduced, and if you could skip forward a few hundred million years and examine a piece of whetstone laid down now, you'd probably find very faint variations in sediment thickness. But whatever the effect is now, it must be insignificant compared to the time when your whetstone was formed. Yet the moon's still there, in what appears to be the same orbit. So what's happened?"

"You tell me, Merlin."

"I don't think it's a moon anymore. I think the original moon got ripped to pieces to make your armored sky. I don't know how much of the original mass got used for that, but I'm guessing it was quite a significant fraction. The question is, what happened to the remains?"

"I'm sure you have a theory."

"I think they made a fake moon out of the leftovers. It sits there in your sky, it orbits Lecythus, but it doesn't pull on your seas the way the old one used to. And because it's new—relatively speaking—it doesn't have the soil chemistry we'd expect of a real moon, one that's been sitting there for billions of years, drinking in solar winds. That's why you didn't find the helium you were expecting."

"So what is it?"

"That's what I'm keen to find out. The thing is, I know what Dowitcher was thinking now. He knew that wasn't a real moon. Which begs the question: what's inside it? And could it make a difference to the survivors you left behind?"

"Hiding inside a shell won't help them," Minla said. "You already told us we'd achieve nothing by digging tunnels into Lecythus."

"I'm not thinking about hiding. I'm thinking about moving. What if the moon's an escape vehicle? An Exodus Ark big enough to take the entire population?"

"You have no evidence."

"I have this." With that, Merlin produced one of Minla's old picture books. Seventy years had aged its papers to a brittle yellow, dimming the vibrancy of the old inks. But the linework in the illustrations was still clear enough. Merlin held the book open to a particular page, letting Minla look at it. "Your people had a memory of arriving on Lecythus in a moon-sized ship," he said. "Maybe that was true. Equally, maybe it was a case of muddling one thing with another. I'm wondering if the thing you were meant to remember was not that you came by moon, but that you could leave by one."

Minla stared at the picture. For a moment, like a breeze on a summer's day, Merlin felt a wave of almost unbearable sadness pass through the room. It was as if the picture had transported her back to her childhood, before she had set her life on the trajectory that, seventy years later, would bring it to this bed, this soundproofed room, the shameful survival of this one ship. The last time she had looked at the picture, everything had been possible, all life's opportunities open to her. She'd been the daughter of a powerful and respected man, with influence and wisdom at her fingertips. And yet from all the choices presented to her, she had selected this one dark path, and followed it to its conclusion.

"Even if it is a ship," she said softly, "you'll never get them all aboard."

"I'll die trying."

"And us? We get abandoned to our fates?"

Merlin smiled: he'd been expecting the question. "There are twelve hundred people on this ship, some of them children. They weren't all party to your schemes, so they don't all deserve to die when you meet the Huskers. That's why I'm leaving behind weapons and a detachment of proctors to show you how to install and use them."

For the first time since his arrival in the room, Minla spoke like a leader again. "Will they make a difference?"

"They'll give your ship a fighting chance. That's the best I can offer."

"Then we'll take what we're given."

"I'm sorry it came to this. I played a part in what you became, of that I've no doubt. But I didn't make you a monster."

"No," she said. "I'll at least take credit for myself, and for the fact that I saved twelve hundred of my people. If it took a monster to do that, doesn't that mean we sometimes need monsters?"

"Maybe we do. But that doesn't mean we should forgive them for what they are, even for an instant." Gently, as if bestowing a gift, Merlin placed the picture book on Minla's recumbent form. "I'm afraid I havc to go now. There won't be much time when I get back to Lecythus."

"Please," she said. "Not like this. Not this way."

"This is how it ends," he said, before turning from her bed and walking to the exit. "Goodbye, Minla."

Twenty minutes later he was in the Waynet, racing back to Lecythus.

There's a lot to tell, and one day I'll get around to writing it up properly. For now it's enough to say that I was right to trust my instincts about the moon. I just wish I'd put the clues together sooner than I did. Perhaps then Minla would never have had to commit her crimes.

I didn't save as many as I'd have wished, but I did save some of the people Minla left behind to die. I suppose that has to count for something. It was close, but if there's one thing to be said for Waymaker-level technology, it's that it's almost childishly easy to use. They were like babies with the toys of the gods. They left that moon there for a good reason, and while it was necessary for them to camouflage it—it had to be capable of fooling the Huskers, or whoever they built that sky to hide from—the moon itself was obligingly easy to break into, once our purpose became clear. And once it started moving, once its great engines came online after tens of thousands of years of quiet dormancy, no force in the universe could have held it back. I shadowed the fleeing moon long enough to establish that it was headed into a sector that appeared to be free of Husker activity, at least for now. It'll be touch-and-go for a few centuries, but with Force and Wisdom on their side, I think they'll make it.

I'm in the Waynet now, riding the flow away from Calliope. The syrinx still works, much to my relief. For a while I considered riding the contraflow, back toward that lone Exodus Ark. By the time I reached them they'd have been only days away from the encounter. But my presence wouldn't have made a decisive difference to their chances of surviving the Huskers, and I couldn't have expected much of a warm welcome.

Not after my final gift to Minla.

I'm glad she never asked me too much about those flowers, or the world they came from. If she'd wanted to know more about Lacertine, she might have sensed that I was holding something back. Such as the fact that the assassin guilds on Lacertine were masters of their craft, known throughout the worlds of the Waynet for their skill and cunning, and that no guild on Lacertine was more revered than the bioartificers who made the sleepflowers.

It was said that they could make them in any shape, any color, to match any known flower from any known world. It was said that they could pass all tests save the most microscopic scrutiny. It was said that if you wanted to kill someone, you gave them a gift of flowers from Lacertine.

She would have been dead not long after my departure. The flowers would have detected her presence—they were keyed to locate a single breathing form in a room, most commonly a sleeper—and when the room was quiet they would have become stealthily animate, leaving their jar and creeping from point to point with the slowness of a sundial's shadow, their movement imperceptible to the naked eye, but enough to take them to the face of the sleeper. Their tendrils would have closed around Minla's face with the softness of a lover's caress. Then the paralyzing toxins would have hit her nervous system.

I hoped it was painless. I hoped it was quick. But what I remembered of the Lacertine assassins was that they were known for their cleverness, not their clemency.

Afterward, I deleted the sleepflowers from the biolibrary.

I knew Minla for less than a year of my life, and for seventy years by another reckoning. Sometimes when I think of her I see a human being in all her dimensions, as real as anyone I've ever known. Other times, I see something two-dimensional, like a faded illustration in one of her books, so thin that the light shines through her.

I don't hate her, even now. But I wish time and tide had never brought us together.

A comfortable number of light-hours behind me, the Waynet has just cut into Calliope's heart. It has already sliced through the photosphere and the star's convection zone. Quite what has happened, or is happening, or will happen, when it touched (or touches, or will touch) the nuclear-burning core is still far from clear.

Theory says that no impulse can travel faster than light. Since my ship is already riding the Waynet's flow at very nearly the speed of light, it seems impossible that any information concerning Calliope's fate will ever be able to catch up with me. And yet. . . several minutes ago I swear that I felt a kick, a jolt in the smooth glide of my flight, as if some report of that destructive event had raced up the flow at superluminal speed, buffeting my little ship.

There's nothing in the data to suggest any unusual event, and I don't have any plans to return to Lecythus and see what became of that world when its sun was gored open. But I still felt something, and if it reached me up the flow of the Waynet, if that impulse bypassed the iron barrier of causality itself, I can't begin to imagine the energies that must have been involved, or what must have happened to the strand of the Waynet behind me. Perhaps it's unraveling, and I'm about to breathe my last breath before I become a thin smear of naked quarks, stretched across several billion kilometers of interstellar space.

That would certainly be one way to go.

Frankly, it would be nice to have the luxury to dwell on such fears. But I still have a gun to find, and I'm not getting any younger.

Mission resumed.

SPLINTERS OF GLASS

MARY ROSENBLUM

H ere's a tense and fast-paced adventure that takes us to
Europa for a deadly game of cat and mouse beneath
its frozen surface, a game where a second's indecision or a
moment of carelessness can make the difference between
life and an especially horrible death...

One of the most popular and prolific of the new writers of
the nineties, Mary Rosenblum made her first sale, to *Asimov's
Science Fiction*, in 1990, and has since become a mainstay
of that magazine, and one of its most frequent contributors,
with almost thirty sales there to her credit. She has also sold
to *The Magazine of Fantasy and Science Fiction, Science
Fiction Age, Pulphouse, New Legends,* and elsewhere.

Rosenblum produced some of the most colorful, exciting,
and emotionally powerful stories of the nineties, earning her
a large and devoted following of readers. Her linked series of
"Drylands" stories have proved to be one of *Asimov's* most
popular series, but she has also published memorable stories
such as "The Stone Garden," "Synthesis," "Flight," "California Dreamer," "Casting at Pegasus," "Entrada," "Rat,"
"The Centaur Garden," "Skin Deep," "Songs the Sirens
Sing," and many, many others. Her novella "Gas Fish" won
the *Asimov's* Readers Award Poll in 1996, and was a finalist

for that year's Nebula Award. Her first novel, *The Drylands,* appeared in 1993 to wide critical acclaim, winning the prestigious Compton Crook Award for Best First Novel of the year; it was followed in short order by her second novel, *Chimera,* and her third, *The Stone Garden.* Her first short story collection, *Synthesis and Other Stories,* was widely hailed by critics as one of the best collections of 1996. She has also written a trilogy of mystery novels under the name Mary Freeman. Her most recent book is a major new science fiction novel, *Horizons.* A graduate of Clarion West, Rosenblum lives in Portland, Oregon.

He wouldn't have seen her arrive if his board hadn't broken down. He wouldn't have known. Qai stepped back against the carved-ice façade of a tea vendor's stall, holding his narrow board like a silver shield in front of him. He caught only a glimpse before she vanished among the passengers disembarking from the monthly shuttle, as they hurried across the gangway to the Ice Palace arrival dock with its tiny customs gate. Most scattered quickly, IDing their way through the "resident" gate, moving with the purposeful skimming strides of travelers returning home. Only a couple of newbies. You could always tell them by the way they walked, high-stepping in slow motion in the thirteen-percent earth-normal gravity—as if walking on a waterbed. And they panted. The nano–red cell transfusions didn't really make up for the low atmospheric pressure and minimal oxygen of Europa's sea-level ice caverns. And of course, they looked up to the vast arch of the Ice Palace dome, its natural ice walls flickering with rainbows in the broad-spectrum light of the Lamp, veined with multicolored moss. Everyone felt it, first time on Europa . . . the enormous weight of the ice shell pressing down on them.

Then the crowd thinned and he saw her clearly: Gerta. Her hair shone like spun gold, just as he remembered. The tiny hardness of the polished ammonite pendant beneath his ice suit and therms seemed to dig into his flesh. He covered it with a palm, instinctively. As if it might call her to him.

She had not changed, after all these years.

That was . . . bad.

She turned as if she had felt the pressure of his stare. Before those blue, blue eyes could pierce his shield, Qai fled around the corner of the tea stall, slipping into a narrow alley, a natural fissure that wandered away from the dome, lined with small shops carved into the ice; low-end food vendors, mostly, selling gray moss tea and sea soup. Get the board fixed, pick up the supplies he needed, and get out, he thought. Do it fast.

She only had one reason to be here.

Him.

Blue moss netted the walls of the fissure, its soft glow brightening as the reflected light from the Ice Palace faded. Finally the alley widened out into the little plaza where Karina had her shop. Starfish lamps shed a soft, silvery light on each side of the carved arch of her doorway, streaking the rough floor of the plaza with dark shadows. A sweeper raked the traffic-polished ice rough for traction, a hunched figure with matted gray hair beneath a gray hooded ice tunic and leggings patched with something that looked like fabric from an EVA suit, maybe an asteroid miner's castoff.

Karina had the only shop on the plaza with lamps. Qai slipped beneath the ornate twined-kelp carvings above her door, wishing briefly that Karina's shop were too poor to afford starfish. But even if Gerta had spotted him she had to clear customs and that was an intricate and complicated dance of bargaining and bribes on the Snow Queen, the Free Port of Europa. She would be lucky if she got through in this day period, and considering it was nearly a meal hour, she'd probably be stuck, forced to share a lavish and hospitable dinner only to pay for the privilege as she tried to clear her luggage.

He'd be out in the ice by then.

"Hey, ice-boy." Karina looked up from the innards of a board lying belly up on her workbench, pulling off her microgoggles. The crimson fiber lights woven into her rows of braids glowed red as blood. "Long time no see." She laughed, her white teeth glittering in her ebony face. "It occurs to me, ice-boy, that I should build a little planned obsolescence into your circuitry. If the only way I get to see you is when your board breaks."

"You busy, Kar?" He tried to keep any trace of urgency out of his voice.

"Why the hurry?" Her eyes narrowed and a hint of anticipation curled the edges of her full lips.

He should have known he couldn't fool Kar. Let her choose between gossip and sex and she'd pick gossip every time. "I spotted a vein of rose moss." He jerked his head vaguely poleward. "I'm afraid Zorn saw me leaving. I wouldn't put it past him to try sniffing out my back trail, dig it out himself. You know Zorn." He jerked his shoulders in an angry shrug. "He's a claim jumper. But I didn't dare stay long enough to dig in and register the site. The power plant was draining." He slapped the board. "Barely made it back as it was."

"Nobody's seen rose for a hundred days." Karina's smile broadened. "But you got the nose, ice-boy. One day you're gonna tell me how you always find the best moss, right?" She spun away from the workbench, her slender arms slipping under his tunic, sliding around his rib cage, her lips rising up to capture his. "I love secrets," she breathed into his mouth. "You know I'll charm it out of you eventually. And you'll love giving it up to me." Her long, strong fingers played his vertebrae like a virtuoso, walking downward to his hips, around and down. . .

"After." He swallowed a groan, caught her wrists. Pushed her away. "Don't lose me this rose, Kar. Or I won't be able to afford you."

"Huh." She spun away, lights flashing in her braids. "You don't buy *me*, honey. Not even with rose moss money. The board work you pay for."

"I didn't mean that." He put his hands on her shoulders, felt lean muscle and bone beneath the slick thermal fabric of her tunic. He dug his thumbs into the muscles along her shoulder blades, heard her deep-within hum of pleasure as he kneaded the knots out of the muscles. "You know I didn't."

He licked the back of her neck, tasting her skin, sweat, the bristling short hairs beneath her braids. "Fix this quick so I can get that rose before Zorn sniffs it out and then we'll celebrate."

"You're so persuasive," she purred, twisting her head back to grin at him. "Okay, ice-boy, clear the decks." She shrugged him off, grabbed his board, and slung it lightly onto the workbench. Opened its access panel with a tap of her finger, pulling the microgoggles onto her face as she bent over the circuitry, probing with a long, tapered fingernail biowired for testing.

Qai held his breath. He had enough credit to buy a new board if he had to.

"Bad regulator chip is all." Karina pushed the goggles up onto her forehead. "Got one in stock, so no biggie." She stepped over a stack of board shells to pull open drawers in her storage wall. "Got it." Ten minutes and she was done, closing up the smart-plastic hull as she straightened. Rose on tiptoes to kiss him. "Go get that rose." She winked. "Then we celebrate."

He pulled her into his arms, mouth covering hers, kissing her hard, so hard that he tasted blood as they separated. Because he might never . . .

Don't think that.

"We'll celebrate." He pretended not to see her surprise and the questions rising in her eyes, grabbed his board before those questions could turn to words. And left.

Forever?

Don't think that.

He hit Ah Zhen's Commodities over on the far side of the Palace, his order already packed into his sled, a blue bullet shape waiting in the hangar like a lost dog . . .

Earth thoughts. Qai shook himself.

Her fault.

He paid Ah Zhen, numbers counting down in his head. If they hadn't made her stay for a fancy meal, if she'd been tough enough to say no and get out . . .

She'd be out in the corridors right now.

He hooked the sled to his board, slipped his foot into

the shoe, and activated the stabilizer field. He ramped up the power and felt the satisfying, bone-humming vibration of power beneath his feet. He toed the board into motion, sliding easily through the corridor, swinging out into one of the narrow naturals that veined the ice all around the Ice Palace, lined with residence holes, cheap shops, sex cribs, and a few pricey freelancers like Karina. Tourists didn't go here, and only the natural glow of the embedded moss lighted the irregular space. A hundred meters ahead, a main drill cut spinward and crossed a big fault that ran three hundred klicks without narrowing. A hundred good secondary faults crossed it. He could be well into the ice in a matter of hours. And because his blood had adapted and was augmented by the nano, he could go high, well above sea level where a tourist couldn't breathe. Out of reach.

Not that it would save him. Not if she had managed to trace him here. *They* would be watching her. They knew where to look, now.

A shadowy figure emerged from a side corridor up ahead, one that led straight from the Ice Palace.

No.

But he knew it was her. Toed the board and it jumped sideways as he leaned into a sharp arc. But she anticipated his evasion and dashed straight into his path, her face a pale oval turned up to his. He kicked the board hard, heard his voice yelling, the sled skidding against the stabilizer's failing grip, dragging his board slantwise.

He hit her.

The edge of the board caught her high in the chest with the sound of an ice ax hitting sludge ice. She flew backward in Europa's minimal G, hitting the wall, sliding along it for meters.

Leaving streaks and flecks of blood. Qai kicked the board into a hard brake, leaped over the skidding sled as it banged into the wall, and skimmed down the corridor in long, flat strides, slamming both palms into the wall to kill his momentum as he reached her, dropping to his knees.

She breathed. Qai let his breath out in a rush even as his fingers probed gently, feeling for the grate of broken bones, wincing at the instant swelling where the sled had struck her, above her small, flat breasts. She had cut her scalp right at the hairline when she hit the wall, and blood gleamed on her face, purplish in the moss-light. Her left collarbone had broken. He felt the small irregularity, checked her shoulders, arms. Didn't find any other breaks, just cuts and scrapes from the rough ice of the wall. Chewing his lip, he rocked back on his heels, thinking hard. As a visitor with a visa chip, she'd get care in the Ice Palace, at the visitors' enclave. But if he brought her there, they'd detain him until she regained consciousness. Just in case he himself had assaulted her or she wanted to press charges. Tourism brought in precious credit and tourists were highly protected. Moss miners were not. He checked her pulse again. He could leave her here and someone would find her. What she would say about the accident, he didn't know. It would be enough.

As Qai started to stand, a flicker of motion at the far reaches of his vision caught his eye, a shadowy figure, nearly invisible in the dim moss-glow. He recognized matted gray hair and the hood of a ragged tunic. The sweeper. From Karina's plaza.

They had followed her, had been working hard while she slept her way up from the platforms, in hibernation in her shielded cocoon. Probabilities spun through his head. If he was accused of killing a tourist, the Ice Palace would sic all of Security on him. They'd start with Karina because too many people knew about them.

Their methods were . . . efficient.

Karina wouldn't know enough to survive the questioning, he guessed. Even as these conclusions clicked into place, he was heaving Gerta's unconscious body onto the sled, securing it with a spare cargo net, arranging her arm so that the collarbone wouldn't take too much stress. Leaping onto his idling board, he toed it into motion, then kicked up the speed. Leaning forward, frigid corridor air whipping tears into his eyes, he fought the erratic tug of the overloaded sled as it tried to pull him into the wall. He didn't dare slow down. The sweeper wouldn't be working alone. He'd have someone on a board. And they'd be armed. They had the power behind them to bring a weapon onto the Snow Queen and get away with it.

He passed a narrow natural ice-crevice patched with yellow moss, began counting as another crevice flashed past on his right. Four . . . five . . . he caught a faint whiff of sulfur and moisture, risked a nanosecond glance behind, saw nothing. He'd have to stay low, near sea level. Gerta couldn't take the ultrathin atmosphere nearer the surface. Qai kicked the board into a slewing turn, braced himself for the jerk of the sled, hoped that she was still unconscious, crouched and rode the board as it bucked, stabilizers whining with strain.

With a centimeter to spare, he made the turn, the sled straightening out behind him, barely kissing the wall as he accelerated down the natural. Blue and green moss patched this one without even a streak of yellow, filling the narrow, wandering natural with a thick, oppressive twilight. Qai took the first secondary fissure antispinward that didn't feel like a dead end, turned north, then spinward, weaving a random path through the fissures that webbed the ice, stretching his senses to the limit, praying that he didn't run out of width before he crossed a big natural. He was lost now, really lost, but that's what it would take to lose their pursuers.

A faint, shimmering hum tickled his awareness. Purple moss. It only grew in naturals that opened to sea, where an upwelling brought warmer water up from the deep vents, exhaling warm, oxygen-laden air into an ice cavern. He eased the board into the narrow fissure, the rippled texture of the ice here glowing a soft blue that slowly darkened to purple. Ahead, open water gleamed like a gash, black as the night between the stars. The natural fissure widened, wall smoothed and pocked from the upwelling warmth and moisture. A wide shelf of smooth ice ringed the open upwell. This was an older, stable upwell then. The cavern had probably reached its mature and stable size and the likelihood of ice falls would be minimal. Qai let his board drift to a halt on the flat and shut it down. As the hum of its power plant faded, the sounds of the Snow Queen filled the thick quiet; the lap and suck of the sea, the deep groan of the ice itself, and the rich, contemplative song of the moss.

Qai stepped off the board, his legs trembling now. Squatting on the ice, forehead against his knees, he drew a long slow breath. Another. Focused on the wandering song of the moss. Yes, this cavern was stable.

"Wilmar?"

He started at her whisper. "Gerta." What do you say? Hello? "Hello." He almost laughed because it was so . . . inappropriate. "I hoped you'd still be out. I'm sorry." He straightened stiffly, his muscles aching with the aftereffects of adrenaline.

"I can't believe . . . I found you." She gasped.

"You've got a broken collarbone." He stumbled to the sled; released the webbing that held her. "I'll give you something for the pain as soon as I can. Here." He slid an arm beneath her shoulders. "Slide off easy. Your ice suit should keep you warm long enough for me to get things set up."

"Wil? How can you be so . . ." She gasped again as he eased her off the sled and onto the ice. "How can you act so . . . so matter-of-fact?"

"I'm not. Just give me some time, okay?" He yanked the main webbing off the sled, tossed it aside. He let himself sink into the familiar routines of setting up camp, inflating the tent, setting up his cookpad, dropping the filter's tube into the midnight sea. As he leaned over the water, a Milky Way of tiny golden stars whirled in slow motion deep within the blackness. Starfish. Way down. Briefly mesmerized, Qai watched the slow spiral of the thousands of distant creatures spinning out their lives in the warm, Europan sea. Then, without warning, they vanished.

Eaten. All at once. Qai shivered. The filter bottle was filling up. He pulled it out of the sea, tipped the liter of clear, drinkable water into his teakettle, and set it on the cookpad. Instantly the droplets of water on its outer surface sputtered into steam. While the water was heating from the focused microwave beam, he found his packet of dried rose moss, measured a generous pinch into his mug. Then he rose, scanning the soft walls and ceiling of the domed space in the purple-lavender glow of the moss.

"What are you doing, Wil?"

He flinched at his name. "I'm Qai now, all right? I'm looking for young purple moss. It stimulates healing . . . it's almost as good as enhanced healing in a hospital." He spied a magenta-purple tracery of a new growth, pulled his ice knife from its sheath and dug a palmful of delicate threads from the spongy ice. The kettle was boiling. He dumped the fresh moss on top of the powdered rose, poured steaming water into the mug, and watched the moss dissolve into a dull lavender liquid. He added a heaping spoon of precious sugar crystals, lifted all the way from the orbital platforms. Hesitated, than added another.

"I'm cold." Gert sucked in her breath as she sat up.

"I need to put a sling on your arm. You have tried moss before, right?" Although it was unlikely she was one of the rare homozygous allergics.

"Of course. Everyone has tried it at least once." She sounded defensive.

"Drink this." Qai knelt beside her with the steaming cup. "It'll make you stop hurting and it'll start the healing process."

She took the cup awkwardly with her left hand, her face paling as the broken collarbone ground. "Damn, it hurts." She sniffed the mug. "Smells like sulfur."

"Everything smells like sulfur here." He smiled in spite of himself because . . . she was Gerta. Still. "In case you hadn't noticed." And fresh moss tasted bad even to him after all his years here. "It's got some rose moss in it too. That blocks pain perception."

"Rose moss?" She blinked. "That's more precious than anything, on Earth. People take it to dream."

"Drink it."

She blinked at his tone, but sipped the brew. Made a considering face, but the heavy lacing with expensive

sugar worked. She lifted her good shoulder in a tiny shrug
and drank it all. Gagged a bit, swallowed hard, and took
a deep breath. "Why did you hit me?" She peered at him
over the rim of the mug, breathing too fast in spite of
the nano–red cells sucking oxygen out of the air in her
lungs.

"Because you ran in front of me, and in case you haven't
noticed, this is an ice world with minimal gravity." He
sighed. "I couldn't just slam on the brakes. Why did you run
in front of me?"

"To stop you." Her blue eyes narrowed.

Ice blue. That memory surfaced with the feel of a kick
to the gut. That's what he would have called the color of
her eyes. But ice had so many more colors. Now it seemed
simplistic, a child's word. But then . . . he had been a child.
"Why did you come here?"

"To find you." Tears finally gathered in the corners of
those blue eyes. "I didn't believe it. When they said you'd
stolen proprietary information, when they said you'd committed murder and sold out to a competing company. That
just isn't you!" Her voice dropped. "And I knew you weren't
dead. Even when they said you were."

Yeah, a part of him had known always that she could not
be fooled.

"What happened, Wil? Why did you come here?"

"Let's get into the tent." He eyed her critically. "You're
shivering and those tourist-weight ice suits aren't really
meant for living out here."

"Wil . . . Qai. This is such a trivial conversation." She
lifted her chin, her eyes already bright with the rose moss's
effect. "Just stop it. Tell me what really happened."

"I will." The weight of that promise settled like stone onto
his shoulders.

He turned his back on her, unsealing the tent and touching the heat to life. The embedded fibers would keep the
small, domed shelter a comfortable ten degrees Centigrade.
That would be too cold for her, he thought, remembering
back across the years to his first months on the ice, when he
never seemed to be warm, never seemed able to catch his

breath. He touched the illumination strip to life, leaving it muted, so that it filled the insulated space with a soft glow like yellow moss. Then he retrieved his med kit from the sled, along with an ice spike and mallet. On the way back to her, he detoured to the edge of the open water, hammering the spike into the ice and pulling his longline pouch from a suit pocket. Gouging a wad of purple moss from the ice, he molded it into a wad in his mouth, barely noticing the rich, sulfurous tang. The protein chains toughened and contracted as they reacted to his alkaline saliva, and he baited the three-pronged hook with the gumlike wad, dropping it into the lightless water.

The weights pulled it down and the bait vanished almost instantly as it sank into the rich world of life below the ice. He filtered more water, and put his little cookpot onto the heating mat to boil. Gerta was drowsing by the time he reached her side, her eyes glittering with moss dreams beneath half-closed eyelids. As he knelt beside her, she smiled at him, with a sleepy waking-up smile that wrenched him back across the years and wrung him with pain. He looked away for a moment, drew a deep breath. "I need to immobilize your arm." He let the breath out, putting her into the context of ice, cold, the heavy, sulfurous sea air. "It's going to hurt some."

"That's okay." She sat up, her lips tightening only a bit. "I can see why that stuff costs so much. Somebody said you can get addicted."

"I don't know." He smiled. "I've never tried to not use it." He touched the med kit's lid, selected "collarbone, simple fracture" from the extensive menu. The lid shimmered, projecting a holo of a woman applying a microfiber sling to a man's arm. He had remembered the procedure correctly. He found the wafer-thin packet of splint fabric in the kit and unfolded it. Wrapping it so that it supported her right arm, he touched the control disk, sending a tiny charge through the fibers so that they stiffened, becoming resilient enough to restrict movement of her arm without the rigidity he'd use for something like a broken leg. She caught her breath once or twice as he worked, but held still, her muscles relaxed. Even when he cleaned her cuts and scrapes with antiseptic, she didn't flinch. The scalp cut had stopped bleeding, at least. He sealed the cut closed with liquid skin.

Gert. Her name meant "warrior." And he smiled. It fit her so well. "Why don't you get into the tent." He resealed the med kit. "It's warm by now."

She got to her feet and crawled awkwardly into the tent. "Cozy." She sat cross-legged on the insulated floor, illuminated by the light strip's glow. "Batteries?" She looked around. "No solar power here, that's for sure." She giggled. "I feel drunk."

"You're not used to the moss, that's all. Here's some water." He put the filter bottle down beside her. "I'm going to go cook us some dinner." He frowned. "Did you get all your inoculations before you left the Ice Palace?"

"I did." She looked up at him. "So I can have dinner with you and the nano in my gut will inactivate all the nasty things that would give me the runs. I feel like I must be about half nano by now. This is so crazy." She laughed giddily. "I search for you for nearly a decade, finally find you, and we sit down and have dinner just as if we were camping out on the tundra. It's even just as cold." Her lips trembled. "Do you even have a reindeer stashed away? Do you remember Whiskers?"

"I. . . I do." He leaned forward suddenly, impelled by the weight of the past that wrung his soul, kissed her lightly on the forehead. Then he fled the tent, fled the memories that fluttered like shadowy bats.

Outside, the moist-sulfur scent of the sea banished the yesterday-bats and he pulled up his fish line. Luck smiled. A fat blue-slug squirmed mindlessly on the end of his line, the hooks embedded firmly in its thick, gelatinous flesh. Good thing Gerta couldn't see it, he thought as he sliced it free of the hook. The severed pieces squirmed on the ice, humping blindly across the pebbled surface with surprising speed. He scooped them up and dropped them into the boiling water. They disintegrated instantly and he added a handful of dried yellow moss, turning the simmering mess an off-green that he suspected would not appeal much to Gerta.

He tidied up the sled, covering it neatly with the cargo net, rebaited his hook, and dropped it back into the water with fresh moss bait. The blue-slug had already digested the original bait. Organisms on Europa were highly efficient at absorbing energy. Any energy. Finally, the slug stew was ready and he had run out of reasons to delay. He set the pot on the ice long enough to cool it to eating temperature, then carried it into the tent along with two spoons.

Gerta was sitting with her back against one wall, her head tilted back. He could see the passage of years in her face, like faint shadows. She was fifty now, ten years older than he. She straightened as he entered. Tears gleamed in the corners of her eyes, but she blinked them away silently as he set the pot on the floor. "I'm afraid it's not going to seem very tasty." He handed her his spare spoon. "I used to buy stuff like garlic essence, curry, spices like that, to sort of hide the taste when I first came here." He shrugged. "It costs a fortune to lift that stuff out here, though, and now the moss . . . tastes fine."

"Golden spoons." She turned it over in her hands, slid a finger along the edge of the wide bowl. "I saw it everywhere in the main port."

"It's sort of like fool's gold on Earth," he said lightly. "Sulfur and iron. Some of the sea life secrete it."

She didn't answer, merely dipped the spoon into the green sludge, lifted it to her lips and sipped at it. Made a face. Sighed, and dipped a full spoon, wincing a bit as she slurped it down. "Does *everything* smell like sulfur here?"

"Pretty much. It drives the energy web. The scientists think that oxygen is a latecomer. It's slowly changing the ecosystem, but it lets us live down here. At least at sea level."

"I don't know if I'd call this living." She drew a deep breath, shook her head. "I feel like I'm half suffocated, like I can't get enough air."

"Yeah, the oxygen content is pretty thin. Eventually, your

body gets used to it . . . you just grow a lot more red blood cells to help out the nano-cells." He scooped up stew, finding himself hungry, but then it had been a full ten-hour since he had eaten last. He had meant to eat with Karina. Closed his eyes briefly, praying to the faceless gods of infinity that his pursuers were too busy looking for him to bother with her.

"You always loved the winter ice." Gerta spoke dreamily, spooning up more stew. "Is that what brought you out here? Is that why you call yourself Qai?" She half smiled. "They call Europa the Snow Queen on the platforms, I found out. They told me she's a cold, evil queen, that she draws the scum of the solar system, that no law can touch anyone here."

"I'd say she draws the misfits and the renegades," Qai said lightly. "The ones that don't fit into the more organized societies. And believe me, we have rules here, even if they aren't laws."

Gerta put her spoon down and faced him, all moss-dream gone from her blue gaze in an instant. "What really happened, Wil? Did she steal your soul? This Snow Queen? Did a splinter of the mirror of evil enter your eye? And did you think I'd care?"

"You always loved that story." He fixed his eyes on his spoon. "Yes, that's why I chose Qai for a new name."

"World Council Security contacted me," she went on doggedly. "They told me that you stole registered experimental software, you killed someone to do it, they had a warrant for your arrest. They said you were hiding, would possibly contact me while you were waiting to sell it." Her voice trembled. "I wouldn't have turned you in. Didn't you *know* that?"

Sweating in his ice suit, Qai pulled the tunic off over his head, stripped off his gloves, and wriggled out of the overall bottoms. He tossed the wad of silken ice fabric aside and sat down cross-legged in his therms. "What are you doing now?" He spoke gently. "When you're not on Europa looking for me?"

"Me?" She blinked. "I've been head of the Education Committee for the World Council. For five years now."

"That was your dream." He smiled. "Congratulations."

"This isn't about me. Wil . . . what happened?"

He sighed again. "Did they show you a warrant? Of course they'd have one," he said as she nodded. "They weren't from the World Council." He lifted a hand as her brow furrowed. Smiled gently. "You can look like anything or anyone if you spend enough credit. You can have all the right credentials. Yes, a splinter of that fairy-tale mirror did get stuck in my eye, Gertrude." He shivered as he said her full name out loud. "I opened my eye and let them put it there. The software was experimental all right. It was clever nanoware. It turned me into a . . . a very efficient computer virus. A human one."

"That kind of nanoware is illegal."

"You're getting it." He nodded, smiling. "I realized what the information I was harvesting had to mean. And I decided . . ." He ran out of words. He wasn't a hero, wasn't a patriot. It just felt . . . wrong. Deeply wrong.

"Oh, my God." She was staring at him, the gold spoon bending in her white-knuckled clutch. "You were running? Wil!" It came out a cry of pain. "Why didn't you let me know? I would have helped you . . ."

He shook his head. "I took the nano voluntarily," he said harshly. "For very good pay, by the way. It's illegal to enter into that kind of transaction, Gerta. No excuses. I didn't want to spend the rest of my life with a supervision collar around my neck." And . . . it would have destroyed her dream of a Council committee chair. Because they had been lovers. The Council was very, very conservative about connections among its highest officers. It would have tainted her forever, her defense of him. "How did you find me?" He pressed the heels of his hands against his eyes, so that red and orange webbed the blackness behind his eyelids. "Nobody has a real name or history here."

"It was a postcard." She laughed, a short, harsh note. "A colleague of mine has a wayward son. And he bought a one-way to Europa. The ultimate act of rebellion." She laughed again. "Or maybe he has his own splinter of that evil mirror. But he sent her a holo clip of the Ice Palace.

She was showing it around, mad at him, sort of proud of him too, I think, for doing something, even if it was just to book transport out to the most godforsaken hole in the solar system. And as I was looking at the holo I saw . . . you." Her voice dropped to a whisper. "I recognized you in a second."

Officially, tourists were supposed to ask . . . read that: *pay* . . . for permission to record locals. Qai closed his eyes. But of course they didn't bother. And he hadn't noticed the holographer. That's partly why he avoided the Ice Palace, he thought bitterly. Because of the occasional tourists and their frenzy of recording. He was the epitome of the patched-and-scruffy Europa moss miner.

"How can you live here?" Gert hunched her shoulders. "I'm not claustrophobic but it gets to me . . . stuck down here under miles of ice. It's awful." She flicked the rim of the cookpot with one fingertip. "Everything stinks, there's no real light, is there? Just that weird glow. I'd go crazy."

"Yeah, you probably would." Qai pried the spoon from her hand, dropped it into the crusted pot along with his own. "You loved the tundra too." He smiled. "But it was the horizon you loved, as I recall."

"So what did you love?" One blond eyebrow rose.

"The quiet voice of the land." He ducked out of the tent, instantly cold in his therms, scooped seawater into the pot and left it for the voracious little microswimmers to scour clean. They'd have it spotless long before the water froze.

She was sitting up straight when he ducked, shivering, back inside. "How can you stand it out there in your underwear?"

"It's pretty warm underwear."

"You can come home." Her eyes blazed with triumph. "I have the power, Wil. I haven't been coasting, you know. I've built a very solid power base in the Council." She was speaking quickly now, her avalanche of logic designed to overwhelm any argument he might offer. It was so . . . *Gerta*. For the first time, tears clenched the back of his throat.

"Yes, you'll be punished, Wil, but I can arrange it so that you're under my official supervision. I have the pull. And that means you'll be under the World Council's authority, so you don't have to worry about any kind of retaliation from your employer, and—"

"Gerta . . . stop." He took her face between his hands, the heat of her skin scorching his palms as he leaned across the distance between them. Her fingers brushed his throat, and, with a small cry, she tugged the pendant from beneath his therms.

"The ammonite. The one I gave you for your birthday." Tears glimmered in her eyes as she took his face between her palms. Her breath smelled of Europa's sea, but her skin, as his lips closed on hers, tasted of Gerta. He groaned softly with memory as her mouth softened beneath his, their bodies melting together, the gulf of years and cold gone in a heartbeat, so that he smelled the cold tundra wind as he rolled onto her, careful of her splinted arm, his mouth and hands remembering yesterday as she arched beneath him. They drowsed after, and he pulled his ice suit over to cover her, curled around her to keep her warm in the air that was warm to him, too cold to her.

He lay on his side, his arm across her splinted arm lightly, remembering nights so long ago, the moss singing softly in his head, in his blood. Rose, purple, yellow, scarlet, he let the voices wash him away, into the ice, spreading his awareness through the veins of the Snow Queen so that he beat with the measure of her heart, breathed with her . . .

. . . woke to claws, started upright, head full of vague dreams of tundra grass.

"You scared me." Gerta let go of his hand, pulled his ice suit tunic around her shoulders. "You didn't wake up."

"Sorry," he mumbled, stretching. He faked a yawn, trying to calm her.

"Your eyes were . . . were white. Rolled clear back." She edged away from him. "I pinched you. Really hard. You didn't even twitch."

"I was just asleep." He smiled, but she retreated a few centimeters more. A vague burn on the back of his bare hand drew his eye. Two tiny red crescents seeped blood. "You pinched hard," he said dryly. "We need to go."

"Go where?" She pulled farther away, good arm folded protectively across her chest. "It was like you were dead. What was that?"

Qai closed his eyes briefly. "Let me tell you about the moss." He opened his eyes, gave her a lopsided smile. "Jupiter's magnetic field here changes direction every five and a half hours. That creates some . . . interesting effects. Mostly it affects the oceans—that's how the original explorers guessed that Europa had water under the surface. The pole changes position every time the field changes." He smiled grimly at her. "But it affects every living creature on the planet too. Most especially . . . the moss."

"The moss?" She looked at him uncertainly.

"Moss is an Earth term." He shrugged. "Because it's fuzzy-looking, I guess." He smiled. "Although I think all Earth moss is green. The stuff here isn't moss." He studied her blue, warrior eyes, so appropriate to her name. "Think of the moss as neurons," he said evenly.

That took a couple of seconds to sink in and then her eyes widened. "But . . ."

"Oh, it's more plant than animal, although I don't think either really apply to Europan life." He laughed softly, although he felt bleak inside. "But yeah, they're like neurons." He waited for her to catch up.

"But it's everywhere . . . the ice." She waved vaguely at the walls of the tent. "So you're saying . . . the planet . . . thinks?"

"Oh, no," he said. "But the moss is aware. And . . . I can hear it sing. Well, that doesn't really describe it . . . it's not a sound." He sighed. "I don't think we have a word for it." He closed his eyes briefly, wanting with a visceral ache to *show* her, to share it with her, that wordless *awareness,* that immensity, that vast, enormous sense of boundless *time*. He opened his eyes and tried to smile. "I think the software I'm carrying does it . . . nobody else I know has ever said that they're aware of the moss voice. It's . . . beautiful." He shook his head, frustrated. The words didn't exist to describe it, she wasn't going to understand, and there wasn't time.

"I can use it," he said crisply. "I can become aware of what's in the ice around me. And we've been followed." He began to pull on his ice suit as he spoke. "I suspect they managed to chip you somehow. They must have decided that I had contacted you or that you are simply a better guesser than they are." He pulled his ice boots on. "We need to start running, Gerta. I don't think they'll let you live if I leave you behind. Even if I hadn't told you, they'd worry that I had."

"You're talking about the corporation that manufactured the nanoware." Gerta's eyes widened with comprehension.

"That's why I brought you out here instead of to the Ice Palace and the hospital. One of them was right behind me." Dressed, he unsealed the tent, letting in a chill breath of sea. "We can't really lose him, but if I can get you back to the Ice Palace, you can check into the tourist hostel there and take the next transport downside. If you're careful, you can avoid them. Just make sure you're always in a very public place and don't let strangers get close to you." He did a quick mental calculation as he slid through the tent opening. "The next transport stops here day after tomorrow. After that, I don't think another one is scheduled for three tendays. Getting you there in time will be cutting it close, but I think we can do it if most of the naturals I know are still open." He slithered backward through the opening of the tent before she could voice the protest rising in her eyes.

Outside, he pulled up his handline, released the purple and orange slug that had digested the bait, and coiled up the line, stowing it and the polished-clean cookpot on the sled. Gerta was crawling out of the tent, awkward with her bad shoulder.

"You're coming back to Earth with me." Still on her hands and knees, she looked up at him with those warrior eyes. "I wasn't kidding when I said I could fix things. It won't hurt my career, Wil, and I won't leave you here in this frozen hell."

"I really wish you'd call me Qai. Touch that red spot on the tent, will you? That deflates it." He skidded the board into position in front of the sled. "We're going to have to run high. The upper ice shifts all the time and maps are pretty useless. And the oxygen pressure is low." He hesitated. "You're going to be pretty uncomfortable, but so will our shadow, if he's not native."

"Don't worry about me," Gerta said grimly.

The tent had finished deflating. He folded it, slipped it into its case, and webbed the load down on the sled. "Here." He handed her an energy bar from his emergency rations. "It should taste a little better than the stew last night, anyway."

"It doesn't," she mumbled with her mouth full.

He took the time to filter his bottles full although the back of his neck tingled with threat. The stranger's presence he'd detected while he was listening to the moss had been huge and loud. Translate that as "close." But they wouldn't have time to stop and melt ice to filter for drinking while they were running.

"I can't believe I'm carrying a chip." She finished the last bites of the bar. "How could someone do that?"

"Oh, it's easy. You probably ate something. Toss the wrapper into the water."

"Littering?"

"Feeding. Watch."

She tossed the crumbled wrapper into the dark water. The surface erupted instantly, boiling like water in a cookpot. The wrapper seemed to melt away in moments, like a flake of ice on a cookpad.

"What happened?" She stared at the now-smooth water.

"Think of that ocean as one huge appetite." He cinched the webbing down tight. "Let's go."

"What if we fall in?"

"Just don't." He stepped onto his board. "Stand behind me and put your arms around my waist. Remember when we used to ride your Uncle Tor's big old Clydesdale? Remember how we had to kind of be the same body or we pulled each other off? Just do that. If we start going fast, close your eyes.

You'll flinch as things rush at you and we might go over. Boards are very responsive."

"Okay." Stress tightened her voice. "Let's hope you're wrong about all this."

Qai kicked the board into start mode. It surged slowly forward as the sled energized, lifting smoothly. He banked into a long curve along the end of the upwell. Their pursuer was behind them. Qai studied the melt-polished walls, searching for a good-sized natural leading up. He spied a likely one, a little narrow for a board towing a sled . . . just as something smacked into the ice wall beside them. Grains of ice stung his face and he caught a glimpse of orange as he heeled the board hard into the natural. Bless Gerta, she had melted to him, her balance shifting with his so that the board didn't even wobble. No more time to be picky. He toed the speed up, leaning forward to counter the nose's rise as the sled dragged at it, praying that this was a good choice as they shot through the blue-green dusk of the moss-lined crevice.

"What happened?" Gerta shouted over the rush of their passage.

"Dart." He leaned into a branch as the natural forked, heading antispinward, toward the Ice Palace. The sled touched the wall and the board shied. For a moment their balance hung by a thread, then he caught it, Gerta balancing flawlessly with him, and they sped down the narrow natural in near-darkness now, because this was a new opening and the first traceries of blue-green moss had barely established.

"It's dark," she yelled.

"Can't risk the floods." He leaned forward, squinting to make out the path of the natural, watching for fractures, for fallen chunks of ice. New naturals like this could be unstable, could shift and close in an instant. "These cracks channel light for hundreds of meters. We hope he takes the wrong branch. Hang on." He kicked the board into a hard brake, the towline slackening for an instant before the sled braked. Got to tell Karina that his synchro was off, he thought as the board kissed the wall of the new branch, the sled hitting it harder. The board slewed wildly and he fought for control as the side-to-side sway slowly damped out. Behind them, ice dust drifted in the blue-green twilight, the heavier particles dropping in slow motion to the floor. Damn. Talk about leaving a sign. A fairly wide natural opened on the left, new enough that no moss yet illuminated the narrow gap. A desperate choice, but hopefully their pursuer would think he was desperate. He slewed the board so that the sled caught the far edge of the opening. More ice exploded from the wall, drifting like a thin veil where the side branch met the main natural.

Perfect. He strained his eyes in the near-darkness. If he was lucky . . . if another leftward branch opened.

It did, not a dozen meters farther down the natural they were traveling. Qai slowed the board this time, eased the sled into the new corridor, so narrow here that they had less than a half meter of clearance on either side of the board. This was an older rift. Traceries of blue-green moss laced the walls, providing just enough light to spot any ice falls ahead. He sped up, blessing their luck.

"What are we doing?" Gerta murmured in his ear.

"He'll see the dust drifting and think we took the last natural." Qai hoped. "If he's scanning you, we're heading in about the same direction as that natural so he may be fooled into taking it." That would give them more time to get lost in the maze of cracks and crevices up here. By the time he backed out of the decoy and found the right natural, they would have had time to make a lot of turns and he'd have a much harder time tracking them.

They were moving fast again, now, and the natural was leading surfaceward. He felt Gerta's shuddering breaths but there was nothing he could do about the air except hope the natural led back down before she passed out. Even he was breathing faster. Qai kept his eyes fixed on the dim limit of visibility, watching for a fall of ice that might block the path. So far so good. They passed another natural, wide enough for the sled. Again, Qai slowed and veered just enough to catch the edge of the opening a glancing blow, this time with the board. Gerta clung to him as it skidded sideways. Behind them, more ice chips swirled in the disturbed air of their passage.

If he knew ice, Qai thought, their pursuer would stop to read the pattern of the settled dust and he'd know they'd cruised on by. If he was a hired assassin, brought to the Queen for this job, he wouldn't know to do that. "Hang on," he murmured and toed the board up to speed. "Next opening to the right we take," he said.

The natural straightened and widened. The younger rift must have caught the tip of this older natural and now they were getting into the main run. The moss thickened, streaked with yellow and pink species so that the light brightened. Qai toed more speed and leaned forward, Gerta moving with him as if they had merged into a single body. They were going to make it, he thought exultantly. He could put a lot of distance between them while their pursuer stopped to check side branches for traces of their passage. They'd have time to get back to the Ice Palace ahead of him.

A wide opening yawned on the left, a new run, the walls where it had broken into this older crevice fractured and buckled. Shards of ice tumbled out across the main crevice and only a few thin patches of moss offered feeble light.

In the depths of that darkness . . . something moved.

Qai looked, the board rocking, nearly losing his balance. Sudden light flared, blinding him. A board's front flood. He wrenched himself straight on the board, stomped it up to top speed. "Hang on," he yelled, his stomach knotting.

So much for luck. Their pursuer had taken the bait, but the decoy natural had connected up to this one. What were the chances? He tasted bile, bent forward, the board rocking with its speed, his eyes fixed on the dim edge of vision. An ice fall coming up. Low enough to get over but . . . "Hang on tight!" He held his breath, watching the tumble of dirty ice speeding toward them . . . twenty meters . . . ten . . . Now! He stomped the nose of the board down, felt Gerta's weight pushing him, then kicked the heel down, leaning forward desperately as the nose leaped up, palm slapping it to keep it from flipping over, cutting the towline loose at the same time. Freed of the sled's drag, the board bucked and he nearly went off, felt Gerta catch her balance, steady him. Then he had his balance back again, slowed, and sneaked a look back.

Miraculously, he had timed it just right. The towline had yanked the sled's nose down and then up just before he cut it loose. It hit the top of the natural and rebounded wildly. Light flashed across the gleaming walls of ice as it either hit their pursuer or he tried to avoid it and hit the ice fall.

He skidded into the next opening they passed, no time to worry about finesse now. Now it was a matter of luck again, and speed. He toed the board's flood, no point in worrying about giving himself away now. All they could do was *go*. Ahead, the natural angled off to the right. Qai fought the board into a hard bank, struggling to stay aboard as it bucked across fragments of shattered ice. Fresh, a part of his mind noticed as they arced into the branch. Ice walls flew past and suddenly... vanished. Utter darkness swallowed the flood beam and Qai caught a gleam of distant ice. Then they were falling.

A cavern. They had burst out into the open space above an upwell. If they landed in the sea... Gerta screamed, her arms locked around him as they fell. Desperately, Qai toed the board to full power. It wouldn't hold them above water, but with luck, if their angle of descent was shallow enough, they might skip across the surface for a few dozen meters.

If the angle was too steep...

The board slammed upward against the soles of his feet and the flood splashed across distant walls of shimmering ice, crusted with flowers of frozen condensation. Wisps of vapor swirled around them. They kept their balance... barely. The board slammed the surface again and water sprayed up this time. The wall loomed closer. Close enough. Another slam and Gerta's balance faltered. Another. She was falling... they were falling... The board flipped and Qai released the toeholds, bracing himself for the shock of icy sea, his mind a black wail of despair.

His shoulder hit ice and he tucked his head without thought, rolling, then flinging out arms and legs to stop his momentum. Slid to rest on his face in darkness, the metallic taste of blood in his mouth, his face burning where he had scraped the ice. "Gerta?" He spat out ice. "Gerta!" The flood had gone out, but the faint glimmer from a thin tracery of yellow and orange moss allowed him to make out the walls of the cavern rising up from the narrow shelf they had crashed on.

Luck. He drew in a shuddering breath. The board had almost slowed enough to drop into the water. "Gerta?"

A soft moan came from his left and Qai sagged with relief. He started to crawl toward the sound, the pocket suddenly turning as pain lanced through his left side. He'd broken something... his left shoulder, felt like. His eyes were adjusting to the moss glow and he spotted her, half a dozen meters from where he'd landed, sprawled facedown less than a meter from the water. He fumbled his headlamp from his ice suit pocket, slipped it on. The soft wash of light from the small flood turned the blood on her face crimson. Ice crusted her hair and her hood had come loose. The cut on her forehead had reopened. He brushed the ice out of her hair with his good hand and wiped the blood from her face with an antiseptic cloth from the tiny emergency aid pack in his suit. Her eyelids fluttered and she groaned.

"We made it." Relief flooded him as her blue eyes focused on his face. Pupils the same size, so no head injury... not a serious one anyway. "Try moving," he murmured.

"I think..." She sucked in a breath and winced. "I don't think anything new got broken." She eased herself into a sitting position. "What happened to your arm?"

"My shoulder." The med kit was back on the sled. He looked up to where the soft glow of the moss vanished into darkness. "This is a young cavern," he murmured.

"How can you tell?"

"Look how sharp all the edges are, and how narrow and steep it is." He tilted his head and the lamp's weak beam faded into the deep darkness above them. "Yellow and orange moss are the first ones to grow in a new cavern and there's hardly any here. No blue-green at all, so this is really new."

"Is that a problem?" She tilted her head at him.

"Not compared to others." He didn't laugh because it would hurt. Slabs and shards of fractured ice lay in piles at the base of the cavern wall, and in many places, the black water lapped sheer, vertical surfaces. Qai shivered at how lucky they had been. Only a few narrow sections of fractured ice shelved the open water. A slightly different trajectory would have dumped them into the water. He swung the lamp's beam around their narrow sanctuary, spotted the board, upended against the wall. "If we can find a natural and get out of here, we might be okay."

"Might." Gerta's voice was dry. "I don't like that word."

Qai lurched to his feet and made his way over to the board. It had shut itself down and he said a small prayer to the Snow Queen's icy heart as he touched the power on. They wouldn't make it back to the Ice Palace on foot without the supplies on the sled. The board hummed to life and relief nearly buckled his knees. "I'll upgrade that 'might' a bit." He shut the board off, frowning. "Be quiet. Come over here. Quick." He illuminated the ice at her feet as she crossed the narrow shelf. "Help me hide the board. Try not to make any sound," he murmured.

"What's wrong?"

"He followed us." The sled trick had slowed him down but that was all.

Between them, one-armed, they managed it, piling chunks and thin fracture-slabs of ice to mask the board. It wouldn't fool a moss miner, Qai thought grimly, but their hunter's choice of the decoy fissure suggested that he wasn't a moss miner.

The moss sang a song of motion that hummed through his flesh as the man and board slid toward them through the ice. The sled trick had had the unintended effect of saving their pursuer from making the same mistake they had and plunging over the lip of the natural. It made him wary. Qai felt his caution through the moss as he slid to the brink of the natural they'd blasted over.

Their luck was still bad.

He stood on the lip of the natural, a shadowy figure barely discernible in the dim moss glow. "I see you." His voice came to them, warped by the ice walls. "You have no options. Step out and I'll make it a clean kill." He paused. "Make me chase you down and it will not be an easy passage, Wilmar."

"If you let her go . . ." Qai winced as she dug her nails into his arm. "I will."

Ice sprayed their faces and Qai rolled away from it, dragging her with him.

Qai scanned the pocket, looking for a safe pathway down to their level, hoping it didn't exist. But it did. Yeah, you could just make it from fracture to fracture; enough ice shelf jutted out to support a board's impeller field. A local would be wary. Even as he looked, their pursuer slid over the lip of the natural and started down, as if he had tracked Qai's stare. He wasn't a local, wasn't wary at all.

Desperately, Qai looked for another hiding place. But the bottom of the pocket was made up of sheer walls and a few ice falls . . . no crevices or narrow naturals to shelter them. Their pursuer had some sort of scanner.

"This is the end, isn't it?" Gerta's face looked waxen in the feeble moss light. "There's no way out, is there?"

He couldn't lie to her, say the false, brave words that the assassin would turn into dust in moments. The assassin skimmed across the final ledge of ice, skipped over a narrow expanse of open water . . . and was on the ledge. He skimmed toward them slowly, his face goggled and invisible within the hood of his ice suit. "I wonder what you did." His voice echoed from the sheer walls. "They're paying me enough. It must have been good. Or you pissed off the wrong person." His goggles tracked them as he glided by, pivoted his board at the far end of the shelf.

Beside him, Gerta's panting breaths emerged in brief puffs of vapor. "I'm sorry," he said softly.

"I brought him here, didn't I?" Gerta kept her eyes fixed

on the ice-suited figure as he drifted his board across the ledge.

"You didn't know." The assassin had turned at the end of the shelf. Yeah, an amateur on a board. He made it move okay, but without the fluid economy of someone who knew what he was doing.

"Final offer on the easy way out." The assassin raised his voice. "The darts are loaded with a neurotranc. It'll leave you paralyzed but conscious." A razored edge of anticipation colored his tone. "I can enjoy my work. Your choice." He toed the board around, aimed straight at them.

Without warning, Gerta leaped into motion.

"No," Qai yelled, grabbing at her. He missed, his gloved fingers scraping her suit.

She charged toward the board and the assassin slewed it only slightly, aiming his weapon almost casually. Qai didn't hear a sound, but Gerta stumbled and lost her footing. Her body tumbled almost in slow motion, sliding finally to rest in a spray of ice crystals.

The assassin hovered his board above her limp body, checking. Then he slewed his board around clumsily and toed it straight at Qai. He leaned forward, assurance etched in every line of his body. Qai jerked his head from side to side, pantomiming panic, turned, and crouched as if in a desperate attempt to hide. He could almost feel the assassin's triumph as the board hummed into maximum speed.

Show-off, Qai thought. He twisted into a spin, the flat plaque of ice he'd selected gripped in both hands. With all the strength in his muscles, he unwound, skimming the plaque on a straight, flat trajectory at the onrushing board. One chance. His feet came off the ground with the force of his throw and he skidded to his knees, his eyes glued on the board.

It flew ruler-straight, dead-on at the nose of the board. A local would have simply ducked it. The assassin ignored it. As the plaque intercepted the impeller field, the board bucked. Caught by surprise, the assassin lost his balance briefly and the board slewed out of control as he overreacted. It bucked again and then nosed straight up. With a cry, the assassin grabbed wildly for the edges, his foot slipping out of the shoe. The board flipped and he fell.

Qai raced toward him, pulling his ice knife from his suit. Before he could reach the assassin, the man skidded across the condensation-slick shelf and splashed into Europa's black sea. He surfaced at once, screaming, grabbing the ledge, then letting go to claw at his exposed face. And sank.

Qai turned away, shuddering at the sounds erupting behind him. If the man was lucky, one of the big eaters would take him quickly.

Gerta lay still and limp on the ice, her breathing light and regular, her muscles slack. Out cold. Qai stood over her for a moment, a tide of memory washing through him. Sun. Tundra grass and reindeer. Making love on a soft-tanned skin on the tangled grass with the scent of northern summer and Gerta's skin dizzying him. Tears stung his eyes. When had he last wept?

He couldn't remember.

She was right. The Snow Queen had frozen him.

He coupled the assassin's board behind his, and lashed Gerta to it one-handed. It only took a few hours to reach the Ice Palace. Karina helped him without question. She put Gerta to bed in her own bed at the back of her shop and steeped the fresh rose moss he had stopped to gather into a potent tea. "I hope she's worth this small fortune, ice-boy." She stood on tiptoes to kiss him lightly on the lips. Her dark eyes searched his. "You going to tell me the truth, one day?"

"Not here."

Karina raised one eyebrow. "Where then?" When he didn't answer, she laughed, a rich sound that always warmed him in a way mere heat could never do and handed him the pot of potent rose-moss tea.

He took it in to where Gerta slept. She was coming out of the drugs. Her eyelids shivered with REM sleep, and as he dripped the tea between her lips, she swallowed reflexively.

He fed her tea until her breathing deepened and slowed and her skin showed the telltale flush of deep rose-moss euphoria. When he judged the dose to be high enough, he set the pot aside and gently arranged her on her side, the way she had always slept when they'd shared a bed, her right arm tucked beneath the pillow, top knee bent, snuggled deep into the covers. He combed her hair back, a bittersweet tide rising in his chest. "Don't you remember?" he murmured. "How we always argued about that story, how I always wondered if Kai maybe hadn't wanted to stay, if the Gert in the story really had been right to drag him home?" He smiled, touched her cheek with one fingertip. "You were so sure she did the right thing. But I fell in love with the Snow Queen, Gerta. I'm sorry. You were wrong about the mirror. It was evil, yes. But that splinter let me see the Snow Queen's beauty. I belong to her, now." He pulled the covers up over her shoulder and tucked her in tenderly.

Karina was waiting for him in her shop, her eyes bright with questions. But she said nothing, merely kissed him again, and this time it wasn't light and it wasn't brief, and the pain from his broken shoulder vanished entirely. "What if I taught you to mine moss?" he breathed as the kiss ended.

"I think I might like that." Karina's white teeth blazed in the dim light of her shop. "I've thought I might like that for a while, ice-boy, but I figured you had to do the offering. Your lover, the Snow Queen, let you go finally?"

"No." He wouldn't lie to her. "But that doesn't mean I can't love you too." He kissed her again, pushed her gently away. Then he reached into the open neck of his therms and pulled out the tiny stone memorial of a creature that had lived on another planet, so many millennia ago. He slipped the braided chain over his head. "Tell her you took it off as a memento. Just before you pushed my body into the sea. With as much moss as I fed her, she's going to believe anything you tell her, and if you tell her just as she's waking up, she'll remember seeing it herself." And she would grieve, but the people who wanted his death would listen for her belief and her grief and hear it. Karina would be safe until she got out into the ice.

"Get yourself set up and start out looking for moss." He ran his fingers lightly over her light-braided hair. "I'll meet you."

"How will you know when I leave?" Karina tilted her head. "How will you find me?"

"The Snow Queen will tell me. She's not a jealous lover." He kissed her one last time and left, slipping out of the shop and into the soft glow of the corridor, heading for Cass, the board seller, to trade the rest of the rose moss he'd gathered for a new outfit. Then he'd visit the healer, get his shoulder taken care of. He could heal out in the ice, waiting for Karina. "Thank you, Gerta," he murmured. "For letting me see what I needed to see."

Beyond the bright and artificial light of the Ice Palace, the moss sang to his blood, and his blood answered.

REMEMBRANCE

STEPHEN BAXTER

Like many of his colleagues here at the beginning of a new century, British writer Stephen Baxter has been engaged for more than a decade now with the task of revitalizing and reinventing the "hard-science" story for a new generation of readers, producing work on the cutting edge of science which bristles with weird new ideas and often takes place against vistas of almost outrageously cosmic scope.

Baxter made his first sale to *Interzone* in 1987, and since then has become one of that magazine's most frequent contributors, as well as making sales to *Asimov's Science Fiction, Science Fiction Age, Analog, Zenith, New Worlds,* and elsewhere. He's one of the most prolific new writers in science fiction, and is rapidly becoming one of the most popular and acclaimed of them as well. In 2001, he appeared on the Final Hugo Ballot twice, and won both *Asimov's* Readers Award and *Analog's* Analytical Laboratory Award, one of the few writers ever to win both awards in the same year. Baxter's first novel, *Raft,* was released in 1991 to wide and enthusiastic response, and was rapidly followed by other well-received novels such as *Timelike Infinity, Anti-Ice, Flux,* and the H. G. Wells pastiche—a sequel to *The Time Machine*—

The Time Ships, which won both the John W. Campbell Memorial Award and the Philip K. Dick Award. His other books include the novels *Voyage, Titan, Moonseed, Mammoth, Book One: Silverhair, Manifold: Time, Manifold: Space, Evolution, Coalescent, Exultant, Transcendent*, and two novels in collaboration with Arthur C. Clarke, *The Light of Other Days* and *Time's Eye, a Time Odyssey*. His short fiction has been collected in *Vacuum Diagrams: Stories of the Xeelee Sequence, Traces, and Hunters of Pangaea*, and he has released a chapbook novella, *Mayflower II*. His most recent books are the novels *Emperor* and *Resplendent*, and coming up is another new novel, *Conqueror*.

Baxter's Xeelee series is one of the most complex sequences in Space Opera, spanning millions of years of time as well as most of the galaxy, and bringing humans into contact (usually hostile contact) with dozens of alien races. Here, in a story that takes place early in the sequence, he points out that while it may be true that those who forget the past are doomed to repeat it, you can't remember the past if you're not *allowed* to remember it . . .

"I am the Rememberer," said the old man. "The last in a line centuries long. This is what was passed on to me, by those who remembered before me.

"Harry Gage was on Earth when the Squeem came . . ."

As he talked, Rhoda Voynet glanced around at her staff. Soldiers all, the planes of their faces bathed in golden Saturn light, they listened silently.

The old man was a Virtual, projected from a police station on Earth, and the sunlight that shone on his face was much stronger than the diminished glow that reached this far orbit. Rhoda felt obscurely jealous of its warmth.

"Harry was born on Mars, in the Cydonia arcology. His great-grandparents were from Earth. There was a lot of that, in those days, before the Squeem. Everybody was mobile. Everything was opened up. Anything was possible.

"Harry's parents brought him to Earth, a once-in-a-lifetime trip to meet great-grandma and grandpa. He never did get to see them."

It had been the year 4874, nearly two centuries past. Harry Gage was ten years old.

And Earth was about to be conquered.

The flitter bearing Harry Gage and his parents had tumbled out of the shimmering throat of the wormhole transit route from Mars to Earthport.

Harry peered out of the cramped cabin, looking for Earth. Mum sat beside him, a bookslate on her lap, and Dad sat opposite, grinning at Harry's reaction. Harry would always remember these moments well.

Earthport was at one of the five gravitationally stable Lagrange points in the Earth-Moon system, leading the Moon in its orbit around Earth by sixty degrees. The flitter surged unhesitatingly through swarming traffic. From here, Earth was a swollen blue disk. Wormhole gates of all sizes drifted across the face of the planet, electric-blue sculptures of exotic negative-energy matter.

The final hop to Earth itself took only a few hours. Soon the old planet, pregnant and green, was approaching, as if surfacing. Huge fusion stations, constructed from ice moons, sparkled in orbit above green-blue oceans. The planet itself was laced with lights, on land and sea. In the thin rim of atmosphere near the north pole, Harry could just make out the dull purple glow of an immense radiator beam, a diffuse refrigerating laser dumping a fraction of Earth's waste heat into the endless sink of space.

Earth was visibly stable, healthy, recovered from the climate-collapse horrors of the past, and managed by a confident mankind.

"Harry's flitter landed in New York," the Rememberer said. "A spaceship coming down in the middle of Manhattan. Imagine that!"

Harry and his parents emerged onto grass, a park, in the sunshine of a New York spring. Harry could see the shoulders of tall, very ancient skyscrapers at the rim of the park, interlaced by darting flitters.

Dad raised his face to the sun and breathed deeply. "Mmm. Cherry blossom and freshly cut grass. I love that smell."

Mum snortcd. "We have cherry trees on Mars."

"Every human is allowed to be sentimental about a spring day in New York. It's our birthright. Look at those clouds, Harry. Aren't they beautiful?"

Harry looked up. The sky was laced by high, fluffy, dark clouds, fat with water, unlike any on Mars. And beyond the clouds he saw crawling points of light: the habitats and factories of near-Earth space. Harry was thrilled to the core.

But Mum closed her eyes. She was used to the pyramids and caverns of Mars, and could not believe that a thin layer of blue air could protect her from the rigors of space.

And as Harry peered up, he saw a line of light cut across the sky, scratched by a spark bright enough to cast faint shadows, even in the sunlight.

New Yorkers looked up, faintly concerned. This wasn't normal, then.

"It was the first strike of the Squeem," the Rememberer said. "Harry never forgot that moment. Well, you wouldn't, would you? It shaped his whole life."

Rhoda and her soldiers listened, trying to understand, trying to decide whether to believe him. Trying to decide what to do about it.

While the old man rested, Rhoda let her staff resume other duties, but summoned Reg Kaser, her first officer.

In her cabin, she powered up her percolator, her one indulgence from her Iowa home. While it chugged and slurped and filled the cabin with sharp coffee scents, she faced her big picture window.

The *Jones* was a UN Navy corvette. It was locked in a languid orbit around Rhea, second largest moon of Saturn. In fact, the *Jones* wasn't far from home; its home base was on Enceladus, another of Saturn's moons.

Rhea itself was unprepossessing, just another ball of dirty ice. But beyond it lay Saturn, where huge storms raged across an autumnal cloudscape, and the rings arched like gaudy artifacts, unreasonably sharp. The Saturn system was like a ponderous ballet, beautiful, peaceful, illuminated by distance-dimmed sunlight, and Rhoda could have watched it forever.

But it was Rhea she had come for. Within its icy carcass were pockets of salty water, kept liquid by the tidal kneading of Saturn and the other moons. That wasn't so special; there were similar buried lakes on many of Sol system's icy moons, even Enceladus.

But within Rhea's deep lakes had been discovered colonies of Squeem, the aquatic group-mind organisms that had, for a few decades, ruled over a conquered mankind, and even occupied Earth itself. The *Jones* was named for the hero who had crucially gained an advantage over the Squeem, a bit of bravery and ingenuity which had ultimately led to the Squeem's expulsion from Sol system—or so everybody had thought, until this relic colony had been discovered. The xenologists were already talking to these stranded Squeem, using antique occupation-era translation devices.

It was Rhoda's task to decide what to do with them. She could have them preserved, even brought back to Earth.

Or she could make sure that every last Squeem in Rhea died. She even had the authority to destroy the whole moon, if she chose, to make sure. She was promised the firepower. Weapons were Reg Kaser's department, and there were a lot of black projects around.

It was a hard decision to make.

And now she had the complication of this old man, the self-styled "Rememberer," and his antique saga of the occupation, which he insisted had to be heard before any decision was made about the Squeem on Rhea.

First Officer Reg Kaser waited silently as she gathered her thoughts.

They were contrasting types. Rhoda Voynet, forty years old, came from an academic background; she had trained as a historian of the occupation before joining the service. Kaser, fifty, scarred, one leg prosthetic, and with a thick Mercury-mine accent, was a career soldier. He had taken part in the counterinvasion a decade ago, when human ships, powered by hyperdrive purloined from the Squeem themselves, had at last assaulted the Squeem's own home-world.

They worked well together, their backgrounds and skills complementary. Kaser had learned to be patient while Rhoda thought things through. And she had learned to appreciate his decisiveness, hardened in battle.

"Tell me what we know of this old man," she said.

Kaser checked over a slate. "His name is Karl Hume. Born and raised on Earth. Seventy-four years old. He's spent his life working for the UN Restoration Agency. Literature section."

Rhoda understood the work well enough. Much of the material she had drawn on in her own research had come from the Restoration's reassembling. The Squeem were traders, not ideological conquerors, but in their exploitation they had carelessly done huge damage to mankind's cultural heritage. A hundred and fifty years after their expulsion, the Restoration was still patiently piecing together lost libraries, recovering works of art, even rebuilding shattered cities brick by brick, like New York, where young Harry Gage had watched the sky fall.

"Hume was a drone," Kaser said, uncompromising. "His work was patient, thorough, reliable, but he had no specific talent, and he didn't climb the ladder. He held down a job, all his life. But nobody missed him when he retired. He had a family of his own. Wife now dead, kids off-Earth. He never troubled the authorities, not so much as a dodgy tax payment."

"Until he tried to abduct a kid."

"Quite."

The boy, called Lonnie Tekinene, was another New Yorker, ten years old—the same age as Harry Gage, Rhoda noted absently, when he had witnessed the Squeem invasion. Hume had made contact with the kid through a Virtual play-world, and had met him physically in Central Park, and had tried to take him off to Hume's apartment. Alert parents had put a stop to that.

As Hume had been processed through the legal system, he had become aware of the discovery of the pocket of

Squeem on Rhea, moon of Saturn, and the deliberation going on within the UN and its military arm as to what to do about it.

Kaser said, "Hume didn't harm a hair of the kid's head. At first, he just denied everything. But when he heard about Rhea, he opened up. He said it was just that his 'time' had come. He was the 'Rememberer' of his generation. But he was growing old. He needed to recruit another to take his place—just as he was recruited in his turn by some other old fossil when *he* was ten."

"He never explained why he chose this kid, this Lonnie. What criteria he used."

Kaser shrugged. "On the other hand, looking at the police files, I don't think anybody asked. Hume was just a nut, to them. A sexual deviant, maybe."

Rhoda said, "And he insisted we have to hear what he has to say. Some truth about the Squeem occupation, preserved only in his head, that will shape our decision."

"But we know all about the occupation," Kaser said. "It was a systemwide event. It affected all of mankind. What 'truth' can this old fool have, locked up in his head, and available nowhere else?"

"What truth so hideous," Rhoda wondered, "that it could *only* be lodged in one man's head? What do you think we should do?"

Kaser shrugged. "Assess the Squeem colony on its own merits. Maybe they're just stranded, left behind in the evacuation. Or this may be a monitoring station of some kind, spying on a system they lost. Maybe it even predates the occupation, a forward base to gather intelligence to run the invasion. Either way, it needs to be shut down."

"But the Squeem themselves don't necessarily need to be eliminated."

"True."

"You think I should just ignore the old man, don't you?"

He grinned, tolerant. "Yes. But you won't. You're an obsessive fact-gatherer. Well, we have time. The Squeem aren't going anywhere." He stood up. "I'll see if the old guy has finished his nap."

Karl Hume, bathed in strong Earth sunlight, spoke of memories passed down through a chain of Rememberers: the memories of ten-year-old Harry Gage.

Before the invasion, humans had diffused out through Sol system and beyond in their bulky, ponderous, slower-than-light GUTships. It was a time of optimism, of hope, of expansion into an unlimited future.

Then the first extrasolar intelligence was encountered, somewhere among the stars.

Only a few years after first contact, Squeem ships burst into Sol system, in a shower of exotic particles and lurid publicity. The Squeem were aquatic group-mind multiple creatures. They crossed the stars using a hyperdrive system beyond human understanding. They maintained an interstellar network of trading colonies. Their human label, a not very respectful rendering of the Squeem's own sonic rendering of their title for themselves— *"Ss-chh-eemnh"*— meant something like the Wise Folk, rather like *"Homo sapiens."*

Communication with the Squeem was utterly unlike anything envisaged before their arrival. The Squeem didn't count in whole numbers, for instance. But eventually, common ground was found. And despite fears that mankind might be overwhelmed by a more technically advanced civilization, trade and cultural contacts were initiated.

Then, in orbit around every inhabited world and moon in Sol system, hyperdrive cannon platforms appeared.

And on Earth, rocks began to fall.

"They came in too fast for the planet's impactor defenses to cope with," the Rememberer whispered. "Rocks from Sol system's own belts of asteroids and comets, sent in at faster than interplanetary speeds. Obviously it was the Squeem's doing.

"And they were targeted.

"Harry and his family, stranded on Earth, got an hour's warning of the Manhattan bolide. Harry's father knew New York. He got Harry off the island through the ancient Queens-Midtown Tunnel.

"The bolide came down right on top of Grand Central Station.

"The impact was equivalent to a several-kiloton explosion. It dug out a crater twenty meters across. Every building south of Harlem was reduced to rubble, and several hundred thousand people were killed, through that one impact alone, on the first day of the invasion. Harry saw it all.

"And Harry's mother didn't make it. Crushed in the stampede for the tunnels. Harry never forgave the Squeem for that. Well, you wouldn't, would you?"

Harry and his father made it to Queens, where a refugee camp was quickly organized.

And the world churned. All Earth's continents were pocked by the impact scars. Millions had died, cities shaken to rubble.

But the damage could have been far worse. The Squeem could have sent in a dinosaur killer. They could have put Earth through an extinction event, just as easily.

"It took a day for their true strategy to be revealed," the Rememberer said. "When people started dying, in great numbers, in waves that spread out like ripples from the impact craters. Of diseases that didn't even have names."

The impactors had been carefully selected. They were all bits of Earth, knocked into space by massive natural impacts in the deep past, and so well preserved that they even carried a cargo of antique life. Spores, still viable.

"Diseases older than grass," the Rememberer whispered, "against which mankind, indeed the modern biosphere, had no defense. They used our own history against us, to cut us back while preserving the Earth itself. Harry lost his father to the plagues. He didn't forgive the Squeem for that either."

Rhoda Voynet listened to this account. She was familiar with the history Hume had outlined so far, at least in summary. It was eerie, though, to hear this tale of immense disaster, eyewitnessed at only a few removes.

The Squeem attack must have been overwhelming, horrifying, for those who lived through it. Incomprehensible in its crudity and brutality.

But since those days, mankind had learned more of the facts of galactic life.

This was the way interstellar war was waged. It wasn't like human war. It wasn't politics, or economics. Though both mankind and Squeem were sentient tool-using species, the conflict between them was much more fundamental than that. It wasn't even ecological, the displacement of one species by another. This was a clash of biospheres.

In such a war, there was no negotiation. You just hit hard, and fast.

Surrender was inevitable.

The Squeem moved quickly.

On Earth, residual resistance imploded quickly.

The more marginal colonies on other planets were subdued even more easily. Harry's home arcology in Cydonia was cracked open like an egg. He never knew about that.

And human space travel was suspended. Wherever the great GUTship interplanetary freighters landed, they were broken up, and the Poole wormhole fast-transit routes were collapsed. Some spaceborne humanity escaped, or hid. Pilots couldn't bear to be grounded. Harry's great-aunt Anna, an AntiSenescence-preserved freighter pilot on the Port Sol run, managed to escape Sol system altogether. Harry never knew about that either. In fact, he never saw any of his family again.

Harry Gage, ten years old when the rocks fell, orphaned in the first few days of the invasion, was a Martian boy stranded on Earth.

He was put to work. In the first weeks, he had to help lug the bodies of plague victims to vast pyres. He always wondered if one of them was his own father. Later, he worked on the construction of labor camps, in the ruins of the shattered cities of mankind.

He grew older and stronger, working hard for the Squeem and their human collaborators, as the aliens began to exploit the worlds they had conquered.

The Squeem had no interest in human technology, too primitive to be useful, still less in the products of human culture. But Earth still had lodes of complex hydrocarbons. The last of the planet's oil and coal was dug up by human muscle, and exported off the planet. Harry worked in the mines, squirming through seams too narrow for an adult.

And some products of Earth's biosphere proved useful for the Squeem, not the bugs or plants or animals themselves, but aspects of their exotic biochemistry. So Harry worked on tramp ships harvesting plankton, and in vast fields of swaying grasses.

Humans themselves could be worth exporting, though they were expensive and fragile. Slave transports lifted off the planet, sundering families, taking their captives to unknown destinations. Even after the eventual expulsion of the Squeem, nobody ever found out what became of them.

And people kept dying, from overwork or hunger or neglect.

The Squeem even shut down AntiSenescence technology. They had no interest in lengthening human lives; fast-breeding generations of servants and slaves were sufficient for them.

Stone-age wars were fought over the last AS supplies. Some of the undying went into hiding, detaching themselves from human history. And other lives centuries old were curtailed in brief agonies of withdrawal.

Amid all this, Harry grew up as best he could. There was no education, nothing but what you could pick up from other workers, and bits of Squeem-collaborator propaganda, about how this wasn't a conquest at all but a necessary *integration* of mankind into a galactic culture. Harry heard little and understood less.

"But," Karl Hume whispered, "Harry never forgave the Squeem, for their murder of his mother and father. And he began to develop contacts with others who were just as unforgiving. It was a dangerous business. There were plenty of collaborators, and the dissident groups were easily infiltrated.

"But a resistance network gradually coalesced. Small acts

of sabotage were committed. Every act was punished a hundredfold. But still they fought back, despite the odds, despite the cost. It was a heroic time."

Lots of untold stories, historian Rhoda thought wistfully.

"Then," said the Rememberer, "Harry was transferred to the Great Lakes."

Lake Superior had the largest surface area of any freshwater lake in the world. It was a grandiose gesture of the Squeem to colonize this great body of water, to symbolize their subjugation of mankind. Harry worked on vast projects to adjust the mineral content of Superior's water to the Squeem's liking, incidentally eliminating much of the native fauna. Then the Squeem descended from the sky in whale-like shuttles.

It was the Superior colony which gave the resistance a real chance to hurt the Squeem.

Rhoda Voynet grew more interested. At last, the Rememberer was talking of incidents she'd never heard of before.

It was easy to kill a Squeem, if you could get near one, as easy as murdering a goldfish. But all Squeem were linked into a mass mind. So the death of a single Squeem affected the totality, but only in a minor way, as the loss of a single neurone from a human brain wouldn't even be noticed. To hurt the Squeem significantly, you had to kill an awful lot of them.

And that was what Harry's resistance cell managed to do. It happened close to Harry's twenty-fifth birthday.

"It was a suicide mission," the Rememberer said. "A volunteer allowed her body to be pumped full of Squeem-specific toxins and pathogens. Harry wasn't the assassin, and neither was he educated enough to have manufactured the toxins. Cells of fifty-somethings, the last generation of preinvasion scientists, labored over that. But Harry was a link in the chain that got the toxins to the assassin, and he helped provide a diversion that enabled the woman to finish the job."

The woman just jumped into Lake Superior, one bright morning, her body weighted with bags of rocks. She slit her own wrists, and cut her throat, and let her crimson blood spill into the crystal waters.

"Every Lethe-spawned Squeem in that lake died," Karl Hume said. "They felt it all the way back to their home-world."

Rhoda saw Reg Kaser clench his fist, the others of her crew shift and murmur. Subtle signs of triumph. It was a story that none of them had heard before; Rhoda, herself a historian, had no idea the invasion-age inhabitants of Earth had been able to mount such an effective assault on the Squeem.

"But of course, it made no difference to the occupation," Hume said. "The Squeem still had Sol system. They still had the Earth. They rounded up everybody even remotely connected with the killing."

"They got Harry," Kaser said.

"Oh, yes. And they put them all in a prison camp, where Harry waited for Earth's punishment.

"To understand what followed," Hume said darkly, "you have to try to see the worldview of the Squeem. For one thing, they aren't instinctive killers, as we are. Their background is a cooperative ecology, not a competitive one, unlike ours. That's how they ended up as a group mind. When they did kill, as in the strikes on the cities, the killing was minimal—if you can call it that—just enough to achieve their objectives, in that case to shatter resistance and subjugate.

"We on the other hand had 'murdered' Lake Superior, in their view. We had rendered a whole body of water uninhabitable. They are aquatic, remember. To them it's as great a crime as if we destroyed an entire world.

"And so they planned a punishment appropriate to the crime they perceived."

In the silent skies above Harry's prison, ships slid into position. Beams of pinkish light connected them, and pulsed down into the ground. It took a full year to assemble the network.

"And when it was ready—"

"Yes?" Rhoda asked, breathless.

"Water is funny stuff," the Rememberer said. "Have you ever heard of hot ice?"

Rhoda had her engineering officers extrapolate what had happened, from the hints in Hume's account.

Ice formed naturally when heat was extracted from a body of water, the hydrogen-oxygen molecules settling into a space-filling solid lattice. But the Squeem had discovered that you can create a particular kind of ice, called polar cubic ice, even at high temperatures, with electricity.

"We know about this too," Reg Kaser said. "All you have to do is pass an electric field through the water—a strong one, a million volts a meter. The two hydrogen atoms in a water molecule have a slight positive charge, and the oxygen atom a negative one, so the electric field makes the molecules line up like fence posts. And there you have it, ice, at as high a temperature as you like. This happens in nature, though on a microscopic scale, wherever there are strong enough electric fields. Such as across the membranes of nerve cells, or in the cavities of proteins. Mini-icebergs riding around inside your cells. Amazing."

Hume said, "The Squeem were masters of this sort of technology. Masters of *water*."

"And so," Rhoda prompted, "on occupied Earth—"

"They froze the water."

"What water?"

"All of it."

Earth's oceans plated over with ice, right down to the equator, and then froze to their beds. And then the hard whiteness crept up the river valleys.

Harry and his codissidents were made to watch, on vast softscreens. Indeed, the Squeem made everybody watch, everybody capable of understanding.

"Even the aquifers froze. Even the moisture in the ground," Hume whispered. "Everybody walked around on permafrost, down to the equator.

"The Squeem controlled it, somehow. After all, humans are just big bags of water. We didn't freeze, nor did the grasses, the animals, the birds, the moisture in the air. Of course, rainfall was screwed, because nothing was evaporating from the oceans.

"They kept it up for a full year. By then, people were dying of the drought and the cold. And Earth blazed white, a symbol of the Squeem's dominance, visible even to all the off-planet refugees and hideouts, visible light-years away.

"Then they released the field. There was a lot of damage as all that ice went away. Coastlines shattered, river valleys gouged out, meltwater floods, climatic horrors. Lots of people died, as usual.

"And the oceans were left sterile. Oh, the Squeem allowed gradual restocking, from samples in climate-crash gene-store facilities, that kind of thing. The oceans didn't stay dead. But still, what followed would always be artificial. The link with the deepest past of life on Earth was cut.

"It was the worst act the Squeem, an aquatic species, could think of," Hume said. "To murder oceans. They thought it would crush human resistance once and for all. And it worked. But not for the reasons they imagined."

"When it was done, they just let Harry and his colleagues go. Harry came out of that prison camp near Thunder Bay, and found himself in an aftermath society.

"It had been by far the worst act of terror ever inflicted on the Earth, by mankind or anybody else.

"And it had cut through some deep umbilical connection we still evidently had with the mother oceans. We came from the oceans. Our deepest cellular origins lie there. When hominids arose, even before we were intelligent, we used the water, river courses and ocean shores, as roadways as we covered the planet. Now all that was gone. Everybody just wandered around stunned."

"I'm not surprised," said Rhoda. She assessed the reactions of her crew to this forgotten crime. Anger, shock, a lust for revenge.

"And," Hume said now, "the Squeem became concerned. A large proportion of mankind was plagued by flashbacks, crippling fear. Productivity was dropping. Birth rates falling. They didn't want to kill off their cheap labor. Maybe they saw they'd gone too far.

"World leaders were summoned to a kind of summit. I say 'leaders.' After two decades of the Squeem, there were no presidents, no UN secretary-general. The 'leaders' were labor organizers, necessary academics like doctors, a few religious types.

"And the Squeem offered, not a restoration, for what they had done could not be put right, but a kind of cure."

Most of humanity was suffering from a deep kind of post-traumatic stress disorder.

The memories of the freezing were etched deeply into every human brain. Like all traumas, the event had produced a rush of adrenaline and noradrenaline, which then forced a brain center called the amygdala to imprint the memories into the hippocampus, the memory center, very deeply. It was essentially a survival mechanism, so that any reminder of the event triggered deep memories and a fast response.

Sometimes such memories were gradually extinguished, the memory pathways overridden if not erased. But in this case, for the majority of mankind, the extinguishing mechanism didn't work well. The event had been too huge, too deep. And global post-trauma stress was the result.

But this could be rectified.

"There are ways to control memory formation," Reg Kaser murmured to Rhoda, taking another briefing from his data slate. "Drugs like beta blockers that inhibit the action of adrenaline and noradrenaline, and so reduce their memory-forming capabilities. A stress-related hormone called cortisol can inhibit memory retrieval. There are drugs that release a brain chemical called glutamate that enhances learning, thereby accelerating the normal memory extinguishing process. And so on."

"You're talking about altering memories with drugs," Rhoda murmured.

"Since the twentieth century, when neuroscience was established as a discipline, human societies have always shied away from memory-changing technology," Kaser said. "There are obvious ethical issues. A memory is part of your identity, after all. Does anybody else have the right to take away part of *you*? And suppose a criminal deliberately erases all her own memory of her crime. If she doesn't remember it, is she any longer responsible? That was used as a defense in a criminal trial during—"

"Never mind," Rhoda said.

"The point is, such technologies have existed in the past. And after a couple of decades of occupation, the Squeem, presumably with human collaborators, were able to come up with a suitable treatment."

"Yes. And this is what they offered us," Hume said. "An engineered virus that would spread through mankind, across the Earth. Eventually moles would carry it through the off-planet populations too. It wouldn't be comfortable. You would have a nightmare, reliving the trauma one last time. But that would make the memory labile again for a short time. And so it could be treated."

"They would delete the memory of the freezing, of this vast crime," Rhoda said. "From everybody's heads."

"That was the idea. There would have to be a subsidiary activity of removing it from various records, but there weren't too many marine biologists at the height of the occupation. It wouldn't be difficult.

"This solution served the Squeem's goals, you see. People would stay pliable. They just wouldn't know why."

Kaser said sharply, "And, since none of us have heard of this freezing before, I take it that these 'leaders' made this supine choice on behalf of the rest of mankind."

"You shouldn't judge them," Hume said. "We had been enslaved from space, for decades already. They could see no way out. The only choice was between a future of terrified subjugation, or a calmer one—vague, baffled, adjusted.

"Even Harry Gage and his resistance colleagues knew they were beaten. They submitted. But," he said, and a smile spread over his leathery face, "there was one last act of defiance."

Everybody alive would forget the terror. Everybody but one.

"It wasn't sophisticated. They would just hide one person away, for a year, perhaps more. Earth's a big planet. There were plenty of places to hide. And not all the biochemists had gone over to the Squeem. Some of them helped out with screens against the virus. And when he or she came out of her hole in the ground—"

Rhoda guessed, "Harry Gage was the first Rememberer."

Hume smiled. "They chose him by lot. It could have been anyone. It's the only reason we remember Harry now, the only extraordinary thing that happened in his life.

"He went into the hole without a word of protest. And when he came back out, he found himself the only one who remembered the freezing. A kind of living memorial to a deleted past.

"Harry just went back to work. But the course of the rest of his life was set out. It must have been hard for him, hard not to talk about what he knew. It's been hard for *me,* and I didn't live through it.

"Harry Gage died in his late forties. It wasn't an age when people grew old. But he fulfilled his last mission, which was to transmit his memories to another.

"The Second Rememberer was in her thirties when the Squeem regime began to crumble—sooner than anybody had expected. She too died young. But she was able to pass on her knowledge to another in turn.

"And so it went. Two centuries after the Squeem conquered Earth, I am the Sixth Rememberer."

Rhoda nodded. "And you tried to recruit Lonnie Tekinene."

Hume sighed. "That was the idea. I left it a bit late in life to be befriending ten-year-olds."

"But," Reg Kaser said, "even though the Squeem fell so long ago, none of you thought to reveal the truth of all this oral history until now."

Hume shrugged. "When would have been right? Each of the Rememberers has had to make that judgment. It was only when I learned of your pocket of Squeem, after the passage of two centuries, that I judged the time was right. You need to know the whole truth about the Squeem in order to deal with them." His face twisted. "But I wasn't *sure*. I'm still not."

Rhoda said gently, "So how do you feel now?"

"Relieved. It's a burden, to be the only one who knows."

It took Rhoda Voynet and her crew another week of data-gathering before she felt ready to make her judgment.

She called Reg Kaser to her cabin, and fired up her percolator once more. Beyond her picture window, Saturn turned, its cloudy face impassive before the turmoil of living things.

"They've started to find proof," she said to Kaser.

"Of what?"

"The freezing. The geologists. The biologists, trawling the seabeds for crushed whale bones. My historian colleagues, finding traces of deleted records. Global evidence of a decade-long glaciation event. It was always there, but unnoticed; it just needed a framing hypothesis to fit it all together."

"So Hume was telling the truth."

"It seems so."

"Meanwhile," Kaser said, "I've been talking to the xenologists, who have been in contact with those Squeem down there under the ice. The Squeem have been making their own case."

"About what?"

"About why we should be lenient. The Squeem say they suffered some deep trauma of their own. After all, they are aquatic, they're functionally fishlike, and it must have taken a huge disjunction to lift them out of their ocean and into space." Kaser scrolled through notes on his slate. "Something about an invasion, by yet another world-conquering species. The Squeem managed to enslave the slavers, and started an empire of their own. Something on those lines. It's complicated."

Rhoda said harshly, "And that justifies them occupying Earth?"

"I suppose that's the argument. But you're the commanding officer."

"I am, aren't I?" She looked him straight in the eye. "I want to know my options. Tell me about the weapon. The one that will destroy the moon."

He looked away. "If you're sure—this is need-to-know only."

"I need to know."

"It's not a human development," Kaser said. "Not even Squeem."

Rhoda glanced beyond Saturn's limb, at the stars. "Something hideous we've found. Out there."

"Yes."

Even under the oppressive Squeem occupation, humans had learned much.

They learned, for example, that much of the Squeem's high technology—such as their hyperdrive—was not indigenous. It was copied, sometimes at second or third hand, based on the designs of an older, more powerful species.

"It was during the occupation," Kaser said, "that the name 'Xeelee' entered human discourse. The primal source of all this good stuff."

Rhoda shuddered. "And is this new weapon a Xeelee artifact?"

"It may be. Stuff gets swapped around out there. Purloined. Modified. We don't know enough about the Xeelee to say."

"Tell me what this thing does."

"Maybe you know that the planet Jupiter is being destroyed. Eaten up from within by a swarm of black holes."

"Yes." In fact, Rhoda knew a little more about it than that.

"If we could make a black hole," Kaser said, "we could throw it at Rhea and demolish it the same way."

"We can't make a black hole."

"No. But we have a technology almost as good." He pulled up graphics on his slate and showed her. "It's a way to create a dark energy black hole."

"A *what*?"

"It's all to do with quantum physics," he said.

"Oh, it would be . . . "

It was another kind of freezing, a phase transition. But this would happen at the quantum level. In a "quantum critical phase transition," ordinary matter congealed into a kind of superconductor, and then into a sluggish stuff in which even subatomic fluctuations died, and mass-energy was shed.

"It's as if time itself is freezing out," Kaser said. He mimed with his hands. "So you have a spherical shell. Just a volume in space. You arrange for matter falling on its surface to go through this quantum phase transition. And as your infalling matter passes into the interior, its mass is dumped, converted to vacuum energy. Dark energy."

"Why doesn't this shell implode?"

"Because dark energy has a repulsive effect. Antigravity. Dark energy is already the dominant component of the universe's mass-energy, and the antigravity force it produces will drive the expansion of the universe in the future. So I'm told by the physicists. Anyhow, the repulsion can balance the infall of matter."

"It *can* balance."

Kaser grinned. "That's the engineering challenge, I guess. If you get it right, you get a stable object which externally looks just like a black hole. Inside, there's no singularity, just a mush of dark energy, but any structure is destroyed just the same. These things are found in nature, apparently."

"And they are easier to make than genuine black holes?"

"So it seems. You do need a big box of exotic matter, that is negative-energy matter, to make it work." He kept grinning.

"Poole wormhole mouths."

"Just the job. The Squeem wrecked the old Poole wormhole transport system, but they left the wormhole mouths in place. There are several still orbiting Saturn. Any one of them will do."

"And if we throw one of these things into Rhea—"

"It will eat up the moon."

"That would get rid of them," Rhoda said.

"That it would. Of course, the Squeem may be useful. We could use them, as they once used us. A galaxy-spanning telepathic network—"

"We don't need them in Sol system for that. We have their homeworld."

"True." Kaser eyed Rhoda. "The technology's in place. The only question remains, do we use it?"

Rhoda thought it through.

The Squeem occupation had changed human perceptions of the galaxy, and humanity's place in it. A historic loss of innocence.

Now humans were tentatively moving out beyond Sol system once more. And everywhere they went, they found life. Intelligences swarming and squabbling. A kind of galactic society, a ramshackle pecking order based on avarice, theft, and the subjugation of junior races.

And for humanity, nothing but threat.

The black holes in Jupiter were clues to a closely guarded secret, which Rhoda hadn't even shared with Reg Kaser. The Squeem invasion hadn't been the first hostile alien incursion into Sol system. Some centuries back invaders called something like "Qax," who would occupy Earth in their turn sometime in the future, had *come back in time* to secure their victory over mankind. In the course of the battle, miniature black holes had been hurled into Jupiter. During the Squeem occupation, knowledge of this event had mostly been lost, and was only now being pieced back together by the historians. But the mortal wound inflicted on Jupiter was unarguable.

Some analysts, poring over the historical reconstructions, argued that the Qax invasion might be only decades away, in the future.

Even beyond the Qax, there was the apparent original source of much of the galaxy's technology (though nobody knew for sure): the Xeelee. Secretive, xenophobic, indifferent. And so far ahead, they made the rest of the galaxy's inhabitants look like tree dwellers.

The future held nothing but peril for mankind. Hierarchies of enemies. And that was the basis on which Rhoda must make her decision.

Rhoda stared down at the ice landscape of Rhea, imagining the stranded Squeem swarming within. "It won't be revenge," she said. "Call it insurance. Look what the Squeem did to us. This will be one danger eliminated."

"We're setting a course for the future, then."

"The future leaves us no choice. And if this makes us harder as a species, good. When the weapon's ready, send Hume up here, would you? He ought to watch this, as the Squeem made Harry Gage watch. Let *this* act be remembered too."

Kaser stood. "I'll call the weapons crew."

THE EMPEROR AND THE MAULA

ROBERT SILVERBERG

Robert Silverberg is one of the most famous SF writers of modern times, with dozens of novels, anthologies, and collections to his credit. As both writer and editor (he was editor of the original anthology series *New Dimensions*, perhaps the most acclaimed anthology series of its era), Silverberg was one of the most influential figures of the Post New Wave era of the seventies, and continues to be at the forefront of the field to this very day, having won a total of five Nebula Awards and four Hugo Awards, plus SFWA's prestigious Grandmaster Award.

His novels include the acclaimed *Dying Inside, Lord Valentine's Castle, The Book of Skulls, Downward to the Earth, Tower of Glass, Son of Man, Nightwings, The World Inside, Born with the Dead, Shadrack in the Furnace, Thorns, Up the Line, The Man in the Maze, Tom O'Bedlam, Star of Gypsies, At Winter's End, The Face of the Waters, Kingdoms of the Wall, Hot Sky at Morning, The Alien Years, Lord Prestimion, Mountains of Majipoor*, and two novel-length expansions of famous Isaac Asimov stories, *Nightfall* and *The Ugly Little Boy*. His collections include *Unfamiliar Territory, Capricorn*

Games, Majipoor Chronicles, The Best of Robert Silverberg, At the Conglomeroid Cocktail Party, Beyond the Safe Zone, and a massive retrospective collection: *The Collected Stories of Robert Silverberg, Volume One: Secret Sharers.* His reprint anthologies are far too numerous to list here, but include *The Science Fiction Hall of Fame, Volume One* and the distinguished Alpha series, among dozens of others. His most recent books are the novel *The Long Way Home,* the mosaic novel *Roma Eterna,* and a massive new retrospective collection, *Phases of the Moon: Stories from Six Decades.* Coming up is a new collection, *In the Beginning.* He lives with his wife, writer Karen Haber, in Oakland, California.

Robert Silverberg is the only author in this book with a writing career long enough that he actually produced some of the *Old* Space Opera, back in the pulp magazines of the fifties, decades before most of the newcomers here even sat down at their first computer keyboard. He's lost none of his chops in the intervening years, though, as he proves with the lush and gorgeously colored story that follows, in which an intrepid human woman dares to penetrate to the heart of a hostile alien empire and confront the all-powerful Emperor himself, armed only with her brains and wit and heart, and enter a contest of wills with everything that's important to her—including her own life—at stake.

BOGAN 17, 82ND DYNASTIC CYCLE (AUGUST 3, A.D. 3001)

The gongs have sounded throughout the ship. We have crossed the invisible line that separates Territorial Space from Imperial Space and now my life is officially forfeit.

And I have chosen to break the code of tiihad that demands my life. We will see what happens when we land on Capital World.

Meanwhile here I am—an Earthborn woman, a mere barbaric *maula*, getting deeper into Imperial Space with each passing light-second. I should be trembling with fear, I suppose.

No. Let the Emperor tremble. Laylah is here!

—From the Diaries of Laylah Walis

1

It was an unusual case. No one at Capital World Starport had ever seen anything like it, which is how it reached the attention, finally, of no one less than the Emperor Ryah VII himself, the High Ansaar, the Supreme Omniscience, the Most Holy Defender of the Race.

The chain that led to the Emperor began with Loompan Chilidor, an arbiter of passenger manifests. He was a short-crested, pale-skinned low-caste person whose job was to check the identity circuits of passengers of newly arrived starships. Routine stuff. But this time, when he ran the transit check on the travelers coming from Seppuldidorior on the starship *Velipok,* jagged incandescent green streaks burst forth on the purple surface of the field.

Tiihad violation!

The highest of the six levels of irregularity—higher even than *vribor,* the carrying of infectious disease, and *gulimil,* the smuggling of dangerous weapons, and *shhtek,* the wearing of medallions of the extinct and proscribed Simgoin Dynasty. Violation of *tiihad* was an assault on the structure of the Empire itself.

Loompan Chilidor's long dangling arms jerked in shock. His small yellow eyes turned orange with surprise. He pressed the red button that sealed the luminance field and summoned his immediate superior, Domtel Tribuso, Manager of Passenger Flow.

Domtel Tribuso, stocky and slow, appeared in due course. The purple luminance field was now a rubbery purple cage. A few dozen travelers were trapped inside.

Domtel Tribuso stared in puzzlement at the green streaks criss-crossing the field. "Green? *Tiihad* violation?"

Most of those in the cage were Ansaar. There were a few Liigachi and some Vrulvruls and a cluster of agitated-looking Zmachs. All those races had held full citizenship in the Imperium for centuries, and surely understood the law.

But one was a creature Domtel Tribuso could not identify at all: a non-Imperial alien, a barbaric life-form from the Territories, a trespasser and transgressor here on this hallowed world. A *maula*. Domtel Tribuso felt amazement and disgust and anger.

The *maula* was thin to the point of gauntness, and its face was as flat as a platter, the features close together, eyes practically next to each other, nose a tiny button just below, its mouth—*was* that its mouth?—a mere slit near its chin. Its legs were much too long and its arms grotesquely short. The creature had no crest, only a short crop of unpleasant dark fur sprouting from its skull. There were two strange round swellings on its chest.

The Manager of Passenger Flow summoned his aides. "Get that *maula* out of there and bring it to Examination Chamber Three."

That was the holding cell for unauthorized life-forms, normally used for unfamiliar pets or trophy animals that a citizen of the Imperium had brought back and that needed to be checked by an Imperial veterinarian before being released from quarantine.

But this was no pet, no trophy, this *maula*. Plainly it was an intelligent life-form—a ticketed passenger in its own right. It stood quite calmly among the passengers of Citizen rank as though it regarded itself as one of them. It was even carrying several pieces of expensive-looking luggage.

How could a *maula* have been able to buy a ticket to Haraar, and why had it been allowed to board the *Velipok,* and why hadn't the *Velipok*'s captain called ahead to say that a *maula* was on board? An investigation was needed. Domtel Tribuso summoned his superior, Graligal Dren, and turned the *maula* over to her.

Graligal Dren, a mid-caste woman of a rich olive hue with a high-peaked sagittal crest of admirable narrowness and delicacy, glowered through the thick glass wall and said, "Are you able to understand Universal Imperial, creature?"

"I speak it quite well, thank you." The *maula*'s voice was clear and high-pitched with a slight West Quadrant accent.

"And do you have a name?"

"My name is Laylah Walis."

An incomprehensible gargling noise, mere sounds. Well, one would expect barbarians to have barbaric names. There it was on the passenger manifest: *LAYLAH WALIS*. The emigration people who had let it board a Haraar-bound ship must have been out of their minds.

"You embarked from Hathpoin in the Seppuldidorior system?"

"That's correct."

"And where did you come from before that?"

"Mingtha, in the Ghair system. Which I reached by way of Zemblano, which is in Briff. And before that—"

"Don't give me your whole itinerary, creature. Just tell me where you are from originally."

"Earth," the *maula* said. "A small world in what you'd call the Northwest Arm. Part of the Empire about twenty years now."

The Northwest Arm was a zone of scruffy worlds inhabited by bestial creatures—frontier worlds, barely civilized, dismal primitive outposts of the Empire. It amazed her that a creature from a world like that spoke Universal Imperial with such precision and force; and with such haughtiness too. You would think that this *maula* had twenty generations of Dynastic blood in its veins.

But it had made no attempt to assume a posture of respect. It simply stared at her in its ugly flat-faced way. Arrogance! Foolishness! But only an arrogant fool of a *maula* would have attempted to come to Haraar. "Tell me, Laylah Walis," said Graligal Dren, "are you aware of where you are now?"

"This is Haraar, the Capital World."

"Yes. The heart and soul of the Empire. And you came knowing that Territorials may not enter any part of Imperial Space?"

"Yes."

Madness. "How did you get a ticket?" Graligal Dren asked.

"A long story," said the *maula*. "I told someone who could get one for me that I wanted to visit Haraar, and it was arranged."

The *maula* had a kind of lunatic self-confidence. "This world is sacred," Graligal Dren said slowly. "The fount and origin of our race. We revere the very dust that blows through its humblest alleyways. We can never let this holy world be desecrated by creatures who are—whom we regard as—who can be defined as—"

"*Maulas*," said Laylah Walis. "Barbarians. Inferior beings."

"Exactly."

"And any *maula* who dares set foot here is put to death."

"You knew that before you came? And you came anyway?"

"It does seem that way," said Laylah Walis.

2

If what this creature wanted was to commit suicide, it had to do it without the help of Graligal Dren. She passed it to the Director of Immigration Facilities, who sent it on to Starport Security. Commissioner Twimat Dulik of Security interrogated the prisoner and confirmed it was a Territorial, native to a conquered world in the West Quadrant. It seemed intelligent enough, for a *maula*, but a *maula* was what it was: subcivilized, contemptible, and unclean by definition. And for desecrating the Capital World it had to die.

The damnable thing was that the *maula* seemed to understand all that, and didn't appear to care.

"Since the *maula* knew the penalty for violating *tiihad*, and chose to trespass anyway, it's obviously insane," said Commissioner Twimat Dulik to his own superior, Justiciar Hwillinin Ma of the Department of Criminal Affairs. "We are civilized beings. Can we put an insane person to death?"

Justiciar Hwillinin Ma, a mid-upper-caste neuter with dusky yellow skin and a lengthy crest, said, "A *maula* isn't a person, Dulik. A *maula* is little more than a brute animal. Point two: our legal definitions of insanity can't be applied to subcivilized beings, any more than to insects or birds or trees. Point three—"

"This isn't an insect or a bird or a tree, Justiciar Ma. This is an alert, intelligent creature that—"

"Point three," said Justiciar Hwillinin Ma sternly, "is that the desecration law is explicit. There's no footnote covering sanity. We must protect the purity of the homeworld and the traditional act of purification is the slaying of the desecrator."

Commissioner Twimat Dulik nodded. "Very well, then, Justiciar Ma. I herewith turn the prisoner over to you for execution." And saluted and went out.

But the Haraar City Department of Criminal Justice, Justiciar Ma learned ten minutes later, would not accept the prisoner.

"Oh, no," said the chief aide to the Prefect of Capital Police. "You can't ship any *maulas* into town, fellow! Don't you realize that that only compounds the desecration?"

"But Justiciar Ma says—"

"Justiciar Ma can *gedoy* his *gevasht*," the aide to the Prefect replied calmly. "Bad enough that this *maula* of yours is polluting the starport, but you think we'd let it be brought into the capital city itself? To have it within a hundred *glezzans* of the High Temple precincts, let alone anywhere near the Imperial Palace? Oh, no, no, no. You keep your *maula* in your own jurisdiction, please."

"But the execution—"

"Take it behind a fuel dump somewhere back of the terminal and blow its head off. Just remember to point your blaster the right way. The long end faces the prisoner."

"The police won't accept the *maula*," the subaltern glumly reported to Justiciar Ma. "They say *we* have to do the execution."

"All right, then. Take care of it."

"Execute the *maula* myself, sir?"

Justiciar Ma stared stonily in the subaltern's direction and said nothing.

"Sir? Sir? Sir?"

3

It was one thing, Justiciar Ma soon discovered, to issue an execution order, and another entirely to get it carried out. No one at the starport could be induced to put the *maula* to death.

"The law clearly states that a *maula* caught anywhere on Haraar must be killed immediately," Justiciar Ma said. He was speaking to his old university classmate Thrippel Vree, a Third Chamberlain to His Imperial Majesty. "We've already held it for something like fourteen hours. Everyone refuses to do the job, and I don't seem to have the legal right to compel anyone. Meanwhile we're all becoming accessories to the desecration."

"You could always kill it yourself," Thrippel Vree suggested. "Ultimately it's your responsibility, right? If you can't find anyone else who—"

"I can't *kill* someone, Thrippel! Even a *maula*!"

"And if it becomes known that you failed to take the appropriate measures—?"

"Be reasonable," Justiciar Ma moaned.

"One quick shot with a blaster would do it. Deep breath, steady hand, ready, aim, fire. File your report. Justice is done."

Justiciar Ma knew that his old friend was merely being playful. Surely Vree couldn't be serious. Surely.

And yet—why *not* do it himself?

No. No. It wasn't that Justiciar Ma was notably merciful, or greatly softhearted. The Ansaar hadn't come to control three fifths of the galaxy by being extraordinarily merciful or tender. But conquering entire solar systems for the greater glory of the Empire was one thing and shooting some hapless subcivilized creature in cold blood was another. Especially when you happened to be a middle-aged bureaucrat of high caste and sedentary nature.

Over the next twelve hours Justiciar Ma grew steadily more convinced that he would pay with his career for the impertinence of this confounded *maula*. A couple of times during those dreary twelve hours he came close to carrying out the execution personally, despite his hesitations, purely to save his own neck.

But meanwhile Third Chamberlain Thrippel Vree managed to save it for him.

The Third Chamberlain chanced to mention the starport episode later that evening to another Third Chamberlain, Danol Giyango. "Perplexing," said Danol Giyango. "It must have known it would have to die for its audacity. Yet it came here anyway. Why, I wonder?"

That was so intriguing that Danol Giyango spoke of it to his wife, a Lady-in-Waiting, who made mention of it to a High Eunuch of the Innermost Chamber, who told a Subsidiary Concubine, who happened to be in attendance later on one of the five Cherished Major Wives, Etaag Thuuyaal. It was her turn that night to be with His Majesty the Emperor Ryah VII, the High Ansaar, the Supreme Omniscience, the Most Holy Defender of the Race.

"I heard the most extraordinary story a little while ago," said Etaag Thuuyaal to the Emperor, as they lay amiably entwined in the Imperial hammock. The Emperor, she knew— as who did not?—was a connoisseur of extraordinary stories, with a voracious appetite for the unlikely and the divertingly strange, a man of intense curiosities and powerful whims.

"And what might that be, my dearest one?"

"Well," said Etaag Thuuyal, "this comes from Subsidiary Concubine Hypoepoi, who heard it from the High Eunuch Sambin, who got it from Lady-in-Waiting Sipyar Giyango, whose husband heard it from somebody whose friend is a Justiciar at the starport. It seems that a starship came in today from the Territories, and it was discovered that one of the passengers was—can you imagine it?—well, the passengers came down the ramp, and most were the usual assortment of tourists and pilgrims and such, but then what do you think marched out of the ship, as blithe and bold as could be—?"

"Tell me," said the Emperor Ryah VII.

Etaag Thuuyaal smiled with deep self-satisfaction. Great benefits, she had learned long ago, accrued to those who were capable of keeping the Emperor amused.

"Well," she said—

The Emperor was startled. And fascinated as well.

A *maula* on Haraar? Of course, the creature would have to die. But why had it come, knowing the risk involved? Barbarians might be uneducated and coarse and crude, but never blind to their own survival. Surely they burned within with the furious species-need to live and reproduce and maintain their species' niche in the great chain of being. An animal might gnaw off its own leg in order to escape a trap it had stumbled into, the Emperor thought, but it would hardly stick its leg in the trap in the first place just to find out if the trap really would close on it.

So why—why—

The Emperor sprang lithely out of the hammock and called for the eunuch on duty. "There's a *maula* at the starport and they haven't executed it yet. Delay carrying out the sentence. Have this *maula* brought here first thing in the morning."

"I hear and obey, O Lord of the Universe."

The Emperor returned to his hammock. Etaag Thuuyaal stretched out her arms to him, amiably, invitingly.

4

Laylah Walis was starting to worry. Everything so far had gone according to plan. She was here and she was still alive.

But it was a wild gamble, a thousand-to-one shot. Sooner or later the port officials might decide that the decree about desecration of the Capital World meant just what it said. And then—

Sounds in the hall. People approaching.

One was the stocky little security chief, Dulik. He had seemed intelligent and sensitive, even sympathetic. With him were two brutish-looking low-caste Ansaar in dull green uniforms. Executioners?

Laylah had studied Ansaar body language well. The posture of these three looked ominous: shoulders up almost to their ears, long arms close to their sides. Eyes retracted, a mark of tension among Ansaar. The vertical slits of their pupils were nearly invisible.

The cell door swung open. "You are summoned, Laylah Walis," the security chief said, in a taut and portentous tone.

"Summoned to what?"

"Not to what, *maula,* but *whom*. The Emperor requests your presence."

A quick smile flitted across her face. Success! Success!

One Ansaar produced a coil of rope and the other yanked her arms roughly behind her back like a beast being trussed for slaughter. They tied her wrists tightly, then her ankles. Seizing her by the elbows, they propelled her across the room and out the door.

Her legs were dragging as they pulled her clumsily along, and their sharp-clawed seven-fingered hands dug miserably into her flesh. She felt stretched and bruised and cramped by the time they had hauled her in a series of bumps and jolts down a long tunnel and out into the bright golden-green light of the Haraar dawn.

A sleek teardrop-shaped car waited. "The Palace," Dulik told the driver. Then, in a muttered undertone: "He delays the *maula's* death. Must speak with her first. Well, who are we to question the Emperor's wishes?"

The car rose and floated down the track toward Haraar City, the fabled capital of the Ansaar Empire.

"The rose-red city half as old as time," a poet had called it—a thousand palaces and five thousand temples, green parks and leafy promenades, shining obelisks and long eye-dazzling colonnades. From here the invincible might of the Ansaar had radiated irresistibly outward over the past ninety thousand years, spreading in ever-widening circles until the Empire's dominion arched across more than a thousand parsecs of space. For eons the wealth of all that vast domain had poured down upon this city of Haraar, making it the most majestic seat of government that had ever existed.

But Laylah sat hunched down between the two Ansaar guards, her long legs sprawling far forward and her head uncomfortably buried in a plush cushion; and all she could see was a glimpse of a golden dome here, a pink minaret there, a great gleaming white obelisk jutting into the sky over yonder.

The car floated to a halt. Ungently they pulled her out.

She had a brief glimpse of the courtyard of an incredible palace, high gleaming porphyry walls inlaid with onyx medallions, delicate many-windowed towers, long boulevards lined by strips of immaculately tended shrubbery, crystalline reflecting pools narrow as daggers. Then a thick furry hood came down over her head and she saw nothing further.

"This is the *maula* that the Emperor asked to see," Dulik said. Her hood was lifted for a moment and yellow Ansaar eyes peered briefly into her own, and then she was swept off her feet. After a time came the sound of a great door being swung back, and the bruising impact of being dropped onto a stone floor.

An intense silence roared in her ears.

She lay bound and hooded on a cold slab of stone. The ropes circling her wrists and ankles chafed and cut cruelly into her skin, and she felt stifled and nauseated by the stale, moist air.

Hours passed. She grew stiff and sore.

Footsteps, finally. People approaching. The hood was lifted. Laylah blinked, gasped eagerly for breath, scratched her chin against her shoulder to gratify the itch that had begun to plague her half a million years before.

It was a bleak, bare, windowless chamber. Around her were armed guards in crimson pantaloons, great green sashes, loose purple tunics with flaring shoulder pads. Like most Ansaar they were short and stocky, with thick chests, long apelike arms, stubby bow legs.

But standing apart from the rest, studying her like some rare zoological specimen, was an Ansaar of such noble mien and grandeur that she knew she was in the presence of the Emperor Ryah VII.

He might almost have been of a different species: tall, well over two meters, perhaps two and a half. His arms reached only as far as his thighs, as a human's arms would. The sagittal crest on his hairless head was the most impressive she had ever seen. Its contours were steep, rising to needle-sharp prominence.

From throat to ankles he was swathed in a brocaded robe of heavy crimson fabric shot through with threads of silver. His face and hands were the color of richest mahogany, with a fiery scarlet undertone. Out of that mask of a face came the gleam of penetrating green eyes—not yellow, like other Ansaar eyes, but *green*, the lustrous heavy green of pure emerald.

Surely this was someone bred for a thousand generations for the Sapphire Throne of the Ansaar Empire. Despite herself, despite the profound and fierce loathing for all things Ansaar that burned within every human, Laylah felt a powerful throb of awe—and an unmistakable, astonishing shiver of immediate physical attraction.

"Lift it up." The Emperor's voice rumbled with authority and sonorous force. "Let me see what this *maula* looks like."

The guards raised her to a standing position. Her eyes met his directly, the upper-caste style of Ansaar social usage, her head inclined at precisely the correct angle to indicate deference to his majestic person while retaining her own personal dignity.

"A she-*maula*, I'd guess. But look at her!" the Emperor cried. "Is that a *maula* expression on her face? Is that the way a *maula* would stand? She holds herself like a countess! She looks right into my eyes as a high-caste woman would!" He smiled a jagged Ansaar smile. "You *are* a female, aren't you, *maula*?"

"That is correct, Majesty," said Laylah coolly.

"And speaks Universal like a lady of the court!" The Emperor's vertical pupils became slits. His brilliant green eyes gleamed brightly with the insatiable curiosity for which he was famed. "How strange you are. Where did you learn such good Universal, *maula*?"

"A long story, O Supreme Omniscience."

"Ah. Ah. A long story." He seemed tremendously amused by her. "Tell me, then. But in shorter form. Three ambassadors wait to see me today, and the Goishlaar of Gozishtandar also. He wants favors from me, as usual, and that always makes him very impatient."

She was silent.

"Go on," he said. "Tell me about yourself. Who are you? Why have you come here? How do you know so much about Ansaar ways?"

Laylah glanced down at her tethered hands. "Telling stories is quite difficult, Majesty, when one is in discomfort. These ropes around me—they bind, they chafe—"

"You're a prisoner, *maula*! Prisoners must be bound!"

"Nevertheless, Sire—if I am to speak of the matters about which you ask—ah, this pain is hard to bear, and the humiliation, besides! I beg you, High One—have my bonds removed from me."

The Emperor's eyes flickered momentarily. But she kept her gaze on him steadily in the deferent-but-not-abased mode, and gradually he seemed to relent.

"Cut the ropes," he ordered.

They were cut away. Laylah rubbed her hands together and shifted her weight from foot to foot.

"Now," the Emperor said. "If you would, my lady—a word or two of explanation from you—"

"In this cold bare room? And without having had anything to eat in almost an entire day?"

Maybe that was going too far. But once again the Emperor let himself be charmed by her impertinence. "Yes," he said, with a flourish. "Certainly, my lady. Some meat and a flask of wine, perhaps? A warm bath?" He seemed not to be speaking sarcastically. "Very well. But then you must tell me what you're all about, agreed? Why you are here—what you thought you could accomplish. Everything. I'll come to you late this afternoon, after I've dealt with the Goishlaar and some of those ambassadors, and you'll answer all my questions, and no more of these little requests of yours. Eh, *maula*?" And once more there was the tone of authority.

"I hear and obey, O Lord of Worlds."

"Good. Good." He stared at her strangely. "How different you are from the other humans I have met. They were in a fury all the time. All they did was shout and rant. And then the other kind, those who cringed and whined and bowed and scraped, crawling in front of me, agreeing with every word I said. They were even worse. But you treat me almost as though we were equals! I see neither defiance nor obsequiousness in your manner. You are very unusual, *maula.* You are extraordinarily unusual."

Laylah said nothing.

The Emperor began to walk away. Then he spun around and said, "Is there a name by which I can call you, *maula*?"

"Laylah. Laylah Walis."

"Which of those is the soul-name, and which the face-name?"

"The face-name is Laylah, Sire. Walis is the soul-name."

"Will it be all right, if I call you Laylah? May the Lord of the Ansaar Empire call a *maula* by her face-name?" Again the wry chuckle. But Laylah knew she was in the hands of a lion toying with his prey. His expression changed once more, turning dark and grim. "You have to die tomorrow, *maula,* and there's no way around that. You know that, don't you? Yes, you do. That's interesting about you, that you know it and you don't seem to care. I want to know more about that. Tonight we talk; and tomorrow morning you die. It is the law, and not even the Most Holy Defender of the Race may trifle with the law." He waved his hand imperiously. "I will speak again with you later, Laylah Walis." And he strode from the room.

5

They took her to what probably was one of the suites of the royal harem. It was said the Emperor had thousands of wives and concubines; and that might not be far from the truth. She was in a separate wing of the palace, set apart by high walls of black brick. Radiating clusters of spokelike hallways jutted in all directions and a maze of brightly lit chambers was visible in the distance. Women and eunuchs in elegant robes glided about softly, dozens of them, scores, not one of them ever meeting Laylah's eye.

"Yours," said the guard who accompanied her, indicating a faintly aromatic door inlaid with strips of ivory.

There were five spacious rooms: a bedroom, a richly curtained sitting room, a bath with a crystal tub, a dining chamber with a table cut from a block of black stone, and a tiring-room for the use of her servants, of whom there were three, two maids and a silent, glum-faced figure with the neuter-sign on his forehead.

They stripped her and bathed her and anointed her body with oils. They would have anointed her hair too, but she stopped them. They gave her robes of a filmy fabric that shifted polarity with every movement of her body, so her nakedness glinted through in quick flashes and then vanished again. They brought her a platter of meat and a bowl of angular purple fruits, and a flask of golden wine shot through with startling red highlights, as if powdered rubies had been mixed into it.

Then they left her alone. She went from room to room. In the storage chambers were robes and diadems, a month's wardrobe for a princess royal who never wore the same thing twice. There was a collection of perfumes and cosmetics and a closet full of liqueurs. Did every member of the royal harem have a suite like this? Say, three hundred concubines and a hundred wives—

The cost was incalculable. Was it for this that the Ansaar had conquered the galaxy, so that their Emperor could squander a planet's ransom on the women who were his toys? Fury coursed through her. But then she grew calm again. What did it matter how the Ansaar chose to waste the profits of their conquests?

She lay down and slept, and dreamed of worlds colliding and smashing asunder, and of blazing stars plummeting through the skies, and of fiery comets with the faces of dragons.

Then she heard a sound and opened her eyes, and saw an Ansaar of immense presence and authority standing over her, a formidably tall and astonishingly handsome Ansaar whom her sleep-fogged mind recognized only after a moment or two as His Majesty Ryah VII.

He took a seat facing her. "Everything is to your liking?"

"Magnificent, Your Highness."

"I told them to give you one of the best available apartments."

"Even though I must die tomorrow?"

He flashed his warmest smile, and then, as before, the smile abruptly turned without any perceptible transition to a grimace of fury. "It is nothing to joke about, my lady."

"You really do intend to put me to death, then?"

"The law is the law. This planet is not only the seat of the Imperial Government, it is sacred as well." His tone was implacable. "There's muttering aplenty already because I've allowed you to live this long. By tomorrow you'll be dead." He leaned toward her. His eyes drilled into her like high-intensity beams. "How could you have been so *stupid*? You're obviously a woman of intelligence and education, as humans go. Why bring certain death down upon yourself? Tell me that! Tell me!"

"It is, as I said, a long story, Majesty."

"Make it no longer than you must, then." He glanced at a pale green jewel on his wrist. "It is the eighth hour of night. At the first hour of morning I must deliver you to the executioner. Between now and then I want to hear all that you have to tell."

"Listen, then, O wise and happy Emperor."

And she leaned back on the divan and commenced her tale.

6

I was born on Earth, in Green River province, one of our most fertile provinces, in our year A.D. 2697—the year Klath 4 of the 82nd Ansaar Imperial Cycle. So I am thirty-four years old by our reckoning; in Ansaar years I am twenty-three. My father was a physician and my mother a scryer, that is, one who studies the nature of the universe.

At the time of the conquest I was a girl just entering womanhood. I had a younger brother who intended to be a healer like my father, and an older sister in training for the scrying arts. I myself had not yet chosen a path to follow.

You should understand, O Supreme Omniscience, that Earth at the time of the Ansaar conquest was a world among worlds, a jewel of the stars, a planet to be envied and admired.

Do you know any of our history? No, of course not, Majesty. The universe is very wide and our world is far away; and the Lord of the Ansaar has much to occupy his mind besides the study of distant and unimportant *maula* planets. But I assure you, Sire, that Earth was no trivial world. To us our little world was the center of the universe, a place of wonder and beauty and nobility.

I tell you that, Omniscience, so that you may see that though to you we are barbarians, we had high regard for our world's civilization. Perhaps some barbarians are content to think of themselves as barbarians, but that was not true of us. Our history went back more than ten thousand of our years. We had surmounted obstacles, transcended our limitations, had built ourselves a society that seemed to us very near perfect.

You smile, O Lord of the Galaxy, at our mere ten thousand years! But consider: at first we were stammering nomads, living on roots and seeds and the beasts of the field; and we rose from that level to conquest not only over the sea and the sky and the darkness of space, but the most difficult of all, triumph over our own selves. We put aside our brutishness and built a great civilization. Has ever a race risen more swiftly from savagery to civilization?

Be aware, O Master of the Ansaar, that we were once a warlike, brutal race, which showed no mercy. I could tell you of great slaughter, the burning of villages and the killing of children, unending cruelties, mindless destruction. A myth of ours tells of the first people, mother, father, two sons, and how one son lifted his hand against his brother and slew him; and that was in the beginning.

For thousands of years there was no peace among us. One family made war upon another, and one town marched against the next, and country against country, and then empires clashed with empires, so that it seemed certain that in time we would turn all the Earth to rubble and ash.

But that did not happen, O Master of the Ansaar. That is perhaps our greatest achievement: that our harsh and irascible nature might have led us to destroy ourselves, and we did not do it, though we had the capability. We did not do it.

You should know, Lord of All, that by the time of my birth the division of the Earth into nations was only a memory, and the populace of the Earth was no greater than the world could sustain; and we had made a green park out of our planet, with fresh, clear air and pure blue seas, and all people lived in harmony and hope.

And then the Ansaar came.

We knew a little by then of the Empire. Not much, for we had chosen not to venture among the stars. It would have been in our power to do it, had we wanted to. But we did not want to.

Those earlier Earthfolk who built nations out of towns and empires out of nations probably looked to the stars as well, and said, "Someday we will rule those also!" But by the time our race knew how to build ships to travel among the stars, we no longer saw reason to do it. We were content to remain on our own small world.

You are probably thinking, O Omniscience, that that is a profound flaw in us; and perhaps you are right. But we were happy enough as we were. Our days of striving were behind us, and it satisfied us to live as we lived, in a balanced, harmonious way.

We knew of the Empire because we could by then detect the messages that pass among the stars, though we didn't understand them; we knew the sky was full of worlds, and we suspected that many of those worlds were under the rule of one dominant race. But we believed that the Empire wanted no part of us.

Of course, we were wrong. The Empire knows no bounds and the spirit of the Ansaar knows no peace; and your people will never rest until your power reaches from one wall of the universe to the other.

The day of the conquest—the Annexation, I should say; I know I should call it that—I will never forget. It was in the time of your father of blessed memory, His Departed Majesty Senpat XIV, may he taste the joys of Paradise forever! It was just two or three years since my breasts had grown. These are breasts, Majesty, these swellings here: if I had a child, they would give milk, for—perhaps you know this?—we humans are mammals. The coming of breasts marks the end of girlhood and the beginning of womanhood for us.

For me the Annexation began at midday in the brightest time of summer, at a time when my life was tranquil and happy, and the future seemed to unfold with limitless promise.

I lived then with my mother, my father, my brother Vann, my sister Theyl, in a house like a golden dome in a village of a thousand people close to the river. To the east were low round hills like green humps; to the west the land tilted as though a giant's hand had lifted it, and mountains of black stone rose to the sky. There once was a great city on our side of the river, back when the Earth had been crowded and noisy; but the city was long gone, and only its traces remained, a gray line of foundations in the grass.

It was a peaceful place and we hoped it would never change. But nothing in the universe is exempt from change, Great One.

Do you know what an Annexation is like? Let me tell you, O great and omnipotent lord.

First there is the Darkness. Then, the Sound. And then, the Splitting of the Sky. And at last the Voice, announcing to the conquered ones the fate that has befallen them.

The Darkness is total—sudden night at midday. Our power sources were orbital satellites whose great wings gathered the sun's energy and sent it to us in laser-steered bundles. In a single moment the Ansaar invaders interrupted the output of every one of our power satellites. The weapon called the Vax did that. It was as if all the satellites in their orbits had been wrapped in blankets of a material impervious to light. Every electrical device on our planet ceased to function. The Darkness had come to us.

I was in the garden. How could I know that the lights were out all over the world and that all our machines, including our weapons of defense, were inoperative? But in the garden there was Darkness. The sun itself had been blotted out. The sky became a black sheet, so black that it was painful to look at. Your Vax had thrown some world-encompassing screen of opaque force, some gigantic barrier, across the sky. It is the great Ansaar weapon, the thing that lets you rule the galaxy: you interpose your might between a planet and its sun, and choke off all light and warmth and energy in a single moment. Who could withstand such a calamity?

I stood staring at the darkened sky and I thought at first I had been struck blind. I held my hand up and could not even see my fingers, not even very faintly, like the shadow of a shadow. I touched my fingers to my eyelids and saw colors, the dancing islands of blue and gold and green that I always saw when I pressed my eyes; but when I opened my eyes again I saw nothing. The world in all its brightness and beauty and wonder was gone.

Yet I was not afraid, not yet. For it all had been so sudden, and so total, that I could not yet take it in.

Next came the Sound, and the Sound was like nothing anyone had ever heard before, a low droning wail, coming from a point near the horizon, that gradually rose in intensity until a dreadful earsplitting screaming was coming down on us, the siren of our doom, a frightful discordant deafening screeching that would not stop, a noise that fell upon us with an almost tangible force.

Now at last I was frightened. This seemed to me to be the end of the world. I fell to my knees and covered my ears. As I think you know already, O Master of All, I am not one easily frightened; and yet I was plunged into an abyss of fear by your Darkness and your Sound. I thought I would never come forth from it.

We were conquered already. But we did not know that yet.

As the Sound grew and grew in strength I saw long belts of light appear, rippling across that curtain of midnight darkness—brilliant horizontal bands of green and yellow and violet and crimson, quivering shimmers of potent brightness that stretched completely across the sky from east to west and vanished beyond the curve of the world's rim. They were like chains encircling a giant's waist. Staring at them in wonder and fright, I felt a sense of *strain,* for I sensed their tense pulsations, as though the giant were breathing in and out, gathering his force, making ready to throw those dazzling shackles off.

The Splitting of the Sky was starting to occur.

The bands of light danced in and out, the green one bending until it seemed to touch the ground and the violet one retracting like a drawn bow, curving far away into the heavens, and the crimson and yellow ones doing the same; then they reversed, snapping inward where they had been out, and out where they were in. And the Sound assailed us with ever more horrendous power. This continued for—five minutes, perhaps? Ten? I became aware, gradually, that the motion of the bands was tearing apart the dense black sheet that lay like a curtain behind them. As they eddied and rippled to and fro, the blackness was strained and stretched to the sundering point.

Then it ripped and the stars came shining through. Thousands, millions, the heavens ablaze with points of light, cold and dazzling, like the reflections of a billion fires in a dark lake.

Then I saw that those myriad lights were moving, moving as stars never move, rapidly growing larger and larger: the ships of the invaders is what they were. The Sound died away, finally. A ghastly stillness took its place, a stillness so total that it was like a roaring in my ears.

And at last came the Voice.

It spoke from the sky, a calm clear deep voice heard everywhere on Earth at once. First in Universal Imperial, of which, naturally, we could not understand a syllable; then again in our own language:

"We bring you the greetings of His Imperial Majesty Senpat XIV, the High Ansaar, the Supreme Omniscience. He instructs us to inform you that you have been gathered this day into the beneficence of the Empire. Thenceforth we of the Empire will shield you from harm, will share with you the greatness of our accomplishments, will guide you toward the attainment of civilization.

"Have no fear. You are in no danger. We come only to offer you the advantages of the Imperial way of life. A new era begins for you this day, people of Earth: an era of security and happiness and prosperity under the benevolent friendship of His Imperial Majesty, the Lord of All, Senpat XIV, may he thrive and prosper."

And so we joined your Empire.

I assumed—we all assumed—that our leaders must already be recovering from the first shock, that defensive measures long held ready were going into action, that everywhere on Earth at this moment the old warlike soul of mankind was awakening from its long slumber and we would begin to take steps to rid ourselves of the unwanted benevolence that the intruders from space were offering us.

But no—no—

Our energy sources remained inoperative. Nothing moved; nothing worked. There was no government, no army, only the two billion baffled citizens of Earth, facing an incomprehensible enemy.

The truth of that landed upon us like a falling mountain. Our souls were numbed; our spirits were crushed. Which is the Ansaar way of conquest: show in the first moments of conquest that resistance is unthinkable, and thus make resistance impossible.

Already the ships of Ansaar were landing in every province of the world, and the Voice of the Imperial Procurator could be heard again everywhere, announcing to us the new order of things.

We were thenceforth under the administration of the Territorial Government of the West Quadrant of the Empire. We would pay taxes to the Territorial Government and would receive the full benefit of membership in the galactic sphere of mutual prosperity that was the Empire. Those with special skills that might be of use to the Empire would be invited to make them available; for the rest, life would go on as it always had, but now an Imperial presence would reside on Earth to insure perpetual peace.

The rioting, the panic, began even before the Voice had finished explaining the changes that had come to our world.

We showed our lack of interest in the benefits of membership in your sphere of mutual prosperity by letting a civilization that had been ten thousand years in the making topple into chaos in a single day.

Once the Voice had stopped speaking I ran for the phone and to call my father at the hospital. Silence came from the speaker grille, the terrible silence of the darkness between the stars.

"Call my mother, then," I told it.

Nothing happened; and it was then that I realized that all communications lines must be dead.

The midday darkness was thinning, now. I saw vague shapes through it, like the shadows of a shadow. Fires blazed in the village. I heard far-off sounds—shouts, cries—

It was the beginning of the Craziness—the Time of Fire.

Demons we had put behind us, monsters and nightmare beings of our bloody past, burst free again now. Our placid society—two billion people neatly spread out across a green planet, quiet villages with tidy homes and pleasing gardens and gentle, law-abiding citizens—went berserk. Nothing mattered except the need to find food, weapons, a secure hiding place. Neighbor turned against neighbor, friend against friend. The world became a jungle again.

Yes, Majesty, I see your smile. *Maulas,* you are thinking. What else could be expected? Mere primitives, with a pitiful ten-thousand-year veneer of civilization—of course they'd turn into savages again the moment things went wrong for them!

Of course!

You are right: we behaved shamefully. But let me put the question to you, Lord of the Ansaar: What if a Darkness were to settle over Haraar, and a Sound were to rend your sky, and starships appeared overhead, and a Voice said that the Ansaar Empire has fallen, that your domain was now a minor province of a far greater empire from another universe, that you have been conquered by a people to whom the mighty Ansaar were no more significant than insects? What would happen, O Emperor of All? The slaves in your palace—eunuchs, concubines, all the lesser and greater wives—would they gather around you and protect you, O Supreme Omniscience? Or would they not fall upon you and tear you into a thousand pieces and run through the palace like beasts?

I mean no disrespect, O Emperor of All. But think of how it would be if a race greater even than yours came without warning and kicked your Empire to pieces the way a boy kicks an insect nest apart—casually, indifferently?

How I managed to live through the first days after the Annexation—the days we called the Craziness, and which now are called by us the Time of Fire—I can hardly say. Thousands died, maybe hundreds of thousands. It was a war of everyone against everyone.

The only rule of law that existed was that of the Ansaar, and in the early days we saw very little of the Ansaar. Sometimes we heard their Voice, but they themselves were all but invisible.

Our government dropped leaflets from the sky urging us to join in a resistance movement; but nothing came of that. At least I was in the safety of my home. I locked the doors and waited, hardly daring to sleep, for my parents or my brother or sister to return.

They never did. I never saw my mother and father again, or my sister. My father, I learned, had died when a mob broke into his hospital looking for medical supplies. My mother was "annexed" herself by the Ansaar, and taken to one of the new depositories where humans with scientific or technical skills were held.

As for my brother and my sister—

My brother Vann, because he pretended to the Ansaar that he was already a trained healer, was taken to the same center as my mother. But soon he was transferred to another Empire world. It would be years before I found him again, and then—but that is another story, Sire, and a very painful one.

Since my sister Theyl was learning to be a scryer, she was, I suppose, annexed and taken to one of the depositories also, or perhaps she was killed during the Time of Fire. But I like to think that she is alive somewhere in this vast Empire.

As for me, I survived. Somehow.

When the food ran out I gathered berries and seeds like any savage. I crept down to the river and filled pots and jars with water. If I had seen small wild animals, I would have tried to kill them by throwing rocks; but wild animals are not common on Earth.

The Darkness was over. The Ansaar once again let the sun shine by day and the moon and stars at night. I would have preferred the Darkness, I think. I would have felt safer moving about in total blackness. Whenever I was outside of the house and spied one of my neighbors I ran desperately and hid in the bushes, like an animal in fear, and crouched there until it seemed safe to come out.

But gradually the Craziness ebbed, and we became accustomed to our new lives. We began to trust each other again and to come together like the civilized beings we once had been.

"The cities have all been destroyed, and their people evacuated into the countryside," I learned from Harron Devoll, the woman who lived just across the stream from me. "And all the government officials are dead." A great weight of loss and sadness descended on me when I heard that.

I heard also that you Ansaar were emptying Earth's museums, taking our treasures to your own main planet; that you were doing something to the oceans and rivers to make Earth's water more agreeable to you; that we would be sent to work in mines on distant worlds; that Ansaar soldiers were raping Earth women.

Was any of it true? Who could say?

But life went on. We formed little groups to raise crops and share such packaged foods as remained to us. We rebuilt much of the village center that rioters had burned the first day. But electrical service still was not restored, nor the communications nets reopened. We had been plunged back into a harsh medieval existence in a single moment.

In the third month of the Annexation three Ansaar came to us in a bronze-colored teardrop-shaped vehicle. They halted in the center of the village and made a tour of inspection, peering at our town hall, at the broken windows of our empty shops, at us.

We had expected demigods; but they were just ugly creatures with crested heads and big-muzzled faces like an animal's, and thick necks, short legs, long arms dangling almost to the ground!

Forgive me, Greatness. They had taken our world in a moment: and surely beings who could do that must be of titanic stature and grandeur. We wanted them to be tall and splendid, with shining eyes and heroic frames. But they were squat, they were coarse, they were ugly. They moved not with the grand swagger of overlords but in the slouching way of those doing a routine job, ordinary troops patrolling an ordinary little conquered planet.

I see you smiling again, Excellency. I know what you are thinking. Such airs this *maula* puts on! She dares complain that the soldiers of the Ansaar weren't grand and awesome enough for her! But I want to speak only the truth. That is how we felt.

"We could kill them," someone suggested. "Only three of them, and so many of us—"

"Perhaps we really could kill these three," someone else answered. "And then others will come and burn the village down to the ground, and burn us with it." And so we did nothing.

The three Ansaar settled in our town hall and made us come before them one by one. I could not stop staring, they seemed so strange to me, so repellent. Yes, Majesty, *repel-*

lent. Yet though I was appalled by them I felt great curiosity too: who are these people who have crossed half the sky to take our world away from us, and why did they want to do it? They had a machine that turned what I said into words they could understand, and what they said into good clear Earth words. They said to me, "What special skill do you have, Laylah Walis?"

"I know how to *learn.* That is my skill."

And as I said it I swore that I would discover for myself all that could be known about our conquerors.

Three days afterward there came a heavy knock at my door, and I heard an Ansaar voice. I was frightened, of course. I was alone. I remembered what I had been told about the Ansaar finding the women of Earth desirable.

But I feared refusing to open the door, so I let him in. He was one of the three from the town hall. I recognized him by a great welt of a birthmark across his face, like a cap worn low on his forehead. He was very short and very wide through the shoulders, and his greenish skin had a pebbled texture.

Can you understand the horror I felt, Majesty? Staring into those alien yellow eyes, seeing that jutting muzzle, imagining those leathery, sharp-clawed hands against my flesh?

And then the Ansaar made a rumbling sound deep in its throat, and took a step toward me, arms outstretched and claws spread wide, and another step, and another—

Abruptly Laylah broke off her tale. "Morning is here, Sire."

The Emperor glanced at the jewel on his wrist and said, "So it is." He frowned. "So our conversation must end. At the first morning hour you have an appointment with the executioner."

She regarded him unwaveringly. "I have not forgotten that either. I hope that I have entertained you at least a little, O Lord of All. And if it is not beneath the dignity of an Emperor of the Ansaar to pray for the repose of a *maula's* soul, I hope you have a good word for me in your prayers this day, Majesty."

"Will you at least finish your tale for me before I go?"

"The first hour is here already, Majesty," said Laylah sweetly. "And my time has come."

"For an Ansaar soldier to assault a woman of an Annexed species is unlawful. And outrageous besides. If any criminal actions occurred, the man will be identified and punished, I promise you that. Tell me exactly what took place. Your execution"—he seemed to have trouble with the word—"can wait."

"Oh, but it is a very long story, Majesty!"

Again the mixture of amusement and annoyance in his expression: "*All* your stories are very long stories, is that not so? Well, leave out those circumstantial details that you paint so well. Simply give me the essence. Did he rape you, yes or no?"

"Majesty—forgive me—it takes time to place the event in its proper context—"

In exasperation the Emperor said, "How much time? An hour? Two? There is no time, woman! The Debin of Hestagar comes to court at the third hour to discuss this year's tribute, and before that I have the morning observances to perform, and then—"

"I could finish the story tonight, then," Laylah suggested.

"For you, lady, there will be no *tonight*."

"Ah. How true," she said.

7

From the puzzled expressions of Laylah's maids that morning and from her scowling neuter chamberlain's long face it was obvious that they were surprised to find her still here past the hour of execution. Her studies of Ansaar culture indicated that the lower castes took *tiihad* with the greatest seriousness. Aristocrats might shrug, but commoners, dreading any collapse of the social order, wanted the rules of behavior to be observed.

She waited to hear the knock of the emissaries of death. Once, when she fell into a sound sleep, she dreamed that the knock had come and that at the door, grinning at her, was a gigantic Ansaar with shoulders like a bull's, holding a gleaming hatchet dripping red with blood.

The day went by, somehow.

Then Laylah's sour-faced chamberlain appeared and announced grandly, "His Majesty the Emperor calls upon you once again!"

"Wine!" the Emperor said brusquely, striding through the ivory-inlaid door of her suite. He clapped his hands. The maids scurried to obey.

"A difficult day, Majesty?" Laylah asked.

He smiled, amused, perhaps, by the intimacy of her tone.

"The Debin," he muttered. "The Goishlar of Gozishtandar. The Great Frulzak of Frist! The Gremb! All day long, princes and princelings of the tributary worlds—whole processions of them, prostrating themselves, murmuring hypocritical words of obscenely overstated praise, shoving heaps of gifts toward me. All of them wanting something from me, wanting, wanting, wanting—" The Emperor took a moody gulp of his wine. "I was third in line for the throne, do you know that? I never expected to inherit. It should have been Senpat. But Senpat loved his little hyperyacht too much; and one day he came out of hyper right in the middle of the sun. Well, there was my brother Iason, the second prince; but when he heard Senpat was dead, he enrolled in a stasis monastery, and there he sits to this day, sealed in beyond all reach for the next ten thousand years, neither dead nor alive but as holy as anyone can possibly be. My father summoned me to the throne chamber—why am I telling you this, I wonder?—he summoned me, tears in his eyes, and he said, 'Ryah, my youngest—Ryah, my dearest—' I thought the tears were for Senpat and for Iason, but I soon saw that they were for me. And so here I am. The wives! The concubines! The grand palaces! The absolute power over a trillion lives! But also—the Debin, the Goishlar! The Great Frulzak of Frist! The Gremb!"

"Kings are like stars," said Laylah. "They rise and set, they have the worship of the world, but no repose."

The Emperor looked up. "Well said! You have the gift of words."

"Oh," she said, smiling. "They are very fine words, yes, but not my own. I quote one of our poets, a man named Shelley."

"Ah. He understood a great deal, your Shelley. Did you have many poets as good as he?"

"A great many, yes."

"So many worlds—so many poets," said the Emperor. "I wish I could study them all. You must recite some work of other poets, Laylah, when there is time."

"But there is no time, Sire. First I must finish my story; and then—and then—"

"Your story, yes," the Emperor said darkly. "And then—then—" He peered into his wine cup. "All day long, between the ambassadors and the potentates and the petitioners, what did I hear from my own people? The *maula,* they said. The *maula,* the *maula,* the *maula*! Where is she? Why has there been no execution?" He glared, a strange tortured look. "Oh, Laylah, Laylah, why did you ever come here? And why did I not have your head cut from your body the moment I learned that you were here?"

"My story, Lord of All—may I resume my story?"

He waved his hand in a fretful, abstracted way. "Yes. Finish your story, yes. And see that you *do* finish this time!"

8

Well, then, O great and glorious Emperor, it is not long after the Annexation. I am alone, and hear the knock, and admit the Ansaar soldier. There I am like one who is frozen, and the soldier is spreading wide his claws and seems about to seize me and do loathsome bestial things to me. But I cannot move.

How could I know, unfamiliar as I was with Ansaar ways, that his outstretched arms and widespread claws, menacing as they seemed, were only a request for a stranger's attention?

"You are Laylah Walis?" He spoke with difficulty in heavily accented English.

"Yes."

He was Procurator-Adjutant Jjai Haunt. He had come here to annex me into the service of the Empire.

"Annexed?" I gasped. "Me? Why?"

"Interfacing duties." Haunt consulted a scrap of paper tucked in his belt. "At your interview you said the ability to learn was your special gift. We need those who can learn. When you have, you will help us to administer the Territory of Earth."

So they would train me to be a traitor. But I was too naïve to realize that, then. In any case, I had been annexed. I had five minutes to choose whatever I wanted to take with me and then he led me outside.

Haunt took me to an Annexation depository on the far side of the mountains. There were at least five hundred humans and about a dozen unarmed Ansaar. The humans all had the same dull, dazed, stunned expression, as though they had been drugged.

But it was the conquest itself that had stunned them, the suddenness of Earth's loss of its ancient independence. It was like living among ghosts, Excellency, to live with these annexed people.

I asked if they knew anything about my mother or my brother or my sister. No one did. For three days I walked the perimeter of the depository and stared at the dark wall of the mountains and counted clouds and tried once more to come to terms with the thing that had happened to our world. On the fourth day Haunt came back for me.

A loose headcloth hid his birthmark. "I am Haunt," he said. "Who was with you before. Your instruction will now begin."

He took me to a three-cornered building on the other side of the camp: our classroom. "First our language," he said, handing me a copper helmet designed for human use, fitting over my head. No Ansaar could have worn it because of the Ansaar crest. I slipped it on and a burst of powerful energy hit me: a sensation like icy daggers plunging into my eardrums, and a wild swirling around me, as if I were in some frightful snowstorm. Choking and gasping, I put my hands to my head to pull the helmet away, but it stuck to me like my own skin.

Haunt removed it. "Now we can begin to teach you our words."

I wondered if the helmet had filled me with your language in one jolt. But no, what I had been given was only the *capacity* to learn Imperial. Your language is so different in basic assumptions, O Lord of All, that our minds must be adjusted in order to grasp them. Such concepts as the unifying divider, the distributive affiliate, the shifter and the reduplicative and the somatic grammatical phase—we find them altogether alien.

Yet—as you see, O Master of the Universe—I speak your language fluently now, thanks to the copper helmet and to Procurator-Adjutant Haunt's patient and effective instruction.

When I could speak well enough he taught me some of the Empire's history: its origins on holy Haraar, its ninety thousand years of constant galactic expansion. He explained the powerful need of your people to introduce order into the turbulence and confusion of the universe; and he showed me the great advantages that have come to the annexed races through their affiliation with the Empire. Even so, I still lamented the loss of our independence, Majesty.

Haunt took me up in a little gravity-thrust vehicle that carried us into the darkness that surrounded the Earth. We traveled the circumference of the Earth, looking down together on the newest of the Ansaar worlds. I stared in wonder and awe at the blue-green bosom of the Earth, at shining fields of white snow and vast tawny wastelands, and at forests so green they seemed black, and the great dark ocean expanses, which hurled blinding sun-blinks back up at us.

And I saw, limned like faint ghost-sketches against the distant ground, the outlines of ancient cities, the dim vestiges and shadowy ruins of the crowded, noisy, brawling Earth of the vanished past. "Tell me what those cities were called," Haunt ordered me. "I want to compile an account of this planet's history over the past fifty thousand years. We already know that Earth once was covered with large cities. Tell me: which was London? Which was Rome? Which was New York? We know the names, but not the locations."

Of course New York and London and Rome were only names to me, vestiges of that troubled era of conflict and irrational hatreds that preceded the tranquility and joy that had been ours. Now, seeing the shadowy outlines of places that had been abandoned for hundreds of years, the stumps of once-majestic buildings, the sketchy hints of what must have been highways and bridges, great amphitheaters and monuments, I could tell him very little.

I studied our archives and taught myself about the Earth that had been, so that I could teach our history to Procurator-Adjutant Haunt. "That one, that was London. And over there, that was Paris, in a country that was called France. You see the spidery metal tower? And the gray building— the cathedral is what that was. For religious ceremonies." I showed him Egypt's Pyramids, rising starkly out of the sands, no more troubled by this latest conqueror than by any earlier ones; I found China's Great Wall for him, zigzagging across the Asian desert; I took him afterward to the sites of other cities, telling him how many millions of people had lived in each: eight million here, I said, and nine million there, and this one, down there, fifteen million, and twenty million in that one in the valley beneath those two lofty mountains.

Haunt was silent much of the time. I desperately wanted him to look up and say to me, "I see now that this was no piddling little world, this Earth of yours!"

I was a naïve child then; and how was I to know that this was Procurator-Adjutant Jjai Haunt's twentieth planetary assignment, that he had helped to conquer at least a dozen huge glittering worlds whose attainments and achievements made those of Earth seem like the doings of children? Well, Haunt had the goodness not to humble my pride. I learned for myself, later on, when I began my travels through the Empire, what *real* planetary magnificence was like. But that was later.

Once Haunt took me right to the edge of our little ship's range to show me how the Ansaar maintain their power over the worlds they annex. We were deep in the darkness above the Earth. He indicated a shining globe floating in orbit nearby that seemed no bigger than my fist. I could have reached out with a boom and gathered it in.

"That is the Vax," said Haunt. "It disrupts all electrical fields not of our own making and severs communications links."

I could see the white whorls of Vax power radiating from it, spinning off in writhing knots through the sky. And I thought I could hear the Vax singing with its own immense power, a slow, heavy, infinitely leisurely song of domination.

"Surely letting me see this is a breach of security," I said. "We could steal one of these ships and come up here and knock your Vax from the sky."

Haunt was amused. "No. Behind this Vax is another, and behind that one a third. They are in—adjacent spaces, well beyond your reach. You could never locate them, or harm them if you did."

I knew it was true; and I knew Haunt had taken me here to show me how futile any treachery would be, that the Ansaar dominion on Earth was unshakable.

I came to like Procurator-Adjutant Haunt very much. How unlikely, a girl of Earth developing warm feelings for one of the invaders. Perhaps it is an overstatement, Majesty, to say that I *liked* Haunt, that my feelings for him were *warm;* but he did come to seem like a friend to me, as much as any Ansaar could have been.

He taught me much. And he was my protector too.

Let me explain, Sire. I have said several times that I was naïve, then, and one mark of my naïveté was that I allowed myself to be turned into a traitor to my people without realizing it.

I know it is difficult for you to see service to the Empire as any kind of treason. But I am a member of an annexed race; and we of Earth are particularly proud and stubborn; and though we had no choice but to accept Annexation, we always resented it. Yet there I was, serving our conquerors.

Without helpers like me they would have had little access to the data that could help them understand this latest conquest. Our language is as alien to the Ansaar as theirs is to us, and as language goes, so goes conceptualization itself. So it was necessary for the Ansaar to turn to guides who could explain human ways.

Though I was inexperienced even in the ways of my own world, I was, as I said, skilled at learning things; and also I am good at explaining what I have learned. So members of the Ansaar high command came to me to ask about Earth and I would answer, and if I did not know the answers, I would find them.

It took me a great deal of time to see that this was treason in the eyes of many of my fellow citizens.

I lived now in New Haraar, the newly built administrative capital, and here I worked at my task of finding answers to Ansaar questions. I had difficulty making friends there. At first I thought it was because I was from a village that they did not know. Then I saw they were deliberately avoiding me.

I was cooperating willingly with our overlords, you see. And my relations with an officer of the occupying force were openly friendly. Most humans at the capital viewed themselves as prisoners of war, serving the Ansaar grudgingly, with hatred in their hearts.

I learned the truth one day when I was walking between my lodging and the Ansaar data repository. I was supposed to meet Haunt and report to him on research I had done on the different racial forms of the human species and the problems that those differences had caused in ancient times. Suddenly a group of people—five, eight, maybe ten—came rushing out of an opening between two buildings and began shouting and shaking their fists at me.

"Ansaar whore!" they cried. "Alien-lover! Traitor!" One spat at me. One pulled my hair. I thought they would kill me.

"Ansaar whore!" they kept yelling. "Whore! Whore! Where's your Ansaar lover, whore?"

I had never fought in my life; but I fought now, trying to hold them off as they punched me, slapped me, tossed me around. "Wait—" I called. "Stop!" They only hit me harder.

My lip was split now. Blood ran down my cheek. One of my eyes felt puffed and swollen.

And then Haunt was there.

He came out of nowhere into the middle of the whirlwind. His claws flashed brightly in the sun and he caught one of my attackers and touched him lightly along the side of his face, and the man fell to the ground. Haunt touched another, and he fell too. Another.

The others stepped back, glaring at Haunt and me with such loathing that it made me tremble.

"You must not harm her," Haunt said. "If you do, you will suffer. Now go. *Go.*" And to me: "Are you all right?"

"Shaken up. Some cuts and bruises. Oh, Haunt, Haunt—were they insane? Why did they jump on me like that?"

"They dislike our—friendship. We are friends, you and I, are we not?"

"Of course."

"They are not pleased by that."

All that day I could hear their angry shouts in my mind. Traitor! Ansaar whore! Where's your Ansaar lover, whore?

Did they think that Haunt and I were—

Yes. A few days later, as I was eating lunch in the commissary, a woman sat down next to me and said in a low voice, "Are you really sleeping with him, girl?"

"What?"

"The Ansaar. Do you and he do it or don't you?"

The image leaped into my mind of Haunt's body pressed against mine, Haunt's clawed hands wandering across my breasts, my thighs, my belly. His jutting muzzle seeking my lips. But of course there had never been any kind of physical contact between us. "How could you imagine such a thing?" I asked her.

"You want to watch your step. One thing to work for them—we all have to do that—but *loving* them?—Oh, no, child, that will not be tolerated. Do you understand me? Will not be tolerated."

Nothing could convince her of my innocence.

When I saw Haunt later that day, I could not bear to tell him what she had said. It was too bizarre, too shameful. I looked at him—the squat little Ansaar officer with the scaly skin and the long dangling arms, the short neck and the protruding jaws, the prickly spines of his crest marching across the top of his head, and I thought, *No, no, we could never be lovers. But he is decent and kindly, and I feel no hatred for him.*

Was I a traitor, though?

Yes. Yes, I was. I saw that now. In my naïveté I had betrayed my people, and they hated me for it. And my life was in jeopardy. If I went on working against my own kind, I would pay for it.

Two days later, I was attacked again in the street.

I never saw my attacker. Someone darted out of the shadows, struck me hard in the face, disappeared. Again my lip was cut. It was as though a white-hot blade had been drawn across it.

"Tell me who it was," Haunt demanded.

I could tell him nothing. He put me under the protection of security robots. Wherever I went I had a robot at my side. I was pointed at, hissed at, jeered at. The robot intercepted things that were thrown at me, but it could not intercept their hatred.

I thought of asking Haunt to release me from my annexation and return me to my village. But I *liked* working for him. I enjoyed helping him learn Earth's history of Earth. And also I felt I was serving the cause of Earth by working with the Ansaar. I was studying them while they were studying us, learning not only their language but their nature. That might be useful someday.

Three indecisive days passed. Then a tall white-haired man halted me outside Haunt's headquarters and said, "Do you recognize me, Laylah?"

I stared at him. "No."

"Dain Italu is my name. I knew your father in medical school." He lowered his voice. "Do you know about the Partisans, Laylah?"

"The Partisans?"

Quietly he said, "We work for Earth's freedom. I'm told that you work willingly with the Ansaar, Laylah, and that you even—" He paused. "Well, there are other charges. They proposed a sentence of death. I spoke out for you. I said no daughter of Tomas Walis could be guilty of such things. I hope I'm right, Laylah."

My face turned red and hot. "I'm not sleeping with an Ansaar, if that's what you were trying to say, Dr. Italu. But I *am* working with one, yes." And I told him that I felt what I was learning about the Ansaar could be valuable to Earth's cause.

"Perhaps. But I warn you, Laylah: get yourself free from this Ansaar of yours. Have nothing further to do with him. Otherwise—when the trouble starts—"

His voice had become ragged and uncertain. And it struck me that he was telling me something I probably should not be hearing, out of friendship that had once existed between him and my father.

He left me standing there, confused, deeply troubled.

I went up to Haunt's office. Ancient documents were spread out before him, texts going back to the era of warring nations.

"Look at these, Laylah. They're fascinating—absolutely fascinating. But there are some things here I don't quite understand. Perhaps you can—"

I have things to tell you, I thought. There's going to be a rebellion. You're at risk, Haunt, and so am I.

But all morning we looked at documents and I said nothing. And that night, when the uprising began—

Ah, Lordship, but morning has come again, I think! And so there is no more time for me to tell my tale!

The Emperor said, "How sly, Laylah! You lead me along and lead me along, and just as I'm caught up in your story, eager to know what happens next, you tell me morning has come again!"

"But morning *has* come again, Sire. And the executioner is waiting."

"Let him wait!" cried the Emperor. "Who rules this Empire, the Emperor or the executioner? There's much that I need to hear. Partisans plotting rebellion—an insurrection against Ansaar rule—why am I learning of these things for the first time? Go on with it. That night, when the uprising began—"

"I have talked all night, Sire. There is so much more to tell; but not now, not now!" Laylah yawned delicately. "I beg your indulgence, for I must sleep now, Excellency. And you—the responsibilities of the throne await you. Tonight, when I resume—"

He smiled wryly. "Tonight! Tonight! And so you buy yourself another day of life!"

"Ah, my lord, so I do. But life as a prisoner. What kind of life is that? I'd gladly tell you all in the next hour, and go at last to the fate reserved for me. But I am so tired now, Majesty."

"I will see you at sundown," said the Emperor Ryah VII, and she could not tell whether his tone conveyed annoyance or amusement, or perhaps some of each. "Rest now, Laylah. And prepare to bring your story to its conclusion this evening." And he was gone.

9

You have ordered me, O Master of the Galaxy and Lord of All, to be concise. And so I will be; for I am a mere barbarian slave and you are the Pillar of the Empire. I will tell you quickly of what happened on that terrible and violent evening in New Haraar.

Ansaar blood was shed that night. Know, O Highest, that Earth has but one moon, large and brilliant. It goes through its phases every twenty-eight days; and so a time comes once a month when the night sky is dark but for the cool sparkle of the stars. On such a night of no moon the Partisans struck their first blow.

You must remember, Excellency, we were once a violent race who with great difficulty had learned the way of peace; but now the buried violence in our souls had come roaring back into us with the vehemence of a beast that had been chained too long.

Two billion of us and only a handful of Ansaar: the Partisans reasoned that if they could pick a few Ansaar off, five here and ten there, the flame of resistance would catch and blaze high, and then the Imperial government might decide we were too fierce, too savage, to take into the Empire.

For weeks the Partisans had gathered weapons—not Ansaar weapons, beyond our poor *maula* skills to understand, but the crude weapons of Earth itself, knives and clubs and such. And they struck in the same instant in a dozen parts of New Haraar. With their knives, their clubs, their simple barbaric weapons.

Jjai Haunt was among those Ansaar who fell in that first onslaught. If I had not left work early that night, I might well have died beside him. He was alone. They came out of the darkness and struck him again and again; and though he fought back bravely—I know he did—there were too many. They struck him down with their knives and their clubs, their simple barbaric weapons; and so they slew an Ansaar who had seen service on twenty worlds of the Empire.

Twelve other Ansaar died in twelve different regions of New Haraar. The moonless night was lit by the red blaze of fifty fires.

Dain Italu came to me. "Get your things together, fast. The Partisans will be here tonight to kill you."

He grabbed a traveling case of mine and threw some things into it; and I collected a few things more—clothing, books, pictures of my mother and father. A floater waited in the street.

"Where are you taking me?" I asked.

"To Sinon Kreish's castle," said Italu.

Sinon Kreish, Majesty, is dead now; but he was the wealthiest man on Earth, of a grandeur that only an Emperor can understand. To me he was legendary.

"Have all the Ansaar been killed?" I asked.

"Only a few, Laylah. The ones who were marked for death."

"And I was marked for death too, then?"

"By one faction, yes. Others argued for saving you. You've been closer to the Ansaar than almost any of us, and you know them in a way that we'll need later on."

We were far from New Ansaar by now. I thought of Jjai Haunt lying dead in the street, and I wanted to cry; but no tears would come. I was too sick at heart, too bewildered.

Pale morning brightness entered the sky. A great black mountain loomed before us.

"Mount Vorn," said Dain Italu. "The estate of Sinon Kreish."

The floater landed on the black, craggy summit. And I knew I had come to a place of wonders and miracles.

Golden sunlight ran in rivers across the iron-blue sky. Sweet morning air rushed into my lungs like fine mellow wine. Ancient sorceries penetrated my soul.

A woman of Sinon Kreish's staff moved toward us with wonderful grace, as though drifting weightless through the strange thin air.

"I am Kaivilda," she said. "Welcome, Laylah Walis."

And I entered the dwelling of Sinon Kreish.

Kreish himself, O Master of All, was complex and sophisticated, wealthy and powerful and shrewd; a personage of splendor and significance. An hour with him, Sire, might have caused you to revise your notions of the barbaric qualities of the *maulas* of Earth.

I wandered through his castle in an ecstasy of amazement. The Keep was a vast, gleaming onyx serpent, looping and leaping along the knifeblade-sharp ridge that is Mount Vorn's highest peak. Its topmost level, a quartz bubble, held Sinon Kreish's bedchamber, with his conjuratorium just alongside. Below—a horn of pure shining platinum boldly cantilevered out over the valley—was his trophy room; and just beside that, a blatant green eye of curving emerald, was the jutting hemisphere of his harmonic retreat.

A white-vaulted passageway led to the apartments of Sinon Kreish's family. A row of razor-keen blades that would rise from the carnelian floor of the passageway at any provocation guarded these.

A second passage opened into a pleasure gallery supported by pillars of golden marble. Here the castle's inhabitants swam in a tank lined with garnet slabs, or drifted in a column of warm air, or made contact with the rhythms and pulses of the cosmos. Here, also, Sinon Kreish maintained patterned rugs for focused meditation, banks of motile light organisms for autohypnosis, and other things whose purposes I did not know.

From there the structure made a swaybacked curve and sent two wings back up the mountain. One contained Sinon Kreish's collection of zoological marvels, the other his botanical garden. Between them were two levels of libraries and chambers for the housing of antiquities and objets d'art, and the castle's dining hall, a single octagonal block of agate thrusting out into the abyss. Below that was the room of social encounter, a cavernous hall whcrc Sinon Kreish entertained guests. A landing stage for visitors' vehicles protruded from the mountain alongside. Behind it, hewn deep into the face of the mountain, were kitchens, waste-removal facilities, power-generation chambers, servants' quarters, and such.

In this miraculous house I spent the next six months, cherished like a member of Sinon Kreish's own family. As for Sinon Kreish himself I saw only an occasional glimpse of a striking, formidable figure moving through the gleaming halls, at least in the beginning. But his kinfolk treated me warmly. It was a time of pure enjoyment— a dream-life, Sire, a time out of time for me. Gradually I began to recover from the shocks and surprises of the time of the Annexation.

They are all dead now, O Lord of All, those sons and daughters of Sinon Kreish, and the castle itself was long ago reduced to rubble by the vengeful armies of the Ansaar. But my stay in that place remains as bright as ever in my memory.

There was no sense there of the Ansaar presence on Earth. The entire Annexation might never have taken place at all.

In time I learned that thc Ncw Haraar uprising had failed. Before dawn of that first night Ansaar forces had arrested nearly all the conspirators. Most were dead now. There had been terrible reprisals everywhere. Some of Earth's greatest monuments were leveled; several of our most productive agricultural zones were systematically ruined. Word went forth that any further attacks against the Ansaar would be met even more stringently. So it was clear that the benevolence of the Ansaar regime was no more than a veneer, that we were in fact slaves, that if we were unruly we would be punished like beasts.

In Sinon Kreish's castle the weeks went by, each much like another. My life was strangely static, leading nowhere, containing no meaning. But then there was a great deal of meaning, indeed.

I was taken to Sinon Kreish's private retreat, the emerald-walled globe at the summit of the entire structure. Sinon Kreish stood rigid and upright as a tree. It was the first time I had ever been alone with him, and I was frightened.

"I will tell you a great secret, girl, that would be worth my life if ever it reached the ears of the Ansaar. I am the leader of the resistance movement here on Earth."

I looked at him in amazement. "The Partisans?"

"In a way. Their goal and mine were the same, to win back our planet's freedom; and so I gave them a certain amount of aid. But the Partisans had no sense, no discretion. They could think only of murder and destruction. What could that gain? We murder ten Ansaar and they kill ten thousand of us. We burn five of their buildings and they destroy five of our provinces." He smiled, the fiercest, most icy smile I had ever seen. "The Partisans were wrong, and paid with their lives. The Empire is stronger and wiser than we are; and it has dealt with rebels before. How many annexed worlds, do you think, have ever won their freedom from the Ansaar?"

I had no idea; and so I said nothing.

Sinon Kreish nodded. "Correct. None. Not one, in the ninety thousand years of the Empire. Revolts, yes. Wars of independence, even. But not a single planet has ever escaped the Ansaar grasp."

"Then we will be Ansaar slaves forever?" I asked.

"Perhaps. We can never *force* the Ansaar to set us free. But maybe someday we can have our freedom as a gift, do you see? Not by resisting, girl, but by freely and willingly cooperating."

I was baffled. Why would the Empire ever relinquish its control over a meek and cooperative world? That was just the sort of world it would want to keep. And how did one resist by cooperating?

He said, as though I had spoken aloud, "I deal with the Ansaar as I would with anyone with whom I am linked by common purpose. The Ansaar don't want to destroy us. They want us to be docile, manageable members of the Empire. I too want to avert Earth's destruction. So we have a common purpose, the Ansaar and I. Therefore I deal with them, do you see? I launch no insurrections. I countenance no assassinations, no arson."

He peered down at me from his great height. "Let's get down to particulars, child. Dain Italu says you speak fluent Ansaar and that you've made a study of their ways and customs."

I nodded. "But I still have a great deal to learn."

"And we want to give you the opportunity to learn it. The more you know about the Ansaar, the more useful you are."

Useful? To whom? I wondered. And how?

Sinon Kreish went on, "I have spoken lately with my friend Antimon Felsert, who is, you know, High Procurator for Earth."

His *friend*? The word took my breath away.

"The High Procurator," he said, "will let a few young people from Earth enter the Empire to study Imperial ways. I've shown him that mankind needs proper knowledge of the society it's joining if it is to be integrated into the Empire." He smiled. "We have been so isolated, so remote from the main currents of galactic life. But if some of our brightest can go forth to travel and study, they'll ultimately serve to explain the ways of the Ansaar to the people of Earth, and to help the Ansaar learn something of our ways as well."

I was thunderstruck. This was all so sudden. I searched desperately for words. "Well—yes—I think—that is—"

"There'd be no possibility of setting foot on the core worlds of the Empire, the ones inhabited by the Ansaar themselves. Entry to Imperial Space is forbidden to *maulas*. You know what that word means, do you?"

Reddening, I said, "Yes, Barbarian."

"Actually it means simply 'those who are not fully civilized.' But yes, 'barbarian' is basically correct. So you could never enter Imperial Space, but that still leaves the vast region of Territorial Space, where non-Ansaar races that are beyond *maula* status but nevertheless not yet entitled to full Imperial citizenship dwell. You'll have plenty to study there."

It was agreed; and I left the castle of Sinon Kreish and traveled back to New Haraar. Where I soon found myself being ushered into the presence of Antimon Felsert, the High Procurator for Earth.

—But I think that morning has come again, Sire. My time is at an end, and I must cease telling my tale.

"This Felsert," said the Emperor. "The name seems familiar."

"It is morning, Sire!"

"Yes, yes, I know. Felsert, Felsert—"

"He was assassinated by terrorists in the last year of your father's reign. Sinon Kreish was charged with the crime and he and his entire family were put to death."

"Yes," the Emperor said, half to himself. "I remember now. The first High Procurator killed by natives in something like four thousand years. There were worldwide reprisals, weren't there?"

"Severe ones, Sire. I was on one of the Bessiral worlds at the time, but I know my world suffered for his death. I was shocked by the assassination, myself, Majesty. It seemed pointless to me."

"Indeed." The Emperor seemed oddly unwilling to leave. Laylah said again, "Is it not morning, Sire?"

He swung around and glared at her. "It is morning, yes!"

"And the executioner—"

"The executioner, the executioner, the executioner! *Vipraint* the executioner! Why are you in such a hurry to die?"

"I'm in no hurry at all, Majesty. But the law requires—"

"Do you presume to teach me the law?"

"A thousand pardons, Sire. I was only reminding you—"

"Yes. Yes. Yes. Yes."

"But if in your great mercy, All-Powerful, you choose to let this poor *maula* remain alive another day, I would offer thanks to the gods of all the worlds."

Sourly the Emperor said, "I asked you to tell me why you had come here although you knew it meant death to do so. So you told me the story of the Annexation of Earth. I asked about what appeared to have been your rape at the hands of an Ansaar soldier, and you told me that the Ansaar had come to you to ask your help, and that he became your friend and protector. I asked for the details of the conspiracy that cost your Ansaar friend his life, and you gave me an account of your visit to the castle of some rich Earthman who eventually was found guilty of treason against the Empire. Three nights have passed in this storytelling, and I have come to know a great deal now about who you are and what you have experienced, and yet I've had no proper answers so far to any of my questions. What am I to do with you, Laylah Walis? What am I to do with you?"

"You are the Guardian of the Law, Majesty. You are free at any time to deliver me up to those who carry out its precepts."

"I want answers from you first!"

"Even so, even so. Come to me again tonight, and I will try to tell you all that you desire to know. But surely you must not stay here any longer this morning. The duties of the court—"

"Yes, the duties of the court," said the Emperor. "The duties of the court! Who but me knows what the duties of the court are like? No wonder my father wept for me when I became the heir. The duties of the court!" His voice was rising. "Today, Laylah: the Twelve Despots of Geeziyangiyang arrive to pay their courtesies. Then the trade delegation of Gimmil-Gib-Huish, with a gift for the Imperial Zoological Gardens: poisonous serpents, most likely. Next the League of the Fertile Womb, presenting the winner of the Imperial Order of the Crystal Egg. Then the Guild of Prophets, with the annual predictions;

the champion *verbish*-breeder of Zabor Province, to get
her medal; the Imperial Architect, to complain about
modifications I want for the Pavilion of the Grand Celestial
Viewing; and then—then—ah, it never ends! What's the
point of absolute power, if you fritter it away on a hundred
ceremonial audiences a day? Lord of All! Master of the
Universe!" The Emperor laughed wildly. Then, his voice
quieter again, almost eerily contained, he said, "The duties
of the court, as you say, must not be shirked. Ah, but if
I could! If I only could! *Thraak* the duties of the court!
Gedoy the duties of the court! I'll go now, and will return at
sundown." He crossed the room, and studied her a moment
at close range. Then his hand reached out—his claws, she
noticed, were elegantly trimmed and rounded—and lightly
touched the curve of her jaw, running his hand up almost
to her ear in a gesture that seemed to be one of tenderness.
In a soft voice he said, "How fascinating you are! And how
maddening. Until later, then, Laylah."

Once more he was gone.

10

If I may resume, Majesty—Light of the Cosmos—Supreme
Monarch of the Million Suns . . .

I was brought into the presence of the High Procurator for
Earth, Antimon Felsert. Never had I beheld an Ansaar even
of the middle castes. High Procurator Felsert was different
from other Ansaar. I saw it in the color of his skin, the shape
and size of his crest, the proportions of his limbs.

He said, in excellent English, "So you're the girl that Sinon
Kreish has sent us for the study program. How old are you,
girl?"

"Sixteen," I said. "Almost seventeen."

"You speak Universal Imperial, girl? And read it? Here,
then. Glance through this." He tossed me a glossy memoran-
dum cube and told me how to activate it. Jjai Haunt's report
on me materialized in bright red letters in the air.

. . . intelligent, eager to please . . . a fast learner . . . almost
suspiciously trustworthy . . . somewhat immature for her age,

considering that human females are capable of reproduction by the time they have lived twelve or thirteen years...

"What do you think he meant, 'almost suspiciously trustworthy'?" the High Procurator asked, speaking in Imperial.

"I have no idea, sir," I replied in the same language.

"And 'eager to please.' Why be eager to please an Ansaar?"

"You are our masters," I said simply.

"Reason enough to hate us, then."

"I hate no one, sir. It seems a waste of emotional energy."

He asked me a few questions more. But they were only routine. My fate had already been decided. My long years of exploration and study were about to begin. Eighteen years, from Earth to this holy world of Haraar and the presence of your majestic self.

Twelve men, seven women, were in the first group sent to the Territories: poets, scholars, scientists. We went forth in groups of three or four. I was sent to Bethareth in the Hklplod system: a golden world of a golden sun, where sleek beautiful creatures, limbless as serpents, worship a monster-god dwelling atop a great mountain. I lived there a year, and watched them as they pressed their jewel-studded foreheads against their god's stone flank. From there I went to Giallo Giallo of the Mirilores, a world of eternal snows and frozen oceans, and traveled with Ansaar explorers into an underground realm of torrid caverns and turbulent lava rivers. It would take me six of these nights to describe that strange world.

Then to Sepulmideine, the World of Chained Moons, where the sky burns with fragrant fires—to Mikkalthrom, where the Emperor Gorn XIX lies buried in a stasis tomb that will not open for fifty thousand Imperial years—to Gambelimeli-dinul, the pleasure world of the Eastern Territories—

Each held more than one could see in a dozen lifetimes; and yet I knew that this was only the edge of the edge of the Empire's myriad Territories, that I could travel forever and never see the whole of them.

The highest moment—and the darkest—came for me on a world called Vulcri of the red sun Kiteil, as I stood staring at the ruins of Costa Stambool, the capital of an empire that had fallen long before the first Ansaar had ever gone forth from Haraar.

I saw layer upon jumbled layer. The crooked streets of the oldest levels, dating from the dying days of an era called the Second Mandala and contemptuously built upon by the glorious successors of that impoverished civilization: its primitive walls were hidden beneath the accretions of a thousand later centuries, and yet they glowed with a proud scarlet phosphorescence. Above were the chalcedony halls of the Concord of Worlds, and above those the streets of the City of Brass, and sprawling over those the remains of the slopes and slideways of gaudy Glissade, the pleasure suburb of Later Costa Stambool. Over everything else was brutally superimposed the final scars inflicted by the vandals who ushered in the climactic Fourth Mandala of Costa Stambool with fire and the sword.

Here were the palaces of obsolete dynasties, the temples of forgotten gods; here were shops that dealt in treasures already incalculably ancient when the Ansaar were young, taverns peddling vintages long turned to dust, parks green with trees and shrubs of species no longer known to the universe. A great marble slab proclaimed in an undecipherable language the glories of an empire that spanned ten solar systems whose name is lost beyond retrieval.

I stood stock-still, letting the splendors of this ancient civilization flood my soul: the palace of the Triple Queen, and the courtyard of the Emperor of All, and the marble cells where the Tribunal of the People, that fifty-minded entity which had governed here for thirty centuries of grimly imposed harmony, lived chin-deep in pools of luminous nutrients drawn from the dissolved bodies of their citizenry, and the celebrated Library of Old Stambool, where books in the form of many-faceted gems, containing in their rigid lattices every word that had ever been written, spilled from iron-bound chests. I peered into the Gymnasium and it seemed that a howling triple-headed beast in fetters was glaring back at me from the Field of Combat with fiery eyes. I entered the Market of All Wonders, where merchandise of a thousand worlds once was laid out in open arcades, everything free for the taking, gift of They-Who-Provide, loving guardians of this greatest of all cities. I was numb with a surfeit of miracle.

Then a voice by my side said, "Someday, perhaps, the capital of the Ansaar will be a ruin like this, eh?"

I whirled. A man—a human!—had quietly come upon me while I still stood in that trance of wonder.

"Are you shocked, Laylah?"

"How do you know my name?"

He laughed. "You don't recognize me, do you?"

I looked—looked—the eyes, the shape of the lips. The curve of the smile. "Vann?" I said, hesitantly.

"Your long-lost brother Vann, yes! Who comes up to you at the edge of nowhere and says hello! Can you believe it, Laylah? Two needles we are, in a haystack a million light-years across!"

We fell into each other's arms, laughing and crying, there beside the ruins of lost Costa Stambool.

I have never known a more wonderful moment, Sire, in my life. But it turned to ashes almost at once. For as we walked back to the visitor lodge, babbling to each other of all that had happened to us since the day of the Darkness and the Sound and the Voice, Vann said something that brought me up short with horror and fright, something so dark and mad that I could scarcely believe he had said it. What my brother said to me—it was utter treason, Majesty.

Ah, but it is time to halt for tonight, eh, Majesty? I have taken so many hours in my descriptions of wonders that I will have to tell you tomorrow of my brother's words, and the effect they had on me, and what happened afterward. So you must spare my life for one more day, if you will. What shall it be, Majesty? The executioner's block for me, or another day and a night of life? For the decision is yours, O Master of All, O Lord of the Universe.

The Emperor was smiling. "You won't *ever* finish the story, will you, Laylah? You'll go on spinning it out for a hundred years, and then a hundred years more, if I allow it."

"There is so much to tell, Majesty!"

"Yes, and you'll insist on telling it all. Whereas all I wanted to know from you was—well, you know what I wanted to find out. And instead you tell me this, you tell me that, you tell me one thing after another—"

"It is all part of the story, Majesty. Everything is linked to everything else. But I do confess that I have been in no hurry to reach the conclusion. If you will grant me one more night, or perhaps two, perhaps then I would be able to—" She glanced sharply at him. "Or if I have begun to bore you, perhaps we should stop for good right here. The executioner's patience was exhausted long ago; and now, I think, yours is also. Very well. I will prolong the story no longer. My tale is over. I bid you farewell forever, Majesty. May you reign and prosper for seven times seven thousand years." And she began to make the Ansaar sign of blessing, that is made only by those who are about to die.

The Emperor caught her hand in mid-gesture and brought it back down to her side. "No," he said.

"No?"

"There'll be no executions today. And there'll be more story-telling tonight. But promise me one thing, Laylah!"

"That I finish it this evening?"

"Yes. Yes. Yes."

She bowed and made the sweeping gesture of submission.

"I will do my best, Majesty. Tonight will see the last of my story. That much I promise you with all my heart, O Light of the Cosmos—O Supreme Monarch of the Million Suns—"

BOGAN 27, 82ND DYNASTIC CYCLE
(AUGUST 15—I THINK—A.D. 3001)

I have him! He's caught good and proper, that much is certain! And he will sit and listen to me—and sit—

and listen—as long as I want him to—as long as I
need him to—and, truth to tell, I would gladly go on
speaking with him forever—

> —From the Diaries of Laylah Walis

11

But this was the night of nights, and she could not bring
herself to begin.

"Tonight," the Emperor prompted at last, "you said you
would tell me what your brother said to you at Costa Stambool, and what effect it had on you."

"Yes." And still she hesitated, for this was the most difficult moment of all. Everything she meant to say tonight had
been arranged properly in her mind, but now, suddenly, for
the first time since her arrival, words would not come.

Again he spoke into her silence: "Let me say it for you.
What he told you was that he was a key member of the
anti-Imperial resistance, that he knew you were expert in
Ansaar language and customs, and that he had come to you
to ask you to make the journey to Haraar, inveigle yourself
into my palace, win my affection with your extraordinary
charm. . . and assassinate me."

He said it quietly, but his words struck her like hammer-
blows. She sat frozen, stunned, lost in a maelstrom of panic.

"Is this not so, Laylah?" He was smiling. "Speak. Or have
you lost your voice?"

Hoarsely she replied, "These are the things I meant to tell
you tonight, yes. But how is it you know them already?"

"From your diary, of course."

"My diary? How could you read my diary? My diary is
in English!"

"Which is the main language of Earth. And Earth is a
world of the Empire." His tone remained gentle. He was
not speaking as an Emperor might speak. "Do you think
we'd annex a world and not learn its language? While you
were asleep an expert in your language entered and read
your little book. But tell me, Laylah: *would* you assassinate me?"

"No. Never. Never!" She was trembling. She could barely get the words out.

"I believe you," he said, and he sounded sincere. "Yet that is what you came to Haraar to do. Is it because you find me so fascinating? Because you have fallen in love with me?" He was playing with her again, the lion toying with his prey. "Or because you have come to see the uselessness of killing me?"

"All of that," she said. Some strength returned to her voice. "Killing you would have been pointless. The Empire has survived the deaths of hundreds of Emperors, and will go on and on regardless of who is on the throne. But why should we discuss this? The game is over, Majesty. Summon your executioner."

"Not just yet. The other part, first: have you really fallen in love with me? With the archenemy of your people?"

His gaze grew fierce. She could not meet his eyes.

"I admit being fascinated by you. That's not quite the same thing as love."

"Agreed. I feel a fascination too. You know that, don't you? Why else do I listen to you, night after night, when I have so much else to do? The lovely *maula* who risks her life to come to Haraar—who talks her way right into the Emperor's presence—who tells him tales of her world that hold him helpless night after night—"

"I played a dangerous game, and I lost." The trembling had stopped. She felt very calm. "Shall we end this little session now? I no longer wish to prolong our conversations."

"But I do, Laylah. What if I were to offer you Earth's freedom from Ansaar rule?"

She gasped. Once again he had caught her unawares and sent her reeling. "Earth's—freedom—?"

"As an autonomous member of the Empire. An end to Ansaar occupation, and freedom for its citizens to travel in Imperial Space. Such a thing is within my power to grant. I saw these lines in your diary too, from one of your ancient poets: 'Titles are shadows, crowns are empty things; the good of subjects is the end of kings.' So I believe, Laylah:

the good of subjects. I am no tyrant, you know. I will set your little world free."

"This is an ugly joke. It's cruel of you to trifle with me like this."

"I'm neither joking nor trifling. The freedom of Earth is yours, Laylah." And, after a moment: "As a wedding gift, that is." His Ansaar hand reached for hers. "'I would gladly go on speaking with him forever,' you wrote. The opportunity is yours. You fascinate me to the point of love, Laylah. I invite you to become one of my Cherished Major Wives."

When she could speak again she said, "One of how many, may I ask?"

"You would be the sixth."

"Ah. The sixth." She was past the first rush of astonishment, almost calm now. But not the Emperor. His eyes were retracted in tension, the vertical pupil-slits barely in view. "Cherished Wife Number Six! What a strange fate for a quiet girl from Earth!" She mused on it while he stared tautly, knotting and unknotting his fingers. "Well, we can discuss it, Majesty. Yes. We can discuss it, I suppose, in the days ahead."

He nodded. "By all means. We can discuss it. I will come to you as before, and you will tell me your tales, and perhaps, by and by—"

"By and by," she said. "Yes. Perhaps."

She forced herself to maintain her eerie calmness, for otherwise she would break loose entirely from her moorings.

Sixth Cherished Wife! And Earth an autonomous world! Yes, but could she? Would she? By and by, perhaps. Perhaps. By and by.

"Tell me the next story, Laylah."

Very well. I must tell you, then, Majesty, that from Costa Stambool I went onward to the forbidden world of Grand Binella, the planet of the Oracle Plain, of which they say that in its shapes and colors are the answers to all the questions that have ever been asked and many that have not yet been framed. Near the Plain are the mountains called the Angelon, where one walks on a carpet of rubies and emeralds. Farther on—almost at the horizon—one sees a body of motionless black water, the Sea of Miaule, with Sapont Island smoldering just offshore, a place of demons and basilisks.

I made my way to this terrifying world, Sire, at my brother's suggestion, because he felt that among those demons and basilisks I might learn certain useful things, things that would stand me in good stead if ever I found myself in the place where I find myself now. And so, upon my arrival there—

THE WORM TURNS

GREGORY BENFORD

Gregory Benford is one of the modern giants of the field. His 1980 novel *Timescape* won the Nebula Award, the John W. Campbell Memorial Award, the British Science Fiction Association Award, and the Australian Ditmar Award, and is widely considered to be one of the classic novels of the last two decades. His other novels include *Beyond Jupiter, The Stars in Shroud, In the Ocean of Night, Against Infinity, Artifact,* and *Across the Sea of Suns, Great Sky River, Tides of Light, Furious Gulf, Sailing Bright Eternity, Cosm, Foundation's Fear,* and *The Martian Race.* His short work has been collected in *Matter's End, Worlds Vast and Various,* and *Immersion and Other Short Novels;* his essays have been assembled in a nonfiction collection, *Deep Time.* His most recent book is a new novel, *Beyond Infinity.* Coming up is another new novel, *The Sunborn.* Benford is a professor of physics at the University of California, Irvine.

In the Galactic Center novels such as *Great Sky River, Tides of Light,* and *Sailing Bright Eternity,* Benford's best-known contributions to the New Space Opera canon, he takes us to the core of the galaxy, where the dwindled remnants of humanity struggle to survive against hostile machine intelligences of immense power. Here, in a story much closer to the present day, at the beginning of humanity's expansion into space (and a direct sequel to his well-known story "A Worm in the Well"), he demonstrates that capturing a black hole is only half of the problem—then you have to *hang on* to it!

⬤ She was about to get whirled into a puree, and all because of tricky accountants.

"Give me infrared," Claire called.

Erma murmured brightly, *I can give you full spectrum,* in Claire's headset and showed a sprawl of color that hurt the eyes.

"You keep trying to get me to look at the world that way, damn it!" Maybe I'm just a touch irritated, Claire thought, under pressure. But software didn't take offense, or so Claire thought. "Uh, I'm just a primate. One spectrum slice at a time. Please."

As you say . . .

Was there an irritated sniff after the words? No matter— Erma obliged.

There were several theorists' terms for the object hovering on her screens: wormring, ringhole. This wormring looked like a blurry reddish doughnut. It spun in a frenzied halo of skating brilliance. Sullen red snakes coiled around its skin. Lightning forked yellow and blue down the northern doughnut hole, but didn't come out on the other side, from this angle. The same fizzing flashes worked around the southern hole too, but there was no answering lightning to the north. Somewhere along that axis lay trouble. And that's where they had to go.

"What's the best trajectory, in theory?"

There is no adequate theory. The best mathematics says there are several entrances, but they all involve acquiring considerable angular momentum.

"Yeah, but there's got to be a best educated guess—"

I do have the latest numerical simulations, which you ordered from Earthside.

"Oh, good. I always feel better after a nice refreshing computer simulation."

It is best to address our safety without stressful sarcasm.

"Sarcasm is just one more service we offer here at *Silver Metal Lugger* Salvage and Loan."

Sarcasm is stressful.

"Stressful for who?"

For us both.

"Do I look like a people person?"

You look anxious.

"I thought you understood rhetorical questions."

You are stalling for time.

"Damn right I am. Look at that wormring on the mass detector."

Erma did. All virtual images that popped up on the screens had a glossy sheen to them that even Erma's teraprocessor couldn't erase. They looked too good to be real. Pristine geometries snarled and knotted into surf around the spinning doughnut. Whorls of spacetime spun away and radiated waves in angry red hisses.

"Does that look safe to you?"

I would point out that I am backed up to Luna every half hour by laser link.

"Yeah, you're immortal as long as I pay your computer fees."

I can find other work—

Claire smiled. Erma didn't often get into a sentence without seeing how it would turn out. Maybe her conversational program was competing with the huge sensor net strung around *Silver Metal Lugger*'s hull. They were measuring everything possible as they gingerly edged closer to the whirling wormring.

"You were saying. . . ?"

I was distracted. And I do have a high opinion of this enterprise. I do not like our probabilities if we hang near this strange object, however.

Could software also get jumpy? Erma hadn't seemed so last time, five years ago, when they had snagged this same wormhole. After that, the astro guys started tinkering with it, trying to expand it so a ship could pass through—and they literally screwed it up. They had nudged and probed and somehow added angular momentum to it. Accidentally, they transformed the entire spacetime around what had been, apparently, a somewhat predictable wormhole. Not that anybody knew what routine was for wormholes. After all, they only had one—this whirling dervish that had already eaten many probes, spitting nothing back out.

We need to go closer, to resolve the possible entrances.

Along the axis of the dervish was a shimmering lump that apparently held some exotic matter. The lump looked to be spinning too. Claire had been warned many times not to touch that lump, or else. Previous probes that had, had got broken down into elementary particles, and not particularly nice ones at that.

"There are basically two ways in, right? North and south poles of this general relativistic merry-go-round. But stay away from that axis."

True. I think our spin matters too. The earlier probes tried varying angular momenta and a few managed to send back coherent signals for a while.

"Sure, for maybe ten seconds. I was kinda counting on my shoot-and-scoot strategy taking about that much time. Our contract says just make some readings and come on home. Didn't one probe get back out?"

If one counts granules of carbon, yes.

"From a ceramic ship?"

Yes, not promising.

In her immersion-work environment, touch controls gave her an abstract distance from the wormring, hovering in space in magnetic clamps a hundred meters away. Whorls of wrenched spacetime slammed into their metallic ship's skin, rattling her teeth, and, on the screens, spraying yellow-white froth of gravitational turbulence around them.

Perhaps the theoretical view would help.

"Doughnuts are doughnuts, Erma. Let's just stick our nose in, real quick."

And all because of tricky accountants.

The thin Luny guys with briefcases got to her before she had even unpacked. She had counted on some ribald bar cruising to rub away the memory of a two-year comet-vectoring job too. She was just about ready to get into the foam shower and run the water a shameful hour or two, to feel really human again, to yammer at somebody other than Erma—and then they rang her door chimes, which played a Bach opening.

She didn't answer. They came right on in, anyway.

"Hey! I'm renting this 'partment."

The taller of them didn't even blink. "We could put you on a perfectly legal formal secure-lock right now."

"The last guy who tried that ended up nearly getting frozen."

The short one, apparently fond of his food, said smugly, "We checked. You didn't prong him at all, just threatened to."

"I could make an exception in your case."

She smiled slowly, slit-eyeing the fat guy—who blinked nervously and took a step backward despite himself. She chided herself for taking on such an easy mark, but hell, she needed a little recreation. It would be fun to deck these two, and, as a bonus, stimulating to a cardiovascular system that had spent too much time in centri-g.

"You are in debt again. Deeply so." Tall Guy's smile was broad but utterly without warmth. "We are a legal officer"— a bow to Fat Guy—"and I am the project accountant. We have orders to duly confiscate your ship."

"The last guy said that too. I dug myself out."

"Yes, very admirable. But your comet-towing business has fallen upon sad times," the tall guy said.

"Look, Second World Corp will vouch for me." *I think. . .*

Fat Guy was still blinking, getting his self-image back in order. It took a fair amount of work for this Horseman of the Esophagus. Tall Guy smiled without a gram of humor and without invitation folded himself into a grav chair. She watched him do this, legs angling like demonstrations of the principle of the lever, and—startled—felt herself moisten. *I've been gone a loooong time.*

"I believe that maneuver will fail," Tall Guy said smoothly.

"Let's try it, shall we?" she said cheerfully. Freezing these guys was getting more attractive. She was tired, still adjusting from their inflight standard Mars grav of 0.38. Their nominals had risen to 1.4 in the comet debacle. Though Moon Standard 0.18 felt great, her reflexes would be off with these two. She might just be getting a bit rickety for this line of work, though sixty-four wasn't all that damn far into middle age anymore.

For the moment, she had better use deflection while she remembered where she had kept her stunner. And maybe just shut down Fat Guy, while she worked her wiles on Tall Guy? The thought intrigued. Pleasure Before Business, her fundamental rule.

"Do not presume to push us." Getting icy now.

Okay, give them lip in return. "How come you can just walk in here?"

Fat Guy launched into a stumbling rendition of how they had used some law that said Financials could access property rights of those with outstanding debt, and at that point she stopped listening. These guys were dead serious. They were used to delivering trouble to people, did it for a living. They probably had other slices of bad news to serve up today.

". . . we trust some accommodation might be arrived at before we are forced to—" Fat Guy was saying.

"Before your heavies come calling?" she asked.

Tall Guy smoothly came in with, "We do hope such methods are not necessary, and had not even considered them."

They were all clichés, straight from business school. And they had probably never been off Luna.

"Look, it wasn't my fault that damn comet nucleus came unglued before we could get it into Lunar orbit. You need all the light elements you can get down here! And tow operations like mine keep you alive, right?"

Tall Guy nodded and with some effort got a diplomatic expression onto his face. "I know you feel that accountants and lawyers are annoying, but—"

"Not all lawyers are annoying. Some are dead."

"My colleague and I are not questioning why you failed—"

"I wasn't in charge of screening the comet ices against that solar flare. We used standard reflecting coating to keep the ice from subliming, routine methods. But that big flare blew off the shadow coating. Not my department! That storm made the whole damn iceberg start boiling off. It developed expansion fractures inside an hour, killed two women who—"

"We are well aware of that." Tall Guy's voice came sliding in like a snake. He had probably laid this conversation out in advance, getting his pitch in shape. To prove his point, he waved a hand and punched a few buttons on his belt. An air display of her account ledgers hung in the air between them, shimmering like a waterfall, the numbers all color-coded so that her debt glared forth in scarlet. A gaudy avalanche of debt. She scowled.

Tall Guy said languidly, "But there . . . may . . . be a way out for you."

She smiled prettily, arched an eyebrow, said nothing. She had learned that if you let people talk, their love of their own voices could lead them into overplaying their hands. They would babble on, and in the course of relating whatever story or moral lesson they imparted, tell you useful things.

She had seen this work before, but the idea came from her famously laconic grandfather. He had squinted at her while she went on at a grand family dinner with a tale that ended in no particular point. Everybody smiled politely and general talk resumed but a few moments later Grandfather leaned over and whispered in his round burr, "Never pass by a chance to shut up." She had blinked and thought furiously about that and learned a lesson that became quite useful.

Tall Guy said with a thin smile, "We can either talk of possibilities or we can seize your ship."

She let out a long breath. "Oh, goody."

"Our offer is quite generous."

"They always are." She was busy looking at his hands. Long fingers too . . .

"Cosmo Corp has asked if you are interested in another expedition?"

"Let me guess. Another wormhole has turned up, stuck in a solar coronal arch? And Cosmo needs somebody to go fetch it. Just like last time."

Another cold, calculating smile. Why did she like guys like this? Okay, it had been a long time, and technology can only do so much for the lonely gal. But still—

"No, alas. Though I might say I thought that an admirably brave and daring act. I heard someone made a 3D about it."

"In case you're wondering, I spent that money too."

His veneer slipped a bit, but he recovered in an eyeblink. "I'm sure for a worthy cause."

"Yeah, spent it all on me. What's the deal?"

Tall Guy looked a bit rushed, as though he liked a lot of foreplay before getting down to business. Well, so did she, but a different kind of business than this character meant.

"It is the same wormhole. But it has changed."

"Escaped?"

"No, it is secured in magnetic fields in free space, held in high Lunar orbit. But Cosmo Corp's experiments to expand its mouth, and thus to bring interstellar travel to mankind, has—"

"Wait, how did Cosmo get the worm?"

"Uh, they exerted stock override options on the holding company consortium that by interplanetary rights had further—"

"Skip the jargon. They bought it?"

"In a manner of speaking."

"I always mind my manners when I speak. What's up?"

Tall Guy was now ignoring Fat Guy, who had found a seat on the other side of the 'partment living room. Claire stayed standing. With guys, who routinely used height to intimidate women, it was just about her only advantage here.

"I am not a technical person." Tall Guy collapsed the glaring account ledger and arched an eyebrow at her. *Damn!* Even *that* got her moist. She really had to get out of here, go barhopping, blow off two years' worth of steam—

"But the wormhole you captured has . . . changed, I do know that. Cosmo Corp was attempting to expand its, ah, mouth size. This is a delicate operation, apparently. I am unsure precisely what the difficulty was, but in making the wormhole mouth large enough to accommodate a substantial ship—such as yours, for example—they somehow added angular momentum to the wormhole. It became another sort of wormhole entirely."

Claire said cautiously, "What sort?"

"One with enough rotation to change the very nature of the spacetime geometry." Tall Guy shrugged, as if altering wormholes were something like the weather. What could one do, after all? Yawn.

"Hey, I'm a contract hauler. I grabbed that wormhole off its perch on the top of a magnetic arch, dragged it back to Earthside. That's what I know, period."

"Yes, but you do have some talent for the unexpected. That is apparently what Cosmo Corp needs. And soon."

"Because. . . ?"

"Because certain governmental entities wish to possess the wormhole."

"The Earthside scientists."

Another *What can one do?* shrug. Very expressive. This guy should have gone on the stage, she thought. "They went through the Planetary Nations."

She let a silence build. This was a critical point. In many negotiations, subtle silences did most of the work. Let the silence run. . . then. . . "Must be tough, dancing around on strings pulled all the way from Earth."

Tall Guy shrugged, not denying it. Lean and muscular, he was the best man she had seen in years. Also the only man she had seen in years. That is, not counting Fat Guy, who might as well be on Pluto. She eyed Tall Guy and wondered if he was an all-business type, or if he was attuned to social signals better than his fat friend. She was wearing slickskin tiger pants and neither of these guys had given that a glance. The oldtime gal rule was that no guy was going to notice what shoes you're wearing, and if he does, he's the wrong guy. Tall Guy was giving nothing away. Poker face, no eye contact, nothing.

Tall Guy said carefully, "The Planetary Nations Scientific Council got a binding injunction which begins in—" Tall

Guy gazed off to the side, probably consulting a clock in his inboard vision. "Seventeen hours."

"Seventeen hours—"

"And forty-eight minutes."

"Nobody can—"

"You can," he said, abruptly urgent. "You have experience with it. And the technical people have tried all they can, without success."

"Anybody get killed?"

He went deadpan. "I can't discuss that. Legal matters—"

"Okay, okay." She felt the fight go out of her. What the hell, she had slept most of the way to Luna, coming back from the comet fiasco. She was rested, well fed. Other hungers, though. . .

She could cut short the shower. Get out to the bars, find a guy, get some sack time in, then back up to *Silver Metal Lugger*—

"Okay, I'm interested." She put both hands on her hips, a commanding stance. "But we have to negotiate."

"There's little time, but we are prepared—"

She sliced a hand through the air, pointed at Fat Guy— who had developed a pout. "No. He goes, you stay. We two negotiate the deal, my fee. And fast. Cosmo Corp needs this done pronto, right?"

"Uh, right." A gleam in Tall Guy's eye? Was she that obvious?

Well, maybe. And that could save them both some time too. Skip cruising the bars, yes. Not the shower, though. She said quickly, "Let's, well, let's do it."

Maybe a shower for two?

We must either go in or out. The ringhole is frame-dragging spacetime itself in its vicinity. Theory predicted this. I can feel its tug. This is not a safe place.

"No place is, when you think about it." She recalled Tall Guy. Some things are better than they look. Maybe this wormring was okay, once you dove through. None of their probes was really savvy, after all. Artificial intelligences had plenty of craft, but little intuition. No animal instincts.

"We can do this. Let's skin about our main axis, dive straight down through the north pole."

We are turning. Hold on.

Claire was at the ship axis anyway, so she felt nothing as the room started to spin. Her fore screen showed them shooting into the wormring. The ship knocked and strummed as they skated by whorls that slammed into their nose.

"Y'know, I kinda hoped I'd have some time to talk to the theory guys about this."

You said you were in the shower a long time.

"Uh, yeah."

Alone?

"You're getting into an area beyond your competence. Y'know, not having a body and all."

Oh, my.

This was in a phony, high-pitched English voice, like a parody of Jane Austen. "Look, skip the gossip! Why's this thing look like a rotating doughnut?"

Wormholes are not tubes, my database says. They present in our space as solid objects. One passes through them by just merging with them. It is not like falling down a pipe.

"This one's spinning."

Apparently. The alterations the scientists carried out to expand it seem to have added angular momentum.

"Wormholes connect parts of spacetime, so—hey, well, it connects both parts of space and. . . uh. . . parts of time?" Not for the first time, she regretted her spotty education. Manual laborers usually did, and realistically, she was just about one grade above that.

I do know from ancillary reading that the philosopher Gödel solved the general field equations in their classical limit, for a rotating universe. He found that time could form loops. Apparently, he did this to illustrate a point about time being eternal in some sense, as Gödel believed, to his friend Einstein. They were, as you would put it, buddies. Physics buddies.

Claire thought, sourly, *I never get a direct answer*

unless I coax. Maybe she should buy a patch into a more masculine software. But then she would have to deal with the male narrow-linear perspective too. There were always trade-offs.

"Very nice, but what's that mean?"

Twist a wormhole, twist space, twist time. I suppose.

"You suppose?"

All wormholes can be made into time machines, by moving them around at high speeds. Apparently, ringholes, with their angular momentum, even more so.

"Um. We need more. What about that big library program I bought you?"

I use it to. . . browse.

"Browse what, porn? I need—"

You have been accessing my routines! And after all my scientific database searchings!

Perfect, Erma; primly change the subject, mix in some offended hauteur. "Show me, with color coding."

On her wall screens, the magnetic grappling strands played and rippled like luminous wheat stirred by a breeze. In their grasp, the ringhole flexed and whirred. Blue lightning snarled and spat. It crushed and curdled light, stirring space with a spoon.

Claire gingerly pulsed *Silver Metal Lugger,* spilling more antimatter into the chambers.

This was more like surfing than flying. They fought their way down. The vortex groped for them. Grabbed.

"In we go." This was lots better than hauling dreary comets, which had come to resemble delivering the milk, door to door. Danger was never boring.

Then the room. . . rippled. Stretched. Boomed. She watched sinusoids flounce through the walls without ripping anything, just flapping steel like waves crossing an ocean.

Her heart pounded. A jittery hum waltzed through her acceleration couch. The couch leather dimpled and puckered as torques warped across it. She could see the rivulets of gravitational stress work across her body too, like tornadoes a centimeter across twisting her uniform. She reminded herself that pilots didn't let their fear eat on them, not while there is flying to be done. And reminded herself again. It became a mantra.

The magnetic catcher's mitt slipped from view and they plunged into the whirl. It felt rubbery, somehow, and then her stomach tried to work up through her throat. Bile rushed into her nose. The acceleration slammed her around like a rag doll. She felt her skin stretching away in several directions. Gravitational stresses seemed to be trying to open her wrapping, to find a Christmas present inside.

"How're . . . we . . . doing . . . getting . . . through?"

I believe we are not.

"What!"

We are stalled in the rotating core of the doughnut.

"I . . . can . . . fly . . . us . . . out . . ." But her fingers moved like sausages.

You are incapable. You have no plan. I believe I must take command.

"You're . . . a program . . . not an . . . officer." Just saying that took all her strength.

The air oozed like greasy hair. "Commit our full antimatter flux. Hammer us out of this."

Inward or outward?

"Which way . . . is outward?"

Something like a peeved sigh came from Erma. *I was hoping you knew.*

"And you wanted to take *command*?" Irritation helped, actually. She could even complete a sentence. "Inward—that way." She jabbed her chin toward the deck. "I guess . . ."

Antimatter howled as it met its enemy in their reaction chamber. The room spun around her so fast it blurred into a fluid. Her teeth rattled. On the screens, there was nothing but dark outside. How big was this thing? Were they squeaking through or in some infinity? "Did you send out laser pulses? Microwaves?"

Of course. Nothing came back.

"Maybe this thing is a perfect absorber? But nothing's perfect."

Something spurted actinic blue and arced big, coming at them. Coming fast. She got a flash image of an oddly shaped ship, far away. Then it was gone. The only thing they had seen. Were they in some murk?

I have an incoming message.

"What? How can—hell, patch it through."

The message says, "Worms can eat their tails and so can you."

"Is this one of your jokes?"

I do not joke. I do not have the software.

"Eat my tail? What's . . . Oh."

Oh?

"Maybe that refers to the Gödel thing? But who *said* it?"

Who is here with us? I am mere software.

Claire sniffed. She was sweating but the ship was cool. Her pulse quickened. This was intriguing, sure, but right now they were in a gravitational whirlwind. The couch adjusted to the tornado violence of their whirl but this could not go on for long. And how long was a wormhole, anyway?

Some glowing stuff zoomed by them—or at least got larger, all she could tell in this dense dark. It looked like neon clotted cream.

"What *was* that?"

My database says that wormrings are held together with exotic material, some kind of matter that has "negative average energy density." Whatever that is, it had to be born in the Blossoming. It threads wormholes, stem to stern.

"Um. Great construction material, if you can get it. No use to us. Are we making any progress out of here?"

I cannot tell.

"And you thought I didn't have a plan."

Wait—I do sense something bright—approaching—

The black outside reddened. Churned.

Suddenly they slammed out—and into a blue storm. A mirror twin of the wormring dwindled behind them now. Brilliant rainbows rimmed it.

They tumbled, ass over entrails. Hot gas rushed by, prickly with blue and ruby glows. A huge gas giant hung between them and a bright, sullen star. The ship rocked and wheeled. A vast wind was driving them outward from the gas giant.

This gas is blowing us away from the wormring. It is mostly molecular hydrogen, quite hot—thus the blue gas. It comes from the planetary atmosphere. We are very near the star, a fraction of Mercury's orbital distance. The star is smaller than ours.

She stared. The slightly reddish star was boiling away the gas giant's surging atmosphere. In its orbit, the world was like a gassy comet, tail pointing outward. The giant was doomed, trapped to circle its tormenter while being slowly shredded.

A vast rosy plume erupted from the gas giant and curled toward *Silver Metal Lugger*. In the streaming gas curled a nasty vortex and they were at its edge.

I cannot navigate in this. My piloting also is not capable of—

"I'll take the helm." Claire fought to turn the ship. Their reaction engines could barely muster enough thrust to compete with the winds here. *Winds in space!* she thought wildly. *This is worse than that coronal arch . . . which we barely survived.*

Even making a turn was hard. It was better to think of the days she had enjoyed sailing. Tacking with the wind, then rounding on it when the vectors and torques allow . . .

She got them to take the billowing gas on their stern, slowing the tumbling pitch and yaw. A knot of angry violet gas shot by them. Flaming debris hit their flank. The screens showed no pressure loss, but plenty of abrasion from the roasting, eating winds. It took a long while to stabilize their course. They still rocked and veered like a sailboat in a hard storm.

"Damn! We're supposed to reconnoiter, then get back home. This stuff is incredible." She had never had an experience of *flying* in space. No way to estimate the damage done to the ship, no clear navigation rules. "But—where's the ringworm?"

I have lost it. We moved quickly, blown away. I tried magnetically attaching a hailer as we departed, but it did not stick.

"It must be hard to glue on to spacetime," Claire said. How do you clip anything to a wormhole?

She was distracted as she banked and turned against the roiling banks of hot hydrogen. "I wonder what happened to the ringworm?"

It may be in a stabilized orbit, a balance of its gravitational forces against this hydrogen wind.

"So it's back there. Somewhere."

They gradually came about and steadied. She took them abroad the gale and worked toward lesser densities. Blue streamers fell behind. The ruddy fog-mist paled. They gradually emerged into fairly open space. The stars reappeared, gleaming reassuringly.

Claire saw the bright sun from an angle now, sighting back along the misty edge of the plume. The eroding giant planet was a round nub against the glaring yellow-white solar disk. Outward from them and surprisingly nearby hung a two-mooned world in crescent. No recognizable constellations in a sky somehow brighter, with more stars—and yes, a globular cluster hovering like an ivory flower between two bright stars.

"Any idea where we are? Can you find galactic reference points?"

I am trying, but none of the local stars are known to me. We're a long way from Earth.

"Keep trying. We may have to walk home."

Another solar system. A long way from Earth. A thrill ran through her and she whispered commands to Erma to take scans of it all. Otherwise, she was speechless, adrift, fears dropping away. Somehow she had thought of this as just another gig. Now the immensity of the ideas Erma went on about, or the biz deals of Tall Guy—all those were details, clues, chatter. This was real.

Something hit them. Hard. The ship rattled.

"What the—"

A large soft mass hit us astern.

"Soft?"

It did little damage but conveyed momentum.

Nothing in Earth's space was soft. Not even comets.

"Distance scan."

I track many small objects. Nearby, approaching.

The screen filled with shapes. A fried-egg jellyfish swooped at them, attached to their skin. Drifting with spines out came a warty cucumber. There were amber pencils in flight, their rear tubes snorting out blue burning gas. Something like an ivory solar sail came at them, reeling its sails in along spars.

"This is crazy."

Disturbing, yes. These cannot be machines—at least, not of metal and ceramics, run by computers. They are alive.

She eyed the many shapes with wonder. Gravity imposed simple geometries—cylinders, boxes, spheres. Here were effortless fresh designs: spokes and beams, rhomboids, fat curves. Rough skins and prickly shells, rubbery rods, slick mirrors—and all in the same twirling creature. "Feeding off that hydrogen, you figure?"

"Get our bots on the skin. Assess the damage. See if they can deal with these living things too."

I have no idea how . . .

Angular shapes came at them, diving close and then veering away, apparently sizing them up. Needle-nosed predators, she would have guessed if this were undersea biology. All these creatures were much smaller than *Silver Metal Lugger,* but she did not like their numbers. More flocked in as she watched. They seemed to come from back toward the pale blue plume, as though they feasted on the hydrogen, hid among the streams, and then came out to forage. Predator/prey ratios in high vacuum? Or more like cloud life?

"Great, we play this by ear. Our bots deployed?"

They are popping out from their hatches.

She could see the clunky forms walking on magnetics across the silvery skin. The teeming ruby sky reflected in the hull and made a double geometry of whirling seethe. The skylife wheeled and darted in gaudy flocks in that sky.

They had backed away once the bots were out. After all, they looked more like kites than birds. The bots were solid, rugged, probably of no interest to these gas-eaters.

The bots followed their grid sweep commands. They found rips and gouges and filled them with quick-fix patches. Claire always liked to do maintenance in case they had a major, subtle problem. It also gave her time to think.

This was a crazy outcome. The theory boys imagined that this ringhole was a gateway, long unused. So by all odds the other end—or ends, because nobody knew if these could have multiple mouths—should be in open space, probably far from a star. They thought this, even though she had caught the wormhole in a coronal magnetic arch on the sun. But then, the original wormhole wasn't an ordinary one either. It had the equivalent of negative mass, since something at its other end had been pouring mass out through it, forcing the curvature of spacetime near the mouth to act as if it held a net negative in its mass budget. Now the thing had stretched and tangled in the tender grasp of techies who didn't know what they were doing—and presto, it had spin and was even more confusing.

Crazy but real, not her favorite category.

"This doesn't feel like progress," Claire mused to herself. Her lips must have shaped the words, because Erma read them and replied,

We are making great discoveries! This is far more interesting than hauling ore and comets around.

"Far more dangerous too. Thing is, we don't know how to get back. That hydrogen column is huge. We can't find our way around in it. The ringhole—what's that? And—"

We can learn more by reconnoitering. Once our repairs—

A bullet-shaped brown thing shot along the hull. This was different, not an airy thing but solid.

It clipped a bot and sent it tumbling into space. The bullet-shape turned in a tight arc and came back. It tossed another bot offhull with a shrug as it passed.

Claire sprang into action. She had two laser cannons on

both ends of *Silver Metal Lugger.* They came online in a moment and she patched in the seek-and-fire software. All this was by the drill, but she was still too late.

The bullet-thing was so fast the utility bots never had a chance. Bots were made to patch and fill, not fend and fight. Within a few moments, the entire crew had spun away into oblivion.

Claire watched in silence. There was nothing more she could do. Another hull crew would get tossed too, and she had skimpy reserves for maintenance.

Erma said nothing. They went after a few of the bots but among the swarming skyline the bots were hard to find on radar. They managed to salvage two, whose carapaces were crumpled in by impact.

Odd. The attacker seems to have lifted out the command module in each.

"Studying us, I guess." Claire frowned.

Silver Metal Lugger drifted for a while and the swarm of living spacecraft simply glided past, as if on patrol—pencils, sails, puffy spheres of malevolent orange. But cautious. None tried to enter the ship through hull ports.

I suggest we get a clear view of that distant planet.

"I want to find the ringhole. I learned that in high school—at a party in a strange place, always find the exits first."

To extend your metaphor, we were not invited to this party at all. The locals seem to be making that point.

"Let's shed them. Accelerate away, take some good long scans of that planet. Then dodge back into the hydrogen column and search it for the ringhole."

Seems plausible. I am accelerating.

The swarm outside started to fall behind. They could trim sails and muster more sunlight, maybe even ride the vagrant hydrogen winds, but *Silver Metal Lugger* outran them in minutes.

"While we're getting set up—that is, while you are— let's think on this. Why is the ringhole down in that gas column?"

I suppose because it got caught there. Much as we found

its other end in a wildly unlikely place, atop a coronal loop. These are not places anyone designing a wormhole transit system would want it.

"And who put it there? Who's in charge here?"

Let me guess. Not someone who wants these wormhole mouths used.

"Yeah, all this fits the opposite of what we thought wormholes were useful for doing."

But anyone who wanted to make a wormhole useless could just throw it into a star.

"But then it would gush hot plasma into your neighborhood."

True. If both mouths were dropped into stars, the two stars would feed each other. If one gained mass that the other lost, that would perturb both stars, affecting their sunlight. I see your point. There may be no good way to rid oneself of a wormhole. . .

Claire snapped her fingers. "So! This system is for limited use. Who around here would want that?"

Not the space life, one assumes.

"Um. Maybe they're part of this, though. . . ."

They were turning, systems running hard. Claire could see the diagnostic panels lighting up with fresh commands. Erma knew her stuff, how to case out a place and make a quick assessment. But for a whole new world? Quite a job for a ship designed to sniff out asteroid ore. Claire watched their long-distance telescopes deploy from their caches, blossoming like astronomical flowers. Dishes and lenses turned and focused like a battery of eyes.

I am beginning an observing run of the planet. Full spectrum. The atmosphere shows obvious biosignatures. I can see the surface in infrared, but cloud cover is thick: oceans, continents, with ice poles rather large. There is minor microwave traffic and radio as well. There appears to be an—wait—

Claire frowned. Seldom did Erma even pause while speaking. Software never used filler words, "ums" and "ahs." But to stop dead was worrisome. The pause lengthened. Nothing appeared on the screens around Claire.

I . . . have just . . . had an unusual experience.

"I could tell."

Another pause.

Something . . . called to me.

"A hail from that planet?" Claire guessed.

Something like that . . . only deeper, with several running lines of discourse I could not follow.

"In what language?"

That was the oddity. It came in my *language.*

"Uh . . . English?"

I do not think in these simple, ambiguous terms that you use. Of course, I know that your internal running systems do not use these "words" you must shape with your mouths. Your brains are much more subtle and dexterous. No, I run in an operating system using complex combinational notations. These carry very dense meanings in packets. I imagine all advanced intelligences do this, for it is efficient. And the message I received was built in this way, perhaps confirming my expectations.

Claire blinked. "But whoever sent it is alien. How could they know . . . Oh. The bots."

I had not thought of that, but yes—it must have captured information from the bot intelligences.

"And reverse engineered it to—wow. And they did it in minutes."

As you say, wow. That word is usefully compact, and so is some of the torrent of signals I am evaluating. But most are not. This is a very strange intelligence.

"I'll take your, uh, word for it. So what did this smart thing say?"

That we must go away. Not approach them.

"And this 'them' is . . . who?"

It says it is the entire planet. An integration of the intelligent species and . . . the biosphere, is the closest I can come to it in a word.

"A living world. Say, some system that somehow lets the oceans talk to the people? That's . . . well, impossible. I'm having trouble here."

So am I. I do not even have a living body, so it is difficult for me to think of this other than abstractly. Like a human conversing with a forest?

"My body talks to me and mostly it's bad news. Stomachaches or sore muscles. Hard to see what a planet might say. 'Don't throw that into me'?And how do you hear it, walking on the beach?"

I suppose you are being too practical.

"I'm a practical kind of gal. Put our lack of imagination aside, then. What's it mean, we should just go away?"

Apparently, it has had some bad experiences with others who came through the ringhole.

"Like who?"

Something that had ideas about recruiting them for something. A quest for God or some odd idea.

"Not humans?"

No, they have not seen the likes of us before.

"Then how'd the original wormhole get anchored near our sun?"

A method of "disposal" I do not comprehend. Apparently, they can whip a wormhole through space by using angular momentum applied at its far end—that is, from here. So they got rid of the God-seekers and then drove the far wormhole mouth out of their neighborhood. They flung it away and it came to rest near our star.

"Even weirder. But those words, 'got rid of.' What's that mean?"

I thought it polite not to ask.

"So world minds have protocols, you figure? We should find out—"

I thought our goal was to get back home.

"So it is, and curiosity killed the cat. How do we get out of here?"

Follow its agents, it said.

"The kite life? They don't seem so friendly."

I suppose they were reconnoitering us.

"Fair enough, though those bots cost me. A small price for a ticket home, though."

Claire gestured at her wall screens, where the many space-born shapes were catching up to them. Each might be a different species, she guessed, deployed by that crescent planet with two moons. What intricate biologies could be at work here, wedding worlds to the spaces around them? How could anything go up against that? Certainly not *Silver Metal Lugger*'s puny lasers—which she discovered, with a quick check, the kites had disabled anyhow.

Now here was an easy decision. "Let's do as they say."

I was holding my breath, hoping you would say that.

"You don't breathe."

Your language is rich in metaphor. The Agency I spoke with spoke like that too, only several orders of magnitude higher in complexity.

"I don't think I can stand to have an example. Save it for our report."

We will report this?

"How do you think I'm going to pay for this? We're under contract."

They—the Agency—may not like to have word spread.

Claire blinked. "Are your conversations monitored by them?"

I had not thought. I am not transmitting, of course, but—

Another atypical pause. Then Erma said, *Apparently, the Agency is listening to us.*

"Planted some tech on our hull, probably."

But they know they cannot control what others say.

"Mighty nice of them. But why are we still alive?"

Perhaps their moral code? Or they may think we are emissaries from another world-mind like theirs. In which case, they will want to be diplomatic.

"I wonder why they don't just put up a NO TRESPASSING sign?"

Do you believe that would work?

"On humans? Not a chance."

The living spacecraft flocked in dense swarms now, as if to be ready for whatever might happen. Claire bit her lip, drew in the ship's dry air, and felt very tired. How long had they been here?

"Y'know, we're mice among elephants here. No, microbes.

And elephants can change their minds, or just make a mis step. Let's run."

I quite agree.

The Planetary Agency, as they decided to call it, spoke through lightning with microwave sizzles while they worked their way into the hydrogen plume. When microwaves from the home planet failed, it used rattles of particle storms on *Silver Metal Lugger*'s hull. The kite life guided them, in odd ways that Claire couldn't follow but Erma found quite natural, somehow. A few hours of turbulent piloting brought them to the whirlpool of gas near the ringhole. The kites backed off and waited to watch them dive in.

"Y'know, we had a weird time in there before . . ."

You are cautious. But recall that we cannot go back out of this plume.

"Meaning?"

I believe that the Agency would take that act rather unkindly.

"Okay. Let's do it." She put a confident tone to the words, though her heart was hammering and she double-checked the straps on her couch.

Silver Metal Lugger started to rattle and hum. Her couch leather dimpled again as torques warped through the ship. Churning red winds outside had snapped into an utter blackness that somehow also writhed. Rivulets of gravitational stress worked at their trajectory. The helm fought her and again she was flying blind.

Pops and pings rang through the ship. She drove them forward with a hard burst of antimatter and saw nothing change ahead at all. Bunches of green mass shot by them and then came around again. That was how she knew that they were in some whirl that grew and grew, pressing her into her couch with a heavy hand, then twisting her around two axes at once. Gs rose and *Silver Metal Lugger* tried to torque around and bite itself.

Bite itself . . . "Say, somebody sent us a message last time we were in here. What was it?"

The message said, "Worms can eat their tails and so can you."

"So... what's it mean?"

You are the pilot, madam.

"Okay, turn us and accelerate opposite to our velocity."

And how do I know our velocity? This is not a Newtonian space, with a fixed spacetime and—

"Do it! Go to low antimatter flux, then come about, then go to max thrust."

Erma made something like a sigh. The swerves and buffeting increased as they made a sluggish turn, as if working against molasses. She felt rather than heard a sound like *whump-whump-whump* through her body. The ship vibrated so badly she had to hold her teeth clamped tight.

They poured on the antimatter and the jarring eased off. Soon they were almost gliding, though she felt the centrifugal press all through her body. "This is working."

At least you feel better. Your stress levels have fallen.

Something came looming out of the blackness. It glowed and soared, alive with amber light. The space around it shimmered with shooting traceries.

"Damn, that looks like an alien craft."

Perceptions are warped here.

"Hail it."

I have an answering echo.

"Maybe they can hear us. Send this: 'Worms can eat their tails and so can you.' That way we can—"

The other ship winked out, gone. They swept on, through churning black. Odd speckles of rainbow light flashed by them. Claire thought she could see snatches of starlit space in the middle of those, but it all went by with a deck-rattling hum, as though they were moving at high speed.

"Go to full flux."

We are. The vector forces are acting to shear us along our main beam. We cannot maintain this level for—

They popped out into clear space. Stars shone brightly— familiar stars!

The ringhole spun away behind. An observer ship hailed them.

"We're back!"

And now we know who sent that message. You did.

Claire stopped, openmouthed. Her whole body ached and she said, "But how . . ."

Let the theorists do the thinking for a while.

That turned out to be a good idea. Claire was glad to leave the hard thinking to people who worked at desks.

Silver Metal Lugger had been gone thirty-one hours in local reference frame. As soon as they returned she felt fatigue fall on her like a weight. On the other side of the ringhole, she had felt lively; now she could not stay awake to debrief them. A gang of physicists were her audience, along with Tall Guy, whose expression varied between awestruck attention and the occasional flickering leer. She got tired of the awestruck pretty quick. Then she fell asleep right in front of them all.

After she awoke, there were more medical exams and she ate three meals in a five-hour period. Her body was getting itself back into its proper time sense. While she slept, Erma was busy answering their questions, so at least she did not have to endure a lot of that. Plus they had the recordings of a whole new world, and a lot of questions to answer.

As it turned out, the star and planet was known—HD209458b, the evaporating planet. That awful name got changed. They used that of the Egyptian god Osiris, who was killed and parts of his body spread over the whole of Egypt. To get him back to life, his sister Isis searched for the pieces, and found all of them but one. So Osiris the planet had been detected from Earth, 150 light-years away. Nobody had suspected an entire civilization there—if that term applied. Maybe they could eavesdrop on their radio signals.

The physicists liked new questions and within hours she was hearing terms like "upwhen" and "time turbulence." These accompanied equations that hurt her eyes. She fell asleep in front of the physicists again, which was embarrassing. But Tall Guy was looking better and better with each meeting.

At a coffee break, Tall Guy came sidling up to her. His ostensible purpose was to negotiate a contract for his employers, locking up her Very Own Personal Story of the voyage. She was ready for that and shot back, "Not in my prior contract. Needs a whole new negotiation."

Subtlety had never been her strong suit. Still, he didn't even blink. He kept up his pitch and just happened to mention that perhaps they could negotiate in private. She opened her mouth to say she needed her own lawyers present and then thought of her grandfather. *Never pass by a chance to shut up.*

She let him keep talking and just gave him a long, slow wink.

SEND THEM FLOWERS

WALTER JON WILLIAMS

Walter Jon Williams was born in Minnesota and now lives in Albuquerque, New Mexico. His short fiction has appeared frequently in *Asimov's Science Fiction*, as well as in *The Magazine of Fantasy and Science Fiction*, *Wheel of Fortune, Global Dispatches, Alternate Outlaws*, and in other markets, and has been gathered in the collections *Facets* and *Frankensteins and Other Foreign Devils*. His novels include *Ambassador of Progress, Knight Moves, Hardwired, The Crown Jewels, Voice of the Whirlwind, House of Shards, Days of Atonement, Aristoi, Metropolitan, City on Fire,* a huge disaster thriller, *The Rift,* and a *Star Trek* novel, *Destiny's Way.* His most recent books are the first two novels in his acclaimed Modern Space Opera epic, "Dread Empire's Fall," *Dread Empire's Fall: The Praxis* and *Dread Empire's Fall: The Sundering.* Coming up are two new novels, *Orthodox War* and *Conventions of War.* He won a long-overdue Nebula Award in 2001 for his story "Daddy's World," and took another Nebula in 2005 with his story "The Green Leopard Plague."

Williams has made his name in New Space Opera circles with novels such as *Aristoi* and the "Dread Empire's Fall" books, but those are not the only strings he has to his bow. In the droll and exciting adventure that follows, he demonstrates that even if you have multiple universes to flee through, the past has an uncomfortable way of *catching up* with you . . .

We skipped through the borderlands of Probability, edging farther and farther away from the safe universes that had become so much less safe for us, and into the fringe areas where stars were cloudy smears of phosphorescent gas and the Periodic Table wasn't a guide, but a series of ever-more-hopeful suggestions.

Our ship was fueled for another seven years, but our flight ended at Socorro for the most prosaic reason possible: we had run out of food. Exchange rates and docking fees ate most of what little money we had, and that left us on Socorro with enough cash for two weeks' food or one good party.

Guess which we chose?

For five months, we'd been running from Shawn, or at any rate the cloaked, dagger-bearing assassins we imagined him sending after us. I'd had nothing but Tonio's company and freeze-dried food to eat, and the only wine we'd drunk had been stuff that Tonio brewed in plastic bags out of kitchen waste. We hadn't realized how foul the air on the *Olympe* had grown until we stepped out of the docking tube and smelled the pure recycled air of Socorro Topside, the station floating in geosynchronous orbit at the end of its tether.

The delights of Topside glittered ahead of us, all lights and music, the sizzle of grilled meats and the clink of glasses. How could we resist?

Besides, freaky Probability was fizzing in our veins. Our metabolisms were pumped by a shift in the electromagnetic fine structure constant. Oxygen was captured and transported and burned and united with carbon and exhaled with greater efficiency. We didn't have to breathe as often as in our home Probability, and still our bodies ran a continuous fever from the boost in our metabolic rate.

Another few more steps into Probability and the multiverse would start fucking with the strong and weak nuclear forces, causing our bodies to fly apart or the calcium in our bones to turn radioactive. But here, we remained more or less ourselves even as certain chemical reactions became much easier.

Which was why Socorro and its Topside had been built on this strange outpost of the multiverse, to create alloys that weren't possible in our home probabilities, and to refine pure chemicals in industrial-sized quantities at a fraction of the energy it would have taken elsewhere.

Probability specialists in the employ of the Pryor corporate gene line had labored hard to locate this particular Probability, with its unique physical properties—some theorists would argue, in fact, that they'd *created* it, like magicians bringing an entire universe into being with their spell. Once the Pryors had found the place, they'd explored it for years while putting together the right industrial base to properly exploit it. When they finally came, they came in strength, a whole industrial colony jigsawing itself into the Socorro system practically overnight.

Once they started shipping product out, they had to declare to the authorities where it came from, and this particular Probability was no longer secret. Others could come and exploit it, but the Pryors already had their facilities in place, and the profits pouring out.

Nobody lived in Socorro permanently. There was something about this reality that was conducive to forming tumors. You came in on a three-year contract and then shipped out, with cancer-preventing chemicals saturating your tissues.

"Oh yisss," Tonio said as we walked down Topside's main avenue. "Scrutinize the fine ladies yonder, my compeer. I desire nothing so much as to bond with them chemically, oh yisss."

The local fashion for women was weirdly modest and demure, covering the whole body and with a hood for the head, and the outfit looked *inflated*—as if they were wearing full-body life preservers, designed to keep them floating even if Topside fell out of orbit and dropped into the ocean.

But even these outfits couldn't entirely disguise the female form, or the female walk. My blood seemed to fizz at the sight, and perhaps, in this quirky Probability, it did.

Music floated out of a place called the Flesh Pit, all suggestive dark windows and colorful electric ads for cheap drinks. "Let us sample the pleasures of this charming bistro," Tonio suggested.

"How about some food first?" I said, but Tonio was already halfway through the door.

The Flesh Pit had alcohol and other conventional stimulants, and also others that were designed for our current reality, taking advantage of the local biochemistry to deliver a packaged high aimed at our pumped metabolisms. The charge was delivered from a pressure cylinder into a cheap plastic face mask. The masks weren't hygienic, but after a few huffs, we didn't much care.

While getting refills at the bar we met a short, brown-skinned man named Frank. He was drinking alcohol, and joined us at our table. After two drinks, he was groping my thigh, but he didn't take it amiss when I moved his hand away.

The Flesh Pit was a disappointment. The music was bottom-grade puti-puti and the women weren't very attractive even after they took off their balloon-suits. After we bought Frank another drink, he agreed to be our guide to Topside's delights, such as they were.

He took us up a flight of stairs to a place that didn't seem to actually have a name. The very second I stepped into the front room, a woman attached herself to me, spreading herself across my front like a cephalopod embracing its prey. My eyes were still adjusting to the dim light and I hadn't seen her until she'd engulfed me.

My eyes adapted and I looked around. We were in what appeared to be a small dance hall: there was a bar at one end and a live band at the other, and benches along the sides where women smoked and waited for partners. There were a few couples shuffling around on the dance floor, each man in the octopus clutch of his consort.

"Buy me a drink, space man?" my partner said. Her name was Étoile and she wore a gardenia above one ear. I looked longingly at the prettier girls sitting on the benches and then sighed and headed for the bar. On my way, I noticed that Tonio had snagged the most beautiful woman in the place, a tall, tawny-haired lioness with a wicked smile.

I bought Étoile an overpriced cocktail and myself a whiff of some exotic gas. We took a turn on the dance floor, then went to the bedroom. Then back to the bar, then to the bedroom. Frank was sent out for food and came back with items on skewers. Then the bar, then the bedroom. I had to pay for clean sheets each time. Étoile was very efficient about collecting. Occasionally I would run into Tonio and his girl in the corridor.

By morning the bar was closed and locked, the dance floor was empty, I was hungry and broke and melancholy, and Tonio's girl had gone insane. She was crying and clutching Tonio's leg and begging him to stay.

"If you leave I'll never see you again!" she said. "If you leave I'll kill myself!" Then she took a bottle from the bar and smashed it on a table and tried to cut her wrist with a piece of glass.

I grabbed her and knocked the broken glass out of her hand, and then I pinned her against the wall while she screamed and sobbed, with tears running down her beautiful face, and Étoile tried to find the management or the bartender or someone to get Tonio's girl a dose of something to calm her down.

I gave Tonio an annoyed look.

He had driven his woman crazy in only one night.

"That's a new record," I told him.

Étoile returned with an irritated and sleepy-eyed manager, who unlocked the bar and got an inhaler. He plastered the mask over the weeping woman's face and cracked the valve and held the mask over her mouth and nose till she relaxed and drifted off to sleep. Then Tonio and I carried her to her room and draped her on the bed.

"She ever done this before?" I asked the manager.

He slapped at the wisp of hair atop his bald head as if it had bitten him. "No," he said.

"You'll have to watch her," I said.

He shrugged his little mustache. "I'm going back to bed," he said.

I looked at Étoile. "Not me," she said. "Unless you pay."

"It is necessary at this juncture," said Tonio, "for me to confess the infortunate condition of our finances."

Infortunate. Tonio was always making up words that he thought were real.

"Then get your asses out of here," said the manager. Étoile glared at me as if it weren't her fault I had no money left.

We dragged ourselves back to the *Olympe*. The ship smelled a lot better with air being cycled in from the station. I wondered if I'd ever be able to pay for the air I was breathing.

"I hope Fanny will recover, yiss," Tonio said as he headed for his rack.

"What did you *do* to her?" I said.

"We did things, yiss. It was Fanny did all the talking."

I looked again at Tonio and tried to figure out yet again why so many women loved him. He wasn't any better-looking than I was, and he was too skinny and he had dirt under his nails. His hands were too big for the rest of him. He had blue eyes, which probably didn't hurt.

Maybe the attraction was the broken nose, the big knot in the center of his face that made it all a little off-center. Maybe that's all it took.

"Listen, Gaucho," he said. He had his sincere face on. "I am aware that this contingency is entirely my fault."

"It's too late to worry about that," I said.

"Yiss, well." He reached down and took the ring off his finger, the one with the big emerald that Adora had given him, and he held it out to me. "This is the only valuable thing I own," he said. "I desire that you take it."

"I don't want your ring," I said.

He took my hand and pressed the ring into it. "If necessity bides, you can sell it," he said. "I don't cognizate how much it's worth, but it's a lot, yiss. It will pay for docking fees and enough food to peregrinate to some other Probability where you might be able to make a success."

I looked at him. "Are you saying goodbye, Tonio?"

He shrugged. "Compeer, I have no plans. But who knows what the future may necessitate?"

He ambled away to his rack. I looked at the ring on my palm—all the intricate little designs on it, the dolphins of the Feeneys and the storks of the Storch line all woven together in little knots.

I went into my stateroom, where I closed the door. I put the ring on my desk and looked at it for a while, and then I went to bed.

When I woke in the morning, the ring was still there, shining like all the unpaid debts in all the multiverse.

I met Tonio when I was working with my wife Karen on a mining concession owned by her family, an asteroid known only by an identification number. We were supervising the robots that did the actual mining, following the vein of gold and sending it streaming out into the void to be caught by the processor that hovered overhead. Gold was a common metal and prices were low. The robots were old and kept breaking down.

Tonio turned up in a draft of new workers, and we became friends. He had his charm, and his strange Andevin accent, and the vocabulary he'd got in prison, where he had nothing to read for months but a dictionary. He said the prison term was the result of a misunderstanding about whether or not he could borrow someone else's blazemobile.

Tonio and I became friends. After Karen and Tonio became friends, I equipped myself with a heavy pry bar and went looking for him. When he opened the door to his little room and saw me standing there, he just looked at me and then shrugged.

"Do whatsoever thou must, compeer," he said, backing away from the door. "For I deserve it in all truth."

I stepped in and hefted the pry bar and realized that I couldn't hit him. I lowered the bar and then Tonio and I talked for about six hours, after which I realized that my marriage hadn't been working in a long time, and that I wanted out and that Tonio could have Karen for all I cared.

After the divorce, when everything had played itself out and there was no point in staying on the claim of a family to which I was no longer tied, I left the scene along with Tonio.

Of the various options, it was the course that promised the most fun.

The *Olympe* isn't a freighter, it's a small private vessel—a yacht in fact, though I'm far from any kind of yachtsman. The boat can carry cargo, but only a modest amount. In practice, if I wanted to carry cargo, there were three alternatives. Passengers. Compact but valuable cargo, which often means contraband. And information, dispatches so private that the sender doesn't want to broadcast them even in cipher. Usually the dispatches are carried by a courier.

Once we docked on Socorro, I advertised *Olympe*—I even offered references—but didn't get any takers, not right away. Fortunately, docking on Socorro was cheap—this wasn't a tourist spot, but an industrial colony with too much docking capacity—and the air was nearly free. So Tonio got a job Upside, selling roasted chestnuts from a little wheeled grill—and with his blue eyes and broken nose working for him, he soon sold more chestnuts than anyone in the history of the whole pushcart business.

I took my aurora onto the station and went looking for work as a musician. I did some busking till I got a job with a band whose aurorista was on vacation in another Probability, and my little salary and Tonio's got us through the first month even though the puti-puti music bored me stiff. Then I auditioned for a band that had a series of regular gigs in upscale bars, and they took me on. I got a full split and a share of tips instead of a tiny salary, and things eased a bit. Even the music was better. We played popular songs while the tables were full of the dinner crowd, but afterward we played what we liked, and when I got a good grind going, I could make the room sizzle the way my blood sizzled in this little corner of the multiverse.

During our flight, I'd had nothing to do but practice, and I'd got pretty good.

A couple of months went by. I didn't see Tonio much—he'd got a girlfriend named Mackey and was spending his free time with her. But he sent a piece of his pay into my account every month, to help pay for *Olympe*.

I didn't have to sell the ring. I put it in the captain's safe and tried not to think about it.

The docking fees got paid, and our air and water bill. I had *Olympe* cleaned and the crudded-up old air filters replaced. I polished the wood and the ornate metalwork in my stateroom till it glistened, and put up some of Aram's old things, in case I wanted to impress a potential passenger with the luxury we could offer. I started stocking the larder against the day it was time to leave.

I began to relax. Perhaps Shawn's vengeance was not quite so hot on our tail. I even spent some dinars on my own pleasures.

Not knowing whether or not it was a good idea, I went back to the place where Frank had taken us that first night. I wanted to find out if Tonio's tawny-haired woman was all right. But I didn't see her, and I had barely started chatting with a couple of the employees when the manager recognized me and threw me out.

Which was an answer, I guess.

There were other places to have fun, though, that didn't come with bad memories. My band played in a lot of them. I met any number of women in them, and we had a good time with the sizzling in the blood and nobody went crazy.

So it went until a friend of Frank's made an offer to hire *Olympe*. Eldridge was a short man with fast, darting hands and genes left over from some long-ago fashion for albinism. His pale hair was shaggy, and his eyes looked at you with irises the color of blood.

Eldridge offered a very generous sum to ship a small cargo out to one of the system's outer moons, a place called

Vantage, where a lot of mining and processing habitats were perched on vast seams of ore. The trip would take five days out and five back, and I was free to take any other cargo on the return trip. Half our fee would be paid in advance, half on delivery. The one condition Eldridge made was that the seals on the packages should not be broken.

I'd been scraping a living aboard *Olympe* long enough to know what that stipulation meant, and I knew what I meant to do about it too.

The band hired a temporary aurora player, and Tonio quit his chestnut-selling job even though his boss offered him a bonus. We had no sooner cleared Upside than the two of us went into the cargo space and broke every seal on every container, digging like maniacs through cushions of spray foam to find exactly what was supposed to be there, bottles of rare brandy or expensive lubricating oil for robots or canister filters for miners' vac suits. We searched until the air was filled with a blizzard of foam and I began to wonder if we'd misjudged Eldridge entirely.

But in what was literally the final container, we found what we were looking for, about forty kilos of blue salt, exactly the stimulant to keep miners working those extra hours to earn that end-of-the-year bonus, to keep them all awake and alert and safe until the salt turned them into sweating, shivering skeletons, every synapse turned to pork cracklings while heavy metals collected in their livers and their zombie bodies ran on chemical fumes.

Well, well, I thought. I looked at Tonio. He looked at me.

Vantage would have been a couple months away except that *Olympe* could shift to a Probability where we could make better time, a place where the stars hung in the sky like hard little pearls on a background of green baize. We made a couple course changes outside our regular flight plan, then docked at Vantage and waited for the police to come and tear our ship apart.

Which they did. It was all part of Eldridge's plan. The griffs would find the blue salt in our cargo hold, and we'd be arrested. The salt would find its way from police lockers to Eldridge's dealers on Vantage, who would sell it and give the griffs a piece. In the meantime, the griffs would collect our fee from Eldridge in fines, and the money would be returned to Eldridge. I'd be coerced into signing over *Olympe* in exchange for a reduced sentence, and *Olympe* would be sold, with the profits split between Eldridge and the griffs.

It's the sort of trap that tourists in the Probabilities walk into all the time. But Tonio and I aren't tourists.

The griffs came in with chemical sniffers and found nothing, which meant they had to break into the cargo containers, and of course found that they'd been broken into already. "A freelance captain's got to protect himself," I told the griff lieutenant. "If I find contraband, it gets spaced."

I wouldn't admit to actually having found the salt. I didn't know the local laws well enough to know whether that admission would implicate me or not, so I refused to admit anything.

The lieutenant in charge of the search just kept getting more and more angry. I was worried that she or one of her cronies would plant some contraband on the ship, so I made a point of telling her that I'd turned on all the ship's cameras, one in every room and cargo space, and was livecasting the whole search back to a lawyer's office on Upside. If she tried to plant anything, it would be caught on camera.

That sent her into a towering rage, and she tossed all the staterooms for spite, ripping the mattresses and blankets off the beds and emptying the closets onto the deck, before she stomped off.

I planned to unload the cargo and leave the second we could get clearance, but thanks to the griff lieutenant's temper tantrum, we had to do some cleanup first. That's why we had time for a passenger to find us. That's how we met Katarina.

Katarina was one of the Pryors, the incorporated gene line that pretty much owned the system, all of Upside and most of Downside, as well as every facility on Vantage. She'd been on some kind of inspection tour of the Pryor facilities on the various moons, but she'd been unexpectedly called back to Socorro and needed a ride.

When the message first came that someone wanted passage to Socorro, I'd been worried that Katarina was a plant from the police or from Eldridge, but as soon as I looked at her I knew that she was going to be a lot more trouble than that.

I don't understand the way the gene lines operate internally, with all the cloning and use of cartridge memories and marriages by cousins to keep all the money and power in the same pedigree, but it was clear from the second she came aboard *Olympe* that she ranked high in the structure. She had that eerie perfection that came with her status. Geneticists had sweated over her body years before she'd ever been born. Flawless complexion, perfect black hair, perfect white teeth, full expressive lips, black eyes that looked at me for a full half-second before they had added up my entire life and riches, found them unworthy of further consideration, and looked away. She wore an outfit that was the opposite of the balloon-suits women wore in Socorro, a dark fabric that outlined perfectly every curve of that genetically ideal body. I got dizzy just looking at her.

She looked at my stateroom—I'd moved my stuff out of it—and spared an extra glance for the painting I'd put over the cabinet door that had been ripped off its hinges by the griffs. The painting was of a nude woman on a sofa, with a black ribbon around her neck and a bangle on her wrist. She has a cat, and a servant bringing her flowers from the admirer that's obviously just walked into the room. She's looking out of the painting at her visitor with eyes hard and objective and cutting as obsidian.

Aram had that painting in the stateroom when he'd died. I'd kept it for a while, but put it away later. It is true that travelers, stuck in their ships for months at a time, like to look at pictures of naked ladies, but not the same lady all the time, and not one who looks back at you the way this one does.

I looked for a startled moment at Katarina and the woman in the painting, and I realized that they had the same look in their eyes, that same hard, indifferent calculation. She turned those eyes to me.

"I'll take it," she said. "There's a room for my secretary?"

"Of course." With a torn mattress and a smashed chair, but I didn't mention that.

She left the stateroom to call for her secretary and her baggage. In the corridor, she encountered Tonio.

He grinned at her, blue eyes set on either side of that broken nose. Those hard black eyes gazed back, then softened.

"Who is *this*?" she asked.

Trouble, I thought.

"I'm the cook," Tonio said.

Of course, she was married. They almost always are.

Tonio and I had first come aboard *Olympe* as crew. Aram was the owner and captain—he was a Maheu and had inherited money and power and responsibility, but after eight hundred years he'd given up everything but the money, and traveled aimlessly in *Olympe,* looking for something that he hadn't seen somewhere before.

He also used massive amounts of drugs, which were sent to him by Maheu's special courier service. To show that the drugs were legitimate he had doctor's prescriptions for everything—he collected them the way he had once collected art.

Physically, he had the perfection of the high-bred gene lines, with broad shoulders, mahogany skin, and an arched nose. It was only if you looked closely that you saw that the eyes were pouchy and vague, that his muscles were wasting away, and that his skin was as slack as his first-rate genetics would permit. He was giving away his body the same way he'd given away his collection.

He was lonely too, because he would talk to Tonio and me, about history, and art, and poetry. He could recite whole volumes of poetry from memory, and it was beautiful even though most of it was in old languages, like Persian, that I'd never heard before and didn't understand.

I asked him about his gene line, his connections, what he did before he'd started his wandering.

"It was prostitution," he said, with a look at the painting on his stateroom wall. "I don't want to talk about it, now I'm trying to regain my virtue."

These conversations took place in the morning, after breakfast. Then he'd put the first patch of the day on his arm and nod off, his head in Maud's lap.

Maud Rain was his girlfriend. She looked about seventeen, and maybe she was. She appeared as if her genetics had been intending to create a lily, or cornflower, or some other fragile blossom, and then been surprised to discover they'd produced a human being. She was blond and green-eyed and blushed easily, and she loved Aram completely. I was a little in love with her, myself.

Life aboard the *Olympe* was pleasant, if somewhat pointless. We wandered around the multiverse without a schedule. We'd stop for a while, and Aram would leave the ship to visit old friends or see something new that he thought might interest him, and we wouldn't hear from him for anywhere between three days and three months, then abruptly we'd be on our way again. Aram paid us well and gave us a good deal of time off, and once he bailed Tonio out of a scrape involving the wife of a Creel station superintendent.

I don't pretend to understand the chemistry between users and their consorts, and I don't know whether Aram talked Maud into using, or whether it was her own idea. I do know that, like all users, Aram wanted to make everyone around him use too. He offered the stuff often enough to me and Tonio, though I never heard him make the same offer to Maud.

Whoever made up Maud's mind for her, she then went on to make a stupid, elementary mistake. She gave herself the same dose that Aram took, without his magic genes and all the immunity he'd built up over the decades, and she screamed and thrashed and went into convulsions. Tonio got his fingers savagely bitten trying to keep the vomit clear of her mouth while I madly shifted the ship through about eight Probabilities to get her to a hospital. By the time we got her there, she didn't have much of a brain left. She still blushed easily, and looked at you with dreamy green eyes. She had the sweet-natured smile, but there was nothing behind it but a void.

We left her in a place where they'd look after her, a stately white building on a pleasant green lawn, and *Olympe* resumed its wanderings. Aram deteriorated quickly. He no longer talked in the mornings. We'd find him alone and crying, the tears pouring down his face in silence, and then he'd put a new patch on his arm and drift away. One afternoon, we found him dead, with six patches on his arm.

In his will, he left all his money to a trust for Maud, and he left *Olympe* and its contents to me. He left Tonio some money. I gave Tonio everything in the pharmacy, and he sold it to someone on Burnes Upside and we gave Aram a long, crazy wake with the profits. The rest of Tonio's money went to lawyers to fix a misunderstanding that occurred during the course of the wake.

When we sobered up, I realized that I had a yacht, but no money to support it.

Tonio was the only crew I ever had, because he didn't expect to be paid. He did the job of a crew, and when he had money, he paid me, as if he were a passenger. When I had money, I shared it with him.

We kept moving, the same kind of random shifts we'd made with Aram.

It was almost enough to keep us out of trouble.

Tonio spent that first night in the stateroom with Katarina Pryor. I tried to console myself with the fact that this was all happening in a whole other Probability from the one Katarina normally lived in. I also tried to concentrate on how I was going to handle Eldridge when I saw him again.

I checked some data sources and inquired about Katarina Pryor. She was about fifty years old, though she looked half that and would for the next millennium, if she so desired. She was one of the Council of Seven that ran Socorro on behalf of the Pryor gene line.

Her husband, Denys, was another one of the Seven.

I let that settle in my brain for a while. Then I sent a message to Eldridge, telling him that I wanted to meet him as soon as *Olympe* docked Topside. He replied that it would be his pleasure to do so.

We'd see how much fun he'd have.

I told Tonio of this development as we were walking to the lounge. As he stepped into the room, he gave me the news. "Katarina has invited me to accompany her to Downside on completion of our returnment. I have accepted, yiss, pending of course my captain's sanction."

Katarina's secretary, a young Pryor named Andrew, happened to be sitting in the lounge as we entered, and he looked as if someone had hit him in the head with a brick.

"It's not as if people are going out of their way to hire us," I said, "so the ship can spare you. But. . . " I hesitated, aware of the presence of Andrew. "Doesn't this *remind* you of anything, Tonio?"

He gave me a look of offended dignity. "The situation of which you speak was on an entirely different plane," he said. "This, on the contrary, is *real.*"

The conversation was taking place in a Probability where stars looked like spinning billiard balls on a felt-green sky, and he and Katarina were traveling to another place where oxygen burned in their blood like naphtha. Who knew how real *anything* could be under such circumstances?

I asked Tonio if he could delay his departure with Katarina until Eldridge came aboard.

"Oh yiss. Most assuredly."

He seemed perfectly confident.

I wish I could have echoed his assurance.

Eldridge was present when *Olympe* arrived at Upside, and he had brought a couple of thick-necked thugs with him. They were hanging back from the personnel lock because there were plainclothes Pryor security present, waiting to escort Katarina and her new beau on the first stage of their planetary honeymoon.

I called Eldridge from the control room. "Come on in," I said. "Leave your friends behind."

When he came on board, he looked as if he were fully capable of dismembering me all by himself, his small size notwithstanding. I escorted him through the lounge, where Katarina and Andrew waited for Tonio to finish his packing job, a job that would not be completed until I gave him the high sign.

Eldridge's eyes went wide as he saw Katarina. She wore a compromise between the local balloon-suits and the form-fitting outfit she'd worn when she came aboard, which amounted to a slinky suit with a puffy jacket on top. But I don't think it was her looks that riveted his attention.

He recognized her.

"This is Miss Katarina Pryor," I told him, redundantly I hoped, "and Mr. Andrew Pryor."

"Pryor," Eldridge repeated, as if he wanted to confirm this striking fact for himself.

Andrew gave him a barely civil nod. Katarina just gave him her stone-eyed stare, let him know he had been measured and found wanting.

I went to the bar and poured myself a cup of coffee. You had to drink coffee quickly here, because in this Probability it cools very fast.

"Eldridge," I remarked. "I haven't received my on-delivery fee."

He gave me a scarlet stare out of his white face. "The cargo did not arrive intact."

"One crate went missing," I said. "It was probably the fault of the loaders, but since I signed for it, you should feel free to deduct its value from the delivery fee." I made a show of looking at the manifest on my pocket adjutant. "What was in that crate—? Ah, jugs of spray foam mix. Value three hundred—would you say that's a correct value, Miss Pryor?"

Katarina drummed her fingers on the arm of the sofa. "Sounds about right, Captain Crossbie," she said, in a voice that said *Don't bother me with this crap.*

I called up my bank account. "Might as well do the transfer now," I said.

Eldridge's eyes cut to Katarina, then cut back. His lips went even whiter than usual.

If the Pryors decided to step on him, he wouldn't leave so much as a grease spot on their shoes. He knew that, as did I.

He got out his own adjutant and tapped in codes with his one long thumbnail. I saw my bank account jump by the anticipated amount, and I put away my adjutant and sipped my coffee. It was already lukewarm.

"Want some coffee, by the way?" I asked.

Eldridge gazed at me out of those flaming eyes. "No," he said.

"We have some other business, but there's no reason to bother Miss Pryor with it," I said.

He followed me into the control room, where I closed the door and gestured him toward a chair.

"Consider that a penalty," I said, "for thinking I was new to the multiverse."

"The Pryors aren't really protecting you," he said. "They can't be."

"They're old family friends," I said. I sat in the padded captain's chair—genuine Tibetan goat hide, Aram had told me—and swiveled it toward him. He just stared at me, his busy fingers plucking at his knees.

"I'm willing to sell you coordinates," I said.

He licked his lips, pink tongue on paper-white. "Coordinates to what?" he asked.

"What do you think?"

He didn't answer.

We had put the blue salt in orbit around an ice moon, one that circled the same gas giant as Vantage.

"The coordinates go for the same price as the cargo." I smiled. "Plus three hundred."

He just kept staring. Probably that agate gaze had frightened a lot of people, but I wasn't scared at all.

Five days around Katarina Pryor had given me immunity to lesser terrors.

"If you don't want the coordinates," I said, "your competition will."

He sneered. "There *is* no competition."

"There will be if Katarina takes you and your tame police out of the equation," I said.

So, in the end, he paid. Once the money was in the account, I gave Eldridge the seven orbital elements that described the salt's amble about its moon. Someone from Vantage could easily hop over and pick up the salt for him, and the strung-out miners would go on getting their daily nerve-searing dose of fate.

I showed Eldridge out, and as he bustled away, he cast a look over his shoulder that promised payback.

I sent a message to Tonio, telling him to solve his packing crisis, and as I returned to the lounge, he came loping out of his quarters, his belongings carried in a rucksack on one shoulder. Andrew raised an eyebrow at the tiny amount of baggage that had taken so long to pack.

Katarina rose to embrace Tonio. I watched as she molded her body to his.

"I am primed, lover mine," Tonio said.

"So am I."

I showed them to the door. "Thank you, Captain," Andrew said, and with an expression like someone passing gas at a funeral, handed me a tip in an envelope.

I looked at the envelope. *This* had never happened before.

"See you later, compeer." Tonio grinned.

"You bet."

I watched them walk toward their waiting transport, arms around each other's waists. People stared. Wary guards circled them. Eldridge and his people were long gone.

I decided it was time to buy and stow a lot of rations. A year's worth, at least.

For two fools, running.

But first I wanted to celebrate the fact that I now possessed more money than I'd ever had in my life, even if you didn't count my tip—which was two thousand, by the way, an inept attempt to buy my silence. I couldn't make up my mind whether Eldridge was going to be a problem or not—if I were him, Katarina would have scared the spleen right out of me, but I didn't know Eldridge well enough to know how stubborn or stupid he was.

While I considered this, it occurred to me to wonder how many years it had been since I'd had a planet under my feet.

Too many, I thought.

I opened my safe and put Tonio's emerald ring in my pocket—no sense in leaving it behind for people like Eldridge to find—and then I followed in the footsteps of Tonio and Katarina and took the next ride down the grapevine to Downside. I looked for tourist resorts and exotic sights, and though I discovered there were none of the former, there were plenty of the latter. There were mountains, gorges, and colossal wildlife—the chemical bonding of the local Probability led to plants, even those with Earth genetics, running amok. I saw rose blossoms bigger than my head, and with a smell like vinegar—chemistry not quite right, you see. Little pine trees grew to the size of Douglas firs. Socorro's internal workings had thrust huge reefs of nearly pure minerals right out of the ground, many of which the miners had not yet begun to disassemble and carry away. For a brief time, wearing a protective raincoat, breathing apparatus, and crinkly plastic overshoes, I walked on the Whitewashed Desert that surrounded Mount Cyanide. I bathed in the Red Sea. Then the Green Sea, the Yellow Sea, and the Winedark Sea. The Yellow Sea stained my skin for days. It looked as if I were dying of cirrhosis.

I kept the ring in a special trouser pocket that would open only to a code from my personal adjutant. After a while, I got used to the feel of it, and days went by before I remembered it was there.

I'd brought my aurora. Along the way there was music, bars, and happy moments. I met women named Meimei, Sally June, and Soda. We had good times together. None of them died, went crazy, or slit their wrists.

Carried away by the sheer carefree joy of it all, I began to think of going back to the *Olympe* and sailing away on the sea of Probability. Tonio was probably still happy with Katarina, and I could leave with his blessing.

I would be safe. Shawn wasn't after *me*. And Tonio, provided he stayed put, would be as safe as he ever was, probably safer.

I contemplated this possibility for a few too many days, because one morning I woke from a dense, velvety dream to the birdlike tones of my adjutant. I told it to answer.

"Compeer," said Tonio. "Wherewhich art thou?"

"Shadows and fog," I said, because the voice seemed to be coming from my dream.

"There's a party on the morrow. Come and share it with me. Katarina would be delighted to see you."

I'll bet, I thought.

The hotel looked like a hovership that had stranded itself on land, a series of swoops and terraces, surrounded by cypress trees the size of skyscrapers, with gardenias as long as my leg tumbling brightly down from the balconies. Katarina had installed Tonio and his rucksack in a five-room suite and given him an expense account that, so far, he'd been unable to dent.

Tonio greeted me as I stepped into the suite. His blue eyes sparkled with joy. He looked well scrubbed and well tended, and his hair was sleek.

"Did you bring your aurora, Gaucho?" he said. "Let us repair to a suitable location, with drinks and the like, and partake of heavenly music."

"I thought we were going to a party."

"That is later. Right now we've got to have you measured for clothes."

A tailor with a double chin and a ponytail stepped out of a side room, had me take off my jacket, and got my measurements with a laser scriber. He vanished. Tonio led me out of the apartment and down a confusing series of stairs and lifts to a subbasement garage. Empty space echoed around us, supported by fluted pillars with lotus-leaf capitals. Tonio whispered a code into his adjutant and turbines began their soft whine somewhere in the darkness. Spotlights flared. A blazemobile came whispering toward us on its cushion of air. I felt its breath on my face and hands. The colors were gray and silver, blending into each other as if they were somehow forged together. The lines were clean and sharp. It looked purposeful as a sword.

"Nice," I said. "Is this Katarina's?" I had a hard time not calling her "Miss Pryor."

"It's mine," Tonio said. "Katarina purchased it for me after, ah, the incident."

I looked at him.

"There was a misunderstanding about another vehicle," Tonio said. "I thought I had the owner's permission to take it."

Ah, I thought. One of *those* misunderstandings.

"Are you driving?" I asked.

"Why don't you drive? You're better than I am."

I settled into the machine gingerly. It folded around me like a piece of origami. Tonio settled into the passenger seat. I drove the car with care till I got out of town, then let the turbines off their leash, and we were soon zooming down a highway under the system's fluorescing, shivering smear of a sun, huge jungle growth on either side of the road turning the highway into a tunnel beneath vines and wild, drooping blossoms.

"There's another car behind us," I said, looking at the displays. I was surprised it could keep up.

"That would be Katarina's security," Tonio said. "It is a mark of her love. They follow me everywhere, to render me safe."

And to prevent, I thought, any of those misunderstandings about who owns what.

A blissful smile crossed Tonio's face. "Katarina and I are so in love," he said. "I sing her to sleep every night."

The thought of Tonio crooning made me smile. "That sounds great," I said.

"We wish to have many babies, but there are complicatories."

"Like her husband?"

"He is obstacular, yiss, but the principal problem is legal."

It turned out that Katarina did not legally own her own

womb, as well as other parts, which belonged to the Pryor family trust. She could not become pregnant without the permission of certain high-ranking members of her line, who alone knew the codes that would unlock her fertility.

"That's . . . not the usual problem," I said, stunned. I don't know much about how the big corporate gene lines work, but this seemed extreme even for them.

"Can you hire a surrogate?" I asked. "Use an artificial womb?"

"It's not the same." He cast a glance over his shoulder. "Those individuals behind us—mayhap you can outspeed them?"

"I'll try."

I set the jets alight. My vision narrowed with acceleration, but oxygen still blazed in my blood. Alarms began to chirp. The vehicle trailing us fell back, but before long we came to a town and had to slow.

It was a sad little mining town, covered with the dust of the huge magnesite reef that loomed over the town. Vast movers were in the process of disassembling the entire formation, while being careful not to ignite it and incinerate the entire county.

Tonio pointed to a bar called the Reefside. "Pull in here, compeer. Mayhap we may discover refreshment."

The bar sat on its tracks, ready to move to another location when the last chunk of magnesite was finally carried away. I put the blazemobile in a side street so as not to attract attention to ourselves. We climbed up into the bar and blinked in its dark, musty-scented interior. We had arrived during an off-peak period and only a few faces stared back at us.

We huffed some gas and shared a bag of crisps. After ten minutes, the security detail barged in, two broad-shouldered, clean-cut, thick-necked young men in city suits. After they saw us, one went back outside, and the other ordered fruit juice.

The regulars stared at him.

I asked the bartender if it was all right to play my aurora.

"You can if you want," he said, "but if the music's shit, I'll tell you to stop."

"That's fair," I said. I opened the case and adjusted the sonics for the room and put the aurora against my shoulder and touched the strings. A chord hung in the air, with just a touch of sourness. The bartender frowned. I tuned and began to play.

The bartender turned away with a grudging smile. I made the aurora sound like chimes, like drums, like brass. Our fellow drinkers began to bob their heads and call for the bartender to refill their glasses. One gent bought us rounds of beer.

The shifts changed at the diggings and miners spilled in, their clothes dusty, their respirators hanging loose around their necks. Some were highly specialized gene types, with sleek skin and implants for remote control of heavy equipment. Others were generalized humans, like us. One woman had lost an arm in an accident, and they were growing it back—it was a formless pink bud on the end of her shoulder.

I played my aurora. I played fierce, then slow. The miners nodded and grinned and tapped their booted feet on the grainy plastic floor. The security man clung unhappily to his glass of fruit juice. I played angry, I played tender, I played the sound of birds in the air and bees in their hive. Tonio borrowed a cap from one of the diggers and passed it around. It came back full of money, which he stuffed in my pockets.

My fingers and mind were numb, and I paused for a moment. There was a round of applause, and the diggers called for more refreshment. A few others asked who we were, and I told them we were off a ship and just traveling around the country.

Tonio had a blazing white grin on his face. "It is *spectacular*!" he said. "This is the true joy!"

"More than with Katarina?"

He shrugged. "With Katarina it is sensational, but she is terribly occupied, and I don't know anyone else in this coincidence of spacetime. People fear to be in my vicinity, and when I corner one, they only speak to me because they are afraid of Katarina. I have nothing in my day but to wait for Katarina to come home."

"Can't she give you a job? Make you her secretary, maybe?"

"She has Andrew."

"Her social secretary, then." I couldn't help but laugh at the idea.

He gave a big grin. "*She* knows the social rules, yiss. I am signally lacking in that area of expertise."

"You could be a prospector. Travel around looking for minerals or whatever."

"For this task they have satellites and artificial intelligences." He gazed for a long moment off into nowhere. "I am filled with gladness that you came to see me, Gaucho."

"I'm glad I came." Though I'm not certain I was telling the truth.

Tonio was getting bored with his life with Katarina. A bored Tonio was a dangerous Tonio.

We talked and drank with the miners till Tonio said it was time to leave. Our guard was relieved to follow us out of the bar. His partner had been guarding our blazemobile all this time.

We were both too drunk to drive, so we got in the car and told the autopilot to take us home. Once we arrived, I had a fitting with the tailor, who had run up my suit while we were off enjoying ourselves. I had this deep blue outfit, all spider silk, with lots of gold braid on my cuffs.

"What's this?" I asked Tonio.

"You are my captain," he said, "and now you are dressed like one."

"I feel ridiculous," I said.

"Wait till you see what *I* am compelled to wear."

The tailor adjusted the suit, then gave me the codes so that I could alter the suit's fit if I wanted to, or add a pocket here or there. In the meantime, Tonio changed. His suit was the latest mode, with ruffles and fringes that seemed to triple the volume of his thin body. He looked unusual, but he carried himself with his usual jaunty style, as if he wanted it made clear to everyone that he was only *pretending* to be the person in the suit.

Katarina arrived and wrapped herself around Tonio without caring if I was there or not. I was reminded of my little limpet-girl, Étoile.

Katarina began tearing at Tonio's ruffles and fringes. They went off to the bedroom for a lust break. I went out onto the balcony and watched the sun set over the jade forest. The sweet smell of flowers rose on the twilight air.

Tonio and Katarina returned. She wore a dark lacy sheath that was as simple as Tonio's suit was elaborate. Gemstones glittered sunset-red about her neck, and a languid postcoital glow seemed to float around her like a halo. I could feel sweat prickling my forehead at her very presence.

"You're looking very well, Captain Crossbie," she said.

"You're looking well yourself," I said. There was a bit more regard in her glance than I usually got. I wondered if Tonio had been telling her stories that made me seem, well, interesting.

We went to the party, which was in the same building. It celebrated the fact that some production quota or other had been exceeded, and the room was full of Pryors and their minions. Katarina took Tonio's arm and pressed herself to him all night, making it clear that they were a couple.

The place was filled with people who were perfectly perfect, perfect everywhere from their dress to their genetics. All the talk I heard was of business, and complex business at that. If I'd been a spy sent by the competition, I would have heard a lot, but it would have been opaque to me.

Don't let anyone tell you that people like the Pryors don't work for their riches and power. They do nothing else.

I was introduced as Captain Crossbie, and people took me for a yachtsman, which technically I suppose I was. People asked me about regattas and famous captains, and I admitted that I only used my yacht for travel. I was then asked where I'd been, and I managed to tell a few stories.

I was talking about yachts to an engineer named Bond— his dream was to buy a ship when he retired, and travel— when a blond man came up to talk to him. I thought the newcomer looked familiar, but didn't place him right away.

He talked to Bond about some kind of bottleneck on the Downside grapevine station that was threatening to interfere with shipments to Upside, and Bond assured him that the problem would be engineered out of existence in a couple weeks. He asked after Bond's family. Bond told him that his son had won some kind of prize from the Pryor School of Economics. It was then that the blond man turned to me.

He had the chiseled perfection that came with his flawless genes, and violet eyes, and around his mouth was a tight-lipped tension that nature—or his designers—had not quite intended for him.

"This is Mister Denys Pryor," Bond said. "Denys, this is Captain Crossbie."

He realized who I was about the same instant that I finally recognized him as Katarina's husband. The violet eyes narrowed.

"Ah," he said. "The accomplice."

"I don't have any response to that," I said, "that I'd expect you to believe."

He gave me a contemptuous look and stalked away. Bond looked after him in surprise, then looked at me. Then the light dawned. Panic flashed across his face.

"If you'll excuse me," he said, and was gone before I could even reply.

That was the last conversation I had at the party. Word about my connection to Tonio flashed through the room faster than lightning, and soon I was alone. I got tired of standing around by myself, so I went out onto the terrace, where a group of women in immaculate white balloon-suits were grilling meats. I was considering chatting up one of them when Tonio came up, carrying a pair of drinks. He handed me one.

"My apologies, compeer," he said. "They are stuck-up here, yiss."

"I've been treated worse."

He looked up at the strangely infirm stars. "I have Katarina by way of compensation," he said. "You have nothing."

"I have *Olympe*," I said. "I've been thinking maybe it's time she and I flew away to the next Probability."

He looked at me somberly. "I will miss your companion-hood," he said.

"You'll have Katarina." I looked at thc sky, where Upside glittered on its invisible tether. "I hope Eldridge isn't still looking for me," I said.

"You don't have to worry about Eldridge," Tonio said. "I told Katarina all about him."

Hot terror flashed through my nerves.

"What did you tell her?" I asked.

"I told her that Eldridge tried to use us to smugglc his salt, and that we found the stuff and spaced it."

I relaxed a little. The scene that Eldridge and I had playcd in front of Katarina might not seem that suspicious, if, of course, she believed her lover.

"You didn't hear the news?" Tonio said. "About that police officer that was found in the vacuum, over on Vantage."

My mouth was dry. "That griff lieutenant?" I asked.

"Her captain. The lieutenant is learning a new job, floating in zero gravity and sucking up industrial wastes with a big vacuum cleaner." He rubbcd his chin. "The Pryors don't like people fucking up their workers with drugs."

"They don't seem to mind all those enhanced production quotas, though," I said. "Do you think those come from workers who aren't spiked up?" There was a moment of silence. The scent of sizzling meat gusted past. "What happened to Eldridge?" I asked.

"Don't know. Didn't bother to ask."

If anything was going to harden my determination to leave Socorro as quickly as I could, it was this.

I turned to Tonio. "I'll miss you," I said. I raised a glass. "To happy endings."

Before Tonio could respond, there was a sudden brilliant radiance in the sky, and we looked up. An enormous structure had appeared in the sky above Socorro, a vast black octahedron covered with thousands of brilliant lights, windows enabling the 1.4 million people aboard to gaze out at the passing Probabilities. To gaze down at *us*.

"It's the Chrysalis," I said aloud.

Surrounding the structure were half a dozen birds, each larger than the habitat, long necks outstretched. The storks that were the emblem of the Storch gene line, each with ghostly white wings flapping in utter silence, holograms projected into space by enormous lasers.

Suddenly, I remembered Tonio's emerald ring, in its special pocket on the old trousers I'd left back at Tonio's flat.

Too late, I thought. Shawn had come for us.

"We can't keep them out," Katarina said. "This Probability isn't a secret any longer, and anyone can exploit it now that it's registered."

I doubted the Pryors could keep the Chrysalis out even if they wanted to. The Pryors maintained a police force here, not an army, and I knew that the Chrysalis had weapons for self-defense. They had those huge lasers they'd used to project their flying stork blazons, for one thing, and those could be turned to military use at any time.

We sat on Tonio's terrace the morning following the Storches' arrival, soaking in the scent of blossoms. The Chrysalis was still visible in daylight, its edges rimmed with silver.

Breakfast was curdling on our plates. Nobody was very hungry.

"The Chrysalis is a state-of-the-art industrial colony," I said. "They can park it here and start exporting materials in just weeks."

Katarina gave me a tell-me-something-I-don't-know look.

"They have also made an official request," she said. "They want the two of you arrested on charges of theft and turned over to them."

I felt myself turn pale, a chill touching my lips and cheeks. "What are we supposed to have stolen?" I asked.

Katarina permitted herself a thin smile. "They haven't said. We have requested clarification." She turned her black eyes to me. "They have also asked that your ship be impounded, until it can be determined whether you obtained it by forging Aram Maheu's will."

"That was all settled in the chancery court on Burnes Upside," I said. "Besides, if I was going to forge a will to give myself a yacht, I'd give myself the money to keep it going."

"The request is a delaying tactic," Katarina said. "It's to tie up your vessel for an indeterminate period and prevent you from escaping."

"Is it going to work?" I asked. Katarina didn't bother to answer.

The previous night's party had ended with the appearance of the Chrysalis, as the Council of Seven went into executive session and their employees scattered to duty stations to do research on the Chrysalis and the implication of its arrival.

Apparently at some point in the night, Tonio had told Katarina about Adora and Shawn, and Katarina must have believed him, because neither of us was being tied to a chair and tortured by Pryor security armed with shock wands.

Katarina rose and gave Tonio a kiss. "I've got a lot of meetings," she said.

"See you tonight, lover mine," Tonio said.

We sat in silence for a while as Socorro's strange sun climbed above the horizon. I turned to Tonio.

"Are you certain," I asked, "that Adora gave you that ring?"

He gave me a wounded look. "Surely I am not hearing what I am hearing, my compeer."

"It wasn't one of those misunderstandings?" I pressed. "Where you're certain she gave it to you, but she doesn't remember doing it?"

"I am certain she told Shawn it was stolen," Tonio said with dignity, "but this is what happened in sooth. He presented her with the ring at their wedding, a sentimental token, I imagine. But later she was angry at Shawn for a scene he'd made, where he was complaining about how she had behaved with me at a certain social function, and out of anger she bestowed the ring upon me."

"And when you left and she went back to Shawn," I said, "she couldn't admit it, so she told him it was stolen."

"That is my postulation."

Or that was the postulation that Tonio wanted me to believe.

Tonio had been to prison, and in prison you learn to manipulate people. You learn to tell them what they want to hear. Is it lying if there is no harm intended? If it's just saying the thing that's most convenient for everyone?

I didn't steal anything. How often in prison do you hear *that*?

I think Tonio was sincere in everything he said and did. But what he was sincere *about* could change from one minute to the next.

In any case, this had to be about more than just the ring. The ring was valuable, but it didn't justify moving over a million Storch employees to this Probability and opening mining operations.

"Why did Shawn and Adora marry in the first place?" I asked.

"Their families told them to. They hadn't met until a few days before the ceremony."

"But *why*? Usually line members marry each other, like Katarina and Denys. It keeps the money in the family. When they merge or take another outfit over, they do it by adoption. But Shawn and Adora were different—each was ordered to marry *out*. The Storches do heavy industry. The Feeneys specialize in biotech and research. What did they have in common?"

Tonio waved a hand in dismissal. "There was a special project. I did not ask for details, no. Why would I? It was connected to Shawn, and when I was with Adora, I had no wish to talk about Shawn. Why spoil a bliss that was so perfect with such a subject?"

"If it was so perfect, why did you leave Adora?" I asked. "When I last saw you together, you seemed so . . . connected."

"She grew too onerous," Tonio said. "Once we began to live together, she began giving orders. *Go here. Do this. Put on these clothes. What do you want to name the children?* Under the oppression my spirit began to chafe, yiss. She loved me, but only as a pet."

"Still," I said, "you had good times."

"Oh yiss." There was a soft light in his eyes. "They were magical, so many of our times. When we were sneaking away together, to make love in an isolated corner of the Chrysalis. . . that was bliss, my compeer."

I looked up at the Chrysalis, hovering over our heads like the Big Heavy Shiny Object of Damocles.

"Do you think she's up there?" I asked. "It was Adora who was the member of the Storch line. Shawn was the Feeney half of the alliance. He could only command the Chrysalis with the permission of his in-laws."

Tonio looked at the sky in wonder. His face screwed up as he tried to think.

I rose and left him to his thoughts. I needed to do a lot of thinking myself.

For the next several days we bounced around the apartment with increasing energy and frustration. The news was grim. Shuttles from the Chrysalis were exploring uninhabited parts of Socorro. There had been one near-miss between a Storch shuttle and a Pryor transport. Fail-safes normally kept ships from getting remotely close to one another, so the miss had been a deliberate provocation.

Guards stood at our door and even on the next terrace, sensors deployed, looking for any assassins lurking on the horizon. Tonio's blazemobile privileges had been revoked, and he wasn't allowed out of the building.

"I love my little Katarina, yiss," he said one day as he stalked about the main room. "But this is growing onerous."

A bored Tonio was a dangerous Tonio. If he walked out on Katarina, we were both just so much dog food.

"She's just trying to protect you," I said. "It'll only last until the business with the Storches is resolved."

He flung out his arms. "But how long will that be?"

I looked at him. "What if Adora's up there, Tonio?"

He gave me an exasperated look. "What if she is?"

"Do you think you can talk to her? Find out what she wants?"

Tonio stopped his pacing. His startled face began to look thoughtful.

"Do you think I can?" he asked.

"If you try it from here, Katarina will be listening in before you can spit."

"But she won't let me *leave* here!"

"Let me work on that."

His adjutant bleeped, and he answered. His face broke into a look of pure joy as he said, "Hello, lover."

Go on pleasing them, Tonio, I thought.

I went to one of the security guards at our door and told him that I needed to speak to Denys Pryor.

"I don't know why I'm even talking to you," said Denys. I had been called into his office, the design of which told me that he liked clean sight lines, no clutter, curved geometries, and a terrace with a water view. He remained at his desk as I entered, and was turned slightly away, so that I saw his perfect chiseled features in three-quarter profile. He wore fewer ruffles in his office than at the party.

There was no chair for me to sit in. Not anywhere in the room. I had a choice of responses—Denys would probably have preferred an awkward shuffle—so instead I leaned on his immaculate white wall.

"I'm here to solve your problems," I said.

He raised an eyebrow.

No wonder Katarina was dissatisfied with him, I thought. She could have conveyed the same suspicion and contempt without twitching a single hair.

"Your Chrysalis problem," I clarified, "and your Tonio problem."

"Tonio Hope," he said, "is welcome to my wife. They deserve each other, and I hope you'll tell them that. But the problem represented by the Chrysalis is rather more urgent." He turned in his chair to face me. "Tell me your scheme, please. Then I can have a good hearty laugh and have you thrown out of here."

Cuckolded husbands, I have observed, are rarely models of courtesy.

"Tell me one thing first," I said. "Is Adora Storch on the Chrysalis?"

"Your friend's former lover? Yes." His tone was bored. "Apparently, he stole something from her, but she's too embarrassed to admit what it was."

"Her heart," I said. He looked away suddenly, toward the distant lake.

"What I would like," I said, "is a secure means of communication between Tonio and Adora." And then, at the sudden, sharp violet-eyed look, I added, "Secure, I mean, from Katarina."

"Start with flowers," I suggested. Tonio contacted a florist on the Chrysalis and sent an extravagant bouquet, with a humble little message. There was no reply. "Just call her," I said finally.

Her secretary kept him waiting for half an hour, while he paced about gripping the adjutant I'd got from Denys. I played quiet, tinkly music on the aurora to keep him calmed down, while I watched the muscles leaping on his face. Finally, I heard Adora's voice.

"Tonio! You have the nerve to call me after the way you walked out on me?"

Adora had taken half an hour to work up sufficient anger to decide to confront Tonio instead of just leaving him hanging. Things had worked out more or less as I'd hoped.

Tonio looked at the adjutant's screen. Over his shoulder I saw Adora's brilliant red hair, her flashing green eyes, her pale rose complexion. He didn't reply.

"What's the matter with you?" she demanded. "Have the lies stuck in your throat for the first time in your life?"

"I—I am but stunned, seeing you again," Tonio said. "I know you're angry and suchlike, but—at least the anger shows you still care."

Adora began screaming at that point, and I left the room. *Just do what you do best,* I told Tonio silently.

I heard Tonio murmur, and more fury from Adora, and then a lot of silence, which meant Adora was doing the talking and Tonio was listening. It went on for nearly two hours.

While it went on, I strummed the aurora, volume at a low setting. I really didn't want to know how Tonio did these things: I didn't think I could be trusted with the knowledge.

After the murmuring stopped, I walked back out into the main room. Tonio sat on the sofa, his hands dangling over his knees. He shook his head.

"I'd forgotten what Adora was like," he said. "How beautiful she is. How passionate."

"You've got to tell Katarina," I said. He looked up in shock.

"Tell her that I—"

"Tell her that you're in touch with Adora. Tell her it was my idea, and I made you do it."

"Why?"

"Because if you don't, Denys will. He'll use it to turn Katarina against you."

He rubbed his face with one of his big hands. "This is complicated."

"Tell Katarina the next time you see her," I said.

Which he did, that night. By morning, he had Katarina thinking this was a good idea, and the three of us plotted strategy over breakfast.

When, later that day, Denys told her of Tonio's supposed treachery, she laughed in his face.

While Denys was fuming, and Tonio and Adora were cooing at each other with Katarina's approval, I decided that it was time to find out as much as I could about the ring. I got free of security by telling them I was going to report to Denys, and took the ring to a jeweler. If I got no answer there, I'd take it to a laboratory.

I could feel my blood sizzle as I walked into the shop. There was a little extra oxygen in the air here, I thought, to make the customers happy and more willing to buy.

The jeweler was a dark-haired woman with a low, scratchy voice and long, elegant hands. She stood amid cases of brilliant splendor, but refused to be distracted by them. Her attention was devoted entirely to the customer.

"Splendid work," she said, gazing at a hologram of the ring as big as her head. "The emerald is a natural emerald, which makes it slightly more valuable than an artificial one."

"How do you know?" I asked. She'd made the judgment a split second after she'd put the ring into the laser scanner.

"Natural gems have flaws," the jeweler said. "Artificial gems are perfect."

Imperfection is worth more. Perhaps that says something about our world. Perhaps that says something about how women relate to Tonio.

"The setting is common gold and platinum," the jeweler continued, "but it's more valuable than the gem, because it's clearly handmade, and by a master. Let me see if it's signed anywhere."

She called up a program that would scan the ring thoroughly for numbers or letters. "No," she said, and then cocked her head. She rotated the image, then magnified it.

"This is curious. There are letters laser-inscribed in the gem, and that's not unusual—most gems are coded that way. But *this* is a type of code I've never seen." She frowned, and her long fingers reached for her keyboard. "Let me check—"

"No," I said quickly. "That's not necessary."

I only recognized the number sequence because I was a pilot. The numbers had nothing to do with the gem. They weren't a code, they were a set of *coordinates*.

For a Probability. And given how badly Shawn wanted it back, it was almost certainly a *brand-new* Probability.

Feeney researchers must have developed it, very possibly a Probability with one of the Holy Grails of Probability research, like a Probability where electromagnetism never broke into a separate force from gravity, or where atoms heavier than uranium have a greater stability than in the Home Universe, thus allowing atomic power with reduced radioactivity. The Feeneys had discovered this new universe, but they needed an industrial combine with the power of the

Storches to exploit it properly. Hence a marriage to seal the bargain. Hence a gem given by one line to the other with the coordinates secretly graven onto it.

I wasn't foolish enough to think the ring held the only copy of the coordinates—the Feeneys wouldn't have been that stupid. But it was the *only copy outside the gene lines' control*. If we gave the coordinates to the Pryors, the Storches would have competition in their new realm before they ever made their investment back.

No wonder something as huge and powerful as the Chrysalis had been sent after us.

I asked the jeweler for an estimate of the ring's worth—"so I know how much insurance to buy"—and then I took the ring and walked out of the shop with billions on my finger. The store's oxygenated atmosphere boiled in my blood.

The ring was the best insurance in the world, I thought. Shawn didn't dare kill us until he got his wedding present back.

That night, Tonio and Katarina had their first fight. She complained about the time he was spending talking to Adora. He pointed out that he was stuck here in the apartment and had nothing else to do. It degenerated from there.

I went to my room and played the aurora, loudly this time, and tried to decide what needed to happen next. It might be a good idea to get Tonio closer to Adora, just in case he needed a fast transfer from one girlfriend to another.

I went to Denys and suggested that we all go up the grapevine to Upside, in case any face-to-face meetings became necessary. He understood my point at once.

And so we all moved off the planet, spending a day and a half in the first-class compartment of a car roaring up the grapevine. Katarina spent the time adhered to Tonio, who looked uncomfortable. Denys kept to a cubicle where he worked, except for his occasional parades through the lounge, where he was all ostentatious about paying no attention to his wife.

The atmosphere on the car was sullen and ominous and filled with electricity, like the air before a thunderstorm. Even the other passengers felt it.

To dispel the lowering atmosphere, I played my aurora, until some pompous rich bastard told me to stop that damned noise or he'd call an attendant. "I'm with Miss Katarina Pryor," I told him. "Take it up with her."

He turned pale. I played on for a while, but the mood, such as it was, had been completely spoiled. I went to my cabin and lay on my bed and tried to sleep.

I needed to get away from Tonio and Katarina and Denys. I needed to get away from this freakish Probability where my blood sizzled all the time and my skin burned with fever. I needed to get *away*.

"I'd like to move onto *Olympe*," I told Katarina. She was curled around the spot on a lounge sofa where Tonio had just been sitting. He had gone to the bar for a cup of coffee, but you could still see his impression on the cushions.

Her cold eyes drifted over me. "Why?"

"I'll be out of your way. And it's where I *live*." When she didn't answer, I added, "Look, I can't leave the dock without your permission. I'm not *going* anywhere."

She turned away, dismissing me. "I'll tell the guards to let you pass," she said.

"There are *guards*?"

The only answer was an exasperated set to her lips, as if she didn't consider the question worthy of answer.

So it was that I showed the guards my ID and moved back onto *Olympe*. The air was stale, the corridors silent. I stepped into the stateroom and told the lights to go on and the first thing I saw was the painting of the naked woman, staring at me. She reminded me too much of some people I'd grown to know, so I put the painting in storage.

I went to the pilot's station, where I'd talked to Eldridge, and checked the ship's systems, which were normal. I wondered what would happen if I powered up the engines, and decided not to find out.

For a few days, I indulged myself in the fantasy that I was going to escape. I filled the larder with food and drink, enough for eight months of flight to whatever Probability struck my fancy. I tuned every system on the ship except the drive. I made plans about where I'd like to travel next.

I thought about putting the ring back in the safe, but I figured that the safe was no real obstacle to people like Denys or Shawn, so I kept the ring in the special pocket in my trousers. Maybe Denys or Shawn was less likely to rip off my pants than rip off the door to the safe.

I went to some of the places I'd enjoyed when I was living Topside the first time. All the bars and restaurants that had seemed so bright and inviting when I was just off a five-month voyage now seemed garish and third-rate. Guards followed me and tried to be inconspicuous. Without a friend, I didn't seem to be having any fun.

It really was time to leave.

I brought a bottle home to the *Olympe* and drank while I worked out a plan. I'd sell the ring's coordinates to Denys in exchange for our safety and a lot of money. Then I'd sell the ring itself back to Shawn for the same thing. I'd split the money with Tonio, and then I'd run for it while the running was good.

I looked at the plan again the next morning, when I was sober, and it still seemed good. I was trying to work out my best approach to Denys when Tonio came aboard. He was a reminder of everything I was trying to escape and his presence annoyed me, but he was exasperated and didn't notice.

"Katarina is more onerous than ever before," he said. He flapped his big hands. "I am watched every moment, yiss. She says she is protecting me but I know it's all because she doesn't want me to speak to Adora. Yet out of every port I see the Chrysalis floating in the sky, with Adora so near."

"You've got to keep Katarina's trust," I said.

"*Olympe* is the only place where I'm free," Tonio said. "Katarina doesn't mind if I come here. And that's why you've got to help me get Adora on board."

"Adora?" I said. "Here?"

"There's no place else."

"But the ship's being watched. So is the Chrysalis. If Adora comes here, they'll see her."

Tonio smiled. "The Pryors and the Storches do not confront each other all the time. Even if they're playing chicken with each other's cargo ships, both the Chrysalis and Socorro possess resources the other finds useful. There are ships coming from the Chrysalis, to purchase certain commodities and sell others and perform transactions of that nature. Adora will come in one of these ships, and when the business is being transacted by her minions she will fly here to me in a vacuum suit, and enter through our very airlock, bypassing those inconvenient guards upon the door."

I was appalled. Tonio smiled. "Adora assures me that it will be perfectly safe."

For whom? I wondered.

"I don't want to be on board when this happens," I said.

When Tonio entertained Adora on my ship, I spent the time shopping for stuff I never bought, and when I got bored with that, I found a bar and huffed some gas. I didn't return to *Olympe* until Tonio sent me a prearranged little beep on my adjutant.

Olympe's lounge still smelled faintly of Adora's flowery perfume. Tonio was splayed on the couch. Energy filled his skinny body. His blue eyes were aglow.

"Such a passion it was!" he said. "Such zealocity! Such a twining of bodies and souls!"

"Glad to know she doesn't want to kill you anymore," I said.

He waved a hand. "All in the past." He heaved a sigh, and looked around the lounge, the old furniture, Aram's brass-and-mahogany trim. "I am glad to bring happiness here," he said, "to counter those memories of sorrow and tragedy."

I looked at him. "What memories are those?"

"The afternoon I spent here with beautiful little Maud. The day before she gave herself that overdose."

I stared at Tonio. Drugs whirled in my head as insects crawled along my nerves.

"You're telling me that—"

He looked away and brushed a cushion with the back of his knuckles. "She was so sweet, yiss. So giving."

I had been off the ship that day, I remembered, making final preparations for departure. Aram was saying goodbye to some of his friends and picking up a new shipment of drugs from the Maheu office. That must have been the time when Maud Rain had finally succumbed to the magic that was Tonio.

And then, in remorse, she'd decided to grow closer to Aram. By becoming a user, like him.

And now she lived in a little white room in the country, her mind as white and blank as the walls that surrounded her.

I stood over Tonio. I felt sick. "Remember you're spending tonight with Katarina," I said.

The glow in his eyes faded. "I know," he said. "It is not that I am not fond of her, but the circumstances—"

"I don't want to hear about the circumstances," I said. "Right now I need to be alone so I can think."

Tonio was on his feet at once. "I know I have made an imposition upon you," he said. "I hope you understand my gratitude."

"I understand," I said. "But I need to be by myself."

"Whatsoever thou desirest, my captain." Tonio rose and loped away.

I went to the captain's station and sat on the goatskin chair and decided that I had better get my escape plan under way. I called Denys's office and asked for an appointment. His secretary told me to come early the next day.

Tonio had been in prison, I thought. In prison, you learn how to handle people. You learn how to tell them what they want and how to please them.

I wondered if Tonio had been playing me all along. Telling me what I wanted in exchange for a place to stay and a tour of the multiverse and its attractions.

I had many hours before my appointment, but alcohol helped.

This reality's blazing oxygen had burned the hangover out of my blood by the time I stepped into Denys's office. The geometries of the room were even more curved than his place Downside, and there were even more windows. Outside the office, the structures of Upside glittered, and beyond them was the ominous octahedron of the Chrysalis, glowing on the horizon of Socorro.

There were two chairs in the room this time, but neither of them were for me. Both were on the far side of Denys's desk. One held Denys, and the other the black-skinned, broad-shouldered form of Shawn Feeney.

Denys raised his brows. "Surprised, Captain Crossbie? Surely you don't imagine that you and Tonio are the only people who employ back-channel communications?"

He was enjoying himself far too much. Cuckolds, as I've stated elsewhere, are rarely models of deportment.

"I'd asked for a private meeting," I said, without hope.

"Shawn and I have decided," Denys said, "that it's time for you and your friend to leave this reality. We know that your ship is provisioned for a long journey, and we intend that you take it."

"How do I know," I said, "that there isn't a bomb hidden somewhere in my ship's pantry?"

The two looked at each other and smirked. Denys answered.

"Because if you and Tonio disappear, or die mysteriously, that makes *us* the villains," he said. "Whereas if you simply abandon this Probability, leaving the two ladies behind. . . " He couldn't resist a grin.

"Then *you* are the bad guys," Shawn finished in his deep voice.

I considered this. "I suppose that makes sense," I said.

"And in exchange for the free passage," Denys said, "I'll take the ring."

"You?" I said, and then looked at Shawn.

"Oh, I'll get it back eventually," Shawn said. "And I'll get the credit for it, too."

"The Storch line," Denys said, "will have at least a couple years to exploit the new Probability before we Pryors arrive in force. But even so, we'll get there years ahead of the rest of the competition. . . and *I'll* get the credit for that."

Shawn smiled at me. "And *you'll* get the blame for selling our secret to our rivals. But by then I'm sure you'll have lots of practice at running."

"I could tell the truth," I said.

"I'm sure you can," Shawn said. He leaned closer to me. "And the very best of luck with that plan, by the way."

"The ring?" Denys reminded.

I thought about it for a moment, and could see no alternative.

"To get the ring," I said, "I have to take my pants off."

Shawn's smile broadened. "We'll watch," he said, "and enjoy your embarrassment."

Tonio was in *Olympe* by the time I returned. Delight danced in his blue eyes.

"I have received a missive from Adora!" he said. "We are to flee together, she and I—and you, of course, my compeer. She has bribed someone in Socorro Traffic Control, yiss, to let us leave the station without alerting the Pryors. We then fly to the coordinates she has provided, where she will join us. From this point on we exist in our own Probability of bliss and complete happiness!"

I let Tonio dance around the ship while I went to the captain's station and began the start-up sequence. Socorro Traffic Control let us go without a murmur. I maneuvered clear of the station and engaged the drive.

As we raced to the coordinates the message had provided, there was no pursuit. No ships came out of some alternate Probability to collide with us. No lasers lanced out of the Chrysalis to incinerate the ship. No bomb blew us to fragments.

As we neared the rendezvous point, Tonio grew anxious. "Where is my darling?" he demanded. "Where is Adora?" His hands turned to fists. "I hope that something has not gone amiss with the plan."

"The plan is working fine," I said, "and Adora isn't coming."

I told him about my meeting with Denys and Shawn, and what I had been ordered to do. Tonio raged and shouted. He demanded I turn *Olympe* around and take him back to his beloved Adora at once.

I refused. I fed coordinates into the Probability drive, and, an instant later, the stars turned to hard little pebbles and we were racing away from Socorro, leaving its quirky electro-magnetic structure in our wake.

Tonio and I were on the run. Again. Trapped with one another in Reality, whether we liked it or not.

I had let Tonio play me, just as he had played Adora and Katarina and Maud and the others. Now we were in a place where we had no choice but to play each other.

Tonio was in despair. "Adora and Katarina will think I deserted them!" he said. "Their rage will know no bounds! They may send assassins—fleets—armies! What can I do?"

"Start," I said, "by sending them flowers."

ART OF WAR

NANCY KRESS

In addition to beauty, Art—and especially the *value* of Art—are things that are most definitely in the eye of the beholder...

Nancy Kress began selling her elegant and incisive stories in the mid-seventies, and has since become a frequent contributor to *Asimov's Science Fiction, The Magazine of Fantasy and Science Fiction, Omni, SCI FICTION,* and elsewhere. Her books include the novel version of her Hugo- and Nebula-winning story, *Beggars in Spain,* and a sequel, *Beggars and Choosers,* as well as *The Prince of Morning Bells, The Golden Grove, The White Pipes, An Alien Light, Brain Rose, Oaths & Miracles, Stinger, Maximum Light, Crossfire, Nothing Human,* and the Space Opera trilogy *Probability Moon, Probability Sun,* and *Probability Space.* Her short work has been collected in *Trinity and Other Stories, The Aliens of Earth,* and *Beaker's Dozen.* Her most recent book is the novel *Crucible.* In addition to the awards for "Beggars in Spain," she has also won Nebula Awards for her stories "Out of All Them Bright Stars" and "The Flowers of Aulit Prison."

"Return fire!" the colonel ordered, bleeding on the deck of her ship, ferocity raging in her nonetheless controlled voice.

The young and untried officer of the deck cried, "It won't do any good, there's too many—"

"I said fire, goddammit!"

"Fire at will!" the OD ordered the gun bay, and then closed his eyes against the coming barrage, as well as against the sight of the exec's mangled corpse. Only minutes left to them, only seconds . . .

A brilliant light blossomed on every screen, a blinding light, filling the room. Crewmen, those still standing on the battered and limping ship, threw up their arms to shield their eyes. And when the light finally faded, the enemy base was gone. Annihilated as if it had never existed.

"The base . . . it . . . how did you do that, ma'am?" the OD asked, dazed.

"Search for survivors," the colonel ordered, just before she passed out from wounds that would have killed a lesser soldier, and all soldiers were lesser than she . . .

No, of course it didn't happen that way. That's from the holo version, available by ansible throughout the Human galaxy forty-eight hours after the Victory of 149-Delta. Author unknown, but the veteran actress Shimira Coltranc played the colonel (now, of course, a general). Shimira's brilliant green eyes were very effective, although not accurate. General Anson had deflected a large meteor to crash into the enemy base, destroying a major Teli weapons store and much of the Teli civilization on the entire planet. It was an important Human victory in the war, and at that point we needed it.

What happened next was never made into a holo. In fact, it was a minor incident in a minor corner of the Human-Teli war. But no corner of a war is minor to the soldiers fighting there, and even a small incident can have enormous repercussions. I know. I will be paying for what happened on 149-Delta for whatever is left of my life.

This is neither philosophical maundering nor constitutional gloom. It is mathematical fact.

Dalo and I were just settling into our quarters on the *Sheherazade* when the general arrived, unannounced and in person.

Crates of personal gear sat on the floor of our tiny sitting room, where Dalo would spend most of her time while I was downside. Neither of us wanted to be here. I'd put in for a posting to Terra, which neither of us had ever visited, and we were excited about the chance to see, at long last, the Sistine Chapel. So much Terran art has been lost in the original, but the Sistine is still there, and we both longed to gaze up at that sublime ceiling. And then I had been posted to 149-Delta.

Dalo was kneeling over a box of *mutomati* as the cabin door opened and an aide announced, "General Anson to see Captain Porter, *ten-hut*!"

I sprang to attention, wondering how far I could go before she recognized it as parody.

She came in, resplendent in full-dress uniform, glistening with medals, flanked by two more aides, which badly crowded the cabin. Dalo, calm as always, stood and dusted *mutomati* powder off her palms. The general stared at me bleakly. Her eyes were shit brown. "At ease, soldier."

"Thank you, ma'am. Welcome, ma'am."

"Thank you. And this is. . . "

"My wife, Dalomanimarito."

"Your wife."

"Yes, ma'am."

"They didn't tell me you were married."

"Yes, ma'am." To a civilian, obviously. Not only that, a civilian who looked. . . I don't know why I did it. Well, yes, I do. I said, "My wife is half Teli."

And for a long moment, she actually looked uncertain. Yes, Dalo has the same squat body and light coat of hair as the Teli. She is genemod for her native planet, a cold and high-gravity world, which is also what Tel is. But surely a general should know that interspecies breeding is impossible—especially *that* interspecies breeding? Dalo is as human as I.

The general's eyes grew cold. Colder. "I don't appreciate that sort of humor, Captain."

"No, ma'am."

"I'm here to give you your orders. Tomorrow at oh five hundred hours, your shuttle leaves for downside. You will be based in a central Teli structure that contains a large stockpile of stolen Human artifacts. I have assigned you three soldiers to crate and transport upside anything that you think has value. You will determine which objects meet that description and, if possible, where they were stolen from. You will attach to each object a full statement with your reasons, including any applicable identification programs—you have your software with you?"

"Of course, ma'am."

"A C–112 near-AI will be placed at your disposal. That's all."

"Ten-hut!" bawled one of the aides. But by the time I had gotten my arm into a salute, she was gone.

"Seth," Dalo said gently. "You didn't have to do that."

"Yes. I did. Did you see the horror on the aides' faces when I said you were half Teli?"

She turned away. Suddenly frightened, I caught her arm. "Dear heart—you knew I was joking? I didn't offend you?"

"Of course not." She nestled in my arms, affectionate and gentle as always. Still, there is a diamond-hard core under all that sweetness. The general had clearly never heard of her before, but Dalo is one of the best *mutomati* artists of her generation. Her art has moved me to tears.

"I'm not offended, Jon, but I do want you to be more careful. You were baiting General Anson."

"I won't have to see her while I'm on assignment here. Generals don't bother with lowly captains."

"Still—"

"I hate the bitch, Dalo."

"Yes. Still, be more circumspect. Even be more *pleasant.* I know what history lies between you two, but nonetheless she is—"

"Don't say it!"

"—after all, your mother."

The evidence of the meteor impact was visible long before the shuttle landed. The impactor had been fifty meters in diameter, weighing roughly sixty thousand tons, composed mostly of iron. If it had been stone, the damage wouldn't have been nearly so extensive. The main base of the Teli military colony had been vaporized instantly. Subsequent shock waves and air blasts had produced firestorms that raged for days and devastated virtually the entire coast of 149-Delta's one small continent. Now, a month later, we flew above kilometer after kilometer of destruction.

General Anson had calculated when her deflected meteor would hit and had timed her approach to take advantage of that knowledge. Some minor miscalculation had led to an initial attack on her ship, but before the attack could gain force, the meteor had struck. Why hadn't the Teli known that it was coming? Their military tech was as good as ours, and they'd colonized 149-Delta for a long time. Surely they did basic space surveys that tracked both the original meteor trajectory and Anson's changes? No one knew why they had not counterdeflected, or at least evacuated. But, then, there was so much we didn't know about the Teli.

The shuttle left the blackened coast behind and flew toward the mountains, skimming above acres of cultivated land. The crops, I knew, were rotting. Teli did not allow themselves to be taken prisoner, not ever, under any circumstances. As Human troops had forced their way into successive areas of the continent, the agricultural colony, deprived of its one city, had simply committed suicide. The only Teli left on 168-Beta occupied those areas that United Space Forces had not yet reached.

That didn't include the Citadel.

"Here we are, Captain," the pilot said, as soldiers advanced to meet the shuttle. "May I ask a question, sir?"

"Sure," I said.

"Is it true this is where the Teli put all that art they stole from humans?"

"Supposed to be true." If it wasn't, I had no business here.

"And you're a . . . an art historian?"

"I am. The military has some strange nooks and crannies."

He ignored this. "And is it true that the Taj Mahal is here?"

I stared at him. The Teli looted the art of Terran colonies whenever they could, and no one knew why. It was logical that rumors would run riot about that. Still. . . "Lieutenant, the Taj Mahal was a building. A huge one, and on Terra. It was destroyed in the twenty-first century Food Riots, not by the Teli. They've never reached Terra."

"Oh," he said, clearly disappointed. "I heard the Taj was a sort of holo of all these exotic sex positions."

"No."

"Oh, well." He sighed deeply. "Good luck, Captain."

"Thank you."

The Citadel—our Human name for it, of course—turned out to be the entrance into a mountain. Presumably the Teli had excavated bunkers in the solid rock, but you couldn't tell that from the outside. A veteran NCO met me at the guard station. "Captain Porter? I'm Sergeant Lu, head of your assignment detail. Can I take these bags, sir?"

"Hello, Sergeant." He was ruddy, spit-and-polish military, with an uneducated accent—obviously my "detail" was not going to consist of any other scholars. They were there to do grunt work. But Lu looked amiable and willing, and I relaxed slightly. He led me to my quarters, a trapezoid-shaped, low-ceilinged room with elaborately etched stone walls and no contents except a human bed, chest, table, and chair.

Immediately, I examined the walls, the usual dense montage of Teli symbols that were curiously evocative even though we didn't understand their meanings. They looked handmade, and recent. "What was this room before we arrived?"

Lu shrugged. "Don't know what any of these rooms were to the tellies, sir. We cleaned 'em all out and vapped everything. Might have been booby-trapped, you know."

"How do we know the whole Citadel isn't booby-trapped?"

"We don't, sir."

I liked his unpretentious fatalism. "Let's leave this gear

here for now—I'd like to see the vaults. And call me Jon. What's your first name, Sergeant?"

"Ruhan. Sir." But there was no rebuke in his tone.

The four vaults were nothing like I had imagined.

Art, even stolen art—maybe especially stolen art—is usually handled with care. After all, trouble and resources have been expended to obtain it, and it is considered valuable. This was clearly not the case with the art stolen by the Teli. Each vault was a huge natural cave, with rough stone walls, stalactites, water dripping from the ceiling, fungi growing on the walls. And except for a small area in the front where the AI console and a Navy-issue table stood under a protective canopy, the enormous cavern was jammed with huge, toppling, six- and seven-layer-deep piles of . . . *stuff.*

Dazed, I stared at the closest edge of that enormous junkyard. A torn plastic bag bearing some corporate logo. A broken bathtub painted in swirling greens. A child's bloody shoe. Some broken goblets of titanium, which was almost impossible to break. A hand-embroidered shirt from 78-Alpha, where such handwork is a folk art. A cheap set of plastic dishes decorated with blurry prints of dogs. A child's finger painting. What looked like a Terran prehistoric fertility figure. And, still in its original frame and leaning crazily against an obsolete music cube, Philip Langstrom's priceless abstract *Ascent of Justice,* which had been looted from 46-Gamma six years ago in a surprise Teli raid. Water spots had rotted one corner of the canvas.

"Kind of takes your breath away, don't it?" Lu said. "What a bunch of rubbish. Look at that picture in the front there, sir—can't even tell what it's supposed to be. You want me to start vapping things?"

I closed my eyes, feeling the seizure coming, the going under. I breathed deeply. Went through the mental cleansing that my serene Dalo had taught me, *kai lanu kai lanu* breathe . . .

"Sir? Captain Porter?"

"I'm fine," I said. I had control again. "We're not vapping *anything,* Lu. We're here to study all of it, not just rescue some of it. Do you understand?"

"Whatever you say, sir," he said, clearly understanding nothing.

But, then, neither did I. All at once, my task seemed impossible, overwhelming. *Ascent of Justice* and a broken bathtub and a bloody shoe. *What* in hell had the Teli considered art?

Kai lanu kai lanu breathe . . .

The first time I went under, there had been no Dalo to help me. I'd been ten years old and about to be shipped out to Young Soldiers' Camp on Aires, the first moon of 43-Beta. Children in their little uniforms had been laughing and shoving as they boarded the shuttle, and all at once I was on the ground, gasping for breath, tears pouring down my face.

"What's wrong with him?" my mother said. "Medic!"

"Jon! Jon!" Daddy said, trying to hold me. "Oh gods, *Jon!*"

The medic rushed over, slapped on a patch that didn't work, and then I remember nothing except the certainty that I was going to die. I knew it right up until the moment I could breathe again. The shuttle had left, the medic was packing up his gear without looking at my parents, and my father's arms held me gently.

My mother stared at me with contempt. "You little coward," she said. They were the last words she spoke to me for an entire year.

"Why the Space Navy?" Dalo would eventually ask me, in sincere confusion. "After all the other seizures . . . the way she treated you each time . . . Jon, you could have taught art at a university, written scholarly books . . ."

"I had to join the Navy," I said, and knew that I couldn't say more without risking a seizure. Dalo knew it too. Dalo knew that the doctors had no idea why the conventional medications didn't touch my condition, why I was such a medical anomaly. She knew everything and loved me anyway, as no one had since my father's death when I was thirteen. She was my lifeline, my sanity. Just thinking about her aboard the *Sheherazade,* just knowing that I would see her again in a few weeks, let me concentrate on the bewildering task in front of me in the dripping, moldy Teli vault filled with human treasures and human junk.

And with any luck, I would not have to encounter General Anson again. For any reason.

A polished marble doll. A broken commlink on which some girl had once painted lopsided red roses. An exquisite albastron, Eastern Mediterranean, fifth century B.C., looted five years ago from the private collection of Fahoud al-Ashan on 71-Delta. A forged copy of Lucca DiChario's *Menamarti,* although not a bad forgery, with a fake certificate of authenticity. Three more embroidered baby shoes. A handmade quilt. Several holo cubes. A hair comb. A music-cube case with holo-porn star Shiva on the cover. Degas's exquisite *Danseuse sur Scène,* which had vanished from a Terran museum a hundred years ago, assumed to be in an off-Earth private collection somewhere. I gaped at it, unbelieving, and ran every possible physical and computer test. It was the real thing.

"Captain, why do we gotta measure the exact place on the floor of every little piece of rubbish?" whined Private Blanders. I ignored her. My detail had learned early that they could take liberties with me. I had never been much of a disciplinarian.

I said, "Because we don't know which data is useful and which not until the computer analyzes it."

"But the location don't matter! I'm gonna just estimate it, all right?"

"You'll measure it to the last fraction of a centimeter," Sergeant Lu said pleasantly, "and it'll be accurate, or you're in the brig, soldier. You got that?"

"Yes, sir!"

Thank the gods for Sergeant Lu.

The location was important. The AI's algorithms were starting to show a pattern. Partial as yet, but interesting.

Lu carried a neo-plastic sculpture of a young boy over to my table and set it down. He ran the usual tests and the measurements appeared in a display screen on the C–112.

The sculpture, I could see from one glance, was worthless as either art or history, an inept and recent work. I hoped the sculptor hadn't quit his day job.

Lu glanced at the patterns on my screen. "What's that, then, sir?"

"It's a fractal."

"A what?"

"Part of a pattern formed by behavior curves."

"What does it mean?" he asked, but without any real interest, just being social. Lu was a social creature.

"I don't know yet what it means, but I do know one other thing." I switched screens, needing to talk aloud about my findings. Dalo wasn't here. Lu would have to do, however inadequately. "See these graphs? These artifacts were brought to the vault by different Teli, or groups of Teli, and at different times."

"How can you tell that, sir?" Lu looked a little more alert. Art didn't interest him, but the Teli did.

"Because the art objects, as opposed to the other stuff, occur in clusters through the cave—see here? And the real art, as opposed to the amateur junk, forms clusters of its own. When the Teli brought back Human art from raids, some of the aliens knew—or had learned—what qualified. Others never did."

Lu stared at the display screen, his red nose wrinkling. How did someone named "Ruhan Lu" end up with such a ruddy complexion?

"Those lines and squiggles"—he pointed at the Ebenfeldt equations at the bottom of the screen—"tell you all that, sir?"

"Those squiggles plus the measurements you're making. I know where some pieces were housed in Human colonies, so I'm also tracking the paths of raids, plus other variables like—"

The Citadel shook as something exploded deep under our feet.

"Enemy attack!" Lu shouted. He pulled me to the floor and threw his body across mine as dirt and stone and mold rained down from the ceiling of the cave. *Die, I was going to die . . .* "Dalo!" I heard myself scream and then, in the weird way of the human mind, came one clear thought out of the chaos: *I won't get to see the Sistine Chapel after all.* Then I heard or thought nothing as I went under.

I woke in my Teli quarters in the Citadel, grasping and clawing my way upright. Lu laid a hard hand on my arm. "Steady, sir."

"Dalo! The *Sheherazade*!"

"Ship's just fine, sir. It was a booby trap buried somewhere in the mountain, but Security thinks most of it fizzled. Place is a mess but not much real damage."

"Blanders? Cozinski?"

"Two soldiers are dead but neither one's our detail." He leaned forward, hand still on my arm. "What happened to you, sir?"

I tried to meet his eyes and failed. The old shame flooded me, the old guilt, the old defiance—all here again. "Who saw?"

"Nobody but me. Is it a nerve disease, sir? Like Ransom Fits?"

"No." My condition had no discoverable physical basis, and no name except my mother's, repeated over the years. *Coward.*

"Because if it's Ransom Fits, sir, my brother has it and they gave him meds for it. Fixed him right up."

"It's not Ransom. What are the general orders, Lu?"

"All hands to carry on."

"More booby traps?"

"I guess they'll look, sir. Bound to, don't you think? Don't know if they'll find anything. My friend Sergeant Andropov over in Security says the mountain is so honeycombed with caves underneath these big ones that they could search for a thousand years and not find everything. Captain Porter—if it happens again, with you, I mean, is there anything special I should do for you?"

I did meet his eyes then. Did he know how rare his gaze was? No, he did not. Lu's honest, conscientious, not-very-intelligent face showed nothing but pragmatic acceptance of the situation. No disgust, no contempt, no sentimental pity, and he had no idea how unusual that was. But I knew.

"No, Sergeant, nothing special. We'll just carry on."

"Aye, aye, sir."

If any request for information came down from General Anson's office, I never received it. No request for a report on damage to the art vaults, or on impact to assignment progress, or on personnel needs. Nothing.

The second booby trap destroyed everything in Vault A.

It struck while I was upside on the *Sheherazade,* with Dalo on a weekend pass after a month of fourteen-hour days in the vault. Lu commlinked me in the middle of the night. The screen on the bulkhead opposite our bed chimed and brightened, waking us both. I clutched at Dalo.

"Captain Porter, sir, we had another explosion down here at oh one thirty-six hours." Lu's face was black with soot. Blood smeared one side of his face. "It got Vault A and some of the crew quarters. Private Blanders is dead, sir. The AI is destroyed too. I'm waiting on your orders."

I said to the commlink, "Send, voice only . . . " My voice came out too high and Dalo's arm went around me, but I didn't go under. "Lu, is the quake completely over?"

"Far as we know, sir."

"I'll be downside as soon as I can. Don't try to enter Vault A until I arrive."

"Yes, sir."

I broke the link, turned in Dalo's arms, and went under. When the seizures stopped, I went downside.

We had nearly finished cataloguing Vault A when it blew. Art of any value had already been crated and moved, and of course, all my data was backed up on both the base AI and on the *Sheherazade.* For the first time, I wondered why I had been given a C–112 of my own in the first place. A near-AI was expensive, and there was a war on.

Vault B was pretty much a duplicate of Vault A, a huge natural cavern dripping water and sediments on a packed-solid jumble of human objects. A carved fourteenth-century oak chest, probably French, that some rich Terran must have had transported to a Human colony. Handwoven *dbeni* from 14-Alpha. A cooking pot. A samurai sword with embossed handle. A holo cube programmed with porn. Mondrian's priceless *Broadway Boogie-Woogie,* mostly in unforgivable tatters. A cheap, mass-produced jewelry box. More shoes. A Paul LeFort sculpture looted from a pleasure craft, the *Princess of Mars,* two years ago. A brass menorah. The entire contents of the Museum of Colonial Art on 33-Delta—most of it worthless, but a few pieces showing promise. I hoped the young artists hadn't been killed in the Teli raid.

Three days after Lu, Private Cozinski, and I began work on Vault B, General Anson appeared. She had not attended Private Blanders's memorial service. I felt her before I saw her, her gaze boring into the back of my neck, and I closed my eyes.

Kai lanu kai lanu breathe. . .

"Ten-hut!"

Lu and Cozinski had already sprung to attention. I turned and saluted. Breathe. . . *kailanukailanu please gods not in front of her.* . .

"A word, Captain."

"Yes, ma'am."

She led the way to a corner of the vault, walking by Tomiko Mahuto's *Morning Grace,* one of the most beautiful things in the universe, without a glance. Water dripped from the end of a stalactite onto her head. She shifted away from it without changing expression. "I want an estimate of how much longer you need to be here, Captain."

"I've filed daily progress reports, ma'am. We're on the second of four vaults."

"I read all reports, Captain. How much longer?"

"Unless something in the other two vaults differs radically from Vaults A and B, perhaps another three months."

"And what will your 'conclusions' be?"

She had no idea how science worked, or art. "I can't say until I have more data, ma'am."

"Where does your data point so far?" Her tone was too sharp. Was I this big an embarrassment to her, that she needed me gone before my job was done? I had told no one about my relationship to her, and I would bet my last chance to see the Sistine Chapel that she hadn't done so either.

I said carefully, "There is primary evidence, not yet backed up mathematically, that the Teli began over time to distinguish Human art objects from mere decorated, utilitarian objects. There is also some reason to believe that they looted our art not because they liked it but because they hoped to learn something significant about us."

"Learn something significant from broken bathtubs and embroidered baby shoes?"

I blinked. So she *had* been reading my reports, and in some detail. Why?

"Apparently, ma'am."

"What makes you think they hoped to learn about us from this rubbish?"

"I'm using the Ebenfeldt equations in conjunction with phase-space diagrams for—"

"I don't need technical mumbo jumbo. What do you think they tried to learn about Humans?"

"Their own art seems to have strong religious significance. I'm no expert on Teli work, but my roommate at the university, Forrest Jamili, has gone on to—"

"I don't care about your roommate," she said, which was hardly news. I remembered the day I left from the university, having spent possibly the most terrified and demoralized first-year ever, how I had gone under when she had said to me—

Kai lanu kai lanu breathe breathe. . .

I managed to avoid going under, but just barely. I quavered, "I don't know what the Teli learned from our art."

She stared at my face with contempt, spun on her boot heel, and left.

That night I began to research the deebees on Teli art. It gave me something to do during the long, insomniac hours.

Human publications on Teli art, I discovered, had an odd, evasive, overly careful feel to them. Perhaps that was inevitable; ancient Athenian commentators had had to watch what they said publicly about Sparta. In wartime, it took very little to be accused of giving away critical information about the enemy. Or of giving them treasonous praise. In no one's papers was this elliptical quality more evident than in Forrest Jamili's, and yet something was clear. Until now, art scholars had been building a vast heap of details about Teli art. Forrest was the first to suggest a viable overall framework to organize those details.

It was during one of these long and lonely nights, desperately missing Dalo, that I discovered the block on my access codes. I couldn't get into the official records of the meteor deflection that had destroyed the Teli weapons base and brought General Anson the famous Victory of 149-Delta.

Why? Because I wasn't a line officer? Perhaps. Or perhaps the records involved military security in some way. Or perhaps—and this was what I chose to believe—she just wanted the heroic, melodramatic holo version of her victory to be the only one available. I didn't know if other officers could access the records, and I couldn't ask. I had no friends among the officers, no friends here at all except Lu.

On my second leave upside, Dalo said, "You look terrible, dear heart. Are you sleeping?"

"No. Oh, Dalo, I'm so glad to see you!" I clutched her tight; we made love; the taut fearful ache that was my life downside eased. Finally. A little.

Afterward, lying in the cramped bunk, she said, "You've found something unexpected. Some correlation that disturbs you."

"Yes. No. I don't know yet. Dalo, just talk to me, about anything. Tell me what you've been doing up here."

"Well, I've been preparing materials for a new *mutomati,* as you know. I'm almost ready to begin work on it. And I've made a friend, Susan Finch."

I tried not to scowl. Dalo made friends wherever she went, and it was wrong of me to resent this slight diluting of her affections.

"You would like her, Jon," Dalo said, poking me and smiling. "She's not a line officer, for one thing. She's ship's doctor."

In my opinion, doctors were even worse than line officers. I had seen so many doctors during my horrible adolescence. But I said, "I'm glad you have someone to be with when I'm downside."

She laughed. "Liar." She knew my possessiveness, and my flailing attempts to overcome it. She knew everything about me, accepted everything about me. In Dalo, now my only family, I was the luckiest man alive.

I put my arms around her and held on tight.

The Teli attack came two months later, when I was halfway through Vault D. Six Teli warships emerged sluggishly from subspace, moving at half their possible speed. Our probes easily picked them up and our fighters took them out after a battle that barely deserved the name. Human casualties numbered only seven.

"Shooting fish in a barrel," Private Cozinski said as he crated a Roman Empire bottle, third century C.E., pale green glass with seven engraved lines. It had been looted from 189-Alpha four years ago. "Bastards never could fight."

"Not true," said the honest Sergeant Lu. "Teli can fight fine. They just didn't."

"That don't make sense, Sergeant."

And it didn't.

Unless...

All that night, I worked in Vault D at the computer terminal which had replaced my freestanding C–112. The terminal linked to both the downside system and the deebees on the *Sheherazade*. Water dripped from the ceiling, echoing in the cavernous space. Once, something like a bat flew from some far recess. I kept slapping on stim patches to stay alert, and feverishly calling up different programs, and doing my best to erect cybershields around what I was doing.

Lu found me there in the morning, my hands shaking, staring at the display screens. "Sir? Captain Porter?"

"Yes."

"Sir? Are you all right?"

Art history is not, as people like General Anson believe, a lot of dusty information about a frill occupation interesting to only a few effetes. The Ebenfeldt equations transformed art history, linking the field both to behavior and to the mathematics underlying chaos theory. Not so new an idea, really—the ancient Greeks used math to work out the perfect proportions for buildings, for women, for cities, all profound shapers of human behavior. The creation of art does not happen in a vacuum. It is linked to culture in complicated, nonlinear ways. Chaos theory is still the best way to model nonlinear behavior dependent on changes in initial conditions.

I looked at three sets of mapped data. One, my multidimensional analysis of Vaults A through D, was comprehensive and detailed. My second set of data was clear but had a significant blank space. The third set was only suggested by shadowy lines, but the overall shape was clear.

"Sir?"

"Sergeant, can you set up two totally encrypted commlink calls, one to the *Sheherazade* and one by ansible to Sel Ouie University on 18-Alpha? Yes, I know that officially you can't do that, but you know everybody everywhere . . . *can* you do it? It's vitally important, Ruhan. I can't tell you how important!"

Lu gazed at me from his ruddy, honest face. He did indeed know everyone. A Navy lifer, and with all the amiability and human contacts that I lacked. And he trusted me. I could feel that unaccustomed warmth, like a small and steady fire.

"I think I can do that, sir."

He did. I spoke first to Dalo, then to Forrest Jamili. He sent a packet of encrypted information. I went back to my data, working feverishly. Then I made a second encrypted call to Dalo. She said simply, "Yes. Susan says yes, of course she can. They all can."

"Dalo, find out when the next ship docks with the *Sheherazade*. If it's today, book passage on it, no matter where it's going. If there's no ship today, then buy a seat on a supply shuttle and—"

"Those cost a fortune!"

"I don't care. Just—"

"Jon, the supply shuttles are all private contractors and they charge civilians a— It would wipe out everything we've saved and—*why*? What's wrong?"

"I can't explain now." I heard boots marching along the corridor to the vault. "Just do it! Trust me, Dalo! I'll find you when I can!"

"Captain," an MP said severely, "come with me." His weapon was drawn, and behind him stood a detail of grim-faced soldiers. Lu stepped forward, but I shot him a glance that said, *Say nothing! This is mine alone!*

Good soldier that he was, he understood, and he obeyed. It was, after all, the first time I had ever given him a direct— if wordless—order, the first time I had assumed the role of commander.

My mother should have been proud.

Her office resembled my quarters, rather than the vaults: a trapezoidal, low-ceilinged room with alien art etched on all the stone walls. The room held the minimum of furniture. General Anson stood alone behind her desk, a plain military-issue camp item, appropriate to a leader who was one with the ranks, don't you know. She did not invite me to sit down. The MPs left—reluctantly, it seemed to me—but, then, there was no doubt in anyone's mind that she could break me bare-knuckled if necessary.

She said, "You made two encrypted commlink calls and one encrypted ansible message from this facility, all without proper authorization. Why?"

I had to strike before she got to me, before I went under. I blurted, "I know why you blocked my access to the meteor-deflection data."

She said nothing, just went on gazing at me from those eyes that could chill glaciers.

"There *was* no deflection of that meteor. The meteor wasn't on our tracking system because Humans haven't spent much time in this sector until now. You caught a lucky break, and whatever deflection records exist now, you added after the fact. Your so-called victory was a sham." I watched her face carefully, hoping for . . . what? Confirmation? Outraged denial that I could somehow believe? I saw neither. And, of course, I was flying blind. Captain Susan Finch had told Dalo only that yes, of course officers had access to the deflection records; they were a brilliant teaching tool for tactical strategy. I was the only one who'd been barred from them, and the general must have had a reason for that. She always had a reason for everything.

Still she said nothing. Hoping that I would utter even more libelous statements against a commanding officer? Would commit even more treason? I could feel my breathing accelerate, my heart start to pound.

I said, "The Teli must have known the meteor's trajectory; they've colonized 149-Delta a long time. They *let* it hit their base. And I know why. The answer is in the art."

Still no change of expression. She was stone. But she was listening.

"The answer is in the art—ours and theirs. I ansibled Forrest Jamili last night—no, look first at these diagrams—no, first—"

I was making a mess of it as the seizure moved closer. Not now *not now* not in front of her . . .

Somehow I held myself together, although I had to wrench my gaze away from her to do it. I pulled the holo cube from my pocket, activated it, and projected it on the stone wall. The Teli etchings shimmered, ghostly, behind the laser colors of my data.

"This is a phase-space diagram of Ebenfeldt equations using input about the frequency of Teli art creation. We have tests now, you know, that can date any art within weeks of its creation by pinpointing when the raw materials were altered. A phase-state diagram is how we model bifurcated behaviors grouped around two attractors. What that means is that the Teli created their art in bursts, with long fallow periods between bursts when . . . no, *wait,* General, this is *relevant to the war!*"

My voice had risen to a shrick. I couldn't help it. Contempt rose off her like heat. But she stopped her move toward the door.

"This second phase-space diagram is Teli attack behavior. Look . . . it inverts the first diagrams! They attack viciously for a while, and during that time *virtually no Teli creates art at all* . . . Then when some tipping point is reached, they stop attacking or else attack only ineffectively, like the last raid here. They're . . . waiting. And if the tipping point—this mathematical value—isn't reached fast enough, they sabotage their own bases, like letting the meteor hit 149-Delta. They did it in the battle outside 16-Beta and in the Q-Sector massacre . . . you were there! When the mathematical value *is* reached—when enough of them have died—they create art like crazy but don't wage war. Not until the art reaches some other hypothetical mathematical value that I think is this second attractor. Then they stop creating art and go back to war."

"You're saying that periodically their soldiers just curl up and let us kill them?" she spat at me. "The Teli are damned fierce fighters, Captain—I know that even if the likes of you never will. *They* don't just whimper and lie down on the floor."

Kai lanu kai lanu . . .

"It's a . . . a religious phenomenon, Forrest Jamili thinks. I mean, he thinks their art is a form of religious atonement— all of their art. That's its societal function, although the whole thing may be biologically programmed as well, like the deaths of lemmings to control population. The Teli can take only so much dying, or maybe even only so much killing, and then they have to stop and . . . and restore what they see as some sort of spiritual balance. And they loot our art because they think we must do the same thing. Don't you see—they were collecting *our* art to try to analyze when we will stop attacking and go fallow! They assume we must be the same as them, just—"

"No warriors stop fighting for a bunch of weakling artists!"

"—as you assume they must be the same as us."

We stared at each other.

I said, "As you have always assumed that everyone should be the same as you. Mother."

"You're doing this to try to discredit me, aren't you," she said evenly. "Anyone can connect any dots in any statistics to prove whatever they wish. Everybody knows that. You want to discredit my victory because such a victory will never come to *you*. Not to the sniveling, backstabbing coward who's been a disappointment his entire life. Even your wife is worth ten of you—at least she doesn't crumple under pressure."

She moved closer, closer to me than I could ever remember her being, and every one of her words hammered on the inside of my head, my eyes, my chest.

"You got yourself assigned here purposely to embarrass me, and now you want to go further and ruin me. It's not going to happen, soldier, do you hear me? I'm not going to be made a laughingstock by you again, the way I was in every officer's club during your whole miserable adolescence and—"

I didn't hear the rest. I went under, seizing and screaming.

It is two days later. I lie in the medical bay of the *Sheherazade,* still in orbit around 149-Delta. My room is locked, but I am not in restraints. Crazy, under arrest, but not violent. Or perhaps the General is simply hoping I'll kill myself and save everyone more embarrassment.

Downside, in Vault D, Lu is finishing crating the rest of the looted Human art, all of which is supposed to be returned to its rightful owners. The Space Navy serving its galactic citizens. Maybe the art will actually be shipped out in time.

My holo cube was taken from me. I imagine that all my data has been wiped from the base's and ship's deebees as well, or maybe just classified as severely restricted. In that case, no one who is cleared to look at it, which would include only top line officers, is going to open files titled "Teli Art Creation." Generals have better things to do.

But Forrest Jamili has copies of my data and my speculations.

Phase-state diagrams bring order out of chaos. Some order, anyway. This is, interestingly, the same thing that art does. It is why, looking at one of Dalo's *mutomati* works, I can be moved to tears. By the grace, the balance, the redemption from chaos of the harsh raw materials of life.

Dalo is gone. She left on the supply ship when I told her to. My keepers permitted a check of the ship's manifest to determine that. Dalo is safe.

I will probably die in the coming Teli attack, along with most of the Humans both on the *Sheherazade* and on 149-Delta. The Teli fallow period for this area of space is coming to an end. For the last several months, there have been few attacks by Teli ships, and those few badly executed. Months of frenetic creation of art, including all those etchings on the stone walls of the Citadel. Did I tell General Anson how brand-new all those handmade etchings are? I can't remember. She didn't give me time to tell her much.

Although it wouldn't have made any difference. She believes that war and art are totally separate activities   one important and one trivial—whose lifelines never converge. The general too will probably die in the coming attack. She may or may not have time to realize that I was right.

But that doesn't really matter anymore either. And strangely, I'm not at all afraid. I have no signs of going under, no breathing difficulties, no shaking, no panic. And only one real regret: that Dalo and I did not get to gaze together at the Sistine Chapel on Terra. But no one gets everything. I have had a great deal: Dalo, art, even some possible future use to humanity if Forrest does the right thing with my data. Many people never get so much.

The ship's alarms begin to sound, clanging loud even in the medical bay.

The Teli are back, resuming their war.

MUSE OF FIRE

DAN SIMMONS

A writer of considerable power, range, and ambition, an eclectic talent not willing to be restricted to any one genre, Dan Simmons sold his first story to *The Twilight Zone Magazine* in 1982. By the end of that decade, he had become one of the most popular and bestselling authors in both the horror and the science fiction genres, winning, for instance, both the Hugo Award for his epic science fiction novel *Hyperion* and the Bram Stoker Award for his huge .horror novel *Carrion Comfort* in the *same year,* 1990. He has continued to split his output since between science fiction (*The Fall of Hyperion, The Hollow Man*) and horror (*Song of Kali, Summer of Night, Children of the Night*). . . although a few of his novels are downright unclassifiable (*Phases of Gravity,* for instance, which is a straight literary novel although it was published as part of a science fiction line), and some (like *Children of the Night*) could be legitimately considered to be either science fiction or horror, depending on how you squint at them. Similarly, his first collection, *Prayers to Broken Stones,* contains a mix of science fiction, fantasy, horror, and "mainstream" stories, as does his most recent collection, *Lovedeath.* Some of his most recent books confirm his reputation for unpredictability, including *The Crook Factory,* a spy thriller set in World War II and starring Ernest Hemingway; *Darwin's Blade,* a "statistical thriller" halfway between mystery and horror; *Hardcase,* a hard-boiled detective novel; and *A Winter Haunting,* a ghost story. Coming up is a new novel, *The Terror.* Born in Peoria, Illinois, Simmons now lives with his family in Colorado.

Simmons has established himself as a force to be reckoned with in the New Space Opera with his glittering, baroque *Hyperion* novels, and his two most recent novels, *Ilium* and *Olympus*, which use the Trojan War as the backdrop for an ambitious space opera duology. In the complex and multifaceted novella that follows, he takes us on a journey of unparalleled scope and scale, in company with a hapless group of actors who find themselves burdened with the responsibility of putting on the single most important theatrical performance in human history . . .

I sometimes think that none of the rest of the things would have happened if we hadn't performed the Scottish Play that night at Mezel-Goull. Nothing good ever comes from putting on the Scottish Play—if we remember any history at all, we know that—and much bad often does.

But I doubt if there have ever been ramifications like this before.

The *Muse of Fire* followed the Archon funeral barge out of the Pleroma into the Kenoma, slipped out of its pleromic wake like a newborn emerging from a caul, and made its own weak-fusion way to our next stop on the tour, a world known only as 25–25–261B. I'd been there before. By this time, I'd been with the Earth's Men long enough to have visited all of the four hundred or so worlds we were allowed to tour regularly. They say that there are over ten thousand worlds in the Tell—ten thousand we humans have been scattered to, I mean—but I'll never know if that's true. *We'll* never know.

I always love the way the *Muse* roars down through cloud and sky on her thundering three-mile-long pillar of fire, especially at night, and the descent to the arbiter community on the coastal plateau below the Archon keep of Mezel-Goull was no disappointment.

We landed on the inner edge of the great stone shelf separating the human villages from the acid-tossed sea cliffs. One glance at the *Muse*'s log had reminded me that 25–25–261B had only three variations in its day and weather: twilight-bright dimness and scalding spray blown in by winds from the crashing black ocean of sulfuric acid for fourteen hours each day; twilight-bright dimness and sandstorms blown to the barely habitable coasts by hot winds from the interior of the continent for another fourteen hours each day; and full darkness when no winds blew for the final fourteen hours. The air was breathable here—all of our tour worlds had that in common, of course, since we only travel to planets where the Archons keep arbeiter and dole slaves—but even in the middle of their twenty-one hours of daytime on this bleak rock, the sky brightened to only a dim, brooding grayness because of the constant layers of clouds, and no one ventured out unprotected during the hours when the scalding spray blew in from the black, sulfuric sea.

The *Muse* touched down during the hours the hot *simoom* winds blew. No one came out from the huddled stone city to meet us. The thousands of arbeiters were either sleeping in their barracks between shifts or working in the mines, dropping down to darkness in rusty buckets and then following veins miles deeper underground to harvest a gray fungus that the Archons considered a delicacy. The few hundred local doles in their somewhat higher huddle of stone hovels were doing whatever doles do: recording, accounting, measuring, file-keeping, waiting for instructions from their masters via the dragomen.

We stayed inside the ship while the hot winds roared, but the *Muse*'s cabiri scrambled out through maintenance hatches like so many flesh-and-metal spiders, opened storage panels, rigged worklights, strung long cables from the hull, pounded k-chrome stakes into solid rock, unfolded steel-mesh canvas, and had the main performance tent up and rigidified within thirty minutes. The first show was not scheduled to begin for another six hours, but it took a while

for the cabiri to arrange the lighting and stage and set up
the many rows of seats. The old Globe Theater in London
during the Bard's time, according to troupe lore, would seat
three thousand, but our little tent-theater comfortably seated
about eight hundred human beings. We expected far fewer
than that during each of our four scheduled performances
on 25–25–261B.

On many worlds we have permission to land at a variety
of arbeiter huddles, but this world had only this single major
human population center. The town has no name, of course.
We humans gave up naming things long ago, abandoning
that habit along with our culture, politics, arts, history, hope,
and sense of self. No one in the troupe or among the arbeiters
and doles here had a clue as to who had named the Archon
keep Mezel-Goull, which apparently meant "Devil's Rest,"
but the name seemed appropriate. It *sounded* appropriate,
even if the words actually had no meaning.

The hulking mass of Archon steel and black stone dominated an overhanging cliff about six miles north of this
plateau upon which the humans were housed. Through binoculars, I could see the tall slits of tower windows glowing
yellow while pale white searchlights stabbed out from the
keep and up to the highlands, then probed down over the
human escarpment and across the *Muse,* then swept out to
the sulfur sea. None of us from the troupe had ever been to
the keep, of course—why would humans, other than dragomen (whom most of us do not consider human), have any
business with Archons? They own us, they control our lives,
they dictate our actions and fates, but they have no interest
in us and we usually return the favor.

There were twenty-three of us in this Shakespearean
troupe called the Earth's Men. Not all of us were men,
of course, although we knew through stage history that
in the Bard's day even the women's roles were acted by
males.

My name is Wilbr. I was twenty SEY old that day we
landed on 25–25–261B and had been chosen for the troupe
when I was ninc and turned out to be good enough at memo-

rizing my lines and hitting my marks to be on stage for most productions, but by age twenty I knew in my heart that I would never be a great actor. Probably not even a good one. But my hope remained to play Hamlet someday, somehow, somewhere. Even if only once.

There were a couple of others about my age in the Earth's Men; Philp was one of them and a good friend. There were several young women in the troupe, including Aglaé, the best and most attractive Juliet and Rosalind I've ever seen: she was a year older than me and my choice for girlfriend, lover, and wife, but she never noticed me; Tooley was our age, but he primarily did basic maintenance engineering on the *Muse,* although he could hold a spear in a crowd scene if pressed to.

Kemp and Burbank were the two real leaders of the troupe, along with Kemp's wife (and Burbank's lover) Condella, whom everyone secretly, and never affectionately, referred to as "the Cunt." I never learned how the nickname got started—some say it was her French accent as Catherine talking to her maid in *Henry V*—but other and less kind guesses would probably have been equally accurate.

Kemp had always been a clown in the most honorable sense of the word: a young arbeiter comic actor and improviser when he was chosen for the Earth's Men by Burbank's father, the former leader of the troupe, more than fifty years earlier. One of Kemp's specialties was Falstaff although he'd lost weight as he aged, so he now had to wear a special suit fitted out with padding whenever he played Sir John. He was a brilliant Falstaff, but he was even more brilliant—frighteningly so—as Lear. If Kemp had had his way, we would have performed *The Tragedy of King Lear* for every second performance.

Burbank had the weight for Falstaff but not the comic timing, and since he was in his early fifties SEY, was not quite old enough—nor impressive enough in personality— to make an adequate Lear. Yet he was now too old to play Hamlet, the role his father had owned and in which this younger Burbank had also excelled. There was something

about the Prince's dithering and indecisiveness and self-pity
that perfectly fit Burbank. Still, it was a frustrating time for
Burbank and he marked it by getting hammier and hammier
in the roles Kemp allowed him and by screwing Kemp's
much younger wife every chance he got.

Alleyn was our young Hamlet now and a wonderful
one at that, especially when set against Burbank's Claudius and Kemp's Polonius. For villains we had Heminges.
Kemp once said to me after a few drinks that our real
Heminges out-Iagoes Iago on and off the stage. He also
said that he wished that Heminges had Richard III's hump
and personality just so things would be more peaceful
aboard the *Muse*.

Coeke was our Othello and was perfect in the role
for more reasons than his skin color. Recca, especially
adept at playing Kate the Shrew, was Heminges's wife
and Coeke's mistress—when she felt like it—and her easy
infidelity had done little in recent years to improve Heminges's personality.

Heminges was also our only revolutionary.

I should explain that.

There were a few men or women out of the billions scattered among the Archon and other alien stars who believed
that humans should revolt, throw off the yoke of the Archons
and reestablish the "human era." As if that were possible.
They were all cranks and malcontents like Heminges.

I was about fifteen and we were in transit in the Pleroma
when I first heard Heminges mutter his suicidal sedition.

"How could we possibly 'rise up' against the Archons?" I
asked. "Humans have no weapons."

Heminges had given me his Iago smile. "We're *in* the most
powerful weapon left to our species, young Master Wilbr."

"The *Muse*?" I said stupidly. "How could the *Muse* be a
weapon?"

Heminges had shaken his handsome head in something
like disgust. "The touring ships are the last artifacts left from
the human age of greatness," he hissed at me. "Think of it,
Wilbr . . . three fusion reactors, a fusion engine that used to
move our ancestors around the Earth's solar system in *days*

and which the Archon cabiri bots... and Tooley... keep tuned for us. Why, the flame tail from this ship is three miles long during early atmosphere entry."

The words had made me cold all through. "Use the *Muse* as a weapon?" I said. "That's . . ." I had no words for it. "The Archons would catch us and put us in a pain synthesizer for the rest of our lives." I assumed this last statement would put an end to the discussion.

Kemp had told me about the Archons' pain synthesizers the first months I'd been with the troupe. The lowest of the four tiers of alien races rarely deigned to deal with us, but when dole or arbeiter disappointed them or disobeyed them in any way, the Archons dropped the hapless people into a pain synthesizer and kept them alive for extra decades. The settings on the synthesizers were reputed to include such pleasures as "crushed testicle" or "hot poker up the anus" or "blade through eyeball". . . and the pain never ended. Drugs in the synthesizer soup kept the prisoner awake and suffering for long decades. And, Kemp had whispered to me, the first thing the Archons do to someone going into the pain synthesizer is to remove their tongue and vocal cords so they cannot scream.

Heminges laughed. "To punish us, the Archon would have to be alive. And so would we. Three fusion reactors make for a very nice bomb, young Master Wilbr."

That thought had kept me awake for weeks, but when I asked Tooley, who was apprenticing with Yerick who was then the ship's engineer, if such a thing were possible, he told me that it wasn't—really—that the reactors could melt and that would be messy, but that they couldn't be turned into what he called "a fusion bomb." Not really. Besides, Tooley said in his friendly lisp, the Archons had long since retrofitted *Muse* with so many of their own posttech safeguards and monitors that no amount of mere human tinkering could cause the reactors to go critical.

"What would we do if we... did... somehow attack the Archons?" I asked Heminges when I was fifteen. "Where would we go? Humans can't transit the Pleroma... only Abraxas can do that, praise be unto His name, and He shares those sacred secrets only with the *Demiurgos,* Poimen, and Archons. We'd be stranded forever in whatever star system we'd started the revolt in."

Heminges had only snorted at that and turned his attention back to his ale.

Still. . . all these years later. . . just the thought of losing the *Muse* made me shiver. She was home to me. She was the only home I'd known in the past eleven SEY and I fully expected to call her home for another fifty SEY until it was time for me to be carted back to Earth on a funeral barge.

We were performing *Much Ado About Nothing* and because I was playing Balthasar, Don Pedro's attendant, I didn't have to go with the supernumeraries as they went out to drum up business with the Circus Parade.

There were twenty cabiri for every human from our troupe, but the parade is hard to ignore. Those not preparing for major roles in *Much Ado* and our huge metal spiders made their way to the dole city on the higher ridges before the cabiri activated their holograms and my friends already in costume began blowing their horns and shouting and singing into their loudhailers.

Only a few doles joined the procession then—they rarely turn out for the Circus Parade—but by the time the line of brightly costumed actors and the procession of free-roaming elephants with red streamers, tigers, dromedaries carrying monkeys wearing fezzes, wolves in purple robes, and even some leaping dolphins got halfway through the arbeiter city, there were several hundred people following them back to the *Muse*.

More trumpets and announcements began blaring from the ship herself. The lower hull is always part of the stage and backdrop, of course, and this night the *Muse* extruded her lower balconies and catwalks and rows of spots and other lights beneath the tent just minutes before the crowd arrived. Holograms and smart paint became the fields and forests and hilltop manse of Leonato while we players in the wings hurried with our last costume and makeup preparations.

We started on time to a final flourish of silencing trumpets. Peering out from behind the arras like Polonius, I could see that there were about six hundred paying customers in their seats. (The chinks were only good in pubs and the few provision outlets, of course, but they were good on all the worlds we visited. Chinks are chinks.)

In the old days, *Much Ado* would have been Kemp's and Condella's tour de force, but a middle-aged Benedick and Beatrice simply didn't work, so after watching Burbank and Recca being merely adequate—and both very bitchy—in the roles for years, on this tour Alleyn and Aglaé were playing the leads.

They were amazing. Alleyn brought to Benedick all the bravado and uncertainty of the sexually experienced young nobleman who remained terrified of love and marriage. But it was Aglaé who dominated the performances—just as the real Beatrice dominated Leonato's compound above Messina with her incomparable and almost frightening wit leavened by a certain hint of a disappointed lover's melancholy. Someone once said that of all of Shakespeare's characters, it was Beatrice and Benedick that one would most want to be seated next to at a dinner party, and I confess that it was a pleasure being onstage with these two consummate young actors in those roles.

Kemp had to satisfy himself with a scene-stealing turn as Dogberry, Burbank blustered as Leonato, and Heminges had to throttle down his ultimate Iago evil to fit into the lesser villain of Don John, a character that Kemp once suggested to me was indeed Shakespeare's early, rough sketch for Iago. Anne played the hapless Hero and Condella was reduced to overacting as Margaret, Hero's waiting gentlewoman attendant. (Condella always created precisely the character here in *Much Ado* that she used for the Nurse in *Romeo and Juliet,* even though I'm certain that the Bard hadn't meant for the two to have any similarities.) And I got to woo her onstage even though I'm twenty SEY younger than she is.

The audience, mostly arbeiters in their brown rawool and a few score doles in their cotton gray, laughed hard and applauded and cheered frequently.

Alleyn and Aglaé were wonderful in their act 1 banter and we'd just gotten into act 2 with Benedick asking me to sing a "divine air"—I don't believe I mentioned that they had me play Balthasar primarily because I was the best singer in the troupe now that Davin had died and left us—and I'd just begun the song when everything changed forever.

> *Sigh no more, ladies, sigh no more,*
> *Men were deceivers ever,*
> *One foot in sea, and one on shore,*
> *To one thing constant never.*
> *Then sigh not so, but let them go,*
> *And be you blithe and bonny,*
> *Converting all your sounds of woe*
> *Into Hey, nonny nonny.*

In the middle of my song, into the tent floated a forty-foot-long heavy iron-gray gravity sledge carrying at least eight carapace-hooded, chitinous, four-armed, ten-foot-tall Archons, each sitting deep in its own iron-gray metal throne. Hanging from the sledge by their synaptic fiberneural filaments, which ran down to their hairless, distended skulls like slim, translucent copper hair, were four naked dragomen. Their oversized, lidless eyes focused on the stage and their cartilage-free ears rotating the better to pick up—and relay to their Archon masters—my singing.

Arbeiters and doles created a racket scrambling out of their seats to get out from under the massive, flat-bottomed gravity sledge. Archons landed their vehicles when and where they pleased and more than a few humans from 25–25–261B certainly had been crushed before this night.

But the sledge did not land. It rose to a point just below the tent roof about forty feet from the stage and hovered there. The doles and arbeiters who'd fled found places to sit in the aisles out from under the sledge's shadow and the dangling bare feet of the dragomen and returned their attention to the stage, their faces pale but attentive.

I'm a professional. I did not miss a beat or drop a note. But I know my voice quavered as I sang the next stanza.

> *Sing no more ditties, sing no more,*
> *Of dumps so dull and heavy.*
> *The fraud of men was ever so,*
> *Since summer first was leavy.*
> *Then sigh not so, but let them go,*
> *And be you blithe and bonny,*
> *Converting all your sounds of woe*
> *Into Hey, nonny nonny.*

Gough, playing Don Pedro, did not miss a beat. "'By my troth, a good song,'" he cried, his eyes never shifting to the sledge and Archons.

"'And an ill singer, my lord,'" was my response. For once I was telling the truth. My voice had cracked or quavered half a dozen times in those eight simple lines of singing.

"'Ha, no, no, faith,'" bellowed Gough/Don Pedro, "'thou sing'st well enough for a shift.'"

My hands were shaking and I *did* sneak a glance at the motionless sledge and the slowly twisting dragomen hanging naked and slick-skinned and hairless and sexless beneath that sledge, the filaments from the four of their skulls running up to red sensory node bundles on the complicated chest carapaces of the eight Archons.

Did the peasant arbeiters and equally peasant doles out there—any of them—have any idea that Gough's use of the ancient word "shift" in his line meant something like "to make do"? Almost certainly not. Almost all of the beauty and subtlety of Shakespeare's language was lost on them. (It had taken me years after the troupe adopted me to begin appreciating it.)

Then what in the hell were the Archons perceiving as they heard these archaic words through the dangling dragomen's ears, saw our colorful costumes and overbright makeup through the dragomen's eyes?

Alleyn caught my eye, forcing my attention back to the play, responded broadly to Don Pedro, and turned to the audience—ignoring the gravity sledge—and gave his chuckling Benedick's reply.

"'An he had been a dog that should have howled thus, they would have hanged him. And I pray God his bad voice bode no mischief. I had as lief have heard the night-raven, come what plague could have come after it.'"

The night-raven, I knew and the arbeiters and doles almost certainly did not know—who in the name of the Gnostic God of All Opposites had any idea what the dragomen and Archons knew?— was the bird of ill omen.

There is always a party after a performance. There was that night.

Some worlds are so dolefully awful that we have to hold the party on the *Muse,* inviting the pretty girls and pretty boys aboard (there are no human dignitaries, mayors, burgomasters, commissars, or officials of importance in human life now, only the gray doles, and they don't know how to party). On the more palatable worlds, and 25–25–261B qualified as such, we tried to move the party to a local pub or barn or similar public space. This rock had a pub in the oldest section of arbeiter town. (Those are the only two public institutions that have survived the end of all human politics and culture after our species' hopeless enslavement—pubs and churches. We'd never partied in a church. At least not yet.)

The drinking with the few adventurous arbeiters and storytelling and drinking and gambling and more storytelling and more drinking went on until the sulfur winds began to howl against the titanium shutters, and then the young ones among us began pairing off with the most attractive locals we could cull from the herd.

Aglaé rarely stayed at these parties for long and never went off with locals, but Philp, Pig (our apprentice Pyk), red-haired Kyder, Coeke, Alleyn, Anne, Pope, Lana, the short Hywo, Gough, Tooley, and some of the rest of us each found someone eager to make the beast with two backs with a rare stranger to their world, and two by two, arbeiter and actor, like randy animals filing toward Noah's

Ark, we began slipping away from the ebbing party and heading for arbeiters' hovels and barracks and outbuildings and barns.

In my case it was a barn.

We did it three times in the loft that night as the acid rains blew against the stone walls. (It would have been more times, but at age twenty, I'm not as young and resilient as I once was.) The barn held five animals (besides us)—a llama, a cow, a goat, and two chickens. None seemed bothered by our exertions or Larli's loud cries.

Larli was the arbeiter girl who'd invited me home to her barrack's barn. She was fairly typical for a postperformance fling girl: very young but old enough for me not to feel too guilty, curly hair, pretty eyes, broad shoulders, more muscles than I'd ever have, and hands so callused and strong that several times when I cried out, it was in pain not ecstasy.

She liked to talk and ask questions also fairly typical for a postplay fling date—and I tried to stay awake and keep up my end of the conversation (since I was too tired to keep anything else up) as the wind and sulfur rain tore at the slate tiles above us.

"You must see a lot of wonderful places," she said, lying back on the blanket on the straw. "Lots of wonderful worlds."

"Uh-huh," I said. I was deciding how to explain that I was going to return to the *Muse* to sleep. I always came home to the *Muse* to sleep after the postperformance. This night was already later than most.

"Have you ever gone to Earth?" she asked. Her voice almost broke on the soft syllable of the last word. They always do.

"I was born on Earth."

I could tell by her silent stare that she didn't believe me.

"A lot of players come from Earth," I said. "I was nine when they chose me."

"There's no one . . . *alive* . . . on Earth," she whispered. I could hear the acid rain outside diminish and the hot winds begin to blow. It would not be long before the terminator crossed this plateau. And it was the Sabbath.

I patted her pale but powerfully muscled leg. "There are thousands of living arbeiters on Earth... um... Larli."

"I thought only the dead lived there." She shook her blond curls, flustered. "You know what I mean."

I nodded in the dim glow of one shielded lantern hanging on a post below this loft. "There are a few thousand living humans on Earth," I said quietly. "My family among them. I was born there. The cabiri tend the tombs and do the heavy work, but there is always some labor for the doles and arbeiters."

"What is it like, Wilbr? Earth, I mean? It must be very beautiful."

"It rains a lot," I said. This was an understatement. Earth had not seen a blue sky in more than a thousand years.

"But the oceans... the *perfecti* tell tales of the great blue seas. Oceans of *water*. They must be gorgeous."

"Yes," I said, thinking only of how I was going to disengage myself so I could get back to my bunk on the *Muse*. The oceans of Earth had been drained by the *Demiurgos* long ago. Everything there now was rock and tombs: metal sarcophagi, tens and hundreds of billions of them, stacked on rocky plains, coastal shelves, deep shadowed mountain ranges that had once been ocean depths. Earth had no ecology, no wild things, no domesticated plants or animals—not even the ubiquitous goats and cows and llamas and chickens and other pathetic livestock scattered among sad arbeiter communities like this around the Tell—and no real towns. The few thousand arbeiters and doles were scattered among the tombs.

"And the sky, so blue," whispered the girl, whose name I'd forgotten again. "It must be *so* lovely."

"Yes," I said and stifled a yawn. My earliest memories were the red sky-scars of descending and ascending Archon funeral barges, carrying millions more of freezedried human corpses to their resting places and then ascending again with the empty sarcophagi, the massive, ugly ship flames clawing across the gray-clouded sky to the backdrop thunder of their booming pulse drives. The only clear areas on Earth were the spaceports where the funeral barges landed and took off, around the clock, while huge service cabiri unloaded the transport sarcophagi, tumbled the brittle corpses into bins, and then reloaded the containers.

The girl started caressing me again. I gently disengaged her hand and began pulling on my clothes.

"Tomorrow's... today's... Sabbath," I whispered. "I'll see you in church."

I actually *was* religious—I was raised that way—and I did see Larli in church later that morning, but only across the crowded heads of the congregation. I was sure that more doles and arbeiters than usual attended services that day just to see the outworlders. As always, the rough stone pews were filled with the usual bands of brown wool homespun work uniforms, slightly less rough gray cotton administrator tunics, and the small cluster of colorful silks and cottons and wools that we dozen or so regularly churchgoing Earth's Men chose to wear to Mass.

The church itself was no cathedral. The locals had cleaned out one of the stone barns erected by the Archon mechs, put rough glass in the windows, converted the hayloft to a choir loft—my loins stirred when I saw the loft and that's when I searched the crowd for Larli—and put some crude stone and canvas images of Gnostic saints and Abraxas him/herself at stations along the wall and behind the altar rail. The icons and paintings were rough but I could make out Saint Valentinius. Saint Sophia, Saint Thomas, Saint Emerson, Saint Blake, Saint Hesse, Saint Caprocates with his wife Alexandra hovering behind and above him, Saint Menander, Saint Basilides, and Simon Magus. That last prophet of the church was always depicted as flying, and in the painting along the north wall, the painted expression of Simon Magus looked as surprised at his sudden flying ability as the poorly rendered faces of the peasants below him.

Abraxas, of course, held center stage, roughly where a huge cross and Jesus might have hung behind the altar long ago during the brief Christian era. The large sculpture carried the traditional whip and shield—showing the conjoined opposites of attack and defense—and had the usual head of a rooster, body of a man, and legs of heavy, coiled snakes. Behind the sculpture on a black, circular stone backdrop were gold stars with varying number of rays as well as the eight-fold symbol of the *ogdoad*, representing the transcending of the seven planets.

The two *perfecti* at the front of the church—one male, one female, as prescribed by the Abraxic requirement of joining of opposites, one in all white with a black collar band, the other wearing the reverse—performed the opening rituals with the usual provincial blend of ineptitude and enthusiasm.

The male *perfectus* gave the sermon. It was the third sermon from Saint Jung's *Seven Sermons to the Dead* and I could have recited it from memory, and with far more feeling than the white-robed *perfectus* could deliver on his best day. Compared to memorizing and delivering the simplest line from Shakespeare, Jung's rhetoric was baby's work.

> *The dead approaches like mist out of the swamps and they shouted: "Speak to us further about the highest god!"*
> *—Abraxas is the god whom it is difficult to know.*
> *His power is the very greatest because man does not perceive it at all. Man sees the* summum bonum, *supreme good, of the sun, and also the* infinum malum, *endless evil, of the devil, but Abraxas, he does not see, for he is undefinable life itself, which is the mother of good and evil alike.*
> *Life appears smaller and weaker than the* summum bonum, *wherefore it is hard to think that Abraxas should supersede in his power the sun, which is the radiant fountain of all life forces.*
> *Abraxas is the sun and also the eternally gaping abyss of emptiness, of the diminisher and dissembler, the devil.*
> *The power of Abraxas is twofold. You cannot see it,*

*because in your eyes the opposition of this power
seems to cancel it out.
That which is spoken by God-the-Sun is life.
That which is spoken by the Devil is death.
Abraxas, however, speaks the venerable and also ac-
cursed word, which is life and death at once.
Abraxas generates truth and falsehood, good and
evil, light and darkness with the same word and in
the same deed. Therefore Abraxas is truly the terrible
one.
He is magnificent even as the lion at the very moment
when he strikes his prey down. His beauty is like the
beauty of a spring morn.
Indeed, he is himself the greater Pan, and also the
lesser. He is Priapos.
He is the monster of the underworld, the octopus with
a thousand tentacles, he is the twistings of winged
serpents and of madness.
He is the hermaphrodite of the lowest beginning.
He is the lord of toads and frogs, who live in water
and come out unto the land, and who sing together at
high noon and at midnight.
He is fullness, uniting itself with emptiness.
He is the sacred wedding;
He is love and the murder of love;
He is the holy one and his betrayer.
He is the brightest light of day and the deepest night
of madness.
To see him means blindness;
To know him is sickness;
To worship him is death;
To fear him is wisdom;
Not to resist him means liberation.
God lives behind the—*

The *perfectus* suddenly fell silent. The priest's gaze was riveted on the rear door of the church and one by one the congregation swiveled their necks to see what or who had interrupted the service.

I'd never seen a dragoman alone and I'd never seen one close up like this. Both new experiences were unsettling.

He—I use the pronoun loosely since dragomen had no sex—was about my height but he had much larger eyes, much larger ears, no lips to speak of, no teeth visible, no real chin, a long tapered nose, and a queerly shaped head, his forehead sloped back along a cranium that seemed to have been malformed rearward until it blended with the long synaptic filaments that trailed on the floor behind now with a faint metallic rustling. His fingers were far too long, as if they had at least one extra joint and perhaps more, and disturbingly spatulate. His feet were flat and too broad—he had no toes and I could hear puckery suckerish sounds as he strode across the broad paving stones of the barn-church. His legs were too long, jointed oddly, and gave the false impression of being almost boneless. He was hairless and naked, of course, and as he passed my pew I saw how his skin glistened wetly, coarsely, like molded wax. He had no nipples. I could see how a waxy fold of loose skin folded down from his lower abdomen to cover whatever orifices he had for urination and excretion; it is common knowledge that dragomen have no real genitals and thus are more *neuter* than hermaphroditic.

He stopped at Kemp's pew and, bending oddly from the waist, leaned toward the leader of our troupe. The dragoman's voice was as high and flat as a young child's without any of a child's charm. "The Heresiarch bids you to perform tonight at the Archon keep. Have your people dressed and prepared for transport at the moment the winds drop on the hour of the third mine shift."

He may have said something else, but if so the words were lost in the explosion of surprised murmuring and shifting in the church.

"This is our chance," whispered Heminges as the men crowded into one of the *Muse*'s two makeup and costuming rooms that afternoon.

"Chance?" said Gough. Kemp and Condella had decided that we were doing the Scottish Play, over Burbank's protests and Alleyn's and Aglaé's indifference.

"To strike," said Heminges. He was costuming himself for the role of Duncan.

Gough rolled his eyes.

"What are you talking about?" I asked. I was already terrified at the thought of performing before the Archons; I didn't need Heminges's revolution fantasies and conspiracies that night.

"I've never heard of a troupe being invited to perform before Archons before... *in their keep,*" whispered Heminges.

"You never heard of it before, because it's never happened before," said Old Adam. He was to be Banquo tonight. His favorite role was as Hamlet's father's ghost. Adam had been to more Bard Rendezvous on Stratford and performed in more competitions there than any of us, even Kemp and Burbank. He knew more lore than anyone else in the Earth's Men.

"Then it *is* perfect," hissed Heminges as he applied his bald wig.

"Perfect for *what,* for Christ's sake? We can't *do* anything up there... but put on the show, I mean. If we did... if we did..."

"The pain synthesizers," rumbled Coeke. "For the rest of our lives and then some."

Heminges showed his thin, tight Iago smile. "When we take the *Muse* to the keep, we set thrust to full burn, then take off before—"

"Oh, shut the fuck up, Heminges," said Burbank, who'd come closer without us noticing. "We're not taking the ship up there. The dragoman told Kemp that we were to be fully dressed and have all our props ready by... less than an hour from now... and a gravity sledge is going to take us the six miles to the castle. Do you *really* think the Archons would let us get a weapon... or anything that could be used as a weapon... anywhere near the keep?"

Heminges said nothing.

"I don't want to hear another word of your silly revolution fantasies," snapped Burbank, his voice as mad-strong as

Hamlet's speaking to Gertrude. "If you play this particular brand of sick make-believe again—one more word—I swear by Abraxas that we'll leave you behind on this godforsaken rock."

It looked as if two thirds of the arbeiters and doles not at work in the mines showed up to watch us leave on the gravity sledge. It was easy to understand why they were curious. In all the centuries they and their ancestors had been on this rock, the only thing that left from the human city to be taken to the keep were dead bodies to be hauled to the Archon spaceport to await transshipment to Earth.

There was a funeral barge up there now. We'd followed it through the Pleroma to this world and had planned to follow it out in three days to the next planet on our tour.

From the look on the silent arbeiters' faces as we floated past the city and up the road carved into rock toward the highlands, they didn't expect us to return from the keep alive. Perhaps we didn't either. But the excitement was real. It had been the unanimous opinion of Kemp, Condella, Burbank, Pope, Old Adam, and the other senior members of the troupe that no traveling Shakespearean group had ever been invited to perform before the Archon before. We had no idea what to expect.

The dragoman who'd come to the church—if it was the same one, they all looked alike to me—was in the control cab of the sledge with various Archon cabiri and we were on the open freight pallet behind, where the human coffins were usually carried, so there was no chance for further conversation with the dragoman. The cabiri that the Archons had designed for the *Muse* and other old human spacecraft I'd seen—Shakespearean troupe, *perfecti,* and physiocrat— were more huge metal-spider than organic, but I noticed more patches of flesh and real hands and even a mouth, more lipped and human-looking than the dragoman's, on the cabiri in the sledge cab. The flesh, lips, teeth, fingers, and the rest looked as if they had come from a human-being parts bin. This was disturbing.

It was also disturbing to be in full costume and makeup so

long *before* the performance. We carried along any changes in costume we'd need and a few props—chairs, a table, daggers, and the like—but no backdrops or scenery. And we assumed we'd have none of the computer-controlled lighting or microphone pickups that were always part of our performances at the *Muse* tents.

The sledge slid two meters above the rock road as it rose toward the keep of Mezel-Goull.

We'd never seen the spaceport or a funeral barge from up close before and we all stared as the sledge reached the cliff ledge and silently floated past the perfectly flat landing area. The barge was as grim as its purpose and huge, a three-siloed gray-black smooth-hulled mass that floated five meters above the scorch-blackened rock. Ramps led down to temperature-controlled storage sheds. More of the disturbing flesh-and-metal cabiri were loading human-sized sarcophagi up dark ramps. The interior of the barge glowed dim red. The ship was large enough to carry tens and tens of thousands of sarcophagi.

There were three other Archon ships at the keep's spaceport. We'd seen such ships before, passing them during our transit from Kenoma to Pleroma or the reverse, but those were always video images, fast glimpses, and fuzzy, distant holos. The close-up reality of the three gray, grim, massive, heavily gunned and blistered and turreted, shaped and shielded vessels reminded all of us that the Archons were a fierce breed. After all these centuries we had no idea who or what their enemies were in the dark light-years beyond the Tell—we knew only that they were subservient to the Poimen, *Demiurgos,* and mythical Abraxi—but these ships were built to fight. They were, all of us were thinking in silence, destroyers of worlds.

The keep loomed larger than we had imagined. From the *Muse,* during our previous visits to the arbeiter town below, we'd guessed the height of the Archon castle to be about a thousand feet, its width about two-thirds that as its shape conformed to the narrow precipice a mile here above the black sulfur sea, but as we approached we realized that it must be more than two hundred stories tall. The gray-black stone was not stone but metal. Everywhere along its walls were blisters and bulges, much like on their warships, but here long rivulets and streaks of rust ran down. The streaks were the color of dried blood.

Some of the window slits far above glowed a dull orange.

"I need to take a piss," said our apprentice Pig. He started to climb down from the slowly moving sledge.

"Stay on," snapped Kemp.

"But . . ." began Pig.

"I need to go as well," said Kyder, costumed well as one of the three weird sisters in the first scene. "I doubt if they'll have lavatories in this Archon heap."

"Stay on the goddamned sledge," shouted Kemp. "If you get left behind, we won't be able to put on the show."

As if the dragoman or cabiri in the cab had heard him, the sledge began spinning and climbing higher then, swirling in the air to fifty feet of altitude, then a hundred, then three hundred. Everyone grabbed everyone, backed away from the open edge of the freight bed, and dropped to at least one knee.

The sledge swung out over the edge of the cliff. Acid breakers crashed onto fang-sharp boulders five thousand feet below us.

"Oh, fuck me!" cried the Pig. I could see the wet stain spreading down his brown tights and I also felt the sudden urge to urinate.

Six hundred feet up on the wall of stained metal-rock, high on the western side of the keep that hung out over the cliff's edge a mile above the sea, there came a great grinding and a trapezoid of light fifty or sixty feet high began to shape itself.

The sledge floated forward and we entered the keep.

The Scottish Play was difficult to do well under the best of conditions, and I would not say that the Archon keep of Mezel-Goull provided the best of conditions.

Our stage was a circular shelf about sixty feet across at the bottom of a giant well at the center of the keep. Or perhaps "well" isn't the proper word here, even though the lightning-roiled sky was visible through the round opening far above, since the rock-steel cliffs on all sides of our circle opened wider the higher they went. I estimated the walls here to be about three hundred feet high. All along the rough circle of stone were small cave openings, and outside these openings, on irregular slabs and ledges, sat the Archons—certainly more than a thousand of them. Perhaps two or three thousand.

Hanging by their filament hair around this almost gladiatorial space were dragomen—I guessed fifty, but there could have been more—attached to the crouching Archons' sensory nerve bundles only by their filaments. Each dragoman's synaptic fibers connected to at least twenty or thirty Archons, who looked more insectoid than ever here in their native habitat, crouched and multilegged on their rock shelves, some holding their red nerve bundle packets away from their bodies with a pair of hands, looking much like an ancient holo I once saw on Earth of a bearded Jesus Christ (or perhaps it was Mohammed; one of the ancient gods at least) holding forth his red heart as if only recently ripped from his chest.

The only bright light was on our solid circle of yellow stone or metal. All the rest of the rising cavernous space was lighted by the dimmest of red glows from the cavern openings. Lightning continued to ripple and tear above us, but something muffled all sound beyond the keep.

Our performance was perhaps the best we'd ever given.

Kemp and Condella played the Thane and his Queen, of course, with Burbank outdoing himself as the drunken Porter. Watching Condella as Lady Ma . . . as the Queen . . . reminded me of why she was one of the most incredible touring actresses in the Tell.

For years I had played Macduff's son but more recently had been upgraded to Lennox, one of the Scottish thanes, so I got to be onstage between the three witches' scenes during the second scene where King Duncan, Malcolm, and the rest of us spy "the bloody man," and I confess that my first line—"What a haste looks through his eyes! So should he look that seems to speak things strange"—came out as more powerful squeak than bold pronouncement.

This unique setting for our performance did not seem to distract the others. Kemp was extraordinary. Condella transcended herself, although—as she once told me bitterly— "The Queen in this damned Scottish Play is just *too* good a role, Master Wilbr. Every time she's onstage everyone else, even the Thane, is thrown into shadow. Shakespeare had to keep her offstage, the same as he had to kill Mercutio early in *Romeo and Juliet* or let him take over the play, like a callower Hamlet wandering loose." And it was true, I noticed back then, that Lady Ma... the Queen... exits in act 3, scene 4, and isn't seen again until she returns, already lost to madness, at the start of act 5.

Aglaé, the most beautiful young actress on this world or any other world, the most beautiful actress in the Tell or beyond, played one of the three Weird Sisters and her makeup was almost, not quite, good enough to hide her beauty behind warts, wrinkles, a fake nose, and a wispy beard.

As I exited... which meant just to walk outside the circle of light onto the dark part of the round slab of floor... Aglaé came on and cried, " 'Where hast thou been, sister?' "

Anne, as the second witch, answered, " 'Killing swine.' "

Standing in the offstage darkness, I peered up at the ungainly slabs and ledges and cavemouths. Did these alien things know what witches were? What swine were? Presumably the latter since they had chosen pigs as one of the few forms of livestock to bring along with their human slaves.

The third witch cried as if blind, " 'Sister, where thou?' "

Aglaé responded, voice husky and ancient, " 'A sailor's wife had chestnuts in her lap. And munched and munched and munched. "Give me," quoth I. "Aroint thee, witch," the rump-fed runnion cries. Her husband's to Aleppo gone, master o' th' *Tiger*. But in a sieve I'll thither sail, and, like a rat without a tail, I'll do, I'll do, and I'll do.' "

Dear Abraxas above, I thought, my heart pounding wildly, *these Archons will not understand a word or thought of this. What help can the soulless dragomen be? They see and hear and maybe translate the words, but how can you translate Shakespeare to alien minds?*

And hard on the heels of that thought came a more terrible certainty: *this is some sort of trial; the Archons are deciding whether to let us live or not.*

We played on. Sans props, sans scenery, sans curtain, sans human audience.

When one act ended, we would all pause outside the circle of light for a few seconds and then begin the next. Kemp later told me that this was more or less the way Shakespeare and his people had done it in their day; that acts and scenes, as separate entities, were a later invention.

One of Kemp's earliest lines, to the witches, was "The Thane of Cawdor lives. Why do you dress me in borrowed clothes."

Dear God, I loved such phrases. "The Thane of Cawdor." It evoked human ages and vital human barbarity long lost to all of us. But what could it possibly mean to the hooded, earless, handless, eyeless, faceless Archons on their bug ledges above?

By the time Kemp choked out these anguished lines, I was sure that we'd already signed our own death warrants through our very incomprehensibility to this chitinous audience:

> *If it were done when 'tis done, then 'twere well*
> *It were done quickly. If th' assassination*
> *Could trammel up the consequence and catch*
> *With his surcease success, that but this blow*
> *Might be the be-all and the end-all here,*
> *But here, upon this bank and shoal of time,*
> *We'd jump the life to come . . .*

When suddenly, from the dark ledges above there came a susurration as of many insect breaths blowing over violin-bow forelimbs, followed by a growing *chrr . . . chrrr . . . ch rrrr . . . chrrrrr.*

Kemp as the Thane did not miss a beat, but offstage in

the dark I leaned on Tooley, one of the soldiers, as I stared up into the dark, straining almost painfully to see. Coeke leaned over and whispered fiercely, "I didn't know the Archons had wings, did you?"

There was more *chrrrring* during the next hour, the loudest—it drowned out the ensuing dialogue and made even our most unperturbable players pause a second—came, for no reason we will ever understand, after Burbank as the Porter gave his "equivocation" speech:

> *Marry, sir, nose-painting, sleep, and urine. Lechery, sir, it provokes, and unprovokes: it provokes the desire, but it takes away the performance. Therefore much drink may be said to be an equivocator with lechery. It makes him, and it mars him; it sets him on and it takes him off; it persuades him and disheartens him; makes him stand to and not stand to; in conclusion, equivocates him in a sleep, and giving him the lie, leaves him.*

The *chrrrring* went on and on for almost three minutes. The drone-hum of wings was so loud I expected to look up to see the Archons flitting about this hive-tunnel space like so many hornets.

Why? What could they possibly know of drunkenness or desire, lechery or impotence? Much less the effect alcohol has on men before, during, or after the sex act?

I looked at Aglaé, still in her witch makeup and costume. As if reading my mind, she shook her head.

In no time, in an eternity, it was over.

Malcolm—Gough—the new King of Scotland, had his final words while Macduff stood there holding a fair likeness of Kemp's head by the hair. It reminded me of the dangling dragomen above.

" 'That calls upon us, by the grace of grace,' " boomed Gough-Malcolm, " 'we will perform in measure, time, and place. So thanks to all at once, and to each one, whom we invite to see us crowned at Scone.' "

Those onstage bowed.

The dead rose and bowed.

Those of us in the darkened wings came into the circle of light and bowed.

Nothing.

No applause. Not a cough. Not even a *chrrring* of wings. Silence.

After a moment of this excruciating nothing, the light in and on our circle went out. We could see that the ledges and slabs above were empty. Even the hanging dragomen were gone.

A trapezoid opened in a solid wall behind us. The gravity sledge floated in.

Kemp, still in makeup, refused to board—or allow us to board—until the dragoman standing by the cab gave us some indication of what the Archons had thought.

The dragoman—I thought it was the same one that had come to the church that morning, but was not sure—said, "You are no longer the Earth's Men."

Kemp opened his mouth but decided not to speak.

"From this moment forward, you are the Heresiarch's Men," said the dragoman.

We rendezvoused in orbit with the Archon warship exactly as instructed. This was to be the first time we ever penetrated the Pleroma following anything but a funeral barge. As far as we knew, it was the first time that any human ship—player troupe, *perfecti,* or physiocrat—had ever entered the Abyss behind anything but a funeral barge.

It was also the first time that anyone other than a member of the troupe had traveled with us in the *Muse.*

I still thought the dragoman was the same one who'd come to the church and driven us to the keep, but I'd seen enough of them in the cone of Mezel-Goull to know they actually all looked alike.

Once we were safely in the Pleroma, surrounded by that objective golden glow, the dragoman had an odd request. He wanted to see the *Muse.* Herself.

Kemp and Condella and Burbank and a few of the co-owners had to confer about that. We had never let an outsider see the true Muse. Except for when we were children trying to frighten each other, we seldom went down there ourselves.

In the end, they relented. What choice did they have? Kemp did ask the dragoman—"Are you still in touch with the Archon? Even though your... ah... hair... isn't connected? Even here in the Abyss?"

The lipless large-eyed man-thing stared in a way that I almost could have interpreted as amusement. "We are always united in the flame of Abraxas," he/it said.

It was from the Fourth Sermon to the Dead.

> Good and evil are united in the flame.
> Good and evil are united in the growth of the tree.
> Life and love oppose each other in their own divinity.

What the hell. They decided to let the dragoman visit the *Muse*.

For some reason, Kemp beckoned me to join the four of them showing the dragoman the way.

The body of the *Muse* slept through eternity in a small compartment past the sleeping level where our bunks lay empty, below the circular common room where a few of the others looked up at us with unanswered questions in their eyes as we passed, beneath the throbbing engine room where Tooley used to let me look in through the thick blue glass at the star-flame of our fusion ship's heart when I was a boy, down a ladder and through two hatches into a space barely large enough for the five of us humans and the dragoman to stand in a circle around the fluid-filled sphere in the center.

She floated there in the thick, blue liquid. Long dead but not dead. Her body mummified. Her eyes long since turned to cobwebs. Her breasts now flattened to wrinkled mummy's dugs. Her sex lost. Her once-red hair mostly gone, the wispy remnants floating like a baby chick's fuzz. Her lips stretched back to reveal all her skull-teeth. Her arms were folded in front of her as she floated, looking as fleshless and fragile as broken bird's wings, her thumbs folded in flat against her fluid-shriveled palms.

"Who was she?" asked the dragoman

"No one knows," said Condella. "Some say she was named Sophia."

"She wouldn't answer if you asked her through the ship?" the dragoman asked.

"She wouldn't understand the question," said Kemp.

"I could ask her directly," said the dragoman. The thought of that made my skin go cold.

The *Muse* spoke then, her voice coming from the walls. I don't know if any of the others jumped, but I did. "We have exited the Abyss and returned to the Kenoma. This system is not numbered. These worlds are unnamed. We are no longer in the Archon warship's pleromic wake. Another craft has taken control and ordered me to follow it until further notice. All imaging surfaces are now active."

"Another craft?" I said, looking from Kemp to Burbank to the dragoman.

The dragoman was clutching his head so fiercely that his ten spatulate fingers compressed white. "They're gone," he gasped.

"Who's gone?" asked Kemp.

"The Archons. For the first time . . . in my . . . existence. There is . . . no . . . contact." The dragoman fell to the deck and wrapped his long arms around his legs as he curled into a tight and rocking fetal position.

"Whose ship is it then?" asked Condella.

Black fluid ran from the dragoman's eyes and open mouth as he gasped. "The Poimen."

In the globe of blue liquid, the mummy of the *Muse* writhed, extended her withered arms, and opened her empty eyes.

We gathered in the common room. Tooley and Pig laid the unconscious dragoman on an old acceleration couch; we could not tell if he was still alive. Black fluid continued to seep from his mouth, ears, eyes, and unseen orifices under his genital flap and none of the rest of us wished to touch him.

Tooley wiped his hands and hurried to unroll viewstrips along the curved outer bulkhead. Within minutes it felt as if we were on a high platform open to three-dimensional space in all directions.

Kemp came down from above. "The *Muse* is not answering questions or responding to navigation requests," he said. "We're not even under power. As far as we can tell, there's no pleromic wake, but we're still under the influence of that ship pulling us toward the gas giant."

The Muse *not answering questions or responding to orders?* We all stared at one another with terror in our eyes. This had never happened. It *couldn't* happen. If the *Muse* failed, malfunctioned, died, we were all dead. I remembered the flailing and stretching and silent gape-mouthed screams of her mummy in the blue sphere below and wondered if somehow we had all killed her by following the Archon warship through the Pleroma.

I realized that the fusion thrum and slight additional weight of in-system thrust was absent for the first time ever in our nonpleromic travels. The only thing keeping us from floating around the room was the sternward pressure of the internal tension fields. At least that meant that some power was still being generated.

Watching the scene through the huge viewstrip windows did nothing to quell our terror.

We were hurtling toward a gas-giant world with a velocity the *Muse* would never have allowed or been able to obtain. Ahead of us was a bluish-gray ship, size impossible to determine without references or radar that the *Muse* would not or could not bring online even after repeated requests. The blue-gray ship seemed solid yet was impossibly malleable, shifting shapes constantly: now an aerodynamic dart, almost winged; now a blue spheroid; now a muscular mass of curves and bubbles that made the missing Archon warship look as crudely made as an iron boomerang.

Then all of us ceased looking at the ship towing us and stared slack-jawed at the approaching world.

Worlds, I should say, because the green and blue and white gas giant—there was no doubt it was a Jovian-sized world—

was accompanied by a dozen or more hurtling moons and a ring.

I'd seen hundreds of gas giants in my travels from Pleroma to the Archon worlds of the Tell, Jupiter and Saturn being only the first and those only briefly glimpsed, but never had I seen a world like this. None of us had.

Instead of the red, orange, yellow, and turqoise methane stripes common to most such giants, this world alternated bands of blue and white. Massive cloud-storms that must have been as large as Jupiter's Red Spot swirled in cyclonic splendor, but these were white storms—Earth-like hurricanes—and they traveled along blue bands that suggested oceans of water thousands of miles below.

This alone would have made us gawk—an Earth-like gas-giant world of such beauty—not to mention the dozen, no fifteen at least, no, now seventeen moons we could see hurtling above the multihued equatorial rings that girdled the big planet some tens of thousands of miles above its shimmering atmosphere, but it was the signs of civilization that kept our mouths open and our eyes wide.

To say the world was obviously inhabited would have been the understatement of all time.

The gas giant was about two-thirds illuminated by its yellow sun, but the dark slice beyond the curve of terminator was as brilliantly lighted as the glaring blue and white daytime side. Straight and winding strings of lights by the millions showed linear communities or highways or flyways or coastlines or spaceports or. . . we did not know what. Constellations of lights, by the billions it seemed, showed cities or, because the constellations were moving, perhaps just the denizens themselves, radiant as gods.

Buildings. . . towers. . . crystalline structures rose out of the clouds and then out of the atmosphere itself; not one or a few, but hundreds of them. They moved with the revolution of the planet. Several rose not only through the atmosphere but up through the orbital rings around the giant world. . . rings which we now could see were made up of artificial moonlets or structures by the million. The myriad of sparkling orbital objects looked as if they were going to crash into the tallest crystal towers with the speed of meteors, of comets, but at the last minute the streams of particles—each object hundreds of times larger than the *Muse*, we realized—parted like a river current around a rock.

The space between the big planet and the moons was filled not only with the countless objects that made up the equatorial rings, and with the fluid-filled cords to the moons, but with more millions of rising and descending flecks catching sunlight and throwing off their own flames. Spacecraft, we presumed, rising and descending from the world.

"Dear Abraxas," whispered Burbank. "How tall are those structures?"

We could see the towers' shadows now, thrown across entire continents below them, across seas of clouds. The base of each tower was invisible beneath the white and blue—perhaps the fluid-filled towers passed through the entire giant world like so many crystalline stakes driven through the planet's heart—but their summits and upper floors rose deep into the vacuum of cislunar space.

"Hundreds of miles high, at least," said Heminges who knew a few technical things. "Thousands, I think."

"That's impossible," said Condella.

The towing ship slowed and we slowed with it as we entered the cislunar system.

"Look at this," said Tooley, who had pushed some of the viewstrips to their maximum magnification.

From farther out we'd seen the writhing strands rising from the world toward the many moons, but now we could see that not only were they continuous—connected all the way from the giant planet to the many hurtling moons, some of which must have been the size of Earth or 25–25–261B, but the cords, each anchored somewhere on the big planet, were transparent and hollow.

"Those must each be three or four hundred miles in diameter," whispered Gough.

"Impossible," said Kemp.

Coeke nodded and rubbed stubble on his massive jaw. "It is impossible, but look . . ." He stabbed a blunt, black finger into the holo of the viewstrip. "There's something moving inside each connecting thread."

"Are those things bridges?" asked Alleyn in hushed tones.

"More like umbilicals, I think," said Hywo. "Conduits. They're filled with liquid. Things are . . . swimming . . . moving both directions in that fluid."

"Not possible," Kemp said.

"We're closing on that tallest tower pretty fast," said Philp.

He was right. Kemp, Tooley, and Burbank, our three most common interlocutors with the *Muse*, began calling to her with some alarm in their voices—if we needed to fire engines to brake, she needed to do it *now*—but the *Muse* did not answer.

"Oh, Abraxas, embracer of all opposites, terror of the sun, heart of the sun, help us," prayed Old Adam.

A blue sphere about twelve feet across floated through the hull. We clambered and leaped to get out of its way.

At first, in my fear and confusion, I thought it was the blue-fluid-filled globe below that held the mummy of the *Muse,* but this was larger and something else. The blue was a different color and the sphere glowed from within. There was a living being in the water or fluid; the creature was golden, vaguely amphibian, and about eight feet long. I could see a face of sorts, eyes of sorts, a slash of a mouth or feeding orifice, large gills, gold and green scales, and two vestigial arms, like those of a malformed fetus, with lovely small hands.

Suddenly the still corpse of the dragoman spoke. "We are sorry we injured this member of your species. He is no longer living. We shall resurrect him to make amends."

None of us spoke until Aglaé managed, "Are you the Poimen?"

"We did not mean to damage this unit while we were taking your ship from the possession of the petty rulers," said the dead dragoman, a black fluid as viscous as ink still running from the corners of his mouth and eyes as he lay there on the couch.

I remembered my catechism, Father teaching me in the glass room through the endless rainy afternoons on Earth. Centuries ago, after our first contact with the Archons and the end of our species' rule of self, Abraxas had revealed four levels of our masters, four stages of our own eternal evolution should our physical bodies be returned to Earth and our *psyche* and *pneuma* be pure enough to ascend the four circles.

The Archons were the petty rulers. The Poimen, whom no humans in our lifetimes had ever glimpsed, were the shepherds. The *Demiurgos* were the half-makers. (It was they who had created our faulty, failed Earth and universe.) The Abraxi were the shattered vessels of Abraxas, the ultimate God of Opposites.

The dragoman sat up on his couch, set his splayed feet on the deck, and wiped ink from his lipless mouth. His synaptic filaments hung down like wet vines. His black-rimmed eyes stared at us with no obvious signs of alarm. "What happened while I was dead?"

Before we could answer, he spoke again, but his voice had that somehow flatter, infinitely more vacant tone it had held a moment before when the Poimen amphibian in the blue globe had spoken through him.

"We will be docking within moments. You will choose one of your *mimesis* episodes for performance in one hour and eleven minutes. An appropriate place will be made ready for you. There will be those there to receive your images and sounds . . . an audience."

"One hour and eleven minutes!" shouted Kemp. None of us had slept for at least thirty-six hours. We'd already performed *Much Ado About Nothing* and the most successful performance of *The Tragedy of Macbe*. . . the Scottish Play . . . that we had ever seen, much less participated in.

"One hour and eleven minutes?" he cried again.

But the Poimen and its sphere were gone, floated back through the hull and out of sight.

The Poimen ship placed the *Muse of Fire* gently in a niche near the top of the crystal tower—we passed through some sort of tough but permeable membrane that held the liquid inside, not to mention its inhabitants, safe and separate from the cold of space—and then other gold and green and reddish and blue-gilled forms piloting small machines, open and delicate jet sledges which they guided with their tiny hands, took us down the thousand miles or two of flooded crystal column at an impossible speed.

"Supercavitation," muttered Tooley.

"What?" snapped Kemp.

"Nothing."

Our one engineer seemed sullen since the *Muse* quit speaking to him.

We spent most of the hour and ten minutes during the descent—the water-scooter Poimen pulled and pushed us through clouds and what seemed like blue and turqoise seas—arguing about what to perform.

"Romeo and Juliet," argued Alleyn and Aglaé. Of course they would argue for that play. It was theirs. Kemp and Condella and Adam and even Heminges were old farts and demoted to secondary and tertiary roles in that play.

Kemp vetoed the idea. "This may be the most important performance we ever do," said the troupe leader. "We have to put on the *best*—the best of the Bard, the best of ourselves."

"You said that yesterday," Alleyn said dryly. "For the Archons."

"Well, it was true then," said Kemp. He was so exhausted that his voice was raw. "It's truer now."

"What then?" asked Burbank. *"Hamlet? Lear?"*

"Lear," decided Kemp.

What a surprise! I thought bitterly. Kemp decides on the play tailored to Kemp on our most important performance ever. The universe ages, Earth loses its oceans, the human race is subjugated and turned into cultureless futureless slaves, but actors still count lines.

"Will I be Cordelia?" asked Aglaé.

Of course she would. She'd been Cordelia in the past twenty performances, with Condella as the infinitely rancid older Goneril.

"No, I will be Cordelia," announced Condella in tones that brooked no opposition. "You will be Regan. Becca can be Goneril."

"But," began Aglać, obviously crushed, "how can you play..." She stopped. How can an actress tell another actress that she's decades too old for a part, even when it would be obvious to the most groundling groundling?

Kemp said, "These are *aliens*. We've never seen these... Poimen... and they've never seen us. They can't tell our ages. They almost certainly can't tell our genders. I'm not sure they can tell our *species*."

"Then how in the hell can they get anything out of the play?" snapped Heminges.

I thought he had something there. But then again, I remembered, the Poimen *were* gods... of a sort.

The ship had been lowered to some appropriate depth, although shafts of sunlight still filtered down through the clear blue waters. It was as if we were in a blue and gold cathedral. Hundreds of the Poimen, who weren't men at all despite that part of their name (or the name Abraxas had given them), swam and shuttled around us, some being pulled by their jet-sled craft, some using other means of propulsion, some inside larger craft and looking out through transparent hulls. The depths were also filled with larger submersibles of varied design, some moving in obvious lanes but others shimmering like gigantic schools of metal fish. Far below us, the waters grew darker and larger things, living things I thought, moved with leviathan slowness.

Kemp gave the assignments. I hoped for Edmund, of course, all of us younger actors did, if we couldn't get Edgar, but received the part of Albany's servant. At least I got to kill and die onstage. (I confess I've never understood that servant's motivation.)

Heminges was to be Edmund, the bastard in every sense. I think I might have cast him as Edgar; Heminges is crazy enough out of character to play Tom o'Bedlam half the time. But Alleyn got Edgar. Pope was the Duke of Cornwall, evil Regan's stupid husband—I could see Pope squinting dubiously at Aglaé (he'd never had such a young Regan). Gough got the good role of the Earl of Kent.

There was a tradition in Shakespeare's day for Lear's Fool, a sort of holy fool, to be played by the same actor who plays Cordelia—the Fool is never onstage when Cordelia is and he disappears completely when her major scenes begin—but this wasn't going to work with tonight's casting.

I would have given my left testicle to play the Fool, but Burbank got it.

Adam got the Old Man—what else?—and Philp was the courtly, brave, and courting Duke of Burgundy. Coeke was to be Curan, Gloucester's retainer, and Hywo Gloucester.

The lesser roles, gentlemen, servants, soldiers, attendants, and messengers, were quickly parceled out. We knew all the parts—or were supposed to.

Pyk came up and tried to get Kemp's attention, but our Fearless Leader was too busy making costume choices and discussing staging—Christ, we hated theater-in-the-round and prayed to Abraxas that this place would not be like Mezel-Goull.

"What is it, Pig?" I whispered.

"The *Muse*," he whispered wetly in my ear.

"What about her?"

"You'd better come see, Wilbr."

I followed him down through the engine room, through the double hatches, down the ladder to the tiny room holding the *Muse*'s sphere and mummy. I admit that I was a little nervous being in there just with Pig after watching the *Muse*'s gyrations and eyes opening an hour or so earlier.

Her eyes were still opened, but no longer empty. They were complete and blue and looking at me. No mummy now. The naked young woman floating in the blue fluid was more beautiful and younger than Aglaé. Her restored red hair floated around her like a fiery nimbus.

She did not quite smile at me but her gaze registered my presence.

I said to Pig, "Jesus Christ and Abraxas's rooster's balls. Let's get the hell out of here." And we did. But what I'd actually thought of in those seconds I stared into the resurrected *Muse*'s eyes was an old catechism line from Saint Jung: "The dream is like a woman. It will have the last word as it had the first."

Saying it was an extraordinary performance of *King Lear* would not be praise enough. It was beyond extraordinary. It would have won the laurel wreath at any gathering of the Bard Troupes on Stratford 111 at any time in the last twelve hundred years or more. The legendary Barbassesserra could not have created a better Lear that night than Kemp did. His very exhaustion lent more credence to the king's age, despair, and madness. And I have to admit that Condella was tragically radiant and perfectly, absurdly stubborn as Cordelia. After a few minutes, I forgot her age—so I had to assume the Poimen never noticed.

The Poimen.

They allowed us to extend and light our own stage from the *Muse*. The ship had recovered sufficiently to handle the stage and basic lighting, although the cabiri were not functional. We were able to use our dressing rooms and regular arras and stage exits. But we did not need a tent where we performed.

Our ship and stage were on a sort of shell within a bubble. I have no idea what energies kept the bubble intact, our air recycled, or the pressures of the alien ocean from rushing in. But the bubble was invisible and it did not distort vision in or out as glass or plastic would. We did not float around or bob; the stage felt as firm beneath us as it had the night before at Mezel-Goull, but this was obviously an illusion since some moments into the performance we realized that our stage and ship and bubble were rotating three hunded and sixty degrees, even turning as they rotated. At times we were completely upside down—the surface of the ocean invisible beneath our feet and stage and stern of the *Muse*—but somehow the stage was always *down*. Our inner ear did not register the changes and gravity did not vary. (In fact, the gravity itself was suspicious, since it felt one-Earth average on such a gigantic planet.) But the turning and rotation were very slow, so if one did not look out beyond the proscenium for any length of time, there was no vertigo involved. When I did look, it took my breath away.

The water—if it was water—was incredibly clear. I could see scores of the huge blue and green crystal towers, each lighted from within, each with a central twin shaft filled with rising and falling liquids and passengers, each rising into sunlight and atmosphere above—where countless more of the Poimen floated and flitted—and then into space above that, each also extending down to the purple depths miles beneath us.

The Poimen floated around us by the thousands or by the tens of thousands. Without staring I couldn't tell, and one can't stare at the audience during a performance, even when the fear of vertigo *isn't* a factor. I could see that they were not all the same. Shafts of sunlight columning down from the rough seas above illuminated a bewildering variety of Poimen sizes, shapes, and iridescent colors. Some of the creatures were as large as Archon spacecraft; others as small as the koi in funeral ponds on Earth. All showed the same sort of flat face, black eyes, throbbing gills, and tiny arms, at least relative to their body size, and delicate hands as our first visitor in the sphere that had come through the *Muse*'s hull.

Kemp and Burbank had gone on about how they hated performing in theater-in-the-round as at Mezel-Goull, but here we were in a theater of three dimensions, with audience above, to the side, and partially beneath us, thousands of pairs of eyes focused on us from all directions, and all of them moving in our constantly rotating field of vision. A lesser troupe would have had trouble going on. We weren't a lesser troupe.

Did the Poimen understand us? Did they get the slightest hint of what our "mimesis episode" was about? Could these sea-space creatures understand the foggiest outline of the themes and depths of Shakespeare's tale of age and loss and ultimate devastation, much less follow the beautiful and archaic song of our language?

I had no idea. I'm sure Kemp and Burbank and Condella

and the others carrying the burden of the performance had no idea. We carried on.

Burbank once told me that his father—who had led the Earth's Men longer than any other person and who was almost certainly the finest actor ever to come out of our troupe—had said to him that *King Lear* precluded and baffled all commentary because the experience of it was beyond theater, beyond even the literature and art and music we had when humans had literature and art and music. *King Lear* and *Hamlet,* the older Burbank had told his son, went even beyond the false but beautiful holy scriptures humans used to have before the Archons and their superiors showed us the truth. The Torah, the Talmud, the New Testament, the Koran, the Upanishads, the Rig-Veda, the Agama, the Mahavastu, the Adi Granth, the Sutta Pitaka, the Dasabhumisvara, the Mahabharata, and the Bible, to name only a few, were false but beautiful, and important for evolving human hearts and minds, said the elder Burbank, but all receded before the unfathomable truths of *Hamlet* and *King Lear.* And where *Hamlet* explored the infinite bounds of consciousness, *Lear* delved the absolute depths of mortality, hopelessness, communication failed, trust betrayed, and the threads of chaos which weave our fates.

I think those are some of the words and phrases Burbank told me his father used. One does get in the habit of memorizing very quickly when traveling with actors.

They'd only been words to me until this night—pleasant theatrical hyperbole (which is redundant, Philp would argue, since all theater, however nuanced, is mimetic hyperbole of life)—but this day, this night, *this* performance of *King Lear* made me understand what Burbank's father had been trying to say.

When Kemp, as Lear gone mad and wearing his crown of weeds and flowers, said to Hywo as the blinded Gloucester

If thou wilt weep my fortunes, take my eyes.
I know thee well enough; thy name is Gloucester.
Thou must be patient. We came crying hither;

Thou know'st the first time that we smell the air
We wawl and cry. I will preach to thee. Mark.

and then Kemp slowly took off his crown not of thorns but of
faded flowers and tangled dry grasses and Hywo/Gloucester
wept

Alack, alack, the day!

only to have mad Kemp/Lear pat his back and console him
with absolute hopelessness—

When we are born, we cry that we are come
To this *great stage of fools.*

I wept.

I'm glad I was offstage and behind the arras, away from
those thousands of staring fish-eyes, because I wept like the
child I don't remember actually being.

By the time Lear carried his dead daughter onstage and
pronounced those five heaviest words in the history of the
theater—"Never, never, never, never, never."—I could no
longer stand. I had to sit down to sob.

And then the play was over.

There was no applause, no noise, no movement, no visible reaction at all from the schools and congregations and
aggregations and flocks of Poimen in the blue beyond our
bubble.

Kemp and the others bowed. We all took our curtain call.

The Poimen moved away in the sea currents and submersibles.

We stood there, exhausted, looking into the wings at
the players who hadn't played but who seemed equally exhausted, and then, almost in unison, we looked at the dragoman where he sat listlessly in the wings, elbows on his knees,
eyes unblinking and seemingly unfocused.

"Well?" demanded Kemp, his voice almost gone and as
old-sounding as the dying Lear's. "Did they like it? Did they
hear it?"

"Why do you ask me?" said the dragoman in his flat squeak.

"Weren't they in *touch* with you?" bellowed Burbank.

"How do I know?" said the dragoman. "Were they in touch with *you*?"

Kemp advanced on the spindly dragoman as though he were going to pummel him, but just then our bubble went dim as surely as if someone had put a towel over a bird's cage.

The dragoman jerked to his feet, not to meet Kemp's charge—he was not even looking at Kemp—and said in a different tone, "You have one hour and eleven minutes to rest. And then you and your ship shall be transported elsewhere."

Our view out the bubble had disappeared with the light. There was no sense of whether we were being moved or not, but we knew from the motion during the performance that something was dampening our sense of inertia in this cage. We went back into the *Muse*.

None of us slept during those seventy-one minutes. Some collapsed on their bunks or just stood in showers letting the hot water run over them—all of the *Muse*'s systems were functioning now—but about half the troupe met in the larger of the two common rooms on the upper deck.

"What's going on?" demanded Pig.

I thought our youngest apprentice had summed up the essential question pretty well with those three words.

"They're testing us," said Aglaé. She'd been a brilliant Regan.

"Testing us?" demanded Kemp. He and Burbank and Condella and the senior members of the troupe were glaring at her.

"What else could it be?" asked my weary and oh-so-lovely Aglaé. "No one's ever heard of a traveling troupe being forced to perform before the Archons before, much less before these . . . *Poimen* . . . if they *are* actually Poimen. We're being tested."

"For what?" asked Heminges. "And why us? And what

happens if we fail?" He should have been as exhausted as
Kemp or Burbank or Condella—he'd had important roles in
all three of the performances we'd done in the last forty-
eight hours—but fatigue just made his face look more hand-
somely gaunt and alert and Iago-cunning.

No one had an answer, not even Aglaé. But I began to
think that she was right—we were being put to the test—but
I could think of no reason, after all these centuries, that a
traveling troupe, or the human race for that matter, should
be tested. Hadn't we been tested and found wanting those
first years when the Archon, on the order of *their* masters we
were made to understand, ended our freedom and cultures
and politics and sense of history and dreams of ever going to
the stars on our own? What more could they take from us if
we failed their goddamned tests?

It made me want to weep, but I'd already blubbered like a
baby enough during that extraordinary, never-to-be-repeated
performance of *King Lear,* so I went up to the topside observation room to talk to Tooley for a few minutes, and then,
when the birdcage towel was lifted and the *Muse* informed
us that we were in the Pleroma again in the wake of the
Poimen ship, I climbed down through all the decks to the
tiny room where the newly resurrected *Muse* floated in her
clear blue nutrient.

I felt like a voyeur.

In my previous eleven years aboard the *Muse,* I'd rarely
come down here to her tiny compartment. There was no real
reason to—the *Muse* spoke to us through the ship, *was* the
ship, and we were no closer to her down here near the mummified husk she'd left behind so many centuries ago than
anywhere else on the ship: less close here really, since she
seemed alive elsewhere. But more than that, I was scared to
come here as a boy. Philp and I used to dare each other to
go down in the dark place to see the dead lady. I rarely came
down here as a man.

But now I had, and I felt like a voyeur.

What had been a brown, wrinkled, eyeless mummy was
now a beautiful young woman, perhaps Aglaé's age, per-

haps even younger, but—I had to admit—even more beautiful. Her red hair was so dark it looked almost black in the blue fluid. Her open eyes—I did not see her blink but at times her eyes were suddenly closed for long periods—were blue. Her skin was almost pure white, lighter than anyone else's aboard. Her nipples were pink. Her lips were a darker pink. The perfect V of her pubic hair was red and curly and dense.

I looked away, thought about going back up to my bunk.

"It's all right," said a soft voice behind me. "She does not mind if you look."

I just about jumped straight up through the hatch eight feet above me.

The dragoman stood there. His fibroneural filaments hung limp on his pale shoulders. There were still black streaks and stains near the corners of his eyes and mouth.

"You're in touch with her?" I whispered.

"No, she's in touch with me."

"What is she saying?"

"Nothing."

"What happened to her?"

The dragoman said nothing. He seemed to be looking at an empty space between me and the blue sphere.

"Who restored her?" I asked, my voice echoing now in the tiny metal room. "The Poimen?"

"No."

"The *Archons*?" It did not seem possible.

"No."

"What does she want?"

The dragoman turned his lipless face toward me. "She tells you that the two of you should come here when it is your turn. Before you act."

"Two of us?" I repeated stupidly. "Which two? Act on what? Why does the *Muse* want me to come here?"

At that moment the ship shook and I felt the familiar ending of the buzz and tingle one feels when transiting the Pleroma, a sort of vibration of the bones and rising of the short hairs on the arm, and then came the slight but perceptible downward shift-shock I'd felt so many times when we transitioned back to the Kenoma of empty forms. Our universe.

"Jesus Christ Abraxas!" came Kemp's voice crashing over the intercom. "Everyone come up to the main common room. *Now!*"

Tooley, Pig, Kemp, and the others had run viewstrips from deck to ceiling around the large common room, and then added more strips across the ceilings. The *Muse*'s external imagers provided and integrated the views. It was as if this deck of the ship were open to space.

There was no Poimen ship ahead of us. We had been flung out of the Pleroma into this system like a stone from a catapult such as the ones we'd seen arbeiters on 30–08–16B9 use to move boulders miles up the mountains to build the Archon's keep.

We were hurtling toward a series of concentric translucent spheres surrounding a blinding blue-white star.

Each sphere was larger than the last, of course, but shafts of brilliant sunlight passed through each sphere to the next and then through the last one out to us. The *Muse* put up deep radar and other readings showing that there were more than a dozen spheres, each one mottled with dark continents and painted with blue seas.

"Eyes of Abraxas!" breathed Heminges. "This is not possible."

"It's not possible in a thousand ways," said Tooley. "According to *Muse*'s data there, we're one hundred and forty-four AU out from this star. There shouldn't be this much light reaching us . . . or this first, last, sphere. Unless each sphere were somehow refracting and refocusing the light . . . or magnifying it . . . or adding to it . . ."

We all stared at Tooley. Usually he spoke only to explain how he was unplugging toilets or greasing gears or some such. This was by far the longest speech any of us had ever heard from him.

I remembered that an AU was an astronomical unit, the distance Earth was from its sun. Most of the Archon worlds we visited lurked at around one AU from their suns.

144 AU out?

"There are a dozen spheres around this sun," came the *Muse*'s strangely young voice. "There are two separate but intersecting spheres at one AU, one at two AU, then others at three AU, five AU, eight AU, thirteen AU, twenty-one AU, thirty-four AU, fifty-five AU, eighty-nine AU, and this outer one at one hundred forty-four AU from the star."

"Fibonacci sequence," muttered Tooley.

"Precisely," said the *Muse*. "But it seems oddly inelegant. A series of orbiting Apollonian circles would have put more spheres of varying diameter within a closer radius to this star without the need for—"

"Muse!" interrupted Kemp. "We're approaching this outer sphere pretty damned quickly. Shouldn't you be firing the engines to slow us?"

"It would not help," said the *Muse*. "Our velocity upon leaving the Pleroma was a significant fraction of C, the speed of light. We have never entered any system from any pleromic wake at anything near this velocity. I do not even understand how we can maintain our integrity at this speed since the collision of isolated hyrdogen particles alone should—"

"You mean you can't slow us?" interrupted Condella.

"Oh, yes, I can," said the *Muse*. "At my full thrust of four hundred gravities, it would take me a little over eight months to bring our velocity down. But we will impact the outer sphere in four minutes and fifteen seconds. Also, the ship's internal fields protect passengers... you... only up to thirty-one gravities. You would be, as the old saying goes, raspberry jam."

"Can you *miss* the outer sphere?" asked Aglaé. "Steer around it?"

The *Muse* only laughed. I had never heard her laugh before and I'm sure that not even the oldest members of the troupe had either.

No one said anything for a while.

Finally, Burbank ordered, "Show clock. Analog. Count-down."

A holographic clock appeared above a viewstrip, showing three minutes and twenty-two seconds until impact. The sweep hand continued moving backward toward zero.

Burbank wheeled on the dragoman who had been silent, great lidless eyes downcast, standing away from the rest of us who were almost forming a circle while staring at the clock and viewstrips. "Do you have any goddamned ideas?" barked Burbank. His tone sounded accusatorial, as if the dragoman had brought us to this end.

It turns out that someone with no lips can still smile. "Pray?" he said softly.

What would you do with three minutes left to live? I didn't pray. I didn't do anything else either, other than to look at Aglaé for a minute with more regret than I thought it possible for a person to hold. I was sorry that she and I would never make love. More than that, I was sorry that I'd never told her I loved her.

"One minute," said the *Muse*.

I suddenly wondered if this was the time the *Muse* had mentioned, through the dragoman, when I should bring Aglaé to the blue sphere with me when—how had she put it?—we should come there when it was our turn, before we act.

. No, it didn't seem that this was what the *Muse* had meant. And it looked as if "our turn," whatever that might have been, would now never come.

The outer sphere filled all viewstrips. We could clearly see the dark undersides of continents and make out the actual turning of the sphere itself. To give us some sense of scale, the *Muse* superimposed an outline of the large continent on 25–25–261B against one of the smaller continents now on the top viewstrip. It was a tiny dot on the huge landmass.

Jaws dropped open but still no one spoke.

"Ten seconds to impact," the *Muse* said calmly. Our speed became apparent as we hurtled at the airless wall ahead of us—a wall that now seemed *flat* because it extended so far in each direction.

We struck.

We did not strike, actually, but passed through the seemingly solid underside, passed through a mile or two of ocean in a blink of an eye, passed through five or eight miles of blue-sky atmosphere above that, and then we were in space again, hurtling toward the next sphere—the eleventh celestial sphere according to the *Muse*'s earlier description, one a mere eighty-nine AU out from this impossible blue-white sun.

"We shed twenty-five percent of our velocity," the *Muse* reported.

"We couldn't . . . that's not . . . how could we . . ." stammered Tooley. "I mean—Abraxas's teeth!—even if the sphere floor were porous, impact with the ocean and atmosphere would have been . . . I mean . . . slowing twenty-five percent from . . ."

"Yes," agreed the *Muse,* "what we just experienced was not possible. We could not have survived. Such a deceleration could not have occurred. That much kinetic energy could not have been dissipated without much violence. Nine minutes until impact with the next sphere."

Thus we passed through the eleventh sphere at eighty-nine AU, and then the tenth at fifty-five AU—although the *Muse* informed us that it should be taking us many weeks to be covering these distances, even at our velocity still some double-digit percentage of light itself, and she suggested that time itself was out of joint in and around the ship, but we did not care about that—and then we approached the ninth sphere rotating at thirty-four AU from the blue-white star.

The *Muse of Fire* bored through an ocean just as the first three times—with Tooley muttering "hypercavitation" to himself as if the word meant anything—but this time we did not tear through the atmosphere and into space again.

The *Muse* rose slowly, reached the top of her arc, hung there a minute like a balloon hovering several thousand feet above a great, almost-but-not-quite flat expanse of green fields and forests and brown mountains, and then began to fall.

The *Muse* fired her engine almost gently. We passed over a coastline and then over wide plains toward a range of mountains.

"We are to land on that mesa," said the dragoman.

"Who's ordering us to land there?" demanded Kemp. "The Poimen?"

The dragoman smiled again and shook his head.

The Archons were the petty rulers according to our Gnostic faith, the Poimen the shepherds (although the gospels never told us *what* or *who* they were shepherds of), the *Demiurgos* were the architects, the fashioners, the true (but flawed and failed) creators of our world and universe, and Abraxas was God of All Opposites, Satan and Savior, Love and Hatred, and all other truths combined.

Now, as we all stood outside our ship in the sweet, rich air of this ninth-sphere world, the *Demiurgos* approached from the direction that might have been north.

None of us had ever set foot on a world as beautiful as this. From our high mesa we could see hundreds if not thousands of square miles of green grasslands, rolling fields golden as if from wheat, thousands of acres of distant tidy orchards, more thousands of acres of apparently wild forest stretching off to the green foothills of a long mountain range, snow on the mountain peaks, a wide blue sky interrupted here and there by bands of clouds with some of the cumulonimbus rising ten miles into the blue sky, rain visibly falling in brushstroke dark bands far to our right, and more, a hint of our just-traversed coastline and ocean far, far to what we decided was the west, and from every direction the sweet scent of grass, growing things, fresh air, rain, blossoms, and life.

"Is this Heaven?" Condella asked the dragoman.

"Why do you ask me?" was the naked dragoman's reply. He added a shrug.

That was when three *Demiurgos* approached from the north.

We'd already seen living things during our minutes alone on the mesa top—huge white birds in the distance, four-

legged grazers that might have been Earth antelope or deer
or wildebeest running in small herds many miles below on
the great green sea of grass surrounding the mesa, large gray
shadows in the faraway forests—elephants? rhinoceroses?
dinosaurs? giraffes? any of Earth's long-extinct large wild
things?

We hadn't brought binoculars out and couldn't tell without
going back into the *Muse* to use her optics and now we didn't
care as the *Demiurgos* approached.

We never doubted that these three were from the race of
our Creators, even though no image of our Demiurge or his
species appeared in our gospels or church windows.

They were six or seven hundred feet tall—above our
height of three or four hundred feet above the lowlands
here on the flat-topped mesa even though the bottoms of
their legs were on the grasslands. They did not seem too
massive for all their height because two thirds of each of
them was in the form of three long, multiply articulated
legs, each glowing a sort of metallic red and banded with
black and dark blue markings, the three legs meeting in
an almost artificial-looking metal-studded triangular disk
of a torso—like a huge milking stool with living legs, was
Tooley's later description.

It was the last hundred feet or so of *Demiurgos* that rose
above the three legs and triangular torso that caught our attention.

Imagine a twenty-story-tall chambered nautilus rising
from that metallic torso—not something *like* a chambered
nautilus, but an actual shell—three shells here, each with its
characteristic bright stripes—and from the lower opening of
each spiraled shell, the living *Demiurgos* itself.

At the center of each shell was the circular umbilicus. Forward of that, over the massive opening, was a huge hood the
color of dried blood. Beneath that hood on each side were
the huge, perfectly round yellow eyes. Each black pupil at
the center of each eye was large enough to have swallowed
me.

And the word "swallow" did come to mind as the three
Demiurgos tripoded their way closer until they hung over

us; the great opening at the front of each shell was a mass of tentacles, tentacle sheaths, orangish-red spotted tonguelike material, horned funnels, and sphinctured apertures that might have been multiple mouths. Each huge yellow eye had its own long, fleshy ocular tentacle with a red-yellow node on its eye-end looking like some gigantic infested sty.

These were our Creators. Or at least one of them had been some twelve to twenty billion years ago. For Creators, I thought, they were very fleshy and organic created things themselves, for all the beauty of their huge spiraled nautilus shells.

We'd all stepped back closer to the open airlocks and ports of the *Muse,* but none of us ran inside to hide. Not yet. I was painfully aware that the *Demiurgos* closest to me could whip down one of those sticky tongue-tentacles and have me in its bony funneled orifice in a second.

"You will perform a play now," said the dragoman. "The best one you know. Perform it well."

Kemp tore his gaze away from the gigantic tripods looming over us and said to the dragoman, "You're in touch with them? They're speaking to you?"

The dragoman did not respond.

"Why won't they speak to *us*?" cried Burbank. "Tell them that we want to talk to them, not perform another play."

"You will perform the best play you know now," said the dragoman, his voice flat in that way it got when he was channeling these other beings. "You will perform it to the best of your ability."

"Is this a test?" asked Aglaé. "At least ask them if this is a test."

"Yes," said the dragoman.

"Yes it's a test?" demanded Kemp.

"Yes."

"Why?" said Burbank.

The dragoman's large eyes were almost closed. The *Demiurgos*'s huge yellow eyes above us never blinked but their ocular tentacles moved in a way that seemed hungry to me.

"What happens if we fail?" asked Aglaé.

"Your species will be extinguished," said the dragoman.

There was a roar of confused noise from all of us at that. The *Demiurgos* leaned farther over the mesa, their mouths and tentacles and eyes coming closer, and I picked up the strong brackish scent of the ocean—salt and reeking mud tidal flats and dead fish in the sun. I had a strong urge to run up the ramp into the *Muse* and hide in my bunk.

"That's just not. . . fucking. . . fair," Kemp said at last, speaking for all of us.

The dragoman smiled and I admit that I wouldn't have minded beating him to death at that moment. He spoke slowly, clearly: "Your species was excused upon first encounter because of Shakespeare. Only because of Shakespeare. His words and the meaning behind his words could not be fully comprehended, even unto the level of the Demiurge who created you. In your world, then, man was Abraxas— you gave birth to and devoured your own worlds and words, embracing eternal weakness even while you blazed with absolute creative power. You sought to build a bridge over death itself. All higher powers beneath the Absence that is Abraxas—the lowly Archons, the preoccupied Poimen, the race of *Demiurgos* themselves—voted that immediate extinction had to be your species' fate. But because of this one dead mind, this Shakespeare, there was a stay of execution on this sentence not to exceed one thousand and nine of your years. That time is up."

We stood silent in the sunlight. There was the sound in my ears of a single, huge, pounding heart, like the surf of a rising sea; I did not know if the pounding beat came from the *Demiurgos* whose shadow fell over me or from me.

"You will perform the best play that you know," repeated the dragoman. "And you will perform it to the best of your ability."

We looked at each other again. Finally Kemp said, *"Hamlet."*

The show went on. It took us half an hour to get into costumes, review roles—although we all knew our roles for *Hamlet* without asking—and slap on makeup, although the idea of the *Demiurgos* noticing our makeup was absurd. Then again, those huge, unblinking yellow eyes did not seem to miss anything, even though they stared through their own waving mass of tentacles when looking forward.

I was Rosenkrantz when we performed *Hamlet* and I enjoyed the part. Philp was Guildenstern. Old Adam had once told us that on Earth, pre-Contact, there had been a derivative play—not by Shakespeare supposedly—which featured Rosenkrantz and Guildenstern, those two lying but playful betrayers. I would have loved seeing it, if it ever did exist. Hell, I would have loved starring in it.

The other parts fell the way you would expect now that you know our troupe—Alleyn as Hamlet, Old Adam as Hamlet's father's ghost (a role our lore says the Bard himself sometimes played), Aglaé as Ophelia, Kemp as Claudius, Burbank as Polonius, Goeke as Horatio, Condella as Hamlet's mother Gertrude, Hywo as Fortinbras... and so on. About the only profound talent in our troupe not fully used in *Hamlet* was Heminges, who carried *Othello* with his powerful Iago, cast as the gravedigger. Now the gravedigger—the official name in our "Persons of the Play" list is "First Clown," the "Second Clown" being the gravedigger's companion played today by Gough—is one of the great roles in all of Shakespeare, but it is relatively brief. Too brief for Heminges's ego. But he made none of his usual protests this time as we rushed to dress and finish our makeup. He even smiled, as if performing for the *Demiurgos* to decide whether our species would be annihilated or not was what he had always looked forward to.

None of us had slept for... I'd lost track of the hours, but seventy-two hours at least and I guessed many more (transiting the Pleroma strangely affects either one's sense of time or time itself)... and we'd performed four daunting plays: *Much Ado About Nothing* for the doles and arbeiters and latecoming Archons, *Macbeth*... shit, I mean "the Scottish Play"... for the Archons, then *King Lear* for the Poimen, and now *Hamlet,* a play that is almost impossible to produce and act in well enough to do it justice at the best of times. One critic, it is said, back in the pre-Contact centuries, suggested that because of all the failed attempts to put on *Hamlet,* we'd do better just to quit trying to perform it and to allow everyone to read it.

Well, the *Demiurgos* did not look as if they were waiting to be handed—tentacled?—copies of the script.

Under the brilliant yellow light of the distant blue-white star, the play went on. Waiting behind the arras with Philp for our characters to enter at the beginning of act 2, scene 2—Hamlet's fellow students and so-called friends confer and conspire with King Claudius and Queen Gertrude before going on to try to trick Hamlet into revealing what the royal couple wants to know—I kept looking up and around.

This ninth sphere-world from the sun we were on was so large that we could not see the upward-curving horizons in any direction, merely a strange glowing haze that might have been the distance-distorted image of the inner wall rising up thousands of miles away from here. But I could see hints of the other eight spheres inward from us toward the sun. That was a sight I have no words for and perhaps Shakespeare would have failed here as well—the size, the crystalline clarity, the turnings within turnings, the shafts of sunlight and quick-caught glimpses of color that might have been continents and blue seas a solar system's leap away—but it made me cry.

I was doing a lot of crying on this trip. I'll blame it on the lack of sleep.

When we had thought our command performance for the Poimen was our last and ultimate test, Kemp and the others had chosen *King Lear* for a variety of reasons, but perhaps because *Lear's* infinitudes and nihilisms are more manageable—by man or any species—than *Hamlet's* ever-expanding paradoxes.

I've seen the play a hundred times and performed in it, usually as Rosenkrantz, more than half that number of times, but it always knocks me on my ass.

In all of Shakespeare's other plays, the characters that are larger than the play being performed—Falstaff, Rosalind, Cleopatra, the night porter in the Scottish Play, Mercutio—are either killed off or contained before they escape the deliberately confined double-sphered space of the play and theater. Not so with Hamlet and *Hamlet*. The play is *about* theater, not revenge, and is both the ultimate experience of theater and the ultimate comment on theater, and the strangely expanding consciousness of Hamlet—who begins as a student character prince about twenty years old and, within a few weeks in the time of the play, ages to a wise man in his fifties at least—makes no pretense of following any story line other than Hamlet's wildly leaping thoughts.

I strutted and fretted my enjoyable moments on the stage. The *Muse*'s caribi bots still were not working (Tooley had found that all their organic parts were missing), so we extended the usual stage and acted on without lighting, which would have been redundant in the bright sunshine anyway—and tried to make our entrances and exits without looking up at the hovering shells and tentacle-mouths of the three *Demiurgos*.

My last scene was one that had been sometimes omitted in our shorter performances of the play—act 4, scene 4, where we encounter Fortinbras's army on our way to the sea to sail to England, where Guildenstern and I are supposed to deliver Hamlet up to his execution but, according to offstage events, Hamlet will steal King Claudius's execution request and substitute Guildie's and my names instead, so presumably this is my swan song, and my last words to Alleyn. . . Hamlet. . . are "Will't please you go, my lord?" but Hamlet is pleased to stay and to give what I call his "even for an eggshell" soliloquy. It's especially odd, and I thought so this day under the shadow of the slowly shifting *Demiurgos,* that Hamlet seems to be praising Fortinbras, who is little more than a quarrelsome killing machine.

> *I see*
> *The imminent death of twenty thousand men*

That for a fantasy and trick of fame
Go to their graves like beds, fight for a plot
Whereon the numbers cannot try the cause,
Which is not tomb enough and continent
To hide the slain? O, from this time forth
My thoughts be bloody or be nothing worth!

In other words, Hamlet—the paragon of human consciousness and occasional conscience (although he showed little enough of that when he stabbed stupid but-innocent Polonius through the arras curtain and announced to his mother that he was going to lug the guts to another room)—was praising bloody action in a thug's nature rather than his own sublime awareness of morality and mortality.

And then the thought hit me like a stab between the ribs—
Where the fuck is Heminges?

Still in Rosenkrantz costume, I ran up the ramp into the *Muse* and began throwing open hull hatches and sliding down ladders without my feet touching the steps.

Heminges was right where I expected him to be, in the *Muse*'s tiny room, but I hadn't expected the heavy spade—the one the gravedigger was to use in his upcoming encounter with Hamlet—in his hands. He'd obviously already taken half a dozen swings at the *Muse*'s blue globe—the metaglass was chipped and a few hairline cracks already extended from the niche where the spadeblade had fallen—and he was winding up to take another overhand swing when I leaped at him.

Heminges was fueled by a fanatic's rage—I could see white froth at the corners of his open mouth—but I was heavier, stronger, and younger than the professional Iago. I grabbed the spade, we whirled, and I forced him back against the bulkhead, but not before I'd glimpsed the *Muse* . . . the physical *Muse,* whoever or whatever she was . . . floating in the red halo of her own hair, her newly young breasts almost touching the metaglass directly beneath the spade's damage, her arms passively down by her naked hips, her palms forward, as if she were awaiting the next and final spade blow almost with anticipation.

Heminges and I lurched around the small compartment with the comic clumsiness of two grown men fighting each other to the death. All four of our hands were gripping the long spade handle chin-high between us. Neither of us spoke; both of us grunted. Heminges's breath smelled of the whiskey we synthesized and broke out only after a successful performance.

Finally my youth and terror-augmented strength—combined with a lucky knee applied briskly to his codpieced balls—turned the tide and I forced Heminges against the bulkhead again and then up, up, the spade handle under his chin, until his toes left the deck. He hung there close to helpless. One final concerted press forward and I'd crush his Adam's apple with the handle, or just choke the fucking fool to death.

Instead of smashing his larynx, I panted, "What are you *doing*?"

His eyes, already wide, grew as round as the dragoman's but much madder. "I . . . break . . . the globe . . ." he panted, breathing whiskey fumes all over me, "and the fusion reactor goes critical. We . . . blow . . . those alien . . . cocksuckers . . . to hell."

"Bullshit," I said, dropping him so his feet hit the deck but not relenting the pressure of the spade handle against his throat. If I slammed it up under his chin, it would snap his neck. "Nothing can make the reactor explode. Tooley told me so."

He tried to shake his head but it only resulted in the spade handle rubbing more skin from his already reddened neck. "*She* . . . told me . . . it would," he gasped. His staring eyes were looking over my shoulder.

I released the pressure and turned to look at the *Muse,* the spade now hefted loosely in my hands. "How did she tell you?" I asked Heminges without turning to look at him. He was no threat. He'd slid down the bulkhead and was sprawled on the deck, panting and wheezing.

"Through dreams," he managed at last. "She gets . . . into

. . . my dreams. If the reactor goes critical, we can blow a hole in this *Demiurgos* sphere and all the air will rush out and. . ."

He stopped. He must have realized then how insane that idea sounded. As if the *Demiurgos*'s home—the ultimate Creation of the Creators—could be so easily damaged.

I did not speak to him then, but looked directly into the *Muse*'s blue eyes when I spoke. "Did you really tell him that? Did you really get into his dreams and tell him he could do this? If you can turn this ship. . . yourself. . . into a hydrogen bomb, you sure don't need this aging Iago to help you do it. What the fuck are you up to, woman?"

The *Muse* smiled sadly at me but no voice came from the speaker grills on the wall.

I turned back to Heminges, stood over him, and handed him the spade. "Claudius, Gertrude, and Laertes are almost finished with their scene," I said. "Gough will be going on with his pickaxe without you. He'd just fucking *love* to take your part and deliver your lines. He's always thought he'd make a better First Clown than you. I doubt if the goddamned *Demiurgos* will notice that there's an assistant gravedigger missing."

It was as if I'd run thousands of amps of current directly into Heminges's ass. He leaped up, steadied himself on the spade, shot an angry look at the *Muse,* and clambered up the steps and out. Actors, I thought, are nothing if not predictable.

My hands empty now, I spent another long moment staring at the naked woman in the blue sphere. I said nothing. This time she did speak through the intercom, her words echoing in the otherwise empty ship.

"That had to be done, Wilbr, or he would have found a real way to damage the ship in his vain attempt at revolution. This way, I would have been the only one injured."

I still stared and said nothing. *Injured?* The *Muse* had been dead for centuries, the solid illusion of her naked young body here notwithstanding.

"Do bring her down here, just the two of you and the dragoman, as soon as we enter the Pleroma," said the *Muse*. Her lips did not move, of course, her mouth did not open, but it was her voice.

I did not say, "Yes." I did not say, "Bring who?" I said nothing.

After a moment I turned my back, scrambled up the ladder, and went out into the sunlight to watch the end of the play.

I'm sorry that I used the word "brilliant" and perhaps even "unprecedented" when I described our performance of *King Lear* earlier . . . and perhaps I even used words like that to describe our performance of the Scottish Play in front of the Archon, or maybe (although I doubt it) our staging of *Much Ado About Nothing* for the arbeiters and doles the day before . . . because now I have no adequate words to describe the *truly brilliant* performance our people achieved with this *Hamlet.* I'd missed a few minutes, to be sure, wrestling with Heminges and the spade down in the storm cellar of the *Muse,* but I'd not missed so much that I didn't realize how truly extraordinary this show had been. Whoever the long-dead critic had been, if he'd been real at all, who said that *Hamlet* should be read rather than seen to be fully appreciated . . . well, he hadn't seen *this* performance.

Our people were half dead with exhaustion and tension by the last line, but somehow that added to the verisimilitude and unique quality of the performance. It was as if we had *lived* these hours—eternities—with the Prince of Denmark and his wit. Even those who hadn't acted or who had simply been onstage as placeholders—the soldiers, attendants, guards, messengers, sailors, followers of Laertes and so forth—seemed as totally wrung out as Alleyn, Aglaé, Kemp, and the other principals.

Heminges, I should mention, was goddamned wonderful. He's the only character in the play—a play in which even the most inconsequential character speaks more artfully than any man or woman now alive—who is a worthy interlocutor to Hamlet. If language is a game—and when is it not with

Shakespeare?—then the gravedigger was the only player who should have been allowed on the court with the fiendishly witty Hamlet. "'Tis a quick lie, sir, 'twill away again from me to you," the gravedigger says once, taking one of Hamlet's serves and smashing it back across the net. (We know about tennis through *Henry V*.)

Even before they are fully engaged in their battle of wits, Hamlet says of the gravedigger to Horatio, "How absolute the knave is. We must speak by the card or equivocation will undo us." Burbank taught me that this is a sailor's card, a shipman's card, that Hamlet is referring to—one on which all thirty-two compass points are clearly marked.

But *Hamlet* is a play in which no clear compass points have ever been marked to guide either the actors or the audiences. It ends, as Hamlet himself does, with far more brilliant questions asked than answered. When Hywo as Fortinbras, his voice husky with exhaustion and emotion, speaks the last words of the play over our rough stage strewn with corpses.

> *Take up the bodes. Such a sight as this*
> *Becomes the field, but here shows much amiss.*
> *Go, bid the soldiers shoot.*

And all the living exited by march, carrying Hamlet's body with them; we did not provide the sound effects of the cannon shooting as we usually did.

There was only silence: a silence broken only by the gentle afternoon breezes blowing across the mesa and the slight creakings and stirring of the *Demiurgos*'s triple legs and metal girdles and many tentacles. Their great yellow eyes did not blink. It was as if they were waiting for an encore.

Our dead sat up onstage. We actors, including Alleyn who was almost staggering from exhaustion and Aglaé, who was as pale as the real drowned Ophelia, came back onstage, joined hands, and bowed.

The *Demiurgos* made no sound or new movement.

"Well," said Kemp at last, still wearing the dead Claudius's crown as he faced the silent dragoman. "Did we pass? Does the human race continue? What's our grade?"

"You are to return to your ship and seal it," said the dragoman.

"Fuck that!" cried Kemp. He was shouting now at the looming ship-sized shells of the *Demiurgos,* I noticed, not at the round-eyed dragoman. "Give us your answer. Give us your verdict. We've done our bleeding best for every race of you alien pricks. Tell us *now.*"

"You are to return to your ship and seal it," repeated the dragoman.

"Arrrrrhh!" screamed Kemp and threw his crown at the tentacled maw of the nearest Demiurge. It did not quite make contact.

We all went into the ship. The hatches were sealed. The viewstrips showed the *Demiurgos* ambling away to the north in their long three-legged strides in the short minute before the mesa rock and grass beneath the ship glowed white, then yellow, then turned into a long metallic funnel, and the ship fell—or was flung—violently down and down and then out. The internal fields all kicked on and we were frozen in place as the *Muse* compensated for the deadly acceleration gravities assailing us. Evidently they were within the thirty-one g's she could handle. A moment later we abruptly transited to the gold nothingness of the Pleroma—the *Demiurgos* had not even bothered flinging us out through their tenth, eleventh, and twelfth spheres before making the transit leap— and Kemp said, "I'll interpret our being allowed to leave as a passing grade."

"Allowed to leave?" said Heminges. "They fucking well booted us out."

Burbank said, "I'm going to get some sleep," and everyone cheered raggedly and we began to head for our bunks. Some were so exhausted that they fell on couches or the deck and were instantly asleep.

I sought out Aglaé before she disappeared up to her bunk cubbie.

"Do you trust me?" I asked when I'd asked her to follow me down to the *Muse*'s level and she'd grudgingly complied. It felt strange to be alone with Aglaé in the dim blue light with the naked female form floating just a few feet away.

"Do you trust me?" I asked again when she did not reply immediately.

"Wilbr, what do you want? I'm tired. Very tired." She had every right to be, I realized. Aglaé had held important parts in all four plays we'd presented in the last three endless, continuous, sleepless days and nights of strangeness. "If you brought me down here for. . ." she began with a warning in her voice.

We were interrupted by the dragoman coming down the ladder after dogging the overhead hatch behind him. I'd not told him to come.

I turned to the *Muse* in her sphere. The tiny cracks where the spade had dented the surface had not spread. My guess was that the metaglass would have survived a thousand spade attacks. "We're here," I said to the naked form.

"In immeasurable distance there glimmers a solitary star on the highest point of heaven," said the dragoman in the *Muse*'s voice, accurate down to her new youthful energy. "This is the only God of this lonely star. This is his world, his Pleroma, his divinity."

I knew the words so well I could have recited them myself. Any of us could have. This was from Saint Jung's Seventh Sermon to the Dead.

"There is nothing that can separate man from his own God, if man can only turn his gaze away from the fiery spectacle of Abraxas," continued the *Muse*'s voice through the dragoman's mouth. I understood that she was communicating with us this way so the rest of the ship would not hear. But why? Why this sermon?

Aglaé looked at me with growing concern in her eyes. She didn't like this sermon coming from the ship's soul, and neither did I. I shook my head to show her my own confusion.

"Man here," said the *Muse*. This was the penultimate verse of the Seventh Sermon, word for word. "God there. Weakness and insignificance here, eternal creative power there. Here is but darkness and damp cold. There all is sunshine."

"*Muse*," began Aglaé, "why have you—"

"Upon hearing this, the dead fell silent," continued the *Muse* as if Aglaé had not spoken, "and they rose up like smoke rises over the fire of the shepherd, who guards his flock by night."

"Amen," Aglaé and I said in unison, out of habit.

"Anagramma," said the *Muse*, her voice lower, completing the Seventh Sermon with its sacred and secret codicil. "Nahtriheccunde. Gahinneverahtunin. Zehgessurklach. Zunnus."

Alarm klaxons began blaring throughout the ship. More alarms rang and bleated and thumped. The *Muse*'s voice— her old voice, probably a recorded voice, her voice in rare alarm even as her face behind the metaglass stayed serene, her eyes watchful—shouted out, "Warning! Warning! The airlocks are opening! The airlocks are opening! We are in Pleroma and all hatches and airlocks are opening! Warning!"

At that moment the dragoman's neurofiber filaments slipped through my skin and flesh and pierced the nerves at the base of my skull. I saw filaments wrapping around Aglaé's lovely neck and doing the same. More filaments shot forward from the dragoman's head, made contact with the metaglass, and then passed through. The *Muse* extended her body so that the filaments pierced her small, white breasts.

"Warning! Airlocks opening. All hatches opening. We are in the Pleroma. Warning! Air pressure dropping. Don protective gear. Warning! All airlocks are..." came the recorded voice at full volume from all speakers, but the words grew tinier and tinnier and then disappeared completely as the last air roared and hissed and flowed out of the ship through all of its open airlocks and hatches and doors, while the golden vacuum of the Pleroma flowed in to fill each compartment and all of our straining lungs with its nothingness.

"Come out!" commanded the voice, but only Aglaé, the dragoman, and I could do so. The others might have been dead, their lungs and eyes and eardrums exploded. Or they could be frozen in the vacuum-thick Pleroma like ancient insects in amber. In either case, they could not move.

Aglaé and I could do so and we did, laboriously climbing the ladder, floating and swimming through the golden medium to the airlock, then out into the Abyss. It seemed to take centuries. But no one was in a hurry. The dragoman followed, his long spatulate fingers and flattened feet pulling him and pushing him through the golden nothing with easy, broad, flick-away swimming motions.

Abraxas was waiting outside. I was not surprised. I could feel that Aglaé was not surprised either, nor the *Muse*—who was watching us somehow, I felt, even though the external imagers no longer worked for those trapped inside.

When I say that we went—or swam—outside into the Abyss, the Pleroma, it gives no real sense of the experience. The Abyss or Void or Pleroma was not absence; it was Fullness beyond all measure. It filled our mouths and lungs and eyes and cells. Moving in it was a matter of will, not locomotion. Once outside, there was no up, no down, no side to side. Aglaé and I willed and swam our way through the golden fullness to the long, gray curve of the outer hull of the ship—the only thing, other than Abraxas and us, that fouled the ineffable absoluteness of the Pleroma. We could use the hull as down if we stood on it; as a wall if we set our backs against it or near it; as a ceiling if we so chose. It gave us reference. Everything else, other than Abraxas waiting, was . . . ineffable.

I had learned that word in my catechisms as a child, but I never understood ineffable until this minute. Even as my mind reeled with vertigo, it remembered the words of our Gnostic prophet Basilides as quoted by Hippolytus some thousands of years before Contact ended all context.

> *For that which is really ineffable is not named Inef-*
> *fable, but is superior to every name that is used...*
> *Naught was, neither matter, nor substance, nor void-*
> *ness of substance, nor simplicity, nor impossibility of*
> *composition, nor inconceptibility, nor imperceptibil-*
> *ity, neither man, nor angel, nor god; in fine, neither*
> *anything at all for which man has ever found a name,*
> *nor any operation which falls within the range either*
> *of perception or conception. Such, or rather far more*
> *removed from the power of man's comprehension,*
> *was the state of nonbeing, when the Deity beyond*
> *being, without thinking, or felling, or determining, or*
> *choosing, or being compelled, or desiring, willed to*
> *create universality.*

This pretty well defined the Pleroma that Aglaé and I found ourselves floating in: a field that was at once bound-less, impersonal, indefinable, and absolutely transcendental. This was the *"Ain Soph Aur"* of the Jewish Kabbalah and the Tibetan and Mongolian and Buddhist "Eternal Parent, wrapped in her Ever-Invisible Robes, asleep in the Infinite Bosom of Duration."

And that pretty well described Abraxas as well.

The Abraxas who waited for us here, the incarnation He chose to show us, held no surprises. This Abraxas was the Heavenly Chanticleer, straight from the paintings in Gnostic churches throughout the Tell: small as far as manifested Ab-solute Gods go—only about six feet tall, a little shorter than me—and matching our images down to his rooster's head, curled serpent legs, and the whip he carried in one inhuman hand and the shield he carried in the other. The stars with their resplendent rays and the *ogdoad* symbol of the tran-scending seven planets were on his shield here rather than floating behind him, but the center of the large gold shield was taken up with a complicated design working the gold of the shield into the face of the sun. Abraxas's eyes were not those of a rooster, but rather the predator orbs of a lion. His mouth was mostly beak, but the teeth and tongue were also those of a lion.

All in all, a modest visible incarnation for the God of Totality, the Lord of Opposites, who not only stands outside of time but rules outside of all mere religions as the reality of the eternally available timeless moment.

"You will perform a play," said the dragoman.

"Yeah, yeah," I said. "What else is new?"

When I tell you "the dragoman said" or "I said," the words are not correct since the medium of the Pleroma, which was not a medium at all, carried no sound. There was no air in my lungs or in Aglaé's lungs. The Pleroma satisfied our brains' and cells' need for oxygen, but it was exactly as if we'd drowned in the Fullness. I know that the other twenty-one members of our troupe were writhing in terror in the ship, trying to move, trying to breathe air that was no longer there, no more concerned about performing a Shakespearean play than a fish out of water would have been about working out multiplication tables as it writhed and flopped on some hostile shore.

But something the *Muse* or the dragoman—or both—had done to Aglaé and me allowed us to think, to move, and, by shaping the words with our mouths and minds even in the golden absence of actual air, to shape our thoughts to be heard as speech.

"Will you perform?" asked the dragoman, presumably speaking for Abraxas who floated before us.

I looked at Aglaé. She nodded, but this was redundant. After whatever we had experienced in the *Muse*'s room, this young woman and I were as in tune as two tuning forks struck to the same pitch and vibration.

"We will do parts of *Romeo and Juliet*," I said. "However much we can do as a troupe of two."

Now, neither Kemp nor Burbank nor any of the other elders of our troupe would have chosen *Romeo and Juliet* as one of Shakespeare's pieces to perform when the future of our species—or even an important performance—was at stake. As appreciated as the old standard was by arbeiter and dole audiences around the Tell—and by the troupe itself, to tell the truth—it was earlier, easier Shakespeare: brilliant in its parts, but never the incomparable artistic achievement that was *King Lear* or *Hamlet* or *Othello* or *The Tempest* or even the Scottish Play.

What were our choices? It would have made more sense to put on *The Tempest* before the God of the Sun and Darkness, dealing as it does with the ultimate magus, magic, enchanted islands, captured races turned into slaves, and the end of control, probably Shakespeare's farewell to the theater if Kemp in his cups is to be believed—literally the drowning of Prospero's Books.

But I couldn't have done Prospero on my best day. I'd never been understudy for Prospero and had had no regular role on the rare occasions when we produced it. And however we might abridge *The Tempest,* it would never make a workable two-person production for Aglaé and me.

Of course, neither would *Romeo and Juliet,* but I regularly played Samson in the opening scenes—"No, sir, I do not bite my thumb at you, sir, but I bite my thumb, sir"—and I'd been understudy for Alleyn as Romeo on multiple occasions. And Aglaé was wonderful as Juliet.

And so we started.

We decided to use the hull as a sort of wall behind us, better to define the stage in our minds and to reach back to touch if the pleromic vertigo became too bad. Other than the absurd rooster-headed Abraxas—solitary King, Bond of Invisibility, Breaker of the Cycles of Bondage, and First Power—there wasn't anything to look at or hold on to out there in the Pleroma except the dragoman and the hull. And Aglaé.

I looked at her, nodded, and floated forward a few yards.

> *Two households, both alike in dignity,*
> *In fair Verona (where we lay our scene),*
> *From ancient grudge break to new mutiny,*
> *Where civil blood makes civil hands unclean.*
> *From forth the fatal loins of these two foes*
> *A pair of star-crossed lovers take their life;*
> *Whose misadventured piteous overthrows*
> *Doth with their death bury their parents' strife.*

Aglaé was watching me intently, wondering, I am sure, if I was going to do the entire Chorus's part, but I wasn't sure of the last part so I broke off there. Then I raised my arms and said conversationally in the direction of Abraxas, who was now seated on a gold throne that had not been there a second before, "Imagine, if you will, two young men, Samson and Gregory, of the house of Capulet, entering in swords and bucklers."

Then I did act out all the parts between Samson and Gregory—I knew these lines well enough—and after that, quickly explaining the situation to the dragoman and the Lord of Light and Darkness in easily improvised phrases, I acted out the entrance of Abraham and a serving man of the House of Montague. In other words, I got to deliver my "but I bite my thumb, sir" line after all.

Aglaé had crossed her arms. I could read her thought. *Will you be doing Juliet as well?*

Instead I improvised a clumsy little summary of Montague and Benvolio's scene—I'd played Benvolio once before when Philp was ill—and then summarized the coming scene between Benvolio and Romeo, stepping into character when it came time for Romeo's major lines and speeches—he was smitten and love-sodden already, you remember—but, we learn, with Fair Rosaline, not Juliet. Shakespeare, never all that interested in logic or verisimilitude, was asking us to believe that in that small town where the Montagues and the Capulets had been entwined with enmity for centuries like a climbing vine on an ancient trellis, Romeo had somehow not seen, or even heard of, Juliet yet.

I stepped—or floated—back. Taking her cue perfectly, Aglaé moved forward facing Abraxas, summarized the scene with old Capulet, Paris, and the clown servingman Peter in just a few words, and then launched into the third scene where she played Capulet's wife, the inimitable Nurse, and Juliet herself. Aglaé's voice was never so beautiful as when she spoke for Juliet—a girl-woman only thirteen years old in Shakespeare's mind. My Romeo was five years younger than I in real life . . . "real life" being the mind of the Bard.

And so our play advanced.

For the next scene, I summarized Benvolio's parts but found that I could do most of Mercutio's amazing lines perfectly from memory. "If love be rough with you, be rough with love: Prick love for pricking, and you beat love down." I'd seen Mercutio performed by the best men of our troupe and now I added my own little bits of business with closed fist and thrust forearm for the pricking lines, picking up Mercutio's madness and Romeo's naïve responses without hesitating a nanosecond between the wide shifts in tone and voice and posture and mannerism.

All my life, I realized, I'd wanted to do the Queen Mab speech, and now I did, babbling on about the tiny fairies' midwife, her wagon's spokes made of spinners' legs, the cover, the wings of grasshoppers, her whip of cricket bone . . . faster and faster, madder and madder, a tortured young man with eloquence rivaling Shakespeare's but none of the solid, business side of the Bard; Mercutio, a man in love with his own words and willing to follow words where they led even as they led him to madness . . .

"'Peace, peace, Mercutio, peace! Thou talk'st of nothing,'" I interrupted myself in my Romeo voice, alarmed now at my much more brilliant friend's frenzy, shifting my body in space through three dimensions as if shaking the space where I'd stood as Mercutio an instant before.

And so the play slid forward in that timeless spaceless space.

I realized almost at once that Aglaé was better at improvising the summaries than I—and she could remember most of the other players' lines and the Chorus's long speeches word for word when she wanted to retrieve any of them—so I let her take the lead, only stepping in as Romeo or Mercutio or Tybalt for key lines, and then only a few. It was as if we were skipping across the surface of a pond, saving ourselves from falling in only through our speed and unwillingness to fall and drown.

Then it was our first encounter, our first scene together as our real characters, all thoughts of Rosaline out of my teenaged mind now, my heart and soul and stirring prick focused forever more on the transcendent image of my Juliet—

"O she doth teach the torches to burn bright!"

We asked the unmoving Abraxas to imagine the party, Tybalt's anger, Capulet's restraint of the young firebrand, the singing, the dancing, the men and women in bright colors and masks, and all the while young Romeo following, almost stalking, young Juliet. Our banter had the urgency of youth and love and lust and of the reality—shared by so few in all of time!—of truly having found the one person in the cosmos meant for you.

"'Good pilgrim, you do wrong your hand too much,'" whispered Juliet/ Aglaé. "'Which mannerly devotion shows in this...'"

A second later I leaned close to her. "'Have not saints lips, and holy palmers, too?'"

"'Ay, pilgrim, lips that they must use in prayer.'"

"'O then, dear saint, let lips do what hands do. They... pray.'" And I sent my palm against hers and we both pressed hard. "'Grant thou, lest faith turn to despair.'"

When we did kiss a few seconds later, it was—for both of us, I could feel—unlike any kiss or physical experience either of us had ever known. It lasted a very long time. I touched her thoughts as well as her lips. Her trust—never fully given before, I understood at that instant, chased by so many men, stolen by a few, betrayed by all others— opened warmly around me.

She floated above me during the balcony scene. It was the first time I'd ever understood the depth and youthful shallowness and hope in those lines I'd heard too many times before.

I was Mercutio and Benvolio and Romeo in coming scenes, even while Aglaé delivered selected lines from the Nurse and from Peter.

She summarized Friar Lawrence's part except for certain responses to her Juliet.

Suddenly I found myself acting out Mercutio's verbal taunts with Tybalt, Benvolio's failed attempts to intervene, Romeo's joyful interruption, the mock fight between Tybalt and Mercutio that led to Mercutio being slain under Romeo's arm.

To an observer—and in a real sense Abraxas was the only observer, since the dragoman's eyes and ears were presumably just conduits to Him—it must have looked as if I were having an epileptic fit in freefall, babbling at myself, twisting, floating, lunging with invisible épées, moaning, dying. "They have made worms' meat of me," cries Mercutio.

"O!" cries Romeo. "I am fortune's fool."

In act 3, scene 5, Aglaé and I made love. We actually made love.

We had not intended to do it, even as our thoughts flew between us like messenger doves during the intimacy of our almost perfect improv. *I* had not thought of doing it.

But as the scene opens but before Juliet says "Wilt thou be gone? It is not yet near day," our stage directions say only that we are both aloft, with a ladder of cords, but Kemp had often staged it with Romeo and Juliet half-dressed on a couch standing in for their marriage bed. Offstage, of course, between scenes, had been Romeo and Juliet's one night of bliss as man and wife—a very few hours of realized love before the lark pierced the fearful hollow of their ears and never, as fate would have it, to be followed by another night or moment of intimacy.

But before Aglaé spoke that first line—she hesitated, her eyes on mine, the God and dragoman forgotten by both of us—I began to undress her. She rushed to undress me.

But the lovemaking was not rushed. I have no need to describe it here and you have no need to hear details, but trust me that there was nothing rushed, nothing self-conscious, no sense of doom or finality, no awareness of other eyes on us—neither divine nor dragomanic—and made love as joyously and slowly and then as impetuously and wildly as Romeo and Juliet would have at their age and in their depths of first-love rapture.

I did love her. Juliet. Aglaé. My love. My life.

We half-dressed afterward, she delivered her "Wilt thou be gone?" line, we laughed and debated whether it was the lark or the nightingale—the former meant death to me from Juliet's family, but I laughed out, "'Let me be ta'en, let me be put to death. I am content, so thou wilt have it so.'"

That wakens her to the morn and danger. She all but shoves me out with protests and final kisses and more final hugs and kisses.

I'd forgotten Abraxas. Forgotten the floating dragoman with the unblinking eyes. I'd forgotten everything but my performance and the truth beneath it—which was my body still vibrating like a struck bell because of my lovemaking with Aglaé and the knowledge that should the human race or universe itself end tomorrow, it was all worth it for these moments.

It was in our final tomb scene together that I realized that we were probably going to die then and there.

Our lovemaking had been spontaneous but real.

Our love was new but real.

The lines we were delivering had never been delivered like this by living actors in all the history of time or theater. Our energies were absolute. Our emotions all real.

I was sure that when I pantomimed drinking the poison in Juliet's tomb, I would feel the cold spread of the true apothecary's poison actually move through my veins like death-ice. And then, a moment later, when Aglaé pantomimed my dagger entering her breast, real blood would flow into the Pleroma and she would die.

"'Here's to my love,'" I whispered anyway, holding up the imaginary bottle and drinking it all down. "'O true apothecary. Thy drugs are quick. Thus with a kiss I die.'"

The kiss was brief. I was dying after all. I fell, floa slowly away from where she floated horizontally
golden glow.

I did not die. Nor did Aglaé's make-believe dagger pierce an all-too-real and beating heart. The show went on. I summarized Friar Lawrence's lines, the Page's, the Watchmen's, then Aglaé reported Capulet's wife's and Montague's sorrow in snippets of dialogue, and then I delivered Balthasar's and the Prince's important lines.

Aglaé floated dead again while I boomed out in a prince's royal voice.

> *A glooming peace this morning with it brings,*
> *The sun for sorrow will not show his head.*
> *Go hence to have more talk of these sad things;*
> *Some shall be pardoned, and some punishèd:*
> *For never was a story of more woe*
> *Than this of Juliet and her Romeo.*

Aglaé floated upright next to me and took my hand. We bowed together in Abraxas's direction.

The God who was also the Devil, the apotheosis of Night and Day combined, did not move. His rooster eyes did not blink. His arms on the throne were still. His serpent legs with their serpent heads and fangs and serpent eyes did not stir or slither.

Aglaé and I looked to the dragoman.

Time did not move in this timeless place, but I could feel Aglaé's heartbeats and my own. We lived.

"Well?" I said to the dragoman at last.

"Return to your ship," he said.

"Not yet," I said. Aglaé and I kicked forward together, floating closer to the throne and the God Above Gods seated on it. We could clearly see the lion teeth in the huge rooster beak as we came closer.

We stopped in front of Him. "Do you have anything to say to us?" I asked.

"_____," said Aglaé to the thing on the throne, "or ___ peace."

___ ot stir or blink.

___st and brought it down hard on the God's ___ticleer coxcomb and skull cracked and fell ___uck again.

Aglaé's small fists pounded His chest. It also cracked and then opened, showing hollowness inside.

The Unlikely Likely One, the All-Powerful in the Realms of Reality and Unreality, was as hollow and fragile as a plaster statue.

We turned to look at the dragoman.

"It's always been you," said Aglaé.

"Of course," said the naked form. "Let's get back into the *Muse* before you catch your death of cold out here."

The *Muse* sealed the airlocks, pumped the Pleroma out, released real air into the ship from storage tanks, and the twenty-one other members of our troupe began gasping and gagging and coughing and retching. All had survived.

"There have been alterations," came the *Muse*'s voice through the intercoms. "I can transit the Pleroma on my own now. To anywhere in the Tell or beyond. Where would you have us go?"

Without really thinking or waiting for Kemp or Burbank or Condella or the others—even my beloved Aglaé—to respond, I said, "25–25–261B."

This transit took less than thirty minutes.

As much as we all wanted to crawl to our bunks and sleep for a month, most of us showered and dressed in our clean ship tunics and gathered in the common room, where Kemp and other older ones—still thinking they commanded the ship or their destinies—demanded to know what had happened in the Pleroma. I let Aglaé tell them.

"What was Abraxas's verdict then?" asked Heminges. "On whether the human race continues or ends?" Aglaé had left out the part where we had found our God to be brittle, dead, false, and hollow.

"Perhaps we'll see on 25–25–261B," I said just as the *Muse* announced that we had exited the Pleroma and were approaching the planet.

The *Muse* roared down through cloud and sky on her thundering three-mile-long pillar of fire. It was daytime and the hot winds were howling in from the high desert above the arbeiters' and doles' plateau.

We suited up in hot condition suits and filter masks and went out anyway.

What we'd seen from orbit was true: the arbeiter barracks were empty, the dole hovels and offices deserted, the mushroom mine works abandoned and silent except for the howling of the wind.

Everyone was gone.

We returned to the ship and I ordered it to rise and hover near the Archon keep.

The stone-steel walls were there, but only a shell now. It looked as if a great fire had consumed every part of the interior. Embers still glowed.

"Where is everyone?" I asked the dragoman.

He showed spatulate fingers in an openhanded gesture even while he gave his small-shouldered shrug. "Perhaps the Archons have gone home—"

"I don't mean the goddamned Archons," I interrupted. "I mean the people. The human beings. The slaves. The people."

If he had shrugged again, or smiled, I would have killed him then—be he dragoman or divinity or both—but he only said, "Perhaps you failed your tests and your people are no more. Gone from the galaxy, with your troupe soon to follow."

"No," I said. It was not a protest, merely a statement of certainty.

"Then perhaps some . . . force . . . has removed them from all worlds in the Tell where they were in bondage and sent them home to Earth," he said.

I shook my head. "There's not room enough on Earth, even without the oceans, even if the goddamned tombs were to be torn down, for the billions upon billions of us from the Tell," I said.

"Then perhaps the oceans are being refilled and the . . . goddamned tombs . . . torn down as we speak," said the dragoman. "And perhaps your kind has been returned also to more Earthlike worlds—beyond the Tell, perhaps even among the Spheres, where they can resume their stumble toward their destiny."

"What in the hell is this . . . *thing* . . . babbling about?" demanded Kemp.

"This *thing* is more God than Abraxas or the Poimen or the Archons were or will ever be," I said tiredly.

Kemp and the others could only stare with their mouths open. I think all of our mouths were open. We were all learning to breathe air again.

"It was never really a test of *us,* was it?" I asked the drago man.

"Only in the sense that every one of your performances is always a test," he said.

"But you were testing *them,*" I said. "The Archons. The Poimen. The *Demiurgos.* Even Abraxas, if there is such a thing."

"Yes," said the dragoman. "There is no Abraxas, but there are the Abraxi. They *are* the Pleroma. Think of them as a sort of primal cosmic zooplankton. They are not very intelligent and make piss-poor gods."

"Did all these species pass?" I asked.

"Not all of them." The dragoman walked past us and looked at the Archon keep a mile below us. "Do you want that to remain?" he asked.

"No," I said. While the others were trying to understand what we were talking about, I said to the *Muse,* "Full fusion thrust, please. Melt that place to slag."

The *Muse* did what I asked. We felt the internal fields press around us as the ship leaped back into space.

"Were you really dead?" I asked the dragoman. "Did the Poimen really resurrect you from the dead?"

"I was. They thought they did. I have allowed others to believe the same in other places and at other times. Illusions are important for children, especially illusions about oneself or one's place in the universe."

"Do they know who you are? What you are?"

"No," said the dragoman. He showed his thin, lipless smile again. "Do you?"

Before I could speak—and I do not know to this day what

I was about to say—the dragoman said to us all. "You will encounter hundreds of other races of sentient and tool-using, if not always intelligent, beings if you cross the Pleroma to places beyond the Tell. None of them are gods. You will have to war with some if you want to survive. Some may have to die out. Some will want to destroy you. Some you may wish to destroy or conquer. You will have to look inside yourselves and to your poetry when those choices are faced."

Aglaé said, "So there are no gods out there?"

"None out there," said the dragoman. "Perhaps one or more in here." He disappeared and we all leaped back as the air rushing into the space where he had been made a small thunderclap.

The *Muse*'s sudden voice from the walls made us all jump again.

> *Were all stars to disappear or die,*
> *I should learn to look at an empty sky*
> *And feel its total dark sublime,*
> *Though this might take me a little time.*

"Which of the Bard's plays is that from?" asked Burbank, his voice hoarse with exhaustion and disbelief that there were lines he did not know.

"It's not Shakespeare," replied the *Muse* in her new, young voice so filled with dark energy. "It's by a man named Wystan Hugh Auden. You people need to learn some new poets."

"Perhaps you'll have time to teach us," I said. "Where are we now, please?" The viewstrips showed only stars, darkness, and arcane coordinates.

"We're approaching pleromic transit-phase velocity," said the *Muse*. "What is your desired destination?"

Only Aglaé spoke, but she spoke for all of us.

"Home."

COPYRIGHT NOTICES

LEGENDS OF THE RIFTWAR

HONORED ENEMY

978-0-06-079284-8

by Raymond E. Feist & William R. Forstchen

In the frozen northlands of the embattled realm of Midkemia, Dennis Hartraft's Marauders must band together with their bitter enemy, the Tsurani, to battle *moredhel*, a migrating horde of deadly dark elves.

MURDER IN LAMUT

978-0-06-079291-6

by Raymond E. Feist & Joel Rosenberg

For twenty years the mercenaries Durine, Kethol, and Pirojil have fought other people's battles, defeating numerous deadly enemies. Now the Three Swords find themselves trapped by a winter's storm inside a castle teeming with ambitious, plotting lords and ladies, and it falls on the mercenaries to solve a series of cold-blooded murders.

JIMMY THE HAND

978-0-06-079299-2

by Raymond E. Feist & S.M. Stirling

Forced to flee the only home he's ever known, Jimmy the Hand, boy thief of Krondor finds himself among the rural villagers of Land's End. But Land's End is home to a dark, dangerous presence even the local smugglers don't recognize. And suddenly Jimmy's youthful bravado is leading him into the maw of chaos . . . and, quite possibly, his doom.